OF LOVE AND LIFE

Three novels selected and condensed by Reader's Digest

CONDENSED BOOKS DIVISION

The Reader's Digest Association Limited, London

With the exception of actual personages identified as such, the characters and incidents in the fictional selections in this volume are entirely the product of the authors' imaginations and have no relation to any person or event in real life.

The Reader's Digest Association Limited
11 Westferry Circus, Canary Wharf, London E14 4HE

www.readersdigest.co.uk

ISBN 0-276-42676-2

For information as to ownership of copyright in the material of this book, and acknowledgments, see last page.

OF LOVE AND LIFE

CONTENTS

Three weeks in Paris
Barbara Taylor Bradford

As students at the prestigious Anya Sedgwick School of Decorative Arts in Paris, best friends Alexa, Kay, Jessica and Maria once shared the challenges and excitement of developing their artistic talents under Anya's caring and demanding guidance. But at the end of their three years at the school, the friends part as enemies, each with strong personal reasons never to return to Paris.

Now, seven years on, for each of them the arrival of an invitation to Anya's eighty-fifth birthday celebrations in Paris means facing up to unfinished business.

Prologue

OUTSIDE ON THE RUE JACOB the man shivered and turned up the collar of his overcoat. It was a bitter February day, icy from the wind that swept down from the Russian steppes and across the plains of Europe to hit Paris with a sharp blast.

The sky was a faded blue, the sun watery as it slanted across the rooftops, almost silvery in this cold northern light, and without warmth. But Paris was always beautiful, whatever the weather; even when it rained it had a special quality all its own.

Spotting a cab, he hailed it, and as it slowed to a standstill he got in quickly and asked the driver to take him to the post office. Once he was there he unwrapped a package of seventy-one stamped envelopes and dropped them into a letterbox, then returned to the cab.

The man now gave the driver the address of the FedEx office, then settled back against the seat, glancing out of the window from time to time. How happy he was to be back in the City of Light, but, nonetheless, he could not help wishing it were a little warmer today.

In the FedEx office, the man filled in the appropriate labels and handed them over to the clerk along with four white envelopes. They would be processed for delivery within the next twenty-four hours, their destinations four cities in distant corners of the world. Back in the taxi he instructed the driver to take him to the Quai Voltaire. Once there, he headed towards one of his favourite bistros on the Left Bank.

And, as he walked, lost in his diverse thoughts, he had no way of knowing that because of his actions, lives were about to be changed irrevocably, and so profoundly that they would never be the same again.

Chapter One

It was her favourite time of day. Dusk. That in-between hour before night descended, when everything was softly muted, merging together. The twilight hour.

Her Scottish nanny had called it 'the gloaming'. She loved that name; it conjured up so much, and even as a little girl she had looked forward to the late afternoon, that period just before supper. As she had walked home from school with her brother Tim, Nanny between them tightly holding on to their hands, she had always felt a twinge of expectancy, as if something special awaited her. This feeling had never changed. Wherever she was in the world, dusk gave her a distinct sense of anticipation.

She stepped away from her drawing table, went to the window of her downtown loft apartment and peered out, looking towards the upper reaches of Manhattan. To Alexandra Gordon the sky was absolutely perfect at this precise moment . . . its colour a mixture of plum and violet toned down by a hint of smoky grey bleeding into a faded pink. The colours of antiquity, reminiscent of Byzantium and Florence and ancient Greece. And the spires and skyscrapers of this great modern metropolis were blurred into timeless images cast against that almost-purple sky.

Alexandra smiled to herself. As far back as she could remember she had believed that this time of day was magical. In the movie business, which she was occasionally a part of these days, dusk was actually called 'the magic hour'. Staring out across the skyline, fragments of her childhood came rushing back to her. For a moment she fell down into her memories . . . memories of the years spent growing up on the Upper East Side of this city . . . of a childhood filled with love and security and the most wondrous of times. Even though their mother had worked, still worked in fact, she and Tim had never been neglected by her, nor by their father. But it was her mother who was the best part of her, and, in more than one sense, she was the product of her mother.

Lost in remembrances of times past, she eventually roused herself and went back to the drawing board, looking at the panel she had just completed. It was the final one in a series of six, and together they composed a winter landscape in the countryside.

She knew she had captured most effectively the essence of a cold, snowy evening in the woods, and bending forward she picked up the panel and carried it to the other side of the studio, where the rest of the panels were aligned. Staring intently at the now-complete set, she pictured them as a giant backdrop on the stage, which was what they would soon become. As far as she was concerned, the panels depicted exactly what the director had requested.

'I want to experience the cold, Alexa,' Tony Verity had told her. 'I want to *feel* the icy night in my bones. Your sets must make me want to rush indoors, to be in front of a roaring fire.'

Stepping back to eye her work from a distance, she thought of the way she had created the panels in her imagination first. She had envisioned St Petersburg in winter, and then focused on an imaginary forest beyond that city. In her mind's eye, the scenery had come alive, almost like a reel of film playing in her head . . . bare trees glistening with dripping icicles, drifts of new snow sweeping up between the trees like white dunes. White nights. White sky. White moon. White silence.

That was the mood she sought, had striven for, and wished to convey to the audience. And she believed she had accomplished that with these panels, which would be photographed later this week and then blown up for the stage.

She had not used any colours except for a hint of grey and black for a few of the skeletal branches. Her final touch, and perhaps her most imaginative, had been a set of lone footprints in the snow. Footprints leading up between the trees, as if heading for a special, perhaps even secret, destination.

The sharp buzzing of the doorbell broke her concentration instantly. She went to the intercom on the wall. 'Hello?'

'It's Jack. I know I'm early. Can I come up?'

'Yes, it's OK.' She pressed the button that released the street door, and then ran downstairs to the floor below to let him in.

A few seconds later Jack Wilton, bundled up in a black duffle coat and carrying a large brown shopping bag, was walking towards her, a grin on his keen, intelligent face. 'Sorry if I'm mucking up your working day, but I was round the corner. At the Cromer Gallery with Billy Tomkins. It seemed sort of daft to go home and then come back here later. I'll sit in a corner down here until you quit.'

'I just did,' she said, laughing. 'I've actually finished the last panel.'

'That's great! Congratulations!' As he stepped into the small hallway of her apartment, he put down the bag, pulled her into his arms and pushed the door closed with his booted foot. He hugged her tightly, and as his lips brushed her cheek, she felt a tiny frisson, a shivery feeling. There was an electricity between them that had been missing for ages. She was startled.

Seemingly, so was he. Jack pulled away, glanced at her quickly and then instantly brought his mouth to hers, kissing her deeply, passionately. After a second, he moved his mouth close to her ear and murmured, 'Let's go and find a bed.'

She leaned back, looking up into his pellucid grey eyes, which were more soulful than ever at this moment. 'Don't be silly.' As she spoke, a small, tantalising smile touched her lips and her sparkling eyes were suddenly inviting.

'Silly? There's nothing silly about going to bed. I think it's a rather serious thing.' Throwing his duffle coat on the floor next to the shopping bag and putting his arm round her, he led her into the bedroom.

He stopped in the middle of the room and taking hold of her shoulders, turned her to face him. 'You went missing for a bit,' he said, sounding more English than ever.

She stared back at him, said nothing.

He tilted her chin, leaned down and kissed her lightly on the mouth. 'But I have the distinct feeling you're suddenly back.'

'I think so.'

'I'm glad, Lexi.'

'So am I,' she answered.

He smiled at her knowingly and led her towards the bed without another word. They sat down together side by side, and he began to unbutton her shirt; she tugged at his tweed jacket, and within seconds they were both undressed, stretched out on the bed.

Leaning over her, he asked, 'And where was it that you went?'

'Not sure. Fell into a deep pit with my work, I suppose.'

He nodded, fully understanding, since he was an artist and tended to do the same at times when he was painting. But he had really missed her, and her remoteness had worried him. Now he brought his mouth down to her, his kisses tender.

Alexandra felt that frisson once more, and she began to shiver slightly under his touch, which was becoming provocative. He continued to kiss her as he stroked her thigh, and to him it soon seemed as though she was opening like a lush flower bursting forth under a warm sun. He loved this woman, and he wanted to bind her to him, and he wanted to make love to her now, be joined with her.

Sliding his hands under her buttocks, he lifted her up, drew her closer to him, calling out her name as he did. 'Come with me, come where I'm going, Lexi!' he exclaimed, his voice harsh, rasping.

And so she did as he demanded, and together they soared, and as he began to shudder against her, he told her over and over how much he loved making love to her.

Afterwards, when they finally lay still, relaxed and depleted, he lifted the duvet up and covered them with it, then took her in his arms. He said against her hair, 'Isn't this as good as it gets?'

When she remained silent, he added, 'You know how good we are together . . .'

'Yes.'

'You're not going to go away from me again, are you?'

'No . . . it *was* the work, the pressure.'

'I'm relieved it wasn't me. That you weren't having second thoughts about me.'

She smiled to herself. 'You're the best, Jack, the very best. Special . . . unique, actually.'

He peered down at her in the dim light of the fading day, wondering whether she were teasing him. Then he saw the intensity in her eyes, and he said softly, 'Let's make it permanent.'

Those lucid green eyes he loved widened. 'Jack . . . I don't know what to say . . .'

'Say yes . . .'

'OK. Yes.'

'I'm talking marriage,' he muttered, a sudden edge to his voice. He focused all his attention on her, his eyes probing.

'I know that.'

'Will you? Will you marry me?'

'Yes, I will.'

A slow, warm smile spread itself across his lean face, and he bent into her, kissed her forehead, her nose, her lips. 'I'm glad. Really so *bloody* glad, Lexi, that you're going to be mine, all mine. Wow, this is great! And we'll have a baby or two, won't we?'

She laughed, happy that he was so obviously delirious with joy. 'Of course.'

They began to roar with laughter, filled with hilarity and pleasure in each other, and the sheer happiness of being young and alive. But after a moment, Jack's face turned serious, and he held Alexandra still. 'You're not going to change your mind, are you, Lexi?'

'Course not, silly.' She touched his cheek lightly, smiled seductively.

'Shall we get to it, then . . . making babies, I mean.'

'Try and stop me—' he began, but paused when the intercom buzzed.

Alexandra scrambled off the bed, took a dressing gown out of the closet, and struggled into it as she ran to the hallway. Lifting the intercom phone, she said, 'Hello?'

'FedEx delivery for Ms Gordon.'

'Thanks. I'll buzz you in. I'm on the fourteenth floor.'

The carbon copy of the original label on the front of the FedEx envelope was so faint she could barely make out the name and address of the sender. In fact, the only part she could read was 'Paris, France'.

She stood holding the envelope, a small furrow crinkling the bridge of her nose. And then her heart missed a beat.

From the doorway of the bedroom, Jack said, 'Who's it from? You look puzzled.'

'I can't make out the name. Best thing to do is open it, I suppose,' she replied, forcing a laugh.

'That might be a good idea.' Jack's voice was touched with acerbity.

She glanced across at him swiftly, detecting at once a hint of impatience, as if it were her fault their lovemaking had been interrupted by the FedEx delivery. Wishing to placate him, she exclaimed, 'Oh, it can wait!' Dropping the envelope on the small table in the hall, she added, 'Let's go back to bed.'

'No, the mood's gone. I'm going to take a shower.' He grinned, kissed the top of her nose. 'Tell you what. Let's take a shower together.' Grasping her hand, he led her across to the bathroom and into the shower stall, turned on the taps, adjusted the temperature and held her close again as the water sluiced over their bodies.

Alexandra leaned against him, closed her eyes, thinking of the envelope she had left on the table. She could well imagine who it was from. It could be only one person . . . the thought terrified her.

But she was wrong. A short while later, when she finally opened the envelope, it was not a letter inside, as she had believed, but an invitation. Her relief was enormous.

She sat on the sofa in her living room, staring at it, and a smile broke through, lighting up her face. Leaping to her feet, she ran across the room to the kitchen, where Jack was cooking, exclaiming, 'Jack, it's an invitation. To a party. In Paris!'

Jack glanced up from the bowl of fresh tomatoes he was stirring, took a sip of his tea, and asked, 'Who's the party for, then?'

'Anya. My wonderful Anya Sedgwick.'

'The woman who owns the school you went to? The Anya Sedgwick School of Decorative Arts, Design and Couture?'

'That's right.'

'And what's the occasion?'

'Her birthday.' Leaning against the doorjamb, she began to read from the engraved invitation. '"The pleasure of your company is requested at a celebration in honour of Anya Sedgwick on the occasion of her eighty-fifth birthday. On Saturday, June the 2nd, 2001. At Ledoyen, Carré Champs-Elysées, Paris. Cocktails at eight o'clock. Supper at nine o'clock. Dancing from ten o'clock on." Hey, isn't that great, Jack? It's a supper dance. Oh, how wonderful!'

'Sounds like it's going to be a super bash. Can you take a friend, do you think?'

Alexandra glanced at the invitation again. Her name had been written across the top in elegant calligraphy, but it was only *her* name. The words 'and guest' were missing. 'I don't think I can. It only has my name on it. I'm sure it's just for her family and former pupils . . .' Alexandra's voice trailed off.

Jack was silent for a moment, then asked, 'Are you going to go?'

'I'm not sure. I don't know. It all depends on work, I guess. I've only one small set to finish for *Winter Weekend*, and then that's it. I'll be out of work, if something doesn't pop up.'

'I'm sure it will, Lexi,' he reassured, glancing at her, smiling. 'Now scoot, and let me finish the pasta pomodoro, and before you can say Jack Robinson I'll have dinner for my lady.'

She laughed, said 'OK,' and went back to the sofa, still holding the invitation in her hand. Sitting down, she stared at it for a moment longer, her mind on Anya Sedgwick, the woman who had been her teacher, mentor and friend. She had not seen her for a year. It would be lovely to be in her company again, to celebrate this milestone in her life. Paris in the spring. How truly glorious it would be . . .

But Tom Conners was in Paris.

When she thought of him she found it hard to breathe.

Alexandra woke with a start. The room was quiet, bathed in silence, but for a long moment she felt as if someone stood nearby, hovered close to the bed. She remained still, pushing the feeling away, knowing this was all it was . . . just a *feeling*, the sensation that he was with her in the room because her dream had been so real.

But then it always was, whenever she dreamed it. Everything that happened had a validity to it, was vivid, lifelike; even now, as she rested against the pillows, she could smell him, smell his body, his hair, the cologne he used. It seemed to her that he had kissed her deeply.

Except that he had not been here tonight. She was alone.

Knowing that sleep would be elusive, Alexa sat up, switched on the bedside lamp and slid her long legs out of bed. Wrapping herself in her pale blue dressing gown, she went into the kitchen, snapping on lights on the way. What she needed was a soothing cup of camomile tea. After filling the kettle with water and putting it on the gas ring, she sat down on a stool, contemplating the dream that she had with such unusual regularity. It was always exactly the same. He was suddenly there with her, cradling her in his arms, telling her he missed her, wanted her, needed her. And always he reminded her that she was the love of his life. His one true love.

And the dream was rooted in such uncanny reality that even her body felt as if it had been invaded by a sensual and virile man. It had been, she muttered under her breath, filling a mug with boiling hot water. At least it had been this afternoon. Jack Wilton made love to me when he arrived here today . . . in the gloaming he loved me well.

Yes, said a voice in her head, but in the dream it's never anybody but Tom Conners loving you, and that's your basic problem.

Sighing to herself, Alexa picked up the mug and walked through to the living room. She turned on a lamp and sat down in the comfortable, overstuffed chair near the fireplace, sipping the camomile tea, staring into the dying embers of the log fire.

What was wrong with her? The question hovered over her like a black cloud.

She had made love with Jack and enjoyed every moment of it, and there had been this unexpected and wonderful renewal of passion between them, a passion sadly absent for months. To excuse this she had blamed tiredness, work, the pressure and stress of designing sets at top speed for the new play. But in all truthfulness, something else had been at work. She had pulled away from having sex with Jack, had avoided it. There had been a strange reluctance in her to be intimate with him, and she had mentally recoiled. But why? He was appealing, good-looking in a quiet way, and had a very endearing personality. He was even funny, and made her laugh hilariously.

So many conflicting thoughts bounced around in her head. She closed her eyes, endeavouring to sort them out, then suddenly she sat up straighter, and thought: My God, I agreed to marry Jack! I'm engaged to him!

This was no joke as far as he was concerned. He was very serious. He had gone on talking about getting married over dinner, constantly touching his glass of red wine to hers. While they hadn't exactly settled on a date, she had sort of acquiesced when he had talked about a winter wedding at the end of the year. 'In New York. A proper wedding,' he had insisted. 'With your family and mine, and all the trimmings. That's what I want, Lexi.' And she had nodded in agreement. Once dinner was over, he had helped her stack the dishwasher, but then he had left, kissing her cheek and whispering that he wanted to get an early start on a large canvas for his forthcoming show.

As for her, she had dreamed about another man, and in the most intimate way possible. Was there something wrong with her? This wasn't normal, was it?

Despite the camomile tea, she was suddenly wide awake. Glancing at the small brass carriage clock on the mantelpiece she saw that it was already ten past six in the morning.

Ten past twelve in Paris.

On an impulse, she lifted the phone on the side table and dialled his office number. Within a split second the number in Paris was ringing.

And then he answered. '*Allô*.'

She clutched the phone tighter. She couldn't speak. She could barely breathe.

'Tom Conners *ici*.' Then again, this time in English, he said, 'Hello? This is Tom Conners. Who is this?'

Carefully she replaced the receiver. Her hands were shaking and her heart was thudding in her chest. She took several deep breaths, leaned against the cushions in the chair, staring into space.

He was there. In his office. He was alive and well in Paris.

And if she went to Paris, to Anya Sedgwick's birthday party, she wouldn't be able to resist. She would call him, and he would say, 'Let's have a drink,' because he was like that, and she would say, 'Yes, that's great,' and she would go and have a drink with him. And after that she would be lost. Floundering about once more. Yes, a lost soul.

Because to her Tom Conners was devastatingly irresistible, a man so potent, so compelling, he lived with her in her thoughts, and in her heart and mind. Even though they had stopped seeing each other three years ago, and he had been the one to break it off, she knew that if she spoke to him he would want to see her.

You're such an idiot, she chastised herself. Anger flooded her. It was an anger at herself and her lingering emotional involvement with Tom Conners. And she knew it had been foolish to make that call, even though she hadn't spoken to him. Just hearing that arresting, mellifluous voice of his had truly unnerved her.

She forced herself to focus on Jack Wilton. He loved her, wanted to make her his wife, and she had actually accepted his proposal. All that aside, he was a truly decent human being, a good man, honourable, kind, loving, and generous to a fault. She knew he adored her, admired her talent as a scenic designer, applauded her dedication and discipline. He encouraged her and was always there for her. And the truth was he had stayed in the relationship and been exceedingly patient with her even when she had been cool towards him these last few months.

Jack would make a wonderful husband, she decided. He loved her, and she loved him. In her own way.

Alexandra purposefully pushed herself up out of the chair and went back to bed. Jack Wilton was going to be her husband and that was that. Sadly, she would have to forgo Anya's eighty-fifth birthday party. For her own self-protection.

Seated at the mahogany table in the elegant dining room of her parents' apartment on East 79th Street, Alexandra was savouring the tomato omelette her mother had just made. 'This is great, Mom,' she said after a moment, 'and thanks for making time for me today. I know you like to have your Saturdays to yourself.'

'Don't be so silly, I'm glad you're here,' Diane Gordon answered, smiling warmly. 'I was just about to call you this morning, when the phone rang and there you were, wanting to have lunch.'

Diane took a sip of water, then asked her daughter, 'Do you want a glass of wine, darling?'

'No, thanks, Mom, not during the day. It makes me sleepy. Anyway, it's fattening . . . all that sugar. I prefer to take my calories in bread.' As she spoke she reached for a piece of the baguette her mother had cut up earlier. She spread it generously with butter and took a bite.

'You don't have to worry about your weight, you look marvellous, really well,' Diane remarked, eyeing her daughter. She couldn't help thinking how young she looked for her age. It didn't seem possible that Alexandra was *thirty*. In fact, in the summer she would be thirty-one, and it seemed like only yesterday that she was a toddler running around her feet. Thirty-one, she mused, and in May I'll be fifty-eight. How time flies, just disappears. Where have all the years gone? David will be fifty-nine in June. Our marriage has lasted so long, so many years, and it's still going strong.

'Mom, what *are* you pondering?' Alexa probed.

'I was just thinking about your father. And our marriage. We've been married for thirty-three years, and the years seem to have passed in a flash. Just like that.' She snapped her fingers.

'You two were lucky,' Alexa murmured, 'so lucky that you found each other.'

'That's absolutely true.'

'You and Dad, you're like two peas in a pod.' She gazed at her mother, thinking how beautiful she was, with her peaches-and-cream skin, her pale golden hair and those extraordinary liquid blue eyes.

'So, what about you, darling? Have you finished those winter sets?'

Alexa's face lit up. 'I completed the last of the panels earlier this week. Yesterday I saw the blowups of them all at the photographic studio, and they're great, Mom, even if I do say so myself.'

'I've told you many times, don't hide your light under a bushel, darling. You're very talented.' She rested her eyes on her daughter thoughtfully. 'And so . . . what's next for you?'

'I have one small set to do for this play and after that my contract's fulfilled.' Alexa laughed a little hollowly, and added, 'Then I'll be out of work, I guess.'

'I doubt that,' Diane shot back, the expression on her face reflecting her pride in her only daughter. 'Not you.'

'To be honest, I'm not worried. Something will turn up.'

Diane nodded, and then her eyes narrowed slightly. 'You said on the phone that you wanted to talk to me. What—'

'Can we do that later, over coffee?' Alexa cut in swiftly.

'Yes, of course, but is there something wrong? You sounded worried earlier.'

'Honestly, there's nothing wrong. I just need . . . a sounding board, a really good one, and you're the very best I know.'

'Is this about Jack?'

'No, and now you're sounding like all those other mothers, which most of the time you don't, thank God. And *no*, it's not about Jack.'

'Don't be so impatient with me, Alexa, and by the way, Jack Wilton is awfully nice.'

'I know he is, and he feels the same way about you. And Dad.'

'I'm glad to hear it. But how does he feel about *you*? That's much more important.'

'He cares.'

'Your father and I both think he would make a good—a very nice son-in-law.'

Alexa did not respond.

Half an hour later Alexandra sat opposite her mother in the living room, watching her as she poured coffee into fine bone-china cups.

'I'm ready to listen, Alexa, whenever you want to start. And whatever it's about, you'll have the best advice I can give.'

'I know that, Mom,' Alexa answered, as she accepted the cup her mother was passing to her. She put it down on the low antique table between them, and settled back against the Venetian velvet cushions on the cream sofa. 'Late yesterday afternoon I got an invitation to go to a party in Paris. For Anya. She's going to be eighty-five.'

A huge smile spread across Diane's face, and she exclaimed, 'Good Lord, I can't believe it! She's a miracle, that woman.'

'I know, and aside from looking so much younger than her age, she's full of energy and vitality. Whenever I speak to her on the phone she sounds as busy as ever, running the school, entertaining and travelling. Only last month she told me she's started writing another book, one on the Art Deco period of design. She's amazing.'

'I'll say she is, and what a lovely trip for you. When is the party?'

'On June the 2nd, at Ledoyen. But, Mom, I'm not sure that I'm going to go.'

Diane was startled. 'Why ever not? You've always been a special favourite of Anya's. Certainly more than the others—' Diane stopped abruptly. 'But of course! That's *it*. You don't want to go because you don't want to see the other three. I can't say I blame you; they turned out to be rather treacherous, those women.'

With a jolt, Alexandra realised that she hadn't even thought about her former best girlfriends, who had ended up her enemies. She had been focused on Tom Conners, but now she realised she must throw them into the equation. Her mother was right, they were an excellent reason to stay away from Paris. They were bound to be at the party . . . Anya would have invited them as well as her. Together, the four of them had been her greatest pride the year of their graduation.

'You're right, Mom, I have no desire to see them,' Alexa said. 'But they're not the reason I don't want to go to Paris. It's someone else. Tom Conners.'

Diane leaned forward slightly, her eyes narrowing. '*Tom Conners*. Isn't he the Frenchman you introduced to us a few years ago?'

'That's right, but Tom's half-French, half-American. His father's an American who went to live in Paris in the early fifties, then married a French girl and stayed. Tom has always lived in France.'

'He's a lawyer, if I remember correctly, and very good-looking. But I didn't realise there was anything serious between the two of you. I thought it was a brief encounter, a sort of fling, if you like.'

'It lasted almost two years, actually.'

'I see.' Diane sat back, wondering how she had missed this particular relationship. On the other hand, that was the period when Alexa had lived in Paris, working with Anya's two nephews in film and theatre. However, her daughter had certainly kept quiet about Tom Conners, had confided nothing. She said slowly, 'Somehow you're still involved with Tom Conners, I think. Is that what you're trying to say?'

'No . . . Yes . . . No . . . Look, Mom, we don't see each other any more, and I never hear from him, he's never in touch, but he's sort of there . . . inside me, in my thoughts . . .' Her voice trailed off lamely and she gave her mother a helpless look.

'Why did you break off with him, Alexa?' Diane asked curiously.

'I didn't. He did. Three years ago now.'

'But *why*?' her mother pressed.

'Because I wanted to get married, and he couldn't marry me.'

'Is he married already?'

'No. Not now, not then.'

'I'm not following this at all. It doesn't make sense to me. I just don't understand what the problem is,' Diane murmured.

Very softly, Alexa said, 'Tom was married very young, to his childhood sweetheart, Juliette. They grew up together, and their parents were friends. Tom and Juliette had a little girl, Marie-Laure, and from what he told me, they were an idyllic couple, very beautiful, very happy together. And then something bad happened.'

Alexa paused, drew a deep breath, and continued, 'In July 1985 they went to Athens. On vacation. Towards the end of the vacation, Tom had to see a client who owned a summer house there. He told Juliette he would meet her and Marie-Laure for lunch at their favourite café, but Tom was delayed and got there late. It was chaotic when he walked into the square where the café was located. Police cars and ambulances were converging in the centre, and the human carnage was horrendous. Only minutes before his arrival, a terrorist bomb had exploded in front of the café where Juliette and Marie-Laure were waiting . . .'

After taking several deep breaths, she went on, 'Tom was frantic as he searched for them. He found them, eventually, under the rubble in the back of the café . . . the ceiling had collapsed on them. They were both dead.' Alexa blinked, and her voice was so low it was almost inaudible as she finished. 'He's never recovered from that . . . nightmare.'

Diane was staring at Alexa in horror, and tears had gathered in her eyes. 'How horrendous! What a terrible, terrible tragedy to happen to them, to him,' she said, and then, looking across at her daughter, she saw that Alexa's face was drained of all colour.

Rising, she went and sat next to her on the sofa, and held her close. 'Oh, darling, you're still in love with him.'

'Am I? I'm not sure, Mom, but he does occupy a large part of me, that's true. He's there, inside, and he always will be, I think. But I'm smart enough to know I have no future with Tom. He'll never marry. Nor will he have a permanent relationship, because he can't. You see, he just can't forget *them*.'

'Or he won't let himself forget,' Diane suggested softly.

'Perhaps that's true. Perhaps he thinks that if he forgets them he'll be riddled with guilt for the rest of his life and wouldn't be able to handle it. But after we broke up, I knew I couldn't moon around yearning for Tom. I understood there was no future in that.'

Diane nodded. 'You were right, and I think you've managed to get on with your professional life extremely well. I'm proud of you, Alexa. You didn't let your personal problems get in the way of your career. So, just as a matter of interest, how old is Tom?'

'He's forty-two.'

Diane nodded, searched her daughter's face intently and wondered out loud, 'Do you love Jack Wilton a little bit at least?'

'Yes, I do love him, in a certain way.'

'Not the way you love Tom?' Diane ventured.

'No.'

'You could make a life with Jack, though?'

'I think so. Jack's got a lot going for himself. He's very attractive and charming, and we get on well. We're compatible, he makes me laugh, and we understand each other, understand where the other is coming from. We admire each other's talents, and respect each other.' She half smiled at her mother. 'He loves me, you know. He wants to marry me.'

'Would you marry him?' Diane asked quietly.

Alexa leaned against her mother, and a deep sigh escaped her. Unexpectedly, tears spilled out of her eyes. Then she swiftly straightened, flicked the tears away. 'I thought I could, Mom, I really did. But now I don't know. Ever since that invitation arrived yesterday, I've been in turmoil.'

'You won't be able to resist seeing Tom if you go to Paris, is that what you're telling me?'

'I guess I am.'

After a short while, Diane said slowly, carefully, 'Here's what your loving and devoted sounding board thinks. You have to forget Tom, as you know you should. He's not for you, Alexa. What happened to his wife and child was unbearable, very, very tragic. But it *was* years ago. And if he's not over it by now—'

'He wasn't over it three years ago, but I don't know about now—'

'—then he never will be,' Diane continued in a very firm voice. 'You can make a wonderful life with Jack. And that's what you should do . . .' Diane stopped, tightened her embrace, and said against her daughter's glossy dark hair, 'There are all kinds of love, you know. And sometimes the great love of one's life is not meant to last . . . perhaps that's how it became the *great love* . . . by ending.' Diane sighed, but after a moment she went on, 'I know it's hard to give someone up. But, in fact, Tom Conners gave you up, Alexa. So why torture yourself? My advice to you is not to go to Paris. That way you won't be tempted to see Tom, and open up all those wounds.'

'I guess you're right, Mom. You usually are. But Anya's going to be really upset if I don't go to the party.'

'I'm sure she will be.' There was a slight pause, and then Diane exclaimed, 'There *is* an alternative! You and Jack could go to Paris together. Obviously, you couldn't go looking for Tom if you were there with another man.'

Want to bet? Alexandra thought, but said, 'The invitation doesn't include a guest. Only my name is written on it.'

'But she wouldn't refuse *you* . . . not if you said you were coming to Paris with your . . . fiancé.'

'I don't know what she'd do, actually. And I have to think about that, Mom, about all of what you've just said.'

The invitation stood propped up on the mantelpiece next to the carriage clock, and the first thing Alexa did when she got home was to pick it up and read it again.

Down in the left-hand corner, underneath the initials RSVP, was the date of the deadline to accept or decline: 'April 1, 2001'. And in the opposite right-hand corner it said: 'Black Tie', and underneath this: 'Long Dress'. So, she had the rest of February and most of March to decide whether to go or not. Deep down she wanted to celebrate this special birthday with Anya. But there was the problem of Tom Conners, and also of her former friends . . . Jessica, Kay and Maria. April the 1st, she mused. An anniversary of sorts, since she had met Tom Conners on April 1, 1996. She had been twenty-five, he thirty-seven.

Placing the invitation back on the mantelpiece, she knelt down in front of the fireplace, struck a match and brought it to the paper and small chips of wood in the grate. Within minutes she had the fire going, the logs catching alight quickly, the flames leaping up the chimney.

Pushing herself to her feet, Alexa turned on a lamp. Along with the fire it helped to bring a warm glow to the living room, already shadowed by the winter light of late afternoon. She sat down on the sofa in front of the fire, staring into the flames flickering and dancing in the grate. Her mind was awash with so many diverse thoughts, but the most prominent were centred on Tom. It was Nicky Sedgwick who had introduced them, when Tom had come out to the studios in Billancourt to see his client Alain Durand, who was producing a movie. It was a French–American co-production, elaborate and costly. Nicky and his brother Larry were the art directors and were designing the sets, and at Anya's suggestion they had hired her as their assistant.

What a challenge the movie had been. It was a historical drama about Napoleon and Josephine, and Nicky, who was in charge, was a stickler for historical detail. He had been thrilled with her . . . with her work, her overall input, and most of all with her set designs.

The day Tom Conners had come out to the studio, shooting was going well. Alain Durand and Tom had invited the Sedgwick brothers to dinner when they wrapped for the day, and she had been included.

She was struck dumb by Tom's extraordinary looks, his charm and sophistication. He treated her with gallantry and grace, and she had been smitten with him before the dinner was over. Later that night she found herself in his arms in his car after he had driven her home. 'Spontaneous combustion' he had called it, but not very long after this he had said it was a *coup de foudre*, clap of thunder, love at first sight. Which they both knew it was.

But that easy charm and effortless grace hid a difficult man of many moods, a man who was burdened with the needless deaths of his wife and child, and by an acute sorrow he was so careful to hide in public.

Nicky had teased her about Tom at times, and once he said, 'I suppose women must find his dark Byronic moods sexy, appealing.' But it was Larry who had been the one to warn her. 'He comes to you dragging a lot of baggage behind him, emotional baggage,' Larry had pointed out. 'So watch out, and protect your flanks.'

Alexa reached for the rug on the arm of the sofa, and stretched out under it. Her thoughts stayed with Tom and their days together in Paris. Despite his moodiness and those awful bouts of sadness, their relationship had always been good, even ecstatic when he shed the burdens of his past. And it had ended only because she had wanted permanence with him. Marriage. Children.

He was forty-two now, and still unmarried, she felt certain of that. What a waste, she thought, and closed her eyes, craving sleep. She wanted to forget Tom and her feelings for him. She was never going back to Paris. Not even for Anya Sedgwick's eighty-fifth birthday.

Chapter Two

I REMEMBER DANCING with him here, right in the centre of this room, under the chandelier, she thought. Her arms outstretched, as if she were holding a man, Kay Lenox turned and whirled to the strains of a waltz playing in her head. She moved gracefully, and the expression on her delicate face was rhapsodic, lost as she was in her thoughts.

Memories flooded her. Memories of a man who had loved and cherished her, a man who had been an adoring husband, but who had changed.

He denied her charge that he was different in his behaviour towards her, insisting that she was imagining things. But she knew she was not. There had been a cooling off in him; it was as if he no longer loved her quite as much as before. Always attentive and solicitous, he now appeared to be distracted, even careless, forgetting to tell her if he planned to work late or attend a business dinner. He would phone her at the very last minute, giving no thought to her, leaving her high and dry for the evening.

Kay had never believed it possible that a man such as Ian Andrews would marry her. But their courtship had been idyllic, and so had the first two and a half years of their marriage, which had been a dream come true. These were the memories that assailed her now as she moved round the room. She recalled his boyishness, his enthusiasm for life, and his charm. He had swept her off her feet and into marriage within a month of their first meeting. Startled though she had been, she had not objected; she had been madly in love with him. It also suited her purpose to marry quickly. She had much to hide.

A discreet cough intruded, brought her out of her reverie and to a standstill. She glanced at the door and gave Hazel, the cook at Lochcraigie, a nervous half-smile.

'Sorry to intrude, Lady Andrews, but I was wondering about dinner.' The cook hesitated. 'Will his lordship be here tonight?'

'Yes, Hazel, he will,' Kay answered, her tone confident. 'Did you see the dinner menu I left?'

'Yes, I did, Lady Andrews.' The cook inclined her head and left.

But *will* he be here? Kay asked herself, walking to the window where she stood looking out across the lawns and trees towards the hills that edged along the pale blue skyline. After breakfast he had announced that he was going into Edinburgh to buy a birthday gift for his sister Fiona, and it was true that it was her birthday tomorrow and they were seeing her for Sunday lunch. But she couldn't help wondering why he hadn't asked her to pick something out, since she went to her studio in the city three days a week.

Turning away from the window, Kay walked across the terracotta tiled floor, heading for the huge stone hearth. She stood with her back to the fire, thinking, as always, what a strange room this was. It was a conservatory that had been added on to one end of the house, and it had been built by Ian's great-great-grandmother in Victorian times. It was airy and light because of its many windows, yet it had a cosiness that was due to the stone fireplace, an unusual addition in a conservatory, but necessary because of the cold winter weather. The potted plants and wicker furniture painted dark brown gave it a garden mood, but a few choice antiques added a sense of permanence.

Kay bit her lip, thinking about Ian. She knew why there had been this moving away . . . it was because she had not conceived. He was desperate for a child, for an heir to this house, where the Andrews family had lived for 500 years. And so far she had not been able to give him one.

'My fault,' she whispered to herself, thinking of what had happened to her when she was a teenager in Glasgow. A shudder passed through her slender frame, and she turned bodily to the fire. Lowering herself onto a leather-topped club fender, she stared into the flames, her face suddenly drawn, her eyes pensive. Yet despite the sadness, there was no denying her exceptional beauty, and with her ivory complexion, eyes as blue as speedwells and red-gold hair that shimmered in the firelight, she was a true Celt. But at this moment Kay Lenox Andrews was not thinking about her beauty, or her immense talent, which had brought her so far in her young life, but of the ugliness and degradation of her past.

When she looked back, growing up in the Gorbals, the slums of Glasgow, had been an education in itself. There were times when Kay wondered whether she might have been a different person if her early environment had not been quite so harsh. When she was a teenager, she was driven by her need to get out of the Gorbals. Fortunately, her mother, Alice Smith, felt the same way, and it was Alice who had pushed her out into the bigger world. 'I want you to have a better life than I've had,' Alice always said. 'You've got looks, brains, and an amazing talent. There's nothing to stop you . . . but yourself. So I'm hoping to make certain you succeed, lass.'

Her mother had plotted, scrimped and saved to fulfil her special plans for her daughter. Eventually, all that striving and sacrifice had paid off. Kay was launched with a new identity—a stunningly beautiful young woman of background, breeding and education, about to become a fashion designer of taste and flair.

I wouldn't have made it to where I am today without Mam, Kay now thought as she left the conservatory and walked towards the front hall. It was a vast open space, with a cathedral ceiling and a double staircase with carved balustrades, which ran up to the wide upper hall. The main feature of the latter was a soaring stained-glass window which bathed the front hall below in multicoloured light.

She took the left-hand side of the staircase, running up to the first floor, where her design studio was located in what had once been the day nursery at Lochcraigie. As she opened the door and went in on this bitter February morning, she was glad to see that Maude, the housekeeper, already had a fire burning brightly in the grate. The high-ceilinged, tall-windowed room was flooded with the cool northern light she loved. In this crystalline light all colours were *true*, and that made her designing so much easier.

Stepping towards the old Jacobean refectory table that served as her desk, she reached over and picked up the phone as it began to ring. 'Lochcraigie House,' she said, walking round to her high-backed chair and sitting down.

'It's me, Kay,' Sophie McPherson, her assistant, said.

'Hello, Sophie. Is something wrong?'

'No, nothing. Why? Oh, you mean because I'm calling on Saturday? No, all's well with the world, as far as I know. At least it is in mine.'

Kay smiled. Sophie was a joy to work with, and at twenty-three she was bursting with talent, enthusiasm and ideas.

Dropping her voice, Sophie now said confidingly, 'I called because I finally got that information for you.'

'What information?'

'About the man my sister Gillian recently heard of . . . You know, we discussed it two weeks ago.'

'Oh, yes, of course. Sorry, Sophie, I guess I'm being a little bit stupid today.' She clutched the receiver more tightly.

'His name is François Boujon, and he lives in France.'

'Where exactly?'

'A place just outside Paris called Barbizon. Do you want to know everything now, or shall I tell you on Monday?'

'Monday's fine, I'll be at the studio by about ten. But tell me one thing now . . . is he difficult to get an appointment with?'

'Yes, a bit, I'm afraid. But Gillian will help.'

'I'm very appreciative, Sophie, I really am. Thank you for going to all this trouble.'

'I was happy to do it. So, I'll see you Monday then.'

'That's right. Have a good weekend.'

'I will, and you do the same.'

'I'll try,' Kay answered, and after saying goodbye, she returned the phone to its cradle. Resting her head against the faded red velvet covering the chair back, she suddenly remembered the letter that had arrived yesterday, and she reached for the decorative wooden box on one end of the desk. Lifting the lid, she took out the envelope with its beautiful calligraphy and slipped out the invitation.

Once again she read it carefully. Anya's party was on June 2, four months away. She wondered whether she could get an appointment with François Boujon for around that time.

It would be perfect if she could, because Ian hadn't been invited, and so she could travel alone to Paris. Kill two birds with one stone, she thought, and then she sat back in the chair with a jerk, frowning hard. *They* would be there and she would have to see them. No, not only see them, but socialise with them, spend time with them. Not possible. And the feeling was mutual.

Alexandra Gordon, the snob from New York. From the elite social set. Always so toffee-nosed with her, stuck up, snubbing *her*.

Jessica Pierce, Miss Southern Belle Incorporated, with her feminine sighs and languor. Poking fun at *her*, teasing her unmercifully.

Maria Franconi, another snob, this one from Italy, with her raven hair and flashing black eyes and fiery Mediterranean temperament, flaunting her money and her connections, treating *her* like a servant.

How miserable they had always made her life. No, Kay told herself, I cannot go to Anya's party.

She knew what she must do. She must go to Paris sooner rather than later, to meet this man François Boujon. With luck she would get an appointment quickly. It did not matter what it cost.

She put the invitation back in the envelope and placed it in the wooden box. Then, once more she leaned back in her chair, her eyes becoming soft and faraway as she thought of Ian. The man she loved. Her husband . . . who must remain her husband at all costs.

Even as a child, Kay had always managed to escape simply by retreating into herself. When the cramped little flat where she lived with her mother and brother, Sandy, became oppressive, she would find a small corner where she could curl up, forget where she really was, and dream. And she always dreamed of beauty—flower-filled gardens, picturesque country cottages with thatched roofs, grassy meadows awash with wild flowers, and grand open spaces with huge, canopied green trees where trilling birdsong came alive.

But as she grew older, Kay replaced her dreams with focus and concentration, and it was these two qualities, plus her unique talent, that helped to make her such a great success in the world of fashion.

Now, as she sat at her desk, thoughts of Ian nagged at the back of her mind. But eventually she let go of her worries about her marriage and became totally engrossed in her work.

After looking through a few sketches for her autumn collection, which she had just finished, she rose and went over to the swatches of fabric hanging on brass hooks attached to the opposite wall. A piece of vermilion wool attracted her attention, and she unclipped it and carried it over to the window, where she scrutinised it intently. In her mind's eye she saw a series of outfits, each one in a different version of vivid vermilion red. She thought of cyclamen first, then deep pink, the colour of peonies, pale pinks borrowed from a bunch of sweet peas, bright red lifted from a pot of geraniums, and all of those other reds sharpened by a hint of blue. And mixed in with them she could see a selection of blues —cerulean, delphinium and aquamarine—as well as deep violet and pansy hues, a softer lilac and the lavender shade of hydrangeas.

That's it, she thought, instantly filling with excitement. A winter collection of clothes based on those two colours—red and blue—interspersed with other tones. What a change from the beiges, browns, greens, taupes and terracottas of her spring season.

Turning away from the window, Kay went over to the other fabric samples and searched through them quickly, looking for the colours she now wanted to use. She found a few and carried them to her desk, where she spread them out. Then she began to match the colour samples to the sketches she had already done for her winter line, envisioning a coat, a suit or a dress in one of the reds, purples or blues.

At twenty-nine Kay Lenox was one of the best-known young fashion designers on both sides of the Atlantic. The clothes she designed were elegant, but in a relaxed and casual manner, and they were extremely well cut and beautifully made.

The fabrics Kay favoured gave her clothes a great sense of luxury—the finest light wools, cashmeres, wool crepes, soft Scottish tweeds, suede, leather, crushed velvet, and a heavy silk which she bought in France. Her flair and imagination were visible in the way she mixed these fabrics with one another in her garments—the result a look unique to her.

Kay worked on steadily through the morning, and so concentrated was she, and focused on her designs, she almost jumped out of her skin when the phone next to her elbow jangled.

Picking it up, she said, 'Lochcraigie,' in a sharpish tone.

'Hello, darling,' her husband answered. '*You* sound a bit snotty this morning.'

'Ian!' she exclaimed, her face lighting up. 'Sorry, I was lost in a dress, figuratively speaking.'

He chuckled. 'Is your designing going well, then?'

'I'll say, and I had a brainstorm earlier. I'm doing the entire winter collection in shades of red running through palest pink to violet.'

'Sounds good to me.'

'Did you find a gift for Fiona?'

There was a moment's hesitation before he said, sounding vague, 'Oh, yes, I did.'

'So you're on your way home now?'

'Not exactly,' he replied. 'Er, well, I'm a bit peckish, so I'm going to have a spot of lunch. I should be back about fourish.'

The brightness in her vivid blue eyes dimmed slightly, but she said, 'All right, then. I'll be here waiting for you.'

'We'll have tea together,' he murmured. 'Bye, darling.'

He hung up before she could say another word. She stared at the receiver in her hand, and then went back to work.

Later that afternoon, when she had eaten a smoked salmon sandwich and drunk a mug of lemon tea, Kay put on a cream fisherman's-knit sweater, thick woollen socks and green Wellington boots. In the cloakroom near the back door she took down her dark green coat of quilted silk, pushed her red-gold hair under a red knitted cap, added a matching scarf and gloves and went outside.

She was hit by a blast of freezing air, and it took her breath away, but her clothes were warm, the coat in particular, and she set out towards the loch, in need of fresh air and exercise.

This was one of her favourite walks on the estate. A wide path led down from the cutting garden just beyond the back door, past broad lawns, and thick woods bordering one side of the lawns. In the distance was the narrow body of glassy water that was Loch Craigie.

At one moment Kay stopped and stood staring across at the distant hills, partially obscured this afternoon by a hazy mist on their peaks and lightly covered in snow. Then she turned her head, her eyes settling on the great stone house where she lived, built in 1559 by William Andrews, the laird of Lochcraigie. From that time onwards, the eldest son had inherited everything through the law of primogeniture, and fortunately there had always been a male heir. An unbroken line for centuries. Ian was the laird now, although only a few old-timers from his grandfather's day, who were still living in the village, addressed him by that title.

Aside from these lands, the Andrews family had interests in manufacturing, publishing and textiles. Everything belonged to Ian, but he was a low-profile millionaire content to lead the quiet country life.

Kay began to walk again, striding out at a steady pace, her eyes thoughtful as she contemplated her own past. She couldn't help wondering what Ian would say if he knew of her mean and poverty-stricken beginnings. He would be horrified, disbelieving . . .

She let these thoughts float away and took several deep breaths. Her troubles had begun when she was a teenager, but she had always known they would end. Now she had everything she had ever wanted, had ever dreamed about . . . a husband who was not only young and handsome but an aristocrat, a big career as a fashion designer, fame, success . . .

But no child.

No heir for Ian.

She sighed under her breath as she approached the loch. The body of water was flat and grey, leaden under the wintry sky, and she did not plan to linger long. The air had grown much colder and there was a hint of snow on the wind. But she walked along the edge of the water for fifteen minutes, enjoying the tranquil view and the all-pervasive sense of peace.

On her way back, she took the paved path that led her past the Dower House where Ian's mother lived. For a moment she thought of dropping in to see her mother-in-law, Margaret, but changed her mind. It was almost four o'clock and Ian would be home soon. She had plans for tonight, big plans, and she wanted him to be in the right frame of mind. If she were absent when he arrived, he could be put out.

She passed the Dower House and climbed the narrow steps, then ran across the lawn to the terrace in front of the conservatory. A second later she let herself into the house.

Kay knew at once that Ian was in a good mood as he walked into the conservatory just after four. When she went to greet him he hugged her close and kissed her cheek. 'You look bonny,' he said.

She smiled. 'Thank you, Ian. Would you like a cup of tea?'

He nodded as he moved away and stood with his back to the fire. 'It was a long drive home, and I thought I was going to hit snow, but so far it's held off.'

'Not quite,' Kay said, and pointedly looked towards the French doors. 'It's just started.'

He followed her gaze, and saw the snowflakes coming down, and heavily. He laughed and said, 'It looks as if we might get snowed in! Let's have that tea.'

They sat down in front of the fire, where the housekeeper had left tea on a tray. Kay poured for them both, looking across at Ian surreptitiously as she did so.

He appeared to be happier and more light-hearted this afternoon than he had for a while. He also looked unusually boyish, but perhaps that was because his fair hair was tousled from the wind. 'Actually, I hope the snow doesn't stick,' he said. 'It really would be quite awful if we had to cancel tomorrow's birthday lunch for Fiona.'

Kay nodded in agreement. 'Let's not worry about the lunch now. I heard a weather report earlier on the radio, and it's supposed to be sunny tomorrow, and also much warmer.'

Ian smiled at her, and surveyed the tray of finger sandwiches and fancy cakes.

'By the way, Ian, what did you end up getting Fiona?'

'What do you mean?'

Kay gave him a baffled look. 'The gift, for her birthday. What is it?'

'Oh, yes . . . a pair of earrings. I'll show them to you later.'

They fell into a companionable silence, sipping their tea and eating the finger sandwiches and cream cakes in front of the blazing fire. Kay couldn't help feeling taut inside, even though Ian appeared to be so relaxed and at ease with himself and with her. She planned to seduce him later, planned a night of lovemaking, and it was important that he be in the right mood.

Kay broke the silence when she confided, 'I received an invitation yesterday . . . an invitation to Anya Sedgwick's eighty-fifth birthday party in Paris.'

'I don't have to go too, do I?' Ian asked, suddenly frowning, looking worried. 'You know how I hate travelling.'

'No, of course not,' she answered quickly. 'I'm not going either.'

Ian stared at her, puzzled and surprised. 'Why ever not?'

'I don't really want to see people I haven't seen for seven years . . . I lost touch with my friends when I graduated.'

'But you've always admired Anya.'

'That's true. She's the most fascinating woman I've ever met.'

'Well, then?' He raised a sandy brow.

'I don't know . . .'

'I think you should go to her party, Kay, just out of respect.'

'Perhaps you're right. I'll think about it.'

By the time they had finished their tea the snow had settled on the ground, and it was continuing to fall steadily. It was growing darker, the dusky twilight of late afternoon long since obliterated, and already a few sparse early stars sprinkled the sky.

But in the snug conservatory, the fire roared in the stone hearth; the table lamps cast a lovely lambent glow throughout and in the background music played softly.

The two of them had been silent for a while, and at one moment Ian looked across at Kay intently, his eyes narrowing. 'You're very quiet this afternoon, and you look awfully pensive. Sad, even. Is something the matter, darling? What are you brooding about?'

Kay roused herself from her thoughts, and shook her head. 'Just thinking . . . people *do* suffer for love, don't they?'

His brows drew together in a small frown, but his expression was hard to read. After a split second he answered her. 'I suppose some do.' He shrugged. 'What exactly are you getting at?'

Kay murmured, 'Your mother once told me that suffering for love is a noble thing. Do you agree with her?'

Ian burst out laughing. 'I'm not so sure I do! My mother is something of a romantic, always has been, always will be, just like you are. But come to think of it, no, I don't want to *suffer* for love. No, not at all. I want to relish it, enjoy it, wallow in it.'

'With me?' A red-gold brow lifted provocatively.

'Is that an invitation?' he asked, eyeing her keenly.

She simply smiled, but beguilingly.

Ian rose and crossed the room, took hold of her hands and brought her to her feet. And then he led her over to the fireplace, pulled her down onto the rug with him. He smoothed his hand over her hair, shimmering in the fire's glow, and held strands of it between his fingers. 'Look at this . . . Celtic gold . . . it's beautiful, Kay.' He removed her cardigan and then began to unbutton her white silk blouse, leaned forward, kissed her cheek, her neck and her mouth.

But after only a moment, Kay pushed him away. 'Ian, stop! We can't. Not *here*! Someone might come in.'

He laughed dismissively. But, nonetheless, he got up and walked over to the door set in the wall, to the right of the fireplace.

Risk, Kay thought. He loves taking risks. And I mustn't fight him now. He wants to make love . . . I must seize this moment. She heard him locking the door, and his footsteps echoing on the terracotta tiles as he came back to her.

Ian knelt on the floor next to Kay. He took her face in both his hands, brought his lips to hers gently, gave her a light kiss.

'What about the French doors?' she asked.

'Nobody's going to be out in this weather.'

Ian had taken off her blouse, and was now fumbling with the hooks on her bra. She helped him to unfasten it, then reached out for him, pulled him into her arms. They fell back on the rug together, and she kissed him deeply. He responded with ardour, and then sat up, pulled off his sweater, struggled out of his shirt, and threw them impatiently to one side. Within a few seconds they were both completely undressed, naked on the rug in front of the fire.

'I want you,' she whispered against his neck, and her long, tapering fingers went up into his hair. 'Take me, take me.'

He wanted her as much as she wanted him, but he also wanted to prolong their lovemaking. And so he kissed her very slowly, almost languorously, and thrilled when her mouth opened under his. He felt her tongue groping for his, and he was more inflamed than ever.

As he began to caress her breasts, her hands moved down over his broad back and settled on his buttocks. Now, as Kay began to move against him, her whole body radiating a desire for him he had not seen in her before, he could hardly contain himself. Excited beyond endurance, he felt every fibre of his being exploding as he tumbled into her warmth and she welcomed him ecstatically.

Well past midnight, Kay curled up in a comfortable chair near the fireplace in the master bedroom. Like the rest of the rooms in this great stone manse, the bedroom had a grandeur and dignity about it.

Of spacious proportions, it had eight windows, one placed on each side of the central fireplace and three set in each end wall. The fireplace itself was also grand and soaring, with an oversized iron grate to hold big logs and slabs of peat. Its mahogany mantelpiece matched the dark beams that floated across the ceiling.

Set against the main wall, and facing the fireplace, stood the mahogany four-poster bed, with its carved posts, rose silk hangings and coverlet. Ian was fast asleep. She could hear the faint rise and fall of his deep breathing; the only other sounds in the room were the crackle of the logs in the grate and the ticking of the old grandfather clock in the corner.

She had been overwhelmed by his passion tonight. He had been unable to get enough of her. She had found herself responding in kind, meeting his passionate sexual needs head-on, as wild and demanding as he was. Hope rose in her that she had conceived.

Kay wanted a child as much as her husband did, not that Ian ever made reference to his longing for a son. But she knew, deep within herself, how much he yearned for an heir, a boy to follow in his footsteps as the Laird of Lochcraigie.

What would happen if she didn't conceive? Not ever? Would he divorce her and find another woman to bear him a son? Or would he shrug and hope that his sister Fiona would marry, and provide a male child to inherit the title and vast family holdings? The awful thing was, she had no idea what Ian would do.

Rising, Kay walked over to the window and looked out. It was still snowing; there was a high wind that sent the crystalline flakes whirling about, and on the ground they were still settling. There was a blanket of white below, and under the pale moon this pristine coverlet seemed woven with silver threads. The wind rattled the windows all of a sudden, but the house stood firm and solid as it always had. Well over four hundred years ago, William Andrews of Lochcraigie had built a manse that had defied time and the harsh Scottish winters.

If only she had someone to talk to, Kay thought, pressing her face against the cold windowpane. She had never discussed their childlessness with Ian, for fear of opening Pandora's box, or with her mother-in-law for the same reason. If only Mam were still alive, she thought, and unexpectedly a surge of emotion choked her. Her mother had made her what she was, and put her where she was, in a sense, but her mam was no longer around to reap the benefits or share the joy. Her brother Sandy was long gone, having emigrated to Australia eight years before, and she never heard from him any more. Sadly.

I have no friends, at least not close friends, she realised, and thought instantly of Alexandra Gordon. They had been so very close once, until their terrible quarrel. Sometimes, when she wasn't closing her mind to those wonderful days at Anya's school, memories of Alexa enveloped her, and she found herself missing the American girl.

A long, rippling sigh escaped from her throat, and she felt a sadness settle over her. But there *was* Anya Sedgwick. She had always been good to her, not only as a teacher and mentor, but as a true friend, almost like a loving mother. Perhaps she should go to Anya's party after all. If she went a few days prior to the party she could meet with Anya privately, unburden herself perhaps. But why wait until June, she now wondered. And thought instantly of François Boujon. Once she had an appointment with him she could make a date for lunch or tea or dinner with Anya, who would be thrilled to see her, she had no doubts about that.

Suddenly, boldly, Kay made a decision. She would go to the party anyway. Out of respect for Anya, as Ian had suggested earlier.

Chapter Three

JESSICA PIERCE WAS IN A FURY. She stood in the elegant den of her Bel-Air house, looking down at her boyfriend Gary Stennis. He was almost falling off the cream velvet sofa, sprawled out across the cushions, dead drunk.

Her cool grey eyes, always keen and observant, swept round the room. Everything looked undisturbed, except for the jumble of things he had managed to accumulate on the low, antique Chinese coffee table in front of the fireplace. The unusual ebony table, beautifully inlaid with mother-of-pearl orange-blossom trees, was littered with highball glasses, one of her best Baccarat crystal goblets, a bottle of Stolichnaya Cristall, half-full, and an empty bottle of her Château Simard Saint-Emilion 1988. One of my better red wines, she thought, as her eyes settled on an antique Lalique crystal dish. With a flash of irritation she saw that it had been used as an ashtray.

A sudden frown furrowed her brow, and she leaned closer to the coffee table, staring at the crystal goblet. It bore traces of lipstick on the rim. But it had been a business meeting, of that she felt sure. Pages of Gary's new script were scattered on the floor, along with a yellow legal pad with scrawled notes in his handwriting.

Straightening, now focusing all of her attention on Gary, she studied him for a long moment through dispassionate eyes. His salt-and-pepper hair was mussed, his face was gaunt and pale, with dark smudges under his eyes. In sleep, he looked curiously old, worn out.

Washed up, she thought, and felt a tinge of sadness.

But no, he wasn't that. At least, not yet.

Gary was still a brilliant screenwriter, and his past was filled with tunes of glory. And Oscars. He had written many of the greatest screenplays ever put on celluloid. He had made and lost several fortunes, married and divorced two movie stars, and, with one, fathered a daughter who no longer spoke to him. Now, he was courting Jessica and entreating her to marry him. When he was sober.

Quite frequently these days he was drunk. And because of this addiction, she knew deep down she would never marry him. On two occasions Jessica had thrown him out, but he had managed to charm his way back into her life. Well, he was charm personified, everyone knew that, and *the* master when it came to words. He had earned millions and millions from his words, hadn't he?

'Don't forget, he's a writer, he knows exactly what to say to press your buttons,' her friend Merle was always saying.

Jessica turned swiftly on her high heels, went out of the den and closed the door quietly behind her. She had been in Santa Barbara for five days, supervising an installation at a client's new house, and Gary had promised her dinner tête-à-tête at home . . . no matter what time she arrived. He was a great chef when he wanted to be, and a great lover when he was sober. But she was furious with him for being in this inebriated state, and the best thing was to let him sleep it off.

When she reached the circular front hall, with its glassy black granite floor and elegant curving staircase, Jessica picked up her bags and headed upstairs. As she went into her dressing room, she caught sight of herself in one of the four mirrors. Stepping closer, she moved her long blonde hair back over her shoulders, then straightened her jacket. What she saw was a tall young woman of thirty-one, not bad-looking, quite elegant in a white gabardine trouser-suit and high-heeled mules, with a string of pearls round her neck and pearl studs on her ears. But it's a tired woman tonight, she muttered, then went back downstairs.

Jessica's brown leather handbag was on a Louis IV bench in the front hall. Picking it up, she hurried down the carpeted corridor to her office.

She turned on the light switch and moved forward to her eighteenth-century bureau in front of the window. The first thing she saw, propped against a Chinese-yellow porcelain lamp, was a FedEx envelope.

Jessica sat staring at the invitation for a long time, lost in her thoughts as she found herself carried back into the past.

A decade fell away. She was young, just twenty-one, and starting out at the Anya Sedgwick School of Decorative Arts, Design and Couture, where she had gone to study interior design. In her mind she could see herself as she was then . . . tall, very thin, with straight blonde hair falling to her shoulder blades. A small-town Texas girl on her first visit to Europe. She had been captivated by Paris, the school, Anya, and the little family *pension* on the Left Bank where she lived. It had all been new and exciting, and far removed from San Antonio.

And it was in Paris that she had met and fallen in love with Lucien Girard. It had been at the end of her first year that she and Lucien were introduced by Larry Sedgwick, Anya's nephew. She was just twenty-two; he was four years older, an actor by profession.

She and Lucien had been a perfect match, completely compatible. They liked the same movies, books, music and art, and got on so well it was almost uncanny. They shared the same philosophy of life, wanted similar things and were ambitious for themselves.

Their days together had been golden, filled with blue skies and sunshine, tranquil days and passion-filled nights.

He had taught her so much . . . about so many different things . . . sex and love . . . the best wines and food, and how to savour them. With him she had eaten mussels in a delicious tangy broth, omelettes so light and fluffy they were like air, soft aromatic cheeses from the countryside, and tiny *fraises de bois*, minuscule wild strawberries fragrant with an indefinable perfume, sumptuous to eat with thick clotted cream.

With him everything was bliss.

He had called her his long-stemmed American beauty, had utterly loved and adored her, as she had him. They had made so many plans . . .

But one day he was gone.

Lucien disappeared.

Teaming up with his best friend Alain Bonnal, Jessica tried to find him. His apartment was undisturbed, nothing had been removed. He was an orphan; they knew of no family member to go to for information. She and Alain checked hospitals, the morgue, listed him as a missing person. To no avail. He was never found.

Suddenly jumping up, Jessica hurried across the office to a large

French *armoire*, opened the drawer at the bottom and pulled out a red leather photograph album. Carrying it back to the desk, she sat down, opened the album and began turning the pages. It was a full and complete record of her three years in Paris studying interior design.

There we are, Lucien and me, she thought, staring down at a photograph of them on the banks of the Seine. She was struck by their similarities; Lucien had been tall and slender also, with fair colouring and bluish-grey eyes. The love of my life, she thought, and turned the page.

Here were she and Alexa, Kay, Maria and Anya, in the garden of Anya's house. And here was a fun picture of Nicky and Larry clowning it up with Alexa, and Maria looking mournful at the back. Jessica experienced a feeling of great sadness . . . Lucien had disappeared and everything had gone wrong after that. They had quarrelled and disbanded. And it had all been so . . . so . . . silly and juvenile.

Jessica closed the album. If she went to Anya's party she would run into her former friends. And could she actually face being in Paris? She didn't know. Paris was Lucien. Lucien no longer existed.

Accept the invitation. Go to Paris, just for the hell of it, she told herself. Then changed her mind instantly. No, decline. You're only going to open up old wounds.

Jessica closed her eyes, leaning back in the chair. Her memories of Paris and Lucien were golden, filled with happiness and a joy she had not experienced since her days with him. Better to keep the memories intact. She would send her regrets.

Gary said from the doorway of her office, 'So you finally decided to come home.'

Startled, Jessica swung round in the chair and stared at him. He was leaning against the doorjamb wearing crumpled clothes and a belligerent expression.

He's an angry drunk, she thought, but said, 'You look as if you've been ridden hard and put away wet.'

He frowned, never having liked her southern Texan humour. 'Why did you get back so late?' he demanded.

'What difference does it make? You had passed out dead drunk on my sofa.'

He let out a long sigh and slid into the room, came to stand by her chair, suddenly smiling down at her. 'I guess we got to celebrating. Harry and Phil were crazy about the first draft of the script, and after making our notes, a few changes, we were pretty sure it was almost good enough to be a shooting script. So . . . we decided to celebrate—'

'I guess it just got out of hand.'

'No. You just got back very late.'

'Nine o'clock isn't all that late.'

'Why *were* you late? Did Mark Sylvester detain you . . . in some way?' He cocked a dark brow and glared.

'Don't be so ridiculous! And I don't like the innuendo. He wasn't even there. I was late because there was a lot of traffic on the Santa Barbara Freeway. And how was Gina?'

'Gina?' Gary frowned, then sat down on the sofa.

'Don't tell me Gina wasn't here tonight, she's always at your script meetings. She drinks my best red wine and leaves her lipstick on the wineglass. Harry hasn't taken to wearing lipstick, has he?'

'Your sarcasm is wasted on me, Jessica. And I fail to understand why you're always so hard on her. Gina's been my assistant for years.'

And partner in bed when you see fit, she thought, then said, 'This ain't my first rodeo . . . I know what's what.'

Gary leapt to his feet, colour flooding his face. He looked apoplectic as he said, 'I can see the frame of mind you're in, and I'm not staying around to get in the way of your whip, missy. I'm going to my place. I'll get my stuff tomorrow. See you around, kid.'

Jessica stared at him coldly, understanding, suddenly, how truly tired she was of having him use her. And misuse her house.

He strode out and slammed the office door behind him. A moment later she heard the front door bang and the screech of wheels as he drove out of her front yard at breakneck speed. And at this moment, Jessica Pierce realised that she didn't care.

She opened the red leather album and turned the pages, glancing through the photographs of her three years in Paris. How young we all looked, she thought. Young, innocent, with life ahead of us . . . how unconcerned we were about the future . . . about our lives.

'Lucien,' she murmured, tracing a finger over his face in the photograph of them together by the Seine. 'What happened to you?'

To Jessica the Pacific had never looked more beautiful. The deepest of blues, glittering brilliantly in the afternoon sunlight, it was dazzling to the eye as it stretched into infinity. It was Monday afternoon, and she was sitting in a small, antique gazebo at the tip of Mark Sylvester's property in Santa Monica.

On a bluff facing the sea, the gazebo was a peaceful spot, a place for reflection and tranquillity, as she had known it would be. Mark loved it, just as he loved the new house. She had been quite certain he would approve, but it was a relief to know he was thrilled with it. He was moving in next weekend, and today she had walked him through for the first time since the furnishings had been installed.

Everything's gone right with the house, everything's gone wrong in my personal life, she thought, her mind settling on Gary. So be it, she decided suddenly. I must get on with my life; move on. Slowly, she stood up and left the gazebo, walking up towards the house, through the beautiful landscaped gardens.

Shimmering in the sunlight was a Palladian villa of incomparable symmetry and style. Built of white stone, it had the classic temple façade of arches and columns made famous by Andrea Palladio, the Renaissance architect. Jessica had worked very closely with the architect to achieve what she knew Mark wanted. Once the house had been completed, she had decorated the interiors in her inimitable and distinctive style, using lots of pastel colours and cream and white, for the most part. Her well-known signature was a room based on a monochromatic colour scheme, the finest antique furniture and art money could buy, combined with luxurious fabrics and carpets. Since Mark had given her carte blanche and an unlimited budget, she had been able to create a house of extraordinary beauty and style, totally lacking in pretension.

Walking along the terrace, Jessica opened the French doors leading into the library, and found herself face to face with Mark.

'Where did you disappear to?' he asked, curiously.

'You became so involved with a business call, I thought I'd better leave you in peace. I went for a walk.'

'You could have stayed,' he replied, and sat down on a sofa.

She took a seat on the opposite sofa, and said, 'I enjoyed a few minutes of perfect quiet, just watching the ocean.'

'It's a great spot.' He eyed her for a moment, before saying, 'You've looked troubled all morning, Jessica. Want to talk?'

'Not sure,' she murmured.

'He's been round the block too many times for you, and he's—' Mark cut himself off, stared at her, suddenly looking chagrined.

She stared back at him, her eyes wide with surprise.

'I'm sorry, Jessica. It's none of my business.'

'No, no, it's OK,' she said, offering him a small smile. 'I was staring at you only because I'd thought the same thing myself yesterday. I'm afraid Gary and I are at odds at the moment, and I'm not sure the situation will change.'

'Leopards and their spots, and all that,' Mark volunteered, and shook his head. 'I guess he's drinking again.'

'No, no, it's not that,' Jessica was quick to say. 'To tell you the truth, it's partially my fault. I've been so involved with my work in the last six months, I'm afraid he's come in for a bit of neglect. Also, I think we've just grown apart.'

'That can happen when there are two careers going strong.' He rose and walked over to the built-in bar at one end of the library.' Would you like something to drink? A Coke? Water?'

'I'll have a cranberry juice, please, Mark.' She laughed. 'I know there's a bottle there, I put it in the refrigerator on Saturday morning.'

He nodded, stood for a moment pouring their drinks, wondering why Jessica had ever become involved with Gary Stennis in the first place. She deserved so much better. Once, in his opinion, Gary had been the greatest scriptwriter, but the booze and the women had taken their toll, laid him out flat at times. Life could be pretty tough on the fast track of Hollywood fame and fortune, accolades and alcohol.

As Mark walked back across the room he couldn't help thinking what a good-looking woman Jessica was. She wore a pale lavender-coloured suit with a shortish skirt and very high-heeled shoes. He had always admired her long silky legs, and her colouring was superb.

'Thanks, Mark,' she said as he put the drink in front of her on the glass-topped coffee table.

His thoughts stayed with her as he went back to the bar to get his ginger ale. Jessica Pierce was one of the nicest people he knew. There was a sweetness and kindness in her nature that were most commendable, and which he admired. He knew that Gary was drinking heavily, and that she had avoided agreeing with him and admitting this to protect Gary in his eyes.

When he returned and sat down opposite her, Mark raised his glass. 'Cheers, Jessica. And thank you for making this place so beautiful. You're just . . . miraculous.'

She smiled at him, her eyes suddenly sparkling with pleasure. 'Thanks, Mark. I'm glad you love your new home. Cheers.' She took a sip of her drink and studied him for a moment. She knew Mark was forty-five, but he didn't look it. In fact, he seemed like a man in his mid-thirties. He was lean, tanned, somewhat athletic in appearance, with a pleasant if angular face, and very knowing, alert brown eyes. She found herself wondering for the umpteenth time why Kelly O'Keefe had left him, had sued for divorce last year. He was such a nice man; fair, reasonable and a pleasure to work with, plus he had a good reputation in Hollywood. She was aware that he was a tough businessman, which was why he was a successful producer.

Mark sat back on the sofa and crossed his long legs. 'So, what are you going to do now, Jessica?'

'I've got a couple of houses to remodel in Beverly Hills and—'

'I meant what are you going to do with your life . . . and with Gary Stennis?'

Letting out a long sigh, she slumped back on the sofa. 'I don't know. Well, that's not true. I know what I should do, and that's end the relationship. It's over really, Mark, it's just a case of easing out of it.'

'I've known Gary for years, and he's always been self-destructive. There's no way you can ease out of this situation. You've got to bail out. Just go. Take a deep breath and jump.'

'I guess you're right about that. Pussyfooting around doesn't solve a thing, and it can be more painful in the long run.'

'You'd better believe it, Jess.'

She nodded, and then changing the subject, she asked, 'And what are you going to do now you've got your new movie in the can?'

'There's a play I want to buy. It's dramatic, and it would make a good movie. My kind of movie. I'll be going to see the playwright in about two weeks. Then I'm going to Paris on some other business.'

'I just received an invitation to go to a party in Paris.'

His eyes lit up, and he exclaimed, 'Will we be there at the same time?'

'I don't know. I don't think so. My party is on June the 2nd. It's for my former teacher, who's going to be eighty-five.'

'Sounds great, but I'll probably have left Paris by then. What a pity.'

She half smiled, then turned her head, looking across at a painting.

Observing her intently, Mark said, 'You've got that sad look on your face again.'

'Receiving the invitation sent me spinning backwards in time, and it opened up old wounds. I haven't been quite the same since.'

'Brought back memories, did it?'

'Yes.' Unexpectedly, tears filled her eyes.

Mark leaned forward. 'Hey, honey, what's all this? Tears? It has to be a man.' A dark brow lifted questioningly.

Jessica could only nod.

'An old love . . . a broken romance . . . yearning for him? Do you want to talk about it? I have a good strong ear for listening.'

Sighing, she said slowly, 'Yes, an old love, a wonderful love. We made so many plans. And then it ended.'

'From the sound of your voice, he broke up with you.'

'No, one day he disappeared. It was just as if he'd dropped off the edge of the world without a trace. I never saw him again.' Speaking slowly and carefully, she told Mark everything there was to tell about Lucien Girard: their first meeting, their relationship, and how she and Alain Bonnal had tried so hard to find him after his disappearance.

When she had finished, Mark said in a thoughtful tone, 'We have two choices here. Either he was killed and his body disposed of remarkably well, or he chose to disappear on purpose.'

'But why would he do that?' she exclaimed.

'Anyone who disappears has their own reasons for doing so. And usually it's hard to find them.'

'Someone who disappears obviously does so because they want to start a new life,' she began, then stopped. Looking across at Mark, she volunteered, 'Alain and I wondered whether he'd been mugged, or killed, and his body taken out to sea.'

'Take me through it again, Jess. The part about him saying he had to go away for a few days.'

'We were having dinner, it was the last time I saw him. Over dinner he said that he was going to Monte Carlo for a few days to shoot a commercial. We made plans for the following week.'

'Did he call you from there?'

Jessica shook her head. 'I didn't really expect him to, since I knew he'd be busy. But after a week's silence I grew anxious. I phoned his apartment, there was no answer. Then I spoke Alain. We went over to Lucien's apartment building and spoke to the concierge. She told us he was still away. And she mentioned that she had seen him leave with his suitcase.'

'And no one else had heard from him?' Mark asked quietly.

'No. Alain and I went to see his agent and he was just as baffled as we were.'

'It's all very odd. And the police never came up with anything?'

'No, they didn't. And neither did the hospitals or the morgue. Alain continued to check with them for a long time, even after I left Paris and came home to America. But there was never anything.'

Mark leaned back against the cushions, and after a split second he asked her in a cautious tone, 'Is there any reason you can think of why Lucien might want to engineer his own disappearance?'

'None at all, Mark. He wasn't that sort of man, he had a true sense of honour. Lucien had more integrity than anyone I knew. Or know.'

'Well, I certainly trust your judgment.' There was a brief pause before he asked her, 'Have you ever been back to Paris since then?'

Jessica shook her head. 'I'm not sure that I'll go to the party. Paris does not hold happy memories for me, Mark. I wouldn't enjoy the trip.'

He said, 'I've got an idea. I could change my plans. Would you like me to come with you in June? Hold your hand?'

So startled was she by this offer, she gaped at him speechlessly. Finally, she answered, 'You'd come to give me courage?'

'If you want to put it that way.'

Jessica fell silent. She and Mark were genuinely good friends; she had designed several of his homes and his offices, and they had become close. That he would want to help make her visit to Paris easier was something that took her breath away. 'Thank you for making such a lovely and generous gesture. I'm grateful, Mark, really I am.' A sigh trickled out of her. 'I do love Anya Sedgwick, and she was an extraordinary influence on my life, but I don't know . . .' She shook her head several times and gave him a helpless look.

'Sometimes having another person with you makes a tough trip much easier. And, as I said, I need to go to Paris anyway, since I'm hoping to shoot part of my next movie there.'

'Well, I haven't made a final decision about attending Anya's party. I only found the invitation waiting for me when I got home on Saturday evening. But whatever I decide, you'll be the first to know.'

Mark gave her a warm smile; he was filled with affection for her. But he did ask himself why he had suddenly insinuated himself into her life. As for Jessica, she was wondering the same thing. And asking herself whether or not she had the guts to go to Paris to confront the past. She simply didn't know.

Chapter Four

HER LIFE HAD CHANGED. Miraculously. Overnight. For the last few days she had felt as though she were walking on air. She was excited and filled with expectation, and in a way she had not been for years.

The change in her had started last Friday, when she had returned to her office after lunch. On her desk was a FedEx envelope from Paris. Momentarily baffled, she had pulled the little tag on the back and taken out the white envelope inside. The way her name was written in beautiful calligraphy told her at once that this was an invitation. When she had removed the card from the white envelope she had been thrilled as she quickly scanned it, reading every word. How wonderful to be invited to this special occasion for Anya.

Anya Sedgwick was a unique person in Maria's life. It was Anya who had taken her under her wing. She had been like a mother to her at times, as well as her champion, and a truly good friend.

When she had first begun to attend the Anya Sedgwick School of Decorative Arts, Design and Couture, Maria had made a lot of other friends as well—besides the three who became her closest friends until the quarrel. In her opinion, it had been about nothing of any consequence. The parting should never have happened. After the break in the friendships, she had been at a loss without the other girls in her life.

She hoped they would be there; she couldn't wait to see them again, whether they wanted to see her or not. Seven years later there could be no animosity left, could there? Maria shrugged. One never knew about people; they could be very strange, as she knew only too well, and to her bitter disappointment.

Maria Pia Francesca Theresa Franconi, called simply Maria by her family and friends, fully intended to go to Paris to celebrate with Anya. In fact, she didn't think about it twice.

The invitation to the party, and the prospect of the trip, were the reasons her depression had fled; she was so buoyed up and excited she could hardly contain herself. Aside from wanting to attend Anya's party, Paris was Maria's favourite place. Also, the idea of escape appealed to her enormously—escape from her domineering family, a job that bored her, a family business she had not the slightest interest in, and a personal life that was dull and uneventful.

It would not be merely a weekend visit to Paris, just to attend the celebration. She planned to take her vacation in June, and she would stay in Paris for a week. Perhaps even two. Or maybe even three. *Three weeks in Paris*. The thought of it took her breath away.

Now on this Thursday evening, almost a week since she had received the invitation, Maria was still soaring. She couldn't wait to tell her brother Fabrizio about the party, and the trip she was planning. Her brother was coming to dinner as he usually did on Thursdays if he was in Milan.

As it was, Fabrizio had been away for the past two weeks, visiting some of their clients in Vienna, Munich and London. He was the head of sales in their company, Franconi and Sons, manufacturers of textiles par excellence since 1870.

With lightness and speed, Maria moved round the kitchen in her modern apartment, checking the pasta she had just freshly made from her own dough, stirring the bolognese sauce she had put in a glass bowl a few minutes before. Moving to the refrigerator, she took out the mozzarella cheese and tomatoes and began to slice them. Once she had done so, she arranged them on two plates, and added basil leaves. Later she would drizzle oil on top.

As she worked, Maria glanced out of the window, thinking what a pretty sky it was. Ink-black, filled with crystal stars and a perfect orb of a moon, it was without cloud. She could see from the delicate, lacy pattern of the frost on the windowpane that it had turned icy outside.

Maria was glad Fabrizio was coming to dinner. He was not only her favourite in the family, but her ally in the business. He took her side whenever she had a strong opinion. Her grandfather usually did not. Frequently her father supported her, since he, too, saw the necessity for a number of their lines to be updated. This was something Maria continually fought for, but she was not always successful.

In the years since she had graduated from Anya's school in Paris, she had become one of the top designers at Franconi, and Fabrizio, in particular, was forever giving her accolades for her textiles. Deep down, though, she felt that she was in a rut.

She sighed under her breath, then immediately clamped down on these negative feelings, focusing instead on her brother. Fabrizio enjoyed her cooking, and they usually had a good time together, no matter what they did. Like her, Fabrizio was single; like her, he was also forever being nagged at by their mother—marriage being the reason for the incessant nagging. Their mother and their Grandmothers Franconi and Rudolfo couldn't wait to bounce *bambinos* on their laps, and were vociferous about it. In fact, none of the older females in the family let the two of them forget that they were in dereliction of their duty.

Their elder brother, Sergio, had been married and divorced and was childless. Obviously he was beyond the pale, as far as the grandmothers were concerned; mostly this was because of his marital history, his taste for the fast track and flashy women. Sergio was the heir apparent. But Maria knew that Fabrizio was the true favourite in the family. He was the best-looking. Tall, blue-eyed and blond, he was a true Franconi in appearance, while she and Sergio were dark and took after the Rudolfos. Fabrizio was the smartest, the brightest, and he worked the hardest. Without trying, he endeared himself to everyone. Even strangers fell under his spell. Fabrizio was the star, and she did not resent this one bit. She loved and admired her brother more than anyone in the world. He had two characteristics she set great store by: honour and integrity.

Ten minutes later, Fabrizio stood leaning against the doorjamb of her kitchen, watching her as she finished cooking, sipping a glass of wine, looking nonchalant.

He was filling her in about his trip, and she turned and smiled at him, glowing inside, when he told her that it was her revamping and updating of their famous Renaissance Collection that was making such a difference to the company. 'The reorders are tremendous, Maria,' he explained. 'And so I toast you, little one, for designing a line that has been such an extraordinary success.'

Picking up her goblet of wine, she touched it to his. 'Thank you, Fab. And won't Grandfather be surprised? He was so against my ideas.' She laughed delightedly. 'I can't wait to see his face when you tell him.'

'Neither can I. Not only that, the customers were really singing your praises. I told them I would be showing them a whole new line next season. A line not based on any of the company's standards.'

'You did!' She stared at him, her dark eyes holding his.

'Yes. And so I am looking to you, Maria, to produce a collection that bears *only* your signature.'

'That's quite a challenge!' She paused for a moment. 'Fabrizio . . .?'

'Yes?' He stared at her alertly, detecting a new note in her voice. 'You sound excited.'

'I am. I got an invitation last week to go to Anya's eighty-fifth birthday party in Paris.'

Fabrizio stiffened slightly, although he endeavoured to disguise this, and his face did not change when he asked, as casually as possible, 'And when is this party?'

'Early June.'

'I see . . .' He let his voice trail off noncommittally, waiting to hear what she had to say.

'I'm going, of course. I wouldn't miss it for the world. I've already sent in the reply card, accepting, and I plan to stay for two or three weeks.'

Her brother frowned. 'Two or three weeks. Whatever for?'

'Because I love Paris, and I want to have my summer holiday there.'

'But we always go to the house in Capri in the summer.'

'Not this year—at least *I* won't be going.'

'They won't like it.'

'I don't care. I'm twenty-nine, almost thirty years old, and I think I can spend a vacation alone for a change. Don't you?'

'But yes, of course, you're an adult.' He smiled at her gently, decided to say no more. Later, after dinner, he would have to tell her she could not go to Paris. He dreaded the thought.

Maria watched her brother surreptitiously, pleased that he was savouring his food, obviously enjoying the dinner she had so painstakingly prepared for him.

After eating a little of the spaghetti bolognese, which was one of her specialities, she put her fork down and reached for her glass of red wine. She took several swallows, then said, 'I'm feeling so much better, Fabrizio, much less depressed. I know it's receiving the invitation to go the party that's cheered me up.'

Lifting his head, he looked at her intently, swallowing his dismay. 'I'm glad you're feeling better. But perhaps this change is really due to the way Father has been backing you and your ideas lately.'

'It's nothing to do with work. Nothing at all!'

'All right, all right, you don't have to get excited.'

'I'm not excited. I'm simply telling you the way it is. And I do know what makes me happy. The thought of going to Paris has been liberating these last few days.'

This was the last thing Fabrizio Franconi wished to hear, and he took a few more forkfuls of the pasta before pushing the plate away. 'That was delicious, Maria. You're the best cook I know.'

'You'd better not let either of our grandmothers hear you say that,' she replied, smiling at him. Then, rising, she took their plates out to the kitchen.

'Can I help you?' her brother called after her.

'No, no, everything's under control.' Maria returned a few seconds later, carrying a plate of cookies. 'I didn't make dessert, because you never eat it. But I did make coffee. Would you like a cup?'

He shook his head. 'No, thanks. I'll savour my wine.'

'How was London?' she asked, sitting down opposite him.

'Cold and wet. But it was good to be back even for a few days. You know, I do have genuinely happy memories about my days at school there. I enjoyed that period of my life. Didn't you enjoy your schooldays in England?'

'Yes, I suppose so. But to be honest, I loved the time I spent at Anya's school so much more.' Her face changed, became animated as she added, 'By the way, her birthday party is black tie. I'll have to get a new evening dress, and I can't wait to go shopping for something special.'

For a second her brother was silent, wondering how to begin. After a few moments of reflection, he said in a soft voice, 'I wish you hadn't already accepted that invitation, Maria.'

'What do you mean?' she asked, her voice rising slightly. She had detected something odd in his voice.

He was silent, staring into his glass of red wine. When he looked up he began very carefully, 'You know you can't go to Paris because—' And then his voice faltered.

She stared at him.

He stared back at her. The face he looked into was one of the loveliest faces he had ever seen. The face of a madonna, worthy of being painted by a great artist. She had huge, soulful eyes as black as obsidian, clouds of thick glossy black hair falling to her shoulders, a perfect oval of a face with dimples in her cheeks when she smiled.

Maria's eyes impaled Fabrizio's as she murmured shakily, '*You* don't want me to go because I'm so . . . heavy. That's what you mean, isn't it?'

'I can't stop you going, if you want to go so badly. After all, to quote your friend Jessica, who *you* are always quoting, you're free, white and twenty-one. But that is just my reason, Maria. *Jessica*. And also Alexandra and Kay. Three very good reasons why you ought not to go to Paris. You are not merely heavy, you are *fat*, and I know you will feel awkward and *humiliated* when you see your friends. Because they are bound to be as svelte as they always were.'

'You don't know that!' she cried, and then closed her eyes. *Of course he was right*. They would look gorgeous, and she would feel like a beached whale. Yet she wanted to go to Paris so much, she couldn't bear the idea of declining the invitation, and so she said, defiantly, 'I can still go. I don't care what they think.'

Fabrizio got up, walked over to the sofa, and said, 'Come and sit here with me, let's talk this out, little one.'

Once she had joined him on the sofa, he took her hand in his, and looked into her eyes lovingly. 'Since you do want to go so badly, there is a way. However, it is going to be tough.'

'What do you mean?'

'First of all, let's talk about your love of cooking. It is an enjoyable hobby, I know, but you do it because you are frustrated about many things. You comfort yourself with food, Maria.'

She did not say a word.

Fabrizio continued: 'If you're going to go to Paris then I suggest you lose some weight. You have a good three months to do that. You will look so much better, and you will feel better.'

'Diets don't really work for me,' she mumbled.

'They would if you really stuck to them,' he shot back swiftly, giving her a penetrating stare. 'You have to stop all this cooking. *Immediately*.'

'Do you think I could stick to a diet, Fab?' she asked, sounding suddenly hopeful.

'I certainly do. I will take you to a nutritionist tomorrow, and she will put you on a regimen that is suitable for you. Then you can enrol at my gym, and start working out every day.'

Later, after Fabrizio had left, Maria stood in front of the full-length mirror. For the first time in years she saw herself as she truly was. Her brother was right. She had put on a lot of weight in the last few years. Yes, I'm fat, she said to herself. No, not just fat. Very fat.

She blinked several times as tears welled, and turned away from the mirror, filled with self-loathing. Reaching for her silk robe, she drew it on quickly and went and lay on her bed, pushing her face into the pillow. She let the tears flow, until finally there were no tears left in her. Exhausted, she lay there, consumed by her longing to go to Anya's party, her weight problem, and her current plight. What to do? What to do? she asked herself repeatedly.

Fabrizio was right. The ideal thing would be to utilise the next few months to get the weight off, but she was so afraid of failure and of the hardship of exercise and dieting.

Ricardo, she suddenly thought. It all began when they pushed Ricardo Martinelli out of my life. How she had loved him, and he her, but her parents had considered him unsuitable, and they had broken up the love affair. He had gone away four years ago, and she had never seen him again.

That was when she had started to put on weight, after Ricardo had exited her life. She pampered herself with food because she had lost him, because her parents and grandparents were domineering, and because she was desperately lonely. She hated her job, was sick and tired of designing textiles.

Escape. That was what she really wanted.

Permanent escape from Milan. From her family. From her job.

But you can't escape from yourself, Maria, she reminded herself, sitting up, pushing her hair away from her face. You have a big, terrible fat body, and you and only you are responsible. You can't blame the family for your eating, at least only indirectly. You and only you are responsible for what you put into your mouth.

She thought of this over and over again as she sat propped up against the pillows, and then after a while she left her bed and sat at her dressing table, staring intently into the mirror.

She saw herself as she really was; it was a beautiful face staring back at her. If only she did not have this awful body. You *can* do it, she insisted in her head. You *can* lose weight. You have great motivation now. Going to Paris to see Anya, to make friends again with Jessica, Alexandra and Kay. And maybe if you get thin enough you can go and see Ricardo. She knew where he was, what he was doing. Perhaps her lover still yearned for her, as she yearned for him.

Chapter Five

ANYA SEDGWICK WAS SO STARTLED she sat back on the sofa and stared at her visitor seated opposite. There was a questioning look in her eyes and her surprise was evident.

After adjusting her back against the antique needlepoint pillows, she frowned slightly and asked, 'But whatever made you do it so . . .so . . . *impetuously*?' She shook her head: 'It's not like you . . .' Her voice trailed off; her eyes remained fixed on his handsome face.

Nicholas Sedgwick cleared his throat several times. 'Please don't be angry with me, Anya.'

'Good heavens, Nicky, I'm not angry.' She gave him the benefit of a warm smile, wanting to reassure him. He was her favourite in the family, and although he was not her child, not even of her blood, she thought of him as a son. He was very special to her.

'All right,' she continued. 'You're giving me a birthday party, and you've already sent out lots of invitations, which perhaps precludes cancelling it. So you'd better tell me about it.'

'I wanted to do something really special for your birthday, Anya,' he replied. 'I know how much you enjoy Ledoyen, so that was my restaurant of choice. I've booked the entire restaurant for the evening. There're going to be a few surprises as well, along the way.'

'I'm sure there'll be lots of surprises in the works, knowing you,' she laughed.

'So far I've invited seventy-five people, but we can have a lot more, double that amount, if you wish.'

'Seventy-five already sounds a few too many!' she exclaimed, but immediately smiled at him when she saw his crestfallen expression. 'I'm only teasing, Nicky. Continue, darling.'

'After I visited the restaurant, I was filled with all kinds of ideas for the party, and I suppose I got overly enthusiastic. I went ahead and created an invitation, which I had printed, and I had a calligrapher address the envelopes. Once they were ready I posted them. But I panicked the day I put them in the post. It struck me that I had pre-empted the rest of the family, that I had taken control, so to speak.'

'As you usually do,' she asserted in a mild tone.

He nodded; he was relieved she sounded so benign. 'You *must* have a celebration for your eighty-fifth birthday, it's such a milestone. And you should be surrounded by everyone you care about.'

'Did you bring the invitation list?'

'Yes, I did.' He smiled wryly as he added, 'I'm afraid I was sneaky. I had Laure take most of the addresses from your files.' Not waiting for a comment from her, he rushed on, 'Here's the list.' Pulling it out of his pocket, he rose to join her on the sofa.

After lunch, when Nicky had finally left, Anya went back to her upstairs sitting room. It was a room she had gravitated to ever since she had come to live here over half a century ago, a place to entertain family and friends, relax and read when she was alone, or listen to the music she loved so much. And it was her preferred place to work. The large antique desk piled with papers, which stood in one corner, was testimony to her lifetime ethic of disciplined hard work.

Walking briskly across the floor, Anya paused briefly at the window, staring down into the yard below, thinking how bleak her garden looked on this cold February afternoon. The trees were skeletal against the pale grey but luminous Paris sky. And the wet cobblestones gleamed with a silvery sheen after the recent downpour.

Mature sycamores and lime trees encircled the house, and there was a lovely old cherry tree in the middle of the courtyard that dominated the scene. Now its bare spreading branches cast an intricate pattern of grey shadows across the yard. But in spring it bloomed softly pink, its branches heavy with cascades of luscious blossoms; in the heat of summer its cool, leafy canopy offered welcome shade.

As bleak as the garden was today, Anya was well aware that in a month or two it would be glowing with verdant grass and banks of ferns, dotted with the variegated pinks of the cherry blossoms and the little impatiens set in borders round the lawn. Now Anya's glance took in the tall, ivy-covered wall which, along with the many trees, made the garden and house so secluded. She had always been enchanted by the garden, the quaint courtyard and the picturesque house with its black and white half-timbered façade. It stood just a stone's throw from the busy Boulevard des Invalides, and round the corner was the rue de l'Université where her school was located.

Anya smiled inwardly, thinking of the surprise most people had when they came in from the street through the great wooden doors and confronted the courtyard. The old house, which had stood here for over a hundred years, and the bucolic setting so reminiscent of Normandy, usually took everyone's breath away.

As it had hers, when she had first visited the house in the summer of 1936, on the day she was celebrating her twentieth birthday. She had come here with Michel Lacoste, to meet his mother. He was the great love of her youth, the man who became her first husband, and the father of her two children, Dimitri and Olga.

This house had belonged to his mother, Catherine, and then to Michel after she died. When Michel died, the house had become Anya's.

Too young to die, she muttered under her breath as she turned away from the window. Of late, so many memories and recollections of the past assailed her. Perhaps that was part of growing old. But she could not dwell on the past. Nicholas Sedgwick, her great-nephew through her second husband Hugo Sedgwick, had forced her to look to the future. To June 2 and the party.

Seating herself at the desk near the fireplace, glad to have the warmth of the blazing logs nearby, she turned her attention to the guest list that he had prepared. She approved of the family and friends he had invited, along with some of her former pupils. In particular, she was pleased to see he had included four brilliant girls from the class of 1994. Jessica Pierce, Kay Lenox, Maria Franconi and Alexandra Gordon. Most especially Alexandra. My special girl, she thought.

Anya sat back in her chair, thinking of Alexandra and her involvement with that poor, bedevilled Tom Conners. All Nicky's fault, since he had introduced them. Well, if she were honest, that wasn't exactly the way it was. Tom had come to the studio to see a client, if she remembered things correctly.

And was it ever anybody's *fault* when lives went awry?

Surely it was fate. She considered her own life and the role fate had played in it. She was certain it was her destiny to end up where she was today, having lived the life she had lived.

Although she enjoyed the milder climate of Provence in the winter months, and frequently went there, Anya was, nevertheless, glad to be back in Paris. And back in the house that meant so much to her, filled as it was with her life's history.

This room in particular told the whole story. Encapsulated within its walls were mementos gathered over the years. Some she had bought, others were gifts, yet more were inherited; certain things she had even created herself.

The decoration of her sitting room depicted a woman of discernment, taste and talent, a woman with an exotic background who had ventured forth courageously when young.

She had followed her heart and her dreams, given free rein to her creativity, believing in her destiny as a woman and an artist. She had lived her life to the fullest, had never regretted anything she had done, only the things she had not found time to do or to accomplish.

After studying the guest list for her birthday party, and making some notes, adding a few names, she had put it to one side. But she had continued to work at her desk, going over papers that had accumulated during the couple of weeks she had been in Provence. Finally growing a little weary, she put down her pen, sat up straighter in the chair, and glanced around.

Anya smiled, thinking that at this moment the room had a lovely golden haze to it, even though dusk was rapidly approaching. But then it had a sunny feeling at all times, as she had fully intended.

Although she had started her professional life as an artist, Anya was talented in many areas, and she had a great flair for interior design. Years ago, wanting to introduce a mood of summer sunshine into this large, high-ceilinged sitting room, she had covered the walls with a yellow-on-yellow striped fabric. This had long since faded from daffodil to a very pale primrose, but it was nonetheless mellow and warm.

In vivid contrast to these now-muted yellow walls were great swaths of scarlet taffeta, which Anya had selected for the full-length draperies at the two windows. They hung on rings from wooden poles, falling straight, but then halfway down they softly billowed out like the skirts of ball gowns.

Anya loved these curtains, the stunning effect they created, and when the bright colour faded she simply replaced them with new ones made of identical fabric. She was forever fussing with them, puffing them up with her hands, and sometimes even stuffing tissue paper behind them for the desired bell shape.

These fabrics were her pride, gave her immense pleasure. Even though Nicky tended to tease her about them, he secretly admired her nerve, knowing that only Anya Sedgwick would have dared to choose them, secure in the knowledge that they were a knockout. She had wanted to surprise, and she had succeeded admirably.

Naturally, Anya paid no attention to his teasing, confident in her own taste and choice of colours. In fact, this whole room was a play on scarlet and yellow, with white accents showing up in the paintwork. Also cooling the strong colours was a pale apple-green silk used on several elegant chairs scattered round the room. Anya believed that these muted tones balanced a room essentially commanding because of its vibrant colours.

In front of the fireplace there was a large, overstuffed chesterfield covered in a scarlet velvet also used to cover two huge chunky armchairs, typical Anya Sedgwick touches. She always opted for comfort as well as style. Even the rectangular coffee table was of her own invention. Originally an old wrought-iron garden gate, which she had found at a local flea market, she had hired a metal worker to weld on short iron legs, and then she had topped it with a thick slab of glass. She was very proud of her unique coffee table, and glanced at it now, nodding her head in approval.

The fire blazing in the hearth added to the sense of warmth and intimacy on this wintry afternoon, and Anya considered herself blessed to have such a wonderful haven; she had been back from Provence for only two days, and she had felt the cold when she had arrived.

Old bones, she muttered as she pushed herself to her feet. Old bones, and getting older. She moved round the desk and went towards the fireplace, but then paused to admire some of her things.

It was as if she had momentarily forgotten how beautiful her possessions were, during her absence in the South, and wanted to reacquaint herself with them, touch them, remember who had given them to her, remember what they meant to her.

That's not in the right spot, she thought, as her sharp eyes settled on a silver samovar. This had been put on a circular table, skirted in a red and yellow *toile de Jouy*, standing between the two windows.

Leaning forwards, she pushed the samovar into the centre of the table, where it was meant to be, then stood back, gazing at it lovingly; it was very special to her. This samovar had been resolutely carried out of Russia by her mother, when they had fled the Bolsheviks and left the country for good. A woman who had been determined that certain precious family objects would not be left behind.

Anya had no recollection of this event, but her mother had recounted it many times to her, and to her siblings, and so it had become part of her family history.

As she walked past a console table she stopped to admire her mother's collection of ancient and valuable icons. At the other end of the table, family photographs from Russia were displayed. These were in gold Fabergé frames encrusted with green malachite and blue lapis stones, and had been deeply treasured by her parents. How they had missed their families, whom they had left behind in Russia; and they had missed Mother Russia, too, despite the country's ills, the turmoil and bloodshed of the Revolution.

These photographs of handsome men, finely dressed, and beautiful women in fashionable gowns and splendid jewels, were poignant reminders of the murdered Romanov monarchy, a lost aristocracy, a vanished world of money, power and privilege, which had once been theirs.

Anya turned away from those evocative family photographs, which had been her parents' legacy to her, along with so many other things they had brought out of Russia. Briefly, her eyes scanned the bookshelves along a wall at the far end of the room. All were filled with a diverse and eclectic mix of books, some of which she had written, while others had been penned by her friends. Soon, she hoped, another of her works would be on a shelf over there, her book on the Art Deco period, which she was finishing at this moment. It would go to the publisher in a month's time.

It was an automatic reaction, the way her eyes then swung to a striking painting, one that exuded dominant force, and hung on the wall adjoining the bookshelves. It was a landscape, all sharp angles and planes, a modern painting awash with deep greens, rich yellows and dark reds, these colours balanced by earthy browns and coppery, autumnal hues. It was a most powerful painting and it was by her father Valentin Kossikovsky, the great Russian artist. It held her eyes, as it always had and always would. She was full of admiration for the extraordinary talent that had been his.

Finally she looked away, moved on.

There were a couple of her own paintings hanging here. One in particular stood out. She had painted it over sixty years ago, and it was the full-length, life-sized portrait of a young woman. Hanging above the fireplace, it was the focus of interest at this end of the room; everyone was drawn towards it, instantly captivated when they caught sight of it.

Anya now approached the fireplace, stood staring up at the canvas, and as usual her eyes were critical. Yet she could never fault this painting, even though it was one of her own works, which she generally had a tendency to excessively criticise.

The painting was of her sister Ekaterina, Katti for short, painted when she was just twenty years old. What a beauty she had been. And there was her own name: Anya Kossikovskaya, together with the date, 1941, in the left-hand corner, at the bottom of the painting.

She herself had been twenty-five when she had asked Katti to sit for the portrait, and reluctantly her sister had agreed. For a great beauty she was singularly without vanity, and modest in her opinion of herself.

When the painting was finally finished, her father had been amazed, and momentarily rendered speechless. And when he had found his voice at last, he had marvelled at Anya's work and had called the painting a treasure. Immediately, he had asked the renowned London art gallery that represented him and handled his own work, to show it, and they had obliged him. They had even gone so far as to give her an exhibition of her other paintings; this had immediately sold out, much to her surprise and delight.

Many people had tried to buy the painting of her sister, which she had called *Portrait of Ekaterina*, because it was so arresting. But she had wanted to keep it for herself. The painting was special to her, meaningful and extremely personal. And over the long years others had tried to buy it, but her answer was always the same: 'Not for sale'.

Anya focused appraising eyes on the painting, wanting to analyse its appeal to so many different people. Here was her darling Katti, blonde, beautiful, with high, slanting cheekbones, a broad forehead, wide-set eyes and an impossibly slender, aristocratic nose. Her sister appeared literally to shimmer in the clear light that she had somehow managed to capture on canvas. The painting virtually glowed with incandescent light, usually a hallmark of her work.

Katti's eyes were a lovely blue, like bits of sky, and they reflected the colour of the blue taffeta gown she was wearing. Even now Anya felt, as she had always felt, that if she reached out to the painting her fingers would touch silk not canvas, so real did the fabric appear to be with its folds and shadows and silvery sheen. She could almost hear it rustle.

Once more, it struck her how English her sister's appearance was. And why not, she asked herself. She had painted the portrait on a sunny afternoon at the height of summer in the garden of a manor house in Kent. The background had a hint of Gainsborough about it, even though she did say so herself. Not that she was comparing herself to the master, but rather to the way he had painted English landscapes of the time.

Were people drawn to this painting because of the girl portrayed in it, she wondered. Or was it for its Englishness? Or perhaps the mood of a bygone age that it seemed to capture? She had no idea. She had never known what it signified to other people, what powerful emotional response it evoked in them.

Turning away, as she now did, her thoughts stayed with her sister. Katti had been born in London, but deep down, Anya believed, she had a truly Russian soul. She was so like their mother, Natasha. Their brother Vladimir, also born in London, was wholly English and did not appear to have a hint of his Russian heritage in him. He was three years younger than Katti.

Both Anya's siblings were alive, and for this she was inordinately grateful. She knew they would be thrilled to come to her birthday party. Despite the fact that Katti and Vladimir still lived in England, all three had remained close and loving over the years. They did not live far away, just across the English Channel in Kent, in the beloved country of their birth.

Obviously Nicky had placed them at the top of the guest list, along with the rest of her extended family. Her sister Katti and her husband Sacha Lebedev, another Russian born in England of émigré parents from Moscow via Paris, and their sons Charles and Anthony, and their daughter Serena. Her brother Vladimir, his wife Lilli, and their three sons Michael, Paul and Peter, and their wives.

And then came her closest family, her children by her first husband, Michel Lacoste. Her daughter Olga and her son Dimitri; there would be Olga's children, her granddaughters Anna and Natalie.

And then there was the Sedgwick tribe, whom she had inherited from Hugo, her second husband, and whom she loved as much as her own. Larry and his wife Stephanie; Nicky, her special favourite, and his wife Constance. But no, perhaps Constance would not come, since she and Nicky were apparently at loggerheads, estranged at the moment.

It was indeed a complex mixture, but they were all members of her family and she cared for each and every one of them. The party's going to be fun, she thought, sitting down on the scarlet velvet sofa. She leaned back against the soft cushions, enjoying the warmth of the fire, the floral smell of the scented candles, the comfort of the surroundings in general, the tranquil atmosphere that prevailed here.

Eighty-five, she thought, I can't believe I'm going to be eighty-five in just three months. I feel so much younger inside.

Anya smiled to herself, and turned back to look at the painting of Katti. She felt as young as that girl there, who gazed back at her with such innocent eyes . . .

She had been born in St Petersburg in 1916, virtually on the eve of the Russian Revolution, although she had no recollection of that city as it was then. Nor had she known of the tumultuous events of 1917 and

1918, which had caused her parents to flee their country. But her father, Prince Valentin Kossikovsky, had recounted everything to her when she was old enough to understand. The politics of these chaotic times was his favourite subject, and besides this he was a mesmerising raconteur.

Her parents were from Russia's most elite and privileged society; her father was a man of ancient lineage, great wealth derived from vast family-owned lands in the Crimea, a variety of industrial holdings in Moscow, and financial interests abroad. Her mother, Nathalie, always called Natasha, was the daughter of Count Ilya Devenarskoe, also a landowner and a man of wealth.

At the time of her birth Anya's father was acquiring a name for himself as an artist of formidable talent. Within fifteen years of his departure from Russia, Valentin would be acclaimed as one of the great Russian painters of the twentieth century. But in 1917 he was not thinking of fame but of escape. He had long anticipated the Revolution and had made certain financial plans.

When the Tsar and his family were brutally murdered, Valentin made his moves with speed. A lot of strings were pulled by a lot of people, and Valentin, Natasha and their baby daughter Anya left Russia six months later, in January 1919. After spending several weeks in Norway, they were able to board a British merchant ship bound for England.

Waiting for them there was Valentin's older sister Olga, who in 1910 had married a wealthy English banker, Adrian Hamilton, and moved to London. Anya's first conscious memories from her childhood were of England, and, in particular, her aunt's beautiful manor house in Kent, Haverlea Chase, where years later she would paint the portrait of Katti on the terrace.

After six months of living in Kent, Valentin and Natasha found a small but attractive house in Chelsea, with a conservatory in the garden. Built almost entirely of glass, this was ideal as a studio in which Valentin could paint. It was here that Anya grew up, surrounded by the possessions and photographs her mother had managed to bring out of Russia.

Anya ate Russian food, and learned Russian history from her father, and the language from her parents who spoke only Russian when they were alone. In essence, she was raised in the same way as a Russian aristocrat would have been brought up in St Petersburg. And yet she was also an English girl who grew up in the ways of her adopted country and became a student at the Royal College of Art. 'I'm a funny mixture,' she said to Michel Lacoste, when she first met him in Paris. 'But deep down I know that my soul is Russian.' And she continued to believe this for the rest of her life, just as her father, the prince, had intended.

Chapter Six

THE RAIN DID NOTHING to dampen Nicholas Sedgwick's good mood as he walked across the Boulevard des Invalides, heading towards the rue de l'Université. He had just finished the sketches of sets for a new movie to be shot at the studios in Billancourt and in the Loire Valley, and the producer and director had liked his designs.

Nothing like a little success to put a man in a happy frame of mind, he thought, as he crossed the boulevard, making for Anya's school.

And then, in a split second, a shadow crossed his handsome face, and settled in his bluish-green eyes. Professionally, he was at a high point; but in his personal life happiness had eluded him. His marriage to Constance Aykroyd, the English stage actress, was over. He had tried to make it work, but he simply became more and more estranged from her as the months went by, and all he wanted now was to end it. But Connie did not want a divorce; she was not about to set him free of her own accord, even though he had moved out many months before.

Nicky sighed to himself, thankful there were no children involved in this disastrous marriage. It would be a clean break, when it finally happened. And he was only thirty-eight. He could start again.

He smiled to himself. Hope springs eternal . . . that was the favourite line of Hugh Sedgwick, his uncle. Hugo, as he was commonly called, had been Anya's second husband, a business genius and the linchpin of the family, the man round whom everyone and everything revolved. Charismatic, reliable and strong, he had been steady as a rock, and the most enduring influence in Nicky's life. Both he and Anya had been devastated by his uncle's death.

Well, at least my work is going well, Nicky thought, as he turned the corner. He and his brother Larry were busier than they had ever been, and their theatrical design company, with offices in Paris and London, was thriving.

Not only that, he was particularly enjoying teaching this season. He gave two classes a week, on set designing and decorating, at Anya's school, and this year he had discovered that he had several brilliant students in his class. He had always found it rewarding to encourage and nurture students who showed promise, and he took pleasure in showing them how to develop their work and achieve their goals.

Halfway down the rue de l'Université he came to the huge, wooden double doors that led into the courtyard of the school. He went in through the small side door designed for pedestrians; as he closed it behind him he hoped Anya would be happy with the designs he had created for her birthday party. He was going to show them to her later today.

Nicky went up in the old-fashioned lift to his office on the third floor. This was in the building where the original school had started, and had been housed from the twenties to the forties, which was when adjoining buildings were acquired.

As he stepped out of the lift and walked along the corridor, he couldn't help thinking about the history of this place. The school would be seventy-five years old later this year, and what a success story it was.

If only walls could talk, he thought, going into his office. He put his umbrella in the cupboard, sat down at his large desk and began to look at the sketches he had made for Anya's party. But his mind drifted off after a while. His thoughts focused on the school and what it had become, all because of Anya Sedgwick.

Originally it had been a modest little school of art run by Catherine Lacoste, Anya's mother-in-law.

The young widow of a renowned French sculptor, Laurent Lacoste, who had started the school in 1926, she had struggled to keep it going after Laurent's death in the early thirties.

Despite being small, it had a good reputation because of the gifted teachers it employed, mostly artists themselves who needed to earn a steady income to support their art. Even in those days it had a certain prestige because of Laurent Lacoste's name.

Incredibly, and to her credit, Catherine had managed to keep the school open even during the war years and the German Occupation of Paris. Then, after the Second World War, the school had begun to blossom more fully once again. But in 1948 Catherine realised she could not run it by herself for much longer. Eventually she had asked her young daughter-in-law to take over the school and run it for her. Anya had agreed, knowing she would have the advice and guidance of her mother-in-law at all times.

Anya and Catherine had been unusually close. They had initially bonded in 1936, when Michel had taken Anya to meet his mother. It had been Anya's twentieth birthday, and Catherine had even predicted, that very afternoon, that Anya and her son would marry one day.

During the war, Michel Lacoste, a journalist by profession, was based in London, where he was a member of the staff of General Charles de Gaulle, leader of the Free French forces, who was headquartered in London. Anya and Michel, who had fallen in love in Paris before the war, continued to see each other in war-torn England. They were married in 1941 during the Blitz. Anya was twenty-five, Michel thirty-one.

In 1946, some months after the war was over, Michel had taken Anya and their two young children, Olga, aged three, and Dimitri, aged two, back to Paris.

Life in France in 1946 was full of postwar problems and shortages. Because of the lack of available housing, and their shaky financial situation, Michel and Anya had moved in with Michel's mother. Catherine had been thrilled; she welcomed them warmly, excited and delighted to have her son's young family with her at long last. The war years had been hard and lonely; she welcomed their company, cherished her beautiful grandchildren.

They had all lived compatibly in the lovely old black and white half-timbered house where Anya still lived. The house was big enough for them all, and the garden a boon, a place for the children to play and run free, especially in the warm weather.

At Catherine's request, Anya had gone to teach part time at the school; much to her amazement, she had discovered that she had a gift for teaching. And then two years later, when Catherine had asked her to take over, she had agreed, confident in her abilities.

Anya was an astute young woman and soon, under her guidance, the school began to prosper. She had a talent for organisation, management and promotion, plus a keen nose for sniffing out exceptional teachers. But, perhaps more importantly, she had a vision. She could see so many marvellous possibilities, exciting ways to expand the little art school by developing its curriculum, adding new courses that taught some of the other important decorative arts. However, she did not make any serious changes until after Catherine's death in 1951.

It was at this time that she slowly and cautiously began to upgrade the school, adding the new courses which taught fashion and textile design, as well as costume and theatrical design. The classes in art and sculpture were still the mainstay of the school, but students began to enrol for the other courses and Michel and Anya were thrilled. They acquired the adjoining building when it became vacant and another a year later.

And then, in 1955, tragedy struck. Michel suddenly and unexpectedly died of a massive heart attack. He was forty-five years old. He and

Anya had been married for fourteen happy years. Stunned and grief-stricken as she was by Michel's untimely death, Anya continued to run the school. When Nicky once asked her how she had managed to do it, she had replied: 'I just kept plodding on. Even though my heart was breaking, I knew I couldn't give in, or collapse. I had so many responsibilities, so many people depending on me for a livelihood, and there were my two young children to raise and educate. I had to keep going. Anyway, I felt I owed it to Catherine's memory to keep the school open.'

Two years after Michel's death, in 1957, Anya met Hugh Sedgwick through mutual friends. An English businessman living and working in Paris, he was a widower and childless. He came from a theatrical family, and in his spare time was a bit of an amateur artist. They seemed to have a lot in common. In 1960 they were married in Paris. When Anya asked him to help her with the financial management of the school, Hugo happily took over these duties. Within a year the school turned yet another corner; it became profitable for the first time in its history.

Not only that, its reputation began to grow in the ensuing years. More than ever before, students were flocking to the school, many of them from abroad. By the mid-sixties it was called the Anya Sedgwick School of Decorative Arts. A few years later the name was changed again, this time to the Anya Sedgwick School of Decorative Arts, Design and Couture. And it went on growing, and turning out exceptional graduates, and Anya had become a legend in her own lifetime.

The shrilling telephone startled Nicky to such an extent he almost jumped out of his skin. He had been so lost in thought it took him a moment to recover and reach for the receiver.

'Nicholas Sedgwick.'

'It's Anya, Nicky.'

'Hello! I was just thinking about you. What time shall I come to your office to show you the sketches for the theme of your party?'

'I don't want to see them, Nicky, that's why I'm phoning you. Frankly, I would much prefer the party to be a total surprise . . . every aspect of it. I'll leave it all to you to make the choices and decisions.'

'But, Anya—'

'No, no,' she cut in. 'I trust you implicitly, darling boy. You have the best taste of anybody I know.'

'That's very flattering, but to be honest, I really was looking forward to seeing you.'

'Then you can take me out to tea. That would be nice, Nicky, and we can have a little chat. We haven't done that lately.'

'What a good idea. It will be my pleasure.'
'Why don't we meet at the Hôtel Meurice, at four o'clock?'
'I'll be there. Four sharp.'

They sat together in the Jardin d'Hiver, the winter garden, just beyond the lobby of the newly refurbished Hôtel Meurice on the rue de Rivoli opposite the Tuileries.

Palm trees in tubs and exotic plants helped to create the garden feeling so prevalent in this charming and comfortable spot. Floating above, was a glass roof in the shape of a dome, interlaced with metalwork. The milky opacity of the glass filtered the natural daylight and gave the room a unique softness.

Anya sat back in her chair and glanced round her. 'My mother-in-law, Catherine Lacoste, always loved this hotel,' she confided after a moment. 'She used to bring me here for tea. Or champagne. It became a favourite of mine, too. Of course, when the war came she never set foot inside the place. During the Occupation, the hotel was the headquarters of the German High Command, you see. How Catherine hated *les Boches*.'

'As did the rest of France.'

'Well, thank God for one thing . . . the Nazis didn't destroy Paris, although they could have done so. Hitler ordered historic buildings destroyed in 1944, when Allied troops were approaching. But General Dietrich von Choltitz, the occupying governor, was not able to perpetrate such sacrilege. He surrendered the city intact to General LeClerc, liberator of Paris.'

'Hugo once told me about that,' Nicholas said and picked up his cup, took a sip of tea, eyed Anya over the rim, thinking how well she looked this afternoon. She was wearing a crisply tailored, pale blue woollen suit, and her softly waved, short dark-blonde hair was as elegantly coiffed as it usually was. She looked positively radiant.

Breaking into his thoughts, Anya asked, 'Have you had many acceptances for my party so far, Nicky?'

'A lot, yes, indeed, and I'm expecting more this week.'

'Have you heard from Alexa? Has she accepted?'

'No, but I'm sure I'll be hearing from her any day now.'

'She might not come. She's not been back to Paris since she broke up with Tom Conners, and if you remember, that was three years ago, just about the time she stopped working with you and Larry. I saw her in New York last year . . .' She paused, gave him a very pointed look, and finished, 'I rather got the impression Alexa was avoiding France, Paris in particular. Because of him.'

Nicky sighed. 'I always warned her about him. Tom's hauling far too much emotional baggage. No woman needs that, Anya.'

'Perhaps he's discarded some of it? By now?' She gave him another penetrating look.

'You'd think so, wouldn't you, but I just don't know . . .' His voice trailed off lamely. 'Tom was always a loner. Kept his thoughts to himself. Stand-offish. Not at all confiding.'

'Don't you ever see him these days?' Anya leaned forward, her light blue eyes focused on him more intently. 'I was under the impression he represented people in show business.'

'That's true, he did. Probably still does. But I haven't run into him for at least a year. Maybe longer even.' His eyes narrowed slightly. 'Why? What are you getting at?'

'I do so want Alexa to be at the party. I was just wondering whether perhaps he's left Paris.'

'I doubt it.' Nicky sat up, an alert expression settling on his face. 'He was born here, it's where he belongs.'

'Some people move, go south to Provence, somewhere like that.'

'Not Tom, take my word for it. Incidentally, I did hear from that nice Italian girl, who was in Alexa's class. Maria Franconi. She was practically the first to accept.'

A wide smile spread itself across Anya's face. 'I'm so glad she's coming! She's such a lovely person. And she has such enormous talent, wasted probably these days.'

'What do you mean?' Nicky asked, frowning.

'She could be doing a lot more than designing textiles for that antiquated family business she's stuck in.' Not giving him a chance to make any kind of comment, she continued, 'Kay Lenox will come, that I am certain of, but not Jessica. I don't think she'll be able to face Paris, in view of what happened to her.'

'You mean Lucien's disappearance?'

'I do. That was a mystery . . . and one that's never been solved.'

'And so you think Jessica will forgo your party because Paris holds bad memories, too much pain for her?'

Anya nodded and sat back in the chair. 'I really do, Nicky. I've never seen anyone so distraught. I remember it so very clearly.' She shook her head. 'I honestly thought she would never recover. It's different when the person you love dies. There's an awful finality to death. But it is final. The end. And there's the funeral, family gatherings, grieving, all of those necessary rituals. And they help, believe me. When the object of your love just *disappears*, there's no way to deal with the grief and pain.'

'Because there's no closure?' Nicky suggested.

'Correct. No body. No burial. No end to the pain. She couldn't come to terms with the loss, and since Lucien Girard had no family there really was no one for her to grieve with, or be consoled by. Lucien's best friend, Alain Bonnal, was wonderful, but like her he was nonplussed, confused and baffled. Still, they were supportive of each other.'

For a moment Nicky did not respond. What a strange story it was. Finally, he asked, 'What actually happened to Jessica, Anya? Did she ever marry? Do you hear from her?'

'Oh yes, I do, I get notes and cards from her from time to time, or a clipping from *Architectural Digest*, when one of the homes she has designed appears in its pages. She hasn't married. She lives in Bel-Air, does a lot of designing for the rich and famous. But she never misses sending me a Christmas card with a lovely message. In fact, I get Christmas cards from Kay and Maria as well.'

'And Alexa?'

'Oh, she's constantly in touch. She has always been devoted to me.'

'I think I was always a bit in love with Alexa.' He took hold of Anya's hand. 'Maybe I still am. Do you know the reason why?'

'No, I don't.'

'It's because Alexandra Gordon is so like you, Anya. She is a reflection of you, and quite by accident. Or maybe she modelled herself on you. In any event, she has a lot of your special talents.'

'I think you might be a bit biased, Nicky,' Anya answered with a small smile. She patted his hand, still holding hers. 'But she does have a lot of talents, you're right.'

Chapter Seven

ALEXA HAD CHANGED HER MIND, and so, here she was, in Paris in the spring. In May, to be exact. Three weeks before the birthday party on June 2. Far too early. On the other hand, she had plenty to occupy herself during this period.

She planned to spend some special time with Anya; she was going to do a lot of shopping and, since she had just agreed to work with Nicky on a new movie, it was imperative that she have meetings with him. And then there was her hidden agenda.

Tom Conners.

She intended to seek him out. She needed to understand where he was at this stage in his life. And how she actually felt about him. After all, she had not seen him for three years; perhaps when they did finally come face to face, her feelings would be quite different.

In her own mind—most of the time anyway—it was over. He *had* ended it, telling her there was no future for her with him, that he could not marry her, would not. Nor anyone else. Seemingly, his past had claimed his future.

And yet, secretly, she still yearned for him. He occupied a large part of her, continually crept into her thoughts. But lately she had come to recognise that none of this was very healthy, and that she could not live with the situation any longer.

Alexa accepted that she had to be emotionally free, in order to move forward. She could not marry Jack Wilton until she had confronted the demons that haunted her. It wouldn't be fair to Jack, who was such a decent human being, or to herself, for that matter.

If she was going to marry Jack, it must be with a free heart, with love in her heart only for him. Anything else would be shoddy.

And so she had come to slay the dragon in his lair.

She had arrived in Paris on Thursday morning, and after unpacking and resting for most of the day she was ready for action. It was eleven o'clock on Friday morning, May 11, and the temptation to call Tom Conners was strong. But Alexa was not ready to face him just yet. And so she picked up her bag, left the suite and headed for the elevator.

A few seconds later she was walking across the elegant, marble-floored lobby of the Hôtel Meurice, which Anya had recommended. Alexa went through the revolving door and down the steps, stood outside in front of the hotel for a moment, undecided what to do. She was invited to Anya's house for lunch at one o'clock, so she had two hours to fill. And lots of options.

She was in her most favourite city in the world, and she knew it well. Since she had not been here for three years she was filled with excitement, nostalgia and the desire to visit much-loved parts of the city.

If she turned left, she could walk down to the Louvre, or she could turn right, walk along the rue de Rivoli, looking in shop windows until she came to the Place de la Concorde, the Champs-Elysées beyond, with the Arc de Triomphe at the top.

Making a snap decision, she set off walking towards the Louvre. What a glorious day it was. Paris shimmered under a brilliant, sunlit sky, which appeared to be high flung, a great arc that looked like an upturned bowl with its inside glazed a soft powder blue.

How magnificent everything looks, she thought, as she glanced around her, walking along the rue de Rivoli at a steady pace. A flood of memories engulfed her. Memories of Tom and the three years they had spent together . . . their sensual lovemaking, their joy in each other. Memories of working on different movies with Nicky and Larry. Such exciting days with them, such exciting nights with Tom . . .

She was assaulted all of a sudden by the fragrant, mouth-watering smell of fresh coffee. Abruptly she came to a stop outside a sidewalk café, and sat down at one of the tables.

'*Café au lait, s'il vous plaît*,' she said to the smiling waiter who had appeared in front of her.

'*Mais oui*,' he said, hurrying off.

Alexa sat back in the metal chair, thinking how wonderful it was to be here; how foolish she had been to stay away for so long.

A few seconds elapsed, and then the waiter was back, placing a pot of coffee and a jug of steaming hot milk in front of her.

'*Voilà, mademoiselle!*' he exclaimed with a nod.

'*Merci*,' she said, smiling back at him as he put a basket of fresh croissants on the table, together with a plate of creamy-looking butter and a dish of dark raspberry jam. She picked up the pot and poured coffee into the large cup, adding the frothy milk.

The first sip was delicious. Then she eyed the basket. She could smell the fresh croissants . . . Oh, what the hell, why not, she thought, and took a croissant, broke a piece off, added a touch of butter and a generous blob of the jam. It seemed to melt in her mouth, and she thought of all those breakfasts she'd had, just like this one, when she had been a student here.

Nine years ago. She had been just twenty-one when she had started at Anya's school. And from the first day to the last she had enjoyed every moment. A feeling of genuine euphoria and excitement enveloped everyone who became students there. Of course, it emanated from Anya, who else? And yet the other teachers were just as inspired, and as inspiring, as she was. They all inculcated a love of learning in her and in the other students, and they were the best, always the greatest experts in their given fields, and specially chosen by Anya Sedgwick for a variety of qualities as well as their talents.

How wonderful those years were, she thought now, leaning back in her chair, letting her mind fill with memories of those days. All her hopes and ambitions had been encouraged here and, thanks to Anya, so many of them had come true.

The woman was so striking and dramatic-looking that heads turned as she passed. She was tall, about five foot ten inches, well built but not overly heavy, and there was a regal air to her posture, fluidity in the way she moved with a measured grace.

But it was her face that made people look at her again. The woman was startlingly beautiful, with a thick mane of jet-black hair falling halfway down her back, perfectly curved black eyebrows above dark eyes that were huge, set wide apart, and a most voluptuous mouth.

Her clothes were simple yet elegant in their cut. She wore a black, light-gabardine trouser-suit, a tailored shirt of white silk, and high-heeled black sandals. A black leather bag was slung over her shoulder and she carried a pair of dark glasses in one hand. This simple elegance was carried through to her jewellery. There was nothing ostentatious about the watch she wore on her left wrist, the gold bracelet on the other, or the small diamond studs in her ears.

This morning she moved at a leisurely pace through the quiet halls of the Louvre. She had plenty of time before she had to leave, to keep her luncheon date at the Ritz Hotel in the Place Vendôme, not far away.

The woman became aware of the stir she was causing, and marvelled to herself. Three months ago she would not have believed it possible, but Maria Franconi had undergone an extraordinary transformation. It had taken her not quite three months to lose forty-eight pounds. During this time she had thrown herself whole-heartedly into a brutal regimen that comprised punishing workouts, and a diet almost free of fat, sugar and carbohydrates; wine and alcohol of any kind were forbidden. One day, halfway through her programme, there was a noticeable change in her face. She had always been very lovely, but now her face had become dramatically beautiful, and she had discovered that being beautiful was really quite addictive.

Even though she was now in Paris, Maria did not let up on her regime. She visited the spa in the hotel every day, swam, did exercises, and worked on the treadmill. She also remained on her strict diet, despite the tempting French food.

Although Fabrizio had been supportive, and had helped her to achieve her goal, he had been against her spending June in Paris. At the beginning of June, the entire family would depart for their villa in Capri, where they would spend most of the summer. Fabrizio was insistent that she should accompany them, and after a great deal of discussion, she finally agreed.

But she was determined to spend three weeks in Paris, and so she had arrived on May 3, and planned to stay until June 5, when she would join the other members of her family in Capri.

Maria had been busy since she had arrived. She had been to visit her beloved Anya several times. She had gone shopping, spent time in art galleries, and been to Versailles. And she had enjoyed every minute away from her job and her domineering family.

I escaped, she thought now, as she slowly began to approach the painting she had come to see. If only I didn't have to go back, if only I could stay in Paris. *Always*. She instantly pushed these longings to one side, not wishing to fall into unhappy thoughts today.

The painting was sublime. Incomparable. Maria stood in front of it for a very long time, gazing at it as if in a trance. It usually had this effect on her . . . it held her spellbound. The *Mona Lisa*. Painted hundreds of years ago by Leonardo da Vinci, the greatest artist there had ever been on this planet, with the exception of Michelangelo, in her opinion, anyway.

To be able to paint like that, she thought, a small sigh escaping her. She stepped closer in order to look more intently at the *Mona Lisa*. As she did so, out of the corner of her eye she caught a glimpse of a woman heading her way. Her heart fell. But she swung her head to make sure she was not mistaken, then swiftly turned back to face the painting.

After one last look, Maria hurried off in the opposite direction.

His table in L'Espadon faced the door, and he saw her the minute she arrived. He pushed back his chair and rose long before she reached the table, a broad smile of welcome on his face. When she came to a standstill he took hold of her arm, almost possessively, kissed her cheek and then stared at her intently for a moment.

Maria smiled at him as she slid into the chair. 'I'm sorry I'm late.'

He sat down opposite her, and shook his head. 'But you're not late, and even if you were, you're certainly worth waiting for. You look very beautiful, Maria.'

'Thank you,' she murmured, dipping her head slightly.

'I ordered grapefruit juice for you,' he went on. 'I hope that's all right.'

'It's perfect, thanks.'

Lifting his wineglass, he said, '*Santé*.'

'*Santé*,' she responded, lifting her glass, touching it to his.

'So what did you do this morning?'

'I went to the Louvre. To see the *Mona Lisa*, in particular. I'm always mesmerised by that painting.'

As I am mesmerised by you, he thought.

The maître d' arrived with the luncheon menus, and they studied them for a few moments. He knew what he was going to order; he assumed Maria did also. Since he was usually on a strict diet, as she was, they seemed to choose the same dishes. The other evening she had told him all about her strenuous dieting and her exercise programme, and had confided a great deal about herself over their second dinner. He had listened attentively and been impressed by her honesty.

He had seen quite a lot of her since her arrival in Paris, and he wanted to continue seeing her. He was smitten with her, and in a way he had not been taken with a woman for years.

'You are staring at me.'

'I'm sorry,' he apologised. 'I just can't help it. Your face is quite . . . *sublime*. That's the only word to describe it.'

Maria laughed lightly, and shook her head. 'I don't know about that. I only use that word when I think of the *Mona Lisa*. Now that truly is a beautiful face.'

'Yes, it is, and actually *you* should be painted by a great artist, a modern-day da Vinci.'

The waiter arrived at the table before she could respond. She ordered oysters on the half-shell and steamed turbot, and so did he.

When they were alone, Maria volunteered, 'I saw Alexandra Gordon at the Louvre this morning.'

His eyes narrowed; he glanced at her alertly. 'How was she? She must have been pleased to see you.'

'I didn't speak to her. I suddenly felt shy, a little nervous, and I slipped away before she spotted me. At least, I don't think I did.' Maria shook her head, added, 'It was foolish perhaps.'

'Was it such a bad rift between the four of you?' he asked.

'It seemed like it at the time. But now it all seems somewhat childish, even silly . . .' Her voice trailed off lamely.

Understanding that she did not wish to pursue the subject, he moved on. 'You're enjoying Paris enormously, aren't you, Maria?'

'Yes, I am. Thanks to you. You've been so wonderful to me.'

Reaching out, he took hold of her hand on the table. After clearing his throat several times, he said in a low voice, 'I'm very smitten with you, Maria. And I am hoping you feel the same way.'

After a moment's silence, she said, 'I do. Oh, Nicky, I *do*.'

They sat holding hands across the table, staring at each other in silence and with great intensity until the oysters were served. Finally releasing her hand, he picked up his oyster fork, and wondered to himself what was happening to him. Here he was, thirty-eight years old, an experienced man of the world, and feeling like a schoolboy. Daft, he thought, I'm daft.

After eating a few oysters, Maria put her fork down, and leaned across the table, levelling her gaze at him again. 'When I came to Paris over a week ago, I thought I'd take the train to London for a day or two. To see Ricardo. As I told you, he's working there. But I don't want to do that, not now, Nicky.'

'Because of me?' he ventured carefully.

'Yes.' She lifted her eyes to his, stared back at him.

Nicky saw desire reflected there, a yearning for him, and his chest tightened. Slowly, he warned himself. Take this very, very slowly.

Coming back to Paris *has* been a mistake, Jessica thought, as she walked up the narrow street alongside the Plaza Athénée Hotel where she was staying. There *were* too many memories here, and most of them were associated with Lucien Girard. They evoked in her an immense sadness for what might have been . . . a marriage that had never happened, children that were never born, a life not lived with the man she had truly loved.

Now she wished she had not phoned Alain Bonnal from Los Angeles last week to make this date for lunch today. She and Alain were friends because of Lucien, but he was not someone she was close to any more. She had seen him only twice in the last few years, when he had been in California on business. On the other hand, she had never forgotten his compassion for her when she had been full of sorrow.

He was a connection to the past—a past she had not been able to let go of apparently, if she were honest with herself. Lucien, and their intense love affair, had haunted her ever since he had disappeared. And haunted any other relationship she had attempted to have. She truly understood that now. Gary Stennis had been a casualty of her past, in certain ways, even though his behaviour had been deplorable. Ultimately, he had given her plenty of reasons to leave him. Not one regret, she thought, I don't have one regret about saying goodbye to Gary.

Of all the men she had known, Lucien had had the most impact on her. It's not a question of unrequited love, she said to herself as she hurried in the direction of Chez André, where she was meeting Alain, but of an unrequited life ever since she had left Anya's school.

She had not had a chance to visit Anya yet, but they had spoken on the phone several times. Perhaps tomorrow she would be able to run over to the house, to have tea or drinks, as Anya had suggested. Jessica had arrived in Paris three days earlier, but her work had taken up all her time. She had accepted a redecorating job for a valued client, who wanted her Bel-Air house to be redone. Jessica had suggested a theme built around French provincial antiques and fabrics, and the client had agreed. For the last couple of days she had been seeing the best of the antique dealers; seeking out fabrics in keeping with French country style; scouring the leading dealers for Aubusson and Savonnerie carpets.

Within a few minutes she was pushing open the door of Chez André, and hurrying into the noisy, bustling bistro, which had a typical old-fashioned Parisian charm, with its marble-topped bar, polished brass and air of bygone days. It was full of patrons at this hour, but as she glanced around swiftly she spotted Alain at once.

He waved when he saw her, pushed himself to his feet and came round the table to greet her. He made a big fuss of her and, after they had embraced and kissed affectionately, they sat down together on the banquette.

Alain exclaimed, 'You are more beautiful than ever, Jessica!' He shook his head wonderingly. 'You never age. Unlike me.'

'Thank you, Alain, for those kind words, but you've always been prejudiced. Anyway, you look pretty good to me.'

'A few grey hairs these days, *chérie*.'

'But a young face, nevertheless,' she shot back, smiling at him, thinking he was just as attractive as ever.

'An apéritif, perhaps?'

'Thanks, that would be nice. I'll have the same as you,' she answered, eyeing his kir royale.

After he had beckoned the waiter and ordered her drink, Alain turned to face her and went on, 'I know you've come to celebrate your former teacher's birthday, but you said something about buying antiques, carpets and art for a client's house. How can I be of help?' A dark brow lifted questioningly as he fastened his pale grey eyes on her.

'It's a house in Bel-Air, actually,' Jessica replied. 'A beautiful house, Alain, and one I believe should be decorated with French country antiques. Now the owner has finally decided to go that route.'

Jessica lifted her glass, which had materialised in front of her while they had been talking. 'Alain, it's nice to see you after all this time.'

'Two years. And *à votre santé*, Jessica. Welcome to Paris.'

'So you're still not married,' she remarked, after taking a sip of champagne mixed with kir liqueur.

He chuckled. 'I'm afraid I'm a confirmed bachelor. Never found the right woman, I suppose.'

She smiled at him, shook her head. 'I have a lot of beautiful women I could introduce you to, when you come to Los Angeles again,' she teased.

He merely smiled, sipped his drink. After a moment, he continued, 'You asked me whether I had any really interesting paintings, and fortuitously we've just received a collection from an estate that is being sold. I think you ought to see it. It is most unusual, and I believe you would make some good purchases.'

'I'd love to see it.'

'Would you like to visit the gallery after lunch today?'

Jessica thought for a moment. 'No, I don't think so, Alain, but only because I'm running out of steam. Jet lag, I guess.'

'Then I must feed you immediately.' He motioned to the waiter hovering nearby, who brought them the menus, recited the day's specials, then left them in peace to make their choices.

'Oh my goodness, my favourite!' Jessica exclaimed, as she stared at the menu. '*Cervelle au beurre*. That's what I'm going to have.'

'I recall how you and Lucien used to love brains. But not for me, I shall have a steak. And what would you like to start with? I see they already have white asparagus.'

'That's for me, Alain. Thank you.'

Once the food had been ordered, Alain asked for two more kir royales, and the wine list.

'Oh, no wine for me, thanks. I'm afraid I can't drink too much during the day,' Jessica explained.

'I will order a dry white wine, a Pouilly-Fumé, and if you wish you can have a glass later.'

'I'll see how I feel. Are you available tomorrow, Alain? Or perhaps the gallery is closed on Saturdays?'

'No, we are open. I will be happy to see you then, and I do think you will be impressed by some of the paintings.'

As they sipped their apéritifs, Jessica talked to Alain about art, and her own preferences, which he enjoyed, since she was knowledgeable. Madame Sedgwick's classes had been worthwhile, he decided, as he listened to her hold forth with confidence.

Alain Bonnal worked with his father and brother in their family-owned gallery. It was one of the best in Paris, and was particularly well known for its Impressionist and post-Impressionist paintings.

As she talked, Alain studied Jessica, thinking how well she looked.

Her face was unlined, and her pale blonde hair fell long and straight to her shoulders. She was slender, had kept her lovely figure. For a moment, he felt as though time had stood still. But it was only a fleeting thought, and then it was gone.

Their orders of white asparagus arrived, and Alain murmured, 'Aren't we lucky it's in season right now?'

Jessica nodded, and began to eat.

When the waiter arrived with the wine, she agreed to have a glass, and later, once their empty plates had been removed, she sat back against the banquette. A reflective look settled on her face.

After a moment or two of growing silence between them, Alain said, 'You're looking pensive, Jessica.'

'Am I? Well, to tell you the truth, I want to talk to you about Lucien.'

He nodded, looked at her attentively, his eyes alert, questioning.

She went on, 'All those years ago, we never considered one thing—that Lucien might have disappeared *on purpose*.'

Alain gaped at her, a look of absolute astonishment crossing his pale face. '*Mais non, non, ce n'est pas possible!*' he cried. 'What possible reason had he to do that?'

'He might have wanted to start a new life.'

'*Ah, non, non!* That is *ridiculous*! You and he had so many wonderful plans. He was an honourable man. No, no, he wouldn't have done anything like that.'

Jessica sat very still, staring at Alain. A vague half-memory stirred at the back of her mind, but she could not make it come to life. 'You know, Alain, I've always had this feeling, deep down inside me—a gut feeling—that Lucien is still alive. Somewhere out there.'

Alain Bonnal sat staring at her, dumbfounded.

When she was back at her hotel, sorting through the samples of the fabrics she had found earlier, Jessica thought about Alain Bonnal's stunned disbelief. Was it an act? *Did* Alain know more than he was saying? Did he know for a fact that Lucien *had* staged his own disappearing act.

'Oh, for God's sake, he's dead!' she cried out loud to the empty room. Move on, she instructed herself, you've got to move on. You've got to get a life. You can't live in the past, or . . .

The shrill ringing of the telephone cut off her thoughts, startled her. Reaching for it, she said, 'Hello?'

'Hi, Jess, it's me. Mark Sylvester.'

'Mark, *hello*! How are you?'

'I'm great. How're you doing?'

'A bit jet-lagged, but OK. Are you in LA? Or London?'

He laughed. 'I'm in Paris.'

He had taken her by surprise and there was a brief silence on her part. Then she said, 'Where are you staying?'

'Next door. Well, I'm not *exactly* next door, but down the corridor. I'm at the Plaza Athénée,' he answered, chuckling. 'How about dinner at La Tour d'Argent tonight? Are you free?'

'Well, yes, I am, as a matter of fact.'

'Then we've got a date. Is eight OK?'

'Yes, it is. I can't wait to see you.'

Chapter Eight

THEY SAT TOGETHER in the garden, under the ancient cherry tree, the old woman and her younger companion. The renowned teacher and her favourite former student. Anya and Alexandra.

Nicky was standing inside Anya's house, staring through the window at the two women. They were drinking their after-lunch coffee at the wrought-iron table, and chatting as animatedly as they always did. They look so comfortable with each other.

His former assistant was still as lovely as ever, he noticed, although her dark hair was cut shorter. It was chic, and she was certainly smartly turned out in her tailored, grey pinstriped jacket and matching short skirt. All the better to see those gorgeous legs, he thought, his eyes sweeping over her. She wore gold earrings and a gold chain round her neck. As always, she dressed with understated elegance during the day.

Next to Alexa, Anya was the *grande dame* personified, so regal in her bearing, and as good-looking as ever with her stylish blonde hair and perfect make-up. Anya was dressed in what she called her working uniform: grey flannel slacks, a white silk shirt and a navy-blue blazer. It makes her look so English, Nicky decided.

Glancing at his watch, he stepped out into the garden, saying, 'Good afternoon, ladies!'

They both stopped talking and looked across at him. Then Alexa leapt to her feet, ran to greet him, and threw her arms round his neck.

'I'm sorry I arrived a bit earlier than expected and interrupted your time with Anya,' Nicky said. He now glanced across at his aunt. 'Sorry, old thing.'

'That's perfectly all right, we'd more or less finished our lovely long discussion anyway. And, Nicholas, darling, please do sit down. I can't stand you hovering there like an anxious waiter.'

Nicky laughed as he strode over to one of the wrought-iron chairs arranged round the table and sat down.

Turning to face Alexandra, touching her arm with a loving hand, Anya said, 'I asked Nicky to do something for me last week, and it has to do with you, Alexa. Now I think he's here to report to me.'

Looking puzzled, Alexa glanced from Anya to Nicky.

'A few weeks ago, Anya had the feeling you probably wouldn't come to her birthday party because of Tom Conners,' Nicky began. 'She suggested I make a few enquiries about Tom, to ascertain what he was doing, what his status was in general.'

'I see,' Alexa murmured, then sat very still. 'He's still in Paris, that I do know. When I received your invitation to the party, I called him at his office. Then I hung up when he answered. I guess I lost my nerve.'

'So he *has* been on your mind,' Anya said. 'I thought as much.' She felt justified at having enlisted Nicky's help.

'Yes, Anya, he has. You see, I want to get rid of this unfinished business of mine. Then perhaps I can move on with my life.'

'Good girl!' Anya exclaimed. 'Well, I suppose we've done your legwork for you. Or Nicky has, at any rate.'

Alexa nodded. She was now eager to hear what he had to say.

'I made a few calls,' Nicky began, giving Alexa a direct look. 'Tom's not married, nor is he seeing anyone special. Although I do hear there are a few women circling him, so to speak. He inherited money from a relative recently, bought an estate in Provence.'

'Does this mean he is leaving Paris?' Alexa ventured.

'I don't know,' Nicky answered her. 'I'm afraid you have the sum total of everything I found out, Alexa, except that he's fit and well and, according to my friend Angélique, a casting director, he's still as good-looking as ever.'

Alexa suddenly felt lighter than she had in ages. As if a weight had been lifted off her chest. She smiled. 'Thanks for doing the legwork, Nicky. I owe you one. And in the meantime, when are we going to get together to discuss the movie? Later today?'

'I'm afraid not,' Nicky said, and glanced at his watch. 'I'm sorry, Alexa, but I have to go home to change. I have a special dinner date tonight.' Rising, he went over to Anya, and kissed her cheek. 'I'm taking Maria to dinner, you'll be glad to hear.'

'I am indeed very pleased, she's a lovely young woman,' Anya responded, and patted his hand.

Moving round the table, he went to Alexa and kissed her. 'We can lunch tomorrow, if you're free,' he said.

'I am, Nicky, that'll be great. Where shall we meet?'

'I'll take you to Le Relais at the Plaza Athénée. Let's meet at one.'

'That's perfect,' Alexa answered.

Anya got up, tucked her arm through his and walked back to the house with him. 'Thank you so much, Nicky, for finding out about Tom. I do appreciate it.'

'I think Alexa does too,' he murmured in a low, confiding voice. 'Don't you think she looks tremendously relieved? Probably to know he's still single.'

'Perhaps,' Anya replied, not quite sure whether this was the case. In her long years as a teacher she had learned one thing: young women could be very tricky.

'I am *so* glad you don't think I'm a meddlesome old woman,' Anya said to Alexa, after she had ushered Nicky out and returned to the table under the cherry tree. 'Some people might, darling girl.'

'First, I never think of you as *old*, and second, you were not meddling,' Alexandra asserted. 'Forewarned is forearmed. I can just hear you thinking that. Am I correct?'

'*Absolutely*.'

'I'm very surprised I didn't get a lecture from Nicky,' Alexa suddenly blurted out. 'He and Larry kept cautioning me about Tom. They both said he would only cause me grief.'

'I know Nicky can be a pain in the neck at times, but he's a good person, and let's face it, Alexa, he wasn't far off the mark, was he? And neither was Larry.'

'You're right, as usual.' Alexa gave Anya a concentrated stare, and asked pointedly, 'A few minutes ago, was Nicky referring to Maria *Franconi*? Is that who he meant?'

'I do believe it is.' Anya sat back, averted her face for a moment, endeavouring to stifle the laughter bubbling in her throat. Alexa had obviously been taken aback by Nicky's announcement about his dinner date. She knew that Alexa and Maria had locked horns at one point, just before their graduation, and there was no love lost there.

'I can't believe it! And certainly I don't get it. He's married. To Connie Aykroyd.' Alexa shook her head.

'Not any more, at least not for much longer. Nicky moved out a long, long time ago, and I suppose he feels he can date other women if he wishes. And if the woman is willing.'

'And obviously Maria Franconi is! Oh, Anya, what a weird *mix*!'

'Oh, I don't know about that. Nicky's quite taken with her.'

'*Really?* How amazing. How is she, anyway?'

'Maria appears to be very well. And pleased that she managed to lose forty-eight pounds.'

'Maria got *fat*?' Alexa exclaimed, and then she laughed. Her eyes narrowed. 'Oh dear, oh dear, all that pasta, I guess.'

Anya bit back a smile. She was amused that for once in her life Alexa was being a little bitchy. She said, 'At least she did something about her weight. But from your tone, I can tell you're still troubled by Maria, and her "treachery". Isn't that what you called it once?'

'She *was* treacherous,' Alexa responded in a hard voice.

'Are you still reluctant to talk to me about it, after all these years?'

'Yes, I am, Anya. It was awful, very unpleasant, and she was most unfair to me.'

Anya knew better than to press the point. Instead, she said, 'Jessica is here also, and I heard from Kay Lenox the other day. She'll be arriving imminently, if she's not already here. I sincerely hope the four of you are going to be able to bury your differences.'

Alexa noticed the slightly plaintive tone in Anya's voice. Reaching out, she patted her hand. 'Of course we are.' She began to laugh, and exclaimed, 'I'll beat them *all* into submission!'

Anya chuckled. 'Oh, Alexa, you can always make me laugh when you want to, especially when you try to be tough.'

'I *am* tough.'

'Not you, darling girl.' Anya shivered slightly, and pushed herself to her feet. 'It's growing cooler, Alexa, let's go inside. Look, the sun is already hidden by the clouds.'

Together they walked towards the lovely old house. Anya led the way, and Alexa followed her into the small library.

Anya went round the room, turning on lamps, saying to Alexa, as she did, 'Darling, do me a favour and light the fire. There's a sudden chill in the air.'

'Right away,' Alexa responded, and knelt down in front of the fireplace. There were rolled pieces of newspaper and chips of wood in the grate, and she found matches in a copper bucket that was filled with logs. The paper caught with a *whoosh*, and she knelt there until the chips also ignited, then she put on several small logs and walked over to a small upholstered chair and sat down.

Anya was already propped up against a pile of pillows on the love seat opposite. 'Thank you, Alexa.'

Picking up their earlier conversation, Anya said, 'So do me a favour, and yourself. Deal with Tom Conners. And if you find it necessary to walk away, then walk away. Get on with your life without him. You'll meet another man one day.' She gave Alexa a hard stare. 'In fact, I'm surprised you haven't done so already.'

'Oh, but I have, Anya. Jack—that's his name—Jack Wilton. He's an artist, very talented and successful. He wants to marry me.'

'And you, Alexa? How do you feel?'

'I like Jack a lot, I love him actually, but . . .' She shook her head. 'It's not the same as it was with Tom.'

She bit her lip and looked away. When she finally brought her eyes back to Anya they were troubled. 'I have too much integrity to marry one man while still yearning for another,' Alexa finished.

'Yes, you always have been a very honourable young woman. But what is honour worth if it is honour without courage? Don't be afraid to confront Tom, *and* Jack, if you have to. Take your courage in both hands and be honest in your confrontations.'

'I know, you're right, Anya.'

Anya smiled at her encouragingly, then glanced at the small desk in one corner of the room. 'There's the telephone. Go on, call Tom now. See how he reacts to hearing from you.'

For a moment, Alexandra found herself shrinking back in the chair. But then she stood up and walked across the room. Her hand shook as she picked up the receiver, but she ignored this, and dialled his private line at the office.

'Tom Conners,' he answered on the second ring.

She found it impossible to breathe. She leaned against the desk, swallowing; her mouth was dry.

'Tom Conners *ici*,' he said again in a level tone of voice.

'Hello, Tom, it's—'

He cut her off. 'Alexa! Where are you calling from?'

'I'm in Paris, Tom. How are you?'

'OK, doing OK. Are you here on business?'

'Sort of,' she answered, glad that she sounded normal. 'But I really came for Anya's eighty-fifth birthday.'

'It's hard to believe Anya's going to be eighty-five,' Tom was saying, laughing. 'I hope I look as great as she does when I'm that age.'

'So do I,' Alexa managed to agree.

'Can we get together, Alexa? Will you have time?'

She felt herself going weak with relief on hearing these words. 'Yes. I'd like to see you. When?'

'What about lunch tomorrow?'

'I can't, I'm afraid. I'm meeting Nicky Sedgwick for lunch. I'm going to be working on a film with him later in the year, and we have quite a lot to go over. So I can't really change it.'

'That's OK. What about tomorrow night? Are you free?'

'Yes.'

'Shall we have dinner?'

'That'll be nice, Tom.'

'Where are you staying?'

'The Meurice.'

'I'll come for you around six thirty, is that all right with you?'

'It's fine. See you then.'

'Great,' he said and hung up.

Alexa stood clutching the phone, staring at Anya.

Anya began to laugh. 'It wasn't so hard after all, was it?'

'Not really, but I *was* shaking. Inside and out. I guess I *am* still in love with him.'

'Perhaps you are. But you won't know how you truly feel until you see him tomorrow night.'

Chapter Nine

KAY WONDERED, as she walked up the Champs-Elysées, how she could have stayed away from Paris all this time. Taking a deep breath, she glanced about her. Paris *was* the most beautiful city, and it was particularly lovely this morning. The sky was a light cerulean blue filled with sweeping white clouds, and bright sunlight washed over the ancient buildings, the stone façades gleaming whitely in the clear light.

Staring ahead, Kay's eyes now fastened on the Arc de Triomphe at the top of the long avenue. Underneath that soaring arch the tricolour, the red, white and blue French flag, fluttered in the light breeze. The sight made her catch her breath. There was something so poetic and moving about that simple flag flaring in the wind. Because it symbolised a country's courage and triumph.

She had once gone up to the top of the arch, where she had stood with Anya, Alexa, Jessica and Maria, looking out across Paris. It was only then that she had truly understood why the area was also called l'Etoile—the star. The arch stood at the centre of twelve avenues which radiated out to form a star. Many were named after famous generals, and had been part of the modernisation of Paris which had begun in 1852.

As she moved through and round the arch, Kay had a sudden, unexpected thought of a woman who, like her, had been unable to give the man she loved an heir—the Empress Josephine. And eventually Napoleon had had to divorce *her* in order to father a son by another woman. He had not been particularly happy with Marie-Louise, daughter of the Austrian emperor, even though she had eventually given birth to a boy. It had been a diplomatic marriage, and Napoleon had forever yearned for Josephine.

Sighing to herself, Kay wandered away from the great arch, crossed over to the other side of the Champs-Elysées, and began to walk down the boulevard, thinking of Dr François Boujon. She had gone to see him yesterday at his rooms on Avenue Montaigne, to discuss her own inability to conceive. She had had an examination and tests, and depending on the results of these tests, she might have to spend a few days at his clinic in Barbizon, near Fontainebleau.

After a while, she came to Avenue George V, and she walked slowly along the street, heading toward the Place de l'Alma. In the distance, dominating the skyline, she could see the Eiffel Tower, and she remembered something Nicholas Sedgwick had once told her. That wherever you looked in Paris you would see either the Eiffel Tower or the great white domes of Sacré-Coeur.

She wondered how Nicky was, and the others. The girls who had been her companions for three years. Would they be able to enjoy Anya's party if they didn't make up? She was doubtful. For a long time she had thought of them as bitchy and unfeeling, but perhaps she was being judgmental after all. Life was too short, wasn't it? There were so many other things infinitely more important than quarrels that had happened seven years ago.

Anya had said this to her last night, when they had spoken on the phone. And Anya was right.

Kay found a table at a small café, on a side street just off the Place de l'Alma. When the waiter came, she ordered a tomato omelette, a green salad and a bottle of sparkling water. Once her order had been taken, she sat back, thinking about her life, and in particular, her husband Ian, whom she loved so much.

He, who was not at all enamoured of travelling, had been forced to fly to New York City the other day, in order to deal with an unexpected business matter to do with the woollen goods they produced at the Scottish mills. He would be gone for ten days, and in that time Kay hoped to finish her tests with Dr Boujon; she also planned to find the perfect premises for a boutique. Sophie McPherson, her assistant, was arriving next week, and together they would work with the estate agent who had been highly recommended.

As she sipped some sparkling water, Kay's thoughts drifted to those years she had lived in Paris. Home had been a small, cosy hotel on the Left Bank, and she had loved her tiny room in it, and the quarter where it was located, just off the Place Saint-Michel.

Kay's time in Paris had been the happiest years for her, and for various reasons. She was far away from the slums of Glasgow; she was safe, *that* most of all; she was attending the famous school she had dreamed about for years, never believing she would actually become a pupil there at the age of nineteen.

Being away from the bad environment in Scotland had given her a sense of enormous relief; she felt secure, not so vulnerable and exposed any more. She missed her mother very much, but her mother never permitted her to come back home. 'Remember this, lassie,' Alice Smith would say. 'There is no such person as Jean Smith. You are Kay Lenox now. New name. New identity. New life. New future. There's no going back, not in any way.'

Her mother's voice seemed to echo in the inner recesses of her mind, always encouraging, always speaking about her new life and her future. And I do have so much, Kay thought. But I'm always afraid of losing it. I can't enjoy what I have. That is the problem.

Things are going to be all right, she told herself firmly. They had to be.

How truly beautiful she has become, Anya thought, staring across at Kay Lenox, who had arrived at her house a few moments before.

It was a warm and sunny day, so Honorine, the housekeeper, had shown Kay to the table in the garden, which had been set for tea. But Kay had obviously immediately risen from her chair and strolled across the cobbled courtyard.

Now she waited under the cherry tree in the garden, gazing into the distance, one hand resting on the trunk, surrounded by the double cherry blossoms of palest pink. She was unaware she was being observed, and her face held a dreamy, faraway expression.

Kay is so tall, long-legged and slender she looks almost ethereal, Anya commented to herself. Sunlight slanted through the branches, turning her hair into a halo of shimmering red-gold fire. She still wore it long, as she had when she had come to the school at nineteen, and from this distance Anya thought Kay did not look as if she had aged a day since then. She wore a tailored outfit of delphinium blue, composed of very narrow trousers worn with high-heeled blue court shoes and a three-quarter-length jacket styled in the manner of a maharajah's tunic. The outfit was the epitome of elegance. Well, she always was enormously talented, a little couturier even when she first came to me, Anya thought to herself.

Stepping into the courtyard, Anya exclaimed, 'Kay, darling, here I am! So sorry to keep you waiting.' She hurried forward, her face radiant with smiles, her joy at seeing Kay after so long reflected in her sparkling eyes.

Kay immediately swung round, then rushed forward at the sight of Anya. She embraced Anya tightly. 'It's wonderful to see you!'

'I might well say the same, Kay. But come, dear, let's go and sit at the table and have a cup of tea. I want to hear all your news.'

Together the two women walked over to the wrought-iron table, where Honorine had covered the surface with a linen cloth, and put out all the accoutrements for afternoon tea. Aside from the big silver teapot, matching milk jug and sugar basin, there was a plate of lemon slices for the tea. On a tiered silver stand, Honorine had arranged an assortment of small nursery-tea sandwiches, as Anya called them, and plain biscuits. There was also a sponge cake filled with jam and whipped cream. Plus an English fruit-cake, dark and rich-looking, its top decorated with blanched almonds.

Picking up the silver pot, Anya poured tea into the china cups, then sat back, staring at Kay.

The young woman was simply spectacular to look at, with her tumbling red hair, cool, polished, ivory skin and blue eyes. 'Kay, you are stunning! What a pleasure it is to see you looking so . . . *fantastic*.'

Kay shared her smile. 'I guess I *was* a bit awkward and gangly even when I graduated, wasn't I?'

'Never quite that,' Anya protested. 'And congratulations on your extraordinary success. You've done the school proud.'

'It's thanks to you that I am where I am today. And of course my mother. Without her I would have been . . . *nothing*.'

Anya noticed the shadow that suddenly blighted Kay's eyes, fading their colour, as she spoke of Alice, dead for some time now. She was well aware that Alice had sacrificed much for Kay.

'We could only guide you, show you the way,' Anya remarked. 'You alone are responsible for your success, Kay.'

Kay nodded, sipped her tea, became silent, her face instantly serious, reflecting her thoughts. She fell down into the past for a few seconds, remembering so many things.

Breaking the silence, Anya said, 'I'm glad you came to Paris well before the party. It gives us a chance to catch up.' Anya chuckled and her eyes were merry. 'The others were of the same mind as you, Kay. Alexa, Jessica and Maria are also here.'

'Oh,' was all Kay could think of to say.

Anya was thinking of Alexa and Jessica who both had unfinished business to deal with. Studying Kay, she wondered about her. Did Kay also have a secret agenda tucked away?

Leaning forward slightly, she focused on the younger woman. 'Did you come early for any special reason, Kay dear?'

'Yes, actually, I did.' Kay turned to face Anya as she spoke, and continued, 'I am thinking of opening a boutique here. Everyone believes my clothes will sell well in Paris.'

'I'm quite certain that's true. And the idea is a marvellous one. I am proud of you.'

'Thank you. Also, I have to go to Lyon to see the textile manufacturer who produces my silks and brocades. I have some special colours I want created for my next collection.'

'You were always so clever with colour. I love this delphinium suit,' Anya murmured. Then she asked, 'And how is your husband?'

Kay sat up straighter. 'He's well.' She shook her head. 'Well, I hope he is. He's in New York on business, and Ian's not very fond of cities. He's probably very depressed and itching to get home to Scotland.'

'Ah yes, the countryman, you once told me.'

'Yes.' There was a slight pause. 'So, the others are here? Have you seen them yet?'

'Maria, several times, and Alexa came to lunch yesterday.'

'Are they both married now?'

'Oh, no.'

'And what about Jessica?'

'I haven't seen her yet. But she's not married. It appears that you are the only member of the quartet who has found the man of her dreams.'

Kay sat back in the metal chair, gaping at Anya, a look of dismay flickering on her face. Unexpectedly, alarmingly, tears gathered in her eyes, were in danger of spilling over onto her cheeks.

'What on earth's the matter?' Anya asked, her surprise and concern apparent.

Kay did not speak. The tears began to fall.

'Darling, what *is* it?' Anya leaned closer across the table, touched Kay's arm, as if to comfort.

Wiping the tears away with her fingertips, Kay said, in a hesitating voice, 'I'm so worried, Anya . . . about my marriage. I haven't become pregnant, and that's what's at the root of it all.'

'Oh, yes, I understand, darling. Ian wants a son and heir. The title . . . the lands . . . *of course*. Yes, I do see.'

Kay swallowed, cleared her throat. 'Ian is a very kind person, and he doesn't talk about it. He never has. But I know it's always at the back of his mind. And it's a kind of *pressure* for me. It's always hanging over me.'

'I know what you mean.'

'I came to Paris to see a Dr François Boujon. Have you heard of him?'

Anya nodded. 'Yes, he is very well respected. I am sure he will be able to help you.'

'Oh, Anya, I *hope* so.'

'Have you seen him yet?'

'Yesterday. I had an examination, and tests—' Kay cut herself off, averted her head, bit her lip.

Anya watched her intently.

Kay brushed her eyes with her fingertips once more; she had begun to weep again.

'Are you all right?'

'I lied to Dr Boujon,' Kay blurted out, turning to Anya. 'He asked me certain questions, and I didn't answer truthfully. I lied.'

'But *why*?' Anya frowned. 'Whatever made you do that? It's not like you.'

Biting her lip again, Kay explained, 'I didn't want to tell him my secrets. I think it's better if people don't know things . . . certain things about me.'

'I see.' Anya leaned back in the chair, looking at her steadily. 'And what exactly are you hiding from Dr Boujon?'

'When he asked me whether I'd ever been pregnant, I said no, I hadn't. But that's not true. I was pregnant once. Do you think he realised that when he examined me?'

'I'm not sure . . .' Anya studied Kay. 'You lost the baby?'

Kay took a deep breath. 'I had an abortion.'

'Oh, *Kay*.'

'Don't look like that, Anya. Please, Anya, please. I was abused when I was very young. When I got pregnant I was only twelve.'

Anya closed her eyes and sat very still for a long moment. When she finally opened them she thought the garden seemed a little less sunny, as if the light had somehow dimmed. Looking at her steadily, she saw that Kay's face was drained. 'Will it help to talk about it, do you think?'

'I've never told anybody. Only Mam knew,' Kay whispered.

Anya squeezed her hand, then poured more tea for them both. She was silent, waiting.

It took Kay a short while to compose herself. She sat back in the chair and took several sips of the tea Anya had just poured. Slowly her agitation and anxiety receded.

Her gaze was level, her voice steady as she looked across at Anya and said, 'I think it's best if I start right at the beginning. My mother worked for a fashion designer in Glasgow called Allison Rawley. Mam ran the shop. Anyway, Allison had a close friend, a titled woman who was English. She sometimes came to stay with Allison, and of course, she bought things at the shop. This woman offered my mother a job running her house. She thought Mam was efficient and capable. I was ten at the time.'

'And your mother accepted the job?'

'Yes. How could she refuse? It sounded fantastic. The house was on the Firth of Forth, about thirty minutes by car from Edinburgh. Her ladyship told Mam there was no problem about us—Sandy and me—that we could go with her and that we'd have our own quarters in the house. My mother saw it as an opportunity to better her position in life, earn more money, get us out of the city and into the countryside.'

Kay paused. 'I don't think I'll ever forget that house, Anya. The grounds were magnificent, and there were views of the Lammermuir Hills and the Firth of Forth. It was magical. But there was a problem in that house, at least for me—his lordship.'

'Was he the one who molested you?' Anya asked softly.

Kay nodded. 'It all started when we'd been living there for about a year. I was ten and a half by then. At first it seemed almost accidental he would brush against me, squeeze my shoulder, stroke the top of my head. But then he began to waylay me in the grounds, and in the woods. He . . . he touched me . . . in the intimate places.'

Not wanting to break the flow of her words, Anya simply nodded.

'After a few really bad incidents, I began to struggle with him. He vowed to sack my mother, send us all away, if I didn't do what he wanted. He said he would send us into penury, and I didn't know what that meant and I was scared. I knew what Mam's job meant to us. Where would we live if we had to leave? And where was Penury? I thought it was some awful place for the longest time.'

'And you never told your mother?' Anya ventured.

'I was too afraid to say anything . . . afraid of him . . . of what he might do to us. He was a powerful man, and we were poor. Dad had been dead for years and we only had Grandma in Glasgow.'

'Oh, Kay dear,' Anya murmured. 'How terrible it must have been for you.' Her face was bleak as she spoke, her eyes pained.

'It was horrendous, and very frightening. Then, as time went on, he became bolder, and he went further with me. I tried to hold him off, but he was strong and persistent. When I was almost twelve he finally went, well, he went the whole way, Anya. He raped me one Saturday afternoon when my mother was in Edinburgh with Sandy.'

Kay stopped again, took a sip of tea. After a few moments, she said, 'That happened several times and I was in panic. Then one day I missed my period, and I knew that what I'd feared had finally happened. I was certain I was pregnant.'

'And so you finally told your mother?'

'I did. I had no alternative. She was wonderful with me, and appalled about what had been going on. She flew into a blind rage when she went to see him. Straight away, she threatened him with the law. She accused him of molesting a minor, said she was going to the police and that she would hire a solicitor in Edinburgh. She vowed to sue him. At first, he denied coming anywhere near me, but there were no other men on the estate and we were in an isolated spot.'

'So your mother went to the police?'

Kay shook her head. 'No, she didn't. She was about to do so when his lordship offered her . . . a deal of sorts. He said he would send us to a doctor in Edinburgh, who would perform an operation on me, and that he would pay for it. He offered my mother three months' severance, and told her that we must all leave. Immediately.'

'What happened? Did your mother accept, Kay?'

'No. She understood she was holding all the cards. His lordship sat in the House of Lords, in London. He and her ladyship moved in all of the top social circles. It struck Mam very forcibly that the last thing he wanted was a scandal. When she realised this she made a counter offer.'

'And what was it?' Anya asked, leaning closer.

'She made sure she had all the information about the doctor in Edinburgh, and had *him* make the appointment. Then she told him that she wanted . . .' Kay took a deep breath. '*A million pounds*.'

Anya gaped at her. For a moment she was speechless. At last she managed to say, 'Did Alice get it?'

'No. In the end he settled for four hundred thousand pounds.'

'Good God!'

Kay nodded, then smiled faintly. 'My mother wouldn't leave until his cheques had cleared. Then we packed and went to Edinburgh where Mam found a small flat for us all.' Kay sat back, shaking her head, then she sighed, stared at Anya.

Everything was very still in the garden. Not a leaf stirred, nor a blade of grass. Nothing moved at all. Even the birds were quiet.

But Anya's head buzzed with all that she had heard.

'The money was used for your education, that's what Alice did with it. Didn't she?'

'Yes, and Sandy's. Mam never used it for herself, except for the rent in the beginning. She always worked hard, and she saved. And the remainder of the money, which she'd put into a savings account at the bank, went to start my fashion business later.'

'Alice was wise, Kay, very wise, and in so many different ways. But the abortion? You haven't spoken about it. Was it botched?'

'I'm not sure. But that's what worries me, Anya. Afterwards, I bled a lot and I was in terrible pain for days. What if the doctor damaged me?'

'I suppose he could have, but I think you would have known. Has everything . . . been all right over the years?'

'Yes, but I'm not sure that means anything.'

Anya rose and went to her, put her arms round her, endeavouring to comfort her as best she could. Kay clung to her, sobbing. Anya soothed her, stroked her head, and eventually she became quieter.

After a few moments, Anya murmured, 'He doesn't know, does he? You've never told Ian anything of this.'

'How could I?' Kay whispered. 'He knows nothing of my past. My mother created a whole new identity for me, and she had the money to back everything up. He'd die if he knew where I came from. And of course he'd divorce me. I know *that*.'

'You can't be sure, Kay, people can be very understanding.'

'I'm not going to take such a chance, rest assured of that, Anya.'

'Words are cold comfort in so many instances,' Anya began gently, stroking Kay's hair again. 'To say I'm sorry this happened to you is just not enough. It doesn't express the pain and hurt I feel for you, darling Kay.' Anya's voice shook slightly with sudden emotion, and she found she was unable to continue.

After a while, Kay pulled away and looked up at her. 'I lived with fear, once he'd started on me. But I was a dreamer. I learned to dream in my very early childhood, and it kept me alive.'

'You've managed very well. I can't imagine what it was like for you.'

'I learned one other thing, Anya.'

'What is that?'

'I learned to arm myself against the world.'

Honorine had come outside to tell Anya that she had a phone call and Anya had gone inside to take it. Kay was alone in the garden.

Her tears had ceased and she sat calmly in the chair, looking at her face in a small silver compact. There were a few mascara smudges round her eyes, and she removed these with a tissue, then powdered the area lightly and refreshed her lipstick. Afterwards, she put the compact and other items back in her handbag and relaxed.

When Anya returned she glanced at her and exclaimed, 'As good as new, my dear. Are you feeling better?'

Kay smiled. 'Yes, and thank you for listening, for being so patient and understanding, Anya. It's helped me.'

'There's just one thing I'd like to say. When you see Dr Boujon again, he might ask you whether you had an abortion, and I do believe you should tell him the truth.'

Kay recoiled slightly and stared at her. 'That would be hard for me—'

'You don't have to give him any of the intimate details,' Anya interrupted. 'I mean about the abuse. Just the bare facts. If you do have some internal problem, he must be told your medical history in order to make a judgment.'

'I suppose so,' Kay reluctantly agreed.

'It's more than likely he'll have good news for you, tell you there's nothing wrong with you, no reason why you can't conceive.' Anya peered at her. 'Then you'll have to try to relax about getting pregnant.'

Kay nodded.

Anya reached across the table and took hold of Kay's hand. 'You've been very brave and strong all your life, Kay, and I'm so proud of you. And I want you to know that I am always here for you, whatever you might need.'

Kay was touched, and she responded, 'Thank you for those words, Anya, and for being my friend, my one *true* friend.'

This remark made Anya frown, and she exclaimed, 'I hope I'm not your only friend, my dear.'

'Well, I'm close to my assistant Sophie, and also to Fiona, Ian's sister, but, well, yes, you are my only really intimate friend.'

How sad that is, Anya thought. She said, 'It's such a pity your little quartet fell apart. I sincerely hope the four of you are going to make an effort to set aside your differences and be friends again.' Anya gave Kay a long and pointed look. 'Take it from an old lady, life is too short to bear grudges.'

'I agree,' Kay answered, thinking that of the four of them she was the least to blame. It was the others who had created the problems.

Chapter Ten

ALEXA LOOKED AT HER WATCH as the phone began to ring. It was exactly six thirty. Snatching up the receiver, she said, 'Hello?' in a tight voice that didn't sound like her own, clutching the phone so hard that her knuckles shone whitely in the lamplight.

'It's Tom. I'm in the lobby.'

'I'll be right down,' she answered, then dropped the phone into the cradle, picked up her bag and shawl, and left the room.

As she waited for the elevator she glanced at herself in a nearby mirror. Her hair was sleek, her make-up perfect; she wore a tailored black linen dress that would go anywhere, her only jewellery was her watch and pearl earrings.

She took a deep breath as she walked into the elevator. She was anxious as it travelled downwards, but she saw him the moment she stepped out. He stood off to one side, near the entrance to the Jardin d'Hiver, but he was looking towards the main lobby and his face was in profile. She saw at once that he was as handsome as ever. He wore a dark blue blazer, grey trousers and a blue shirt. His tie was silk, a blue and silver-grey stripe; his brown loafers gleamed.

She swallowed, trying to get a grip on herself, and then started in surprise as he turned his head abruptly and saw her at once.

His face was serious as he walked towards her, his step and his demeanour full of confidence. Then he smiled suddenly, showing his perfect white teeth. His eyes were very blue. She saw too that his hair was now grey at the sides.

'Alexa,' he said, taking hold of her arm, kissing her cheeks.

She pulled away, almost at once, afraid he would hear the pounding of her heart. Swallowing, her mouth dry, she said, 'Hello, Tom.'

His vivid blue eyes searched her face for a split second, and he frowned. Taking hold of her arm again, he said, 'Let's have a drink, shall we?' They went into the Bar Fontainebleau that faced out through bay windows onto the Rivoli arches, positioned in front of the main entrance of the hotel.

He guided her to a small table near a window in a corner, where they both sat down. A waiter was with them in an instant.

Tom looked across at her and raised a dark brow. 'The usual?'

She nodded.

'*Deux coupes, s'il vous plaît.*'

As the waiter disappeared, Tom looked at her intently. 'You haven't changed. You look exactly the same, except for your hair.'

'I cut it.'

'I can see that. It suits you. *Très chic.*'

She said nothing.

After a slight pause, Tom went on, 'I've read a lot about you, Alexa. You've been having great success with your theatrical sets.'

'Yes, but I've been lucky in many ways.'

'I would say it has much more to do with talent.'

She smiled at him weakly, wishing her heart would stop clattering in the way it was.

The waiter was back at the table, depositing the two flutes of champagne in front of them.

Once they were alone again, Tom picked up his glass and clinked it to hers. '*Santé.*'

'*Santé*,' she said, and gave him a wide smile.

He put down his drink. 'At last,' he murmured. 'I thought that grim look was never going to disappear.'

'I didn't know I was looking grim.'

'Take it from me, you were.' He leaned across the table, the expression in his eyes more intense than ever. 'I'm glad you called. And I'm glad to see you, Alexa.' When she remained silent, he asked, 'Aren't you pleased to see me?'

'Yes.'

He laughed. 'Such a poor little "yes". So timid.'

'Not at all. I *am* happy to see you, Tom. I wanted to see you, otherwise I wouldn't have called.'

He reached out, took hold of her hand, held it in his, scrutinising her carefully. Then he glanced down at her hands. 'Not married or engaged or otherwise taken?'

Alexa shook her head, not trusting herself to speak.

'There must be someone,' he probed. 'Or is every man blind where you live?'

She began to laugh—he had always managed to make her do that—and she shared his sense of humour. She was about to tell him there was no one special, but she changed her mind. Instead, she said, 'I have one friend. An artist. He's very nice. English.' The words came out in a staccato delivery.

'Is it serious?'

'I—I—don't know,' she began. 'Well, perhaps *he* is serious.'

'And what about you?'

'I'm . . . uncertain. Is there someone special in your life?'

'No,' he answered laconically.

'I can't imagine you haven't had, don't have, a girlfriend around.'

'Of course. But you can make that plural. And none of them means much to me.'

She experienced such a surge of relief her whole body went slack. She hoped he hadn't noticed this, and said quickly, 'I saw Nicky Sedgwick at Anya's the other day. He mentioned that you'd bought a place in Provence. At least, that's what he'd heard.'

'It is true. My French grandmother died. She left me a little money. I bought a small farm outside Aix-en-Provence, an olive farm.'

'How great! Is it actually operating?'

'Limping.' He grinned at her. 'But I'm going to put a bit of money into it, hire extra help for the manager who runs it for me. But it will be a hobby, nothing more serious, *naturellement*.'

'So you're not giving up your law practice? Or leaving the city?'

'Now, who could leave Paris? Certainly not I. And surely you know I'm not cut out to be a country boy.'

'I do.'

He took a sip of his champagne, and continued, 'I booked a table at L'Ambroisie. In the Place des Vosges. But first I thought we could take a drive around Paris. It's such a beautiful evening, and you haven't been here for a long time.'

A short while later he was leading her down the front steps of the hotel, his hand under her elbow, guiding her. As they moved along the sidewalk, he raised a hand, signalling to a driver a little further along who was standing next to a car.

A moment later, Tom was helping her into the back seat of a maroon Mercedes and climbing in after her. Alexa slid along the seat, positioned herself in the corner; Tom took the other corner, and she placed her shawl and bag between them, as a barrier.

She noticed him glance down at them, saw his mouth twitch as he attempted to swallow a smile. She suddenly felt foolish, and racked her brain for some kind of small talk, but without success. She was shaking inside and once more felt as though she couldn't breathe. But this was not unusual. He had always had an extraordinary effect on her.

He was talking to the driver in rapid French, explaining where he should drive them—round the Place de la Concorde, up the Champs-Elysées, back down to the Seine, over to the Left Bank. Once he had finished giving the driver instructions he settled back in the corner, looked at her and began to talk in an effortless manner. 'So how is Nicky? I haven't run into him for a long time.'

'He looks great, and he and Larry are more successful than ever.'

'So I hear. And you're going to be working with them?'

'Nicky only. We had our first meeting today over lunch. And of course he always loves to rope me in when it's a costume picture . . . he knows I don't mind the historical research involved.'

'And what's the movie?'

'It's about Mary, Queen of Scots.'

'To be made in France?'

'Well, yes, and in England and Ireland.' Alexa broke off, exclaimed, 'Oh, Tom, how beautiful the Place de la Concorde looks tonight under this perfect sky.'

He glanced out of the window and murmured, 'Yes, there is such a marvellous clarity of light this evening. The city looks magnificent at this hour.'

'A little bit later than the magic hour, but nothing to complain about,' she said.

'You and your magic hour! Dreamed up when you were a child,' Tom laughed.

'You remember?'

'I remember everything.'

He reached for her hand, but she quickly put it on her lap and glanced out of the window again, pretending she had not realised he wanted to hold hers in his. She knew if he touched her she would fall apart or leap on him.

'So, tell me more about your movie,' he suddenly said, turning towards her. 'Do you know when the film starts shooting?'

'Not exactly. At the end of the summer, I think. Why?'

'I like the idea of having you here in Paris.'

'Oh,' was all she could say. She was at a loss for words.

Not long after this conversation the car came to a standstill on the Place Saint-Michel. 'Come on,' Tom said, and opened the door, reached in to help her out. To the driver he said, '*Cinq minutes*, Hubert,' slammed the car door shut, and took hold of her hand.

Striding out, he led her down the rue de la Huchette and up into the rue de la Bûcherie with its little cafés. Going towards the Seine, Tom exclaimed, 'Look, Alexa! You always said this was your favourite view in Paris.' Together they stood staring across at the Ile de la Cité, one of the small islands in the Seine, on which stood the Cathedral of Notre Dame. Alexa turned to glance up at Tom, just as he looked down at her. Their eyes met and held; she nodded, then turned to face Notre Dame. Its imposing Gothic towers were silhouetted against the deep blue sky, and the taller spire shone in the last rays of the fading sun.

She glanced up at him again and said, 'Yes, it does have a very special meaning for me, this view.'

'And for me, too. Do you think I don't remember that we came and stood here the first night we had a date.'

She opened her mouth to speak but no words came out. He bent towards her and kissed her softly. Then he pulled her into his arms, held her tightly against him, his kisses growing more passionate.

Her arms went round him, and she clung to him.

When they drew apart, he looked deeply into her eyes, and gently stroked one side of her face with his hand.

'Why did you bring me here, Tom?'

'So that you would know I haven't forgotten anything.'

'Neither have I,' she whispered. Her heart clenched as she thought of the pain he had caused her and the happiness they had shared.

At last she said, 'I don't think I could ever come to Paris without calling you.'

'And I couldn't bear it if you were here and I didn't see you.' Placing his arm round her shoulders, he walked her back to the car, and at one moment, he said quietly, 'I've missed you . . . a lot.'

'So have I . . . you.'

Tom took a deep breath, blew out air, glanced around him, and then after a moment, he ventured, 'Your friend. The Englishman. Does he want to make the relationship permanent?'

'He's talked about it, yes.'

'That's what *you* want, isn't it? Marriage, children, a family life?'

'I did want that, with you, yes.'

'And not with him?'

Alexandra shrugged, looked up at the sky, shook her head. 'I just don't know. Actually, I don't want to talk about it.'

'So sorry, I *am* prying . . .' His voice trailed off, and he led her towards the Mercedes parked just ahead.

They hardly spoke on the way to the restaurant, but sat quietly in their respective corners, although the silence between them was not angry but amicable. They were compatible, and comfortable with each other, even when they did not want to talk.

Alexa was in a quandary inside. She couldn't for the world figure out why he was asking questions about her love life. After all, it had been Tom who had broken it off three years ago. Then again, he wasn't acting as if it were over. He had pulled her into his arms and kissed her with growing passion a few minutes ago. She was glad it was he who had made the first move and not her. He had acted suddenly, unexpectedly, and she was so taken by surprise she had fallen into the trap . . . and into his arms. And willingly so. She had clung to him and kissed him back, and her heart had been clattering as erratically as his. So it wasn't over for him either, was it? She tried to pull her swimming senses together; she knew, only too well, that it wasn't over for her and she doubted that it ever would be.

For his part, Tom Conners was silently chastising himself for falling prey to his emotions in the way he had. From the moment he had seen her standing in the hotel lobby, he had wanted to kiss her long and hard. And he had spoken the truth when he said that he had missed her, and that he remembered everything about their time together. The problem was, he hadn't meant to start a relationship with her once more. It wasn't that he didn't want to make love to her, of course he did. But he was well aware that he had nothing to offer her . . . not in the long run. And he did not want to hurt her again.

'I'd forgotten how charming the Place des Vosges is,' Alexa said, breaking into his thoughts, and he roused himself quickly, pushed a smile onto his face.

'It really is the most beautiful old square in Paris, and you know it's seventeenth-century,' he said. 'And I think I told you once, my mother grew up in an apartment in one of the old houses at the other side of the gardens over there.'

'How is she? And your father?'

'They're both well, thanks, and yours?'

'The same, they're great.'

Hubert, the driver, was suddenly opening the door of the Mercedes, and after Tom alighted, he helped her out. They went into L'Ambroisie together, blinking slightly as they entered the dim interior. Tom was greeted warmly, and they were shown to a table for two in a quiet corner of a medium-sized room.

Alexa glanced around, once they were seated, taking note of the mellow old panelling on the walls, the high ceiling, the ancient tapestries, the silver candlesticks with white candles, the big stone urns filled to overflowing with fresh flowers.

'It has the feeling of an old house, a private home,' she murmured, leaning across the table towards Tom.

'And that's what it was, of course. There are several rooms for dining, and it's very hard to get a table unless you're famous or a politician. Or a noted lawyer.' He winked at her. 'And its undeniable charm is matched only by its delicious food. The chocolate dessert is sublime, and they have one of the best *caves* in Paris.'

'You know I'm not a big drinker.'

'But you'll have a glass of champagne, won't you?'

'That'll be nice.'

After he had ordered the champagne, Alexa said, 'You haven't told me anything about yourself. How have *you* spent these last few years?'

He leaned back in the chair, eyeing her thoughtfully, pondering.

She thought his eyes had never looked more blue; he was very handsome, debonair in his demeanour, and irresistible.

'I still represent a number of people in the film industry. In fact, I'm now head of the show business division of the law firm. The firm's become rather prestigious in the last two years. And my own work has been going well.' He gave her a lopsided smile. 'But nothing special has been happening. I lead a rather humdrum sort of life, Alexa.'

'I wouldn't call it that, Tom.'

The waiter arrived with two extra-tall crystal flutes of champagne, pale blond in colour and sparkling, and he was saved the trouble of answering her. He wondered why they were here; he wanted her at home in his bed.

Suddenly the maitre d' was standing next to the table, talking to Tom about the menu. It was obvious Tom was a favoured client.

Alexa sat back, half listening, her eyes riveted on Tom, mesmerised by him. Humdrum life, she thought at one moment, and wished she could live it with him. And then she thought of Jack and was sad.

The only man she wanted was Tom Conners.

'I hope you don't mind, but I've ordered for both of us,' Tom said, breaking into her thoughts. 'White asparagus, a taste of the langoustine in pastry leaves, which is their speciality, to be followed by . . .'

'Lamb,' Alexa interrupted peremptorily. 'I think you must have forgotten I speak French.'

'No, I haven't.' He sat back in his chair, his gaze steady as he studied her. If only she knew what he remembered. Images of her and their time together were indelibly printed on his brain, and she existed inside him, in his heart.

Alexa said, 'And you've ordered your favourite wine, Chateau Pétrus, which you once told me should be drunk only on special occasions. Is tonight special, Tom?' She gazed at him, the expression in her light green eyes as serious as her face.

'Absolutely. We're celebrating your return to Paris.'

'I'm just visiting. And not for long.'

He threw her an odd look, frowning, and murmured, 'Don't talk about leaving, Alexa, you've only just arrived. And you're coming back for the film.' His blue eyes quickened. 'How long will you be here on the movie?'

'I don't know. Nicky hasn't said. But quite a few months, I'm fairly certain of that.' She lifted her glass, took a sip of champagne, and asked curiously, 'You've never been to New York in the past three years?'

'No. I was in Los Angeles two years ago to meet a client.' He shook his head. 'I should have phoned you.'

'Why didn't you?'

He put his hand over hers. 'I didn't feel I had the right. I was the one who brought our relationship to an end. I was positive you had fallen in love with someone else and made a new life. Moved on.'

Alexa gaped at him, her eyes opening wider, and she thought: Fallen in love, moved on. How can he possibly think that? Doesn't he know how much I loved him? With all my heart and soul, with every fibre of my being? She held herself very still in her chair. Her eyes welled with tears and she wanted to look away but discovered that she couldn't. She blinked back her tears.

'I've upset you. What is it? What's wrong?' His fingers tightened on hers and he leaned closer over the table, his eyes troubled.

'I guess I'm surprised, that's all . . . that you think I could move on so quickly.'

'It's been a long time—three years.'

'You haven't moved on. Or have you?'

He did not want to answer at first, and then he admitted, 'No, Alexa,

I haven't.' He hesitated and then asked, 'But what about your friend? The Englishman? You must have a relationship with him, since you said he wants to make it permanent.'

'Yes, I do, but I have always been uncertain about the situation.' Alexa gave a strange little laugh. 'Some people would think I'm crazy for telling you this, feeding your ego, I guess.' She took a deep breath and finished softly. 'I love you, Tom. I always have, from the first moment we met, and I suppose I always will.'

He nodded, continuing to hold her hand very tightly in his. His blue gaze fastened on hers. 'I've spent the last few years having meaningless sex with women who meant nothing at all to me. They're a blur. You see, Alexa, I didn't want anyone else but you.'

She stared hard at him, her eyes narrowing. 'Why didn't you call me? Weren't you ever tempted?'

'Of course I was! I must have picked up the phone a hundred times. But I felt I did not have the right, as I just told you. I also knew I had problems to work out in my own head.'

'You said that you had nothing to offer, and you were setting me free. But you didn't do that. I've been for ever bound to you, Tom.'

There was a moment of silence.

He sat looking at her, his eyes searching her face, that face he loved. Slowly, in a low voice, he said, 'I've waited a long time for the call you made yesterday. I could hardly believe it was you.'

The waiter arrived with the white asparagus; he took a few moments serving it and drizzling the vinaigrette dressing before stepping away.

Alexa ate a few spears and then sat back in the chair.

Tom looked up from his plate, and frowned. 'Is something wrong? You're not eating.'

'I'm not really hungry.'

'Neither am I.'

They stared at each other, exchanging an intimate look full of yearning, fully aware of what they really wanted.

Tom said, 'We cannot leave now, not until the entire meal has been served. If we go, I won't ever be able to come here again.' He sighed, reached for her hand. 'I'll be *persona non grata*.'

'I understand. And after all this time, what's another hour?'

By the time the langoustine was served they had both adopted a more relaxed demeanour. At one moment, picking up his goblet of red wine, Tom toasted her. 'Here's to you, Alexa. Welcome back.'

'I'm glad to be back,' she said, touching her glass to his. She took a sip of wine. 'Smooth as silk, this Chateau Pétrus of yours.'

He laughed, looked pleased.

Alexa toyed with the lamb on her plate, took a forkful, ate a bite, then put the fork down. Looking across at him, she said, 'You mentioned your problems just now. Have you worked them out finally?'

'I believe I have, Alex, yes,' he replied, took a long swallow of the wine, and leaned back in his chair. His face had changed slightly in that moment. 'It's taken me a long time to settle things in my mind, to come to terms with everything, but I have.'

'I'm glad. It must make you feel better.'

'It does. I do have my moments, when I'm sad, but for the most part I'm much better than I ever was. I slayed the demons.'

'How did you manage to do that?' she asked, and then cringed inside when she saw the look on his face. 'I'm sorry,' she added quickly. 'I don't want to pry.'

'If I can't talk to you about it, then I don't know who I can talk to. I did it on my own, no psychiatrists, no tranquillisers to get me through. I just faced up to what had happened and, most importantly, managed to stop feeling guilty.'

'That must have been very difficult, Tom.'

'It was, but I had enormous incentive. I wanted to be the Tom Conners I was before Juliette and Marie-Laure died. When I told you there was no future for you with me, and you left Paris, I sort of fell apart. I began drinking. A lot.' He glanced at the glass of wine on the table. 'And not that mother's milk either. Hard liquor. Vodka, mostly, because it tastes of nothing. For six months. But one day I hated what I had become and I stopped. I also did something else.'

'What was that?'

'I decided to do some research.'

'*Research*? About what?'

'Terrorism. My wife and child were murdered by terrorists on a warm, sunny day in Athens. Like everyone else in that square that day, they were innocent. I wanted to know *who* and *why*, and so I spent a whole year reading, talking to experts, learning about Muslim fundamentalism and terrorist groups. And about four months ago I realised I was finally free of guilt. *I* hadn't killed my wife and child by being late that day. They had been blown to smithereens by those brutal cowards who fight a guerrilla war in the name of Islam.'

Alexa was very quiet for a moment or two, and then she reached out, touched his hand. 'Did you find out which group blew up the bus of Americans that day?'

'I have a good idea, and so do various governments. But what good does that do?' He sighed. 'The main thing is, I managed to rid myself of guilt, and I've felt like a normal person ever since.'

'I really am so happy for you, Tom, happy that you have been able to ease your pain . . .' Alexa broke off as the waiter came to the table and began to clear away their plates.

Once they were alone, Tom leaned forward and said quietly, 'Will you come home with me?'

'You know I will. Where else could I possibly want to go?'

They stood in the hall of Tom's apartment, alone at last as they had longed to be for the last few hours, but curiously silent now as they stared at each other intently. Although they had been more at ease with each other in the restaurant, the tension between them had returned once they were sitting on the back seat of the Mercedes.

Acutely conscious of each other, they had hardly spoken a word as Hubert had driven the car through the evening traffic, heading in the direction of the Faubourg Saint-Germain where Tom lived. Now the electricity between them was a palpable thing once more, and they both moved forward, coming together in the middle of the floor.

Tom gathered Alexa close, and she held on to him tightly, her body instantly welded to his. He bent down, began to kiss her fervently, and she matched his ardour. Alexa was shaking, her long pent-up desire for Tom flooding her entire body. Her bag and her shawl fell from her hands, but she ignored them as he led her away from the hall and into the bedroom.

He pulled her down onto the bed with him, and began to kiss her once more. His hand went to her breast and he stroked it. A small groan escaped her throat; her hands went up into his thick, dark hair and she felt his scalp with her fingertips. They were lost in their raging desire for each other, wanting only to possess and be possessed.

Alexa was overwhelmed by him, and her feelings for him, as she had been from the first moment they met. Her throat tightened. Nothing had changed, she knew that now. She felt undone, helpless, and so in love with him nothing else, no one else, mattered.

Tom touched her mouth with one finger, leaned into her, said softly, 'Take your clothes off, darling.'

She slid off the bed, did as he asked, quickly shedding everything, and then moved back onto the bed again.

Tom did the same, undressed with swiftness, and she watched him in the dim light of the bedroom, shivering slightly as he came back to her. He was so tall, long-legged, broad-shouldered, the most handsome and masculine man she had ever known. She longed for him to take her to him.

Tom lay down next to her, covered her body with his own, held her in his arms. Against her hair, he said, 'I've never stopped wanting you, and only you, Alexa.'

'Oh, Tom, darling Tom,' she whispered.

He stopped her words with his kisses, his mouth firm yet gentle on hers. As one of his hands moved down to smooth and fondle her rounded breast, he brought his mouth to it, smothered it with kisses.

Wanting to touch and kiss every inch of her, his mouth moved on, fluttered across her stomach, to those erotic secret parts of her. Her excitement fed his own arousal and he knew he needed to possess her totally, to make her his own.

Tom pushed himself up on his arms and looked down into Alexa's light green eyes. Her emotions were explicit on her face, and as his gaze lingered for a moment longer his heart clenched. He knew, all of a sudden, what she truly meant to him. He also knew what a fool he had been to ever let her go. As he entered her, she cried his name again and he told her finally, and with absolute certainty, that he loved her, that she was the love of his life.

They lay amid rumpled pillows and tangled sheets, resting quietly. The impact of seeing each other again had been devastating to them both, and they had fallen into their own thoughts.

For Alexa, their passionate lovemaking on this bed was merely a confirmation of what she already knew, had known deep down inside herself for the last few years. She loved Tom, always had, always would.

Endeavouring to move on, because he had been unable to make a commitment to her, she had striven for a successful career, a good life, and eventually she had even enjoyed a relationship with another man . . . Jack Wilton. The thought of Jack made her heart sink. She was going to have to tell him she couldn't marry him; she hated the thought of hurting him. But even though there might not be a future with Tom, she could not marry Jack or anyone else. Her heart belonged to this man cradling her in his arms.

He loved her; she had always known he did. Yet he couldn't take that final step. At least, not in the past. Now he might. He had told her he no longer felt guilt about the tragic deaths of his wife and child. And yet she wondered . . . had he really conquered it?

As he lay next to her, Tom was contemplating the dichotomy in his nature. How he loved her, this woman in his arms, with all his heart.

They were perfectly matched. Her passion, ardour and sensuality in bed had echoed his since their first night together years ago. She truly satisfied him and he knew he satisfied her. Yet despite all this he was afraid to make the relationship permanent, afraid he might somehow hurt her in the long run . . . But if he lost her again, where would he be?

Alexa moved in his arms, and turned to face him. Her cool green eyes looked deeply into his. 'I want to tell you something, Tom.'

'Then tell me.' He held his breath, wondering what was coming.

'I want to be with you, and being married doesn't really matter to me any longer. Just so long as we're together.'

He searched her face; his eyes, fastened on hers, were filled with love. 'And I want to be with you, Alexa. But we're so far away from each other; you're in New York, I'm here.'

'I know, but I'm coming back soon, to do the movie.'

'And after that?'

'I think we can work it out.'

'I know we can, darling.' He kissed her, and they both knew a bargain had been sealed. 'You're my one true love, Alexa.'

Reaching out, she touched his cheek very gently, and leaned into him, kissed him lightly on the lips. 'Everything will be all right. *We're* going to be all right, Tom.'

Tom relaxed, closing his eyes, and he realised then that the pain had finally stopped. That awful pain he had lived with all these long years had miraculously ceased to exist, and he was at peace.

'Why do you have this photograph in your album?' Tom asked, looking up at Alexa as she came out of the bathroom in her hotel room. It was Sunday morning. As he waited for her, Tom had seen the small red leather album and picked it up.

'Which one are you referring to?'

'This one,' he said, holding the album out to her.

Alexa took it from him and stared down at the photograph he was indicating. It was of Jessica and Lucien on the Pont des Arts, and she had taken it just a few weeks before graduation.

'It's Jessica Pierce,' Alexa explained as she looked up at Tom. 'She was at Anya's school with me.'

'No, no, it's the man I'm talking about. I didn't know you knew him. He's a neighbour of my parents.'

Alexa was gaping at Tom. 'That can't be. Lucien disapp—'

'Why do you call him that?' Tom interrupted.

'That was his name . . . Lucien Girard.'

'No, no, Alexa,' Tom argued, shaking his head. 'The man with Jessica is Jean Beauvais-Cresse, and he lives in the Loire Valley.'

Alexa was speechless for a second, and she sat down heavily on the chair opposite Tom. 'Are you sure about what you're saying?'

He leaned back on the sofa, a reflective expression crossing his face. 'Well, I'm pretty certain this *is* Jean Beauvais-Cresse. I could be wrong, but I don't think I am.'

Tom took the album and carefully studied the photograph of Jessica and Lucien on the bridge. Placing it on the coffee table, he said, 'The man in the picture appears to be in his mid-twenties. When did you take it?'

'About seven or eight years ago.'

'The man I know, well, I shouldn't say I know him, I'm acquainted with him, that's all. Anyway, he's in his mid-thirties now.' Tom focused his eyes on her. 'It's Jean when he was younger.'

Alexa bit her lip and shook her head. 'Then at a certain time he led a double life. Or he led a different life as Lucien Girard.'

'Tell me about him and Jessica, Alexa.'

'There's not a lot to tell. Jessica and Lucien met, started to date. Soon they were in love. She told me they wanted to marry. And then one day Lucien disappeared. She and a friend of Lucien's did everything they could to find him, but without success. In the end she just gave up and went back to the States.'

Tom nodded. 'And what was this Lucien Girard doing at the time? Was he a student also? Or was he working? Or what?'

'He wasn't a student, Tom. He was an actor. Not well known, he only had small roles, but he was quite good, from what I heard.'

Alexa rose, went to the window, and stood looking out at the Tuileries across the street. After a short while she came back to her chair and looked across at Tom. 'If Lucien and Jean *are* the same person, Jessica has a right to know.'

Tom inclined his head. 'I've barely met Jean Beauvais-Cresse, but I could phone my father and ask him what he knows.'

Alexa's face quickened. 'Would you mind?'

'No, I'll call him after lunch.'

Alexa rose suddenly. 'I'd better finish dressing, then we can leave for Anya's. We mustn't be late for Sunday lunch. It's a sort of ritual with her.'

Alexa was quiet in the taxi on the way to Anya's house, and several times Tom glanced at her out of the corner of his eye. She seemed preoccupied, and so he knew it was wisest to keep silent.

Settling back against the seat, he thought about their morning together. They had woken early and prepared breakfast in the kitchen. Later Alexa had wandered around, exclaiming about the changes he had made in the apartment since she had last been there, showing her approval. Then she had called her hotel for messages. The only one was from Anya, inviting her to Sunday lunch. He had heard her on the phone, asking whether she could bring him, and then the whoop of jubilation as she had hung up the phone. 'She can't wait to see you, Tom! You're invited too.'

On their way to lunch they had stopped off at the hotel, so Alexa could put on make-up and change. He glanced at her now, thinking that her clothes stamped her nationality on her. She could only be an American in her blue jeans, white silk shirt, and brown loafers worn with white woollen socks. A dark blue cashmere sweater was tied round her neck. He loved her looks.

Instinctively, Tom knew that Alexa was going to tell Anya about the resemblance between Lucien Girard and Jean Beauvais-Cresse. He had seen Alexa put the leather album into her bag before they had left the hotel suite, and he wondered what Anya would have to say.

Chapter Eleven

ANYA SEDGWICK GLANCED AROUND her upstairs sitting room through appraising eyes and decided that it looked particularly warm and welcoming this morning.

Red and yellow tulips made stunning pools of vivid colour in various parts of the room, and a fire burned brightly in the hearth. Although it was another sunny May day there was a nip in the air, and she had asked Honorine to make a fire. She had always liked to see one burning in this room, even in spring and summer.

Moving around, her bearing as elegant as always, her eagle eyes sought anything that might be out of place; she found little amiss, except for a crooked photograph frame on the skirted table. After straightening this, she went and sat down behind her large desk in the corner near the fireplace.

As she waited for her luncheon guests to arrive, she once again looked at the list of acceptances for her birthday party. It had grown, and the number now reached a hundred and fifty. She put the list down and sat back in her chair, staring into space for a moment, her eyes as clear and bright as they had always been. She truly was looking forward to her eighty-fifth birthday party and had carefully planned what she would wear.

Anya knew she didn't look her age, and she certainly didn't feel it. I've been on this earth eighty-five years and I've lived every one of those years to the full, with energy, zest and enthusiasm. I've never been bored or jaded, and my mind has always been active, alert and filled with optimism. She smiled inwardly, as she added to herself: And I aim to be around for a long time yet.

The telephone rang, and she picked it up. 'Hello?'

'It's Nicky, Anya, good morning. I'm sorry, but—'

'Don't tell me you're not coming to lunch.'

'There's a problem.'

'What is it?'

'Maria. She's very nervous about coming face to face with Alexa.'

'Well, she'd better get over it, because she's going to have to do exactly that and very soon, even if she doesn't do it today. I want this mess cleaned up before the party, Nicky!' she exclaimed. 'Actually, I was planning on having a lunch for those four later in the week, so this makes a good beginning.'

'Oh, are the other women coming today?' he asked quickly.

'No, no, just Alexa and Tom, as I told you.'

'Are they back together?'

'I don't know. I understand they had dinner last night.'

Nicky sighed. 'Well, I hope I can persuade her.'

'Don't sound so weak-kneed, Nicky. Be firm. Wait, put her on the phone, I'll speak to her myself.'

'Oh, I'm not . . .'

'Don't stonewall me. I know she's with you, either at your flat or her hotel. You're having an affair with Maria, and more power to the two of you. Please, put Maria on the phone. *Now*.'

'Yes, OK, and calm down, Anya.'

A moment later, Maria said meekly, 'Good morning, Anya.'

'Good morning, my dear. I expect you for lunch at one o'clock. It is extremely important to me that you are present today.'

'Yes, we will come,' Maria promised, and hung up the phone.

Anya rose, walked round the desk to the fireplace, stood with her back to it for a few moments, thinking about Nicky and Maria. She had seen them on quite a few occasions since Maria's arrival in Paris, and it was very apparent to her that they were completely absorbed in each other. Infatuated, she thought, and then amended that. No, they're in love, she corrected herself, and she just hoped Nicky would be able to sort out his problems with Constance, and as quickly as possible. Maria and Nicky were ideally suited, and they should be together on a permanent basis.

As for Alexandra and Tom Conners, there was no question that these two had connected again last night. When Alexa had returned her phone call, earlier this morning, she had asked her whether this was so. Alexa had answered in the affirmative, adding, 'big time'. Anya loved this expression, and she smiled to herself. With a sudden flash of intuition, Anya knew that these two *were* going to be together for the rest of their lives, even if they didn't know that yet.

Ten minutes later Alexa was rushing into the room, her face filled with smiles, followed closely by Tom, who was also smiling broadly.

'Good morning, Anya!' Alexa cried, hurrying over to the fireplace, hugging Anya tightly. In her ear, she whispered, 'I'm so glad you made me call him. He's been wonderful.'

'I'm happy you're here, Alexa, and you too, Tom,' Anya said as Alexa stepped away from her. She stretched out her hand to Tom, who took it, and shook it with a firm grip.

'It's wonderful to see you again after so long.'

'You're looking well, Tom,' Anya responded, still smiling. 'Now, what would you both like to drink?' As she spoke she glanced over at a chest in the far corner, where bottles of liquor and glasses were lined up on a tray. There were also two silver buckets filled with ice, one containing a bottle of white wine, the other champagne.

'I know Alexa will have champagne, Anya, and so will I. Why don't I pour it, and what about you? What will you drink?'

'The Veuve Clicquot also, thank you, Tom.'

He nodded and moved across the room. She watched him as he poured champagne into tall flutes. He had always been well dressed, and today he wore a pale blue checked shirt, navy tie, navy blazer and blue jeans, impeccably tailored. Custom-made, Anya thought, and then accepted a glass of champagne from him.

The three of them stood in front of the fireplace, and clinking their glasses, they said, 'Cheers,' in unison. Looking up at Tom, Anya found his eyes blinding for a split second. They were the bluest eyes she had ever seen. If only I were fifty years younger, she thought, and then smiled inwardly, amused at herself. Imagine fancying a man at my age, she thought, and focused on Alexa.

'Is Nicky coming to lunch by any chance?' Alexa asked.

'He is, as a matter of fact, and he's bringing Maria Franconi.'

'Oh no!' Alexa exclaimed before she could stop herself.

'Oh yes,' Anya shot back. 'And I think you'd better get used to it, Alexa, since you'll be working with Nicky. Those two have become . . . well, an item is the best way to put it. That aside, I am hoping you, Maria, Kay and Jessica are going to be civil to one another. I'm planning a lunch later in the week, so you can all have it out. None of you has ever told me what caused you to blow your friendships apart.' She raised an eyebrow questioningly.

'It just so happens that it all started with Maria,' Alexa volunteered after a moment or two. 'But since she's coming for lunch we'd better not get into it now.' Moving towards the sofa, Alexa sat down, and Anya joined her.

Tom lowered himself into the armchair next to them, and put his glass on the coffee table. Turning to Anya he said, 'I think Alexa wants to talk to you about something important. Don't you, Alexa?'

Taken aback for a moment, knowing he was referring to Jessica and Lucien, she could only nod. Finding her voice at last, she said, 'I think Tom ought to tell you what happened this morning, and then I'll take it up from there.' She put her glass down, reached for her bag on the floor, and opened it.

Tom said, 'I was waiting for Alexa to change at the hotel, and I happened to pick up a photo album. As I went through it, I saw a picture of a man who's a neighbour of my parents in the Loire. In the photo he looked about eight years younger than he does today. I didn't understand why Alexa would have a picture of him.'

Alexa handed Anya the album open at the photograph of Jessica with Lucien Girard.

Anya took the album, gazed at the picture for a second, then looking at Tom, she said, 'It's Lucien. But who do *you* think he is?'

'Jean Beauvais-Cresse, a man in his mid-thirties who lives near my parents. I don't know much about him.'

'He could be a relative,' Anya pointed out.

'Indeed he could,' Tom agreed. Taking a deep breath, he said, 'Alexa feels she ought to talk to Jessica. What do you think, Anya?'

'Not at the moment!' Anya exclaimed. 'Jessica shouldn't be told anything about this. It would only upset her terribly.'

Nodding, Alexa said, 'Anya, you might think I'm being fanciful, but I have a really weird feeling about this photo. I think Jean Beauvais-Cresse and Lucien Girard are the same person. I can't explain—' She stopped as Nicky walked into the room with Maria Franconi.

'I hope we're not *very* late,' Nicky said. After kissing Anya and squeezing Alexa's shoulder, he shook Tom's hand. 'Tom, it's great to see you! And this is Maria Franconi, I don't think you've met.'

Maria smiled, shook Tom's hand. 'I am pleased to meet you.'

'It's a pleasure,' Tom replied, smiling at her.

After kissing Anya on the cheek, Maria looked towards Alexa, now seated on the sofa, and forced a smile. 'Hello, Alexa.'

'Hi, Maria,' Alexa responded coolly, without smiling.

'Do be a darling, Nicky, and pour Maria a glass of champagne,' Anya said.

'Oh no, Anya, thank you, but I'd prefer water,' Maria announced.

'Coming right up, sweetie,' Nicky said as he crossed the room to the drinks tray. 'But I think *I'll* have a drop of bubbly myself.'

'Sit down, Maria dear.' Anya indicated the chair next to her, and went on, 'I haven't had a chance to tell you this before, but I've studied the photographs Nicky gave me the other day. Maria, your paintings are extraordinary. But then you were an enormously talented artist when you were at the school.'

Maria looked extremely pleased when she spoke. 'Thank you, Anya. Hearing those words from you is very important to me.'

Nicky carried the water to Maria, and then stood in front of the fire, regarding all of them. After a moment he took a sip of his champagne, and said, 'Cheers, everybody.'

'Cheers,' Tom answered.

'*Santé*, Nicky darling,' Anya murmured.

Alexa simply raised her glass to him, and smiled, and then eyed Maria out of the corner of her eye. She was indeed a beautiful woman now.

Glancing across at Alexa, Nicky said, 'Did I hear you mention Lucien Girard just now?'

The room went quiet.

Tom glanced at Alexa and they exchanged pointed looks.

Anya said swiftly, 'Oh, it was nothing important, Nicky, just a casual remark on Tom's part. Now, Honorine's daughter, Yvonne, came in to cook for me today, and I know she's making something very special for the first course. So drink up, Nicky.'

Everyone finished their drinks and trooped down the stairs and into the dining room which overlooked the cobbled courtyard and the garden. To reflect the outside, which was so visible through the windows and the French doors, Anya had used a colour scheme of light and dark greens, accented with touches of white. With its billowing white organdie curtains at the windows, dark parquet wood floor and masses of white flowering plants, the room looked fresh, airy and cool.

Pausing at the circular table, made of highly polished yew wood and surrounded by five Louis XV chairs upholstered in a green and white checked fabric, Anya rested one hand on a chair and said, 'Maria, come and sit at my left, and Tom, please take the chair at my right. Alexa dear, sit down next to Tom, and Nicky, you can sit between Alexa and Maria.'

Smiling, she lowered herself into her chair. 'I think that works very well,' she continued, and looking across at Nicky she said, 'Would you pour the white wine for those who want it, and there's a very nice red to have with the main course.'

Nicky did as he was asked as Honorine came into the room carrying a large tray. She was followed by her daughter Yvonne who held a smaller tray in her hands. Within minutes they had all been served with an individual cheese soufflé and were soon exclaiming about it. At one moment Nicky announced, 'It's as light as a baby's breath.' Everyone laughed at this expression, and the ice was broken a little, but Anya noticed as this first course was being eaten that Alexa and Maria avoided speaking to each other. However, Tom and Nicky had lost no time in getting reacquainted, and they were now chatting enthusiastically about the movie industry in general.

After the empty soufflé dishes had been cleared away, Nicky served the Mouton Rothschild to everyone except Maria, and Tom poured the mineral water. Not long after this, Honorine came back with a platter of roast leg of lamb, followed by Yvonne with a dish of steamed vegetables and roasted potatoes. The conversation at the table was rather mundane as the main course was eaten and enjoyed, the red wine savoured, the water drunk.

Once lunch was over, Anya asked everyone upstairs for coffee, and once again they moved en masse to the floor above.

Anya was pouring the coffee when Tom, hovering over her, asked, 'May I use your phone, please, Anya?'

'But of course,' she said, and glancing at Alexa, she went on: 'Show Tom into that little den down the corridor, Alexa, please. He can use the phone in there.'

Alexa nodded, took hold of Tom's hand and accompanied him out of the room. Once they were in the corridor, close by the den, Tom pulled her into his arms, and kissed her deeply. As he released her, Alexa smiled up at him adoringly. Pushing open the door of the den, she whispered, 'Don't be too long.'

As she walked back to the sitting room, Alexa wondered whether to say anything to Nicky about Lucien Girard. Normally she would have done so, but she didn't trust Maria. How she had changed in her appearance, though. With a tendency to overeat, she had looked slightly plump all the time she had attended Anya's school. Her face had been lovely but her body too fleshy for a young woman.

Maria was standing near the window, looking casually elegant in burgundy slacks and matching woollen jacket, her black hair streaming down her back; her face, in profile, was stunningly beautiful.

No wonder Nicky fell for her, Alexa thought, sitting down next to him on the sofa. She picked up her coffee cup and took a sip, then glanced at Nicky. 'I can't wait to see the script, and once I've read it, Tom will drive me down to the Loire. He feels sure there are any number of houses that would be a perfect setting for the film.'

'Maybe we'll all go down for a weekend,' Nicky suggested.

Alexa gaped at him. 'You've got to be kidding!'

Nicky exclaimed, 'Oh I know you're angry with Maria. She's told me all about it. And frankly I think it's about time you both grew up and behaved like the mature young women you are.'

'Hear! Hear!' Anya exclaimed. 'It's time to move on.'

Maria walked slowly towards the fireplace, looking nervous. Then she sat down on the edge of a chair, and said in a low voice, 'I'm sorry, Alexa, for causing you so much trouble. Truly regretful. But I was young, I didn't mean . . .'

'You betrayed me!' Alexa snapped.

'I didn't mean to! It was an accident. An error on my part. I've always been . . . so very sorry, Alexa.'

Alexa glared at her. 'I was never interested in Ricardo. That was all your imagination. And you blew it into something so enormous you incited Jessica to action, and she told me off in the most awful way. She took your side and she stopped being my friend.'

'I'm so very, very sorry, Alexa,' Maria apologised again. Her face had turned a ghastly white, and she appeared contrite, worried.

'You were jealous of our friendship,' Alexa shot back.

'I wasn't. That's not true.' Maria now looked as if she were on the verge of tears.

'That's enough, girls,' Anya said in a firm voice. 'I want you both to come over here for coffee tomorrow morning. And I'll have Jessica and Kay here as well, and we'll straighten this out once and for all. So let us shelve the matter. This is not an appropriate time.'

At this moment Tom walked back into the room, and from the look on his face Alexa realised his father had told him something he found interesting.

She said, 'It's all right, Tom, you can talk freely here in front of Nicky and Maria.'

Surprised, he raised a brow questioningly.

Alexa nodded, then focused her attention on Maria. 'We're going to talk about Lucien Girard. But you cannot breathe a word of it to Jessica. Do you understand that, Maria?'

'Yes. I wouldn't say anything to Jessica . . . or anyone.'

Nicky, intrigued, asked, 'What's all this about then, Tom?'

Tom explained, telling them about the photo in Alexa's album. 'The whole thing is a bit flimsy, I must admit, although a couple of things my father said intrigued me. The two men *could* be one and the same.'

Nicky sat up straighter on the sofa, frowning. 'I didn't know Lucien all that well, Tom, but I don't think he was the kind of man to lead a double life. Anyway, who is it that so resembles him?'

'A man called Jean Beauvais-Cresse, who's in his mid-thirties. Earlier, I'd thought he might be related to Lucien. Perhaps Lucien was a brother using a stage name. However, my father told me that Jean's only brother died about seven years ago.'

Maria and Alexa exchanged glances.

'What else did your father say?' Anya asked.

'He told me that the brother was the eldest son, and that he was killed in a terrible accident. The brother's untimely death caused the father to have a stroke. Apparently he was very attached to the son who died. He was the heir to the title, the lands, the chateau. Jean had been living in Paris, but came back when his father was stricken, to look after him. He inherited everything when the old man died.'

'But don't you think it sort of fits in with Lucien's disappearance?' Alexa asked.

Tom nodded. 'The time frame is certainly right.'

Nicky said, 'Let's just go over it. Seven years ago, Lucien Girard disappears. Seven years ago Jean's elder brother dies unexpectedly, so that Jean becomes the heir. But what if Lucien, working in Paris as an actor, were the eldest son and met a terrible fate?'

'I thought of that,' Tom answered. 'But my father said the eldest son was much older than Jean. By about fifteen years.'

'So Lucien and Jean *could* be the same person,' Anya stated.

Tom sat down in a chair, and continued, 'My father said he'd make a few discreet enquiries, and I'll talk to him tomorrow. In the meantime, no one should say a word to Jessica. It wouldn't be fair. Either to her or to Jean Beauvais-Cresse.'

Anya settled back against the sofa, closing her eyes for a moment. Something had stirred at the back of her mind but she couldn't quite put her finger on it. And so she let it go. For the moment.

'Let's go for a walk,' Tom said, as they left Anya's house.

'Great idea,' Alexa agreed, falling into step with him. 'This is my favourite part of town.'

Tom smiled, and took hold of her hand, tucked her arm through his, and together they headed in the direction of the rue de Solférino and the quays running parallel to the River Seine.

It was warmer now and sunny, and the sky above was a clear blue arc, unblemished, without cloud, and benign on this May Sunday afternoon. For a short while they walked along the Quai Anatole France, enjoying each other, the weather, and the charming views of the Seine. Its rippling waters glittered in the sunlight, and suddenly a faint breeze blew up, rustled through the trees that grew alongside the Seine, made the leaves flutter and dance in the silvery light.

They paused for a moment, looking down, and Alexa smiled at the sight of the colourful *bateaux-mouches* smoothly moving down the river, leaving frothy trails in their wake.

She had always enjoyed the trips she had taken on them, especially those in the evenings with Tom years ago. Paris at night was romantic and magical when seen from the river in a slow-moving boat, the glittering lights of the city illuminating the inky sky. There was nowhere like it in the world.

Hand in hand, they walked on, heading towards the Quai Voltaire. Ahead, reaching into the sky, were the great towers of Notre Dame, hazy now in the soft afternoon light of Paris, a light loved by artists over the centuries and so frequently captured on canvas.

As they reached the Quai Malaquais, Tom said, 'Let's head down into Saint-Germain-des-Prés for coffee before going home.'

Alexa nodded in agreement, and still holding hands they strolled down the rue Bonaparte, and into a huddle of quaint old cobbled streets. At the Café Voltaire, they found a table outside and settled into chairs under the awning, relaxing after their walk. After ordering coffee for them both, Tom loosened his tie and opened the neck of his shirt. 'It's become quite warm,' he said, glancing at her. 'Do you want to take off your sweater?'

'Yes, I will.' She loosened the cashmere sweater tied round her neck and laid it across her knees. Turning to Tom, she added, 'Did your father tell you anything else?'

'Not exactly. He did tell me that Jean Beauvais-Cresse was married, and that there was a child. But that's about it. My parents haven't lived in the Loire all that long, and much of what he knows is gossip anyway.'

'I understand.' Alexa paused, looked off into the distance.

After a moment or two of watching her, Tom said quietly, 'Is there something wrong, Alexa? You're looking somewhat pensive.'

A little sigh escaped her. 'I was just thinking about Lucien Girard. If he *is* Jean Beauvais-Cresse and he just decided to go back to his old life one day, he must be a truly cruel man. Imagine doing something like that to Jessica, or any woman. She's probably been carrying a torch for Lucien all these years.'

He frowned. 'Do you really think so?'

'Yes, I do.' She sighed. 'It makes me so mad.'

'I can understand why. But if my father has no additional information, I think we just have to forget I ever mentioned Jean.'

'Not so easy.' Again Alexa stared ahead, and after a moment or two of thoughtful reflection, she turned to Tom, put her hand on his arm. 'I think I have a way of finding the truth.'

'You do?' Tom sounded surprised.

The waiter arrived with their cups of coffee, and once he was out of earshot, Alexa said carefully, 'You and I, with Jessica, should drive down to the Loire Valley one day next week. Once we arrive at Jean's house, Jessica and I will remain in the car while you go to the door. If Jean answers the door, you tell him you have a client who wants to shoot a movie, and is looking for appropriate chateaux in which to film the interior scenes. Once you get him engaged in conversation, Jessica and I will get out of the car and walk over to join you. If he *is* Lucien, we'll know. He'll be in shock.'

Tom nodded. 'I'm following you. And if he's not Lucien, he won't recognise either of you, is that what you're trying to say?'

'Correct.'

'But, Alexa, you will have to tell Jessica, and that could open up her old wounds.'

'It will. But look, if we solve a seven-year-old mystery and she can finally put the whole thing to rest, that's a good thing, isn't it?'

Tom saw the sense in what she was saying, and told her so, adding, 'Quarrel or no quarrel, you really are being a good friend to Jessica. I admire you for that.'

'When Lucien disappeared her life changed radically,' Alexa replied. 'Never to be the same again, that I surely know. And if I have a chance to help her, as I now think I do, why wouldn't I?'

Tom searched her face and said softly, 'I see into your heart, my sweet Alexa, and you are truly a good person.' She did not answer, and he thought: She fills the empty places in my heart, she makes me whole.

Chapter Twelve

'I'M SO GLAD you could come early, darling,' Anya said, smiling across at Alexa. 'I just want to go over a couple of things, before the others arrive.'

'And I have something to tell you,' Alexa responded, settling in the chair opposite Anya. The two women were sitting in the small library which opened onto the gardens. It was another beautiful day, and the French doors were wide open to reveal a view of the cobbled courtyard and the cherry tree.

'What is it you wish to tell me?' Anya probed.

Alexa shook her head. 'Tell me first why you wanted me to come earlier than the others, and then I'll explain something to you, an idea I've had.'

'All right.' Anya sat up a little straighter in the chair and continued. 'I want everything ironed out between the four of you today, Alexa, and I'm looking to *you* to create harmony among you.'

'I'll do my best, and I agree with you. After yesterday's confrontation with Maria, I don't like the thought of any more of them. They're too upsetting. Let's face it, we're all around thirty and we should know better by now.'

Anya nodded. 'I'm glad you feel you want to be conciliatory. That's the way to go, and once you've talked it through I'm going to take you all out to lunch.'

'Oh, that'll be nice!' Alexa exclaimed. 'But you should let *us* take *you*. To somewhere chic and expensive. We can all afford it now.'

Laughing, Anya said, 'There's something else I want to mention. I would like Nicky to invite Tom to my party. Would he come?'

'I'm sure he would.' Alexa flashed her a wide smile.

'That's what I thought. I'll tell Nicky to send him an invitation. I'm also going to tell Kay to invite her husband, and naturally Maria will be accompanying Nicky. But I don't know what to do about Jessica. I've no idea if she's in Paris alone or with someone.'

'You still haven't seen her?'

'No, darling girl, I haven't. I asked her several times to come and have a drink, or lunch, but I think she's staying away on purpose.'

'But why?'

Anya made a *moue* with her mouth, and then explained, 'Jessica identifies me with the past, in particular the last few months when Lucien went missing. I think she's a little bit afraid to see me, for fear of the memories it will evoke. Remember, Jessica hasn't seen me since you all graduated. It's been *seven years*. And she links that time to him.'

'I know. But I'm sure she'll open up today, and we can find out whether she's here alone or not. I'll do everything I can to make her feel at ease, and Kay too.'

'And Maria. Don't forget Maria, Alexa. She was awfully nervous yesterday. Afraid of you, I do believe.'

'I suppose I was a bit fierce,' Alexa admitted, looking shamefaced. 'I'll be nice, I promise.'

'Now, what is the idea you said you had? An idea for what exactly?'

'Finding the truth.' Alexa took a deep breath, and shifted her body in the chair. 'I think Jessica and I, along with Tom, should go down to the Loire, seek out this Jean fellow, and confront him.'

'Alexa darling, you can't go rushing around the countryside accusing people of leading a double life.'

'I didn't say we'd be doing that. I said we'd go over to his house just to see him, let him see us. Get his reaction or non-reaction.'

'I think I'd like to hear what Tom has to say.'

A moment later Anya was standing up, walking across to the door, a huge smile illuminating her face.

'Hello, Jessica,' she exclaimed. 'It's wonderful to see you.'

'And you, Anya, after so long.'

The two women embraced and then Anya stepped back, and stared at Jessica, an appraising look in her eyes.

What a lovely woman Jessica had become, elegant in her well-tailored black trouser-suit and white silk shirt, her long, pale blonde hair falling round her tanned face. She was still as pretty as she was seven years ago. But there was a sadness in her eyes, and Anya was sure that deep within her soul Jessica still yearned for Lucien. She was thirty-one and still not married. Anya had immediately noticed there were no rings on her fingers. Maybe Alexa was right about going to the Loire to discover the truth. Might it not set Jessica free?

'Come in, come in, don't let's stand here in the doorway!' Anya exclaimed, taking Jessica's arm, leading her into the room. 'Here's Alexa. And the others should be here any moment.'

Alexa had risen, her hand outstretched. 'Hello, Jessica, it's been a long time,' she said striving for genuine cordiality.

Jessica inclined her head, and took her hand. 'Hello, Alexa.'

Alexa recoiled slightly; there was such coldness in Jessica's voice and her demeanour was equally icy.

Anya had noticed Jessica's extreme coldness and she instantly filled with dismay and just a little trepidation. 'Jessica, do sit down,' she said, and lowered herself onto the sofa.

Jessica did as she was asked, glancing around, and then said in a softer tone, 'I'd forgotten how lovely the library is, Anya. It's just charming, the way you've redecorated it.'

'And I must tell you how proud I am of your work, Jessica. The houses and apartments you've designed are simply superb. I've loved seeing them in the magazines over the years. Congratulations, my dear.'

'Thanks, Anya. Everything I know I learned at your school.'

'The school can't teach anyone taste and style, and you have an inbred sense of those qualities,, Jessica. I always told you that.'

'Yes, you did, and you helped to make my dreams come true, professionally. I had the best training in the world, and what's stood me in great stead is my knowledge of history, English, French and European furniture through the centuries, antique fabrics, and classical architecture. You taught me so much, Anya.'

'Well, thank you for those kind words.' Anya settled back against the cushions, and asked, 'Are you by any chance in Paris alone, Jessica?'

'I'm alone, yes.'

'I see. The reason I ask is that I thought you might wish to bring someone with you to my party, to be escorted by a friend that evening. And if that *is* the case, I will have Nicky send him an invitation.'

Jessica blinked and nodded in a positive manner, her face softening. 'I think I *would* like to have an escort that night. One of my clients happens to be in Paris. His name is Mark Sylvester, and he's a movie producer from Hollywood. He's working on a picture, shooting here and in London. He told me that he'll be backwards and forwards between the two cities for the next month or so. I'm sure he would love to come.'

'I'm delighted. May I ask where he's staying, my dear?'

'The Plaza Athénée, and I'll tell him to expect the invitation. Thanks so much for being so considerate, Anya.'

Suddenly, Maria was gliding into the room looking stunning in an ankle-length black skirt and matching jacket. Underneath the jacket she wore a low-cut black silk blouse. Her long neck was enhanced by a gold necklace of ancient coins, and she wore matching earrings. Her black shoes had very high heels and she actually looked willowy this morning, Anya thought.

But when Maria spotted Jessica seated on a chair near the fireplace, she came to a sudden halt, looked hesitant, and appeared uncertain whether to enter the room or not.

Anya, detecting this at once, pushed herself to her feet and hurried to her, embraced her. 'You're looking wonderful,' she said, wanting to imbue confidence in her. 'We're just waiting for Kay now.'

The words had hardly left Anya's mouth when Kay came walking in from the front portico, exclaiming, 'Oh dear, am I late? So sorry.'

Swinging round, Anya smiled at Kay and shook her head. 'No, you're not late at all. But now that you are here, my dear, I would like to get down to business.' Escorting Maria and Kay into the room, Anya continued, 'The business being solving your problems with one another.' She threw Alexa a pointed look as she returned to her seat on the sofa.

Understanding what was expected of her, Alexa rose, walked over to the fireplace and stood in front of it. 'Hi, Maria, hi, Kay.'

Both women acknowledged her, although neither sounded friendly.

Alexa said, 'Anya asked me to speak to you about our falling out with one another just before graduation. She doesn't want any bad feelings between us during her birthday party. She thinks we should sort out our differences. In order to do that I think we must all talk about our feelings, get things off our chests, so to speak.'

'I want the air cleared,' Anya murmured.

Alexa unbuttoned the jacket of her black trouser-suit, pushed her hands into her pockets, and went on, 'Yesterday Maria and I did begin talk about the problem, so I'm going to let Maria explain how she and I fell out. Then perhaps Jessica could respond.'

Maria was totally taken aback as she looked round at everyone. After a moment, she said haltingly, 'Alexa blamed *me* yesterday. She said I told Jessica lies about her. But that's not correct . . .'

'Yes, it is!' Alexa cut in peremptorily, and then took a step back. 'I'm sorry for interrupting, Maria. Please continue.'

Looking at Jessica, Maria said, 'I didn't tell you any lies. I told you what I believed to be the truth—that Alexa had been flirting with my boyfriend, Ricardo Martinelli, and that she was trying to steal him.'

Alexa had to bite off another exclamation, this time of denial. She was infuriated with Maria again but forced herself to remain calm.

Jessica was nodding. 'Yes, I remember that. You explained that you were worried that Ricardo was going to become involved with Alexa. Because of *her* behaviour. That you thought she was after him. You cried a lot. And yes, I *did* believe you.' Jessica glanced at Alexa. 'And I did take Maria's side, there's no question about that.'

'But it wasn't true!' Alexa protested. 'And don't you think you owed me the benefit of the doubt, plus a chance to defend myself?'

Jessica bit her lip. 'I guess that's true, but I did see you flirting with Ricardo at the party Angélique's mother gave. You were draped all over him when you were dancing, clinging to him, pressing into him. That's what clinched it for me.'

Alexa felt bright colour flame in her face, and she said, 'I *was* dancing with him, and quite intimately, I suppose. I admit that. But we were *only* dancing. And *I* wasn't flirting with him. *He* was flirting with me. He had a tendency to do that, as you well know, Jessica. And *you* also know it, Maria.' Alexa gave Kay a very direct look and added, 'I saw Ricardo flirting with *you*, Kay, the Sunday night we all went to Les Deux Magots for coffee. After your birthday dinner.'

Kay sighed. 'Yes, that's perfectly correct, Alexa.' Kay turned to Maria. 'He did flirt with me. He was after all of us. I wasn't interested in him, though, and I don't think Alexa was either. I have to take her side in that.'

'Listen to me, Maria,' Alexa cried. 'You were putting on weight, and you knew it and you weren't at all happy with yourself or your relationship with Ricardo. So you dreamed up this idea of my trying to steal him, when all along *he* was at fault, not I. You took it out on me. You went running off to Jessica, because you were jealous of our friendship, and you turned her against me.'

Maria was stunned and she gaped at Alexa. But she said nothing.

Alexa went on, '*Why?* Why didn't you come to me? You were really sneaky, and you genuinely hurt me. I was heartbroken about losing Jessica's friendship.'

Maria seemed about to burst into tears, and did not respond. She threw Jessica a helpless look and said in a plaintive voice, 'I know I accused Alexa, Jessica, but I did believe she was trying to steal Ricardo from me. Now I realise that accusing her was an error, and I apologised to Alexa yesterday. I said I was sorry, and I say that to you, too.'

'Maria *was* jealous of our friendship,' Alexa announced to Jessica, staring hard at her.

Jessica exclaimed, 'Oh, I don't know about that . . .'

Maria interrupted, when she admitted, 'I think I *was* envious of your relationship. You seemed to have so much in common. You laughed a lot. At the same things. Sometimes I felt shut out . . .'

'But we're both Americans!' Jessica cried. 'Of course we had a lot in common—like growing up in the same country, for one thing. But I never thought we were excluding you. Or Kay.'

'But you were!' Kay shot back. 'And you did it a lot.'

'Let's finish with Maria and Jessica,' Alexa instructed firmly.

Jessica shook her head, blew out air. 'Gee whiz, I guess I did the wrong thing, seven years ago, Alexa. I listened to Maria, a very tearful Maria, I might add, and I made a judgment. A flawed judgment, as it turns out. I guess I should have talked it out with you.'

'Yes, you should have, but you didn't want to,' Alexa snapped. 'You were caught up with Lucien's disappearance. I realised that then, and I acknowledge it now. However, you just stopped speaking to me . . .'

'I did, yes, and that was wrong. My only excuse is that I *was* extremely upset about Lucien, heartbroken. And I would like to point out that you weren't very helpful or sympathetic at the time.' She gave Alexa a hard stare. 'I expected more from you.'

'You expected sympathy, and I gave it to you! But you weren't receptive. You were far too busy condemning me for being a man-snatcher, as you put it. You didn't want my help, only Alain Bonnal's.'

Jessica sat back. She looked suddenly haggard, and her eyes filled with tears. 'I think you might have a point,' she admitted finally.

Alexa nodded and then looked at Maria, and said, 'And thank you, Maria, for being so honest yesterday, and again today.'

Anya said, 'Well, it certainly does help to clear the air. And what about you, Kay? Do you have anything to add to this?'

'I . . . well, I don't know. I don't think so.'

'Why not?' Jessica suddenly demanded. 'You certainly had enough to say about us behind our backs! You gossiped about us.'

'I did not!' Kay cried. Reminding herself that she was now Lady Andrews, she took several deep breaths. Then she said, 'I never talked about any of you behind your backs.'

'You're a *liar*, Kay. You did badmouth us—Alexa, Maria and me,' Jessica accused in an icy voice.

'How dare you call me a liar!' Kay looked at Alexa. 'She's the one who's lying. Not me.'

Jessica half rose in the chair. 'You did talk about us. I was informed of everything you said, and by a very good source. You said Alexa was superior and a snob, that she was always snubbing you. That Maria was a *rich* snob and treated you like a servant, and that I was a la-di-da southern belle, forever taunting you, putting you down. You called us the three bitches. Not very nice, *Lady* Andrews.'

A bright scarlet flush rose from Kay's pale neck to suffuse her face; she blinked back the tears that suddenly filled her eyes. A moment later she fumbled in her bag for a handkerchief.

There were a few seconds of quiet in the library. None of the women spoke. Anya glanced from one to the other, suddenly worried about Kay. She looked as though she was about to faint.

And then Kay finally spoke, breaking the silence. 'It's true that I did harbour a few grudges against all of you. We had been so close and happy together for three years, and then a few months before graduation you all changed towards me. I thought you didn't like me any more because I didn't have your upbringing, your family backgrounds. You all slighted me.'

Alexa stared hard at her, frowning, totally nonplussed. 'But we didn't slight you, and certainly we didn't think you were any different from us. Did we, Jessica?'

'No.'

'Did we, Maria?'

'No, Alexa, not at all.'

'But I felt the change in you,' Kay protested.

Alexa said quietly, 'I think we changed for the reasons we've just discussed. The problems were about me, Maria and Jessica.' She let out a small sigh. 'Sadly, you just imagined we had changed towards you, but we hadn't. *Honestly*.'

'We never knew much about you, or your background, Kay,' Maria volunteered. 'You never confided. But you had beautiful clothes, plenty of money, an air of breeding. We did not think of you as being different.'

'But I was,' Kay said slowly. '*I was different*.' She stopped, looked across at Anya.

Anya nodded, encouraging her to continue.

'I was a poor girl from the Glasgow slums,' Kay confided in a fading voice. 'But my mother worked hard to give me a good education in England. And then she sent me here to Anya's school.'

'We didn't know,' Jessica said. 'And we really wouldn't have cared. We loved you for being *you*, Kay, and for your talent and caring ways.'

Kay nodded. 'I'm sorry,' she said in a regretful tone. 'But I felt you'd cut me out, that's why I said the things I did.' She groped again for the handkerchief and wiped her eyes.

The four women sat quietly, saying nothing to one another, each one lost in her own thoughts for a few minutes.

Anya had listened to their words very attentively, and she understood that Alexa had told the truth. It *had* all started with Maria, but Jessica had not helped the situation. In a sense, Alexa had been a victim of Maria's jealousy and muddled thinking, as well as Jessica's readiness to condemn her. As for Kay, she had allowed her insecurity and sense of inferiority to get the better of her. What a loss of true friendship, she thought. Such a waste of those years when they could have given one another moral support and helped in other ways. What a shame they hadn't been able to communicate better, more explicitly, when they were here at the school.

Alexa broke into her thoughts, when she said, 'Let's bury this . . . *garbage*! Seven years have passed. We've all grown up. And yes, we're truly lucky women. Let's be friends again.'

Alexa offered her hand to Maria, who took hold of it and joined her near the fireplace. Jessica then stood up and came over to them. The three women put their arms round each other and looked across at Kay.

'Come on!' Jessica exclaimed, smiling at her. 'Make the quartet complete again.'

Kay pushed herself to her feet and rushed into their arms. The four of them stood in a huddle, half laughing, half crying. Then, breaking the circle they made, Jessica said, 'We're missing one . . . come on, Anya. You belong here with us. For what would we be without you?'

Chapter Thirteen

ANYA TOOK THEM to Le Grand Véfour for lunch.

The ancient restaurant, dating back to before the French Revolution, was situated beneath the arches of the Palais-Royal, and it was a historical landmark.

Now the five of them sat at one of the best tables in the restaurant, sipping champagne, surrounded by the distinctive decor of the eighteenth and nineteenth centuries.

Red velvet banquettes were balanced by simple, clean-lined chairs in black and gold, and a richly patterned black and gold carpet. Scarred antique mirrors in old gold frames were affixed to the ceiling and to some of the walls; on other walls were neoclassical paintings of nymphs entwined with flowers and vines, set under glass.

'What a fabulous place this is,' Jessica said, her keen eyes taking in every detail of the decor. 'I just love the paintings, they look as if they come from ancient Rome.'

'I noticed a brass plaque on one of the banquettes bearing the name of Victor Hugo,' Alexa said. 'And another one with Colette's name. She must have been a regular client too.'

Anya nodded. 'A lot of writers came here, and also politicians. Why, even Napoleon used to bring Josephine here to dine.'

'*Really!*' Kay exclaimed, her ears pricking up. 'I hadn't realised the place was that old!'

'Oh yes, it dates back to 1784, but at that time it was called the Café de Chartres. Anyway, I must admit, I never tire of its charm and refined elegance,' Anya said. 'And I know you're going to enjoy the food as much as you're enjoying the ambiance.' Glancing at Maria, she added, 'They offer a very nice sole, my dear, so you don't have to worry about your diet.'

'You're always so considerate, Anya,' Maria answered, and took a sip of her mineral water.

Soon the maitre d' was hovering next to the table, telling them about the specialities of the house, and handing round the menus. After studying them for a while, they all settled for the sole except for Anya, who had decided to indulge herself. 'I'm going to have the pigeon stuffed with foie gras,' she announced with a wide smile. 'And no one is going to make me feel guilty.'

It was a warm and happy lunch. All of the women were at ease with one another once again; as Anya studied them from time to time she felt the quarrel might never have happened. They were as sweet and loving as they had been in their early years at the school. And this pleased her . . . it was the best birthday gift she could ever have.

Before they knew it, the lunch was over and they were trooping out into the street. Alexa began to chastise Anya, complaining that she should not have signed the bill, that they had wanted to take her to lunch. 'It should have been our treat,' she insisted.

'Don't be silly, darling. It was my pleasure to have you all together again, and so *tranquil*, too. I'm very happy the quarrel is behind us.'

As they waited for Anya's car and driver, Alexa drew Jessica under the arches for a moment and said to her quietly, 'I need to talk to you about something really important, Jessica. Can you spare me half an hour?'

Jessica looked at her swiftly, then nodded, glanced at her watch. 'Let's find a cab. We can talk on the way to the Bonnal Gallery. I have an appointment there with Alain, about a painting for a client.'

Alexa was staring at her intently.

Jessica frowned. 'You remember him, don't you? He was a good friend of Lucien's.'

'Oh yes, I remember him,' Alexa murmured.

A week later, very early on a warm Saturday morning, they drove to the Loire Valley. Tom was at the wheel of his Mercedes, with Mark Sylvester sitting next to him in the front. In the back seat were Alexa, Jessica and Alain Bonnal.

Although it was balmy weather, the sun was hidden by dark clouds that floated across the horizon. Tom hoped it would not rain, wanting a fast run down to his parents' house near Tours.

Once they arrived there they planned to freshen up and have breakfast before heading over to Montcresse, the chateau that was the family home of Jean Beauvais-Cresse. Only Tom, the two women and Alain would go there; this had been decided over dinner the previous evening. They had agreed that Mark would remain with Tom's parents. As soon as the meeting with Jean had taken place, the others would return for lunch and then head back to Paris.

Because it was so early in the morning, it seemed to Tom that no one wanted to talk. He slipped a disc into the player on the dashboard, and soon the car was filled with the soothing background themes from great Hollywood movies.

Jessica's eyes were closed, but she was not dozing. She was wide awake, simply feigning sleep in order to sink down into her diverse thoughts. She had been determined to come and see this man in the Loire who looked so much like Lucien, but now she felt a bit queasy about it.

Could it be Lucien? Was he alive and well and living in the Loire? Alexa had told her about the photograph album, Tom's reaction to the photograph of her and Lucien standing on the Pont des Arts. And although she had been momentarily startled, it had not come as a great shock. In one sense, she had half expected to hear something like this over the years. Then again, Mark had put the idea in her head in February, when he had suggested that Lucien might have vanished on purpose.

She needed to go to Chateau Montcresse to close this chapter in her life. If the man who lived there with his wife and child was not Lucien, no harm would be done. But if it was Lucien, she would finally have answers.

She had voiced all this to Mark yesterday, before they had gone to meet the others for dinner. He had encouraged the trip, and asked her to allow him to come along. 'I care about you, Jessica,' he had said. 'And I'd like to be there for you, in case you need me. I'm your friend, you know.' She had smiled and squeezed his arm, and said she would be relieved if he went with them.

Not long after he had left the motorway at the exit to Tours, Tom took a secondary road going towards Loches. 'We'll soon be there,' he said, and everyone sat up, looking out of the car windows eagerly.

Fifteen minutes later Tom slowed down and turned into a driveway through iron gates which stood open and welcoming. At the end of a short drive stood a lovely old manor house made of local Loire stone which was renowned for turning white as it aged over the years. The manor looked pale and elegant set against a backdrop of dark green trees and an azure sky. As Tom pulled up outside the house, his father came hurrying out of the front door.

After embracing his son, Paul Conners hugged Alexa with great affection, and then Tom made the introductions all round.

'Come on, let's go inside and have breakfast,' Paul said, leading the way into the circular front hall with a terracotta tiled floor and white stone walls hung with antique tapestries.

Christiane Conners, Tom's mother, appeared at this moment, and greeted Tom and Alexa and their companions. 'Perhaps you would like to freshen up,' Christiane said, turning to Alexa and Jessica, and then heading towards the staircase, beckoning to them. 'And Paul and Tom, I'll leave you to look after Mark and Alain.'

Christiane led the way up the curving staircase to the floor above, and showed them both into a pretty guest room decorated with a pale blue *toile de Jouy* used throughout. It covered the walls, the bed, and was hanging at the windows as curtains.

'You will find everything you need here, Alexa,' Christiane said, waving her hand around the room and then indicating the bathroom.

'Thank you, Christiane.' Alexa turned to Jessica. 'Why don't you tidy up first, Jessica, I want to talk to Tom's mother for a moment.'

'Thanks,' Jessica replied and disappeared into the bathroom.

Once they were alone, Christiane rushed over to Alexa and hugged her. 'I was so happy when I heard you were in Paris, *ma petite*, and that you and Tom were back together.'

'We're meant to be together,' Alexa answered, 'and I think Tom knows that now.'

'I hope so, *chérie*. You are important for him, good for him.'

When Jessica came out of the bathroom, Christiane looked at her intently and said, 'Tom wished me to tell you about Jean Beauvais-Cresse, but there is not much to tell, Jessica.'

'He is the mystery man, according to Tom,' Jessica responded, sitting down on the chair opposite Christiane while they waited for Alexa.

'Mystery man?' Tom's mother repeated, and shook her head. '*Non, non*.' She thought for a moment, before continuing. 'I think of him as a recluse. We do not see much of him in public. Nor his wife. They keep to themselves.'

'Perhaps that's an indication of something peculiar,' Alexa said as she came out of the bathroom. 'I think so, anyway.'

'I hope we'll soon have some answers,' Jessica muttered.

Christiane nodded. 'Let us go downstairs and have a little refreshment. I am sure you are anxious to be on your way to Montcresse.'

Despite her preoccupation, the designer in Jessica surfaced a couple of times as she followed Tom's mother and Alexa down the stairs, across the entrance hall and into an unusual circular room. This was at the back of the house, and had many windows that looked out onto lawns, gardens and a stand of trees. Beyond she could see a stretch of the river.

'How beautiful!' she exclaimed as she glanced around, noting the tasteful decorations, the mellow antiques, the displays of porcelain plates on the walls.

'This is the summer dining room,' Christiane explained, ushering them towards the circular table in the middle of the room.

They sat down just as Tom, his father and the other two men came into the room. 'Sit anywhere you wish,' Paul said. He took a seat next to Alexa, grasped her hand in his and squeezed it. 'Penny for your thoughts, Alexa?'

She laughed. 'I couldn't possibly tell you.'

'Then I'll tell you,' he said with a small, knowing smile. Leaning closer he whispered in her ear, 'You want to be with him for the rest of your life.'

Alexa stared at Paul Conners. 'How did you know?'

'It's written all over your face, my dear.'

Christiane poured coffee, and Tom offered a basket of breads to everyone, moving round the table slowly. 'What would you like, Alexa?' he asked when he finally stopped next to her chair.

'You,' she mouthed silently, as she took a croissant.

Tom kissed the top of her head, and made no comment.

Paul focused on Alain, and said, 'Tom explained to me that you used to know Lucien Girard when Jessica did.'

'*Oui, oui*,' Alain said, nodding.

'And he was a nice guy, then?'

'*Ah, bien sûr*,' Alain exclaimed. 'A man of integrity. I find it hard to accept this theory that he disappeared on purpose.'

Mark interjected, 'It wouldn't be the first time a man has done that. Or a woman, for that matter.'

Paul nodded. 'And there's usually a good reason when this happens. I can't imagine what his family suffered.'

'He told me that he was an orphan. That his parents were dead,' Jessica volunteered.

Alain added, 'And he told me the same thing. No parents, no siblings.'

'And seemingly no past,' Mark remarked, turning to Paul.

'If you're intent on leading a double life it's always best to keep the story and the details very simple. That way you can't make too many mistakes,' Paul responded.

'That is true,' Christiane murmured.

Alexa, studying Tom's mother, thought how lovely she looked, but then she usually had in the past. Christiane Conners was one of those well-groomed Frenchwomen who could manage to look chic in a plain cotton shirt and trousers, which is what Christiane was wearing this morning. She admired her for looking the way she did at her age, and she was glad Tom's mother was her ally.

Jessica had been listening to them all, quietly sipping her coffee, saying nothing very much. But once she thought everyone had finished, she asked, 'Do you think we can drive over there, Tom? I'm awfully nervous, and as long as I sit here I'm prolonging the agony.'

'Of course we can go,' Tom said. He and Alexa both leapt to their feet. Taking hold of Alexa's hand, he told his parents he would see them later and moved away from the table. Alain did the same, then ushered Jessica out of the dining room.

Mark pushed back his chair and hurried out after Jessica. He caught up with her on the front steps, took hold of her arm, drew her towards him. 'Remember that whatever happens over there doesn't really matter, Jessica darling.'

Jessica tried to smile but it faltered. 'You're right, Mark, I know that. I'm just nervous, queasy.'

He held her close, and said against her hair, 'You're going to be all right, Jessica. I'm going to make sure of that.'

Tom and Alain sat in the front of the Mercedes; Alexa and Jessica took the back seat. No one spoke on the way to Montcresse, but at one moment Alexa reached out, grabbed Jessica's hand and held it tightly in hers, wanting to comfort and reassure her.

Jessica sat very still on the back seat, anxious to get to the chateau. Already she was wishing the confrontation were over, and that they were on their way back to Paris.

Tom broke the silence in the car when he said, 'That's Montcresse straight ahead of us.'

Jessica and Alexa strained to get a better glimpse.

What they saw was a truly grand chateau, standing proudly on a rise not far from the River Indre—a tributary of the Loire. Its white stone walls gleamed in the bright morning sunlight, while the black, bell-shaped roofs atop the numerous circular towers gave the massive edifice a fanciful air.

As Tom drove up the rise, Jessica noticed the well-kept grassy lawns edging the sand-coloured gravel driveway, and behind the chateau there was a dense wood of tall, dark trees. Two more circular towers with bell-shaped roofs and thin spires flanked the drawbridge leading into the interior courtyard.

Tom slowed down as he rolled over the drawbridge, went under the arch and into the yard, heading towards the front door.

Jessica felt her stomach lurch, and for a second she thought she could not go through with this encounter. She almost told Tom to turn round and leave; she looked at Alexa, opened her mouth to speak but no words came out.

At once, Alexa saw the expression of anxiety mingled with fear on Jessica's pale face, and she tightened her grip on Jessica's hand, murmuring, 'It'll be fine.'

Still unable to say anything, Jessica merely nodded.

Tom parked close to the chateau's walls, a short distance from the huge front door. Half turning in his seat, he said to the two women, 'One of the staff might answer the door, and in that case I'll be invited inside. Should that happen, wait five minutes and then come looking for me. You'll be allowed inside if you say you're with me.'

Now glancing at Alain, Tom went on, 'You should take charge if I go inside. It will be quicker and easier for you to deal with any members of staff.'

'Of course, Tom, don't worry,' Alain answered.

Alexa asked, 'But what if Jean answers the door?'

'I'll engage him in conversation for a few minutes, then I'll glance at the car, wave to you. At that moment you should join me . . . join us. Everything clear?'

'Yes,' Alexa said, and Jessica nodded.

Tom alighted, and walked across the cobbled courtyard, heading for the front door made of nail-embellished wood. When he came to a stop he saw that it stood ajar. Nonetheless, he knocked and waited.

A moment later an elderly, grey-haired man wearing a striped apron over his trousers, shirt and waistcoat suddenly appeared in the entrance hall. He was carrying a silver tray, and he stepped forward when he saw Tom. He inclined his head, '*Bonjour, monsieur*.'

'*Bonjour. Je voudrais voir monsieur le Marquis.*'

'*Oui, oui, attendez une minute, s'il vous plaît.*'

These words had hardly left the man's mouth when Tom heard footsteps on the cobblestones and he glanced down towards the stables.

Jean Beauvais-Cresse was walking towards him. He wore black riding boots, white jodhpurs and a black turtleneck sweater. He raised a hand in recognition, and a second later the two men were greeting each other and shaking hands.

Tom then went on, 'I apologise for intruding like this, without telephoning first, but as we passed the chateau my clients asked me to stop the car. They were intrigued by Montcresse. You see, they're making a movie about Mary, Queen of Scots and plan to shoot in the Loire. I've been showing them possible locations for the film . . .'

'*Ce n'est pas possible*,' Jean cut in with a small, regretful smile. 'Many people have wanted to film here in the past. But it doesn't work. The chateau's not the best place to shoot a film, I'm afraid.'

'I see,' Tom responded. 'But what about outside? There are quite a lot of exterior scenes, and perhaps you would consider allowing them access to the property.'

Unexpectedly, Jean appeared to be considering this idea. At the same time, he moved forward, stepped inside the chateau, stood regarding Tom from the entrance hall. 'Perhaps there might be a way to film on the estate,' he said finally.

Tom was listening attentively, but out of the corner of his eye he saw Alexa, Alain and Jessica walking towards him. Wishing to keep the other man totally engaged as they approached, Tom leaned forward slightly, and continued, 'There would be a very good fee involved, and the crew would have instructions to be extremely careful on your land. Also, the production company is insured anyway.'

'I understand. But I must think about it—' Jean broke off abruptly. Shock was registering on his narrow face, and he had paled. As if undone, he staggered slightly, then leaned against the doorjamb, his eyes wide with surprise and panic.

Jessica now stepped forward, staring at Jean. Immediately, she recognised him, just as he had recognised her. It *was* him. Shaking inside, she swallowed hard. 'I often thought you must be alive somewhere out there in the world.' Her eyes welled with tears.

Jean stared at her, then his gaze settled on Alain and finally Alexa. His eyes acknowledged them but he said nothing.

He shook his head slowly. Sighing heavily, he opened the door wider. 'You'd better come inside.'

Jessica was still shaking and her legs felt weak, but she managed to hold herself together as the four of them followed Jean across the huge stone hall. It was baronial, hung with dark tapestries and stags' heads; a huge chandelier hung down from the high ceiling. Their footsteps echoed on the stone floor.

He led the way down three steps into a long, spacious book-lined room with French windows opening onto a terrace. Jessica only vaguely noticed the dark wood furniture, the faded fabrics, the air of shabby elegance.

Jean paused in the centre of the room, and waved his hand at a grouping of chairs and sofas. 'Please,' he murmured. He did not sit himself, but moved away, went and stood near the stone fireplace.

Once the others were seated, he glanced at Tom and asked, 'Did we know each other in Paris years ago?'

'No.'

'How did you . . . make the connection?'

'My friend Alexa has a photograph of Jessica with you. When I mentioned your name, she said the man in the picture was Lucien Girard. Then she told me the story of . . . of your disappearance.'

'I see.' He shifted on his feet, blinked several times.

No longer able to contain herself, Jessica leaned forward slightly, and asked in a tight voice, '*Why?* Why did you do it? Vanish the way you did, without a trace?'

He did not respond.

No one else spoke. The room was very quiet.

Outside, a light wind rustled through the trees and in the distance a bird trilled. Through the windows the scent of roses and other flowers floated inside, filling the air with sweetness. There was a sense of tranquillity in this long, narrow library, an air of timelessness, of gentleness. But there was also a good deal of emotion.

Jessica exclaimed, 'I think you owe me an explanation. And Alain. We tried so hard to find you, and when we couldn't, we thought you were dead. We grieved for you!' She shook her head, and tears gathered again in her eyes. 'I think I've been grieving for you right until this very moment.' Her voice broke and she could not continue.

'I think you should tell Jessica why you disappeared, Lucien. You owe that to Jessica, if not to me,' Alain interjected.

'Yes, I do owe you both an explanation.' He sat down on a chair near the fireplace and slowly began to speak. 'I said I was going to Monte Carlo to work because I couldn't tell you the truth, Jessica.'

'And what was the truth?' she asked, still tearful.

'That I was not really Lucien Girard. This name was my stage name. I was, I am, Jean Beauvais-Cresse. But twelve years ago I left this house after a bad quarrel with my father. He disapproved of my desire to be an actor, and washed his hands of me. In any case, my older brother Philippe was his favourite, and he was the heir to the title and the lands. Seven years ago, just before you graduated, Philippe was tragically killed in an accident. He was flying on a private plane to Corsica, to join his fiancée and her family, when the plane went down in a bad thunderstorm. Everyone on board was killed.

'When he received the terrible news of Philippe's death, my father had a stroke. My mother, who was an invalid, summoned me to return to Montcresse. I had a funeral to arrange, and other matters to attend to, as well as my mother and father to care for.'

'But why didn't you tell me?' Jessica demanded. 'I could have come with you, helped you.'

'It was far too complicated. I did not have time for long explanations. I was suddenly needed immediately. Urgently. Anyway, I believed I would be here in the Loire for only a week, at the most.' Jean paused, leaned back in his chair, took a deep breath.

Scrutinising him intently, Jessica thought he looked older than thirty-five. His narrow face was lined and his fair hair was sparse. He had always been slender, but now he was really thin. He seemed undernourished, and it struck her that he had lost his looks.

For his part, Jean Beauvais-Cresse was fully aware of her fixed scrutiny, and he flinched under it. His discomfort was profound. Seeing her again had sent shock waves through him. She had never looked more beautiful, and her allure for him was as potent as ever. He still loved her deeply. He would always love her until the day he died. She had been, still was, the love of his life. But it was not meant to be, could not be. Not any more.

Jean was filled with regret. A deep sense of loss overwhelmed him, and his emotions ran high. He had to steady himself, take hold of his swimming senses. For one awful moment he thought he would weep. Breathing deeply, taking hold of himself with steely determination, he rose, moved to the fireplace once more, took up a stance there.

Clearing his throat, he said, 'I truly did intend to tell you everything when I returned to Paris, Jessica. Please believe that.'

'And then what?' Jessica asked, her voice still shaking.

'I hoped we could continue as we were, make a life together. Somehow. But then something else occurred, just after the funeral of my brother.'

Alain, frowning intently, asked quickly, 'What happened?'

'I became ill. Extremely ill. I had been fighting what I thought was flu. A scratchy throat, aches and pains, night sweats, fever were the symptoms. I mentioned this to my father's doctor, the day after the funeral, when he came to Montcresse to see my parents. At once, he insisted I go to his office for an examination . . .' Jean stopped, cleared his throat, seemed for a moment hesitant to continue.

Jessica's eyes were riveted on Jean. Even before he spoke she knew he was about to tell them something quite terrible.

Jean continued, 'Dr Bitoun sent me to see a cancer specialist in Orléans. I had X-rays, a CAT scan, and a biopsy of a node under my arm. Everyone's worst fears were confirmed when the results of the tests came back. I had Hodgkin's disease.'

'But you were so young, only in your mid-twenties!' Jessica cried, her eyes wide with shock.

'That is true. It often does strike young men in their twenties, sometimes even in their teen years,' Jean answered, and went on to explain, 'Hodgkin's disease is cancer of the lymphatic system, and once I was diagnosed, the oncologist at the clinic in Orléans admitted me to hospital at once, and started radiation treatment. Aside from—'

'But why didn't you call me?' Jessica interrupted heatedly. 'I would have come to you at once. I loved you.'

'I know, and I love . . .' He coughed behind his hand before saying, 'I loved you, too, Jessica. However, I suddenly realised I had nothing to offer you. I believed I was going to die. I also had an invalid mother, a stricken father, and the responsibility of running the estate. It seemed too much to burden you with at the time. You were so young. And I really did not think I would live for very long.'

'But you did live,' Alain said, staring hard at Jean.

Jean nodded. 'I did, yes. After a number of agonising treatments, I went into remission after about eight months. Even so, the oncologist warned me the cancer would probably come back.' He looked across at Jessica. 'Marriage was no longer a possibility.'

'But you *did* marry. And you have a child,' she responded quietly, hurting inside.

'That is true, yes. I married three years ago. I had a childhood friend living nearby, and once I came out of the hospital she came here to Montcresse to help me handle things. Then my father died suddenly, and I inherited. My responsibilities increased. Sadly, my mother died a few months after my father. I was overwhelmed. Annick, my dear friend, was my rock at the time. Slowly, we became involved, but I had no plans to marry.'

'Then why did you marry her?' Jessica asked. 'And not me? I would have come here. I, too, could have been your rock.'

'Because Annick became pregnant,' Jean answered. 'I had not thought this possible, because often the treatment for cancer renders a man sterile. Annick loved me, wanted to marry me, and so I did the correct thing. She was going to give me an heir to the title and the lands, someone to follow me when I died. She knew that I would probably not live to see the boy grow up, but she and I accepted that.'

'How old is the child?' Alexa asked.

Jean looked at her, a faint smile flickering on his mouth. 'Three.'

'And you are in remission now, are you?' Alain asked.

'No. I'm undergoing treatment again. Chemotherapy this time.'

'I'm sorry,' Alain responded. 'I'm sorry it has come back.'

Jessica, her eyes still moist, said slowly, 'I would have understood all this. I would have come to you, Lucien. You were my life.'

Jean's light, bluish-grey eyes filled with tears. He opened his mouth to reply, but found he could not say a word.

Jessica rose and walked across the room, her step firm. When she drew closer to him, Jean reached out to her. As she came to a standstill in front of him, Jessica saw the tears on his cheeks, the grief and sorrow in his eyes.

He was aware of no one else in the room but her. He took hold of her gently, brought her into his arms. She clung to him, rested her head against his chest, her face wet with tears. And she forgot every other question she had meant to ask him. They no longer mattered.

Against the top of her head, he said in a low voice, 'I thought I was doing the right thing. The best for you. Forgive me, Jessica.'

'I do,' she whispered against his chest. 'I do forgive you, Lucien.' She blinked back fresh tears.

There was a sudden rustling noise, the sound of running feet, and as the two of them drew apart, a small boy came hurtling into the library through the French doors. '*Papa! Papa! Je suis là!*' he cried, and then stopped when he saw that there were other people with his father.

Jean walked over to him, took hold of his hand, and led him over to Jessica. 'This is my son . . . Lucien,' Jean told her, looking deeply into her eyes.

She gazed back at Jean, nodding, understanding. Then she knelt down in front of the child, touched his soft, round baby cheek with one finger, and smiled at him. '*Bonjour. Je suis Jessica*,' she said.

The boy smiled back at her. '*Bonjour*,' he answered, in his high child's voice, his little face radiant with happiness and good health.

Swallowing her emotions, Jessica stood up, looked across at Alexa and the two men. 'I think perhaps we should go,' she said to them, and turning to Jean, she added, 'Thank you for explaining everything.'

'And I believe you understand *everything*.'

'I do.'

Dropping his voice, he said, 'So you are not married, Jessica?'

'No.'

He sighed, looked at her sadly. 'I'm sorry. *C'est dommage*.'

'It's all right.'

Jean escorted them out of the library, one hand on Jessica's shoulder, the other holding his son's hand as he crossed the stone hall to the front door. When they stepped out into the courtyard, he leaned into her, kissed her cheek.

'*Au revoir*, Jessica. *Bonne chance*.'

'Goodbye.'

She walked away from him, heading for the car. She heard the others taking their leave, hurrying after her. Jessica paused at the car; turning round, she looked back.

He stood where she had left him near the door, holding the child's hand in one of his. With the other he blew a kiss to her, and then waved. So did Lucien.

She blew kisses back and waved to them, then got into the car, her heart full.

No one spoke as they drove away from Montcresse.

Alexa held Jessica's hand, and once they had left the chateau behind, she finally asked, 'Are you all right?'

'Oh yes, I'm fine,' Jessica replied in a soft voice. 'Now that I know what happened to Lucien I can be at peace with myself.'

'It was so sad,' Alexa said. 'My heart went out to him.'

'I also felt sorry for him,' Alain murmured, turning to look at them. 'What a pity the cancer has come back. But perhaps . . . well, let us hope he will go into remission again.'

'I honestly think he believes he made the right choice. For you, Jessica. He thought he was protecting you,' Tom told her.

'I know he did. But he did my thinking for me. That's not really fair.' Jessica let out a deep sigh. 'All these years I have been in love with a memory of Lucien, a memory of my first love. But he is different now and *I* am different now. I just wish he had trusted me. Trusted our love enough to tell me the truth seven years ago, when all these terrible things were happening to him.'

'What would you have done?' Alexa ventured, looking at her intently.

'I would have gone to him immediately,' Jessica asserted. 'There is no question in my mind about that.'

'And would it have worked, do you think?' Tom asked.

'I don't know, I really don't. But I am relieved I did finally see him again. Now I can move on at last.'

But part of me will always love him, Jessica thought to herself as she leaned back and closed her eyes. And part of me will always belong to him, as I know part of him belongs to me. He made that so very clear, just as he made it clear that he still loves me.

Chapter Fourteen

KAY SAT STARING AT HERSELF in the mirror, wondering whether she needed just a touch more blusher. It seemed to her that her face was paler than usual, and she wanted to look her best tonight.

Leaning back in the small chair, she turned her attention to her hair. It fell round her face in a tumble of red-gold waves and curls; she mussed it a little more with her hands, combed the front and sprayed it lightly. 'There, that's the best I can do,' she said out loud, again peering at herself in the dressing-table mirror.

'You look beautiful, Kay,' Ian said from behind her, placing a hand on her shoulder.

'You surprised me!' she exclaimed, craning her neck to look up at him towering above her.

'Close your eyes,' he instructed.

'Why?'

'Just do as I say.'

Once her eyes were tightly shut, Ian reached into the pocket of his dressing gown and pulled out a necklace. Very carefully, he fastened it round Kay's long, slender neck. 'Now you can open your eyes.'

When Kay did so she gasped in delight. Round her neck her husband had placed the most beautiful diamond and topaz necklace she had ever seen. Loops of diamonds formed a lacy bib, and set along the front in the loops of the diamonds were eight large topaz stones. 'Ian, it's exquisite!' she exclaimed, gazing at him in the mirror. 'Thank you, oh, thank you so much.'

'I'm glad you like it, darling. I fell in love with it the moment I saw it, in just the same way I fell in love with you.'

She laughed, and then her eyes widened as he handed her a small black velvet box.

'These will add the finishing touch,' he said.

Again she gasped as she lifted the lid. Lying on the black velvet were a pair of topaz earrings, each large stone encircled by diamonds. 'Ian, how extravagant you've been,' she cried. 'But they're so beautiful. Darling, thank you.'

A wide smile spread across his face. 'Put them on,' he said.

'Right away,' she answered and clipped an earring on each ear, staring at herself. 'They're just . . . *magnificent*,' she said.

'As is my beautiful wife.'

'Thank you for the compliment and for these beautiful pieces. But it's not Christmas, nor is it my birthday.'

'It doesn't have to be a special day for me to give you a present, does it?'

She laughed. 'No. And you're quite incorrigible.'

'I truly hope so.' He stroked her shoulder, then said, 'Do you remember when I went into Edinburgh, that Saturday in February? The day before Fiona's birthday?'

'Yes, very well. You seemed a bit mysterious.'

'I know. The reason being the necklace and earrings. I'd asked old Barnes, the manager of Codrington's, the jewellers, to keep his eyes open for a diamond necklace. Imagine my delight when he phoned to say he had a diamond and topaz necklace, very rare, very old, and would I like to see it.' Ian paused, touched a strand of her hair. 'I really went into Edinburgh to look at the necklace, although I did need to buy something for my sister.'

'And you've had those pieces all these months?'

He nodded. 'Actually, Kay, I was going to give them to you for Christmas, but suddenly I realised that now would be as good a time as any. So I brought them with me on Thursday.'

She nodded and rose, went to him, put her arms round his neck and kissed him firmly on the mouth. 'You are the most wonderful husband a girl could ever want.'

'Likewise, my pet.' As he spoke he untied the belt of her robe, slipped it off her shoulders. It fell to the floor, a pool of blue round her feet. He held her away from him, gazing at her. 'Look at you, Kay. So beautiful.'

Slipping off his own robe, Ian brought her into his arms, held her tightly, kissing the hollow of her neck, and then her breasts. Lifting his head he looked deeply into her eyes and said, 'Come to bed with me. I promise I won't mess your face and hair.'

She laughed lightly. 'As if I really care. I can do it all again.'

They lay down together, clasped in each other's arms, their mouths meeting again. Kay let her tongue brush Ian's lips and then she opened her mouth slightly, tasting him, their tongues meeting. His kisses became more passionate, more intense, and his hands roamed over her delicately, touching, stroking, exploring. Her long tapering fingers went into his hair, and then moved down to stroke his back.

Leaning over her, Ian kissed her on her mouth, slowly, lingeringly, and then he lay on top of her, pushed his hands under her buttocks and brought her closer. He entered her swiftly, and she groaned; instantly the two of them fell into a rhythm they had made their own long ago. As she moved her body against him, breathing harder, clutching at his shoulders, he felt as though he were going to explode. A moment later, they were carried along on a wave of rising passion, lost in their shared ecstasy.

At last, when they lay still, Ian raised himself up on an elbow, gazed down at her, moving a strand of hair away from her face. 'Perhaps we just made that baby you want so badly,' he murmured, a smile playing around his generous mouth. 'But if we haven't, it doesn't matter. You do understand that now, don't you, darling?'

'Yes, I do.' She returned his smile. 'As Dr Boujon told me, I have to relax, and we have to just keep on trying. And as he mentioned, there are always ways he can help.'

Ian laughed. 'That won't be necessary, I'm sure of that. Don't forget, I'm a full-blooded Scotsman from the Highlands.'

Fifteen minutes later, Kay was sitting at the dressing table again, smoothing a make-up sponge across her face. As she outlined her mouth with a lip pencil, she thought about the last five days. Ian had arrived in Paris unexpectedly, responding to her invitation to join her for Anya's birthday party tonight.

He had come a few days early, he explained, because he felt they needed a few days together, alone, away from Lochcraigie.

And on that first night, after they had made passionate love in her suite at the Meurice, she had found herself telling him about her visits to Dr Boujon. There was nothing physically wrong with her; now that she knew this she had been able to confide her worries about not getting pregnant to her husband. The doctor had recommended that she do this, and it had been worth it.

After Ian had listened to her concerns, he had told her to stop worrying, that it didn't trouble him at this moment.

His kindness and understanding had given her the courage to tell him about all the terrible things that had happened to her when she was a child. When she had finished he had taken her in his arms and held her close. 'Now you have me to look after you, Kay darling, and I'll never let anyone hurt you again.'

She had held on to him tightly, loving him more than ever for being such a good man. She also understood that he had never changed towards her. All of that had been in her head. And at that moment, she vowed never to doubt him or his love for her ever again.

Now, Kay rose from the dressing table and moved across the bedroom. Tall, slender, long-limbed and elegant. She was already wearing stockings and high heels, and she took the champagne-coloured chiffon dress from its hanger and stepped into it.

Suddenly, as if she had summoned him, Ian was standing in the doorway, looking handsome in his tuxedo. 'Shall I zip you up?'

Turning her head, she smiled. 'Thanks, Ian.'

Once she had smoothed the dress down, and adjusted it on her body, she swung round to face him. 'Do you like it?'

'It's wonderful on you, so frothy and light, and the necklace and earrings are perfect with it.'

'Thank you again for those beauties. And now I think we'd better go down to the bar. I'm sure the others are waiting.'

Kay spotted Alexa the moment they entered the Bar Fontainebleau. She and Tom were seated at a table in a corner near the window, and she raised her hand and waved.

As Kay and Ian drew closer, Kay saw that Alexa was also wearing a chiffon dress; it looked as if it was cut on the bias and it was composed of variegated greens. To Kay it was the perfect choice. The mingled greens matched Alexa's eyes, set off her dark hair.

Tom jumped up and greeted them, and, once they were seated, the waiter brought them glasses of champagne. A moment after this, Jessica arrived with Mark Sylvester. Jessica had chosen to wear a pale blue organza gown delicately patterned with trailing darker blue flowers and, like Kay's and Alexa's, it floated gently around her as she moved.

As soon as Mark and Jessica drew to a standstill at the table, Alexa said, with a light laugh, 'Well, I see we all had the same idea about a June party in Paris, and what to wear.'

Mark, his eyes roving over them, said, 'You're going to be the belles of the ball.'

'Oh no!' Kay exclaimed, her eyes sparkling. 'That role is reserved for Anya.'

Alexa, glancing from Tom to Ian to Mark, exclaimed, 'But one thing is certain, girls, we have the most handsome escorts.'

'Thanks for the rather nice compliment, Alexa,' Ian responded. He liked Kay's girlfriends, and the men in their lives, all of whom he had met last night. Tom had taken everyone to dinner at the beautiful L'Ambroisie in the Place des Vosges. It had been the kind of evening Ian had not had in a long time, and he had appreciated every moment of it.

But most of all he had enjoyed meeting Anya Sedgwick, and he had listened to her raptly as she had extolled Kay's virtues, acclaimed her talent, and confided how much she loved his wife. 'Cherished her' was the way she had put it. He had been bursting with pride and love for his wonderful Kay.

Nicky Sedgwick had been charming, friendly and amusing. While the fourth member of the quartet, Maria Franconi, had been such a knockout in her simple black dress and pearls that none of the other diners had been able to take their eyes off her.

Now Ian said, 'I suppose Nicky and Maria are not coming for drinks with us. I rather got the impression they were going to collect Anya and take her to the party directly.'

'Anya didn't want to be late,' Alexa explained. 'She wanted to be there first, to greet the guests as they arrived.'

More flutes of champagne arrived at the table for Jessica and Mark, and the six of them now clinked glasses and toasted one another. And then they settled down to chat together for a short while before leaving for Ledoyen.

Anya, flanked by Nicky and Maria, stood in the entrance foyer of Ledoyen, glancing about her.

A look of enchantment crossed her face, brought a sparkle to her eyes, a glow to her face. 'Oh, Nicky, my darling boy, you've outdone yourself!' she exclaimed, turning to him, clutching his arm. 'This is simply beautiful!'

He smiled with pleasure and gratification. 'I'm glad you like it. I wanted you to feel . . . at home.'

Anya laughed her light tinkling laugh that was ageless, and took a step forward, her eyes everywhere. What Nicky had done was to re-create the front façade of her black and white, half-timbered manor house in Paris, with its trellis and ivy growing up part of the façade. This replica was actually a trompe l'oeil, the style of painting that gave an illusion of reality, like a photograph, and the giant canvas was attached to a long wall at one side of the hall. This entire area had been designed to look like the cobbled courtyard of her house; the cherry tree in full bloom was there, with the four metal garden chairs standing underneath its laden branches. And her flower garden, enclosed within a white picket fence, took pride of place at the other side of the hall.

Taking hold of her arm, Nicky said, 'Come along, Anya, I've more surprises for you.'

Still smiling broadly, Anya allowed herself to be propelled up the staircase. 'Where are we going?' she asked.

'For cocktails,' Maria said, beaming at her.

Anya nodded, glanced at Maria out of the corner of her eye, thinking how elegant she looked in a midnight-blue chiffon gown with a strapless top and a flowing skirt, her only jewellery a thin strand of diamonds round her neck and diamond studs in her ears.

'Maria, you're simply exquisite,' Anya murmured, momentarily awed by the girl's staggering beauty tonight.

'It's thanks to Nicky, he chose my dress. It's from Balmain,' Maria said.

'Oh, it's not the dress I'm talking about, but you, my dear.'

Maria flushed slightly, smiled with pleasure. 'And you look wonderful in your signature red, Anya.'

Anya said, 'Well, you know I've always loved red. It makes me feel happy. Not that I need a colour to do that for me tonight. I'd be happy whatever colour I was wearing.'

When they reached the first-floor landing, Nicky took hold of Anya's hand and led her towards large double doors. He opened them, ushered her inside, and exclaimed, '*Voilà!*'

Anya gasped, truly surprised.

She stood staring at another replica, this time of the sitting room of her house in Provence, the house Hugo had bought for her years ago, and where they had spent so many happy times together. Nicky had used Provençal country furniture, many bright colours reminiscent of the real room, and in doing so had created a perfect copy. Waiters and waitresses, dressed in the local costumes of the area, stood around smiling, ready to serve drinks.

'Nicky, oh Nicky,' was all Anya could manage to say as he guided her through the room and into an adjoining one.

Now she found herself in a Russian dacha filled with rustic peasant furniture, and here, to make it completely authentic in mood, were waiters wearing scarlet and gold Cossack tunics, with baggy trousers tucked into black boots.

She stood stock-still, glancing around, endeavouring to take everything in, but Nicky would not permit her to linger long. He took her hand in his, moving her onwards, and into a third room.

Anya was startled, amazed and touched all at the same time, and she experienced a rush of emotion. Here she stood, in the living room where she had grown up in London with her parents. Nicky had re-created it down to the last detail. Tears suddenly sprang into her eyes.

Turning to him, she asked a little tremulously, 'How on earth did you manage this?'

'With your sister Katti's help. She had some old photographs of your parents' living room, which were a great help. But most importantly, she has a photographic memory, and it's not dimmed by age at all.'

Blinking back her tears, Anya walked round the room, noting the samovar, and the icons on velvet-skirted tables. Nicky had found so many objects similar to the things her parents had owned, as well as photographs of her family in old Fabergé frames, and of her when she was a young girl. The colour scheme of pale blue and gold was the one her mother had so loved.

Slowly, she walked back to Nicky and embraced him. 'Thank you, thank you,' she said, her voice choked. 'Thank you for bringing so many of my very cherished memories to life tonight.'

A waiter dressed as an English butler now came forward with a tray of drinks, and the three of them took flutes of champagne. They clinked glasses and said cheers at the same time, and Nicky added, 'I want you to have the most wonderful evening, Anya.'

'I know I will, and what you've done is quite extraordinary.'

He laughed. 'There are still a few surprises in store for you, Anya.'

'I can't believe you can top this! Such as what?' she probed.

'Oh, you'll just have to wait and see,' he teased. 'Now, where do you want to greet your guests? Which room?' Nicky asked.

'I'm not sure, darling boy, each room is so very special.'

'Perhaps we should wait in the first room, because everyone enters there,' Maria suggested.

'Good idea, my sweet,' Nicky said and together they walked back to the Provençal sitting room with its small tables covered with the cheerful red, green and yellow tablecloths from Provence. Brown ceramic jugs filled with tall sunflowers stood on a long sideboard, and the scent of lavender filled the air.

As they entered, one of the waitresses wearing a Provençal costume came over to them holding a tray, and Anya smiled when she saw all her favourite things. Warm pirozhki, the small Russian pastries filled with chopped meat; dollops of caviar atop tiny baked potatoes; smoked salmon on toast; and miniature sausage rolls.

'Well!' she exclaimed, 'I can't resist these. I must sample one of each.'

'I hoped you would,' Nicky said. 'I'll join you.'

And then a few minutes later the guests began to arrive.

Anya was suddenly surrounded by family.

Her sister and brother-in-law, Katti and Sacha, and all the Lebedevs, kissing her, congratulating her. And then her brother Vladimir and his wife Lilli, and their children, so warm and loving. And behind them came her own children, Olga and Dimitri, and their families, hugging her, wishing her a happy birthday, their faces smiling and happy.

After them came so many old friends from across the years, and the students who had passed through the school and remained close to her for thirty years or more.

And then at last her special girls. Her four favourites from the class of '94. Alexa, Jessica, Kay and Maria. How beautiful they all looked as they now walked towards her, escorted by the men in their lives, elegant in their dinner jackets.

Alexa, Kay and Jessica greeted her, and so did Tom, Ian and Mark, and then with Nicky the three men stepped back so that she was left alone with the quartet.

'It goes without saying that you all look gorgeous!' Anya exclaimed, beaming at them. 'And before we go any further, I want to thank you all for your gifts. Kay, this antique shawl is exquisite, I couldn't resist wearing it tonight. And as you see, it's the same red as my gown. And, Jessica, the icon is a prize, and it has pride of my place in my sitting room. And so does your lacquered box, Alexa. The painting of St

Petersburg on its lid is a little jewel. Thank you, thank you.' Anya smiled at Maria, and finished, 'As for your painting, Maria, it is absolutely extraordinary, and it is now hanging in my bedroom. I thank you so much for it.'

Maria blushed and smiled but remained silent.

Anya's eyes swept over them again, and she said softly, in the most intimate of voices, 'I am so happy you all came to Paris early, so that we had time to be together and you had the chance to air your differences and make up.'

'It's like old times,' Alexa said. 'We're here for one another. For ever. Through thick and thin. Aren't we, girls?'

They all agreed with her, and Kay said, 'It doesn't seem like seven years at all, only yesterday that we were here at your school, Anya.'

'You taught us so much, nurtured our talents, helped us to realise our dreams,' Jessica told her. 'You helped to make us what we are, Anya. And for that we'll be for ever grateful.'

Anya nodded. 'You all came to Paris for some other reasons as well, I realise that. You had unfinished business. Each one of you had a quest. And I'm so very happy you found what you were seeking.' She focused on Alexa. 'You and Tom got back together . . . permanently?'

Alexa nodded, her face glowing as she showed Anya her left hand. A diamond ring sparkled on it. 'We got engaged tonight. Tom slipped the ring on my finger as we were being driven over here.'

'I'm so happy for you, Alexa darling.'

Looking closely at Maria, Anya continued, 'And you and Nicky seem to be ideally suited.'

'Yes, we are, Anya, and Nicky wants us to marry. When he's free, after he is divorced. And I'm not going back to Milan. I'm going to live in Paris with Nicky and be an artist. No more textile designing for me,' Maria announced.

Anya clapped her hands together softly. 'Thank God for that, Maria. It would be a waste of your talent if you kept your job at home. And congratulations to you, too. I shall give the wedding for you when you marry. It will be my great pleasure. And, Kay, what about you? Everything seems to be working with you and your lovely Ian.'

'It is, Anya, and as I told you, there's nothing wrong with me physically. There's no reason why I can't have a baby.' Kay laughed lightly. 'But Ian doesn't care. He says it's me he wants.'

'And why wouldn't he feel that way? He's a lucky man to have you,' Anya replied. Her eyes rested finally on Jessica, and she noticed yet again that there was still a wistfulness to her, a sadness in her eyes.

'I'm relieved you found Lucien, and that you had a chance to see him, Jessica,' Anya began. 'I know what a shock it was for you, but now you can finally close this chapter, my dear.'

'Close the book, actually, Anya,' Jessica answered. 'It's not often a person gets a second chance in life, but I'm lucky because I have Mark. He thinks we have a future together, and I have a feeling he's right.'

'I know he is. And he's a lovely man. Why, they're all lovely men.'

A short while after this they all went downstairs to dinner.

Nicky and Maria escorted Anya, and as they led her into the dining room she was unexpectedly blinded by tears.

The room had been transformed into the most beautiful garden she had ever seen. Masses of flowering plants were banked high round the room. Orange trees in tubs decorated corners. Stone fountains sprayed arcs of shimmering water up into the air. There were stone statues and stone sundials in strategic places, and bowers and arches of fresh roses entwined with ivy leaves. And each table was skirted in pale pink with low bowls of pink roses in the centre, and votive candles flickered brightly . . . hundreds of tiny lights round the room that added to the magic.

'Oh, Nicky,' Anya said, and was unable to say another word. She shook her head and clutched his arm as he led her forward to the main table, where she was to sit with her immediate family. 'Thank you, thank you, darling,' she whispered hoarsely, still choked, as he pulled out her chair for her.

'It was my pleasure, my very great pleasure, Anya,' he said, and moved away, holding Maria's hand as they went to join the others at their intimate table for eight.

I'm so very lucky, a most fortunate woman, Anya thought, as she sipped her water, waiting for the table to fill up with her children and her beloved sister, Katti. What a life I've had. Eighty-five wonderful years. Love and happiness. Pain and suffering. And quite a lot of grief. But I've always come through my troubles. I've endured. Perhaps that's what life is all about. Enduring. Being a survivor.

And my four girls are survivors. Anya turned in her chair, focused her eyes on the dance floor. The table next to hers had emptied, and its occupants were on the dance floor . . .

Maria was in Nicky's arms. He was moving her slowly round the room, whispering in her ear.

Kay's head was against Ian's shoulder, her expression dreamy, and he had a look of absolute contentment in his eyes.

Jessica was holding on to Mark very tightly, and her face was no longer sad. She was looking up at him, her eyes sparkling.

Alexa and Tom were not dancing at all, merely swaying to the music. At one moment he looked down at her, and kissed her lightly on the lips. 'Let's get married as soon as possible,' he said softly. 'I can't wait for you to be my wife. I love you so much.'

'And I love you, Tom. For always,' Alexa said, and she held him closer to her. All she wanted was to share that humdrum life of his, as he called it. She smiled a small, secret smile. Humdrum indeed, she thought.

Anya, still watching them, wished she knew what they were saying to one another. And then she laughed out loud. Of course they were telling each other beautiful things, making promises, making commitments . . . just as she had done so many years ago. First with Michel Lacoste and then with Hugo Sedgwick.

Love, she thought. There's nothing like it in this world. It's the only thing that really matters in the end.

BARBARA TAYLOR BRADFORD

'I always like to write about strong, independent career women,' says Barbara Taylor Bradford and, like her heroines, she is a woman whose zest for life goes hand in hand with a willingness to work hard to achieve her dreams.

Born in Upper Armley, Leeds, Barbara was the only child of Winston (named after Churchill) and Freda Taylor. Her mother, a former children's nurse and nanny, was an enormous influence on her daughter, introducing her to the wonders of books at the tender age of four. After leaving school at the age of fifteen, Barbara began work as a typist for the *Yorkshire Evening Post*. Within six months she was promoted to cub reporter in the newsroom. 'It was because I was such a bad typist and was ruining so much of their expensive paper!' she jokes. Nevertheless, at eighteen she became editor of the *Post*'s woman's page and by the age of twenty she had graduated to London's Fleet Street where, in 1961, she met American film producer Robert Bradford on a blind date and fell in love at first sight. They were married in 1963 and Barbara moved to America, where she continued her career as a journalist until her first novel, *A Woman of Substance*, was published in 1976 and became an instant best seller. Since then, the author has never looked back and is

now published in eighty-nine countries and in thirty-nine languages, with sales figures in excess of sixty-two million copies.

Barbara Taylor Bradford loves her adopted homeland and, in particular, New York, where she lives with Robert in a landmark building in Manhattan, overlooking the East River. The couple share their home with their two Bichon Frise dogs, Beaji and Chammi, who sit beneath Barbara's desk while she writes. The view is spectacular but Barbara seldom gets to enjoy it, spending, as she does, up to eight hours a day, five days a week, creating her latest blockbusters. The apartment boasts possessions that reflect Robert's and Barbara's passionate and personal tastes: collections of Art Deco antiques, Biedermeier furniture, teapots (one of which was a wedding gift to Barbara's parents in the 1920s), contemporary Impressionist paintings, and Winston Churchill memorabilia.

Another city much-loved by the author is Paris—the setting for her latest best seller, *Three Weeks in Paris*. The food, the atmosphere, the pulse of the city sparkle into life in the novel, as does the world of haute couture. Barbara confesses to having 'a passion for fashion' and wryly admits to having 'known a lot of designers and a lot of clothes!'

Jane Eastgate

THE SECRET LIFE OF BEES

SUE MONK KIDD

Lily has grown up believing that she accidentally killed her mother, a fact her cruel father does not dispute. Overwhelmed by guilt, Lily struggles to discover the mother she hardly knew, but all she has is a photograph, a pair of white cotton gloves and a picture of a black Madonna with the words *Tiburon, S.C*, written on the back.

The only person who loves Lily is her black servant, Rosaleen, and when racial tension erupts in the local community and Rosaleen is arrested and beaten, the pair run away together. But where in 1960s South Carolina can a black woman and a white teenager hide?

CHAPTER ONE

AT NIGHT I WOULD lie in bed and watch the show, how bees squeezed through the cracks of my bedroom wall and flew circles around the room, making that propeller sound, a high-pitched *zzzzzz* that hummed along my skin. I watched their wings shining like bits of chrome in the dark and felt the longing build in my chest. The way those bees flew, just for the feel of the wind, split my heart down its seam.

During the day they tunnelled through my bedroom walls, sounding like a radio tuned to static in the next room, and I imagined them turning the walls into honeycombs, with honey seeping out for me to taste.

The bees came the summer of 1964, the summer I turned fourteen and my life went spinning off into a whole new orbit. Looking back now, I want to say the bees were sent to me. I want to say they showed up like the angel Gabriel appearing to the Virgin Mary, setting events in motion I could never have guessed. I know it is presumptuous to compare my small life to hers, but I have reason to believe she wouldn't mind; I will get to that. Right now it's enough to say that despite everything that happened that summer, I remain tender towards the bees.

July 1, 1964, I lay in bed, waiting for the bees to show up, thinking of what Rosaleen had said when I told her about their nightly visitations.

'Bees swarm before death,' she'd said.

Rosaleen had worked for us since my mother died. My daddy—who I called T. Ray because 'Daddy' never fitted him—had pulled her out of the peach orchard, where she'd worked as one of his pickers. She had a big round face and a body that sloped out from her neck like a tent, and she was so black that night seemed to seep from her skin. She lived alone in a little house in the woods, not far from us, and came every day to cook, clean and be my stand-in mother. Rosaleen had never had a child herself, so for the last ten years I'd been her pet guinea pig.

Bees swarm before death. She was full of crazy ideas that I ignored, but I lay there thinking about this one, wondering if the bees had come with my death in mind. I wasn't that disturbed by the idea. Those bees could have descended on me like a flock of angels and stung me till I died, and it wouldn't have been the worst thing to happen. People who think dying is the worst thing don't know a thing about life.

My mother died when I was four years old. It was a fact of life, but if I brought it up, people would suddenly get interested in distant places in the sky, and seem not to hear me. Once in a while, though, some caring soul would say, 'Just put it out of your head, Lily. It was an accident. You didn't mean to do it.'

That night I lay in bed and thought about dying and going to be with my mother in paradise. I would meet her saying, 'Mother, forgive. Please forgive,' and she would kiss me and tell me I was not to blame. She would tell me this for the first ten thousand years.

The next ten thousand years she would fix my hair. She would brush it into such a tower of beauty, people all over heaven would drop their harps to admire it. You can tell which girls lack mothers by the look of their hair. My hair was constantly going off in eleven wrong directions, and T. Ray refused to buy me bristle rollers, so I had to roll it on Welch's grape juice cans, which had nearly turned me into an insomniac.

I would take four or five centuries to tell her about the special misery of living with T. Ray. He had an orneriness year-round, but especially in summer, when he worked his peach orchards daylight to dusk. Mostly I stayed out of his way. His only kindness was for Snout, his bird dog, who got her stomach scratched any time she rolled onto her wiry back. I've seen Snout pee on T. Ray's boot and it not get a rise out of him.

I had asked God repeatedly to do something about T. Ray. He'd gone to church for forty years and was only getting worse. It seemed like this should tell God something.

I kicked back the sheets. The room sat in perfect stillness, not one bee anywhere. Every minute I looked at the clock on my dresser and wondered what was keeping them.

Finally, some time close to midnight, when my eyelids had nearly given up the strain of staying open, a purring noise started over in the corner, low and vibrating. Moments later shadows moved like spatter paint along the walls, catching the light when they passed the window so I could see the outline of wings. The sound swelled till the entire room was pulsating, till the air became matted with bees. They lapped around my body, making me the perfect centre of a whirlwind cloud.

The sight was a true spectacle. Suddenly I couldn't stand not showing it off to somebody, even if the only person around was T. Ray. I slid from the covers and dashed through the bees for the door. I woke him by touching his arm with one finger, softly at first, then harder and harder till I was jabbing into his flesh.

T. Ray bolted from bed in his underwear. I dragged him towards my room, him shouting how this better be good, how the house damn well better be on fire, and Snout barking like we were on a dove shoot.

'Bees!' I shouted. 'There's a swarm of bees in my room!'

But when we got there, they'd vanished back into the wall like they knew he was coming.

'Goddamn it, Lily, this ain't funny.'

I looked up and down the walls. I got down under the bed and begged the very dust and coils of my bedsprings to produce a bee.

'They were here,' I said. 'Flying everywhere.'

'Yeah, and there was a goddamn herd of buffalo in here, too.'

'Listen,' I said. 'You can hear them buzzing.'

He cocked his ear towards the wall. 'I don't hear any buzzing,' he said, and twirled his finger beside his temple. 'I guess they must have flown out of that cuckoo clock you call a brain. You wake me up again, Lily, and I'll get out the Martha Whites, you hear me?'

Martha Whites were a form of punishment only T. Ray could have dreamed up. I shut my mouth instantly.

Still, I couldn't let the matter go entirely—T. Ray thinking I was so desperate I would invent an invasion of bees to get attention. Which is how I got the bright idea of catching a jar of these bees, presenting them to T. Ray, and saying, 'Now who's making things up?'

My first and only memory of my mother was the day she died. I tried for a long time to conjure up an image of her before that, just a sliver of something, like her tucking me into bed, reading the adventures of Uncle Wiggly, or hanging my underclothes near the heater on ice-cold mornings. Even her picking a switch off the forsythia bush and stinging my legs would have been welcome.

The day she died was December 3, 1954. The furnace had cooked the air so hot my mother had peeled off her sweater and stood in short sleeves, jerking at the window in her bedroom, wrestling with the stuck paint. Finally she gave up and said, 'Well, fine, we'll just burn the hell up in here, I guess.'

Her hair was black and generous, with thick curls circling her face, a face I could never quite coax into view, despite the sharpness of everything else.

I raised my arms to her, and she picked me up, saying I was way too big a girl to hold like this, but holding me anyway. The moment she lifted me, I was wrapped in her smell.

The scent got laid down in me in a permanent way and had all the precision of cinnamon. I used to go regularly into the Sylvan Mercantile and smell every perfume bottle they had, trying to identify it. Every time I showed up, the perfume lady said, 'My goodness, look who's here.' Like I hadn't just been in there the week before and gone down the entire row of bottles. Shalimar, Chanel No. 5, White Shoulders.

I'd say, 'You got anything new?'

She never did.

So it was a shock when I came upon the scent on my fifth-grade teacher, who said it was nothing but plain ordinary Pond's Cold Cream.

The afternoon my mother died, there was a suitcase open on the floor, sitting near the stuck window. She moved in and out of the closet, dropping this and that into the suitcase, not bothering to fold them.

I followed her into the closet and scooted beneath dress hems and trouser legs, into darkness and wisps of dust and little dead moths. I stuck my hands inside a pair of white high heels and clapped them together.

The closet floor vibrated whenever someone climbed the stairs below it, which is how I knew T. Ray was coming. Over my head I heard my mother, pulling things from the hangers, the swish of clothes, wire clinking together. *Hurry*, she said.

When his shoes clomped into the room, she sighed, the breath leaving her as if her lungs had suddenly clenched. This is the last thing I remember with perfect crispness—her breath floating down to me like a tiny parachute, collapsing without a trace among the piles of shoes.

I don't remember what they said, only the fury of their words, how the air turned raw and full of welts. I inched backwards, deeper into the closet, feeling my fingers in my mouth, the taste of shoes, of feet.

I didn't know at first whose hands pulled me out, then I found myself in my mother's arms, breathing her smell. She smoothed my hair, said, 'Don't worry,' but I was peeled away by T. Ray. He carried me to the door and set me down in the hallway. 'Go to your room,' he said.

'I don't want to,' I cried, trying to push past him, back into the room, back where she was.

'Get in your goddamned room!' he shouted, and shoved me. I landed against the wall, then fell forwards onto my hands and knees. Lifting my head, looking past him, I saw her running across the room. Running at him, yelling. 'Leave. Her. Alone.'

I huddled on the floor beside the door and watched him take her by the shoulders and shake her, her head bouncing back and forth. I saw the whiteness of his lip. And then—though everything starts to blur now in my mind—she lunged away from him into the closet, away from his grabbing hands, scrambling for something high on a shelf.

When I saw the gun in her hand, I ran towards her, clumsy and falling, wanting to save her, to save us all.

Time folded in on itself then. What is left lies in clear yet disjointed pieces in my head. The gun shining like a toy in her hand, how he snatched it away and waved it around. The gun on the floor. Bending to pick it up. The noise that exploded around us.

This is what I know about myself. She was all I wanted. And I took her away.

T. Ray and I lived just outside Sylvan, South Carolina, population 3,100. Peach stands and Baptist churches, that sums it up.

At the entrance to the farm we had a big wooden sign with OWENS PEACH ENTERPRISES painted across it in the worst orange colour you've ever seen. I hated that sign.

T. Ray didn't believe in slumber parties, which wasn't a big concern as I never got invited to them anyway, but he refused to drive me to town for football games or pep rallies, which were held on Saturdays. He did not care that I wore clothes I made for myself in home economics class, cotton print shirtwaists with crooked zippers and skirts hanging below my knees, outfits only the Pentecostal girls wore.

I needed all the help that fashion could give me, since no one, not a single person, had ever said, 'Lily, you are such a pretty child,' except for Miss Jennings at church, and she was legally blind.

I watched my reflection not only in the mirror, but in store windows and across the television when it wasn't on, trying to get a fix on my looks. My hair was black like my mother's but basically a nest of cowlicks, and it worried me that I didn't have much of a chin. I kept thinking I'd grow one the same time my breasts came in, but it didn't work out that way. I had nice eyes, though, what you would call Sophia Loren eyes, but still, even the boys who wore their hair in ducktails dripping with Vitalis and carried combs in their shirt pockets didn't seem attracted to me, and they were considered hard up.

Matters below my neck had shaped up, not that I could show off that part. It was fashionable to wear cashmere twinsets and plaid kilts midthigh, but T. Ray said hell would be an ice rink before I went out like that—did I want to end up pregnant like Bitsy Johnson whose skirt barely covered her ass? How he knew about Bitsy is a mystery, but it was true about her skirts and true about the baby. An unfortunate coincidence is all it was.

Rosaleen knew less about fashion than T. Ray did, and when it was cold she made me go to school wearing long britches under my Pentecostal dresses.

There was nothing I hated worse than clumps of whispering girls who got quiet when I passed. I started gnawing the flesh around my fingernails till I was a bleeding wreck. I worried so much about how I looked and whether I was doing things right, I felt half the time I was impersonating a girl instead of really being one.

I had thought my chance would come from going to charm school at the Women's Club last spring, Friday afternoons for six weeks, but I got barred because I didn't have a mother, a grandmother, or even a measly aunt to present me with a white rose at the closing ceremony. Rosaleen doing it was against the rules. I'd cried till I threw up in the sink.

'You're charming enough,' Rosaleen had said, washing the vomit out of the sink. 'You don't need to go to some high-falutin school to get charm.'

'I do so,' I said. 'They teach everything. How to walk and pivot, what to do with your ankles when you sit in a chair, how to get into a car, pour tea, take off your gloves . . .'

Rosaleen blew air from her lips. 'Good Lord,' she said.

'Arrange flowers in a vase, talk to boys, tweeze your eyebrows, shave your legs, apply lipstick . . .'

'What about vomit in a sink? They teach a charming way to do that?' she asked.

Sometimes I purely hated her.

The morning after I woke T. Ray, Rosaleen stood in the doorway of my room, watching me chase a bee with a mason jar. Her lip was rolled out so far I could see the little sunrise of pink inside her mouth.

'What are you doing with that jar?' she said.

'I'm catching bees to show T. Ray. He thinks I'm making them up.'

'Lord, give me strength.' She'd been shelling butter beans on the porch, and sweat glistened on the pearls of hair around her forehead. She pulled at the front of her dress, opening an airway along her bosom, big and soft as couch pillows.

The bee landed on the state map I kept tacked on the wall. I watched it walk along the coast of South Carolina on Highway 17. I clamped the mouth of the preserving jar against the wall, trapping it between Charleston and Georgetown. When I slid on the lid, it went into a tail-spin, throwing itself against the glass over and over with pops and clicks.

I'd made the jar as nice as I could with fat, felty petals, and more than enough nail holes in the lid to keep the bees from perishing.

I brought the jar level with my nose. 'Come look at this thing fight,' I said to Rosaleen.

When she stepped in the room, her scent floated out to me, dark and spicy like the snuff she packed inside her cheek. She held her small jug with its coin-size mouth and a handle for her to loop her finger through. I watched her press it along her chin, her lips fluted out like a flower, then spit a curl of black juice inside it.

She stared at the bee and shook her head. 'If you get stung, don't come whining to me,' she said, ''cause I ain't gonna care.'

That was a lie.

I was the only one who knew that, despite her sharp ways, her heart was more tender than a flower skin and she loved me beyond reason.

I hadn't known this until I was eight and she bought me an Easter-dyed biddy chick from the mercantile. I found it trembling in a corner of its pen, the colour of purple grapes, with sad little eyes that cast around for its mother. Rosaleen let me bring it home, right into the living room, where I strewed a box of Quaker Oats on the floor for it to eat and she didn't raise a word of protest.

The chick left dollops of violet-streaked droppings all over the place, due, I suppose, to the dye soaking into its fragile system. We had just started to clean them up when T. Ray burst in, threatening to boil the chick for dinner. He started to swoop at the biddy with his tractor-grease hands, but Rosaleen planted herself in front of him. 'There is worse things in the house than chicken shit,' she said and looked him up and down. 'You ain't touching that chick.'

His boots whispered down the hall. I thought, *She loves me*, and it was the first time such a far-fetched idea had occurred to me.

Her age was a mystery, since she didn't possess a birth certificate. She would tell me she was born in 1909 or 1919, depending on how old she felt at the moment. She was sure about the place: McClellanville, South Carolina, where her mama had woven sweet-grass baskets and sold them on the roadside.

'Like me selling peaches,' I'd said to her.

'Not one thing like you selling peaches,' she'd said back. 'You ain't got seven children you gotta feed from it.'

'You've got *six* brothers and sisters?' I'd thought of her as alone in the world except for me.

'I did have, but I don't know where a one of them is.'

She'd thrown her husband out three years after they married, for carousing. 'You put his brain in a bird, the bird would fly backwards,' she liked to say. I often wondered what that bird would do with Rosaleen's brain. I decided half the time it would drop shit on your head and the other half it would sit on abandoned nests with its wings spread wide.

I used to have daydreams in which she was white and married T. Ray, and became my real mother. Other times I was a Negro orphan she found in a cornfield and adopted. Once in a while I had us living in a foreign country like New York, where she could adopt me and we could both stay our natural colour.

My mother's name was Deborah. I thought that was the prettiest name I'd ever heard, even though T. Ray refused to speak it. If I said it, he acted like he might go straight to the kitchen and stab something. Once when I asked him when her birthday was and what cake icing she preferred, he told me to shut up, and when I asked him a second time, he picked up a jar of blackberry jelly and threw it against the kitchen cabinet. We have blue stains to this day.

I did manage to get a few scraps of information from him, though, such as my mother was buried in Virginia where her people came from. I got worked up at that, thinking I'd found a grandmother. No, he tells me, my mother was an only child whose mother died ages ago. Naturally. Once when he stepped on a roach in the kitchen, he told me my mother had spent hours luring roaches out of the house with bits of marshmallow and trails of graham-cracker crumbs, that she was a lunatic when it came to saving bugs.

The oddest things caused me to miss her. Like training bras. Who was I going to ask about that? And who but my mother could've understood the magnitude of junior cheer-leader tryouts? I can tell you for certain T. Ray didn't grasp it. But I missed her most the day I was twelve and woke up with the rose-petal stain on my panties. I was so proud of that flower and didn't have a soul to show it to except Rosaleen.

Not long after that I found a paper bag in the attic stapled at the top. Inside it I found the last traces of my mother.

There was a photograph of a woman smirking in front of an old car, wearing a light-coloured dress with padded shoulders. Her expression said, 'Don't you dare take this picture,' but she wanted it taken, you could see that. You could not believe the stories I saw in that picture, how she was waiting for love to come to her, and not too patiently.

I laid the photograph beside my eighth-grade picture and examined every possible similarity. She was more or less missing a chin, too, but even so, she was above-average pretty, which offered me genuine hope for my future.

The bag contained a pair of white cotton gloves stained the colour of age. When I pulled them out, I thought, *Her very hands were inside here.* I feel foolish about it now, but one time I stuffed the gloves with cotton balls and held them through the night.

The end-all mystery inside the bag was a small wooden picture of Mary, the mother of Jesus. I recognised her even though her skin was black, only a shade lighter than Rosaleen's. It looked to me like somebody had cut the black Mary's picture from a book, glued it onto a sanded piece of wood about two inches across, and varnished it. On the back an unknown hand had written 'Tiburon, S.C.'

For two years now I'd kept these things of hers inside a tin box, buried in the orchard. There was a special place out there in the long tunnel of trees no one knew about, not even Rosaleen. I'd started going there before I could tie my shoelaces. At first it was just a spot to hide from T. Ray and his meanness or from the memory of that afternoon when the gun went off, but later I would slip out there, sometimes after T. Ray had gone to bed, just to lie under the trees and be peaceful.

I'd placed her things in the tin box and buried it out there late one night by flashlight, too scared to leave them in my room. I was afraid T. Ray might go up to the attic and discover her things were missing, and turn my room upside-down searching for them. I hated to think what he'd do to me if he found them hidden among my stuff.

Now and then I'd go out there and dig up the box. I would lie on the ground with the trees folded over me, wearing her gloves, smiling at her photograph. I would study 'Tiburon, S.C.' on the back of the black Mary picture, and wonder what sort of place it was. I'd looked it up on the map once, and it wasn't more than two hours away. Had my mother been there and bought this picture? I always promised myself one day, when I was grown-up enough, I would take the bus over there. I wanted to go every place she had ever been.

After my morning of capturing bees, I spent the afternoon in the peach stand out on the highway, selling T. Ray's peaches. It was the loneliest summer job a girl could have, stuck in a roadside hut with three walls and a flat tin roof.

I sat on a Coke crate and watched pick-ups zoom by till I was nearly poisoned with exhaust fumes and boredom. Thursday afternoons were usually a big peach day, with women getting ready for Sunday cobblers, but not a soul stopped.

T. Ray refused to let me bring books out here, and if I smuggled one out under my shirt, somebody, like Mrs Watson from the next farm, would see him at church and say, 'Saw your girl in the peach stand reading up a storm. You must be proud.' And he would half kill me.

What kind of person is against *reading*? I think he believed it would stir up ideas of college, which he thought a waste of money for girls, even if they did, like me, score the highest number a human being can get on their verbal aptitude test. Math aptitude is another thing, but people aren't meant to be overly bright in everything.

I was the only student who didn't groan when Mrs Henry assigned us another Shakespeare play. Well actually, I did *pretend* to groan, but inside I was as thrilled as if I'd been crowned Sylvan's Peach Queen.

Up until Mrs Henry came along, I'd believed beauty college would be the upper limit of my career. Once I told her if she was my customer I would give her a French twist that would do wonders for her, and she said—and I quote—'Please, Lily, you are insulting your fine intelligence. Do you have any idea how smart you are? You could be a professor or a writer with actual books to your credit. Beauty school. *Please*.'

It took me a month to get over the shock of having life possibilities. You know how adults love to ask, 'So . . . what are you going to be when you grow up?' I can't tell you how much I'd hated that question, but suddenly I was going around volunteering to people, people who didn't even want to know, that I planned to be a professor and a writer of actual books.

I kept a collection of my writings. For a while everything I wrote had a horse in it. After we read Ralph Waldo Emerson in class, I wrote 'My Philosophy of Life', which I intended for the start of a book but could get only three pages out of it. Mrs Henry said I needed to live past fourteen years old before I would have a philosophy.

She said a scholarship was my only hope for a future and lent me her private books for the summer. Whenever I opened one, T. Ray said, 'Who do you think you are, Julius Shakespeare?' The man sincerely thought that was Shakespeare's first name, and if you think I should have corrected him, you are ignorant about the art of survival.

Without books in the peach stand, I often passed the time making up poems, but that slow afternoon I didn't have the patience for rhyming words. I just sat out there and thought about how much I hated the peach stand, how completely and absolutely I hated it.

The day before I'd gone to first grade, T. Ray had found me in the peach stand sticking a nail into one of his peaches.

He walked towards me with his thumbs jammed into his pockets and his eyes squinted half shut from the glare. I watched his shadow slide over the dirt and weeds and thought he had come to punish me for stabbing a peach. I didn't even know why I was doing it.

Instead he said, 'Lily, you're starting school tomorrow, so there are things you need to know. About your mother.'

For a moment everything got still and quiet, as if the wind had died and the birds had stopped flying. He squatted down in front of me.

'It's time you knew what happened to her, and I want you to hear it from me. Not from people out there talking.'

We had never spoken of this, and I felt a shiver pass over me. The memory of that day would come back to me at odd moments. The stuck window. The smell of her. The clink of hangers. The suitcase. The way they'd fought and shouted. Most of all the gun on the floor, the heaviness when I'd lifted it.

I knew that the explosion I'd heard that day had killed her. The sound still sneaked into my head once in a while and surprised me. Sometimes it seemed that when I'd held the gun there hadn't been any noise at all, that it had come later, but other times, sitting bored and alone on the back steps, or pent up in my room on a rainy day, I felt I *had* caused it, that when I'd lifted the gun, the sound had torn through the room and gouged out our hearts.

It was a knowledge that would overwhelm me, and I would take off running—even if it was raining out—down the hill to my special place in the peach orchard. I'd lie on the ground and it would calm me.

Now, T. Ray scooped up a handful of dirt and let if fall out of his hands. 'The day she died, she was cleaning out the closet,' he said. I could not account for the strange tone of his voice, an unnatural sound, how it was almost, but not quite, *kind*.

Cleaning the closet. I had never considered what she was doing those last minutes of her life, what they had fought about.

'I remember,' I said. My voice sounded small and far away to me, like it was coming from an ant hole in the ground.

His eyebrows lifted. 'You *what*?'

'I remember,' I said again. 'You were yelling at each other.'

His face tightened. 'Is that right?' he said. His lips had started to turn pale, which was the thing I always watched for. I took a step back.

'Goddamn it, you were four years old!' he shouted. 'You don't know what you remember.'

In the silence that followed, I considered lying to him, saying, *I take it back, I don't remember anything*, but there was such a powerful need in me, pent up for so long, to speak about it, to say the words.

I looked down at my shoes, at the nail I'd dropped when I'd seen him coming. 'There was a gun.'

'Christ,' he said.

He looked at me a long time, then walked over to the bushel baskets stacked at the back of the stand. He stood there a minute with his hands balled up before he turned round and came back.

'What else?' he said. 'You tell me right now what you know.'

'The gun was on the floor—'

'And you picked it up,' he said. 'I guess you remember that.'

The exploding sound had started to echo around in my head. I looked off in the direction of the orchard, wanting to break and run.

'I remember picking it up,' I said. 'But that's all.'

He leaned down and held me by the shoulders, gave me a little shake. 'You don't remember anything else? You're sure? Now, think.'

I paused so long he cocked his head, looking at me, suspicious.

'No, sir, that's all.'

'Listen to me,' he said, his fingers squeezing into my arms. 'We were arguing like you said. We didn't see you at first. Then we turned around and you were standing there holding the gun. You'd picked it up off the floor. Then it just went off.'

He let me go and rammed his hands into his pockets. I could hear his hands jingling keys and nickels and pennies. I wanted so much to grab on to his leg, to feel him reach down and lift me to his chest, but I couldn't move, and neither did he. He stared at a place over my head. A place he was being very careful to study.

'The police asked lots of questions, but it was just one of those terrible things. You didn't mean to do it,' he said softly. 'But if anybody wants to know, that's what happened.'

Then he left, walking back towards the house. He'd gone only a little way when he looked back. 'And don't stick nails into my peaches again.'

It was after 6.00pm when I wandered back to the house from the peach stand, having sold nothing, not one peach, and found Rosaleen in the living room. Usually she would've gone home by now, but she was wrestling with the rabbit ears on top of the TV, trying to fix the snow on the screen. President Johnson faded in and out, lost in the blizzard. I'd never seen Rosaleen so interested in a TV show that she would exert physical energy over it.

'What happened?' I asked. 'Did they drop the atom bomb?'

'No,' she said. 'Just come here and see if you can fix the TV.' Her fists were burrowed so deep into her hips they seemed to disappear.

I twisted tin foil round the antennae. Things cleared up enough to make out President Johnson taking his seat at a desk, people all around.

Rosaleen dragged the footstool in front of the set and sat down, so the whole thing vanished under her. She leaned towards the set, holding a piece of her skirt and winding it around in her hands.

'What is going on?' I said, but she was so caught up in whatever was happening she didn't answer me. On the screen the President signed his name on a piece of paper, using about ten ink pens to get it done.

'Rosaleen—'

'Shhh,' she said, waving her hand.

I had to get the news from the TV man. 'Today, July 2nd, 1964,' he said, 'the President of the United States signed the Civil Rights Act into law in the East Room of the White House . . .'

I looked over at Rosaleen, who sat there shaking her head, mumbling, 'Lord have mercy,' just looking so disbelieving and happy.

I didn't know whether to be excited for her or worried. All people ever talked about after church were the Negroes and whether they'd get their civil rights. Who was winning—the white people's team or the coloured people's team? When that minister from Alabama, Reverend Martin Luther King, got arrested last month in Florida for wanting to eat in a restaurant, the men at church acted like the white people's team had won the pennant race. I knew they would not take this news lying down, not in one million years.

'Hallelujah, Jesus,' Rosaleen was saying. Oblivious.

Rosaleen had left dinner on the stove top, her famous smothered chicken. As I fixed T. Ray's plate, I considered how to bring up the delicate matter of my birthday, something T. Ray had never paid attention to in all the years of my life, but every year I got my hopes up thinking *this* year would be the one. I had the same birthday as the country, which made it even harder to get noticed.

I wanted to tell T. Ray that any girl would love a silver charm bracelet, that last year I'd been the only girl at Sylvan Junior High without one, that the whole point of lunchtime was to stand in the cafeteria line jangling your wrist, giving people a guided tour of your charm collection.

'So,' I said, sliding his plate in front of him, 'my birthday is this Saturday.'

I watched him pull the chicken meat from the bone with his fork.

'I was just thinking I would love to have one of those silver charm bracelets they have down at the mercantile.'

The house creaked like it did once in a while. Outside the door Snout gave a low bark, and then the air grew so quiet I could hear the food being ground up in T. Ray's mouth. He ate his chicken breast and started on the thigh, looking at me now and then in his hard way.

I started to say, *So then, what about the bracelet?* but I could see he'd already given his answer, and it caused a fresh sorrow to rise in me that had nothing, really, to do with the bracelet. I think now it was sorrow for the sound of his fork scraping the plate, the way it swelled in the distance between us, how I was not even in the room.

That night I lay in bed listening to the flicks and twitters and thrums inside the bee jar, waiting till it was late enough so I could slip out to the orchard and dig up the tin box that held my mother's things. I wanted to lie down in the orchard and let it hold me.

When the darkness had pulled the moon to the top of the sky, I got out of bed, put on my shorts and sleeveless blouse, and glided past T. Ray's room in silence. I didn't see his boots, how he'd parked them in the middle of the hall. When I fell, the clatter startled the air so badly T. Ray's snore changed rhythm. At first it ceased altogether, but then the snore started back with three piglet snorts.

I crept down the stairs, through the kitchen. When the night hit my face, I felt like laughing. The moon was a perfect circle, so full of light that all the edges of things had an amber cast. The cicadas rose up, and I ran with bare feet across the grass.

To reach my spot I had to go to the eighth row left of the tractor shed, then walk along it, counting trees till I got to thirty-two. The tin box was buried in the soft dirt beneath the tree, shallow enough that I could dig it up with my hands. When I brushed the dirt from the lid and opened it, I saw first the whiteness of her gloves, then the photograph wrapped in waxed paper, just as I'd left it. And finally the funny wooden picture of Mary with the dark face. I took everything out, and, stretching out among the fallen peaches, I rested them across my abdomen.

When I looked up through the trees, the night fell over me, and for a moment I felt like the sky was my skin and the moon was my heart beating up there in the dark. Lightning came, not jagged but in soft, golden licks across the sky. I undid the buttons on my shirt and opened it wide, just wanting the night to settle on my skin, and that's how I fell asleep, lying there with my mother's things, with the air making moisture on my chest and the sky puckering with light.

I woke to the sound of someone thrashing through the trees. *T. Ray!* I sat up, panicked, buttoning my shirt. I heard his footsteps, the fast, heavy pant of his breathing. Looking down, I saw my mother's gloves and the two pictures. I stopped buttoning and grabbed them up, fumbling with them, unable to think what to do, how to hide them. I had dropped the tin box back in its hole, too far away to reach.

'Lileeee!' he shouted, and I saw his shadow plunge towards me across the ground.

I jammed the gloves and pictures under the waistband of my shorts, then reached for the rest of the buttons with shaking fingers.

Before I could fasten them, light poured down on me and there he was without a shirt, holding a flashlight. The beam swept and zagged, blinding me when it swung across my eyes.

'Who were you out here with?' he shouted, aiming the light on my half-buttoned top.

'N-no one,' I said, gathering my knees in my arms, startled by what he was thinking.

He flung the beam into the darkness. 'Who's out there?' he yelled.

'Please, T. Ray, no one was here but me.'

'Get up from there,' he yelled.

I followed him back to the house. He didn't speak till we reached the kitchen and he pulled the Martha White grits from the pantry. 'I expect this out of boys, Lily—you can't blame them—but I expect more out of you. You act no better than a slut.' He poured a mound of grits the size of an anthill onto the pine floor. 'Get over here and kneel down.'

I'd been kneeling on grits since I was six, but still I never got used to that powdered-glass feeling beneath my skin. I walked towards them and lowered myself to the floor, determined not to cry, but the sting was already gathering in my eyes.

T. Ray sat in a chair and cleaned his nails with a pocketknife. I swayed from knee to knee, hoping for a second or two of relief, but the pain cut deep into my skin. I bit down on my lip, and it was then I felt the wooden picture of black Mary underneath my waistband. I felt the waxed paper with my mother's picture inside and her gloves stuck to my belly, and it seemed all of a sudden like my mother was there, up against my body, like she was bits and pieces of insulation moulded against my skin, helping me absorb all his meanness.

The next morning I woke up late. The moment my feet touched the floor, I checked under my mattress where I'd tucked my mother's things—just a temporary hiding place till I could bury them back in the orchard. Satisfied they were safe, I strolled into the kitchen, where I found Rosaleen sweeping up grits.

I buttered a piece of bread.

She jerked the broom as she swept. 'What happened?' she said.

'I went out to the orchard last night. T. Ray thinks I met some boy.'

'Did you?'

I rolled my eyes at her. 'No.'

'How long did he keep you on these grits?'

I shrugged. 'Maybe an hour.'

She looked down at my knees and stopped sweeping. They were swollen with hundreds of red welts, pinprick bruises that would grow into a blue stubble across my skin. 'Look at you, child. Look what he's done to you,' she said.

My knees had been tortured like this enough times in my life that I'd stopped thinking of it as out of the ordinary; it was just something you had to put up with from time to time, like the common cold. But the look on Rosaleen's face cut through all that. *Look what he's done to you.*

That's what I was doing—taking a good long look at my knees—when T. Ray stomped through the back door.

'Well, look who decided to get up.' He yanked the bread out of my hands and threw it into Snout's food bowl. 'Would it be too much to ask you to get out to the peach stand and do some work? You're not Queen for a Day, you know.'

This will sound crazy, but up until then I thought T. Ray probably loved me some. I could never forget the time he smiled at me in church when I was singing with the hymn book upside-down.

Now I looked at his face. It was despising and full of anger.

'As long as you live under my roof, you'll do what I say!' he shouted.

Then I'll find another roof, I thought.

'You understand me?' he said.

'Yes, sir, I understand,' I said, and I did, too.

Late that afternoon I caught two more bees. Lying on my stomach across the bed, I watched how they orbited the space in the jar, round and round like they'd missed the exit.

Rosaleen poked her head in the door. 'You all right?'

'Yeah, I'm fine.'

'I'm leaving now. You tell your daddy I'm going into town tomorrow instead of coming here.'

'You're going to town? Take me,' I said.

'Why do you wanna go?'

'*Please*, Rosaleen.'

'Ain't nothing much gonna be open but firecracker stands and the grocery store.'

'I don't care. I just wanna get out of the house some on my birthday.'

Rosaleen stared at me. 'All right, but you ask your daddy. I'll be by here first thing in the morning.' She was out of the door.

I called after her. 'How come you're going to town?'

She stayed with her back to me a moment, unmoving. When she turned, her face looked soft and changed. Her hand dipped into her pocket, where her fingers crawled around for something. She drew out a folded piece of notebook paper and came to sit beside me on the bed. I rubbed my knees while she smoothed out the paper across her lap.

Her name, Rosaleen Daise, was written twenty-five times at least down the page in large, careful cursive. 'This is my practice sheet,' she said. 'For the 4th of July they're holding a voters' rally at the coloured church. I'm registering myself to vote.'

An uneasy feeling settled in my stomach. Last night the television had said a man in Mississippi was killed for registering to vote, and I myself had overheard Mr Bussey, one of the deacons, say to T. Ray, 'Don't you worry, they're gonna make 'em write their names in perfect cursive and refuse them a card if they forget so much as to dot an i.'

I studied Rosaleen's R. 'Does T. Ray know what you're doing?'

'T. Ray,' she said. 'T. Ray don't know nothing.'

At sunset he shuffled up, sweaty from work. I met him at the kitchen door, my arms folded across the front of my blouse. 'I thought I'd walk to town with Rosaleen tomorrow. I need to buy some sanitary supplies.'

He accepted this without comment. T. Ray hated female puberty worse than anything.

That night I looked at the jar of bees on my dresser. The poor creatures perched on the bottom barely moving, obviously pining away for flight. I thought about the way my mother had built trails of graham-cracker crumbs and marshmallow to lure roaches from the house rather than step on them. I doubted she would've approved of keeping bees in a jar. I unscrewed the lid and set it aside.

'You can go,' I said.

But the bees remained there, like planes on a runway not knowing they'd been cleared for takeoff. They crawled on their stalk legs around the curved perimeters of the glass as if the world had shrunk to that jar. I tapped the glass, even laid the jar on its side, but those crazy bees stayed put.

The bees were still in there the next morning when Rosaleen showed up. She was bearing an angel food cake with fourteen candles.

'Here you go. Happy birthday,' she said. We sat down and ate two slices each with glasses of milk. The milk left a moon crescent on her upper lip, which she didn't bother to wipe away. Later I would remember that, how she set out, a marked woman from the beginning.

Sylvan was miles away. We walked along the ledge of the highway, Rosaleen moving at the pace of a bank-vault door, her spit jug fastened on her finger. Haze hung under the trees, and every inch of air smelled overripe with peaches.

'You limping?' Rosaleen said.

My knees were aching to the point that I was struggling to keep up with her. 'A little.'

'Well, why don't we sit down on the side of the road awhile?' she said.

'That's OK,' I told her. 'I'll be fine.'

A car swept by, slinging scalded air and a layer of dust. Rosaleen was slick with heat. She mopped her face and breathed hard.

We were coming to Ebenezer Baptist Church, where T. Ray and I attended. The steeple jutted through a cluster of shade trees; below, the red bricks looked shadowy and cool.

'Come on,' I said, turning in the drive.

'Where're you going?'

'We can rest in the church.'

The air inside was dim and still, slanted with light from the side windows, not those pretty stained-glass windows but milky panes you can't really see through. I led us down front and sat in the second pew, leaving room for Rosaleen. She plucked a paper fan from the hymnbook holder and studied the picture on it—a white church with a smiling white lady coming out of the door.

Rosaleen fanned and I listened to little jets of air come off her hands. She never went to church herself, but on those few times T. Ray had let me walk to her house back in the woods, I'd seen her special shelf with a stub of candle, creek rocks and a reddish woodpecker feather, and right in the centre a picture of a woman, propped up without a frame.

The first time I saw it, I'd asked Rosaleen, 'Is that you?' since I swear the woman looked exactly like her, with woolly braids, blue-black skin, narrow eyes, and most of her concentrated in her lower portion.

'This is my mama,' she said.

The finish was rubbed off the sides of the picture where her thumbs had held it. Her shelf had to do with a religion she'd made up for herself, a mixture of nature and ancestor worship. She'd stopped going to the House of Prayer Full Gospel Holiness Church years ago because it started at ten in the morning and didn't end till three in the afternoon, which is enough religion to kill a full-grown person, she'd said.

T. Ray said Rosaleen's religion was plain wacko, and for me to stay out of it. But it drew me to her to think she loved rocks and feathers, that she had a single picture of her mother just like I did.

One of the church doors opened and Brother Gerald, our minister, stepped into the sanctuary.

'Well, for goodness' sake, Lily, what are you doing here?'

Then he saw Rosaleen and started to rub the bald space on his head with such agitation I thought he might rub down to the skull bone.

'We were walking to town and stopped in to cool off.'

His mouth formed the word 'oh,' but he didn't actually say it; he was too busy looking at Rosaleen in his church, Rosaleen who chose this moment to spit into her snuff jug.

It's funny how you forget the rules. She was not supposed to be inside here. Every time a rumour got going about a group of Negroes coming to worship with us on Sunday morning, the deacons stood locked-arms across the church steps to turn them away. We loved them in the Lord, Brother Gerald said, but they had their own places.

'Today's my birthday,' I said, hoping to send his thoughts in a new direction.

'Is it? Well, happy birthday, Lily. So how old are you now?'

'Fourteen.'

'Ask him if we can have a couple of these fans for your birthday present,' said Rosaleen.

He made a thin sound, intended for a laugh. 'Now, if we let everybody borrow a fan that wanted one, the church wouldn't have a fan left.'

'She was just kidding,' I said, and stood up. He smiled, satisfied, and walked beside me all the way to the door, with Rosaleen tagging behind.

Outside, the sky had whited over with clouds, and shine spilled across the surfaces. When we'd cut through the parsonage yard and were back on the highway, Rosaleen produced two church fans from the bosom of her dress, and, doing an impersonation of me gazing up sweet-faced, she said, 'Oh, Brother Gerald, she was just kidding.'

We came into Sylvan on the worst side of town. Old houses set up on cinder blocks. Dirt yards. Women in pink curlers. Collarless dogs.

After a few blocks we approached the Esso station on the corner of West Market and Park Street, generally recognised as a catchall place for men with too much time on their hands.

I noticed that not a single car was getting gas. Three men sat in dinette chairs beside the garage with a piece of plywood balanced on their knees. They were playing cards.

'Hit me,' one of them said, and the dealer slapped a card down in front of him. He looked up and saw us, Rosaleen fanning and swaying side to side. 'Well, look what we got coming here,' he called out. 'Where're you going, nigger?'

Firecrackers made a spattering sound in the distance. 'Keep walking,' I whispered. 'Don't pay any attention.'

But Rosaleen, who had less sense than I'd dreamed, said in this tone like she was explaining something real hard to a kindergarten student, 'I'm going to register my name so I can vote, that's what.'

'We should hurry on,' I said, but she kept walking at her slow pace.

The man next to the dealer, with hair combed straight back, put down his cards and said, 'Did you hear that? We got ourselves a model citizen.'

I heard a slow song of wind drift along the gutter. We walked, and the men pushed back their makeshift table and came to the kerb to wait for us, like they were spectators at a parade and we were the prize float.

'Did you ever see one that black?' said the dealer.

And the man with his combed-back hair said, 'No, and I ain't seen one that big either.'

The third man looked at Rosaleen sashaying along, holding her white-lady fan, and he said, 'Where'd you get that fan, nigger?'

'Stole it from a church,' she said. Just like that.

I had gone once in a raft down the Chattooga River with my church group, and the same feeling came to me now—of being lifted by currents, by a swirl of events I couldn't reverse.

Coming alongside the men, Rosaleen lifted her snuff jug, which was filled with black spit, and calmly poured it across the tops of the men's shoes, moving her hand in little loops like she was writing her name—Rosaleen Daise—just the way she'd practised.

For a second they stared down at the juice dribbled across their shoes. They blinked, trying to make it register. When they looked up, I watched their faces go from surprise to anger, then outright fury. They lunged at her, and everything started to spin. There was Rosaleen, grabbed and thrashing side to side, swinging the men on her arms, and the men yelling for her to apologise and clean their shoes.

'Clean it off!' That's all I could hear, over and over. And then the cry of birds overhead, sweeping from trees, stirring up the scent of pine.

'Call the police,' yelled the dealer to a man inside.

By then Rosaleen lay sprawled on the ground, pinned, twisting her fingers around clumps of grass. Blood ran from a cut beneath her eye. It curved under her chin the way tears do.

When the policeman got there, he said we had to get into the back of his car. 'You're under arrest,' he told Rosaleen. 'Assault, theft, and disturbing the peace.' Then he said to me, 'When we get down to the station, I'll call your daddy and let him deal with you.'

Rosaleen climbed in, sliding over on the seat. I moved after her, sliding as she slid, sitting as she sat.

The door closed. So quiet it amounted to nothing but a snap of air, and that was the strangeness of it, how a small sound like that could fall across the whole world.

CHAPTER TWO

THE POLICEMAN DRIVING US to jail was Mr Avery Gaston, but the men at the Esso station called him Shoe. A puzzling nickname since there was nothing remarkable about his shoes, or his feet so far as I could see.

The three men followed us in a green pick-up with a gun rack inside. They drove close to our bumper and blew the horn every few seconds. I jumped each time, and Rosaleen gave my leg a pat. In front of the Western Auto the men started a game of pulling alongside us and yelling things out the window, mostly things we couldn't make out because our windows were rolled up. People in the back of police cars were not given the benefit of door handles or window cranks, I noticed, so we were blessed to be chauffeured to jail in smothering heat, watching the men mouth things we were glad not to know.

Rosaleen looked straight ahead and acted as if the men were insignificant houseflies buzzing at our screen door. I was the only one who could feel the way her thighs trembled.

'Mr Gaston,' I said, 'those men aren't coming with us, are they?'

His smile appeared in the rearview mirror. 'I can't say what men riled up like that will do.'

Before Main Street they tired of the amusement and sped off. I breathed easier, but when we pulled into the empty lot behind the police station, they were waiting on the back steps. The dealer tapped a flashlight against his hand. The other two held our church fans.

When we got out of the car, Mr Gaston put handcuffs on Rosaleen, fastening her arms behind her back. I walked so close to her I felt heat vapour trailing off her skin. She stopped ten yards short of the men and refused to budge.

'Now, look here, don't make me get out my gun,' Mr Gaston said. Usually the only time the police in Sylvan got to use their guns was when they got called out to shoot rattlesnakes in people's yards.

'Come on, Rosaleen,' I said. 'What can they do to you with a policeman right here?'

That was when the dealer lifted the flashlight over his head, then down, smashing it into Rosaleen's forehead. She dropped to her knees.

I don't remember screaming, but the next thing I knew, Mr Gaston had his hand clamped over my mouth. 'Hush,' he said.

'Maybe now you feel like apologising,' the dealer said. Rosaleen tried to get to her feet, but without her hands it was hopeless. It took me and Mr Gaston both to pull her up.

'Your black ass is gonna apologise one way or another,' the dealer said, and he stepped towards Rosaleen.

'Hold on now, Franklin,' said Mr Gaston, moving us towards the door. 'Now's not the time.'

'I'm not resting till she apologises.'

That's the last I heard him yell before we got inside, where I had an overpowering impulse to kneel down and kiss the jail-house floor.

The only image I had for jails was from Westerns at the movies, and this one was nothing like that. For one thing, it was painted pink and had flower-print curtains in the window. It turned out we'd come in through the jailer's living quarters. His wife stepped in from the kitchen, greasing a muffin tin.

'Got you two more mouths to feed,' Mr Gaston said, and she went back to work without a smile of sympathy.

He led us round to the front, where there were two rows of jail cells, all empty. Mr Gaston removed Rosaleen's handcuffs and handed her a towel. She pressed it against her head while he filled out papers at a desk, followed by a period of poking around for keys in a file drawer.

The cells stank with the breath of drunk people. He put us in the first cell on the first row. Nothing seemed real. *We're in jail*, I thought.

When Rosaleen pulled back the towel, I saw an inch-long gash across a puffy place high over her eyebrow. 'Is it hurting bad?' I asked.

'Some,' she said, sinking down onto the bench.

'T. Ray will get us out,' I said.

'Uh-huh.'

She didn't speak another word till Mr Gaston opened the cell door about a half hour later. 'Come on,' he said. Rosaleen looked hopeful for a moment. She actually started to lift herself up. He shook his head. 'You ain't going anywhere. Just the girl.'

At the door I held on to a cell bar like it was Rosaleen's arm. 'I'll be back. All right? . . . All right, Rosaleen?'

'You go on, I'll manage.'

The caved-in look of her face nearly did me in.

The speedometer needle on T. Ray's truck wiggled so badly I couldn't make out whether it pointed to seventy or eighty. The poor truck was rattling to the point I expected the hood to fly off and decapitate a couple of pine trees.

I imagined that T. Ray was rushing home so he could start right away constructing pyramids of grits all through the house, where I would go from one pile to the next, kneeling for hours with nothing but bathroom breaks. I didn't care. I couldn't think of anything but Rosaleen in jail.

I squinted at him. 'What about Rosaleen? You have to get her out—'

'You're lucky I got *you* out!' he yelled.

'But she can't stay there—'

'She dumped snuff juice on three white men! And on Franklin Posey, for Christ's sake. She couldn't pick somebody normal? He's the meanest nigger-hater in Sylvan. He'd as soon kill her as look at her.'

'But not really,' I said. 'You don't mean he would *really* kill her.'

'What I mean is, I wouldn't be surprised if he flat-out killed her.'

My arms felt weak in their sockets. Franklin Posey was the man with the flashlight, and he was gonna kill Rosaleen. But then, hadn't I known this inside even before T. Ray ever said it?

He followed me up the stairs. I moved with deliberate slowness, anger building in me. How could he leave Rosaleen in jail like that?

As I stepped inside my room, he stopped at the doorway. 'I have to go settle the payroll for the pickers,' he said. 'Don't you leave this room. You understand me? You sit here and think about me coming back and dealing with you. Think about it real hard.'

'You don't scare me,' I said, mostly under my breath.

He'd turned to leave, but now he whirled back. 'What did you say?'

'You don't scare me,' I repeated, louder this time. A brazen feeling had broken loose, a daring something that had been locked up in my chest.

He stepped towards me, raising the back of his hand like he might bring it down across my face. 'You better watch your mouth.'

'Go ahead, try and hit me!' I yelled. When he swung, I turned my face. It was a clean miss.

I ran for the bed and scrambled onto the middle of it, breathing hard. 'My mother will never let you touch me again!' I shouted.

'*Your mother?*' His face was bright red. 'You think that goddamn woman gave a shit about you?'

'My mother loved me!' I cried.

He threw back his head and let out a forced, bitter laugh.

'It's—it's not funny,' I said.

He lunged towards the bed then, pressing his fists into the mattress, bringing his face so close I could see the tiny holes where his whiskers grew. I slid back towards the headboard.

'Not funny?' he yelled. '*Not funny?* Why, it's the funniest goddamn thing I ever heard: you thinking your mother is your guardian angel.' He laughed again. 'The woman could not have cared less about you.'

'That's not true,' I said. 'It's *not*.'

'And how would you know?' he said, still leaning towards me. A left-over smile pulled the corners of his mouth.

'I hate you!' I screamed.

That stopped his smiling instantly. He stiffened. 'Why, you little bitch,' he said. The colour faded from his lips.

I felt an ice-cold tremor slide along my spine.

'You listen to me,' he said, his voice deadly calm. 'The truth is, your mother ran off and left you. The day she died, she'd come back to get her things, that's all. Hate me all you want, but *she's* the one who left you.'

The room turned absolutely silent.

He brushed at something on his shirtfront, then walked to the door.

After he left, I didn't move. The sound of his boots banging down the stairs drifted away, and I took the pillows from underneath the bed-spread and placed them around me like I was making an inner tube that might keep me afloat. I could understand her leaving him. But leaving *me*? This would sink me for ever.

The bee jar sat on the bedside table, empty now. Some time since this morning the bees had finally got around to flying off. I reached over and took the jar in my hands, and out came the tears I'd been holding on to, it seemed like for years.

The day she died, she'd come back to get her things, that's all.

The memory settled over me. The suitcase on the floor. The way they'd fought. My shoulders began to shake in a strange, uncontrollable way. I held the jar pressed between my breasts, hoping it would steady me, but I couldn't stop shaking, couldn't stop crying, and it frightened me, as though I'd been struck by a car I hadn't seen coming and was lying on the side of the road, trying to understand what had happened.

I sat on the edge of the bed, replaying his words over and over. Each time there was a wrench in what felt like my heart.

I don't know how long I sat there feeling broken to pieces. Finally I walked to the window and gazed out at the peach trees stretching halfway to North Carolina. The rest was sky and air and lonely space. *How could she have left me*? I stood there several minutes looking out on the world, trying to understand. Little birds were singing, so perfect.

That's when it came to me: *What if my mother leaving wasn't true? What if T. Ray had made it up to punish me?*

I felt almost dizzy with relief. That was it. That had to be it. I mean, my father was Thomas Edison when it came to inventing punishments. Once after I'd back-talked him, he'd told me my rabbit had died, and I'd cried all night before I discovered her the next morning healthy as anything in her pen. He had to be making this up, too. Some things were not possible in this world. Children did not have two parents who refused to love them. One, maybe, but for pity's sake, not two.

It had to be like he'd said before: she was cleaning out the closet the day of the accident. People cleaned out closets all the time.

I took a breath to steady myself.

You could say I'd never had a true religious moment, the kind where you know yourself spoken to by a voice that seems other than yourself. But I had such a moment right then, standing in my own ordinary room. I heard a voice say, *Lily Melissa Owens, your jar is open.*

In a matter of seconds I knew exactly what I had to do. I had to get away from T. Ray, who was probably on his way back this minute to do Lord-knows-what to me. And I had to get Rosaleen out of jail.

The clock read 2:40. I needed a plan, but I didn't have the luxury of sitting down to think one up. I grabbed my pink canvas duffel bag, the one I'd planned to use for overnights the minute anyone asked me. I took the thirty-eight dollars I'd earned selling peaches and stuffed it into the bag with my seven best pairs of panties, the ones that had the days of the week printed across the backside. I dumped in socks, shorts, tops, a nightgown, shampoo, brush, toothpaste, toothbrush, all the time watching the window. *What else?* Catching sight of the map tacked on the wall, I snatched it down, not bothering to prise out the tacks.

I reached under the mattress and pulled out my mother's picture, the gloves, and the wooden picture of black Mary, and tucked them down in the bag, too.

Tearing a sheet of paper from last year's English notebook, I wrote a note, short and to the point: *Dear T. Ray, Don't bother looking for me. Lily. P.S. People who tell lies like you should rot in hell.*

When I checked the window, T. Ray was coming out of the orchard towards the house, fists balled, head ploughed forward like a bull wanting to gore something.

I propped the note on my dresser and stood a moment in the centre of the room, wondering if I'd ever see it again. 'Goodbye,' I said, and there was a tiny sprig of sadness pushing up from my heart.

Outside, I spied the broken space in the latticework that wrapped around the foundation of the house. Squeezing through, I disappeared into violet light and cobwebbed air.

T. Ray's boots stomped across the porch.

'Lily! Li-leeeee!' I heard his voice sailing along the floor of the house.

All of a sudden I caught sight of Snout sniffing at the spot where I'd crawled through. I backed deeper into the darkness, but she'd caught my scent and started barking her mangy head off.

T. Ray emerged with my note crumpled in his hand, yelled at Snout to shut the hell up, and tore out in his truck, leaving plumes of exhaust all along the driveway.

Walking along the weedy strip beside the highway for the second time that day, I was thinking how much older fourteen had made me. In the space of a few hours I'd become forty years old.

The road stretched empty as far as I could see, with heat shimmer making the air seem wavy. If I managed to get Rosaleen free—an 'if' so big it could have been the planet Jupiter—just where did I think we'd go?

Suddenly I stood still. *Tiburon, South Carolina.* Of course. The town written on the back of the black Mary picture. Hadn't I been planning to go there one of these days? It made perfect sense: my mother had been there. Or else she knew people there who'd cared enough to send her a nice picture of Jesus' mother. And who would think to look for us there?

I squatted beside the ditch and unfolded the map. Tiburon was a pencil dot beside the red star of Columbia. T. Ray would check the bus station, so Rosaleen and I would hitchhike. How hard could that be?

A short distance past the church, Brother Gerald whizzed by in his white Ford. I saw his brake lights flicker. He backed up.

'I thought that was you,' he said through the window. 'Where're you headed?'

'Town.'

'Again? What's the bag for?'

'I'm . . . I'm taking some things to Rosaleen. She's in jail.'

'Yeah, I know,' he said, flinging open the passenger door. 'Get in, I'm heading there myself.'

I'd never been inside a preacher's car before. It's not that I expected a ton of Bibles stacked on the back seat, but I was surprised to see that, inside, it was like anybody else's car.

'You're going to see Rosaleen?' I said.

'The police called and asked me to press charges against her for stealing church property. They say she took some of our fans. You know anything about that?'

'It was only two fans—'

He jumped straight into his pulpit voice. 'In the eyes of God it doesn't matter whether it's two fans or two hundred. Stealing is stealing. She asked if she could take the fans, I said no, in plain English. She took them anyway. Now that's sin, Lily.'

Pious people have always got on my nerves.

'But she's deaf in one ear,' I said. 'I think she just mixed up what you said. She's always doing that. T. Ray will tell her, "Iron *my two* shirts," and she'll iron the *blue* shirts.'

'A hearing problem. Well, I didn't know that,' he said.

'Rosaleen would never steal a thing.'

'They said she'd assaulted some men at the Esso station.'

'It wasn't like that,' I said. 'See, she was singing her favourite hymn, "Were you there when they crucified my Lord?" I don't believe those men are Christians, Brother Gerald, because they yelled at her to shut up with the blankety-blank Jesus tune. Rosaleen said, "You can curse me, but don't blaspheme the Lord Jesus." But they kept right on. So she poured the juice from her snuff cup on their shoes. Maybe she was wrong, but in her mind she was standing up for Jesus.' I was sweating through my top and all along the backs of my thighs as I told him these lies.

Brother Gerald dragged his teeth back and forth across his lip. I could tell he was actually weighing what I'd said.

Mr Gaston was in the station alone, eating boiled peanuts at his desk, when Brother Gerald and I came through the door.

'Your coloured woman ain't here,' he said, looking at me. 'I took her to the hospital for stitches. She took a fall and hit her head.'

Took a fall, my rear end. I wanted to throw his boiled peanuts against the wall. I could not keep myself from shouting at him. 'What do you mean, she fell and hit her head?'

Mr Gaston looked over at Brother Gerald, that all-knowing look men give each other when a female acts the least bit hysterical. 'Settle down, now,' he said to me.

'I can't settle down till I know if she's all right,' I said, my voice calmer but still shaking a little.

'She's fine. It's only a little concussion. I expect she'll be back here later this evening. The doctor wanted her watched for a few hours.'

While Brother Gerald was explaining how he couldn't sign the warrant papers seeing as how Rosaleen was nearly deaf, I started for the door.

Mr Gaston shot me a warning look. 'We got a guard on her at the hospital, and he's not letting anybody see her, so go home. Understand?'

'Yes, sir. I'm going home.'

'You do that,' he said. ''Cause if I hear you've been anywhere near that hospital, I'm calling your daddy again.'

Sylvan Memorial Hospital was a low brick building with one wing for whites and one for blacks.

I stepped into a deserted corridor clogged with smells. Carnations, rubbing alcohol, bathroom deodoriser. Air conditioners poked out from the windows in the white section, but back here there was nothing but electric fans moving the hot air from one place to another.

At the nurses' station a policeman leaned on the desk. He looked like somebody just out of high school. He was talking to a girl in white. A nurse, I guess, but she didn't look much older than I was. 'I get off at six o'clock,' I heard him say. She stood there smiling, tucking a piece of hair behind her ear.

At the opposite end of the hall an empty chair sat outside one of the rooms. It had a policeman's hat underneath it. I hurried down there to find a sign on the door. NO VISITORS. I went right in.

There were six beds, all empty except the one over by the window. The sheets rose up, trying hard to accommodate the occupant. I plopped my bag on the floor. 'Rosaleen?'

A gauze bandage the size of a baby's diaper was wrapped round her head, and her wrists were tied to the bed railing.

When she saw me standing there, she started to cry. In all the years she'd looked after me, I'd never seen a tear cross her face. Now the levee broke wide open. I patted her arm, her leg, her cheek, her hand.

When her tear glands were finally exhausted, I said, 'What happened to you?'

'After you left, that policeman called Shoe let those men come in for their apology.'

'They hit you again?'

'Two of them held me by the arms while the other one hit me—the one with the flashlight. He said, "Nigger, you say you're sorry." When I didn't, he came at me. He hit me till the policeman said that was enough. They didn't get no apology, though.'

I wanted those men to die in hell begging for ice water, but I felt mad at Rosaleen, too. *Why couldn't you just apologise? Then maybe Franklin Posey would let you off with just a beating.* All she'd done was guarantee they'd come back.

'You've got to get out of here,' I said, untying her wrists.

'I can't just *leave*,' she said. 'I'm still in jail.'

'If you stay here, those men are gonna come back and kill you, like those coloured people in Mississippi got killed. Even T. Ray said so.'

When she sat up, the hospital gown rode up her thighs. She tugged it towards her knees, but it slid right back like a piece of elastic. I found her dress in the closet and handed it to her.

'This is crazy—' she said.

'Put on the dress. Just do it, all right?'

She pulled it over her head and stood there with the bandage sloped over her forehead.

'That bandage has got to go,' I said. I eased it off to find two rows of catgut stitches. Then, signalling her to be quiet, I cracked the door to see if the policeman was back at his chair.

He was. It was too much to hope he'd stay off flirting long enough for us to float out of here. I stood there a couple of minutes, trying to think, then opened my bag and dug out a couple of dimes. 'I'm gonna try and get rid of him. Get in the bed, in case he looks in here.'

She stared at me, her eyes shrunk to mere dots. 'Baby *Jesus*,' she said.

When I stepped out into the hall, he jumped up. 'You weren't supposed to be in there!'

'Don't I know it,' I said. 'I'm looking for my aunt. I could have sworn they told me Room One-oh-two, but there's a coloured woman in there.' I shook my head, trying to look confused.

'You're lost, all right. You need to go to the other side of the building. You're in the coloured section.'

I smiled at him. 'Oh.'

Over on the white side of the hospital I found a payphone next to a waiting area. I got the hospital number from Information and dialled it up, asking for the nurses' station in the coloured wing.

I cleared my throat. 'This is the jailer's wife over at the police station,' I said to the girl who answered. 'Mr Gaston wants you to send the policeman who we've got over there back to the station. Tell him the preacher is on his way in to sign some papers, and Mr Gaston had to leave. So if you could tell him to get over here right away . . .'

Part of me was saying these actual words, and part of me was listening to myself say them, thinking how I belonged in a reform school or a juvenile delinquent home for girls, and would probably soon be in one.

She repeated it all back to me, making sure she had it straight. Her sigh passed over the receiver. 'I'll tell him.'

She'll tell him. I couldn't believe it.

I crept back to the coloured side and hunched over the water fountain as the girl in white relayed all this to him. I watched as the policeman put on his hat and walked down the corridor and out of the door.

When Rosaleen and I stepped from her room, I looked left, then right. We had to go past the nurses' desk to get to the door, but the girl in white was preoccupied, sitting with her head down, writing something.

'Walk like a visitor,' I told Rosaleen.

Halfway to the desk, the girl stopped writing and stood up.

'Shitbucket,' I said. I grabbed Rosaleen's arm and pulled her into a patient's room.

A tiny woman was perched in the bed, old and birdlike. Her mouth opened when she saw us. 'I need a little water,' she said.

Rosaleen went over and poured some from a pitcher and gave the woman the glass, while I peeped out of the door. I watched the girl disappear into a room a few doors down carrying some sort of glass bottle.

'Come on,' I said to Rosaleen.

'Y'all leaving already?' said the tiny woman.

'Yeah, but I'll probably be back before the day's out,' said Rosaleen.

This time we didn't walk like visitors, we tore out of there. Outside, I took Rosaleen's hand and tugged her down the sidewalk.

'Since you got everything else figured out, I guess you know where we're going,' she said, and there was a tone in her voice.

'We're going to Highway Forty and thumb a ride to Tiburon, South Carolina. At least we're gonna try.'

I took us the back way, cutting through the city park, down a little alley to Lancaster Street, then three blocks over to May Pond Road, where we slipped into the vacant lot behind Glenn's Grocery.

We waded through Queen Anne's lace and thick-stalked purple flowers, into the smell of Carolina jasmine so thick I could almost see it circling in the air. She didn't ask me why we were going to Tiburon. What she did ask was 'When did you start saying "shitbucket"?'

I'd never resorted to bad language, though I'd heard my share of it from T. Ray. 'I'm fourteen now. I guess I can say it if I want to.' And I wanted to, right that minute. 'Shitbucket,' I said.

'Shitbucket, hellfire, damnation and son of a bitch,' said Rosaleen, laying into each word like it was sweet potatoes on her tongue.

We stood on the side of Highway 40 in a patch of shade provided by a faded billboard for Lucky Strike cigarettes. I stuck out my thumb while every car on the highway speeded up the second they saw us.

A coloured man driving a beat-up Chevy truck full of cantaloupes had mercy on us. I climbed in first and Rosaleen settled herself by the window. The man said he was on his way to visit his sister in Columbia, that he was taking the cantaloupes to the state farmers' market. I told him I was going to Tiburon to visit my aunt and Rosaleen was coming to do housework for her. It sounded lame, but he accepted it.

'I can drop you three miles from Tiburon,' he said.

We rode a long time in the sad glow of sunset, everything silent except for the crickets and the frogs who were revving up for twilight. I stared through the windshield as the burned lights took over the sky.

The farmer flicked on the radio and the Supremes blared through the truck cab with 'Baby, baby, where did our love go?' There's nothing like a song about lost love to remind you how everything precious can slip from the hinges where you've hung it so careful. I laid my head against Rosaleen's arm. I wanted her to pat life back into place, but her hands lay still in her lap.

Ninety miles after we'd climbed in his truck, the farmer pulled off the road beside a sign that read TIBURON 3 MILES. It pointed left, towards a road curving away into silvery darkness. Climbing out of the truck, Rosaleen asked if we could have one of his cantaloupes for our supper.

'Take yourself two,' he said.

We waited till his taillights turned to specks before we spoke or even moved. I was trying not to think how sad and lost we really were. I was not so sure it was an improvement over living with T. Ray, or even prison. There wasn't a soul anywhere to help us. But I felt painfully alive, like every cell in my body had a little flame inside it.

'At least we got a full moon,' I told Rosaleen.

We walked along, pretending it was a regular day. Rosaleen said it looked like that farmer who'd driven us here had had a good crop of cantaloupes. I said it was amazing the mosquitoes weren't out.

When we came to a bridge with water running beneath, we decided to pick our way down to the creek bed and rest for the night. It was a different universe down there, the water shining with moving light and kudzu vines draped between the pine trees like giant hammocks.

Rosaleen broke open the cantaloupes against a creek stone. We ate them down to their skins, then scooped water into our hands and drank, not caring about algae or tadpoles or whether the cows used the creek for their toilet. Then we sat on the bank and looked at each other.

'I just wanna know, of all the places on this earth, why you picked Tiburon,' Rosaleen said. 'I've never even heard of it.'

Even though it was dark, I pulled the black Mary picture out of my bag and handed it to her. 'It belonged to my mother. On the back it says Tiburon, South Carolina.'

'Let me get this straight. You picked Tiburon 'cause your mother had a picture with that town written on the back—*that's it?*'

'Well, think about it,' I said. 'She must have been there some time in her life to have owned this picture. And if she was, a person might remember her, you never know.'

Rosaleen held it up to the moonlight to see it better. 'Who's this supposed to be?'

'The Virgin Mary,' I said.

'Well, if you ain't noticed, she's coloured,' said Rosaleen, and I could tell it was having an effect on her by the way she kept gazing at it with her mouth parted. She handed it back. 'I guess I can go to my grave now, because I've seen it all.'

I pushed the picture down in my pocket. 'You know what T. Ray said about my mother?' I asked, wanting finally to tell her what had happened. 'He said she left me and him way before she died. That she'd just come back for her things the day the accident happened.'

I waited for Rosaleen to say how ridiculous that was, but she squinted straight ahead as if weighing the possibility.

'Well, it's not true,' I said, my voice rising. 'And if he thinks I'm going to believe that story, he has a hole in his so-called brain. He only made it up to punish me. I know he did.'

I could have added that mothers have instincts and hormones that prevent them leaving their babies, that even pigs didn't leave their offspring, but Rosaleen, having pondered the matter, said, 'You're probably right. Knowing your daddy, he could do a thing like that.'

'And my mother could never do what he said she did,' I added.

'I didn't know your mama,' Rosaleen said. 'But I used to see her from a distance sometimes when I came out of the orchard. She'd be hanging clothes on the line or watering her plants, and you'd be there beside her, playing. I only saw her one time when you weren't under her feet.'

I had no idea Rosaleen had ever seen my mother. I felt suddenly light-headed. 'What was she doing that time you saw her alone?' I asked.

'She was out behind the tractor shed, sitting on the ground, staring off at nothing. When we walked by, she didn't even notice us. I remember thinking she looked a little sad.'

'Well, who wouldn't be sad living with T. Ray?' I said.

The light bulb snapped on in Rosaleen's face then. 'Oh,' she said. 'I get it. You ran off 'cause of what your daddy said about your mother. It didn't have nothing to do with me in jail. And here you got me worrying myself sick about you running away and getting in trouble over me, and you would've run off anyway. Well, ain't it nice of you to fill me in.' She poked out her lip and looked up towards the road. 'So what are you planning to do?' she said. 'Go from town to town asking people about your mother? Is that your bright idea?'

'If I needed somebody to criticise me around the clock, I could've brought T. Ray along!' I shouted. 'And I don't exactly have a plan.'

'Well, you sure had one back at the hospital, coming in there saying we're gonna do this and we're gonna do that, and I'm supposed to follow you like a pet dog. You act like you're my keeper. Like I'm some dumb nigger you gonna save.' Her eyes were hard and narrow.

I rose to my feet. 'That's not fair!' Anger sucked the air from my lungs.

'You meant well enough, and I'm glad to be away from there, but did you think once to ask me?' she said.

'Well, you *are* dumb!' I yelled. 'You have to be dumb to pour your snuff juice on those men's shoes. And then dumber not to say you're sorry, if it'll save your life. They were gonna come back and kill you. I got you out of there, and this is how you thank me. Well, fine.'

I stripped off my sneakers, grabbed my bag and waded into the creek. The coldness cut sharp circles around my calves. I didn't want to be on the same planet with her, much less the same side of the creek.

'You find your own way from now on!' I yelled over my shoulder.

On the opposite side I plopped onto the mossy dirt. We stared across the water at each other. In the dark she looked like a boulder shaped by five hundred years of storms. I lay back and closed my eyes.

In my dream I was back on the peach farm, sitting out behind the tractor shed, and even though it was broad daylight, I could see a huge, round moon in the sky. It looked so perfect up there. I gazed at it awhile, then leaned against the shed and closed my eyes. Next I heard a sound like ice breaking, and, looking up, I saw the moon crack apart and start to fall. I had to run for my life.

I woke with my chest hurting. I searched for the moon and found it all in one piece, still spilling light over the creek. I looked across the water for Rosaleen. She was gone.

My heart did flip-flops. *Please, God. I didn't mean to treat her like a pet dog. I was trying to save her. That's all.*

Fumbling to get my shoes on, I felt the same old grief I'd known in church every single Mother's Day. *Mother, forgive.*

Rosaleen, where are you? I gathered up my bag and ran along the creek towards the bridge. Tripping over a dead limb, I sprawled through the darkness and didn't bother to get up. I could picture Rosaleen miles from here, tearing down the highway, mumbling, *Shitbucket, damn fool girl.*

Looking up, I noticed that the tree I'd fallen beneath was practically bald. Only little bits of green here and there, and lots of grey moss dangling to the ground. Even in the dark I could see that it was dying. That was the way of things. Loss takes up inside of everything sooner or later and eats right through it.

Humming drifted out of the night. It wasn't a gospel tune, but it carried all the personality of one. I followed the sound and found Rosaleen in the middle of the creek, not a stitch of clothes on. Water beaded across her shoulders, shining like drops of milk, and her breasts swayed in the currents. It was the kind of vision you never get over. I couldn't help it, I wanted to go and lick the milk beads from her shoulders.

I opened my mouth. I wanted something. Something, I didn't know what. *Mother, forgive*. That's all I could feel.

Off came my shoes, my shorts, my top, my underpants.

The water felt like a glacier melting against my legs. I must have gasped at the iciness, because Rosaleen looked up and seeing me come naked through the water, started to laugh. 'Look at you strutting out here. Jiggle-tit and all.'

I eased down beside her, suspending my breath at the water's sting. 'I'm sorry,' I said.

'I know,' she said. 'Me, too.' She reached over and patted the roundness of my knee like it was biscuit dough.

Leaning back on my elbows, I slid down till the water sealed over my head. I held my breath and listened to the scratch of river against my ears, sinking as far as I could into that shimmering, dark world. But I was thinking about a suitcase on the floor, about a face I could never quite see, about the sweet smell of cold cream.

I woke the next morning beside the creek in a bed of kudzu vines. A barge of mist floated along the water, and dragonflies, iridescent blue ones, darted back and forth like they were stitching up the air. It was such a pretty sight for a second I forgot the heavy feeling I'd carried since T. Ray had told me about my mother. *Day one of my new life*, I said to myself. *That's* what this is.

Rosaleen slept with her mouth open and a long piece of drool hanging from her bottom lip. I could tell by the way her eyes rolled under her lids she was watching the silver screen where dreams come and go. Her swollen face looked better, but in the bright of day I noticed purple bruises on her arms and legs as well. Neither one of us had a watch on, but going by the sun we had slept more than half the morning away.

I hated to wake Rosaleen, so I pulled the wooden picture of Mary out of my bag and propped it against a tree trunk in order to study it properly. A ladybug had crawled up and sat on the Holy Mother's cheek, making the most perfect beauty mark on her.

I lay back and tried to invent a story about why my mother had owned a black Mary picture. I drew a big blank, probably due to my ignorance about Mary, who never got much attention at our church. According to Brother Gerald, hell was nothing but a bonfire for Catholics. We didn't have any in Sylvan—only Baptists and Methodists. The only Mary story we talked about was the wedding story—the time she persuaded her son to manufacture wine out of plain water. This had been a shock to me, since our church didn't believe in wine or, for that matter, in women having a lot of say about things. All I could really figure was my mother had been mixed up with the Catholics somehow, and—I have to say—this secretly thrilled me.

I stuffed the picture into my pocket while Rosaleen slept on, blowing puffs of air that vibrated her lips. I decided she might sleep into tomorrow, so I shook her arm till her eyes slit open.

'Lord, I'm stiff,' she said. 'I feel like I've been beaten with a stick.'

'You *have* been beaten, remember?'

'But not with a stick,' she said.

I waited till she got to her feet, a long, unbelievable process of grunts and moans and limbs coming to life.

'What did you dream?' I asked when she was upright.

She rubbed her elbows. 'Well, let's see. I dreamed the Reverend Martin Luther King, Jr., knelt down and painted my toenails with the spit from his mouth, and every nail was red like he'd been sucking on red hots.'

I considered this as we set off for Tiburon, Rosaleen walking like she was on anointed feet, like her ruby toes owned the whole countryside.

We drifted by grey barns, cornfields in need of irrigation, and clumps of Hereford cows, chewing in slow motion. In the distance I could see farmhouses with wide porches and tractor-tyre swings suspended from nearby trees; windmills sprouted up beside them, their giant silver petals creaking when the breezes rose.

The asphalt ran out, turned to gravel. I listened to the sound it made scraping under our shoes. Perspiration puddled in the notch where Rosaleen's collarbones came together. I didn't know whose stomach was carrying on more about needing food, mine or hers, and since we'd started walking, I'd realised it was Sunday, when the stores were closed. I was afraid we'd end up eating dandelions, digging wild turnips and grubs out of the ground to stay alive.

The smell of fresh manure floated out from the fields and took care of my appetite then and there, but Rosaleen said, 'I could eat a mule.'

'If we can find some place open when we get to town, I'll go in and get us some food,' I told her.

'And what're we gonna do for beds?' she said.

'If they don't have a motel, we'll have to rent a room.'

She smiled at me then. 'Lily; child, there ain't gonna be any place that will take a coloured woman. I don't care if she's the Virgin Mary, nobody's letting her stay if she's coloured.'

'Well, what was the point of the Civil Rights Act?' I said, coming to a full stop in the middle of the road. 'Doesn't that mean people have to let you stay in their motels and eat in their restaurants if you want to?'

'That's what it means, but you gonna have to drag people kicking and screaming to do it.'

I spent the next mile in deep worry. I had no plan, no prospects of a plan. Until now I'd mostly believed we would stumble upon a window somewhere and climb through it into a brand-new life. Rosaleen, on the other hand, was out here biding time till we got caught. Counting it as summer vacation from jail.

What I needed was a sign. I needed a voice speaking to me like I'd heard yesterday in my room saying, *Lily Melissa Owens, your jar is open.*

I'll take nine steps and look up: Whatever my eyes light on, that's my sign. When I looked up, I saw a crop duster plunging his little plane over a field of growing things, behind him a cloud of pesticides. I couldn't decide what part of this scene I represented: the plants about to be rescued from the bugs or the bugs about to be murdered by the spray. There was an offchance I was the plane zipping over the earth creating rescue and doom everywhere I went. I felt miserable.

The heat had been gathering as we walked, and it now dripped down Rosaleen's face.

'Too bad there's not a church around here where we could steal some fans,' she said.

From far away the store on the edge of town looked about a hundred years old, but when we got up to it I saw it was older. A sign over the door said, FROGMORE STEW GENERAL STORE AND RESTAURANT SINCE 1854.

The front of the store was a forgotten bulletin board: Studebaker Service, Live Bait, Buddy's Fishing Tournament, Rayford Brothers' Ice Plant, Deer Rifles $45, and a picture of a girl wearing a Coca-Cola bottle cap on her head. A sign announced a gospel sing at the Mount Zion Baptist Church that took place back in 1957.

In the side yard a coloured man lifted the top of a barbecue pit made from an oil drum, and the smell of pork lathered in vinegar and pepper drew so much saliva from beneath my tongue I actually drooled onto my blouse.

A few cars and trucks were parked out front, probably belonging to people who cut church and came here straight from Sunday school.

'I'll go in and see if I can buy some food,' I said.

'And snuff. I need some snuff,' said Rosaleen.

While she slumped on a bench near the barbecue drum, I stepped through the screen door into the mingled smells of pickled eggs and sawdust, beneath dozens of hams dangling from the ceiling. The restaurant was situated in a section at the back while the front of the store was reserved for selling everything from sugarcane stalks to turpentine.

'May I help you, young lady?' A small man wearing a bow tie stood on the other side of a wooden counter. His voice was high-pitched, and he had a soft, delicate look to him.

'I don't believe I've seen you before,' he said.

'I'm not from here. I'm visiting my grandmother.'

'I like it when children spend time with their grandparents,' he said. 'You can learn a lot from older folks.'

'Yes, sir,' I said. 'I learned more from my grandmother than I did the whole eighth grade.'

He laughed like this was the most comical thing he'd heard in years. 'Are you here for lunch? We have a Sunday special—barbecue pork.'

'I'll take two of them to go,' I said. 'And two Coca-Colas, please.'

While I waited for our lunch, I wandered along the store aisles, stocking up for supper. Salted peanuts, buttermilk cookies, pimiento-cheese sandwiches and a can of Red Rose snuff. I piled it on the counter.

When he returned with the plates and drinks, he shook his head. 'I'm sorry, but it's Sunday. I can't sell anything from the store, just the restaurant. Your grandma ought to know that. What's her name anyway?'

'Rose,' I said, reading it off the snuff can.

'Rose Campbell?'

'Yes, sir. Rose Campbell.'

'I thought she only had grandboys.'

'No, sir, she's got me, too.'

He touched the bag of cookies. 'Just leave it all here. I'll put it back.'

The cash register pinged, and the drawer banged out. I rummaged in my bag for the money and paid him.

'Could you open the Coke bottles for me?' I asked, and while he walked back towards the kitchen, I dropped the Red Rose snuff in my bag and zipped it up.

Rosaleen had been beaten up, gone without food, slept on the hard ground, and who could say how long before she'd be back in jail or even killed? She deserved her snuff.

I was speculating how one day, years from now, I would send the store a dollar in an envelope to cover it, when I found myself looking at a picture of the black Mary. I do not mean a picture of just any black Mary. I mean the very same one as my mother's. She stared at me from the labels of a dozen jars of honey. BLACK MADONNA HONEY, they said.

The door opened, and a family came in fresh from church, the mother and daughter dressed alike in navy with white Peter Pan collars. Light streamed in the door, blurred with drizzles of yellow. The little girl sneezed, and her mother said, 'Come here, let's wipe your nose.'

I looked again at the honey jars, at the amber lights swimming inside them, and breathed slowly. I realised it for the first time in my life: there is nothing but mystery in the world; it hides behind the fabric of our poor, browbeat days, shining brightly, and we don't even know it.

I thought about the bees that had come to my room at night, how they'd been part of it all. And the voice I'd heard the day before, saying, *Lily Melissa Owens, your jar is open*, speaking as plain and clear as the woman in navy speaking to her daughter.

'Here's your Coca-Colas,' the bow-tied man was saying.

I pointed to the honey jars. 'Where did you get those?'

He thought the tone of shock in my voice was really consternation. 'I know what you mean. A lot of folks won't buy it 'cause it's got the Virgin Mary pictured as a coloured woman, but see, that's because the woman who makes the honey is coloured herself.'

'What's her name?'

'August Boatwright,' he said. 'She keeps bees all over the county.'

Keep breathing, keep breathing. 'Do you know where she lives?'

'Oh, sure, it's the darndest house you ever saw. Painted like Pepto-Bismol. Your grandmother surely's seen it—you go through town on Main Street till it turns into the highway to Florence.'

I walked to the door. 'Thanks.'

'You tell your grandma hello for me,' he said.

Rosaleen's snores were making the bench slats tremble. I gave her a shake. 'Wake up. Here's your snuff, but put it in your pocket, 'cause I didn't exactly pay for it.'

'You stole it?' she said.

'I had to, 'cause they don't sell items from the store on Sunday.'

'Your life has gone straight to hell,' she said.

I spread our lunch out like a picnic on the bench but couldn't eat a bite of it till I told her about the black Mary on the honey jar and the beekeeper named August Boatwright.

'Don't you think my mother must've known her?' I said. 'It couldn't be just a coincidence.'

She didn't answer, so I said louder, 'Rosaleen? Don't you think so?'

'I don't know what I think,' she said. 'I don't want you getting your hopes up too much, is all.' She reached over and touched my cheek. 'Oh, Lily, what have we gone and done?'

Tiburon was a place like Sylvan, minus the peaches. In front of the domed courthouse someone had stuck a Confederate flag in the mouth of their public cannon. South Carolina was Dixie first, America second.

Strolling down Main Street, we moved through long blue shadows cast from the two-storey buildings that ran the length of the street. At a drugstore, I peered through the plate glass at a soda fountain with chrome trim, where they sold cherry Cokes and banana splits, thinking that soon it would not be just for white people any more.

We walked past the Amen Dollar Store, which had hulahoops, swimming goggles, and boxes of sparklers in the window with SUMMER FUN spray-painted across the glass. A few places, like the Farmers Trust Bank, had GOLDWATER FOR PRESIDENT signs in their windows.

At the Tiburon post office I left Rosaleen on the sidewalk and stepped inside to where the post office boxes and the Sunday newspapers were kept. As far as I could tell, there were no wanted posters in there of me and Rosaleen, and the front-page headline in the Columbia paper was about Castro's sister spying for the CIA and not a word about a white girl breaking a Negro woman out of jail in Sylvan.

I dropped a dime into the slot and took one of the papers, wondering if the story was inside somewhere. Rosaleen and I squatted on the ground in an alley and spread out the paper, opening every page. It was full of Malcolm X, Saigon, the Beatles, tennis at Wimbledon, and a motel in Jackson, Mississippi, that closed down rather than accept

Negro guests, but nothing about me and Rosaleen.

Sometimes you want to fall on your knees and thank God in heaven for all the poor news reporting that goes on in the world.

CHAPTER THREE

THE WOMAN MOVED along a row of white boxes that bordered the woods beside the pink house, a house so pink it remained a scorched shock on the back of my eyelids after I looked away. She was tall, dressed in white, wearing a pith helmet with veils that floated across her face, settled around her shoulders and trailed down her back. She looked like an African bride.

Lifting the tops off the boxes, she peered inside, swinging a tin bucket of smoke back and forth. Clouds of bees rose up and flew wreaths around her head. Twice she disappeared in the fogged billows, then gradually re-emerged like a dream rising from the bottom of the night.

We stood across the road, Rosaleen and I, temporarily mute. Me out of awe for the mystery playing out and Rosaleen because her lips were sealed with Red Rose snuff.

'She's the woman who makes the Black Madonna Honey,' I said. I was unable to take my eyes off her, the Mistress of Bees, the portal into my mother's life. *August*.

Rosaleen spat a stream of black juice. 'I hope she makes honey better than she picks out paint.'

'I like it,' I announced.

We waited till she went inside, then crossed the highway and opened the gate in the picket fence that was about to topple over from the weight of Carolina jasmine. Add that to all the chive, dillweed and lemon balm around the porch and the smell could knock you over.

We stood on the porch in the pink light shining off the house. June bugs flickered all around, and music notes floated from inside, sounding like a violin, only a lot sadder.

I asked Rosaleen if she could hear my heart beating, it was that loud.

'I don't hear nothing but the Good Lord asking me what I'm doing here.' She spat what I hoped was the last of her snuff.

I knocked on the door while she muttered a slew of words under her breath: *Give me strength . . . Baby Jesus . . . Lost our feeble minds.*

The music stopped. In the corner of my eye I caught a slight movement at the window, a venetian blind slit opened, then closed.

When the door opened, it was not the woman in white but another one wearing red, her hair cut so short it resembled a little grey, curlicue swimming cap pulled tight over her scalp. Her face stared at us, suspicious and stern. I noticed she carried a musical bow tucked under her arm like a riding whip. It crossed my mind she might use it on us.

'Yes?'

'Are you August Boatwright?'

'No, I'm June Boatwright,' she said, her eyes sweeping over the stitches on Rosaleen's forehead. 'August Boatwright is my sister. You came to see her?'

I nodded, and simultaneously another woman appeared, with bare feet. She wore a green and white sleeveless gingham dress and short braids that stuck straight out all over her head.

'I'm May Boatwright,' she said, 'I'm August's sister, too.' She smiled at us, one of those odd grins that let you know she was not an altogether normal person.

I wished June would grin, too, but she only looked annoyed.

'Is August expecting you?' she said, directing her words to Rosaleen.

Of course Rosaleen jumped in ready to spill the whole story. 'No, see, Lily has this picture—'

I broke in. 'I saw a honey jar back at the store, and the man said . . .'

'Oh, you've come for honey. Well, why didn't you say so? Come on in the front parlour. I'll get August.'

I shot a look at Rosaleen that said, *Are you crazy? Don't tell them about the picture*. We were going to have to get our stories straight, that was for sure.

Some people have a sixth sense. I believe I must have it, because the moment I stepped into the house I felt a trembling along my skin, a current that moved up my spine, down my arms, pulsing out from my fingertips. The body knows things before the mind catches up to them. I was wondering what my body knew that I didn't.

I smelt furniture wax everywhere. Somebody had gone over the entire parlour with it, a big room with fringed throw rugs, an old piano and cane-bottom rockers, each with its own little velvet stool sitting before it. I went over and rubbed my hand across one of them. Next I walked over to a drop-leaf table and sniffed a beeswax candle that sat in a star-shaped holder. It smelt precisely like the furniture wax. A milk bottle filled with gladioli was perched on another table under the window. The curtains were silver-grey organdie, so the air came through with a slightly smoky shimmer. I counted five mirrors, each one with a big brass frame round it.

Then I turned around and looked back towards the door where I'd come in. Over in the corner was a carving of a woman nearly three foot tall. She was one of those figures that had leaned out from the front of a ship in olden times, so old she could have been on the *Santa María* with Columbus for all I knew. She was black as she could be, twisted like driftwood, her face a map of all the storms and journeys she'd been through. Her right arm was raised, as if she was pointing the way, except her fingers were closed in a fist. It gave her a serious look, like she could straighten you out if necessary.

Even though she wasn't dressed up like Mary and didn't resemble the picture on the honey jar, I knew that's who she was. She had a faded red heart painted on her breast and a yellow crescent moon, worn down and crooked, painted where her body would have blended into the ship's wood. A candle inside a tall red glass threw glints and glimmers across her body. She was a mix of mighty and humble all in one. Her lips had a beautiful, bossy half-smile, the sight of which caused me to move both my hands up to my throat. Everything about that smile said, *Lily Owens, I know you down to the core.*

I felt she knew what a lying, murdering, hating person I really was. How I hated T. Ray, and the girls at school, but mostly myself for taking away my mother. I wanted to cry, but then, in the next instant, I wanted to laugh, because the statue also made me feel like Lily the Smiled-Upon, like there was goodness and beauty in me, too. Like I really had all that fine potential my teacher Mrs Henry said I did. Standing there, I loved myself and I hated myself. That's what the black Mary did to me, made me feel my glory and my shame at the same time.

I stepped closer to her and caught the faint scent of honey coming from the wood. May walked over and stood beside me, and I could smell nothing then but the onions on her hands. Her palms were pink like the bottoms of her feet, her elbows darker than the rest of her, and for some reason the sight of them filled me with tenderness.

August Boatwright entered, wearing a pair of rimless glasses and a lime-green chiffon scarf tied to her belt. 'Who've we got here?' she said, and the sound of her voice snapped me back to my ordinary senses.

She was almond-buttery with sweat and sun, her face corrugated with a thousand caramel wrinkles and her hair looking flour dusted, but the rest of her seemed decades younger.

'I'm Lily, and that's Rosaleen,' I said, hesitating as June appeared in the doorway behind her. I opened my mouth without any sense of what I would say next. What came out couldn't have surprised me more. 'We ran away from home and don't have any place to go,' I told her.

Any other day of my life I could have won a fibbing contest hands down, and that, *that* is what I came up with: the pathetic truth. I watched their faces, especially August's. She took off her glasses and rubbed the depressions on each side of her nose. It was so quiet I could hear a clock ticking in another room.

August replaced her glasses, walked to Rosaleen, and examined the stitches on her forehead, the cut under her eye, the bruises along her temple and arms. 'You look like you've been beaten.'

'She fell down the front steps when we were leaving,' I offered, returning to my natural fibbing habit.

August and June traded looks while Rosaleen narrowed her eyes, letting me know I'd done it again, speaking for her like she wasn't there.

'Well, you can stay here till you figure out what to do. We can't have you living on the side of the road,' said August.

The intake of June's breath nearly sucked the air from the room. 'But, August—'

'They'll stay here,' she repeated in a way that let me know who the big sister was and who the little sister was. 'It'll be all right. We've got the cots in the honey house.'

June flounced out, her red skirt flashing round the door.

'Thank you,' I said to August.

'You're welcome. Now, sit down. I'll get some orangeade.'

We got situated in the rockers while May stood guard, grinning her crazy-woman grin. She had big muscles in her arms, I noticed.

'How come y'all have names from a calendar?' Rosaleen asked her.

'Our mother loved spring and summer,' May said. 'We had an April, too, but . . . she died when she was little.' May's grin dissolved, and she started humming 'Oh! Susanna' like her life depended on it.

Rosaleen and I stared at her as her humming turned into hard crying. She cried like April's death had happened only this second.

Finally August returned with a tray of four glasses, orange slices stuck real pretty on the rims. 'Oh, May, honey, you go on out to the wall and finish your cry,' she said, nudging her towards the door.

August acted like this was the sort of normal behaviour happening in every household in South Carolina. 'Here you go—orangeade.'

I sipped. Rosaleen, however, downed hers so fast she let out a belch that the boys in my old junior high would have envied.

August pretended that she didn't hear it while I stared at the velvet footstool and wished Rosaleen could be more *cultured*.

'So you're Lily and Rosaleen,' August said. 'Do you have last names?'

'Rosaleen . . . Smith, and Lily . . . Williams,' I lied, then launched in. 'See, my mother died when I was little, and then my father died in a tractor accident last month on our farm in Spartanburg County. I don't have any other kin around here, so they were going to send me to a home.'

August shook her head. Rosaleen shook hers too, for a different reason.

'Rosaleen was our housekeeper,' I went on. 'She doesn't have any family but me, so we decided to go up to Virginia to find my aunt. Except we don't have any money, so if you have any work for us to do while we're here, maybe we could earn a little before heading on. We aren't really in a hurry to get to Virginia.'

Rosaleen glared at me. For a minute there was nothing but ice clinking in our glasses. I hadn't realised how sweltering the room was, how stimulated my sweat glands had become. I could actually smell myself. I cut my eyes over to the black Mary in the corner and back to August.

She put down her glass. I had never seen eyes that colour, eyes the purest shade of ginger.

'I'm from Virginia myself,' she said, and for some reason this stirred up the current that had moved in my limbs when I'd first entered the room. 'All right, then. Rosaleen can help May in the house, and you can help me and Zach with the bees. Zach is my main helper, so I can't pay you anything, but at least you'll have a room and some food till we call your aunt and see about her sending some bus money.'

'I don't exactly know her whole name,' I said. 'My father just called her Aunt Bernie; I never met her.'

'What were you planning to do, child, go door to door in Virginia?'

'No, ma'am, just Richmond.'

'I see,' said August. And she did. She saw right through it.

That afternoon heat built up in the skies over Tiburon, finally it gave way to a thunderstorm. August, Rosaleen and I stood on the back porch and watched the clouds bruise dark purple over the treetops and the wind whip the branches. We were waiting for a let-up so August could show us our new quarters in the honey house, a converted garage in the back corner of the yard painted the same hot-flamingo shade as the house.

Now and then sprays of rain flew over and misted our faces. Every time I refused to wipe away the wetness. It made the world seem so alive. I couldn't help but envy the way a good storm got everyone's attention.

August went back into the kitchen and returned with three aluminium pie pans and handed them out. 'Come on. Let's make a run for it. These will keep our heads dry, at least.'

August and I dashed into the downpour, holding the pans over our heads. Glancing back, I saw Rosaleen holding the pie pan in her hand, missing the whole point.

When August and I reached the honey house, we huddled in the door to wait on her. Rosaleen glided along, gathering rain in the pan and flinging it out. She walked on puddles like they were Persian carpets, and when a clap of thunder boomed around us, she looked up at the drowned sky, opened her mouth, and let the rain fall in. Ever since those men had beaten her, her face had been so pinched and tired, her eyes dull like they'd had the light knocked out of them. Now she was returning to herself, looking like an all-weather queen out there.

If only she could get some manners.

The inside of the honey house was one big room filled with strange honey-making machines—big tanks, gas burners, troughs, levers, white boxes, and racks piled with waxy honeycombs. My nostrils nearly drowned in the scent of sweetness.

Rosaleen made gigantic puddles on the floor while August ran for towels. I stared at a side wall that was covered with shelves of mason jars. Pith helmets with netting, tools and wax candles hung from nails near the front door, and a thin veneer of honey lay across everything. The soles of my shoes stuck slightly as I walked.

August led us to a tiny corner room in the back with a sink, a full-length mirror, one curtainless window, and two wooden cots made up with clean white sheets. I placed my bag on the first cot.

'May and I sleep out here sometimes when we're harvesting honey round the clock,' August said. 'It can get hot, so you'll need to turn the fan on.'

Rosaleen reached up to where it sat on a shelf along the back wall and flipped the switch, causing cobwebs to blow off the blades and fly all over the room. She had to pick them off her cheekbones.

'You need dry clothes,' August told her.

'I'll air-dry,' Rosaleen said, and she stretched out on the cot, making the legs on it bow.

'You'll have to come into the house to use the bathroom,' August said. 'We don't lock the doors, so just come on in.'

Rosaleen's eyes were closed. She had already drifted off and was making little puff noises with her mouth.

August lowered her voice. 'So she fell down the steps?'

'Yes, ma'am, she went down headfirst. Caught her foot in the rug at the top of the stairs, the one my mother hooked herself.'

The secret of a good lie is don't overly explain, and throw in one good detail.

'Well, Miss Williams, you can start work tomorrow,' she said. I stood there wondering who she was talking to, who was Miss Williams, when I remembered *I* was Lily Williams now. That's the other secret to lying—you have to keep your stories straight.

'Zach will be away for a week,' she was saying. 'His family has gone down to Pawley's Island to visit his mama's sister.'

'If you don't mind my asking, what will I be doing?'

'You'll work with Zach and me, making the honey, doing whatever needs doing. Come on, I'll give you the tour.'

We walked back to the large room with all the machines. She led me to a column of white boxes stacked one on top of the other.

'These are called supers,' she said, setting one on the floor in front of me and removing the lid.

From the outside it looked like a regular old drawer pulled out of the dresser, but inside it were frames of honeycomb hung in a neat row. Each frame was filled with honey and sealed over with beeswax.

She pointed her finger. 'That's the uncapper over there, where we take the wax off the comb. Then it goes through the wax melter over here.'

I followed her, stepping over bits and pieces of honeycomb. She stopped at the big metal tank in the centre of the room.

'This is the spinner,' she said. 'Go on up there and look in.'

I climbed up the two-step ladder and peered over the edge, while August flipped a switch and a motor on the floor sputtered and cranked. The spinner started slowly, gaining speed like the cotton-candy machine at the fair, until it was sending heavenly smells into the atmosphere.

'It separates out the honey,' she said. 'Takes out the bad stuff, leaves in the good. I've always thought how nice it would be to have spinners like this for human beings. Just toss them in and let the spinner do its work.'

I looked back at her, and she was staring at me with her ginger-cake eyes. Was I paranoid to think that when she'd said human beings, what she really meant was me?

She turned off the motor and the humming stopped with a series of ticking sounds. Bending over the brown tube leading from the spinner, she said, 'From here it goes into the baffle tank, then over to the warming pan, and finally into the settling tank. That's the honey gate, where we fill the buckets. You'll get the hang of it.'

I doubted it. I'd never seen such a complex situation in my life.

'Well, I imagine you'll want to rest up like Rosaleen. Supper is at six.

You like sweet-potato biscuits? That's May's speciality.'

When she left, I lay on the cot while rain crashed on the tin roof. I felt like I'd been travelling for weeks, like I'd been dodging lions in the Congo, trying to get to the Lost Diamond City, which happened to be the theme of the last matinée I'd seen in Sylvan. I felt that somehow I belonged here, but I *could* have been in the Congo for how unfamiliar it felt. Staying in a coloured house with coloured women, eating off their dishes, lying on their sheets—it was not something I was against, but I was brand-new to it, and my skin had never felt so white to me.

T. Ray did not think coloured women were smart. Since I want to tell the whole truth, which means the worst parts, I thought they could be smart, but not as smart as me, me being white. Lying on the cot in the honey house, though, all I could think was *August is so intelligent, so cultured*, and I was surprised by this. That's what let me know I had some prejudice buried inside me.

When Rosaleen woke from her nap, before she had a chance to raise her head off the pillow, I said, 'Do you like it here?'

'I guess I do,' she said, working herself to a sitting position. 'So far.'

'Well, I like it, too,' I said. 'So I don't want you saying anything to mess it up, OK?'

She crossed her arms over her belly and frowned. 'Like what?'

'Don't say anything about the black Mary picture I got in my bag, OK? And don't mention my mother.'

She reached up and started twisting some of her loose braids back together. 'Now, how come you wanna keep that a secret?'

I hadn't had time to sort out my reasons. I wanted to say, *Because I just want to be normal for a little while—not a refugee girl looking for her mother, but a regular girl paying a summer visit to Tiburon, South Carolina. I want time to win August over, so she won't send me back when she finds out what I've done*. And those things were true, but even as they crossed my mind, I knew they didn't completely explain why talking to August about my mother made me so uneasy.

I went over and began helping Rosaleen with her braids. My hands were shaking a little. 'Just tell me you aren't gonna say anything,' I said.

'It's your secret,' she said. 'You do what you want with it.'

The next morning I woke early and walked outside. The rain had stopped and the sun glowed behind a bank of clouds.

Pinewoods stretched beyond the honey house in every direction. I could make out about fourteen beehives tucked under the trees in the distance, the tops of them postage stamps of white shine.

The night before, during dinner, August had said she owned twenty-eight acres left to her by her granddaddy. A girl could get lost on twenty-eight acres. She could open a trap door and disappear.

Light spilled through a crack in a cloud, and I walked towards it along a path that led from the honey house into the woods. I passed a child's red wagon loaded with garden tools. It rested beside a plot of tomatoes mixed in with orange zinnias and lavender gladioli.

Where the grass gave way to the woods, I found a stone wall crudely cemented together, not even knee high but nearly fifty yards long. It curved on round the property and abruptly stopped. It didn't seem to have any purpose to it. Then I noticed tiny pieces of folded-up paper stuck in the crevices around the stones. I walked the length of the fence, and it was the same all the way, hundreds of these bits of paper.

I pulled one out and opened it, but the writing was too blurred to make out. I dug out another one. *Birmingham, Sept 15, four little angels dead.* I folded it and put it back, feeling like I'd done something wrong.

Stepping over the wall, I moved into the trees, picking my way through ferns, careful not to tear the designs the spiders had worked so hard on all morning. I began to hear the sound of running water. It's impossible to hear that sound and not go searching for the source. I pushed deeper into the woods. The growth turned thick, and sticker bushes snagged my legs, but I found it—a little river, not much bigger than the creek where Rosaleen and I had bathed.

Taking off my shoes, I waded in. The bottom turned mushy, squishing up through my toes. A turtle plopped off a rock into the water right in front of me. There was no telling what other invisible creatures I was out here socialising with—snakes, frogs, fish, a whole river world of biting bugs, and I could have cared less.

When I put on my shoes and headed back, the light poured down in shafts, and I wanted it to always be like this—no T. Ray, no Mr Gaston, nobody wanting to beat Rosaleen senseless. Just the rain-cleaned woods and the rising light.

The first week at August's was a consolation, a pure relief. The world gives you that once in a while, a brief time-out; the bell rings and you go to your corner, where somebody dabs mercy on your beat-up life.

All that week no one brought up my father, supposedly dead in a tractor accident, or my long-lost Aunt Bernie in Virginia. The calendar sisters just took us in.

The first thing they did was take care of Rosaleen's clothes. August got into her truck and went to the Amen Dollar Store, where she bought

Rosaleen four pairs of panties, a blue cotton nightgown, three waistless, Hawaiian-looking dresses, and a bra that could have slung boulders.

'This ain't charity,' said Rosaleen when August spread them across the kitchen table. 'I'll pay it all back.'

'You can work it off,' said August.

May came in with witch hazel and cotton balls and began to clean up Rosaleen's stitches. 'Somebody knocked the daylights out of you,' she said, and a moment later she was humming 'Oh! Susanna' at that same frantic speed she'd hummed it before.

June jerked her head up from the table, where she was inspecting the purchases. 'You're humming the song again,' she said to May. 'Why don't you excuse yourself?'

May dropped her cotton ball on the table and left the room.

I looked at Rosaleen and she shrugged. June finished cleaning the stitches herself; it was distasteful to her, I could tell by the way she held her mouth, how it drew into a tight buttonhole.

I slipped out to find May: I was going to say, *I'll sing 'Oh! Susanna' with you start to finish*, but I couldn't find her.

It was May who taught me the honey song:

Place a beehive on my grave and let the honey soak through.
When I'm dead and gone, that's what I want from you.
The streets of heaven are gold and sunny,
but I'll stick with my plot and a pot of honey.
Place a beehive on my grave and let the honey soak through.

I loved the silliness of it. Singing made me feel like a regular person again. May sang the song in the kitchen when she rolled dough or sliced tomatoes, and August hummed it when she pasted labels on the honey jars. It said everything about living here.

We lived for honey. We swallowed a spoonful in the morning to wake us up and one at night to put us to sleep. We took it with every meal to give us stamina and prevent disease. We swabbed ourselves in it to disinfect cuts or heal chapped lips. It went in our baths, our skin cream, our raspberry tea and biscuits. Nothing was safe from honey. In one week my skinny arms and legs began to plump out and the frizz in my hair turned to silken waves.

I spent my time in the honey house with August while Rosaleen helped May around the house. I learned how to run a steam-heated knife along the super, slicing the wax cap off the combs, how to load them into the spinner. I adjusted the flame under the steam generator and changed the nylon stockings August used to filter the honey in the settling tank. I caught on so fast she said I was a marvel.

My favourite thing was pouring beeswax into the candle moulds. August used a pound of wax per candle and pressed tiny violets into them, which I collected in the woods. She had a mail-order business to stores in places as far away as Maine and Vermont. People bought so many of her candles and jars of honey she couldn't keep up with it, and there were tins of All-Purpose Beeswax for her special customers. August said it could make your fishing line float, your button thread stronger, your furniture shinier, your stuck window glide, and your irritated skin glow like a baby's bottom. Beeswax was a cure for everything.

May and Rosaleen hit it off right away. May was simple-minded. I don't mean retarded, because she was smart in some ways and read cookbooks nonstop. I mean she was naive and unassuming, a grown-up and a child at the same time, plus she was a touch crazy. Rosaleen liked to say May was a bona fide candidate for the nuthouse, but she still took to her. I would come into the kitchen and they would be standing shoulder to shoulder at the sink, holding ears of corn they couldn't get shucked for talking.

It was Rosaleen who figured out the mystery of 'Oh! Susanna'. She said if you kept things on a happy note, May did fine, but bring up an unpleasant subject—like Rosaleen's head full of stitches or the tomatoes having rot-bottom—and May would start humming 'Oh! Susanna'. It seemed to be her personal way of warding off crying. It worked for things like tomato rot, but not for much else.

A few times she cried so bad, ranting and tearing her hair, that Rosaleen had to come get August from the honey house. August would calmly send May out back to the stone wall. Going out there was about the only thing that could bring her round.

May didn't allow rat traps in the house, as she couldn't even bear the thought of a suffering rat. But what really drove Rosaleen crazy was May catching spiders and carrying them out of the house in the dustpan. I liked this about May, since it reminded me of my bug-loving mother. I went around helping May catch granddaddy longlegs, not just because a smashed bug could send her over the edge but because I felt I was being loyal to my mother's wishes.

The one it was hard to get a fix on was June. She taught history and English at the coloured high school, but what she really loved was music. If I got finished early in the honey house, I went to the kitchen and watched May and Rosaleen cook, but really I was there to listen to June play the cello.

She played music for dying people, going to their homes and even to the hospital to serenade them into the next life. I would sit at the table drinking sweet iced tea, wondering if this was the reason June smiled so little. Maybe she was around death too much.

I could tell she was still bristled at the idea of me and Rosaleen staying; it was the one sore point about our being here.

I overheard her talking to August one night on the back porch as I was coming across the yard to go to the bathroom in the pink house. Their voices stopped me beside the hydrangea bush.

'You know she's lying,' said June.

'I know,' August told her. 'But they're in some kind of trouble and need a place to stay. Who's gonna take them in if we don't—a white girl and a Negro woman? Nobody around here.'

For a second neither spoke. I heard the moths landing against the porch lightbulb.

June said, 'We can't keep a runaway girl here without letting somebody know.'

August turned towards the screen and looked out, causing me to step deeper into the shadows. 'Let who know?' she said. 'The police? They would only haul her off some place. Maybe her father really did die. If so, who better is she gonna stay with for the time being than us?'

'What about this aunt she mentioned?'

'There's no aunt and you know it,' said August.

June's voice sounded exasperated. 'What if her father *didn't* die in this so-called tractor accident? Won't he be looking for her?'

A pause followed. I crept closer to the edge of the porch. 'I just have a feeling about this, June. Something tells me not to send her back to some place she doesn't want to be. Not yet, at least. She has some reason for leaving. Maybe he mistreated her. I believe we can help her.'

'Why don't you ask her point-blank what kind of trouble she's in?'

'Everything in time,' August said. 'The last thing I want is to scare her off with a lot of questions. She'll tell us when she's ready.'

'But she's *white*, August.'

This was a great revelation—not that I was white but that June might not want me here because of my skin colour. I hadn't known this was possible—to reject people for being *white*.

'Let's see if we can help her,' August said as June disappeared from my line of sight. 'We owe her that.'

'I don't see we owe her anything,' June said. A door slammed. August flipped off the light and let out a sigh that floated into the darkness.

I walked back towards the honey house, feeling ashamed that August had seen through my hoax but relieved, too, that she wasn't planning on calling the police or sending me back—*Yet. Yet*, she'd said.

Mostly I felt resentment at June's attitude. As I squatted on the grass at the edge of the woods, the pee felt hot between my legs. I watched it puddle in the dirt, the smell of it rising into the night. There was no difference between my piss and June's. That's what I thought when I looked at the dark circle on the ground. Piss was piss.

Every evening after supper we sat in their tiny den round the television set with the ceramic bee planter on top. You could hardly see the screen for the philodendron vines that dangled round the news pictures.

Walter Cronkite filled us in on an integration parade in St Augustine that got attacked by a mob of white people, about white vigilante groups, fire hoses and teargas. We got the totals. Three civil rights workers killed. Two bomb blasts. Three Negro students chased with axe handles.

Since Mr Johnson signed that law, it was like somebody had ripped the side seams out of American life. We watched the lineup of governors coming on the TV screen asking for 'calm and reason'. August said she was afraid it was only a matter of time before we saw things like that happen right here in Tiburon.

I felt white and self-conscious sitting there, especially with June in the room. Self-conscious and ashamed.

Usually May didn't watch, but one night she joined us, and midway through she started to hum 'Oh! Susanna'. She was upset over a Negro man named Mr Raines, who was killed by a shotgun from a passing car in Georgia. They showed a picture of his widow, holding her children, and suddenly May started to sob. Everybody jumped up like she was an unpinned grenade and tried to quieten her, but it was too late.

May rocked back and forth, slapping her arms and scratching at her face. I had never seen her like this, and it frightened me.

August and June each took one of May's elbows and guided her smoothly through the door. A few moments later I heard water filling the claw-footed tub where twice I'd bathed in honey water. One of the sisters had put a pair of red socks on two of the tub's feet—who knows why. I supposed it was May, who didn't need a reason.

Rosaleen and I crept to the door of the bathroom. It was cracked open enough for us to see May sitting in the tub in a cloud of steam, hugging her knees. June scooped up handfuls of water and drizzled them across May's back. Her crying had eased off now into sniffling.

August's voice came from behind the door. 'That's right, May. Let all that misery slide right off you. Just let it go.'

Each night after the news, we all knelt down on the rug in the parlour before black Mary and said prayers to her, or rather the three sisters and I knelt and Rosaleen sat on a chair. August, June and May called the statue 'Our Lady of Chains', for no reason that I could see.

Hail Mary, full of grace, the Lord is with thee. Blessed art thou among women . . .

The sisters held strands of wooden beads and moved them in their fingers. In the beginning Rosaleen refused to join in, but soon she was going right along with the rest of us. I had the words memorised after the first evening. That's because we said the same thing over and over till it went on repeating itself in my head long after I stopped mouthing it.

It was some kind of Catholic saying, but when I asked August if they were Catholic she said, 'Well, yes and no. My mother was a good Catholic, but my father was an Orthodox Eclectic.'

I had no idea what sort of denomination Orthodox Eclectic was, but I nodded like we had a big group of them back in Sylvan.

She said, 'May and June and I take our mother's Catholicism and mix in our own ingredients. I'm not sure what you call it, but it suits us.'

When we finished saying Hail Mary about three hundred times, we said our personal prayers silently, which was kept to a minimum, since our knees would be killing us by then. I shouldn't complain, since it was nothing compared to kneeling on the Martha Whites. Finally the sisters would cross themselves, and it would be over.

One evening, after everyone had left the room but me and August, she said, 'Lily, if you ask Mary's help, she'll give it.'

I didn't know what to say to that, so I shrugged.

She motioned me to sit next to her in the rocking chair. 'I want to tell you a story,' she said. 'It's a story our mother used to tell us when we got tired of our chores or out of sorts with our lives.'

'I'm not tired of my chores,' I said.

'I know, but it's a good story. Just listen.'

I situated myself in the chair and rocked back and forth.

'A long time ago, across the world in Germany, there was a young nun named Beatrix who loved Mary. She got sick and tired of being a nun, though, what with all the chores she had to do and the rules she had to go by. So one night she took off her nun outfit, folded it up, and laid it on her bed. Then she crawled out the convent window and ran away.'

OK, I could see where we were headed.

'She thought she was in for a wonderful time.' August said. 'But life wasn't what she imagined it would be for a runaway nun. She roamed around feeling lost, begging in the streets. After a while she wished she could return to the convent, but she knew they'd never take her back.'

We weren't talking about Beatrix the nun, that was plain as day. We were talking about me.

'What happened to her?' I asked, trying to sound interested.

'Well, one day, after years of wandering and suffering, she disguised herself and went back to her old convent, wanting to visit one last time. She went into the chapel and asked one of her old sisters, "Do you remember the nun Beatrix, who ran away?" "What do you mean?" the sister said. "Beatrix didn't run away. Why, there she is over near the altar, sweeping." Well, you can imagine how this floored the real Beatrix. She marched over to the sweeping woman to get a look at her and discovered it was none other than Mary. Mary smiled at Beatrix, then led her back to her room and gave her back her nun outfit. You see, Lily, all that time Mary had been standing in for her.'

The creaking in my rocker died away as I slowed to a stop. Just what was August trying to say? That Mary would stand in for me back home in Sylvan so T. Ray wouldn't notice I was gone? That was too outlandish even for the Catholics. I think she was telling me, *I know you've run away—everybody gets the urge to do that some time—but sooner or later you'll want to go home. Just ask Mary for help.*

I excused myself, glad to be out of the spotlight. After that I started asking Mary for her special help—not to take me home, like the poor nun Beatrix, but to see to it that I never went back. I asked her to draw a curtain round the pink house so no one would ever find us. I asked this daily, and it seemed to be working. No one knocked on the door and dragged us off to jail. Mary had made us a curtain of protection.

CHAPTER FOUR

ON OUR FIRST Friday evening there, after prayers were finished and orange and pink swirls still hung in the sky from sunset, I went with August to the bee yard.

I hadn't been out to the hives before, so to start off she gave me a lesson in what she called 'bee yard etiquette'. She reminded me that the world was really one big bee yard, and the same rules worked fine in both places: Don't be afraid, as no life-loving bee wants to sting you. Still, don't be an idiot; wear long sleeves and trousers. Don't swat. If you feel angry, whistle. Anger agitates, while whistling melts a bee's temper. Act like you know what you're doing, even if you don't. Above all, send the bees love. Every little thing wants to be loved.

August had been stung so many times she had immunity. They barely hurt her. In fact, she said, stings helped her arthritis, but since I didn't have arthritis, I should cover up. She made me put on one of her long-sleeved white shirts, then placed one of the white helmets on my head and adjusted the netting.

If this was a man's world, a veil took the rough beard right off it. Everything appeared softer, nicer. When I walked behind August in my bee veil, I felt like a moon floating behind a night cloud.

She kept forty-eight hives strewn through the woods around the pink house, and another 280 were parcelled out on various farms, in river yards and upland swamps. The farmers loved her bees, thanks to all the pollinating they did, how they made the watermelons redder and the cucumbers bigger. They would have welcomed her bees for free, but August paid every one of them with five gallons of honey.

She was constantly checking on her hives, driving her old flat-bed truck from one end of the county to the other. The 'honey wagon' was what she called it. Bee patrol was what she did in it.

I watched her load the red wagon, the one I'd seen in the back yard, with brood frames, those little slats that slip down in the hives for the bees to deposit honey on.

'We have to make sure the queen has plenty of room to lay her eggs, or else we'll get a swarm,' she said.

'What does that mean, a swarm?'

'Well, if you have a queen and a group of independent-minded bees that split off from the rest of the hive and look for another place to live, then you've got a swarm. They usually cluster on a limb somewhere.'

It was clear she didn't like swarms.

'So,' she said, getting down to business, 'what we have to do is take out the frames filled with honey and put in empty ones.'

August pulled the wagon while I walked behind carrying the smoker stuffed with pine straw and tobacco leaves. Zach had placed a brick on top of each hive telling August what to do. If the brick was at the front, the colony had nearly filled the combs and needed another super. If the brick was at the back, there were problems like wax moths or ailing queens. Turned on its side, the brick announced a happy bee family.

August struck a match and lit the grass in the smoker. Her face flared with light, then receded into the dimness. She waved the bucket, sending smoke into the hive. The smoke, she said, worked better than a sedative.

Still, when August removed the lids, the bees poured out in thick black ropes, breaking into strands, a flurry of wings moving around our faces. The air rained bees, and I sent them love, just like August said.

She pulled out a brood frame, a canvas of whirling blacks and greys, with rubbings of silver. 'There she is, Lily, see her?' said August. 'That's the queen, the large one.'

I made a curtsy like people do for the Queen of England, which made August laugh. I wanted to make her love me so she would keep me for ever. If I could make her love me, maybe she would forget about Beatrix the nun going home and let me stay.

When we walked back to the house, darkness had settled in and fireflies sparked around our shoulders. I could see Rosaleen and May through the kitchen window finishing the dishes.

August and I sat in collapsible lawn chairs beside a crepe myrtle that kept dropping blossoms all over the ground. Cello music swelled out from the house.

I gazed at the stone wall that edged the back yard. 'There are pieces of paper in the wall out there,' I said, as if August didn't know this.

'Yes, I know. It's May's wall. She made it herself.'

'May did?' I tried to picture her mixing cement, carrying rocks around in her apron.

'She gets a lot of the stones from the river that runs through the woods back there. She's been working on it ten years or more.'

So that's where she got her big muscles—rock lifting. 'What are all those scraps of paper stuck in it?'

'It's a long story,' August said. 'I guess you've noticed—May is special.'

'She sure does get upset easy,' I said.

'That's because May takes in things differently than the rest of us do.' August reached over and laid her hand on my arm. 'See, Lily, when you and I hear about some misery out there, it might make us feel bad for a while, but it doesn't wreck our whole world. It's like we have a built-in protection that keeps the pain from overwhelming us. But May doesn't have that. Everything just comes into her—all the suffering out there—and she feels as if it's happening to her. She can't tell the difference.'

Did this mean if I told May about T. Ray's mounds of grits, his dozens of small cruelties, about my killing my mother—that hearing it, she would feel everything I did? I wanted to know what happened when *two* people felt it. Would it divide the hurt in two, make it lighter to bear?

Rosaleen's voice drifted from the kitchen window, followed by May's laughter. May sounded so normal and happy right then, I couldn't imagine how she'd got the way she was—one minute laughing and the next overrun with everybody's misery.

'Was she born like that?' I asked.

'No, she was a happy child at first.'

'Then what happened to her?'

August focused her eyes on the stone wall. 'May had a twin. Our sister April. The two of them were like one soul sharing two bodies. I never saw anything like it. If April got a toothache, May's gum would plump up red and swollen just like April's. Those two had no separation between them.'

'The first day we were here May told us that April died.'

'And that's when it all started with May,' she said, then looked at me like she was trying to decide whether to go on. 'It's not a pretty story.'

'My story's not pretty either,' I said, and she smiled.

'Well, when April and May were eleven, they walked to the market with a nickel each to buy an ice cream. They'd seen the white children in there licking their cones and looking at cartoon books. The man who owned the market gave them the cones but said they had to go outside to eat them. April was headstrong and told him she wanted to look at the cartoon books. She argued with the man, like she used to do with Father, and finally the man took her arm and pulled her to the door, and her ice cream dropped to the floor. She came home screaming that it wasn't fair. Our father was the only coloured dentist in Richmond and he'd seen more than his share of unfairness. He told April, "Nothing's fair in this world. You might as well get that straight right now."'

I was thinking how I myself had got that straight long before I was eleven. I blew a puff of air across my face, bending my neck to behold the Big Dipper. June's music poured out, serenading us.

'I think most children might have let that roll on by, but it did something to April,' August said. 'It opened her eyes to things she might not have noticed, being so young. She started having stretches when she didn't want to go to school or do anything. By the time she was thirteen, she was having terrible depressions, and of course the whole time, whatever she was feeling, May was feeling. And then when April was fifteen, she took our father's shotgun and killed herself.'

I hadn't expected that. I sucked in my breath, then felt my hand go up and cover my mouth.

'I know,' said August. 'It's terrible to hear something like that.' She paused a moment. 'When April died, something in May died, too. She never was normal after that. It seemed like the world itself became May's twin sister.'

August's face was blending into the tree shadows. I slid up in my chair so I could still see her.

'Our mother said she was like Mary, with her heart on the outside of her chest. Mother was good about taking care of her, but when she died, it fell to me and June. We tried for years to get May some help. She saw doctors, but they didn't have any idea what to do with her except put her away. So June and I came up with this idea of a wailing wall.'

'A what kind of wall?'

'Wailing wall,' she said again. 'Like they have in Jerusalem. The people go there to mourn. It's a way for them to deal with their suffering. They write their prayers on scraps of paper and tuck them in the wall.'

'And that's what May does?'

August nodded. 'All those bits of paper you see out there stuck between the stones are things May has written down—all the heavy feelings she carries around. It seems like the only thing that helps her.'

I looked in the direction of the wall, invisible now in the darkness. *Birmingham, Sept 15, four little angels dead.*

'Poor May,' I said.

'Yes,' said August. 'Poor May.' And we sat in the sorrow for a while, until the mosquitoes collected around us and chased us indoors.

In the honey house Rosaleen was on her cot with the lights out and the fan going full blast. I stripped down to my panties and sleeveless top, but it was still too hot to move.

My chest hurt from feeling things. I wondered if T. Ray was pacing the floors, telling himself what a rotten excuse for a father he was for not treating me better, but I doubted it. Thinking up ways to kill me was more like it.

I turned my pillow over and over for the coolness, thinking about May and her wall and what the world had come to that a person needed something like that.

The worst thing was lying there wanting my mother. That's how it had always been; my longing for her nearly always came late at night when my guard was down. I tossed on the sheets, wishing I could crawl into bed with her and smell her skin. I could just see her, propped in bed. My mouth twisted as I pictured myself climbing in beside her and putting my head against her breast. I would put it right over her beating heart and listen. *Mama*, I would say. And she would look down at me and say, *Baby, I'm right here*.

I could hear Rosaleen trying to turn in her cot. 'You awake?' I said.

'Who can sleep in this oven?' she said.

I wanted to say, *You can*, as I'd seen her sleeping that day outside the Frogmore Stew General Store and Restaurant, and it had been at least this hot. She had a fresh Band-Aid on her forehead. Earlier, August had boiled her tweezers and fingernail scissors in a pot on the stove and used them to pluck out Rosaleen's stitches.

'How's your head?'

'My head is just fine.' The words came out like little jabs in the air.

'Are you mad or something?'

'Why would I be mad? Just 'cause you spend all your time with August now, ain't no reason for me to care.'

I couldn't believe it; Rosaleen sounded jealous.

'I don't spend *all* my time with her.'

'Pretty much,' she said.

'Well, what do you expect? I work in the honey house with her. I have to spend time with her.'

'What about tonight? You out there working on honey sitting on the lawn?'

'We were just talking.'

'Yeah, I know,' she said, and then she rolled towards the wall, turning her back into a great hump of silence.

'Rosaleen, don't act like that. August might know things about my mother.'

She raised up on her elbow and looked at me. 'Lily, your mama's gone,' she said softly. 'And she ain't coming back.'

I sat straight up. 'How do you know she isn't alive right in this very town? T. Ray could've lied about her being dead, just like he lied about her leaving me.'

'Oh, Lily. Girl. You got to stop all this.'

'I feel her here,' I said. 'She's been here, I know it.'

'Maybe she was. I can't say. I just know some things are better left alone.'

'What do you mean? That I shouldn't find out what I can about my own mother?'

'What if—?' She paused and rubbed the back of her neck. 'What if you find out something you don't wanna know?'

What I heard her say was *Your mother left you, Lily. Let it alone*. I wanted to yell how stupid she was, but the words bunched in my throat. I started hiccuping instead. 'You think T. Ray was telling me the truth about her leaving me, don't you?'

'I don't have any idea about that,' Rosaleen said. 'I just don't want you getting yourself hurt.'

I lay back on the bed. My hiccups ricocheted around the room.

'Hold your breath, pat your head and rub your tummy,' Rosaleen said.

I ignored her. Eventually I heard her breathing shift to a deeper place.

I pulled on my shorts and sandals and crept to the desk where August filled honey orders. I tore a piece of paper from a tablet and wrote my mother's name on it. Deborah Owens.

When I looked outside, I knew I would have to make my way by starlight. I crept across the grass, back to the edge of the woods, to May's wall. Hiccuping all the way. Placing my hands on the stones, all I wanted was not to ache so much.

I wanted to let go of my feelings for a little while. I pressed the paper with her name into a cranny that seemed right for her, giving her to the wailing wall. Somewhere along the way my hiccups disappeared.

I sat on the ground with my back against the stones and my head tilted back so I could see the stars. I started thinking maybe I should find out what I could about my mother, before T. Ray or the police came for us. But where to start? I couldn't just pull out the black Mary picture and show it to August without the truth wrecking everything, and she might decide that she was obliged to call T. Ray. And if she knew that Rosaleen was a true fugitive, wouldn't she *have* to call the police?

The night seemed like an inkblot I had to figure out. I sat there and studied the darkness, trying to see through it to some sliver of light.

The next morning in the honey house, I woke to banging in the yard. When I pulled myself off the cot and wandered outside, I found the tallest Negro man I'd ever seen working on the truck, bent over the motor, tools scattered around his feet. June handed him wrenches and what-have-you, cocking her head and beaming at him.

In the kitchen May and Rosaleen were working on pancake batter. The electric percolator bubbled into the tiny glass nozzle on top of it. *Bloop, bloop*. I loved the way it sounded, the way it smelt.

'Who's the man out there?' I asked.

'That's Neil,' said May. 'He's sweet on June.'

'It looks to me like June is sweet on him, too.'

'Yeah, but she won't say so,' said May. 'She's kept that poor man strung along for years. Won't marry him and won't let him go.'

May drizzled batter on the griddle in the shape of a big L. 'This one's yours,' she said. L for Lily.

Rosaleen set the table and warmed the honey in a bowl of hot water. I poured orange juice into glasses.

'How come June won't get married to him?' I asked.

'She was supposed to get married to somebody else a long time ago,' said May. 'But he didn't show up for the wedding.'

I looked at Rosaleen, afraid this situation of jilted love might be unfortunate enough to send May into one of her episodes, but she was intent on my pancake. It struck me for the first time how odd it was that none of them was married.

I heard Rosaleen make a sound like *Hmmmph*, and I knew she was thinking about her own sorry husband, wishing he hadn't shown up for *their* ceremony.

'June swore off men and said she would never get married, and then she met Neil when he came to be the new principal at her school. He has tried every which way to get June to marry him, but she won't do it. Me and August can't convince her either.'

A wheeze welled up from May's chest, and then out came 'Oh! Susanna'. *Here we go.*

'Lord, not again,' said Rosaleen.

'I'm sorry,' May said. 'I just can't help it.'

'Why don't you go out to the wall?' I said, prising the spatula out of her hand. 'It's OK.'

'Yeah,' Rosaleen told her. 'You do what you gotta do.' We watched from the screen door as May cut past June and Neil.

A few minutes later June came in with Neil behind her. I worried that his head wouldn't clear the door.

'What started May off?' June wanted to know. Her eyes followed a roach that darted beneath the refrigerator. 'You didn't step on a roach in front of her, did you?'

'No,' I said. 'We didn't even see a roach.'

She opened the cabinet under the sink and dug into the back for a pump can of bug killer. I thought about explaining to her my mother's ingenious method of ridding the house of roaches—cracker crumbs and marshmallow—but then I thought, *This is June, forget it.*

'Well, what upset her, then?' June asked.

I hated to come out and say it with Neil standing there, but Rosaleen didn't have any problem with it. 'She's upset you won't marry Neil.'

I had never considered until then that coloured people could blush, or maybe it was anger that turned June's face such a dark plum colour.

Neil laughed. 'See there. You should marry me and quit upsetting your sister.'

'Oh, get out of here,' she said, and gave him a push.

'You promised me pancakes, and I'm gonna have them,' he said. He wore blue jeans and an undershirt with grease smears on it, along with horn-rimmed glasses. He looked like a very studious mechanic.

He smiled at me and then Rosaleen. 'So are you gonna introduce me or keep me in the dark?'

June's eyes turned dull and hard when she looked at me. 'This is Lily and Rosaleen,' she said. 'They're visiting for a while.'

'Where do you come from?' he asked me.

'Spartanburg County,' I said, having to pause and remember what I'd said earlier.

'And you?' he said to Rosaleen.

She stared at the copper moulds that hung on either side of the window over the sink. 'Same place as Lily.'

'What's that burning?' said June.

Smoke poured off the griddle. The L-shaped pancake had burned to a crisp. June yanked the spatula from my fingers, scraped up the mess, and dropped it into the trash.

'How long are you planning on staying?' Neil asked.

June stared at me. Waiting. Her lips pinched tight along her teeth.

'A while longer,' I answered, looking into the garbage can. L for Lily. I could feel the questions gathering in him, knew I could not face them.

'I'm not hungry,' I said, and walked out of the back door.

Crossing the back porch, I heard Rosaleen say to him, 'Have you registered yourself to vote?'

On Sunday I thought they would go to church, but no, they held a special service in the pink house, and people came to them. It was a group called the Daughters of Mary, which August had organised.

The Daughters of Mary started showing up in the parlour before 10.00am. First was an old woman named Queenie and her grown daughter, Violet. They were dressed alike in bright yellow skirts and white blouses, though they wore different hats. Next came Lunelle, Mabelee and Cressie, who wore the fanciest hats I'd ever laid eyes on.

It turned out Lunelle was a hatmaker without the least bit of shyness. I'm talking about purple felt the size of a sombrero with fake fruit on the back. That was Lunelle's. Mabelee wore a creation of tiger fur wrapped with gold fringe, but it was Cressie who carried the day in a crimson smokestack with black netting and ostrich feathers. If this was not enough, they wore clip-on earbobs of various coloured rhinestones and circles of rouge on their brown cheeks. I thought they were beautiful.

In addition to all these Daughters, it turned out Mary had one son besides Jesus, a man named Otis Hill, in an oversize navy suit, so technically the group was the Daughters and Son of Mary. He'd come with his wife, who was known to everyone as Sugar-Girl. She wore a white dress, turquoise cotton gloves and an emerald green turban.

August and June, hatless, gloveless, earbobless, looked practically poverty-stricken next to them, but May, good old May, had tied on a bright blue hat with the brim up on one side and down on the other.

August had brought in chairs and arranged them in a semicircle facing the statue of Mary. When we were all seated, she lit the candle and June played the cello. We said the Hail Marys together, Queenie and Violet moving strings of wooden beads through their fingers.

August stood up and said she was glad me and Rosaleen were with them; then she opened a Bible and read, '"And Mary said . . . Behold, from henceforth all generations shall call me blessed. For he that is mighty hath done to me great things . . . He hath scattered the proud . . . He hath put down the mighty from their seats, and exalted them of low degree. He hath filled the hungry with good things; and the rich he hath sent empty away."'

Laying the Bible in her chair, she said, 'It's been a while since we've told the story of Our Lady of Chains, and since we have visitors who've never heard the story of our statue, I thought we'd tell it again.'

One thing I was starting to understand was that August loved to tell a good story.

'Stories have to be told or they die,' she said, 'and when they die, we can't remember who we are or why we're here.'

Cressie nodded, making the ostrich feathers wave through the air. 'That's right. Tell the story,' she said.

August pulled her chair close to the statue and sat facing us. When she began, it didn't sound like August talking at all but like someone from another time and place, talking through her. Her eyes looked off towards the window, like she was seeing the drama play out in the sky.

'Well,' she said, 'back in the time of slaves, when the people were beaten down and kept like property, they prayed every day and every night for deliverance. On the islands near Charleston, they would go to the praise house and sing and pray, and someone would ask the Lord to send them rescue. To send them consolation. To send them freedom.'

I could tell she had repeated those opening lines a thousand times, that she was saying them the exact way she'd heard them coming from the lips of some old woman, the way they came out like a song, with rhythms that rocked us to and fro.

'One day,' August said, 'a slave named Obadiah was loading bricks onto a boat when he saw something washed up on the bank. Coming closer, he saw it was the wooden figure of a woman. Her body was growing out of a block of wood, a black woman with her arm lifted out and her fist balled up.'

At this point August stood up and struck the pose herself. She looked just like the statue standing there, her right arm raised and her hand clutched into a fist.

'Obadiah pulled the figure out of the water,' she went on, 'and struggled to set her upright. Then he remembered how they'd asked the Lord to send them rescue. To send them consolation. To send them freedom. Obadiah knew the Lord had sent this figure. He knelt down in the marsh mud before her and heard her voice speak plain as day in his heart. She said, "It's all right. I'm here. I'll be taking care of you now."'

This story was ten times better than Beatrix the nun. August glided back and forth across the room as she spoke. 'Obadiah tried to pick up the waterlogged woman whom God had sent to take care of them, but she was too heavy, so he went and got two more slaves, and between them they carried her to the praise house and set her on the hearth.

'By the time the next Sunday came, everyone had heard about the statue washing up from the river, how it had spoken to Obadiah. The praise house was filled with people spilling out of the door and sitting on the window ledges. Obadiah told them he knew the Lord God had sent her, but he didn't know who she was.'

'He didn't know who she was!' cried Sugar-Girl. Then all the Daughters of Mary broke loose, saying over and over, 'Not one of them knew.'

I looked over at Rosaleen, who I hardly recognised for the way she leaned forward in her chair, chanting along with them.

When everything had quieted down, August said, 'Now, the oldest of the slaves was a woman named Pearl, and when she spoke, everyone listened. She got to her feet and said, "This here is the mother of Jesus."

'Everyone knew the mother of Jesus was named Mary, and that she'd seen suffering of every kind. That she was strong and constant and had a mother's heart. And here she was, sent to them on the same waters that had brought them here in chains. It seemed to them she knew everything they suffered.'

I stared at the statue, feeling the fractured place in my heart.

'And so,' August said, 'the people cried and danced and clapped their hands. They went one at a time and touched their hands to her chest, wanting to grab on to the solace in her heart. They did this every Sunday in the praise house, and eventually they painted a red heart on her breast so the people would have a heart to touch.

'Our Lady filled their hearts with fearlessness and whispered to them plans of escape. The bold ones fled, finding their way north, and those who didn't lived with a raised fist in their hearts. And if ever it grew weak, they would only have to touch her heart again.

'She grew so powerful she became known even to the master. One day he hauled her off on a wagon and chained her in the carriage house. But then, without any human help, she escaped during the night and made her way back to the praise house. The master chained her in the barn fifty times, and fifty times she loosed the chains and went home. Finally he gave up and let her stay there.'

The room grew quiet as August stood there a minute, letting everything sink in. When she spoke again, she raised her arms out beside her. 'The people called her Our Lady of Chains. They called her that not because she *wore* chains but because *she broke them*.'

June wedged the cello between her legs and played 'Amazing Grace', and the Daughters of Mary got to their feet and swayed together like colourful seaweed on the ocean floor.

I thought this was the grand finale, but no, June switched over to the piano and banged out a jazzed-up version of 'Go Tell It on the Mountain'. Then August started a conga line. She danced over to Lunelle, who latched on to August's waist. Cressie hooked on to Lunelle, followed by Mabelee, and off they went round the room. When they swung back by, Queenie and Violet joined them, then Sugar-Girl. I wanted to be part of it, too, but I only watched, and so did Rosaleen and Otis.

June seemed to play faster and faster. I fanned my face, trying to get a little air, feeling light-headed.

When the dance ended, the Daughters stood panting in a half-circle before Our Lady of Chains, and what they did next took my breath away. One at a time they went and touched the statue's fading red heart.

Queenie and her daughter went together and rubbed their palms against the wood. Lunelle pressed her fingers to Mary's heart, then kissed each one of them in a slow, deliberate way. Otis pressed his forehead to the heart, like he was filling up his empty tank.

June kept playing while each of them came, until there was only Rosaleen and me left. May nodded to June to keep on with the music and took Rosaleen's hand, pulling her to Our Lady of Chains, so even Rosaleen got to touch Mary's heart.

I wanted to touch her red heart, too, as much as anything I'd ever wanted. As I rose from my chair, my head was still swimming some. I walked towards black Mary with my hand lifted. But just as I was about to reach her, June stopped playing. She stopped right in the middle of the song, and I was left in the silence with my hand stretched out.

Drawing it back, I looked around me, and it was like seeing everything through a train's thick window. A blur passed before me. A moving wave of colour. *I am not one of you*, I thought.

My body felt numb. I thought how nice it would be to grow smaller and smaller—until I was a dot of nothing. I called to the Lady of Chains, but maybe I wasn't really saying her name out loud, only hearing myself call on the inside. That's the last I remember. Her name echoing through the empty spaces.

When I woke, I was lying on August's bed across the hall with an ice-cold flannel folded over my forehead and August and Rosaleen staring down at me. Rosaleen was fanning me with the skirt of her dress.

'Since when have you started fainting?' she said, and sat down on the edge of the bed, causing me to roll into her side. She scooped me into her arms. For some reason this caused my chest to fill with more sadness than I could bear, and I wrestled myself free.

'Maybe it was the heat,' August said. 'I should've turned on the fans. It must've been ninety degrees in there.'

'I'm all right,' I told them, but to tell the truth I was bewildered. I felt I'd stumbled upon an amazing secret—it was possible to close your eyes and exit life without actually dying. You just had to faint. Only I didn't know how to make it happen, how to pull the plug when I needed to.

My fainting spell had broken up the Daughters of Mary and sent May to the wailing wall. June had gone upstairs to her room and locked the door, while the Daughters huddled in the kitchen.

We chalked it up to heat. Heat, we said. Heat would make a person do strange things.

You should have seen how August and Rosaleen fussed over me the rest of the evening. You want some root beer, Lily? How about a feather pillow? Here, swallow this spoon of honey.

We sat in the den, where I ate supper off a tray, which was a privilege in itself. June was in her room, not answering August's calls at the door, and May was in the kitchen clipping recipes from *McCall's* magazine.

On the television Mr Cronkite said they were going to send a rocket ship to the moon. 'On July 28th, the United States of America will launch *Ranger 7* from Cape Kennedy, Florida,' he said. It was going to take a 253,665-mile flight before it crash-landed onto the moon. The whole point was to take pictures of the surface and send them back.

'Well, baby Jesus,' said Rosaleen. 'A rocket to the moon.'

August shook her head. 'Next they'll be walking around up there.' She cut off the TV set. 'I need some air.'

We all went, Rosaleen and August holding on to my elbows in case I started to keel over again.

It was the in-between time, before day leaves and night comes, a time I've never been partial to because of the sadness that lingers in the space between going and coming. August gazed at the sky where the moon was rising, large and ghostly silver.

'Look at her good, Lily,' she said. 'You're seeing the end of something.'

'I am?'

'Yes, you are, because as long as people have been on this earth, the moon has been a mystery to us. Think about it. She is strong enough to pull the oceans, and when she dies away, she always comes back again. My mama used to tell me Our Lady lived on the moon and that I should dance when her face was bright and hibernate when it was dark.'

August stared at the sky a long moment and then turned towards the house. 'Now it won't ever be the same, not after they've landed up there and walked around on her. She'll be just one more big science project.'

I thought about the dream I'd had that night Rosaleen and I slept by the pond, how the moon had cracked to pieces.

August disappeared into the house, and Rosaleen headed for her cot in the honey house, but I stayed on and stared at the sky, imagining *Ranger 7* blasting away for it.

I knew one day I would go into the parlour when no one was around and touch the Lady's heart. Then I would show August the picture of my mother and see if the moon broke loose and fell out of the sky.

CHAPTER FIVE

I JUMPED EVERY time I heard a siren. It might have been an ambulance off in the distance or a police chase on television—it didn't matter. Part of me was always braced for T. Ray or Mr Shoe Gaston to drive up and end my charmed life. We had been at August's house eight whole days. I didn't know how long black Mary could keep the curtain drawn.

On Monday morning, July 13, I was walking back to the honey house after breakfast when I noticed a strange black Ford parked in the driveway. I lost my breath for a moment, till I remembered Zach was coming back to work today.

It would be me and August *and* Zach. I'm not proud of it, but I resented the intrusion.

He was not what I expected. I found him inside holding a honey drizzle like a microphone, singing 'Blueberry Hill'. I watched unseen from the doorway, not making a sound, but when he launched into 'Viva Las Vegas', slinging his hips around Elvis-style, I broke out laughing.

He whirled round, knocking a tray of brood frames to the floor.

'I was just singing,' he said, like this was news to me. 'Who are you anyway?'

'Lily,' I said. 'I'm staying with August and them for a while.'

'I'm Zachary Taylor,' he said.

'Zachary Taylor was a president,' I told him.

'Yeah, so I've heard.' He fished out a dogtag suspended on a chain under his shirt and held it up to my nose. 'See right there. Zachary Lincoln Taylor.' He smiled then, and I saw he had a one-sided dimple. It's a feature that has always got to me.

He cleaned up the floor. 'August told me about you being here and helping us out, but she didn't say anything about you being . . . white.'

'Yep, I'm white, all right,' I said. 'White as can be.'

There was nothing white about Zachary Lincoln Taylor. Even the whites of his eyes weren't exactly white. He had broad shoulders and a narrow waist and short-cropped hair like most of the Negro boys wore, but it was his face I couldn't help staring at. If he was shocked over me being white, I was shocked over him being handsome.

At my school they made fun of coloured people's lips and noses. I had laughed at these jokes, hoping to fit in. Now I wished I could pen a letter to my school to be read at opening assembly that would tell them how wrong we'd all been. You should see Zachary Taylor, I'd say.

I wondered how August could forget to tell him a thing like the fact that I was white. She'd told *me* plenty about *him*. I knew she was his godmother. That his daddy had left him when he was small, that his mama worked as a lunchroom lady at the school where June taught. He was about to be a junior at the black high school, where he made all A's and played halfback on the football team. She'd said he ran like the wind, which might be his ticket to a college up north. This had struck me as better than I would manage, since I was probably headed for beauty school now.

I said, 'August went out to the Satterfield farm to check on some hives. She said I should help you in here. What do you want me to do?'

'Grab some frames from the hive boxes over there and help me load the uncapper, I guess.'

'So who do you like best, Fats Domino or Elvis?' I asked, dropping in the first frame.

'Miles Davis,' he said.

'I don't know who that is.'

'Of course you don't. But he's the best trumpet player in the world. I'd give anything to play like him.'

'Would you give up football?'

'How do you know I play football?'

'I know things,' I said, and smiled at him.

'I can see that.' He was trying not to smile back.

I thought, *We're going to be friends.*

He flipped the switch, and the extractor started to spin, building speed. 'So how come you're staying here?'

'Me and Rosaleen are on our way to Virginia to live with my aunt. My daddy died in a tractor accident, and I haven't had a mother since I was little, so I'm trying to get to my family up there before I get put in an orphanage or something.'

'But how come you're *here*?'

'Oh, you mean at August's. We were hitchhiking and got let out at Tiburon. We knocked on August's door, and she gave us a bed. That's it.'

He nodded like this made some kind of actual sense.

'How long have you worked here?' I asked, happy to change the subject.

'All through high school. I come after school when it's not football season, every Saturday and all summer. I bought a car with the money I made last year.'

'That Ford out there?'

'Yeah, it's a '59 Ford Fairlane,' he said.

He flipped the switch on the extractor again, and the machine groaned while it came to a stop. 'Come on, I'll show you.'

I could see my face in the surface of it. I figured he stayed up nights polishing it. I walked along giving it the white-glove inspection.

'You can teach me to drive,' I said.

'Not in this car.'

'Why not?'

'Because you look like the kind of girl who'll wreck something.'

I turned to face him, ready to defend myself, and saw he was grinning. And there was the one-sided dimple again.

Every day Zach and I worked in the honey house. August and Zach had already extracted most of the honey from her bee yards, but there were still several stacks of supers on pallets sitting around.

We ran the warmer and caught the wax in a tin tub, then loaded the frames into the extractor and filtered the honey through brand-new nylon hose. August liked to keep a little pollen in her honey because it was good for people, so we saw to that, too. Sometimes we broke off pieces of comb and pushed them down into the jars before we filled them. You had to make sure they were new combs with no brood eggs in them, since nobody wanted to have baby bee larvae in their honey.

And if we weren't doing all that, we were filling candle moulds with beeswax and washing mason jars till my hands turned stiff as corn husk from detergent.

The only part of the day I dreaded was dinner, when I had to be around June. You'd think anybody who played music for dying people would be a nicer person. I couldn't understand why she resented me so much. Somehow even me being white and imposing on their hospitality didn't seem enough reason.

'How are things with you, Lily?' she'd say every night at the table. Like she'd rehearsed this in the mirror.

I'd say, 'Things are fine. And how are they with you, June?'

She would glance at August, who would be following all this like she was overcome with interest. 'Fine,' June would say.

Having got that out of the way, we would do our best to ignore each other the rest of the meal.

One night after the Hail Marys, August said, 'Lily, if you wish to touch Our Lady's heart, you're welcome, isn't she, June?'

I glanced at June, who gave me a forced smile.

'Maybe some other time,' I said.

If I was dying on my cot in the honey house and the only thing that could save me was June's change of heart, I would meet my death and shoot straight to heaven. Or maybe hell. I wasn't even sure any more.

The best meal was lunch, which Zach and I ate under the cool of the pine trees. May fixed us bologna sandwiches nearly every day. And candlestick salad, which meant half a banana standing up in a pineapple slice. 'Let me light your candle,' she'd say, and strike an imaginary match. Then she'd fasten a bottled cherry on the tip of the banana with a toothpick. Like Zach and I were still in kindergarten. We'd go along with her, acting excited over her lighting the banana. For dessert we crunched cubes of lime Kool-Aid, which she'd frozen in ice trays.

One day we sat on the grass after lunch, listening to the wind snap the sheets Rosaleen had hung out on the clothes line.

'What's your favourite subject in school?' Zach asked.

'English.'

'I bet you like to write stories,' he said, rolling his eyes.

'As a matter of fact I do. I was planning on being a writer and an English teacher in my spare time.'

'*Was* planning?' he said.

'I don't think I have much of a future now, being an orphan.' What I meant was being a fugitive from the law. Considering the state of things, I didn't know if I'd even get back to high school.

He studied his fingers. I could smell the sharp scent of his sweat. He had patches of honey on his shirt, which were attracting a horde of flies and causing him to swat incessantly.

After a while he said, 'Me neither.'

'You neither *what*?'

'I don't know if I'll have much of a future either.'

'Why not? *You're* not an orphan.'

'No,' he said. 'I'm a Negro.'

I felt embarrassed. 'Well, you could play football for a college team and then be a professional player.'

'Why is it sports is the only thing white people see us being successful at? I don't want to play football,' he said. 'I wanna be a lawyer.'

'That's fine with me,' I said, a little annoyed. 'I've just never heard of a Negro lawyer, that's all. You've got to hear of these things before you can imagine them.'

'Bullshit. You gotta imagine what's never been.'

I closed my eyes. 'All right then, I'm imagining a Negro lawyer. You are a Negro Perry Mason. People are coming to you from all over the state, wrong-accused people, and you get at the truth at the very last minute by tricking the real criminal on the witness stand.'

'Yeah,' he said, laughing. 'I bust their ass with the truth.'

I started calling him Zach the ass-busting lawyer. 'Oh, look who's here, Zach the ass-busting lawyer,' I'd say.

It was about this point Rosaleen started asking me what did I think I was doing—auditioning myself to get adopted by the calendar sisters? She said it was living in a dream world to pretend we had a regular life when there was a manhunt going on, to think we could stay here for ever, to believe I would find out anything worth knowing about my mother.

Every time I shot back, *What's wrong with living in a dream world?* And she'd say, *You have to wake up*.

One afternoon when I was alone in the honey house, June wandered in looking for August. Or so she said. She crossed her arms over her chest. 'So,' she said, 'you've been here—what? Two weeks now?'

How obvious can you get?

'Look, if you want us to leave, me and Rosaleen will be on our way,' I said. 'I'll write my aunt, and she'll send us bus money.'

She raised her eyebrows. 'I thought you didn't remember your aunt's last name, and now you know her name *and* her address.'

'Actually, I knew it all along,' I said. 'I was just hoping for a little time before we had to leave.' It seemed like her face softened some when I said that, but it could've been wishful thinking on my part.

'Heavens to Betsy, what's this talk about you leaving?' said August from the doorway. Neither of us had seen her come in. She gave June a hard look. 'Nobody wants you to leave, Lily, till you're good and ready.'

Standing beside August's desk, I fidgeted with a stack of papers.

June cleared her throat. 'Well, I need to get back and practise,' she said, and breezed out of the door.

August walked over and sat down in her desk chair. 'Lily, you can talk to me. You know that, don't you?'

When I didn't answer, she caught my hand and drew me to her, pulling me right down onto her lap.

I wanted nothing more than to come clean with her. Go pull my bag from under the cot and bring out my mother's things. Produce the black Mary picture and say, *This belonged to my mother, this exact same picture you put on your honey jars. And it has Tiburon, South Carolina, written on the back so I know she must've been here.* I wanted to hold up her photograph and say, *Have you ever seen her? Take your time. Think carefully*.

But I hadn't yet pressed my hand to the black Mary's heart in the parlour, and I was too afraid to say all this without having done at least that. I leaned against August's chest, pushing aside my secret wanting, too afraid she'd say, *No, I never saw this woman in my life*. And that would be that. Not knowing anything at all was better.

I struggled to my feet. 'I guess I'll go help in the kitchen.' I crossed the yard without a glance back.

That night, when the darkness was weighed down with singing crickets and Rosaleen was snoring right along with them, I had myself a good cry. I couldn't even say why. Just everything, I guess. Because I hated lying to August when she was so good to me. Because Rosaleen was probably right about dream worlds. Because I was pretty sure the Virgin Mary was not back there on the peach farm standing in for me the way she'd stood in for Beatrix.

Neil came over most evenings and sat with June in the parlour while the rest of us watched television in the den. During commercials I pretended to go for water and instead crept down the hall, where I tried to make out what June and Neil were saying.

'I'd like you to tell me why not,' I heard Neil say one evening. And June, 'Because I can't.'

'That's not a reason.'

'Well, it's the only one I've got.'

'Look, I'm not gonna wait around for ever,' Neil said.

I was anticipating what June would say to that, when Neil came through the door without warning and caught me pressed against the wall listening. He looked for a second like he might turn me over to June, but he left, banging the front door behind him.

I hightailed it back to the den, but not before I heard the beginnings of a sob in June's throat.

One morning August sent Zach and me six miles out in the country to bring in the last of the supers to be harvested. Zach drove the honey wagon as fast as it would go, which was about thirty miles an hour. The wind whipped my hair and flooded the truck with a new-mown smell.

The roadsides were covered with fresh-picked cotton, blown from the trucks carrying it to the cotton gin in Tiburon. Scattered along the highway, it looked for all the world like snow, which made me wish for a blizzard to come cool things down.

I went off into a daydream about Zach pulling the truck over because he couldn't see to drive for the snow and us having a snowball fight, blasting each other with soft white snow cotton. I imagined us building a snow cave, sleeping with our bodies twined together to get warm, our arms and legs like black and white braids. This last thought shocked my system so bad I shivered.

'You all right?' asked Zach.

'Yeah, why?'

'You're shaking over there.'

'I'm fine. I do that sometimes.'

I turned away and looked out of the window, where there was nothing but fields and now and then a falling-down wooden barn or some old, abandoned coloured house. 'How much further?' I said in a way that suggested the excursion could not be over too soon.

'You upset or something?'

I refused to answer him, glaring instead through the dirty windshield.

When we turned off the highway onto a beat-up dirt road, Zach said we were on property belonging to Mr Clayton Forrest, who kept Black Madonna Honey and beeswax candles in the waiting room of his law office so his customers could buy them. Part of Zach's job was delivering honey and candles to places that sold them on consignment.

'Mr Forrest lets me poke around his law office,' he said.

'Uh-huh.'

'He tells me about the cases he's won.'

We hit a rut and bounced on the seat so hard our heads rammed into the truck roof, which flipped my mood upside-down. I started to laugh. The more my head slammed against the truck, the worse it got, till I was having one big, hilarious seizure. I laughed the way May cried.

At first Zach aimed for the ruts just to hear me, but then he got nervous because I couldn't seem to stop. He cleared his throat and slowed way down till we were bounce-free.

Finally it drained out of me, whatever it was. I remembered the pleasure of fainting that day during the Daughters of Mary meeting and thought now how much I would like to keel over right here in the truck.

I was conscious of Zach's breathing, his shirt pulled across his chest, one arm draped on the steering wheel. The hard, dark look of it. The mystery of his skin.

It was foolish to think some things were beyond happening, even being attracted to Negroes. I'd honestly thought such a thing couldn't happen, the way water could not run uphill or salt could not taste sweet. A law of nature. Maybe it was a simple matter of being attracted to what I couldn't have. Or maybe desire kicked in when it pleased without noticing the rules we lived and died by. *You gotta imagine what's never been*, Zach had said.

He stopped the honey wagon beside a cluster of twenty hives tucked in a thicket of trees. He climbed out and dragged a load of equipment off the back of the truck—helmets, extra supers, fresh brood frames, and the smoker, which he handed me to light. I moved through camphorweed and wild azalea, stepping over fire-ant mounds and swinging the smoker while he lifted the lids off the hives and peered inside.

He moved like a person with a genuine love of bees. I could not believe how gentle and softhearted he could be. One of the frames he lifted out leaked honey the colour of plums.

'It's purple!' I said.

'When the weather turns hot and the flowers dry up, the bees start sucking elderberry. It makes a purple honey. People will pay two dollars a jar for purple honey.'

He dipped his finger into the comb and, lifting my veil, brought it close to my lips. I opened my mouth, let his finger slide in, sucking it clean. The sheerest smile brushed his lips, and heat rushed up my body. He bent towards me. I wanted him to lift back my veil and kiss me, and I knew he wanted to do it, too, by the way he fixed his eyes on mine. We stayed like that while bees swirled around our heads with a sound like sizzling bacon, a sound that no longer registered as danger. Danger, I realised, was a thing you got used to.

But instead of kissing me, he turned to the next hive and went right on with his work. The smoker had gone out. I followed behind him, and neither of us spoke. We stacked the filled supers onto the truck like the cat had our tongues, and neither of us said a word till we were back in the honey truck passing the city-limits sign.

TIBURON POPULATION 6,502
Home of Willifred Marchant

'Who is Willifred Marchant?' I said, desperate to break the silence and get things back to normal.

'You mean you've never heard of Willifred Marchant?' he said. 'She is only a world-famous writer who wrote three Pulitzer Prize books about the deciduous trees of South Carolina.'

I giggled. 'They didn't win any Pulitzer Prizes.'

'You better shut your mouth, because in Tiburon Willifred Marchant's books are way up there with the Bible. We have an official Willifred Marchant Day every year, and she always comes wearing a big straw hat and carrying a basket of rose petals, which she tosses to the children.'

'She does not,' I said.

'Oh, yes. Miss Willie is very weird.'

'Deciduous trees are an interesting topic, I guess. But I myself would rather write about people.'

'Oh, that's right, I forgot,' he said. 'You're planning on being a writer.'

'You act like you don't believe I can do it.'

'I didn't say that.'

'You implied it.'

'What are you talking about? I did not.'

I turned to concentrate on things beyond the window. Zach crossed the intersection. I could feel his eyes bore into the back of my head.

'You mad at me?' he said.

I meant to say, *Yes, I most certainly am, because you think I will never amount to anything*. But what came out of my mouth was something else, and it was embarrassingly stupid. 'I will never throw rose petals to anybody,' I said, and then I broke down, the kind of crying where you're sucking air and making heaving sounds like a person drowning.

Zach pulled over on the side of the road, saying, 'Holy moly. What's the matter?' He wrapped one arm round me and pulled me across the seat to him.

I'd thought the whole thing was about my lost future, the one Mrs Henry encouraged me to believe in by plying me with books and reading lists and talk about scholarships to Columbia College, but sitting there close to Zach, I knew I was crying because he had that one-side dimple I loved, because every time I looked at him I got a hot, funny feeling that circulated from my waist to my kneecaps, because I'd been going along being my normal self and the next thing I knew I'd passed into a place of desperation. I was crying, I realised, for Zach.

I laid my head on his shoulder and wondered how he could stand me. In one short morning I had exhibited insane laughter, hidden lust, pissy behaviour, self-pity and hysterical crying. If I'd been *trying* to show him my worst sides, I could not have done a better job than this.

He gave me a squeeze and spoke into my hair. 'It's gonna be all right. You're gonna be a fine writer one day.' I saw him glance behind us, then across the road. 'Now, you go back over to your side of the truck and wipe your face,' he said, and handed me a rag that smelt like gasoline.

When we got to the honey house, it was deserted except for Rosaleen, who was gathering up her clothes so she could move up to May's room. I'd been gone two slim hours, and our whole living arrangement had been overturned.

'How come you get to sleep over there?' I asked her.

''Cause May gets scared at night by herself.'

Rosaleen was going to sleep in the extra twin bed, get the bottom drawer of May's dresser, and have the bathroom at her fingertips.

'I can't believe you're leaving me over here by myself!' I cried.

Zach grabbed the hand truck and wheeled it out as fast as he could to start unloading the supers from the honey wagon. I think he'd had enough female emotion for the time being.

'I'm not leaving you. I'm getting a mattress,' she said, and dropped her toothbrush and the Red Rose snuff into her pocket.

I crossed my arms over my blouse that was still damp from all the crying I'd been doing. 'Fine then, go on. I don't care.'

'Lily, that cot is bad on my back. And if you ain't noticed, the legs on it are all bent out of whack now. Another week and it's gonna collapse on the floor. You'll be fine without me.'

My chest closed up. Fine without her. Was she out of her mind?

'I don't wanna wake up from the dream world,' I said, and mid-sentence my voice cracked, and the words twisted in my mouth.

She sat on the cot and pulled me down beside her. 'I know you don't, but I'll be here when you do. I might sleep up there in May's room, but I'm not going anywhere.'

She patted my knee like old times. She patted, and neither of us said anything. We could've been back in the policeman's car riding to jail for how I felt. Like I would not exist without her patting hand.

I followed Rosaleen as she carried her few things over to the pink house, intending to inspect her new room. We climbed the steps onto the porch. August sat on the porch swing that was suspended from two chains in the ceiling. She was rocking back and forth, having her orangeade break and reading her new book, which she'd got from the bookmobile. I turned my head to read the title. *Jane Eyre*.

May was on the other side of the porch running clothes through the rubber rollers on the wringer washing machine, which they kept out on the porch because there was no room in the kitchen. She smiled as Rosaleen went by with her things.

'Are you OK with Rosaleen moving over here?' August said, propping the book on her stomach.

'I guess so.'

'May will sleep better with Rosaleen in there,' she said. 'Won't you, May?' I glanced over at May, but she didn't seem to hear over the washer.

Suddenly the last thing I wanted was to follow Rosaleen and watch her tuck her clothes into May's dresser. I looked at August's book.

'What are you reading about?' I asked.

'It's about a girl whose mother died when she was little,' she said. Then she looked at me in a way that made my stomach tip over, the same way it'd tipped over when she'd told me about Beatrix.

'What happens to the girl?' I asked, trying to make my voice steady.

'I've only just started the book,' she said. 'But right now she's feeling lost and sad.'

I turned and looked out towards the garden, where June and Neil were picking tomatoes. I stared at them while the crank on the washer squeaked. *She knows*, I thought. *She knows who I am*.

When I glanced back at August, she was still staring at me, like she expected me to say something.

'Well, I guess I'll go see Rosaleen's new bed,' I said.

August picked up her book, and that was that. The moment passed, and so did the feeling that she knew who I was. I mean, it didn't make sense: how could August Boatwright know anything about me?

It was around this time that June and Neil started a fight out in the tomato garden. June shouted something, and he shouted back.

'Uh-oh,' said August. She put down the book and stood up.

'Why can't you just let it be?' yelled June. 'Why does it always come back to this? Get this through your head: I'm not getting married. Not yesterday, not today, not next year!'

'What are you scared of?' Neil said.

'For your information, I'm not scared of anything.'

'Well, then, you're the most selfish bitch I ever met,' he said, and started walking towards his car.

'Oh, Lord,' said August under her breath.

'How dare you call me that!' said June. 'You come back here. Don't you walk off when I'm talking to you!'

Neil kept right on walking. Zach, I noticed, had stopped loading supers onto the hand truck and was watching, shaking his head.

'If you leave now, don't plan on coming back!' she yelled.

Neil climbed into his car, and suddenly June came running with tomatoes in her hands. She reared back and threw one, *smat*! right into the windshield. The second one landed on the door handle.

'Don't come back!' she yelled as Neil drove off. Trailing tomato juice.

May sank down onto the floor, crying and looking so hurt inside I could almost see soft, red places up under her rib bones. August and I walked her out to her wall, and for the umpteenth time she wrote *June and Neil* on a scrap of paper and wedged it between the rocks.

We spent the rest of the day working on the supers that me and Zach had hauled in. Stacked six high, they made a miniature skyline all through the honey house. We ran twelve loads through the whole system. August didn't like her honey to sit around too long, because the flavour got lost. We had two days to finish it up, she said. At least we didn't have to store the honey in a special hot room to keep it from crystallising, because every room we had was hot. Carolina heat turned out to be good for something.

Just when I thought we were done for the day and could go and eat dinner, August had us load up the empty supers and haul them out to the woods so the bees could come and do the big cleanup. She would not store her supers for the winter until the bees had sucked out the last remaining bits of honey from the combs. She said that was because honey remnants attracted roaches. But I'm sure it was because she loved throwing a little end-of-the-year party for her bees.

The whole time we worked, I marvelled at how mixed up people got when it came to love. I myself, for instance. It seemed like I was now thinking of Zach forty minutes out of every hour. Zach, who was an impossibility. That's what I told myself five hundred times: impossibility.

That night it felt strange to be in the honey house by myself. I missed Rosaleen's snoring the way you'd miss the sound of ocean waves after you've got used to sleeping with them. I didn't realise how it had comforted me. Quietness has a strange, spongy hum that can nearly break your eardrums.

I didn't know if it was the emptiness, the stifling heat or the fact it was only nine o'clock, but I couldn't settle into sleep despite how tired I was. I peeled off my top and my underwear and lay on the damp sheets. I liked the feel of nudeness. It was a smooth, oiled feeling on the sheets. A set-free feeling.

I imagined then that I heard a car pull into the driveway. I imagined it was Zach, and the thought of him moving in the night just outside the honey house caused my breath to speed up.

I rose and slipped across to the wall mirror. Pearled light poured through the open window behind me, moulding to my skin, giving me a halo, not just around my head but across my shoulders, along my ribs and thighs. I studied the effect, cupping my hands under my breasts, studying my nipples, the thin curves of my waist, every soft and glowing turn. It was the first time I'd felt like more than a scraggly girl.

I closed my eyes, and the balloon full of craving finally burst open in my chest, and when it did, wouldn't you know—one minute I was dreaming of Zach and the next I was hungering for my mother, imagining her calling my name, saying, *Lily, girl. You are my flower*.

When I turned to the window, there was no one there. Not that I had expected there would be.

Two days later, after we had run ourselves into the ground harvesting the rest of the honey, Zach showed up with the prettiest notebook—green with rosebuds on the cover. He met me coming out of the pink house. 'This is for you,' he said. 'So you can start on your writing.'

That's when I knew I would never find a better friend than Zachary Taylor. I threw my arms round him and leaned into his chest. He made a sound like *Whoa*, but after a second his arms folded round me, and we stayed like that, in a true embrace. He moved his hands up and down my back, till I was almost dizzy.

Finally he unwound my arms and said, 'Lily, I like you better than any girl I've ever known, but you have to understand, there are people who would kill boys like me for even looking at girls like you.'

I couldn't restrain myself from touching his face, the place where his dimple caved into his skin. 'I'm sorry,' I said.

'Yeah. Me, too,' he said.

For days I carried the notebook everywhere. I wrote constantly. A made-up story about Rosaleen losing eighty-five pounds, looking so sleek nobody could pick her out of a police lineup. One about August driving a honeymobile around, similar to the bookmobile, only she had jars of honey to dispense instead of books. My favourite, though, was one about Zach becoming the ass-busting lawyer and getting his own television show like Perry Mason. I read it to him during lunch one day, and he listened better than a child at story hour.

'Move over Willifred Marchant,' was all he said.

CHAPTER SIX

AUGUST TORE THE PAGE for July from the wall calendar by her desk in the honey house. It was still July for five more days, but I figured it was a case of her wanting it over with so she could start into August, her special month. Like June was June's month and May belonged to May.

August had explained to me how when they were children and their special month came round, their mother excused them from chores and let them eat all their favourite foods and stay up an hour later at night doing whatever their heart desired. August said her heart had desired to read books, so the whole month she got to prop on the sofa in the quiet of the living room reading after her sisters went to bed.

After hearing this, I'd spent a good amount of time trying to think up which month I would have liked to have been named for. I picked October, as it is a golden month with better-than-average weather, and my initials would be O.O. for October Owens, which would make an interesting monogram. I pictured myself eating three-tiered chocolate cake for breakfast throughout the entire month, staying up an hour after bedtime writing high-calibre stories and poems.

I looked over at August, who stood by her desk with the July calendar page in her hand. She wore her white dress with the lime-green scarf tied on her belt, just like she was wearing the first day I showed up. She hummed their song: 'Place a beehive on my grave and let the honey soak through.' I was thinking what a good, fine mother she must've had.

'Come on, Lily,' she said. 'We've got all these jars of honey to paste labels on, and it's just me and you.'

Zach was spending the day delivering honey all over town and picking up money from the previous month's sales. 'Honey money', Zach called it. Even though the big honey flow was over, the bees were still out there sucking nectar. Zach said August's honey brought fifty cents a pound. I figured she must be dripping in honey money. I didn't see why she wasn't living in a hot pink mansion somewhere.

August opened a box containing the new shipment of Black Madonna labels, then reached inside for them. Next she pulled a fat envelope from her desk drawer and poured out dozens of a smaller label with printed letters: BLACK MADONNA HONEY—Tiburon, South Carolina. I was supposed to swipe the backs of both labels with a wet sponge and hand them to August to position on the jars, but I paused a minute to take in the Black Madonna's picture, which I'd studied so many times glued onto my mother's little block of wood. It always caused a tiny jump in my chest, thinking that my own mother had stared at this same picture.

I hated to imagine where I might have ended up if I hadn't seen the Black Madonna's picture that day in the Frogmore Stew General Store and Restaurant. Probably sleeping on creek banks all over South Carolina. Drinking pond water with the cows.

'I hope you don't take this the wrong way,' I said. 'But I never thought of the Virgin Mary being coloured till I saw this picture.'

'A dark-faced Mary is not as unusual as you think,' August said. 'There are hundreds of them over in Europe, places like France and Spain. The one we put on our honey is old as the hills. She's the Black Madonna of Breznichar in Bohemia.'

'How did you learn about all that?' I asked.

She rested her hands and smiled, like this had dredged up a sweet, long-lost memory. 'I guess it started with my mother's prayer cards. She used to collect them, the way good Catholics did back then—you know, those cards with pictures of saints on them. She'd trade for them like little boys traded baseball cards.' August let out a big laugh at that. 'I bet she had a dozen Black Madonna cards. I used to love to play with her cards, especially the Black Madonnas. Then, when I went off to school, I read everything I could about them. That's how I found out about the Black Madonna of Breznichar in Bohemia.'

I tried to say Breznichar, but it didn't come out right. 'Well, I can't say her name, but I *love* her picture.' I swiped the back of the label and watched August fix it on the jar, then fasten the second label beneath it.

'What else do you love, Lily?'

No one had ever asked me this before. What did I love? I wanted to say I loved the picture of my mother, leaning against the car with her hair looking just like mine, plus her gloves and her picture of the black Mary with the unpronounceable name, but I had to swallow that back.

I said, 'Well, I love Rosaleen, and I love writing stories and poems.' After that, I really had to think. 'This may be silly, but after school I love Coca-Cola with salted peanuts poured in the bottle. And I love the colour blue—bright blue like the hat May had on at the Daughters of Mary meeting. And since coming here, I've learned to love bees and honey.' I wanted to add, *And* you, *I love* you, but I felt too awkward.

'Did you know there are thirty-two names for love in one of the Eskimo languages?' August said. 'We just have this one. We're so limited; you have to use the same word for loving Rosaleen as you do for loving a Coke with peanuts. Isn't it a shame we don't have more ways to say it?'

I nodded, wondering where was the limit of her knowing things. Probably one of those books she'd read after bedtime during the month of August had been about Eskimos.

'I guess we'll just have to invent more ways to say it,' she said. Then she smiled. 'Do you know I love peanuts in my Coke, too? And blue is my favourite colour?'

You know that saying, 'Birds of a feather flock together'? That's how I felt.

We were working on the jars of tupelo-tree honey, which Zach and I had gathered out there on Clayton Forrest's land, plus a few jars of purple honey from the hive where the bees had struck it rich on elderberries. It was a nice colour coordination the way the Bohemian Madonna's skin was set off by the golds in the honey. Unfortunately, the purple honey didn't do a whole lot for her.

'How come you put the Black Madonna on your honey?' I asked. I'd been curious about this from day one.

August grew still, looking into the distance like she'd gone in search of the answer and that finding it had been the bonus of the day. 'I wish you could've seen the Daughters of Mary the first time they laid eyes on this label. Because when they looked at her, it occurred to them for the first time in their lives that what's divine can come in dark skin. You see, everybody needs a God who looks like them, Lily.'

I only wished I'd been there when the Daughters of Mary had made this big discovery. I pictured them whooping it up in their glorious hats. Feathers flying.

'So how did you get the black Mary statue in the parlour?' I asked.

'I can't say, exactly. I only know she came into the family at some point. You remember the story about Obadiah taking the statue to the praise house, and how the slaves believed it was Mary?'

I nodded.

'Well,' August said, going right on with her pasting, 'you know, she's really just the figurehead off an old ship, but the people needed comfort and rescue, so when they looked at it, they saw Mary, and so the spirit of Mary took it over. Really, her spirit is everywhere, Lily, just everywhere. Inside rocks and trees and even people, but sometimes it will get concentrated in certain places and just beam out at you in a special way.'

I had never thought of it like that, and it gave me a shocked feeling, like maybe I had no idea what kind of world I was actually living in. I started thinking about the world loaded with disguised Marys sitting around all over the place and hidden red hearts tucked about that people could rub and touch, only we didn't recognise them.

August arranged the jars she'd labelled so far in a cardboard box and set it on the floor, then dragged out more jars. 'I'm just trying to explain to you why the people took such care with Our Lady of Chains, passing her one generation to the next. The best we can figure, some time after the Civil War she came into the possession of my grandmother's people.

'When I was younger than you, me and June and May—and April, too, because she was still alive then—all of us would visit our grandmother for the summer. We'd sit on the rug in the parlour, and Big Mama—that's what we called her—would tell us the story. When she finished, May would say, "Big Mama, tell it again," and she'd repeat the whole thing. I swear, if you listen to my chest with a stethoscope, what you'd hear is that story going on and on in my Big Mama's voice.'

I was so caught up in what August was saying I had stopped wetting labels. I was wishing I had a story like that one inside me, so loud you could pick it up on a stethoscope, and not the story I did have about ending my mother's life and sort of ending my own at the same time.

'You can wet the labels and listen,' August said, and smiled. 'So, after Big Mama died, Our Lady of Chains was passed to my mother. She stayed in Mother's bedroom. My father hated her being in there. He wanted to get rid of the statue, but Mother said, "If she goes, I go." I think the statue was the reason Mother became a Catholic, so she could kneel down before her and not feel like she was doing anything peculiar. We would find her in there talking to Our Lady like they were two neighbours having iced tea. Mother would tease Our Lady; she'd say, "You know what? You should've had a girl instead!"'

August set down the jar she was working on, and there was a mix of sorrow and amusement and longing across her face, and I thought, *She is missing her mother*.

I stopped wetting the labels, not wanting to get ahead of her. When she picked up the jar again, I said, 'Did you grow up in this house?'

She shook her head. 'No, this is where I spent my summers,' she said. 'You see, the house belonged to my grandparents, and all this property around it. Big Mama kept bees, too, right out there in the same spot they're in today. Nobody around here had ever seen a lady beekeeper till her. She liked to tell everybody that women made the best beekeepers, ''cause they have a special ability built into them to love creatures that sting. "It comes from years of loving children and husbands," she'd say.' August laughed, and so did I.

'Was your Big Mama the one who taught you to keep bees?'

August took off her glasses and cleaned them on the scarf at her waist. 'She taught me lots more about bees than just how to keep them. She used to tell me one tall bee tale after another.'

I perked up. 'Tell me one,' I said.

August thumped her finger on her forehead like she was trying to tap one of them off some shelf in her head. Then her eyes lit up, and she said, 'Well, one time Big Mama told me she went out to the hives on Christmas Eve and heard the bees singing the words of the Christmas story right out of the Gospel of Luke.' August started to sing then in a humming sort of way, '"Mary brought forth her firstborn child and wrapped him in swaddling clothes and laid him in the manger."'

I giggled. 'Do you think that really happened?'

'Well, yes and no,' she said. 'Some things happen in a literal way, Lily. And then other things, like this one, happen in a not-literal way, but they still happen. Do you know what I mean?'

I didn't have a clue. 'Not really,' I said.

'What I mean is that the bees weren't *really* singing the words from Luke, but still, if you have the right kind of ears, you can listen to a hive and hear the Christmas story inside yourself. You can hear silent things on the other side of the everyday world. Big Mama had those kind of ears. My mother didn't. I think it skipped a generation.'

I was itching to know more about her mother. 'I bet your mother kept bees, too,' I said.

She seemed amused at that. 'Goodness no, she wasn't interested at all. She left here as soon as she could and went to live with a cousin up in

Richmond. Got a job in a hotel laundry. You remember the first day you got here, I told you I grew up in Richmond? Well, that's where my father was from. He was the first coloured dentist in Richmond. He met my mother when she went to see him with a toothache.

'I loved Richmond, but my heart was always right here,' she said. 'Growing up, I couldn't wait to get here and spend the summers, and when Big Mama died, she left all this property to me, June and May. I've been here keeping bees nearly eighteen years now.'

Sunlight gleamed against the honey-house window, flickering now and then with a shifting cloud. We sat in the yellowish quiet for a while and worked without talking. I was afraid I'd tire her out with all my questions. Finally I couldn't hold myself back. I said, 'So what did you do in Virginia before you came here?'

She gave me a teasing look that seemed to say, *My goodness, you sure do wanna know a lot of things*, but then she dived right in, her hands not slowing down one bit pasting labels.

'I studied at a Negro teachers' college in Maryland. June did, too, but it was hard to get a job, since there weren't that many places for Negroes to teach. I ended up working nine years as a housekeeper. Eventually I got a job teaching history. It lasted six years, till we moved down here.'

'What about June?'

She laughed. 'June—you wouldn't catch her keeping house for white people. She went to work at a coloured funeral home, dressing the bodies and doing their hair.'

That seemed like the perfect job for her. It would be easy for her to get along with dead people.

'May said June almost got married one time.'

'That's right. About ten years ago.'

'I was wondering—' I stopped, looking for a way to ask her.

'You were wondering if there was a time when I almost got married.'

'Yeah,' I said. 'I guess I was.'

'I decided against marrying altogether. There were enough restrictions in my life without someone expecting me to wait on him hand and foot. Not that I'm against marrying, Lily. I'm just against how it's set up.'

'Weren't you ever in love?' I asked.

'Being in love and getting married, now, that's two different things. I was in love once, of course I was. Nobody should go through life without falling in love.'

'But you didn't love him enough to marry him?'

She smiled at me. 'I loved him enough,' she said. 'I just loved my freedom more.'

We glued labels till we ran out of jars. Then, for the heck of it, I moistened the back of one more and pressed it onto my T-shirt, in the gully between my breasts.

August looked at the clock, announcing we'd done so good with our time we had a whole hour left before lunch.

'Come on,' she said. 'Let's do bee patrol.'

Though I'd done bee patrol with Zach, I hadn't been back to the hives with August since that first time. I pulled on long cotton trousers that used to be June's, and August's white shirt, which needed the sleeves rolled up about ten turns. Then I placed the jungle helmet on my head, letting the veil fall down over my face.

We walked to the woods beside the pink house with her stories still pulled soft around our shoulders like a shawl.

'There is one thing I don't get,' I said.

'What's that?'

'How come if your favourite colour is blue, you painted your house so pink?'

She laughed. 'That was May's doing. She was with me the day I went to the paint store to pick out the colour. I had a nice tan colour in mind, but May latched on to this sample called Caribbean Pink. She said it made her feel like dancing a Spanish flamenco. I thought, Well, this is the tackiest colour I've ever seen, and we'll have half the town talking about us, but if it can lift May's heart like that, I guess she ought to live inside it.'

'All this time I just figured you liked pink,' I said.

She laughed again. 'You know, some things don't matter that much, Lily. Like the colour of a house. How big is that in the overall scheme of life? But lifting a person's heart—now, *that* matters. The whole problem with people is—'

'They don't know what matters and what doesn't,' I said, filling in her sentence and feeling proud of myself for doing so.

'I was gonna say, The problem is they *know* what matters, but they don't *choose* it. You know how hard that is, Lily? I love May, but it was still so hard to choose Caribbean Pink. The hardest thing on earth is choosing what matters.'

I couldn't locate a stray bee anywhere. The hives looked like an abandoned neighbourhood, the air groggy with heat. You got the impression the bees were inside having a big siesta.

'Where are they?' I said.

August placed her finger to her lips. She lifted off her helmet and laid the side of her face flat against the top of the hive box. 'Come listen,' she whispered.

I removed my hat, tucking it under my arm, and placed my face next to hers so that we were practically nose to nose.

'You hear that?' she said.

A sound rushed up. A perfect hum, high-pitched and swollen.

'They're cooling the hives down,' she said. 'That's the sound of one hundred thousand bee wings fanning the air.'

She closed her eyes and soaked it in the way you imagine people at a fancy orchestra concert drinking up highbrow music. We had our ears pressed to a giant music box.

Then the side of my face started to vibrate as if the music had rushed into my pores. When we stood back up, my cheek prickled and itched.

'You were listening to bee air-conditioning,' August said. 'Most people don't have any idea about all the complicated life going on inside a hive. Bees have a secret life we don't know anything about.'

I loved the idea of bees having a secret life, just like the one I was living.

'What other secrets have they got?' I wanted to know.

'Well, for instance, every bee has its role to play.'

She went through the whole thing. The nest builders were the ones that drew the comb. Field bees had good navigation skills and tireless hearts, going out to gather nectar and pollen. There was a group called mortician bees whose job it was to rake the dead bees out of the hive and keep everything clean. Nurse bees had a gift for nurturing, and they fed all the baby bees. They were probably the self-sacrificing group, like the women at church socials who said, 'No, you take the chicken breast. I'm just fine with the neck and gizzard, really.' The only males were the drones who sat around waiting to mate with the queen.

'And of course,' August said, 'there's the queen and her attendants.'

'She has attendants?'

'Oh, yes, like ladies-in-waiting. They feed her, bathe her, keep her warm or cool—whatever's needed. You can see them always circled around her, fussing over her. I've even seen them caress her.' August returned her helmet to her head. 'I guess I'd want comfort, too, if I did nothing but lay eggs all day long, week in and week out.'

'That's all she does—lay eggs?'

'Egg laying is the main thing, Lily. She's the mother of every bee in the hive, and they all depend on her to keep it going. Whatever their job is, they know the queen is their mother. She's the mother of thousands.'

The mother of thousands.

I put on my helmet as August lifted the lid. The way the bees poured out, rushing up in spirals of chaos and noise, caused me to jump.

'Don't move an inch,' said August. 'And remember, don't be scared.'

A bee flew straight at my forehead, collided with the net, and bumped against my skin.

'She's giving you a little warning,' August said. 'When they bump your forehead, they're saying, *I've got my eye on you, so you be careful*. Send them love and everything will be fine.'

I love you, I love you, I said in my head. *I LOVE YOU*. I tried to say it thirty-two ways.

August pulled out the brood frames not even wearing her gloves. While she worked, inspecting the frames, looking for wax buildup on the comb, the bees spun round us, gathering strength till they made soft wind on our faces. It reminded me of the way the bees had flown out of my bedroom walls, stranding me at the centre of a bee whirlwind.

The bees began to light on my shoulders the ways birds sit on telephone wires. They sat along my arms, speckled the bee veil so I could scarcely see through it. *I love you. I love you.*

My breath came faster, and something coiled round my chest and squeezed tighter and tighter, until suddenly, like somebody had snapped off the panic switch, I felt myself go limp. My mind became unnaturally calm, as if part of me had lifted right up out of my body and was sitting watching the spectacle from a safe distance. The other part of me danced with the bees. I wasn't moving a lick, but in my mind I was spinning through the air with them.

I sort of forgot where I was. With my eyes closed, I slowly raised my arms, weaving them through the bees, until I stood with them stretched out from my sides in a dreamy place I'd never been before, somewhere that didn't rub too close against life. Lost in the bees, I felt dropped into a field of enchanted clover that made me immune to everything, as if August had doused me with the bee smoker and quietened me down.

Then, without warning, all the immunity wore off, and I felt the hollow, spooned-out space between my navel and breastbone begin to ache. The motherless place. I could see my mother in the closet, the stuck window, the suitcase on the floor. I heard the shouting, then the explosion. I almost doubled over. I lowered my arms, but I didn't open my eyes. How could I live the whole rest of my life knowing these things? What could I ever do that would make them go away? How come we couldn't go back and fix the bad things we did?

But here, surrounded by stinging bees on all sides and the motherless place throbbing away, it felt like the queen's attendants were out here in a frenzy of love, caressing me in a thousand places. *Look who's here, it's*

Lily. She is so weary and lost. Come on, bee sisters. I was the stamen in the middle of a twirling flower. The centre of all their comforting.

'Lily . . . Lily.' My name came across the blue distances. '*Lily!*'

I opened my eyes. August stared through her spectacles. The bees had shaken the pollen dust off their feet and were starting to settle back into the hive. I could see tiny grains of it drifting in the air.

'Are you OK?' August said.

I nodded. Was I? I had no idea.

'You know, don't you, that the two of us need to have a good talk. And this time not about me. About you.'

I wished I could just bump her forehead with a warning like the bees, tap it with my finger. *I got my eye on you. Be careful. Don't go any further*.

'I suppose,' I answered.

'What about right now?'

'Not right now.'

'But, Lily—'

'I'm starved,' I said. 'I think I'll go on back to the house and see if lunch is ready.'

I didn't wait for her to speak. Walking to the pink house, I could almost see the end of the line. I touched the place on my shirt where I'd stuck the black Mary. She was starting to come unglued.

The whole house smelt like fried okra. Rosaleen was setting the table in the kitchen while May dipped down in the grease and brought up the golden brown kernels. I didn't know what had brought on the okra, since it was usually bologna sandwiches and more bologna sandwiches.

May had not had a crying bout since June's tomato-throwing fit, and we were all holding our breath. After going this long, I worried that even something as simple as burnt okra might send her over the edge.

I said I was hungry, and Rosaleen said to hold my wild horses. Her lower lip was plumped out with Red Rose snuff. The smell followed her round the kitchen: a combination of allspice, fresh earth and rotten leaves. Between the okra and the snuff I could not get a decent breath. Rosaleen walked across the back porch, leaned out the door, and spat a tiny jet stream across the hydrangeas.

Zach shuffled into the kitchen behind August.

'My, my. Okra and pork chops for lunch. What's this about?' August asked May.

May sidled over to her and said in a low voice, 'It has been five days since I've been to the wall,' and I could see how proud of this fact she was, how she wanted to believe her days of hysterical crying were behind her, how this okra lunch was a celebration.

August smiled at her. 'Five days, really? Well, that deserves a feast,' she said. And May, she beamed.

Zach plopped down in a chair.

'Did you finish delivering the honey?' August asked him.

'Everywhere but Mr Clayton's law office,' he said. He was fidgeting with everything in sight. First the place mat, then a loose thread on his shirt. Like he was bursting to say something.

August looked him over. 'You got something on your mind?'

'You won't believe what people downtown are saying,' he said. 'They're saying Jack Palance is coming to Tiburon this weekend and bringing a coloured woman with him.'

We all stopped what we were doing and looked at each other.

'Who's Jack Palance?' Rosaleen asked.

'He's a movie star,' said Zach.

June snorted, 'Well, how dumb is *that*? What would a movie star be doing in Tiburon?'

Zach shrugged. 'They say his sister lives here, and he's coming to visit and intends to take this coloured woman to the movie theatre this Friday. Not to the balcony, but downstairs in the white section.'

August turned to May. 'Why don't you go out to the garden and pick some fresh tomatoes to go with our lunch?' she said, then waited till May was out of the door. 'Are people stirred up about this?' she asked Zach. Her eyes looked serious.

'Yes, ma'am,' he said. 'In Garret's Hardware there were white men talking about standing guard outside the theatre.'

'Lord, here we go,' said Rosaleen.

June made a *pffff* sound with her lips while August shook her head, and it washed over me just how much importance the world had ascribed to skin pigment. Ever since school let out this summer, it had been skin pigment every livelong day. In Sylvan we'd had a rumour about a busload of people from New York City showing up to integrate the city pool. Talk about a panic. We had a citywide emergency on our hands, as there is no greater affliction for the southern mind than people up north coming down to fix our way of life. After that was the whole mess with the men at the Esso station. It seemed to me it would have been better if God had deleted skin pigment altogether.

As May came back into the kitchen, August said, 'Let's enjoy our meal,' which meant Jack Palance was not a lunch topic.

May plopped down three big tomatoes, and while she and Rosaleen sliced them up, August went to the den and put a Nat King Cole record on the player. She was crazy about Nat King Cole, and she returned, with the volume up, frowning in that way people do when they bite into something and it tastes so delicious they appear to be in pain over it. June turned up her nose. She only cared for Beethoven and that whole group. She went and turned the sound down. 'I can't think,' she said.

August said, 'You think too much. It would do you a world of good to stop thinking and just go with your feelings once in a blue moon.'

June said she would take her lunch in her room, thank you.

That was just as well, because I'd been looking at the tomatoes May and Rosaleen were slicing and rehearsing in my head how I would say, *So will you have some tomatoes, June?* Now I would be saved from that.

We ate till we were tired out from eating. Zach pushed back from the table, saying he was heading to Clayton Forrest's office to leave a dozen jars of honey.

'Can I go?' I asked.

August knocked over her sweet tea, a thing so unlike her. You did not associate spills with August. With May, for sure, but not August. Tea ran across the table and onto the floor. I thought this might set May off, the tragedy of a spilt drink. But she only got up, humming 'Oh! Susanna' without real urgency, and grabbed a towel.

'I don't know, Lily,' August said.

'Please.' All I really wanted was some time with Zach and to expand my world by visiting the office of a real-life lawyer.

'Well, all right,' she said.

The office was one block off Main Street, where Rosaleen and I had paraded into town that Sunday more than three weeks ago. It didn't look like my idea of a law office. The whole operation was really a large house, white with black shutters and a wraparound porch with big rocking chairs. A sign on the lawn said CLAYTON FORREST, ATTORNEY AT LAW.

His secretary was a white lady who looked about eighty years old. She sat at a desk in the reception area, putting on fire-red lipstick. Her hair was permed into tight curls that had a faint blue cast.

'Hi, Miss Lacy,' Zach said. 'I brought more honey.'

She worked the lipstick back into the tube, looking mildly annoyed. 'More honey,' she said, shaking her head. She let out an overdone sigh and reached into a drawer. 'The money for the last batch is in here.' She dropped an envelope onto the desk.

She looked me over. 'You're new.'

'I'm Lily,' I said.

'She's staying with August,' Zach explained.

'You're staying in her *house*?' she said.

'Yes, ma'am, I'm staying there.'

'Well, I'll be,' she said. She stood up. 'I've got an appointment at the dentist. Put the jars over there on the table.'

I pictured her whispering the news to all the people in the waiting room who were about to get their cavities drilled. 'This white girl, Lily, is staying with the Boatwright sisters. Doesn't that seem strange to you?'

As she left, Mr Forrest came out of his office. He had sandy hair, and bushy eyebrows that curled towards his blue eyes, and smile crinkles in his face that signalled a good person. So good that apparently he couldn't bring himself to get rid of Miss Lacy.

He looked at me. 'And who would this pretty young lady be?'

'Lily uh—' I couldn't remember what last name I was using. I think it was because he'd referred to me as pretty, which had been a shock to my system. 'Just Lily.' I stood there looking gawky, one foot tucked behind the other. 'I'm staying with August till I go live with my aunt in Virginia.'

'How nice. August is a good friend of mine,' he said. 'I hope you're enjoying your stay?'

'Yes, sir. Very much.'

'What case are you working on?' asked Zach, stuffing the envelope of honey money into his pocket and setting the box of jars on the side table by the window. It had a framed HONEY FOR SALE sign on it.

'Run-of-the-mill stuff. Deeds, wills. I got something for you, though. Come on back to the office and I'll show you.'

'I'll just wait out here and arrange the honey,' I said, hating to intrude.

'You sure? You're welcome to come, too.'

'I'm sure. I like it out here.'

They disappeared down a hallway. I heard a door close. A car horn on the street. The blast of the window air conditioner that dripped water into a dog bowl on the floor. I stacked the jars in a pyramid. Seven on bottom, four in the middle, and one on top, but it looked misshapen, so I took it apart and settled for plain rows.

I went over and inspected the pictures that covered one wall. First was a diploma from the University of South Carolina and then another one from Duke University. Next was a picture of Mr Forrest on a boat, holding a fish about my size. After that, Mr Forrest shaking hands with Bobby Kennedy. Last, Mr Forrest and a small blonde-headed girl, standing in the ocean. She was jumping over a wave. The spray made a blue fan behind her, a peacock tail of water, and he was helping her, lifting her over it, smiling down on her. I bet he knew her favourite colour, what she ate for afternoon snacks, everything she loved.

I went and sat on one of the two red sofas in the room. Williams. My made-up last name finally came to me. I counted the floorboards from the desk to the front door. Fifteen. Closing my eyes, I pictured the ocean, the white froth on it, light scattering everywhere. I saw myself jumping a wave. T. Ray held my hand, pulling me up and over. I had to concentrate so hard to make this happen.

Thirty-two names for love.

Was it unthinkable he could speak one of them to me, even the one reserved for lesser things like peanuts in your Coke? Was it so out of the question that T. Ray knew I loved the colour blue? What if he was home missing me, saying, '*Why oh why didn't I love her better*?'

Miss Lacy's telephone sat right there on her desk. I picked up the receiver and dialled 0 for operator. 'I am making a collect call,' I told her, and gave her the number. Almost faster than I would've believed, I heard the phone in my house ringing. I stared down the hallway at the closed door and counted the rings. Three, four, five, six.

'Hello.' His voice caused my stomach to pitch into my throat. I was unprepared for the way it buckled my knees. I had to sit down in Miss Lacy's chair spraddle-legged.

'I have a collect call from Lily Owens,' the operator said. 'Will you accept the charge?'

'You're goddamn right I'll accept it,' he said. Then he launched right in. 'Lily, where the hell are you?'

I had to hold the phone from my eardrum for fear of him rupturing it. 'T. Ray, I'm sorry I had to leave, but—'

'You tell me where you are right now, do you hear me? Do you have any idea the trouble you're in? Busting Rosaleen out of the hospital—holy shit, what were you thinking?'

'I was only—'

'I'll tell you what you were. You were a goddamn fool who went looking for trouble and found it. I've had to stop everything and search for you all over creation, and meanwhile the peaches have gone to hell.'

'Well, quit yelling, all right? I said I was sorry.'

'Your sorry ain't worth a shitload of peaches, Lily. I swear to God—'

'I called because I was just wondering something.' I squeezed the arm of the chair till my knuckles hurt. 'I was wondering, do you know what my favourite colour is?'

'Jesus Christ. What are you talking about? You tell me where you are.'

'I said, do you know what my favourite colour is?'

'I know one thing, and that's I'm gonna find you, Lily, and when I do, I'm gonna tear your behind to pieces—'

I lowered the receiver back to the cradle and sat on the sofa again. I sat in the brightness of the afternoon and watched the hem of light under the venetian blinds. I told myself, *Don't you cry. Don't you dare cry. So what if he doesn't know the colour you love best? So what?*

Zach returned holding a big brown book that looked half mouldy with age. 'Look what Mr Clayton gave me,' he said, and you would have thought it was a six-pound baby he'd birthed by the proud look of him.

He turned it over so I could read the binding. *South Carolina Legal Reports 1889*. Zach rubbed his hand across the front, and little flecks of it fell off onto the floor. 'I'm starting my law library.'

'That's nice,' I said.

Mr Forrest stepped closer, staring at me with such intensity I thought I must need to wipe my nose.

'Zach says you're from Spartanburg County, that your parents both died?'

'Yes, sir.' One thing I didn't want was to get on the witness stand right here in his office and have him fire lawyer questions at me. An hour from now Rosaleen and I could be packing for prison.

'What brings you—?'

'I really do need to get back.' I put my hand low on my stomach. 'I'm having a little female trouble.' I tried to look mysterious, troubled by internal things they could not imagine and did not want to. It had been my experience for nearly a year that uttering the words 'female trouble' could get me into places I wanted to go and out of places I didn't.

'Oh,' said Zach. 'Well, let's go.'

'Nice to meet you, Mr Forrest,' I said. Clutching my abdomen. A small wince. Walking slowly to the door.

'Believe me, Lily,' he said, calling after me, 'the pleasure was all mine.'

That night, when the pink house was sound asleep, I came creeping in, needing the bathroom. I never worried about finding my way, as August left a trail of night-lights on from the kitchen to the bathroom.

I had come barefoot, collecting dew on the soles of my feet. Sitting on the toilet, trying to pee quietly, I could see crepe myrtle petals stuck to my toes. Over my head, Rosaleen's snores sifted through the ceiling. It is always a relief to empty your bladder. Better than sex, Rosaleen said. As good as it felt, though, I sincerely hoped she was wrong.

I headed towards the kitchen, but then something made me turn around; your guess is as good as mine. I walked in the opposite direction to the parlour. Stepping inside, I heard a sigh so deep and satisfying that for a moment I didn't realise it had come from my own lungs.

The candle in the red glass beside the Mary statue still burned, looking like a tiny red heart in a cave of darkness, pulsing out light to the world. August kept it going night and day.

Our Lady of Chains looked so different late at night, her face older and darker, her fist bigger than I remembered. I wondered about all the places she'd travelled out there on the waters of the world, all the sad things that had been whispered to her, the things she'd endured.

Sometimes, after we'd done our prayers, I could not remember how to cross myself right, getting it mixed up like you would expect any Baptist-raised person to do. Whenever that happened, I just put my hand over my heart, and that's what happened now—my hand just went automatically to my heart and stayed there.

I told her, *Fix me, please fix me. Help me know what to do. Forgive me. Is my mother all right up there with God? Don't let them find us. If they find us, don't let them take me back, keep Rosaleen from being killed. Let June love me. Let T. Ray love me. Help me stop lying. Make the world better. Take the meanness out of people's hearts.*

I moved closer, so now I could see the heart on her chest. In my mind I heard the bees fanning their wings down in the dark music box. I remembered August's voice the first time she told the story of Our Lady of Chains. *Send them rescue, send them consolation, send them freedom.*

I reached out and traced black Mary's heart with my finger. I stood with the petals on my toes and pressed my palm hard against her heart.

I live in a hive of darkness, and you are my mother, I told her. *You are the mother of thousands.*

CHAPTER SEVEN

JULY 28 WAS A DAY for the record books. At eight o'clock in the morning it hit 94 degrees, with the ambitious plan of reaching 103 before noon. I woke up with August shaking my shoulder, saying it was gonna be a scorcher, get up, we had to water the bees.

I climbed into the honey wagon with my hair uncombed, with May handing me buttered toast and orange juice through the window and

Rosaleen sticking in Thermoses of water, both of them practically running alongside the truck while August rolled out of the driveway. I felt like the Red Cross springing to action to save the bee queendom.

In the back of the truck August had gallons of sugar water already made up. 'When it gets over a hundred,' she said, 'the flowers dry up and there's no food for the bees. They stay in the hives fanning themselves. Sometimes they just roast.'

I felt like we might roast alive ourselves. You could not touch the door handle for fear of a third-degree burn. Sweat ran between my breasts and sopped my underwear band. August turned on the radio for the weather, but what we heard was how *Ranger 7* had finally landed on the surface of the moon in a place called the Sea of Clouds, how police were looking for the bodies of those three civil rights workers in Mississippi, and the terrible things that had happened in the Gulf of Tonkin. It ended with a story about what was happening 'closer to home', how black people from Tiburon, Florence and Orangeburg were marching today all the way to Columbia asking the governor to enforce the Civil Rights Act. August turned it off. Enough was enough. You cannot fix the whole world.

'I've already watered the hives around the house,' she said. 'Zach is taking care of the hives on the east side of the county. So you and I've got the west side.'

Rescuing bees took us the entire morning. Driving into remote corners of the woods, we would come upon twenty-five beehives up on slats. We lifted the covers and filled the feeders with sugar water. As a bonus, we sprinkled dry sugar on the rims.

I managed to get stung on my wrist while replacing a lid onto a hive box. August scraped out the stinger.

'I was sending them love,' I said, feeling betrayed.

August said, 'Hot weather makes the bees out of sorts, I don't care how much love you send them.' She pulled a small bottle of olive oil and bee pollen from her free pocket and rubbed my skin—her patented remedy. It was something I'd hoped never to test out.

'Count yourself initiated,' she said. 'You can't be a true beekeeper without getting stung.'

A true beekeeper. I would add that to my list of careers. A writer, an English teacher, *and* a beekeeper.

'Do you think I could keep bees one day?' I asked.

August said, 'Didn't you tell me one of the things you loved was bees and honey? If that's so, you'll be a fine beekeeper. Actually, you can be bad at something, Lily, but if you love doing it, that will be enough.'

The sting shot pain all the way to my elbow, causing me to marvel at how much punishment a minuscule creature can inflict. I'm prideful enough to say I didn't complain. After you get stung, you can't get unstung no matter how much you whine about it. I just dived back into the riptide of saving bees.

When we had watered all the hives of Tiburon and sprinkled enough sugar to cause a human being to gain fifty pounds, we drove home hot, hungry, and nearly drowned in our own sweat.

Pulling into the driveway, we found Rosaleen and May sipping sweet tea on the back porch. May said she'd left our lunches in the refrigerator, cold pork-chop sandwiches and slaw. While we ate, we heard June upstairs in her room playing the cello like something had died.

We scoffed down every morsel without talking, then pushed back from the table. We were wondering how to get our tired selves to a standing position when we heard squealing and laughing—the kind you're apt to hear at a school recess. August and I dragged ourselves to the porch to see. And there were May and Rosaleen running through the water sprinkler, barefoot and fully clothed. They had gone berserk.

Rosaleen's dress was sopped and plastered to her body, and May was catching water in the bowl of her skirt and tossing it up across her face. Sunlight hit the hair sheen on her braids and lit them up.

'Well, isn't this the living end?' August said.

When we got out there, Rosaleen picked up the sprinkler and aimed it at us. 'You come over here and you gonna get wet,' she said, and *splat*! we were hit full in the chest with ice-cold water.

Rosaleen turned the sprinkler head down and filled May's dress. 'You come over here and you gonna get wet,' May echoed, and she came after us, pitching the contents of her skirt across our backs.

I can tell you this much: neither of us protested that loudly. In the end we stood there and let ourselves be drenched by two crazy women.

All four of us turned into water nymphs and danced around the cool spray, just the way it must have been when Indians danced circles around blazing fires. Squirrels and Carolina wrens hopped as close as they dared and drank from the puddles, and you could almost see the blades of brown grass lift themselves up and turn green.

Then the porch door banged, and here came June with her dander up. I must have been drunk with water and air and dancing, because I picked up the sprinkler and said, 'You come over here and you're gonna get wet.' Then I hosed her.

She began to holler. 'Damn it to hell!' I knew this was going down the wrong path, but I couldn't stop. I was seeing myself as the fire department and June as the raging inferno.

She yanked the sprinkler out of my hands and turned the spray on me. Some of the water rushed up my nose and burned. I yanked at the sprinkler, and each of us held on to one side of it while it blasted away at our stomachs and chins. We went to our knees, wrestling for it, the geyser weaving between us, her eyes staring at me, close and bright with beads of water on her eyelashes. I heard May start to hum 'Oh! Susanna'. I laughed to let her know it was all right, but I wouldn't let go. I would not let June Boatwright win.

Rosaleen said, 'They say if you aim the hose on two locked dogs, they'll turn loose, but I guess that ain't always so.'

August laughed, and I saw the softening come round June's eyes. She was trying not to laugh, but the minute she softened her eyes, the whole thing collapsed. I could almost see her smack her forehead, thinking, *I am wrestling with a fourteen-year-old girl over a garden sprinkler. This is ridiculous.*

She let go and sprawled back on the grass in convulsions of laughter. I plopped down next to her and laughed, too. We could not stop. I wasn't exactly sure of everything we were laughing about—I was just glad we were doing it together.

When we got up, June said, 'Lord, I feel woozy, like somebody has pulled the plugs in my feet and drained me out.'

Rosaleen, May and August had returned to the business of being water nymphs. I looked back down at the ground where our bodies had lain side by side, the wet grasses pressed down, perfect depressions on the earth. I stepped over them with the utmost care, and, seeing how careful I was, June stepped over them, too, and then, to my shock, she hugged me. June Boatwright hugged me while our clothes made sweet, squishy sounds up and down our bodies.

If the heat goes over 104 degrees in South Carolina, you have to go to bed. It is practically the law. Some people might see it as shiftless behaviour, but really, when we're lying down from the heat, we're giving our minds time to browse around for new ideas, wondering at the true aim of life, and generally letting things pop into our heads that need to.

If you lie down now and then and get still as you can, your mind will slide open like elevator doors, letting in all the secret thoughts that have been standing around so patiently, pushing the button for a ride to the top. The real troubles in life happen when those hidden doors stay closed for too long. But that's just my opinion.

August, May, June and Rosaleen were supposedly over in the pink house in their rooms, lying under the fans with the lights out. In the honey house I reclined on my cot and told myself I could think about anything I wanted, except my mother, so naturally she was the only thing that I wanted on the elevator.

I could feel things unravelling around me. All the fraying edges of the dream world. Pull one wrong thread and I'd be standing in wreckage to my elbows. Ever since I'd called T. Ray, I'd wanted to tell Rosaleen about it. To say, *If you've been wondering whether my leaving has caused T. Ray to examine his heart, or change his ways, don't waste your time.* But I couldn't bring myself to admit to her that I'd cared enough to call him.

What was wrong with me that I was living here as if I had nothing to hide? I lay on the cot and stared at the square of window, exhausted. It takes so much energy to keep things at bay. *Let me on*, my mother was saying. *Let me on the damn elevator*.

Well, fine. I pulled out my bag and examined my mother's picture. The wanting-her was still in me, but it wasn't nearly so fierce and raging as before. Pulling on her gloves, I noticed how tight they fitted all of a sudden. By the time I was sixteen, they would feel like baby gloves. My palms would split the seams, and I would never wear them again.

I peeled the gloves from my sweaty hands and felt a wave of jitteriness, the old saw-edged guilt, the necklace of lies I could not stop wearing, the fear of being cast out of the pink house.

'No,' I breathed. The word took a long time to work its way to my throat. A scared whisper. No, I will not think about this. I will not feel this. I will not let this ruin the way things are. *No*.

I decided that lying down from the heat was a hick idea. I gave up and walked to the pink house for something cold to drink. When I came into the kitchen, May was sitting on the floor with her legs straight out and a box of graham crackers in her lap.

'I saw a roach,' she said, reaching into a bag of marshmallows that I hadn't noticed was there. She pulled one out and pinched off little pieces of it. Crazy May.

I opened the refrigerator and stood there staring at the contents like I was waiting for the grape-juice bottle to jump into my hand. I could not seem to register what May was doing. Sometimes things of magnitude settle over you with excruciating slowness.

I had nearly finished a glass of juice before I let myself look at the little highway of broken graham crackers and marshmallow bits that May was constructing, how it started at the sink and angled towards the door, thick with golden crumbs and smudges of sticky white.

'The roaches follow this out the door,' May said. 'It works every time.'

I don't know how long I stared at the line on the floor, at May's face turned towards mine, eager for me to say something, but I couldn't think what to say. The room filled with the steady whir of the refrigerator motor. I felt a strange, thick feeling inside. A memory. I stood there waiting, letting it come . . . *Your mother was a lunatic when it came to bugs*, T. Ray had said. *She used to make trails of graham cracker crumbs and marshmallows to lure roaches outside.*

I looked again at May. *My mother couldn't have learned the roach trick from May*, I thought: *Could she?*

Ever since I'd set foot in the pink house, some part of me had kept believing that my mother had been here. No, not believing it so much as daydreaming it and running it through a maze of wishful thinking. But now that the actual possibility seemed to be right in front of me, it seemed so far-fetched, crazy. *It couldn't be*, I thought again.

I walked over and sat down at the table. Shadows from late afternoon pushed into the room, peach tinted, fading in and out, and the kitchen was completely silent. Even the refrigerator hum had died away. May had turned back to her work. She seemed oblivious to me sitting there.

My mother could have learned it from a book, maybe from her mother. How did I know that households everywhere didn't use this particular roach-ridding method? I stood up and walked over to May. I felt a trembly feeling at the back of my knees. I put my hand on her shoulder. *OK*, I thought, *here goes*. I said, 'May, did you ever know a Deborah? Deborah Fontanel? A white woman from Virginia? It would have been a long time ago.'

There wasn't a trace of cunning in May, and you could depend on her not to overthink her answers. She didn't look up, didn't pause, just said, 'Oh, yes, Deborah Fontanel. She stayed out there in the honey house. She was the sweetest thing.'

And there it was. There it all was.

For a moment I felt light-headed. I had to reach for the countertop to steady myself. Down on the floor the trail of crumbs and marshmallows looked half alive.

I had a million more questions, but May had started humming 'Oh! Susanna'. She set down the box of crackers and got up slowly, starting to sniffle. Something about Deborah Fontanel had set her off.

'I think I'll go out to the wall for a little while,' she said. And that's how she left me, standing in the kitchen, the world tilted under me.

Walking to the honey house, I concentrated on my feet touching down on the hard-caked dirt, the fresh-watered grass, how the earth felt solid, alive, ancient, right there every time my foot came down. There and there and there, always there. The things a mother should be.

Oh, yes, Deborah Fontanel. She stayed out there in the honey house. She was the sweetest thing.

In the honey house I sat on the cot, hugging my knees with my arms. I looked at the floor and the walls with brand-new eyes. My mother had walked about in this room. A real person. Not somebody I made up, but a living, breathing person.

The last thing I expected was to fall asleep, but when there's a blow to the system, all the body wants to do is go to sleep and dream on it.

I woke an hour or so later in the velvety space where you don't yet remember what you've dreamed. Then suddenly the whole thing washed back to me.

I am constructing a spiralling trail of honey across a room that seems to be in the honey house one minute and the next my bedroom back in Sylvan. I start it at a door I've never seen before and end it at the foot of my bed. Then I sit on the mattress and wait. The door opens. In walks my mother. She follows the honey, making twists and turns across the room until she gets to my bed. She is smiling, so pretty, but then I see she is not a normal person. She has roach legs protruding through her clothes, six of them, three on each side.

I couldn't imagine who sat in my head making this stuff up. The air was now dusky rose and cool enough for a sheet. I pulled it round my legs. My stomach felt icky, like I might throw up.

If I told you right now that I never wondered about that dream, never closed my eyes and pictured her with roach legs, never wondered why she came to me like that, with her worst nature exposed, I would be up to my old habit of lying. A roach is a creature no one can love, but you cannot kill it. It will go on and on and on. Just try to get rid of it.

The next few days I was a case of nerves. I jumped out of my skin if somebody so much as dropped a nickel on the floor. At the dinner table I poked at my food and stared into space like I was in a trance. Sometimes the picture of my mother with roach legs would leap into my head, and I would have to swallow a spoonful of honey for my stomach.

I walked round the house, pausing here and there to picture my mother in the various rooms. Sitting with her skirt spread over the piano bench. Kneeling beside Our Lady. Studying the recipe collection that May clipped from magazines and kept taped on the refrigerator. I would stare at these visions with my eyes glazed over, only to look up and see August, or June, or Rosaleen watching me. They clucked their tongues and felt my face for fever.

They said, 'What's wrong? What's got into you?'

I shook my head. 'Nothing,' I lied. 'Nothing.'

In truth I felt as if my life was stranded out on the high dive, about to leap into unknown waters. I only wanted to postpone the plunge awhile, to feel my mother's closeness in the house, to pretend I wasn't afraid of the story that had brought her here or that she might go and surprise me the way she had in the dream, turning up six-legged and ugly.

I wanted to march up to August and ask why my mother had been here, but fear stopped me. I wanted to know, and I didn't want to know. I was all hung up in limbo.

Late Friday afternoon, after we'd finished cleaning and storing the last of the supers, Zach went out to take a look under the hood of the honey wagon. It was still overheating, in spite of Neil having worked on it.

I wandered back to my room and sat on my cot. Heat radiated from the window. I considered getting up to turn on the fan but only sat there staring through the panes at the milky-blue sky, a sad, ragged feeling catching hold inside. I could hear music coming from the truck radio, Sam Cooke singing 'Another Saturday Night', then May calling across the yard to Rosaleen, something about getting the sheets off the clothes line. And I was struck all at once how life was out there going through its regular courses, and I was suspended, caught in a terrible crevice between living my life and not living it. I couldn't go on biding time like there was no end to this summer. I felt tears spring up. I would have to come clean. Whatever happened . . . well, it would just happen.

I went over to the basin and washed my face.

Taking a deep breath, I stuffed my mother's black Mary picture and her photograph into my pocket and started towards the pink house to find August. I thought we would sit down on the end of her bed, or out in the lawn chairs if the mosquitoes weren't bad. I imagined August would say, *What's on your mind, Lily? Are we finally gonna have our talk*? I would pull out the wooden picture and tell her every last thing, and then she would explain about my mother.

If only that had happened, instead of what did.

As I strode towards the house, Zach called to me from the truck. 'Wanna ride to town with me? I've gotta get a new radiator hose before the store closes.'

'I'm going to talk to August,' I said.

He slammed down the hood and smeared his hands front and back on his trousers. 'August is with Sugar-Girl in the parlour. She showed up crying. Something about Otis using their life savings to buy a secondhand fishing boat.'

'But I've got something really important to talk to her about.'

'You'll have to get in line,' he said. 'Come on, we'll be back before Sugar-Girl leaves.'

I hesitated, then gave in. 'All right.'

The auto-parts store sat two doors down from the movie theatre. As Zach pulled into a parking space in front, I saw them—five or six white men standing by the ticket booth. They glanced up and down the sidewalk like they were waiting for someone, all of them so nicely dressed, wearing ties. One man held what looked like the handle from a shovel.

Zach turned off the honey wagon and stared at them through the windshield. A dog, an old beagle with an age-white face, wandered out of the auto-parts store and began to sniff at something on the sidewalk. Zach drummed his fingers on the steering wheel and sighed. And I suddenly realised: it was Friday, and they were out here waiting for Jack Palance and the coloured woman.

We sat there a minute not speaking, the sounds in the truck magnified. The squeak in a spring under the seat. The tapping of Zach's fingers. The sharp way I was breathing.

Then one of the men yelled, causing me to jump and bang my knee against the glove compartment. He gazed across the street and shouted, 'What are you staring at over there?'

Zach and I both turned and looked through the back window. Three teenaged coloured boys stood on the sidewalk, drinking R.C. Colas out of the bottle and glaring over at the men.

'Let's come back another time,' I said.

'It'll be OK,' Zach said. 'You wait here.'

No, it won't be OK, I thought.

As he slid out of the honey wagon, I heard the boys call Zach's name. They crossed the street and came over to the honey wagon. Glancing through the window at me, they gave Zach a few playful shoves. One of them waved his hand in front of his face like he'd bitten into a Mexican pepper. 'Who you got in there?' he said.

I looked at them, tried to smile, but my mind was on the men, who I could see were watching us.

The boys saw it, too, and one of them—who I would later find out was named Jackson—said real loud, 'You gotta be dumb as dirt to believe Jack Palance is coming to Tiburon,' and all of them laughed. Even Zach.

The man holding the shovel handle walked up to the truck bumper and stared at the boys with that same half-smile, half-sneer I had seen on T. Ray's face a thousand times, and he yelled, 'What did you say, boy?'

The murmuring noise on the street fell away. The beagle slunk off under a parked car. I saw Jackson bite down, causing a tiny ripple across his jaw. I saw him raise his R.C. Cola bottle over his head. And throw it.

I closed my eyes as it flew out of his hand. When I opened them again, there was glass sprayed across the sidewalk. The man with the shovel handle had dropped it and had his hand over his nose. Blood seeped through his fingers.

He turned back to the other men. 'That nigger busted open my nose,' he said, sounding more surprised than anything. He looked around, confused for a moment, then headed into a nearby store, dripping blood all the way.

Zach and the boys stood by the truck door in a little knot, stuck to the pavement, while the rest of the men walked over and formed a half circle around them, hemming them in against the truck. 'Which one of you threw that bottle?' one man said.

The boys didn't open their mouths.

'Bunch of cowards,' another man said. This one had picked up the shovel handle from the sidewalk and was jabbing it in the air in the boys' direction every time they moved. 'Just tell us which one of you it was, and you other three can go,' he said.

Nothing.

People had started coming out of the stores, gathering in clumps. I stared at the back of Zach's head, waiting to see what he would do. I knew that a snitch was considered the lowest sort of person, but I wanted him to point his finger and say, *The one over there. He did it.* That way he could climb back into the honey truck and we would be on our way.

Come on, Zach.

He turned his head and looked at me from the corner of his eye. Then he shrugged his shoulder and I knew it was over. He would never open his mouth. He was trying to say to me, *I'm sorry, but these are my friends.*

He chose to stand there and be one of them.

I watched the policeman put Zach and the other three boys in his car. Driving away, he turned on his siren and red light, which seemed unnecessary, but I guess he didn't want to disappoint the audience on the sidewalk.

I sat in the truck like I had frozen and the world had frozen round me. The crowd faded away, and all the cars downtown went home one by one. People closed up their stores. I stared through the windshield as if I was watching the test pattern that came on television at midnight.

After the shock wore off some, I tried to think what to do, how to get home. Zach had taken the keys, or I might've tried driving myself, even though I didn't know gears from brakes. There wasn't a store open now to ask to use a phone, and when I spotted a payphone down the street, I realised I didn't have a dime. I got out of the truck and walked.

When I got to the pink house a half-hour later, I saw August, June, Rosaleen, Neil and Clayton Forrest gathered in the long shadows near the hydrangeas. Their voices floated up into the dying light. I heard Zach's name. I heard Mr Forrest say the word 'jail'. I guessed that Zach had called him with his one phone call, and here he was, breaking the news.

Neil stood next to June, which told me they hadn't really meant all that *don't you come back* and *you selfish bitch* that they'd hurled at each other. I walked towards them, unnoticed. Someone down the road was burning grass clippings. Stray pieces of ash flicked over my head.

Coming up behind them, I said, 'August?'

She pulled me to her. 'Thank goodness. Here you are. I was about to come looking for you.'

I told them what had happened as we walked back to the house. August's arm was round my waist like she was afraid I'd keel over again in a blind faint, but I had never been more present. The blue in the shadows, the white parting in Clayton Forrest's hair, the weight of our caring strapped round our ankles. We could hardly walk for it.

We sat in the ladder-back chairs round the kitchen table, except for Rosaleen, who poured glasses of tea and set a plate of pimiento-cheese sandwiches on the table, as if anybody could eat.

'Now, what about bail?' August said.

Clayton cleared his throat. 'Judge Monroe is out of town on vacation, so nobody is getting out before next Wednesday, it looks like.'

Neil stood up and walked over to the window. His hair was cut in a neat square at the back. I tried to concentrate on it to keep from breaking down. Next Wednesday was five days from now. *Five days*.

'Well, is he all right?' asked June. 'He wasn't hurt, was he?'

'They only let me see him for a minute,' said Clayton. 'But he seemed all right.'

Outside, the night sky was moving over us. I was aware of it, aware of the way Clayton had said *he seemed all right*, as if we all understood he wasn't but would pretend otherwise.

August used her fingers to smooth out the skin on her forehead. I saw a shiny film across her eyes—the beginning of tears. But I could see a fire inside them. It was a hearth fire you could depend on, you could get warm by if you were cold. I felt like we were all adrift in the world, and all we had was the wet fire in August's eyes. But it was enough.

Rosaleen looked at me, and I could read her thoughts. *Just because you broke me out of jail, don't get any bright ideas about Zach.* I understood how people became career criminals. The first crime was the hardest. After that you're thinking, *What's one more?* A few more years in the slammer. Big deal.

'What are you gonna do about this?' said Rosaleen, standing beside Clayton, looking down at him. Her fists were planted in her hips. She looked like she wanted us all to fill our lips with snuff and go directly to the Tiburon jail and spit on people's shoes. It was plain Rosaleen had fire in her, too. Not hearth fire, like August, but fire that burns the house down, if necessary, to clean up the mess inside it. Rosaleen reminded me of the statue of Our Lady in the parlour, and I thought, *If August is the red heart on Mary's chest, Rosaleen is the fist.*

'I'll do my best to get him out,' said Clayton, 'but I'm afraid he's got to stay in there a little while.'

I reached into my pocket and felt the black Mary picture, remembering the things I'd planned to say to August about my mother. But how could I do that now, with this terrible thing happening to Zach? Everything I wanted to say would have to wait.

'I don't see why May needs to know about this,' June said. 'It will do her in. You know how she loves that boy.'

Every one of us turned to look at August.

'You're right,' she said. 'It would be too much for May.'

'Where is she?' I asked.

'In her bed, asleep,' Rosaleen said. 'She was worn out.'

I remembered I had seen her in the afternoon, out by the wall, pulling a load of stones in the wagon. Building onto her wall. As if she sensed a new addition was called for.

The jail in Tiburon did not have curtains like the one in Sylvan. It was concrete-block grey, with metal windows and poor lighting. I told myself it was an act of stupidity to go inside. I was a fugitive from justice, and here I was breezing into a jail where there were probably policemen trained to recognise me. But August had asked if I wanted to come with her to visit Zach. How was I going to say anything but yes to that?

The policeman inside had a crew cut and was very tall. He didn't seem especially glad to see us. 'Are you his mother?' he asked August.

I looked at his name tag. Eddie Hazelwurst.

'I'm his godmother,' August said, standing very erect, like she was having her height measured. 'And this is a friend of the family.'

His eyes passed over me. The only thing he seemed suspicious about was how a girl as white as me could be a friend of the family.

'All right, you can have five minutes,' he said.

He opened a door into a corridor that led to a single row of four jail cells, each of them holding a black boy. The smell of sweating bodies and sour urinals almost overpowered me. I wanted to bring my fingers up to pinch my nose, but I knew that would be the worst insult. They couldn't help that they smelt.

They sat on benchlike cots hooked along the wall, staring at us as we passed. Mr Hazelwurst led us to the last cell.

'Zach Taylor, you got visitors,' he said, then glanced at his watch.

When Zach stepped towards us, I wondered if he'd been handcuffed, fingerprinted, photographed, pushed around. I wanted so much to reach through the bars and touch him, because it seemed that only then could I be sure all this was actually happening.

When it was apparent Mr Hazelwurst wasn't leaving, August began to speak. She spoke about one of the hives she kept over on the Haney farm, how it had up and swarmed. 'You know the one,' she said. 'The one that had trouble with mites.'

She went into minute detail about the way she'd searched high and low, into the dusk hours, combing the woods out past the watermelon fields, finally finding the bees in a magnolia sapling. 'I used the funnel to drop them in a swarm box,' she said, 'then I hived them again.'

I think she was trying to put it in Zach's mind that she would never rest till he was back home. Zach listened with his eyes watery brown. He seemed relieved to keep the conversation on the level of bee swarms.

I'd worked on lines I wanted to say to him, too, but in the moment I couldn't remember them. I stood by while August asked him questions—how was he doing, what did he need?

I watched him, filled with tenderness and ache, wondering what it was that connected us.

When Mr Hazelwurst said, 'Time's up, let's go,' Zach cast his eyes in my direction. A vein stuck out above his temple. I watched the blood pulsing through it. I wanted to reach through the bars and touch it.

'Are you writing in your notebook?' he asked, his face and voice suddenly, oddly, desperate.

I looked at him and nodded. In the next cell, the boy—Jackson—made a noise, a kind of catcall, that caused the moment to seem silly and cheap. Zach shot him an angry look.

'Come on, you've had your five minutes,' the policeman said.

August placed her hand on my back, nudging me to leave. Zach seemed to want to ask me something. He opened his mouth, then closed it.

'I'll write this all down for you,' I said. 'I'll put it in a story.'

I don't know if that's what he wanted to ask me, but it's something everybody wants—for someone to see the hurt done to them and set it down like it matters.

We went around not bothering to smile, even in front of May. When she was in the room, we didn't talk about Zach, but we didn't act like the world was fine and rosy either. June resorted to her cello, the way she always did when sorrow came along. And walking to the honey house one morning, August stopped and stared at the tyre ruts in the driveway left by Zach's car. The way she stood there, I thought she might cry.

Everything I did felt heavy and difficult—drying the dishes, kneeling for evening prayers, even pulling down the sheets to get into bed.

On the second day of the month of August, after the supper dishes were washed up, and the Hail Marys had been done, August said, 'No more moping tonight, we're going to watch Ed Sullivan.' And that's what we were doing when the phone rang. To this day August and June wonder how our lives would have been different if one of them had answered the phone instead of May.

I remember that August made a move to answer it, but May was closest to the door. 'I'll get it,' she said. No one thought a thing about it. We fixed our eyes on the television, on Mr Sullivan, who introduced a circus act involving monkeys that rode tiny scooters across a high wire.

When May stepped back into the room a few minutes later, her eyes zigzagged from face to face. 'That was Zach's mother,' she said. 'Why didn't you tell me about him getting put in jail?'

She looked so normal standing there. For a moment none of us moved. We watched her like we were waiting for the roof to cave in. But May just stood there, calm as she could be. I started thinking maybe some sort of miracle had taken place and she'd somehow been cured.

'You all right?' said August, easing to her feet.

May didn't answer.

'May?' June said.

I even smiled over at Rosaleen and nodded, as if to say, *Can you believe how well she's taking this*?

August, though, turned off the television and studied May, frowning.

May's head was angled to the side, and her eyes were fixed on a cross-stitched picture of a birdhouse that hung on the wall. It struck me that her eyes weren't actually seeing the picture. They had glazed over.

August went over to May. 'Answer me. Are you all right?'

In the silence I heard May's breathing grow loud and a little ragged. She took several steps back, until she came to the wall. Then she slid down onto the floor without making a sound.

Rosaleen bent over May and spoke in a loud voice. 'Zach is gonna be all right. You don't need to worry any. Mr Forrest is getting him out of jail on Wednesday.'

May stared straight ahead like Rosaleen wasn't even there.

'What's happened to her?' June asked, and I could hear a note of panic in her voice. 'I've never seen her like this.'

May was here but not here. Her hands lay limp in her lap, palms up. No sobbing into her skirt. No rocking back and forth. No pulling at her hair braids. She was so quiet, so different.

I turned my face to the ceiling, I just couldn't watch.

August went to the kitchen and came back with a dish towel filled with ice. She pulled May's head to her so it rested against her shoulder, and then she lifted her sister's face and pressed the towel to May's forehead and temples and neck. She kept on doing this for several minutes, then put the cloth down and tapped May's cheeks with her hands.

May blinked a time or two and looked at August. She looked at all of us, huddled above her, as if she were returning from a long trip.

'You feel better?' said August.

May nodded. 'I'll be OK.' Her words came out in an odd monotone.

'Well, I'm glad to see you can talk,' said June. 'Come on, let's get you in the bathtub.'

August and June pulled May to her feet.

'I'm going to the wall,' May said.

June shook her head. 'It's getting dark.'

'Just for a little while,' May said. She moved into the kitchen, with all of us following her. She opened a cabinet drawer, took out a flashlight, her tablet, a stub of a pencil, and walked onto the porch. I pictured her writing it down—*Zach in jail*—and pushing it into a crevice in the wall.

'I'll go with you,' said August.

May spoke over her shoulder. 'No, please, August, just me.'

August started to protest. 'But—'

'Just me,' said May, turning to face us. 'Just me.'

We watched her go down the porch steps and move into the trees. In life there are things you can't get over no matter how hard you try, and that sight is one of them. May walking into the trees with the little circle of light bobbing in front of her, then swallowed up by the dark.

CHAPTER EIGHT

I SAT IN THE kitchen with August, June and Rosaleen while the night spread out round the house. May had been gone a whole five minutes when August got up and began to pace. She walked out to the porch and back and then stared out towards the wall.

After twenty minutes she said, 'That's it. Let's go get her.'

She got the flashlight from the truck and struck out for the wall, while June, Rosaleen and I hurried to keep pace. A night bird was singing from a tree branch, urgent and feverish.

'Ma-a-a-a-y,' called August. June called, too, then Rosaleen and me. We went along shouting her name, but no sound came back. Just the night bird singing.

After we walked from one end of the wailing wall to the other, we went back and walked it again, like this time we were going to get it right. Walk slower, look closer, call louder. This time May would be there kneeling with the flashlight batteries burnt out. We would think, *My goodness, how did we miss her here the first time?*

That didn't happen, though, so we walked into the woods behind the wall, calling her name louder and louder, but not one of us would say, *Something is terribly wrong.*

Despite the night, the heat had lingered on bad as ever, and I could smell the hot dampness of our bodies as we combed the woods with a spot of light four inches across. Finally August said, 'June, you go to the house and call the police. Tell them we need help to find our sister. When you hang up, you kneel before Our Lady and beg her to watch over May, then you come back. We're going to walk towards the river.'

June took off running. We could hear her crashing through the brush as we turned towards the back of the property where the river flowed. August's legs moved faster and faster. Rosaleen struggled to keep up.

When we reached the river, we stood there a moment. I'd been in Tiburon long enough for the full moon to fade away and grow back full again. It hung over the river, sliding in and out of clouds. I stared at a tree on the opposite bank, where the roots were exposed and twisted, and felt a metallic-dry taste rise from the back of my throat.

I reached for August's hand, but she had turned right and was moving along the bank, calling May's name.

'Ma-a-a-ay.'

Rosaleen and I moved close behind her in our clumsy knot. I was surprised when the prayer we said after dinner each night, the one with the beads, started up of its own accord and recited itself in the back reaches of my head. I could hear each word plainly. *Hail Mary, full of grace, the Lord is with thee. Blessed art thou among women, and blessed is the fruit of thy womb, Jesus. Holy Mary, mother of God, pray for us sinners, now and at the hour of our death. Amen.*

It wasn't till August said, 'Good, Lily, we should all pray,' that I realised I'd been repeating it out loud. I couldn't tell if I was saying it as a prayer or muttering it as a way to push down the fear. August said the words with me, and then Rosaleen did, too. We walked along the river with the words streaming behind us like ribbons in the night.

When June came back, she was holding another flashlight she'd dug up somewhere at the house. The puddle of light wobbled as she came through the woods.

'Over here,' called August, aiming her flashlight up through the trees. We waited for June to reach the riverbank.

'The police are on their way,' June said.

She shouted May's name and ploughed up the riverbank into the dark, followed by Rosaleen, but August moved slowly now, carefully. I stayed close behind her, saying Hail Marys to myself, faster and faster.

Suddenly August stopped in her tracks. I stopped, too. And I didn't hear the night bird singing any more.

I watched August, not taking my eyes off her. She stood tense and alert, staring down at the bank. At something I could not see.

'June,' she called in a strange, whispery voice, but June and Rosaleen had pushed farther up the riverbank and didn't hear. Only I heard.

The air felt thick and charged. I stepped over beside August, letting my elbow touch her arm, needing the weight of her next to me; and there was May's flashlight, shut off and sitting on the wet ground.

August didn't speak. A wind rose up, hitting our faces like an oven blast, like the sudden breezes of hell. August looked at me, then moved her flashlight beam out to the water.

The light swept across the surface, making a spatter of ink-gold splotches before it stopped, abruptly. May lay in the river, just beneath the surface. Her eyes were wide open and unblinking, and the skirt of her dress fanned out and swayed in the current.

I heard a noise come from August's lips, a soft moan.

I clutched frantically at August's arm, but she pulled free of me, threw down her flashlight, and waded into the river.

I splashed in after her. Water surged round my legs, causing me to fall once on the slippery bottom. I grabbed for August's skirt, just missing. I came up sputtering.

When I reached her, August was staring down at her baby sister. 'June,' she shouted. '*June*!'

May lay in two feet of water with a huge river stone on top of her chest. It weighted her body, holding it on the bottom. I wanted to reach down and touch her, shake her shoulder a little. She couldn't have died out here in the river. That would be impossible.

The only parts of her not submerged were her hands. They floated, her palms little ragged cups bobbing on the surface, the water weaving in and out of her fingers. Even now that's the picture that will wake me up in the night, not May's eyes, open and staring, or the stone resting on her like a grave slab. Her hands.

June came thrashing into the water. When she reached May, she stood beside August, panting, her arms dangling beside her body. '*Oh, May*,' she whispered and looked away, squeezing her eyes closed.

Glancing towards the bank, I saw Rosaleen standing ankle deep in the river, her whole body shaking.

August knelt down in the water and shoved the stone off May's chest. Grabbing May by the shoulders, she pulled her up. Her body made a sucking sound as it broke the surface. Her head rolled back, and I saw that her mouth was open and her teeth were rimmed with mud. River reeds clung to her braids. I looked away. I knew then. *May was dead*.

August knew, too, but she put her ear to May's chest, listening. After a minute, though, she drew back and pulled May's head to *her* breast, and it almost seemed like she wanted May to listen now for *her* heart.

'We've lost her,' August said.

I started to shiver. I could hear my teeth crashing against each other. August and June scooped their arms under May's body and struggled to carry her to the bank. She was saturated. I grabbed her ankles and tried to steady them. The river, it seemed, had carried away her shoes.

When they laid her down on the bank, water gushed from her mouth and nostrils. *Look at her fingers, her hands,* I thought. *They are so precious*.

I imagined how May had rolled the rock from the bank out into the river, then lay down, pulling it on top of her. She had held it tight and waited for her lungs to fill. I wondered if she had flailed and jerked towards the surface at the last second, or did she go without fighting, embracing the rock, letting it soak up all the pain she felt?

June and August, sopping wet, stooped on either side of her, while mosquitoes sang in our ears and the river coiled off into the darkness. I was sure they pictured May's last moments, too, but I did not see horror on their faces now, just a heartbroken acceptance. They'd been waiting for this for half their lives without even realising it.

August tried to close May's eyes with her fingers, but they would only stay half shut. 'It's just like April,' June said.

'Hold the flashlight on May for me,' August said to her. The words came out quiet and steady.

By the small beam of light, August plucked out the tiny green leaves stuck in the plaits in May's hair and tucked each one into her pocket.

August and June scraped off every piece of river debris there was from May's skin and clothes, and Rosaleen, poor Rosaleen, who I realised had lost her new best friend, stood, not making a sound, but with her chin shaking so awful I wanted to reach up and hold it for her.

Then a long, bubbling sigh whooshed out of May's mouth, and we all looked at each other, confused, with a second of actual hope, as if the miracle of miracles was about to take place after all, but it was only a pocket of swallowed air that had suddenly been released. It swept across my face, smelling like the river.

I looked down at May's face and felt a wave of nausea. Stumbling off into the trees, I bent over and vomited.

Afterwards, as I wiped my mouth on the hem of my shirt, I heard a sound break through the darkness, a cry so piercing it made the bottom of my heart drop. Looking back, I saw August framed in the light of June's flashlight, the sound coming from deep in her throat. When it faded away, she dropped her head straight down onto May's soggy chest.

I reached for the limb of a small cedar and held tight, as though everything I had was about to slip from my hands.

'So you're an orphan?' the policeman said. It was that tall, crewcut Eddie Hazelwurst who'd escorted August and me in to see Zach in jail.

Rosaleen and I sat in the rocking chairs in the parlour, while he stood before us holding a small notebook. The other policeman was outside searching around the wailing wall, for what I couldn't imagine.

My chair rocked so fast I was in danger of being pitched out of it. Rosaleen's, however, remained motionless—her face closed down.

When we'd first got back to the house after finding May, August had met both policemen and then sent me and Rosaleen upstairs. 'Go on up there and get dried off,' she said to me.

I'd peeled off my shoes and rubbed myself with a towel while we stood at the upstairs window. We'd watched the men from the ambulance bring May back from the woods on a stretcher, then listened as the two policemen asked August and June all sorts of questions. Their voices had floated up the stairwell. *Yes, she's been depressed lately. Well, actually, she was depressed on and off all the time. She had a condition. She couldn't seem to distinguish other people's suffering from her own. No, we didn't find a note. An autopsy? All right, we understand.*

Mr Hazelwurst had wanted to talk to everyone, so here we were. I'd told him what happened from the time May answered the telephone to the moment we found her in the river. Then he started with the personal questions. Wasn't I that girl who came to the jail last week to see one of the coloured boys? What was I doing staying here? Who was Rosaleen?

I explained everything about my mother dying when I was small, my father going to his Maker earlier this summer after a tractor accident, which was the story I was sticking with. Rosaleen, I said, was my nanny.

'I guess you could say I'm an orphan,' I told him. 'But I've got family in Virginia. It was my father's dying wish for me to go live with my Aunt Bernie. She's expecting me and Rosaleen both. She'll be sending us bus fare or driving down here and picking us up herself. She keeps saying, "Lily, I can't wait for you to get here." I tell her, "Just so we're there before school starts." I'll be a sophomore, which I cannot believe.'

He narrowed his eyes like he was trying to follow all this. I was breaking every rule of successful lying. *Do not talk so much*, I told myself. I was only glad August and June were not present to hear it. They had left to follow the ambulance in the honey wagon, wanting to see May's body delivered safe and sound to wherever it was going. It was bad enough Rosaleen was in the room. I was afraid she was going to give us away, say something like *Actually we came here right after Lily broke me out of jail*. But she sat drawn into herself, a complete mute.

'Now, what was your last name again?' he said.

'Williams,' I said. I had told him this twice already.

He drew up even taller. 'Well, what I don't understand is, if you're going to live with your aunt in Virginia, what are you doing here?'

I took a breath. 'Well, my Aunt Bernie had to have an operation. It was female trouble. So Rosaleen said, "Why don't me and you stay with my friend August Boatwright in Tiburon till Aunt Bernie gets on her feet again?" It was no sense us going up there while she was in hospital.'

He was actually writing this down. *Why*? I wanted to yell at him, *This is not about me and Rosaleen and Aunt Bernie's operation. This is about May. She is dead, or haven't you noticed?*

I should've been in my room right then crying my eyeballs out, and here I was having the stupidest conversation of my life.

'Didn't you have any white people back in Spartanburg you could stay with?'

'No, sir, not really. I didn't have that many friends. For some reason I didn't fit in that well with the crowd. I think it was because I made such good grades. One lady at church said I could stay there till Aunt Bernie got well, but then she got shingles, and there went that.'

Lord God, somebody stop me.

He looked at Rosaleen. 'So how did you know August?'

I held my breath.

'She's my husband's first cousin,' Rosaleen said. 'Me and her kept up after my husband left me. August was the only one of his family who knew what a sorry jackass he was.' She cut her eyes at me as if to say, *See? You aren't the only one who can concoct lies at the drop of a hat.*

He flipped his notebook shut and, crooking his finger at me, motioned me to follow him to the door. After he stepped outside, he said, 'Take my advice and call your aunt and tell her to come on and get you, even if she isn't a hundred per cent well. These are coloured people here. You understand what I'm saying?'

I wrinkled up my forehead. 'No, sir, I'm afraid I don't.'

'I'm just saying that you shouldn't be . . . well, lowering yourself.'

'Oh.'

'I'm gonna come back soon, and I better not find you still here. OK?' He smiled and put his gigantic hand on my head like we were two white people with a secret understanding.

'OK.'

I closed the door behind him. Whatever glue had kept me together throughout all that cracked then. I walked back into the parlour, already starting to sob. Rosaleen put her arm round me, and I saw tears coming down her face, too.

We walked up the stairs to the room she'd shared with May. Rosaleen pulled down the sheets on her bed. 'Go on, get in,' she told me.

'But where will you sleep?'

'Right over here,' she answered, pulling back the covers on May's bed. She climbed in and pushed her face into the creases of the pillow. I knew she was smelling for May's scent.

You'd think I would have dreamed about May, but when I fell asleep, it was Zach who came. I can't even tell you what was happening in the dream. I woke up, and I knew it had been about him. He seemed close and real, like I could sit up and touch my fingertips to his cheek. Then I remembered where he was, and an unbearable heaviness came over me.

I pictured his cot with his shoes sitting under it, how he was probably lying awake this very moment, listening to the other boys breathe.

Across the room a rustling noise startled me. Only half awake, I'd thought I was in the honey house, but it came to me now that the sound was Rosaleen turning over in bed. And then, then I remembered May. I remembered her in the river.

I had to get up, slip into the bathroom and throw water on my face. I was standing there with the night-light casting its small brightness when I looked down and saw the claw-footed tub wearing the red socks May had put on its porcelain feet. I smiled then; I couldn't help it. It was the side of May I never wanted to forget.

I closed my eyes, and all the best pictures of her came to me. I saw her corkscrew braids glistening in the sprinkler, her fingers arranging the graham-cracker crumbs, working so hard on behalf of a single roach's life. And that hat she wore the day she danced the conga line with the Daughters of Mary. Mostly, though, I saw the blaze of love and anguish that had come so often into her face.

In the end it had burned her up.

After the autopsy, after the police made her suicide official, after the funeral home had fixed May up as pretty as they could, she came home to the pink house. First thing Wednesday morning, August 5, a black hearse pulled up in the driveway, and four men in dark suits lifted out May's coffin and brought it right into the parlour. When I asked August why May was coming through the front door in her coffin, she said, 'We're going to sit with her till she's buried.'

I hadn't expected this, as all the people I knew in Sylvan had their dead loved ones go straight from the funeral home to the graveyard.

August said, 'We sit with her so we can tell her goodbye. It's called a vigil. Sometimes people have a hard time letting death sink in, they can't say goodbye. A vigil helps us do that.'

If the dead person is right there *in* your living room, it would certainly make things sink in better. It was strange to think about a dead person in the house, but if it helped us say goodbye better, then OK, I could see the point of it.

August had them roll the coffin, which sat on its own table with wheels, in front of Our Lady of Chains and then open it up. After the funeral home men drove away, August and Rosaleen walked up to the coffin and stared down at May, but I hung back. I was walking around, inspecting myself in the mirrors, when June came down with her cello and began to play. She played 'Oh! Susanna', which made all of us smile.

There is nothing like a small joke at a vigil to help you relax. I walked up to the coffin and stood between August and Rosaleen.

It was the same old May, except her skin was pulled tight across her face bones. The lamplight spilling into the coffin gave her a kind of glow. They had her wearing a royal blue dress I had never seen, with pearl buttons and a boat-neck collar, and her blue hat. She looked like any second she would pop open her eyes and grin at us.

This was the woman who'd taught my mother everything there was to know about getting rid of roaches in a nice way. It was six days since May had told me about my mother staying here. It seemed like six months.

I still wanted so badly to tell August what I knew. Standing at the coffin, looking up at her, I had a powerful urge to tell her right then. Just blurt it out. *I'm not Lily Williams, I'm Lily Owens, and it was my mother who stayed here. May told me.* And then it would all come out. When I peered up at her, though, she was brushing tears off her face, looking for a handkerchief in her pocket, and I knew it would be selfish to pour this into her cup when it was already to the brim with grief.

June played with her eyes closed, as if May's spirit getting into heaven depended solely on her. You have never heard such music, how it made us believe death was nothing but a doorway.

August and Rosaleen finally sat down, but once I was up at the coffin, I found I couldn't leave. May's arms were crossed over her chest, wings folded in on themselves, a pose I did not find flattering. I reached in and held her hand. It was waxy-cool, but I didn't care. *I hope you will be happier in heaven*, I told her. *I hope you will not need any kind of wall up there.* For some reason I felt like May's spirit was hovering in a corner of the ceiling hearing every word, even though I wasn't speaking out loud.

And I wish you would look up my mother, I said. *Say this to her: 'Lily would appreciate a sign letting her know that you love her. It doesn't have to be anything big, but please send something.'*

I let out a long breath, still holding her dead hand. *So I guess this is goodbye*, I told her. A shudder went through me, a burning along my eyelashes. Tears fell off my cheeks and spotted her dress.

Before I left her, though, I rearranged her a little. I folded her hands together and tucked them under her chin like she was thinking seriously about the future.

At ten o'clock that morning, while June was playing more songs for May, and Rosaleen was poking around in the kitchen, I sat on the back-porch steps with my notebook, trying to write everything down, but really I was watching for August. She had gone out to the wailing wall. I pictured her out there working her pain into the spaces around the stones.

By the time I spotted her coming back, I'd stopped writing and was doodling in the margins. She paused halfway across the yard and stared towards the driveway, shielding her eyes from the sun. 'Look who's here!' she yelled, breaking into a run.

I had never seen August run before, and I could not believe how quickly she crossed the grass with her loping strides, her long legs stretched out under her skirt. 'It's Zach!' she shouted at me, and I dropped my notebook and flew down the steps.

I heard Rosaleen behind me in the kitchen shouting to June that Zach was here, heard June's music stop in the middle of a note. When I got to the driveway, he was climbing out of Clayton's car. August wrapped him up in her arms. Clayton stared at the ground and smiled.

When August turned Zach loose, I saw how much skinnier he looked. He stood there watching me. I couldn't read the expression on his face. I walked up to him, wishing I knew the right thing to say. A breeze tossed a piece of my hair across my face, and he reached out and brushed it away. Then he pulled me hard against his chest and held me for a few moments.

'Are you all right?' June said, rushing up and cupping his jaw in her hand. 'We've been worried sick.'

'I'm fine *now*,' Zach said. But something I couldn't put my finger on had evaporated from his face.

Clayton said, 'The girl who sells tickets at the theatre—well, apparently she saw the whole thing. It took her long enough, but she finally told the police which one of the boys threw the bottle. So they dropped the charges against Zach.'

'Oh, *thank God*,' said August, and every one of us seemed to breathe out all at once.

'We just wanted to come by and say how sorry we are about May,' Clayton said. He embraced August, then June. When he turned to me, he placed his hands on my shoulders, not an embrace, but close. 'Lily, how nice to see you again,' he said, then looked at Rosaleen, who was hanging back by the car. 'You, too, Rosaleen.'

August took Rosaleen's hand and pulled her over, then went on holding it, the way she used to hold May's sometimes, and it struck me that she loved Rosaleen. That she would like to change Rosaleen's name to July and bring her into their sisterhood.

'I couldn't believe it when Mr Forrest told me about May,' said Zach.

We walked back to the house so Clayton and Zach could take their turns beside the coffin, then we all gathered round May. Clayton bowed his head, but Zach stared into her face.

We stood there and stood there. Rosaleen made a little humming sound, I think out of awkwardness, but eventually she stopped.

I looked over at Zach, and the tears were pouring down his cheeks.

'I'm sorry,' he said. 'It was all my fault. If I'd turned in the one who threw the bottle, I wouldn't have got arrested and none of this would've happened.'

I had thought maybe he would never find out it was his arrest that sent May to the river. But that had been too much to hope for.

'Who told you?' I said.

He waved his hand like it didn't matter. 'My mother heard it from Otis. She didn't want to tell me, but she knew I'd hear it from somewhere, sooner or later.' He wiped his face. 'I just wish I'd—'

August reached over and touched Zach's arm. She said, 'Well, now, I guess I could say if I'd told May from the beginning about you getting arrested, instead of keeping it from her, none of this would've happened. Or if I'd stopped May from going out to the wall that night, none of this would've happened. What if I hadn't waited so long before going out there and getting her—' She looked down at May's body. 'It was May who did it, Zach.'

I was afraid, though, the blame would find a way to stick to them. That's how blame was.

'I could use your help right now to drape the hives,' August said to Zach as they started to leave.

'Sure, I can stay and help,' said Zach.

'You wanna come, Lily?' August asked.

'Yes, ma'am.' Draping the hives—I had no idea what that was, but you couldn't have paid me fifty dollars to miss it.

After Clayton said goodbye, we fastened on our hats and veils and went out to the hives, bearing giant squares of black crepe material. August showed us how to drape a square over each hive box, securing it with a brick and making sure we left the bees' entrance door open.

I watched how August stood a moment before each hive with her fingers knitted together under her chin. *Exactly what are we doing this for*? I wanted to know, but it seemed like a holy ritual I shouldn't interrupt.

When we had all the hives covered, we stood under the pines and gazed at them, this little town of black buildings. A city of mourning.

August pulled off her hat and walked to the lawn chairs in the back yard with me and Zach tagging behind her. We sat with the sun behind us, staring out towards the wailing wall.

'A long time ago beekeepers always covered their hives when someone in their family died,' said August.

'How come?' I asked.

'Covering the hives was supposed to keep the bees from leaving. You see, the last thing they wanted was their bees swarming off when a death took place. Having bees around was supposed to ensure that the dead person would live again. The kings in Greece made their tombs in the shape of beehives for that very reason.'

My eyes grew wide. 'Really?'

Zach stared at the grass. 'When a bee flies, a soul will rise,' he said.

'It's an old saying,' August said. 'It means a person's soul will be reborn into the next life if bees are around.'

I shoved my hands under my thighs and sat up. 'Do you think putting black cloths over the hives will help May get to heaven?'

'Goodness no,' August said. 'Putting black cloths on the hives is for us. I do it to remind us that life gives way into death, and then death turns round and gives way into life.'

I leaned back in my chair, gazing at the sky, how endless it was, the way it fit down over the world like the lid of a hive. I wished more than anything we could bury May in a beehive tomb. That I could, myself, lie down in one and be reborn.

When the Daughters of Mary showed up, they were loaded down with food. Queenie and her daughter, Violet, had left off their hats completely. Lunelle, Mabelee, Cressie and Sugar-Girl each wore a black hat, which they took off and lined them up on the piano as soon as they came in, so that you wanted to say, *What's the use*?

They got under way slicing ham, laying out fried chicken, shaking paprika on the devilled eggs. We had green beans, turnips, macaroni cheese, caramel cake—all kinds of funeral foods. We ate from paper plates, standing in the kitchen, saying how much May would have liked everything.

When we were so full that what we needed was a nap, we went to the parlour and sat with May. The Daughters passed round a wooden bowl full of something they called manna. A salted mixture of sunflower, sesame, pumpkin and pomegranate seeds drizzled with honey and baked to perfection. They ate it by the handfuls, saying they wouldn't dream of sitting with the dead without eating seeds. Seeds kept the living from despair, they explained.

Mabelee said, 'She looks so good—doesn't she look good?'

Queenie snorted. 'If she looks that good, maybe we ought to put her on display in the drive-by window at the funeral home.'

'Oh, *Queenie*!' cried Mabelee.

Cressie noticed Rosaleen and me sitting there in the dark and said, 'The funeral home in town has a drive-by window. It used to be a bank.'

'Nowadays they put the open coffin right up in the window where we used to drive through and get our cheques cashed,' said Queenie. 'People can drive through and pay their respects without having to get out. They even send the guest book out in the drawer for you to sign.'

'You ain't serious?' said Rosaleen.

'Oh, yeah,' Queenie said. 'We're serious.'

They might've been speaking the truth, but they didn't look serious. They were falling on each other laughing, and there was May, dead.

I turned to August, who was wiping her eyes from tears of hilarity. I said, 'You won't let them put May in the bank window, will you?'

'Honey, don't worry about it,' said Sugar-Girl. 'The drive-by window is at the white people's funeral home. They're the only ones with enough money to fix up something that ridiculous.'

They all broke down again with hysterics, and I could not help laughing, too, partly with relief that people would not be joyriding through the funeral home to see May and partly because you could not help laughing at the sight of all the Daughters laughing.

But the thing that brought me the most cause for gladness was how Sugar-Girl said what she did, like I was truly one of them. They didn't even think of me being different.

I thought of that policeman, Eddie Hazelwurst, saying I'd lowered myself to be in this house of coloured women, and for the life of me I couldn't understand how it had turned out this way, how coloured women had become the lowest ones on the totem pole. You only had to look at them to see how special they were.

I felt so warm inside towards them I thought to myself that if I should die, I would be glad to go on display in the bank window and give the Daughters of Mary a good laugh.

On the second morning of the vigil, long before the Daughters arrived, even before June came downstairs, August found May's suicide note caught beneath the roots of a live oak, not ten yards from the spot she'd died. The woods had buried it under fresh-sprouted leaves.

Rosaleen was making banana cream pie, and I was sitting at the table trying to find something decent on the transistor radio when August burst into the kitchen holding the note with two hands, like the words might fall off if she wasn't real careful.

She yelled up the stairs, 'June, come down. I found a note from May.'

August spread it out on the table and stood over it with her hands pressed together. I turned off the plastic radio and stared at the crinkle-stiff paper, saw how the words were faded from being outside.

June's bare feet slapped the stairs, and she broke into the room. 'Oh, God, August. What does it say?'

'It's . . . so May,' August said. She lifted up the note and read it to us.

Dear August and June,

I'm sorry to leave you like this. I hate you being sad, but think how happy I'll be with April, Mama, Papa and Big Mama. Picture us up there together, and that will help some. I'm tired of carrying around the weight of the world. I'm just going to lay it down now. It's my time to die, and it's your time to live. Don't mess it up.

Love, May

August laid the note down and turned to June. She opened her arms wide, and June walked into them. They clung to each other—big sister to little sister, bosom to bosom, their chins wrapped round each other's necks. They stayed that way long enough for me to wonder—should Rosaleen and I leave the room?—but finally they unwound themselves, and we all sat with the smell of banana cream pie.

June said, 'Do you think it was really her time to die?'

'I don't know,' said August. 'Maybe it was. But one thing May was right about is that it's our time to live. It's her dying wish that we do that, June, so we need to see to it. All right?'

'What do you mean?' said June.

August walked over to the window, put her hands on the countertop, and gazed out at the sky. It was aquamarine and shiny as taffeta. You had the feeling she was making a big decision.

June pulled out a chair, sat down. 'August, *what*?'

When August turned back, her jaw was set. 'I'm going to say something to you, June.' She walked over and stood in front of her. 'You've been halfway living your life for too long. May was saying that when it's time to die, go ahead and die, and when it's time to live, live. Don't sort-of-maybe live, but live like you're going all out, like you're not afraid.'

'I don't know what you're talking about,' June said.

'I'm saying marry Neil.'

'What?'

'Ever since Melvin Edwards backed out of your wedding all those years back, you've been afraid of love, refusing to take a chance. Like May said, it's your time to live. Don't mess it up.'

June's mouth sat open in a circle, and not a word crossed her lips.

Suddenly the air was coated with the smell of burning. Rosaleen yanked the pie from the oven to find every last meringue tip scorched.

'We'll eat it like that,' said August. 'A burn taste never hurt anybody.'

Every day for four days straight we kept the vigil. August had May's note with her at all times, tucked in her pocket or slipped under her belt. June seemed quieter since August had lowered the boom on her about Neil. I would catch her sitting beside the coffin leaning her forehead against it, and you could tell she was doing more than saying goodbye to May. She was trying to find her own answers to things.

One afternoon August and Zach and I went out to the hives and took off the black cloths. August said we couldn't leave them on too long, since the bees had memorised everything about their hive and a change like that could make them disorientated. They might not find their way home again, she said. *Tell me about it*, I thought.

The Daughters of Mary showed up each day just before lunch and sat in the parlour with May through the afternoon, telling stories about her. We cried a good bit also, but I could tell we were starting to feel better about saying goodbye.

Neil stayed at the house nearly as much as the Daughters, and seemed downright confused by the way June stared into his face. She could barely play the cello, because it meant turning loose of his hand. To tell the truth, the rest of us spent nearly as much time watching June and Neil as we did seeing May into the next life.

On the afternoon that the funeral home came to pick up May for the burial, bees buzzed around the front-window screens. As the coffin was loaded into the hearse, bee hum swelled and blended into the late-afternoon colours. Yellow-gold. Red. Tinges of brown.

I could still hear them humming at the graveside, even though we were miles away in a coloured cemetery with crumbled markers and weeds. The sound carried on the breezes while we watched them lower May's coffin into the ground. August passed around a paper bag full of manna, and we scooped up handfuls and threw the seeds into the hole with the coffin, and my ears were filled with nothing but bee hum.

That night, in my bed in the honey house, when I closed my eyes, bee hum ran through my body. Ran through the whole earth. It was the oldest sound there was. Souls flying away.

CHAPTER NINE

AFTER MAY'S BURIAL August shut down honey making, honey selling, even bee patrol. She and June took the meals that Rosaleen cooked to their rooms. I barely saw August except in the mornings when she crossed the yard headed towards the woods. She would wave at me, and if I ran over and asked where she was going, could I come, too, she would smile and say not today, that she was still doing her mourning. Sometimes she would stay out in the woods past lunch.

I had to fight an impulse to say, *But I need to talk to you*. Life was so funny. I'd spent over a month here dillydallying around, refusing to tell August about my mother when I could have done it so easy, and now that I really needed to tell her, I couldn't. You just don't interrupt somebody's mourning with your own problems.

I helped Rosaleen some in the kitchen, but mostly I was free to lie around and write in my notebook. I wrote so many things from my heart that I used up all the pages.

It surprised me no end how much I missed our ordinary, routine life—the simple act of pouring wax into a candle mould or repairing a broken hive box. Kneeling for evening prayers to Our Lady.

I walked in the woods in the afternoon when I was sure August wasn't out there. I would pick a tree and say, *If a bird lands in that tree before I count to ten, that is my mother sending her sign of love*. When I got to seven, I would start counting real slow, dragging it out. I would get to fifty sometimes, and no bird.

I studied my map of South Carolina at night when everyone was asleep, trying to figure where me and Rosaleen might head next, but it nearly crushed me to think of leaving.

Sometimes I didn't even feel like getting out of bed. I took to wearing my days-of-the-week panties out of order. It could be Monday and I'd have on underwear saying Thursday. I just didn't care.

The only time I saw June was when Neil came over, which was every single day. She would come out wearing hoop earrings, and off they'd go, taking long rides in his car, which, she said, did her a world of good. The wind rearranged her thoughts, and the countryside made her see all the life still left out there waiting to be lived. Neil would get behind the wheel, and June would slide over on the front seat so she was practically under the wheel with him. Honestly, I worried for their safety.

Zach showed up a few times just to visit and found me in the lawn chair with my legs tucked under me, reading back over my notebook. Sometimes when I saw him my stomach went through a series of sudden drops and lurches.

'You are one-third friend, one-third brother, one-third bee partner, and one-third boyfriend,' I told him. He explained to me I had one too many thirds in the equation, which, of course, I knew, as I am bad in math but not *that* bad. We stared at each other as I tried to figure out which third would get deleted.

I said. 'If I was a Negro girl—'

He placed his fingers across my lips. 'We can't think of changing our skin,' he said. 'Change the world—that's how we gotta think.'

All he could talk about was going to law school and busting ass. He didn't say *white* ass, but I believe that's what he meant. There was a place inside him now that hadn't been there before. Heated, charged, angry. Coming into his presence was like stepping up to a gas heater, to a row of blue fire burning in the dark, wet curve of his eyes.

His conversations were all about the race riots in New Jersey, policemen taking their nightsticks to Negro boys who threw stones, about Molotov cocktails, sit-ins, Malcolm X, and the Afro-American Unity group giving the Ku Klux Klan a taste of their own medicine.

I wanted to say to Zach, *Remember when we ate May's Kool-Aid ice under the pine trees? Remember when you sang 'Blueberry Hill'? Remember?*

After nonstop mourning all week, just when I thought we would go on for ever in our private, grieving worlds and never again eat another meal together or work side by side in the honey house, I found Rosaleen in the kitchen laying the table for four, using the Sunday-china plates with pink flowers and lacy scallops round the edge. I broke out with happiness because life seemed headed back to normal.

Rosaleen put a beeswax candle on the table, and I believe that was the first candlelit meal of my life. Here was the menu: smothered chicken, rice and gravy, butter beans, sliced tomatoes, biscuits, and *candlelight*.

We had barely started in when Rosaleen said to June, 'So are you gonna marry Neil or not?'

August and I both stopped chewing and sat up.

'That's for me to know and you to find out,' June answered.

'How are we supposed to find out, if you won't tell us?' said Rosaleen.

When we'd finished the food, August produced four bottles of ice-cold Coca-Colas from the refrigerator, along with four little packages of salted peanuts. We watched her pop the tops off the Cokes.

'What the heck is *this*?' said June

'It's Lily's and my favourite dessert,' August told her, smiling over at me. 'We like to pour our peanuts straight into the bottle, but you can eat yours separately if you prefer.'

'I think I prefer mine separate,' said June, rolling her eyes.

'I wanted to make a cobbler,' Rosaleen told June, 'but August said it was gonna be Cokes and peanuts.' She said 'Cokes and peanuts' the way you might say 'snot and boogers'.

August laughed. 'They don't know a delicacy when they see one, do they Lily?'

'No, ma'am,' I said, shaking the peanuts into my bottle, where they caused a little reaction of foam, then floated on the brown liquid. I drank and munched with the glory of salt and sweet in my mouth at the same time, all the while looking towards the window, at birds flying home to their nests and moonlight just starting to pour down on the midlands of South Carolina, this place where I was tucked away with three women whose faces shone with candle glow.

When we had drained the Cokes, we went to the parlour to say our Hail Marys together for the first time since May had died.

I knelt on the rug by June, while Rosaleen, as usual, helped herself to the rocker. August stood beside Our Lady and folded May's suicide letter so it resembled a tiny paper airplane. She wedged it into a deep crevice that ran down the side of Our Lady's neck. Then she patted black Mary's shoulder and let out a long sigh that made the airless room feel alive again. And said, 'Well, that's that.'

I'd been staying up in May's room with Rosaleen ever since May died, but when Rosaleen and I started to climb the stairs that night, on impulse I said, 'You know what? I think I'll move back into the honey house.' I found out I'd missed having a room to myself.

Rosaleen put her hands on her waist. 'Good Lord, all that fuss you made about me moving out and leaving you, now here you are wanting to leave me.'

Actually, she didn't care one bit that I wanted to move out; she just couldn't pass up a chance to give me a hard time. 'Come on, I'll help you carry your stuff over there,' she said.

'You mean, *now*?'

'No time like the present,' she told me.

I guess she'd missed having a room to herself, too.

After Rosaleen left, I looked round my old room in the honey house—it was so quiet. All I could think was how this time tomorrow the truth would be out, how everything would change.

I got my mother's photograph and the black Mary picture from my bag, ready to show August. I slid them under my pillow, but when I turned out the light, fear filled up my hard, narrow bed. It told me all the ways life could go wrong. It had me in a girls' prison camp in the Florida Everglades. Why the Everglades, I don't know, except I've always thought that would be the worst place to be in prison. Think of all the alligators and snakes, not to mention heat worse than we had here. I could not imagine breathing in Florida. I would be down there suffocating and never see August again.

It was fear all night long. I would've given anything to be back in May's room, listening to Rosaleen snore.

The next morning I slept late, considering the on-and-off night I'd had, plus I'd been falling into lazy habits without the honey house to keep me industrious. The smell of fresh-baked cake wafted all the way from the pink house to my cot, curled into my nostrils, and woke me up.

When I got to the kitchen, there were August, June and Rosaleen, dusted with flour, baking small cakes the size of honey buns. They were singing while they worked, singing like the Supremes, like the Marvelettes, like the Crystals wiggling their butts to 'Da Doo Ron Ron'.

'What are y'all doing?' I said, grinning from the doorway.

They stopped singing and giggled, giving each other little nudges.

'Well, look who's up,' said Rosaleen.

June had on lavender pedal pushers with daisy buttons up the sides, the likes of which I'd never seen before. She said, 'We're baking cakes for Mary Day. It's about time you got over here and helped us. Didn't August tell you this was Mary Day?'

I glanced at August. 'No, ma'am, she didn't.'

August, who was wearing one of May's aprons, wiped her hands across the front and said, 'I guess I forgot to mention it. We've been celebrating Mary Day around here every August for fifteen years. Come on and get your breakfast, and then you can help us. We've got so much to do I don't know whether we're gonna make it.'

I filled a bowl with Rice Krispies and milk, trying to think over the snap-crackle conversation it was having with itself. How was I supposed to have a life-altering talk with August with all *this* going on?

'A thousand years ago women were doing this exact same thing,' said

August. 'Baking cakes for Mary on her feast day.'

June looked at my blank face. 'Today is the Feast of the Assumption. August fifteenth. Don't tell me you never heard of that.'

I shook my head. 'We didn't really allow Mary at our church except at Christmas.'

August smiled and dunked a wooden drizzle into the vat of honey, which sat on the counter by the toaster oven. While she spun honey across the tops of a fresh pan of cakes, she explained to me in detail how the *Assumption* was nothing less than Mary rising up to heaven.

'May is the one who started calling it Mary Day,' said June.

'It's not just about the Assumption, though,' August said, shovelling the cakes onto the wire racks. 'It's a remembrance for our own Lady of Chains. We reenact her story. Plus we give thanks for the honey crop. The Daughters of Mary come. It's our favourite two days of the year.'

'You do this for two days?'

'We start this evening and finish tomorrow afternoon,' said August. 'Hurry up with your cereal, because you've got to make streamers and garlands, hang the Christmas lights, put out the candleholders, wash the wagon, and get out the chains.'

I was thinking, *Whoa, back up*. Wash the wagon? Hang Christmas lights? Get out the chains? The chains?

The knock on the back door came as I was putting my bowl in the sink. 'If this isn't the best-smelling house in Tiburon, I'll be a monkey's uncle,' said Neil, stepping inside.

'Well, I guess you're saved from that special relationship,' June said.

She offered him a honey cake, but he shook his head, which was a dead giveaway right there that he had something on his mind. Neil did not refuse food. Ever. He stood in the middle of the floor, shuffling from one foot to the other.

'What are you doing here?' June asked.

He cleared his throat, rubbed his sideburns. 'I—I came over here hoping for a word with you.'

This sounded so stiff coming out of his mouth that June narrowed her eyes and studied him a second. 'Are you all right?'

'I'm fine.' He put his hands in his pockets. Took them out. 'I just want a word with you.'

She stood there waiting. 'Well, I'm listening,' she said.

'I thought we could take a drive.'

She looked around the kitchen. 'If you haven't noticed, I'm up to my ears in work, Neil.'

'I can see that, but—'

'Look, just tell me what it is,' June said, starting to get into one of her huffs. 'What is so all-fired important?'

I glanced at August, who had her lips screwed over to the side, trying to look busy. Rosaleen, on the other hand, had stopped all semblance of work and looked from June to Neil. Back to June.

'Hell,' he said, 'I came over here planning to ask you, for the hundredth time, to marry me.'

I dropped my spoon in the sink. August laid down the honey drizzle. June opened her mouth and closed it without anything coming out. Everyone just stood there.

Come on. Don't mess up your time to live.

The house creaked, like old houses do. Neil glanced at the door. I felt my shirt dampen all under my arms. I had the feeling that Neil was going to walk out of the door before June could answer.

Rosaleen said, 'Well, don't just stand there with your mouth open, June. Say something.'

June stared at Neil, and I could see the struggle in her face. The surrender she had to make inside. Not just to Neil, but to life. Finally she let out a long, sighing breath. 'All right,' she said. 'Let's get married.'

Rosaleen slapped her thigh and burst out with a whoop, while August broke into the biggest smile I believe I'd ever seen on her face. Me, I just looked from one person to another, trying to take it in.

Neil walked over and kissed June right on the mouth. I didn't think they were ever going to come up for air.

When they did, Neil said, 'We're going to the jewellery store this minute and pick out a ring before you change your mind.'

June cast a look back at August. 'Well, I hate to leave them with all this work,' she said, but I could tell she didn't mind a bit.

'Go on,' August said.

When they'd left, August, Rosaleen, and I sat down and ate honey cake while it was still hot, talking over what had just happened. We had all these chores facing us, but some things you have to sit and mull over before you can go on. We said, 'Did you see the look on Neil's face?' . . . 'Can you believe that kiss?' Mostly we just stared at each other, saying 'June's getting married!'

Getting ready for Mary Day was nonstop work. First August got me started on the streamers. I cut packages of thick blue and white crepe paper into strips till I had blisters on both thumbs. I formed little twists in the edges with my fingers to give them a curled effect, then dragged the stepladder into the yard and hung them from the myrtle trees.

I clear-cut the gladiolus bed and made a six-foot garland by wiring the blossoms to a piece of string, which I thought I never would get right. When I asked August what I was supposed to do with it, she said, 'Drape it round the wagon.' Well, of course. Why didn't I think of that?

Next I rummaged around the hall closet for the Christmas lights, which she had me wind round the bushes by the back-porch steps, not to mention all the extension cords I had to rig.

As I worked, Zach pushed the lawn mower, shirtless. I set up the card tables beside the myrtle trees so the streamers would drift over and tickle our faces while we ate. I tried not to look at him, his skin sparkling with sweat, his shorts slung low on his hips, the little tuft of hair starting under his navel.

He hoed up a big infestation of cabbage weeds, without even being asked to. He swung the hoe with a blaze of angry grunts, while I sat on the steps and dug candle wax out of two dozen glass holders. I refilled them with fresh candles and set them all around on the grass, under the trees, mostly in the little holes where the cabbage weeds had grown.

Up on the back porch August cranked the ice-cream churn. Beside her feet sat a coil of chains. I stared at it. 'What's that for?'

'You'll see,' she said.

At 6.00pm I was exhausted from Mary Day goings-on, and the real part hadn't even started. I got the last thing on my list done and was headed to the honey house to get dressed, when June and Neil pulled into the driveway.

June waltzed up with her hand stuck out so I could admire her ring. I looked it over, and I have to say Neil had outdone himself. It wasn't that big, really, it was just so pretty. The diamond was tucked inside a scalloped silver setting.

'That's the most beautiful ring I've ever seen,' I said.

She kept her hand stretched out, turning it, letting the diamond catch the light. 'I think May would have loved it, too,' she said.

The first carload of the Daughters drove up then, and June sauntered towards them with her hand outstretched.

Inside the honey house I lifted up my pillow to be sure my mother's photograph and her black Mary picture were still underneath. Feast Day or not, tonight *had* to be the night I got the truth from August. The thought set off a nervous quiver through me.

Heading back to the pink house, wearing clean shorts and a top, my hair combed, I stopped to behold everything. August, June, Rosaleen, Zach, Neil, Otis and all the Daughters of Mary stood around on the mowed grass beside the card tables, their laughter low and vibrating. Piles of food. Blue and white streamers rippling in the breezes. The Christmas lights glowed in spirals of colour around the porch, and the candles were lit, even though the sun was still working its way down.

I said to myself, *I love this place with my whole heart.*

The Daughters fussed over me—how good I smelt, how exceptional my hair was when it was combed. Lunelle said, 'Would you like me to make you a hat, Lily?'

'Really? You'd make me a hat?' Where I would wear a Lunelle-created hat was a mystery, but I wanted one all the same. At the least, I could get buried in it one day.

'Of course I'll make you a hat. I'll make you a hat you won't believe. What colour would you like?'

August, who was listening in, said, 'Blue,' and winked at me.

First we ate. By now I'd learned eating was a high priority with the Daughters. When we finished, the redness had seeped from the day and night was arranging herself around us. Cooling things down, staining the evening blue-black. Rosaleen brought out the platter of honey cakes and set them on one of the tables. August motioned us to stand round the table in a circle. The Mary Day programme was under way.

'These are Mary's honey cakes. Cakes for the Queen of Heaven,' August said. She took one of them in her hand and, pinching off a piece, held it before Mabelee, who stood next to her in the circle. August said, 'This is the body of the Blessed Mother.' Mabelee closed her eyes and opened her mouth, and August laid the cake on her tongue.

After Mabelee had swallowed, she did the same thing August had done—snipped off a piece and gave it to the next person in the circle, who happened to be Neil. Mabelee, who could not have measured five feet tall in spike heels, practically needed a stepladder to get up to his mouth. Neil crouched down and opened wide. 'This is the body of the Mother,' Mabelee said, and popped it in.

I did not know one thing, really, about the Catholic Church, but somehow I felt sure the Pope would have keeled over if he'd seen this.

Me, I had never seen grown-ups feed each other, and I watched with the feeling I might burst out crying. I don't know what got to me about it, but that circle of feeding made me feel better about the world.

The one who fed me turned out to be June. Opening my mouth, closing my eyes, and waiting for the body of the Mother, I heard June's whisper brush my ear—'I'm sorry for being hard on you when you first got here'—and then the sweetness of honey cake spread through my mouth.

I wished it could have been Zach standing next to me so I could lay the cake on his tongue. I would have said, *I hope this softens you towards the world. I hope it brings you a tender feeling.* Instead I got to give the pinch of cake to Cressie, who ate it with her eyes closed.

After we were all fed, Zach and Neil went to the parlour and returned carrying Our Lady of Chains. Otis followed them, lugging the pile of chains. They stood her upright in the red wagon. August leaned over to me. 'We're going to reenact the story of Our Lady of Chains. We're taking her to the honey house and chaining her in there for the night.'

I thought, *Our Lady is spending the night in the honey house. With me.*

As August pulled the wagon slowly across the yard, Zach and Neil braced Our Lady with their hands. If I do say so, the flower garland around the wagon set the whole thing off.

June carried her cello, while the Daughters trailed the wagon single file, carrying burning candles. They sang, 'Mary, star of the sea, Mary, brightest moon, Mary, comb of honey.'

Rosaleen and I brought up the rear, toting candles, too, trying to hum along, since we didn't know the words. I cupped one hand round the flame of my candle to be sure it didn't blow out.

At the door of the honey house, Neil and Zach lifted the statue out of the wagon and carried her inside. Otis stepped up and helped them get her situated between the extractor and the baffle tank.

'All right,' August said. 'Now we'll start the last part of our service. Why don't you stand in a semicircle right here around Our Lady.'

June played us a gloomy-sounding song on the cello while August retold black Mary's story start to finish. When she got to the part about the slaves touching Our Lady's heart and how she filled them with fearlessness and plans of escape, June turned up the volume.

'Our Lady became so powerful,' said August, 'that the master was forced to put her under house arrest, to chain her in the carriage house. She was cast down and bound up.'

Neil and Otis took the chains and started wrapping them round Our Lady.

August went on. 'But each time the master chained Mary in the carriage house, she would break the chains and return to her people.'

August paused. She went round the circle and looked at us one by one, letting her eyes settle on each face like she wasn't in any rush.

Then she lifted her voice. 'What is bound will be unbound. What is cast down will be lifted up. This is the promise of Our Lady.'

'Amen,' said Otis.

June began to play again, this time a more joyful tune. I gazed at Mary, wrapped head to toe in rusted chain. Outside, heat lightning pulsed across the sky. They all seemed to be sunk in their meditating, or whatever it was they were doing. Everyone's eyes were closed, except Zach's. He stared right at me.

I glanced at poor, shackled Mary. I couldn't bear seeing her like that. 'It is only a reenactment,' August had said. 'To help us remember. Remembering is everything.' Still, the whole idea wrapped me in sadness. I hated remembering.

I turned and walked out of the honey house, into the hush of night.

Zach caught up with me as I reached the tomato garden. He took my hand, and we kept walking, stepping over May's wall, walking into the woods without speaking. The cicadas were going crazy, filling the air with their strange singing. Twice I walked into a spider's web, feeling the fine, transparent threads across my face, and I liked them there. A veil spun from the night. Beneath the trees, moonlight trailed down.

I wanted the river. Its wildness. I wanted to strip naked and let the water lick my skin. Even May's death had not ruined the river for me. The river had done its best, I was sure, to give her a peaceful ride out of this life. I steered us towards the water.

Water can be so shiny in the dark. We stood on the bank and watched the moving pockets of light. We were still holding hands, and I felt his fingers tighten round mine.

'There was a pond near where I used to live,' I said. 'Sometimes I would go there to wade in the water. One day the boys from the next farm were there fishing. They had all these little fish they'd caught fastened onto a stringer. They held me down on the bank and hooked it round my neck, making it too small to pull over my head. I was shouting, "Let me up, get that off me," but they laughed and said, "What's the matter, don't you like your fish necklace?"'

'Goddamn boys,' Zach said.

'A few of the fish were already dead, but most of them flapped around with their eyes staring, looking scared. I realised if I swam out into the water up to my neck, they could breathe. I got as far as my knees, but then I turned back. I was too afraid to go any further. I think that was the worst part. I could've helped them, but I didn't.'

'You couldn't have stayed out there in the pond for ever,' Zach said.

'But I could've stayed a long time. All I did was beg them to undo the stringer. *Begged*. They said to shut up, I was their fish holder, so I sat there till all the fish died against my chest. I dreamed about them for a year. Sometimes I would be hooked on the chain along with them.'

'I know that feeling,' he said.

I looked as far into his eyes as I could see. 'Getting arrested—' I didn't know how to put it.

'What about it?' he said.

'It changed you, didn't it?'

He stared at the water. 'Sometimes, Lily, I'm so angry I wanna kill something.'

'Those boys who made me wear the fish—they were angry like that, too. Angry at the world, and it made them mean. You have to promise me, Zach, you won't be like them.'

'I don't want to,' he said.

'Me either.'

He bent his face close to mine and kissed me. At first it was like moth wings brushing my lips, then his mouth opening on mine. I gave way against him. He kissed me gently but hungrily, and I liked how he tasted, the scent of his skin, the way his lips opened and closed, opened and closed. I was floating on a river of light. Escorted by fish. Jewelled with fish. And even with so much beautiful aching inside my body, with life throbbing beneath my skin and the rushing ways of love taking over, even with all of that, I could feel the fish dying against my heart.

When the kiss was over, he looked at me with burning in his face. 'Nobody will believe how hard I'm gonna study this year. That jail cell is gonna make me earn grades higher than I ever got. And when this year is over, nothing can keep me from leaving here and going to college.'

'I know you'll do it,' I said. 'You will.' And it wasn't just words. I'm good at sizing up people, and I knew he would make himself into a lawyer. Changes were coming, even to South Carolina—you could smell them in the air—and Zach would help bring them. He would be one of those drum majors for freedom that Martin Luther King talked about.

He faced me, and shifting around on his feet, he said, 'I want you to know that I—' He stopped and looked up into the tree-tops.

I stepped nearer to him. 'You want me to know what?'

'That I—I care about you. I think about you all the time.'

It crossed my mind to say there were things he didn't know about me, that he might not care so much if he knew them, but I smiled and said, 'I care about you, too.'

'We can't be together now, Lily, but one day, after I've gone away and become somebody, I'm gonna find you, and we'll be together then.'

'You promise?'

'I promise.' He lifted the chain with his dogtag from around his neck and lowered it over my head. 'So you won't forget, OK?'

The silver rectangle dropped down under my shirt, where it dangled cold and certain between my breasts. Zachary Lincoln Taylor, resting there, along my heart.

Wading in up to my neck.

CHAPTER TEN

I WAITED FOR AUGUST in her room. Waiting was a thing I'd had tons of experience doing. Waiting for the girls at school to invite me somewhere. For T. Ray to change his ways. For the police to show up and drag us off to prison. For my mother to send a sign of love.

Zach and I had hung around outside till the Daughters of Mary finished in the honey house. We'd helped them clean up the yard, me stacking plates and cups and Zach folding up card tables. Queenie had smiled and said, 'How come you two left before we finished?'

'It got too long,' said Zach.

'So that's what it was,' she teased, and Cressie giggled.

When Zach left, I slipped back into the honey house and retrieved my mother's photograph and her black Mary picture from underneath my pillow. Clutching them in my hands, I glided past the Daughters as they finished up the dishes in the kitchen. They called to me, 'Where're you going, Lily?'

I hated to be rude, but I couldn't answer, couldn't speak a word. I wanted to know about my mother. I didn't care about anything else.

I marched straight into August's room, a room filled with the smell of beeswax. I switched on a lamp and sat on the cedar chest at the end of her bed, where I folded and unfolded my hands eight or ten times, then stuck them under my thighs.

The only other time I'd been in August's room was the time I'd fainted during the Daughters of Mary meeting and woken in her bed. I must have been too muddled then to see it, because it all seemed new to me.

For starters, everything was blue. Bedspread, curtains, rug, chair cushion, lamps. She had ten different shades of it. Sky blue, lake blue, sailor blue, aqua blue—you name a blue. I had the feeling of scuba diving through the ocean.

On her dressing table, August had a fish aquarium turned upside-down with a giant piece of honeycomb inside it. Honey had oozed out and formed puddles on the tray underneath. On her bedside tables were beeswax candles, melted into brass holders. I wondered if they could be the ones I'd personally created. It gave me a little thrill to think so.

I walked over and inspected the books arranged neatly on her bookshelf. *The Language of Beekeeping, Apiary Science, Bee Pollination, Bulfinch's Age of Fable, The Cultivation of Honey, Bee Legends Around the World, Mary Through the Ages*. I pulled the last one off the shelf and opened it across my lap, thumbing through the pictures. Sometimes Mary was brunette and brown-eyed, other times blonde and blue-eyed, but gorgeous every time. She looked like a Miss America contestant.

The big shock, though, was all the pictures of Mary being presented with a *lily* by the Angel Gabriel. In every one, where he showed up to tell her she was going to have the baby of babies, even though she wasn't married yet, he had a big white lily for her. As if this was the consolation prize for the gossip she was in for. I closed the book and put it back on the shelf.

A breeze moved through the room from the open window. I walked to it and stared out at the dark fringe of trees by the edge of the woods, a half-moon wedged like a gold coin into a slot, about to drop through the sky with a clink. Voices filtered through the screen. Women's voices. They rose in chirps and melted away. The Daughters were leaving.

I sat down on the cedar chest again.

Footsteps landed on the floorboards in the hallway, precise, unhurried steps. August steps. I sat up straighter, taller, my heart starting to beat so I could hear it in my ears. When she stepped into the room, she said, 'I thought I might find you here.'

I had a desire to bolt past her through the door. *You don't have to do this*, I told myself, but the wanting rose up. I had to know.

'Remember when . . .' I said. My voice came out barely a whisper. I cleared my throat. 'Remember when you said we should have a talk?'

She closed the door. A sound so final. *No turning back*, it said.

'I remember it very well.'

I laid out the photograph of my mother on the cedar chest.

August walked over and picked up the picture. 'You are the spitting image of her.' She turned her eyes on me, her big, flickering eyes with the copper fire inside them. I wished I could look out at the world through them just one time.

'It's my mother,' I said.

'I know, honey. Your mother was Deborah Fontanel Owens.'

I looked at her and blinked.

She dragged the chair from her dressing table over to the cedar chest and sat down facing me. 'I'm so glad we're finally going to talk this out.'

A full minute passed without either of us saying a word. She held the picture, and I knew she was waiting for me to break the silence.

'You knew she was my mother all along,' I said, uncertain whether I felt anger, or betrayal, or just plain surprise.

She placed her hand on mine and brushed her thumb back and forth across my skin. 'The first day you showed up, I took one look at you and all I could see was Deborah when she was your age. I knew Deborah had a daughter, but it was too much to believe that Deborah's daughter would turn up in my parlour. Then you said your name was Lily, and right that minute I knew who you were.'

Probably I should have expected this. I felt tears gather in the back of my throat, and I didn't even know why. 'But—but—you never said a word. How come you didn't tell me?'

'Because you weren't ready to know about her. I didn't want to risk you running away again. I wanted you to have a chance to get yourself on solid ground, get your heart bolstered up first. There's a fullness of time for things, Lily. You have to know when to prod and when to let things take their course. That's what I've been trying to do.'

It grew so quiet. How could I be mad at her? I had done the same thing. Held back what I knew, and my reasons were not the least bit noble like hers.

'May told me,' I said.

'May told you what?'

'I saw her making a trail of graham crackers and marshmallows for the roaches to follow. My father told me once that my mother used to do the same thing. I figured she'd learned it from May. So I asked her, "Did you ever know a Deborah Fontanel?" and she said yes she did, that Deborah had stayed in the honey house.'

August shook her head. 'Goodness, there's so much to tell. You remember I told you I worked as a housekeeper back in Richmond, before I got my teaching job? Well, that was in your mother's house.'

My mother's house. It seemed odd to think of her with a roof over her head. A person who lay on a bed, ate food at a table, took baths in a tub.

'You knew her when she was little?'

'I used to take care of her,' August said. 'I ironed her dresses and packed her school lunch in a paper bag. She loved peanut butter. That's all she wanted. Peanut butter Monday through Friday.'

I let out my breath, realising I'd been holding it. 'What else did she love?'

'She loved her dolls. She would hold little tea parties for them in the garden, and I would make these teeny-tiny sandwiches for their plates.' She paused, like she was remembering. 'What she didn't like was schoolwork. I had to stay after her all the time about it. One time she climbed a tree, hiding up there so she wouldn't have to memorise a poem. I found her and climbed up there with the book and wouldn't let her come down till she could say the whole thing by heart.'

Closing my eyes, I saw my mother perched beside August on a tree limb. I let my head drop.

'Lily, before we talk any more about your mother, I want you to tell me how you came to be here. All right?'

I opened my eyes and nodded.

'You said your father was dead.'

I glanced down at her hand still on mine, afraid she might move it. 'I made that up,' I said. 'He's not really dead.' *He just deserves to be dead.*

'Terrence Ray,' she said.

'You know my father, too?'

'No, I never met him, only heard about him from Deborah.'

'I call him T. Ray.'

'Not Daddy?'

'He's not the Daddy type.'

'What do you mean?'

'He yells all the time.'

'At you?'

'At everything in the world. But that's not the reason I left.'

'Then what was it, Lily?'

'T. Ray . . . he told me my mother . . .' The tears rushed up, and my words came out in high-pitched sounds I didn't recognise. 'He said she left me, that she left both of us and ran away.' A wall of glass broke in my chest, a wall I didn't even know was there.

August slid up to the edge of her chair and opened her arms. I leaned into them, felt them close around me. I was pressed so close to her I felt her heart like a small throbbing pressure against my chest. Her hands rubbed my back. She didn't say, *Come on now, stop your crying, everything's going to be OK*, which is the thing people say when they want you to shut up. She said, 'It hurts, I know it does. Let it out. Just let it out.'

So I did. With my mouth pressed against her dress, it seemed like I drew up my whole lifeload of pain and hurled it into her breast, heaved it with the force of my mouth, and she didn't flinch.

She was wet with my crying. Up around the collar her dress was plastered to her skin. I could see her darkness shining through the wet places. She was like a sponge, absorbing what I couldn't hold any more.

Every time I paused to sniff and gasp for a little air, I heard her breathing. Steady and even. As my crying wound down, I let myself be rocked in her breathing. Finally I pulled back and looked at her, dazed by the force of what had erupted. She ran her finger along the slope of my nose and smiled a sad kind of smile.

'I'm sorry,' I said.

'Don't be sorry,' she said. She went to her dresser and pulled a white handkerchief from the top drawer. It had 'A.B.' monogrammed on the front in silvery threads. She dabbed softly at my face.

'I want you to know,' I said, 'I didn't believe T. Ray when he told me that. I know she never would've left me like that. I wanted to find out about her and prove how wrong he was.'

I watched her move her hand up under her glasses and pinch the place between her eyes. 'And that's what made you leave?'

I nodded. 'Plus, Rosaleen and I got in trouble, and I knew if I didn't leave, T. Ray was gonna half kill me, and I was tired of being half killed.'

'What sort of trouble?'

I wished I didn't have to go on. I looked at the floor.

'Are you talking about how Rosaleen got the cut on her head?'

'All she wanted to do was register her name to vote.'

August squinted like she was trying to understand. 'All right, now, start at the beginning. Just take your time and tell me what happened.'

The best I could, I told her the miserable details, careful not to leave anything out: Rosaleen practising writing her name, the three men taunting her, how she poured snuff juice on their shoes.

'A policeman took us to jail,' I said.

'Jail?' she said. 'They put you in *jail*? What was the charge?'

'The policeman said Rosaleen assaulted the men, but I was there, and she was only protecting herself. That's all.'

August's jaw tightened, and her back went ramrod straight. 'How long were you in there?'

'Me, I didn't stay long. T. Ray came and got me out, but they wouldn't let Rosaleen go, and then those men came back and beat her up.'

'Mother of God,' said August. The words hovered over us. 'Well, how did she finally get out?'

I took a deep breath. 'I went to the hospital where they'd taken her to get stitches, and I—I sneaked her past the policeman.'

'Mother of God,' she said for the second time. She stood up and walked one loop around the room.

'I never would have done it, except T. Ray said the man who beat her was the meanest hater of coloured people anywhere, and it would be just like him to come back and kill her. I couldn't leave her there.'

It was scary, my secrets spilled out across the room, like a garbage truck had backed up and dumped its contents across the floor. But that wasn't what frightened me most. It was the way August leaned back in her chair with her gaze skimming the top of my head, looking at nothing but the sticky air, her thoughts a nerve-racking mystery.

A fever broke along my neck. 'I don't mean to be a bad person,' I said, my hands folded together like hands in prayer. 'I can't seem to help it.'

You would think I was totally cried out, but tears beaded again along my lids. 'I do all the wrong things. I tell lies, all the time. And I hate people. Not just T. Ray but lots of people. The girls at school, and they haven't done anything except ignore me. I hate Willifred Marchant, the poet of Tiburon, and I don't even know her. Sometimes I hate Rosaleen because she embarrasses me. And when I first came here, I hated June.'

A flood of silence now. It rose like water; I heard a roar in my head.

Look at me. Put your hand back on mine. Say something.

I was sniffling, wiping my cheeks, unable to stop my mouth from spewing out every horrible thing I could drum up about myself, and once I was finished . . . well, if she could love me then, maybe I would be able to look in the mirrors in her parlour and see the river glistening in my eyes, flowing on despite the things that had died in it.

'But all of that, that's nothing,' I said. I was on my feet needing to go someplace, but there was no place to go. We were on an island. A floating blue island where I spilled out my guts and then hoped I wasn't tossed out to sea to wait for my punishment.

'I—'

August was looking at me, waiting. I didn't know if I could say it.

'It was my fault she died. I—I killed her.' I sobbed and dropped down onto my knees on the rug. It was the first time I'd ever said the words to another person, and the sound of them broke open my heart.

Probably one or two moments in your whole life you will hear a dark whispering spirit, a voice coming from the centre of things. It will have blades for lips and will not stop until it speaks the one secret thing at the heart of it all. Kneeling on the floor, unable to stop shuddering, I heard it plainly. It said, *You are unlovable, Lily Owens. Unlovable. Who could love you? Who in this world could ever love you*?

I sank further down, onto my heels, hardly aware of myself mumbling the words out loud. 'I am unlovable.' When I looked up, I saw dust particles floating in the lamplight, August standing, looking down at me. I thought she might try to pull me to my feet, but instead she knelt beside me and brushed the hair back from my face.

'Oh, Lily,' she said. 'Child.'

'I accidentally killed her,' I said, staring straight into her eyes.

'Listen to me now,' said August, tilting my chin to her face. 'That's a terrible, terrible thing for you to live with. But you're *not* unlovable. Even if you did accidentally kill her, you are still the most dear, most lovable girl I know. Why, Rosaleen loves you. May loved you. It doesn't take a wizard to see Zach loves you. And every one of the Daughters loves you. And June, despite her ways, loves you, too. It just took her a while longer because she resented your mother so much.'

'She resented my mother? But why?' I said, realising that June must have known who I was all along, too.

'Oh, it's complicated, just like June. She couldn't get over me working as a maid in your mother's house.' August gave her head a shake. 'I know it wasn't fair, but she took it out on Deborah, and then on you. But even June came around to loving you, didn't she?'

'I guess,' I said.

'Mostly, though, I want you to know, *I* love you. Just like I loved your mother.'

August stood up, but I stayed where I was, holding her words inside me. 'Give me your hand,' she said, reaching down. Getting to my feet, I felt dizzy around the edges, that feeling like you've stood up too fast.

All this love coming to me. I didn't know what to do with it.

I wanted to say, *I love you, too, I love you all.* The feeling rose up in me like a column of wind, but when it got to my mouth, it had no voice, no words. Just a lot of air and longing.

'We both need a little breather,' August said, and she plodded towards the kitchen.

August poured us glasses of iced water from the refrigerator. We took them to the back porch, where we sat in the porch swing, taking little gulps of coolness and listening to the chains creak. It's surprising how soothing that sound can be.

After a few minutes August said, 'Here's what I can't figure out, Lily—how you knew to come here.'

I pulled the wooden picture of black Mary from my pocket and handed it to her. 'It belonged to my mother,' I said. 'I found it in the attic, the same time I found her photograph.'

'Oh my Lord,' she said, her hand going up to the side of her mouth. 'I gave this to your mother not long before she died.'

She set her water glass on the floor and walked across the porch. I waited for her to say something, and when she didn't, I went and stood beside her. She had her lips tight together and her eyes scanning the night. The picture was clutched in her hand, which dangled by her side. It took a full minute for her to pull it up so we could both stare at it.

'It has "Tiburon, S.C." written on the back of it,' I said.

August turned it over. 'Deborah must have written that.' Something close to a smile passed over her face. 'That would've been just like her.'

She handed me the picture. I stared at it, letting my finger move across the word 'Tiburon'.

'Who would've thought?' August said.

We went and sat in the swing, where we rocked back and forth. She stared straight ahead. Her slip strap had fallen down to her elbow, and she didn't even notice.

Thunder rumbled over the trees. I thought of my mother's tea parties, tiny sandwiches for a doll's mouth, and it washed me in sadness. Maybe because I would've loved so much to have attended something like that.

I gave a sideways glance at August. I forced my mind back to that moment in her bedroom when I'd confessed the worst of human things. Upon hearing it, she'd said, 'I love you. Just like I loved your mother.'

'All right then,' said August, like we'd never stopped talking. 'The picture explains how you came to Tiburon, but how did you find *me*?'

'That was easy,' I said. 'We hadn't been here any time before I spotted your Black Madonna Honey, and there was the same picture on it as my mother had. The Black Madonna of Breznichar of Bohemia.'

'You said that real nice,' August told me.

'I've been practising.'

'Where did you see the honey?'

'I was in that Frogmore Stew General Store out on the edge of town. I asked this man in a bow tie where he got it. He's the one who told me where you lived.'

'That would be Mr Grady.' She shook her head. 'I swear, it makes me think you were *meant* to find us.'

I *was* meant to, I didn't have a doubt about it. I just wish I knew where I was meant to end up.

'So why don't we talk some more about your mother?' she said.

I nodded. Every bone in my body was cracking with the need to talk about her.

'Any time you need to stop and take another break, you just tell me.'

'All right,' I said. What was coming, I couldn't imagine. Something that required *breaks*. Breaks for what? So I could dance for joy? Or so I could let the bad news sink all the way in?

A dog started barking way off in the distance. August waited for it to stop, then said, 'I started working for Deborah's mother in 1931. Deborah was four years old. The cutest child, but a real handful. For one thing, she used to walk in her sleep. One night she walked outside and climbed a ladder the roofers had left leaning against the house. Her sleepwalking nearly drove her mother crazy.' She laughed.

'And your mother had an imaginary friend. You ever had one?' I shook my head. 'She called hers Tica Tee. She would talk to her out loud like she was standing right there in front of us, and if I forgot to set a place for Tica Tee at the table, Deborah would throw a fit. Once in a while, though, I'd set a place and she'd say, "What are you doing? Tica Tee's not here. She's off starring in the movies."'

'Tica Tee,' I said, wanting to feel that on my tongue.

'Whatever Deborah struggled with, Tica Tee could do it perfectly,' August said. 'Tica Tee made hundreds on her school papers, got gold stars in Sunday School, made her bed, cleaned her plate. People told your grandmother—Sarah was her name—that she ought to take Deborah to this doctor in Richmond who specialised in children with problems. But I told her, "Don't worry about it. She's just working things out in her own way. She'll grow out of Tica Tee in time." And she did.'

Where had I been that I didn't know about imaginary friends? I could see the point of it. How a lost part of yourself steps out and reminds you who you could be with a little work.

'It doesn't sound like me and my mother were anything alike,' I said.

'Oh, but you were. She had a streak in her like you do. Suddenly she would up and do something other girls wouldn't dream of.'

'Like what?'

August smiled. 'One time she ran away from home. I can't even remember what she was upset about. We looked for her long past dark. Found her curled up in a drainage ditch, sound asleep.'

The dog had started barking again, and August grew quiet. We listened like it was some kind of serenade, while I sat with my eyes closed, trying to picture my mother asleep in a ditch.

After a while I said, 'How long did you work for—my grandmother?'

'A good long time. Over nine years. Until I got that teaching job I told you about. We still kept up after I left, though.'

'I bet they hated it when you moved down here to South Carolina.'

'Poor Deborah cried and cried. She was nineteen by then, but she cried like she was six.'

The swing had slowed to a stop, and neither one of us thought to rev it back up.

'How did my mother get down here?'

'I'd been here two years,' August said. 'Had started my honey business and June was teaching school, when I got a long-distance phone call from her. She was crying her eyes out, saying her mother had died. "I don't have anybody left but you," she kept saying.'

'What about her father? Where was he?'

'Oh, Mr Fontanel died when she was a baby. I never even met him.'

'So she moved down here to be with you?'

'Deborah had a friend from high school who'd just moved to Sylvan. She convinced Deborah it was a good place to be. Told her there were jobs and men back from the war. So Deborah moved. I think it was a lot because of me, though. I think she wanted me nearby.'

The dots were all starting to connect. 'My mother came to Sylvan,' I said, 'met T. Ray, and got married.'

'That's right,' August said.

When we'd first come out onto the porch, the sky had been clotted with stars. But now a damp fog rolled into the yard and settled over the porch. A minute later a light rain fell out of it.

I said, 'The part I will never figure out is why she married *him*.'

'I don't think your father was always like he is now. Deborah told me about him. She loved the fact he was decorated in the war. He was so brave, she thought. Said he treated her like a princess.'

I could have laughed in her face. 'This isn't the same Terrence Ray, I can tell you that right now.'

'You know, Lily, people can start out one way, and by the time life gets through with them they end up completely different. I don't doubt he started off loving your mother. In fact, I think he worshipped her. And your mother soaked it up. Like a lot of young women, she could get carried away with romance. But after six months or so it started wearing off. One of her letters talked about Terrence Ray having dirt under his fingernails, I remember that. Next thing I knew she was writing me how she didn't know if she could live way out on a farm, that kind of thing. When he proposed, she said no.'

'But she married him,' I said, genuinely confused.

'Later on she changed her mind and said yes.'

'Why?' I said. 'If the love had worn off, why did she marry him?'

August cupped her hand on the back of my head and smoothed my hair with her fingers. 'I've thought hard about whether I should tell you, but maybe it'll help you understand everything that happened a lot better. Honey, Deborah was pregnant, that's why.'

The instant before she said it, I knew what was coming, but still her words fell like a hammer.

'She was pregnant with *me*.' My voice sounded tired.

'That's right, pregnant with you. She and Terrence Ray got married around Christmastime. She called long distance to tell me.'

Unwanted, I thought. *I was an unwanted baby*. Not only that, my mother had got stuck with T. Ray because of *me*. I was glad it was dark, so August couldn't see my face. You think you want to know something, and once you do, all you can think about is erasing it from your mind.

I listened to the hiss of rain. The spray floated over and misted my cheeks while I counted on my fingers. 'I was born seven months after they got married.'

'She called me right after you were born. She said you were so pretty it hurt her eyes to look at you.'

Something about this caused my own eyes to sting like sand had flown into them. Maybe my mother had cooed over me after all. Made embarrassing baby talk. Twirled my newborn hair like the top of an ice cream cone. Done it up with pink bows. Just because she didn't plan on having me didn't mean she hadn't loved me.

August went on talking while I leaned back into the familiar story I'd always told myself, the one about my mother loving me beyond reason. I'd lived inside it the way a goldfish lives in its bowl, as if that was the only world there was. Leaving it would be the death of me. I sat there with my shoulders slumped, staring at the floor.

'Are you all right?' August said. 'You want to go to bed now and sleep on all this, talk about the rest in the morning?'

'No' burst out of my lips. I took a breath. 'I'm fine, really,' I said, trying to sound unruffled. 'I just need some more water.'

She took my empty glass and went to the kitchen. When she returned with the water, she had a red umbrella hooked over her wrist. 'In a little while I'll walk you over to the honey house,' she said.

As I drank, the glass shook in my hand and the water would hardly go down. The sound of my swallowing grew so loud it blotted out the rain for several seconds.

'Are you sure you don't want to go to bed now?' August asked.

'I'm sure. I need to know . . . everything.'

August settled beside me on the swing. 'All right then,' she said.

'I know she only married him because of me, but do you think she was just a little bit happy?' I asked.

'I think for a while she was. She tried, I know that. I got a dozen or so letters and at least that many phone calls from her over the first couple of years, and I could see she was making an effort. Mostly she wrote about you, how you were sitting up, taking your first steps, playing patty-cake. But then her letters came less and less often, and when they did come, I could tell she was unhappy.

'One day she called me up. It was around the end of August—I remember because we'd had Mary Day not long before. She said she was leaving T. Ray. She wanted to know if she could stay with us here till she figured out where to go. Of course, I said, that would be fine. When I picked her up at the bus station, she didn't even look like herself. She had got so thin and had these dark circles under her eyes.'

My stomach did a slow roll. I knew we'd come to the place in the story I feared the most. I began to breathe fast. 'I was with her when you picked her up at the bus station. She brought me along, didn't she?'

August leaned over and whispered against my hair. 'No, honey, she came by herself.'

I realised I'd bitten the skin inside my cheek. The taste of blood made me want to spit, but I swallowed it instead. 'Why?' I said. 'Why didn't she bring me?'

'All I know, Lily, is that she was depressed, kind of falling apart. The day she left home, nothing unusual happened. She just woke up and decided she couldn't be there any more. She called a lady from the next farm to baby-sit, and she drove Terrence Ray's truck to the bus station. Up until she got here, I thought she'd be bringing you with her.'

The swing groaned while we sat there smelling warm rain, wet wood, rotted grass. *My mother had left me.*

'I hate her,' I said. I meant to shout it, but it came out unnaturally calm, low and raspy like the sound of cars crunching slowly over gravel.

'Now, hold on, Lily.'

'I do, I hate her. She wasn't anything like I thought she was.' I'd spent my life imagining all the ways she'd loved me, what a perfect specimen of a mother she was. And all of it was lies. 'It was easy for her to leave me, because she never wanted me in the first place,' I said.

August reached for me, but I got to my feet and pushed open the screen door leading to the porch steps. I let it slam behind me, then sat on the rain-sopped steps, hunched up under the eave.

I heard August move across the porch, felt the air thicken as she stood behind me on the other side of the screen. 'I'm not going to make excuses for her, Lily,' she said. 'Your mother did what she did.'

'Some mother,' I said. I felt hard inside. Hard and angry.

'Will you listen to me for a minute? When your mother got here to Tiburon, she was practically skin and bone. May couldn't get her to eat a thing. All she did was cry for a week. Later on we called it a nervous breakdown, but while it was happening we didn't know what to call it. I took her to the doctor here, and he gave her some cod liver oil and asked where her white family was. He said maybe she needed to spend some time on Bull Street. So I didn't take her back to him again.'

'Bull Street. The mental institution?' The story was getting worse by the minute. 'But that's for crazy people,' I said.

'I guess he didn't know what else to do for her, but she wasn't crazy. She was depressed, but not crazy.'

'You should've let him put her in there. I wish she'd rotted in there.'

'Lily!'

I'd shocked her, and I was glad.

My mother had been looking for love, and instead she'd found T. Ray and the farm, and then me, and I had not been enough for her. She'd left me with T. Ray Owens.

The sky was split by a zigzagged path of lightning, but even then I didn't move. I stared at a dollop of bird shit on the bottom step, the way the rain was smearing it into the crevices of the wood.

'Are you listening?' August said.

'I hear you.'

'Depressed people do things they wouldn't ordinarily do.'

'Like what?' I said. 'Abandon their children?'

Letting out a loud breath, August walked back to the swing and sat down. It seemed like maybe I'd disappointed her, and something about that punched a hole in me. Some of my pridefulness drained out.

I eased off the steps and went back inside, onto the screened porch. As I sat down beside her on the swing, she laid her hand on mine, and the heat flowed out from her palm into my skin. I shuddered.

'Come here,' she said, pulling me over to her. It was like being swept under a bird's wing, and that's how we stayed for a while, rocking back and forth with me tucked under there.

'What made her so depressed like that?' I said.

'I don't know the whole answer, but part of it was her being out on the farm, isolated from things, married to a man she really didn't want to be married to.'

The rain picked up, coming down in large, silver-black sheets. I tried, but I couldn't make heads or tails of my heart. One minute I hated my mother, the next I felt sorry for her.

'OK, she was having a nervous breakdown, but how could she leave me behind like that?' I said.

'After she'd been here three months and was feeling a little better, she started talking about how much she missed you. Finally she went back to Sylvan to get you.'

I sat up and looked at August. 'She came back to get me?'

'She planned to bring you here to Tiburon to live. She even talked to Clayton about filing divorce papers. The last time I saw her, she was on a bus waving at me through the window.'

I leaned my head on August's shoulder and knew exactly what had happened next. I closed my eyes, and there it was. The long-gone day that would never leave—the suitcase on the floor, how she'd tossed clothes into it without folding them. *Hurry*, she'd kept saying.

T. Ray had told me she came back for her things. But she'd come back for me, too. She'd wanted to bring me here, to Tiburon, to August's.

If only we'd made it. I remembered the sound of T. Ray's boots on the stairs. I wanted to pound my fists against something, to scream at my mother for getting caught, for not packing faster, for not coming sooner.

At last I looked up at August. When I spoke, my mouth tasted bitter. 'I remember it. I remember her coming back for me.'

'I wondered about that,' she said.

'T. Ray found her packing. They were yelling and fighting. She—' I stopped, hearing their voices in my head.

'Go on,' August said.

I looked down at my hands. They were trembling. 'She grabbed a gun from inside the closet, but he took it away from her. It happened so fast it gets mixed up in my brain. I saw the gun on the floor, and I picked it up. I don't know why I did that. I—I wanted to help. To give it back to her. Why did I do that? Why did I pick it up?'

August slid out to the edge of the swing and turned to face me. 'Do you remember what happened next, after you picked it up?'

I shook my head. 'Only the noise. The explosion. So loud.' The chains on the swing twitched. I looked over and saw August frowning. 'How did you find out about—my mother dying?' I asked.

'When Deborah didn't come back like she said, I called your house. A woman answered, said she was a neighbour. She said Deborah had been killed in an accident with a gun. That's all she would say.'

I turned and looked out at the night. 'You didn't know that I was the one, who—who did it?'

'No, I never imagined such a thing,' she said. 'I'm not sure I can imagine it now.' She laced her fingers together, then laid them in her lap. 'I tried to find out more. I called again, and Terrence Ray answered, but he wouldn't talk about it. He kept wanting to know who I was. I even called the police station in Sylvan, but they wouldn't give any information either, just said it was an accidental death. So I've had to live with not knowing. All these years.'

We sat in the stillness. The rain had nearly stopped, leaving us with all this quiet and a sky with no moon.

'Come on,' August said. 'Let's get you in bed.' We walked into the night, into the blurring song of katydids, the thud-splat of raindrops on the umbrella, all those terrible rhythms that take up inside when you let your guard down. *Left you*, they drummed. *Left you. Left you.*

Knowing can be a curse on a person's life. I'd traded in a pack of lies for a pack of truth, and I didn't know which one was heavier. Which one took the most strength to carry around? It was a ridiculous question, though, because once you know the truth, you can't ever go back and pick up your suitcase of lies. Heavier or not, the truth is yours now.

In the honey house, August waited till I crawled under the sheets, then bent over and kissed my forehead.

'Every person on the face of the earth makes mistakes, Lily. We're all so human. Your mother made a terrible mistake, but she tried to fix it.'

'Good night,' I said, and rolled onto my side.

'There is nothing perfect,' August said from the doorway. 'There is only life.'

CHAPTER ELEVEN

HEAT COLLECTED IN THE CREASES of my elbows, in the soft places behind my knees. Lying on top of the sheets, I touched my eyelids. I'd cried so much they were puffed out and half shut. If it hadn't been for my eyelids, I might not have believed any of the things that had passed between me and August.

I hadn't moved since August left, only lay there staring at the flat surface of the wall, at the array of night bugs that wander out and crawl around for fun after they think you're asleep. When I grew tired of watching them, I placed my arm across my eyes and told myself, *Sleep, Lily. Please, just go to sleep.* But of course, I couldn't.

More than once I'd thought of Our Lady. I wanted to talk to her, to say, *Where do I go from here*? But when I'd seen her earlier, she didn't look like she could be of service to anybody, bound up with all that chain around her. You want the one you're praying to at least to *look* capable.

I dragged myself out of bed and went to see her anyway. I decided that even Mary did not need to be one hundred per cent capable all the time. The only thing I wanted was for her to understand.

Right off I smelt the chain, its thick, rusty odour. I had the urge to unwrap her, but of course that would have ruined the whole reenactment August and the Daughters had going. The red candle flickered at Mary's feet. I plopped onto the floor and sat cross-legged in front of her.

The terrible thing was the anger in me. I didn't want to be angry. I told myself, *You don't have any right to be angry. What you did to your mother is a lot worse than what she did to you*. But you can't talk yourself out of anger. Either you are angry or you're not.

The room was hot and still. In another minute I would not be able to breathe for the anger filling me up. My lungs went out only so far before they struck against it and closed back in.

I got to my feet and paced in the darkness. Behind me on the worktable half a dozen jars of Black Madonna Honey waited for Zach to deliver them somewhere in town.

How dare she? How dare she leave me? I was her child.

I looked towards the window, wanting to smash the panes out of it. I wanted to throw something all the way to heaven and knock God clean off his throne. I picked up one of the honey jars and hurled it as hard as I could. It missed black Mary's head by inches and smashed against the back wall. I picked up another one and threw it, too. It crashed on the floor. I threw every last jar on the table, until honey was spattered everywhere. I stood in a gooey room full of broken glass, and I didn't care. My mother had left me. Who cared about honey on the walls?

I grabbed a tin bucket next and, letting out a grunt, threw it with so much force it left a dent in the wall. My throwing arm was nearly worn out, but I picked up a tray of candle moulds and flung that, too.

Then I stood still, watching the honey slide down the wall. There was a trickle of bright blood on my left arm. I had no idea how it had got there. My heart beat wildly. The room turned like a carousel, with my stomach gliding up and down. I felt a need to touch the wall with both hands to make it still again.

I walked back to the table where the honey jars had been and braced my hands against it. I couldn't think what to do. I felt a powerful sadness, not because of what I'd done, but because everything seemed emptied out—the feelings I'd had for her, the things I'd believed, all those stories about her I'd lived off like they were food and water and air. Because I was the girl she'd left behind. That's what it came down to.

Looking around at the wreck I'd made, I wondered if someone in the pink house might have heard the honey jars hit the wall. I went to the window and stared across the gloom in the yard. The panes in August's bedroom window were dark. I felt my heart in my chest. It hurt so badly. Like it had been stepped on.

'How come you left me?' I whispered, watching my breath make a circle of fog on the glass.

I stayed pressed against the window for a while, then went and cleared off a few pieces of glass from the floor in front of Our Lady. I lay down on my side, drawing my knees towards my chin. Above me, black Mary was flecked with honey and seemed not at all surprised. I lay in the emptiness, in the tiredness, with everything—even the hating—drained out. There was nothing left to do. No place to go. Just right here, right now, where the truth was.

I woke to Rosaleen's big hands shaking me and opened my eyes to a terrible brightness. Her face was bent over mine, the scent of coffee and grape jelly coming from her mouth. 'Lily!' she yelled. 'What in the Sam Hill happened in here?'

I'd forgotten there would be dried blood caked across my arm. I looked at it, at a piece of glass, small as a stub of diamond, burrowed in a puckered setting of skin. Around me, jagged pieces of jars and puddles of honey. Blood dotted the floor.

Rosaleen stared at me, bewildered-looking. I stared back, trying to make her face come into focus. Sunlight fell down around us.

'Answer me,' Rosaleen said.

I squinted in the light. My mouth couldn't seem to open up.

'Look at you. You've been bleeding.'

My head nodded. I looked at the wrecked room. I felt embarrassed, ridiculous, stupid. 'I—I threw some jars of honey.'

'*You* made this mess?' she said, like she couldn't quite believe it, like what she'd expected me to say was that a roving band of house wreckers had come during the night. 'Lord God in heaven,' she said.

I got to my feet, waiting for her to bawl me out, but she took her thick fingers and struggled to pluck the piece of glass from my arm. 'You need some Mercurochrome on this before you get infected,' she told me. 'Come on.' She sounded exasperated, like she wanted to take me by the shoulders and shake me till my teeth fell out.

I sat on the side of the tub while Rosaleen dabbed my arm with a stinging icy swab. She plastered a Band-Aid across it and said, 'There, you won't die from blood poisoning at least.'

She closed the medicine cabinet over the basin, then shut the bathroom door. I watched her take a seat on the commode, how her belly dropped down between her legs. I perched on the side of the tub and thought how glad I was August and June were still in their rooms.

'All right,' she said, 'why did you throw all that honey?'

I went over to the window ledge and picked up a seashell, a pretty white one, flat with yellow around the edges.

Rosaleen sat there watching me. 'Any time now,' she said.

'T. Ray was right about my mother,' I said. 'She left me. It was just like he said it was. She left me.' For a second the anger flared up, and it crossed my mind to slam the shell against the tub, but I took a breath instead. Throwing stuff wasn't that satisfying, I'd found out.

Rosaleen shifted her weight, and the toilet lid squeaked. 'So your mother did leave after all,' she said. 'Lord, I was afraid of that.'

I lifted my head. I remembered that first night after we ran away, down by the creek, when I'd told Rosaleen what T. Ray had said. I'd wanted her to laugh at the very idea of my mother leaving me, but she'd hesitated.

'You knew already, didn't you?' I said.

'I didn't know for sure,' she said. 'I just heard things.'

'What things?'

She let out a sigh. 'After your mama died,' she said, 'I heard T. Ray on the phone talking to that neighbour lady, Mrs Watson. He was telling her he didn't need her to watch after you, that he'd got one of the pickers out of the orchard. He was talking about me, so I listened.'

I knew Mrs Watson from church, from all the times she stopped to buy peaches from me. She was kind as she could be, but she'd always looked at me like there was something indescribably sad written across my forehead, like she wanted to come over and scrub it off.

I clutched the side of the tub as Rosaleen went on, not sure I wanted her to. 'I heard your daddy tell Mrs Watson, "Janie, you've done more than your share, looking after Lily these past months. I don't know what we would've done without you."' Rosaleen looked at me and shook her head. 'I always wondered what he meant by that. When you told me what T. Ray said about your mother leaving you, I guess I knew then.'

'I can't believe you didn't tell me,' I said and folded my arms across my chest.

'So how did you find out?' Rosaleen asked.

'August told me,' I said. I thought of all that crying I'd done in her room. The monogram on her handkerchief, scratchy against my cheek.

'August?' Rosaleen repeated, looking dumbfounded.

'She knew my mother back when she was a little girl in Virginia,' I explained. 'August helped raise her.' I waited a few seconds, letting it soak in. 'This is where my mother came when she left. When . . . Mrs Watson took care of me,' I said. 'She came right here to this house.'

Rosaleen's eyes grew even narrower. 'Your mother—' she said, then stopped. I could see that her brain was struggling to fit it all together. My mother leaving. Mrs Watson watching me. My mother returning, only to get killed.

'My mother stayed here three months before she went back to Sylvan,' I said. 'I guess one day it finally dawned on her: *Oh, yeah, that's right, I've got a little girl at home. Gee, maybe I'll go back and get her now.*'

I heard the bitter tone in my voice, and it came to me how I could lock that tone into my voice for ever.

Rosaleen got to her feet. I stood up, too, and we were sandwiched together between the tub and the toilet, staring at each other.

'I wish you'd told me what you knew about my mother,' I said. 'How come you didn't?'

'Oh, Lily,' she said, and there was gentleness in her words, like they'd been rocked in a little hammock of tenderness down in her throat. 'Why would I go and hurt you with something like that?'

Rosaleen walked beside me to the honey house with a mop flung over her shoulder and a spatula in her hand. I carried a bucket of rags and the Spic and Span. We used the spatula to scrape off the honey. Some of it had got all the way over onto August's adding machine.

We wiped off the floors and the walls, then went to work on Our Lady. We picked the place up and turned it back the way it was, and the entire time we didn't speak a word.

I worked with heaviness inside, with my spirit emptied out. There was my breath curling in hard puffs from my nostrils. There was Rosaleen's heart so full towards me it broke through into her sweating face. There was Our Lady talking with her eyes, saying things I could not make out. And there was nothing else.

The Daughters and Otis arrived at noon, lugging in all manner of potluck dishes, as if we hadn't eaten ourselves sick the night before. They tucked them into the oven to keep warm and stood around in the kitchen sneaking bites of Rosaleen's corn fritters, saying they were the finest fritters they'd ever had the pleasure of eating, which caused Rosaleen to swell up with pride.

'Stop eating up all Rosaleen's fritters,' June said. 'They're for lunch.'

'Oh, let 'em eat,' said Rosaleen, which floored me, since she'd been known to smack my hand for pinching a single crumb off her fritters before dinner. By the time Neil and Zach arrived, the fritters were nearly gone, and Rosaleen was in danger of floating off into the atmosphere.

I stood numb and plaster-stiff in the corner of the kitchen. I wanted to crawl on my knees back to the honey house and ball up in the bed. I wanted everybody to shut up and go home.

Zach started towards me, but I turned away and stared down the sink drain. From the corner of my eye I grew aware of August watching me. She walked over and touched her hand to my cheek. I didn't think August knew about me turning the honey house into a disaster zone, but she had a way of figuring things out. Maybe she was letting me know it was OK.

'I want you to tell Zach,' I said. 'About me running away, about my mother, about everything.'

'Don't you want to tell him yourself?'

My eyes started to fill up. 'I can't. Please, you do it.'

She glanced in his direction. 'All right then. I'll tell him the first chance I get.'

She led the group outside for the last of the Mary Day ceremony. We paraded into the back yard, where June was waiting for us, sitting in an armless kitchen chair, playing her cello. We gathered round her while the lights of noontime bore down. The music she played was the kind that sawed through you, cutting into the secret chambers of your heart and setting the sadness free. Listening to it, I could see my mother sitting on a Trailways bus, riding out of Sylvan, while my four-year-old self napped on the bed, not yet knowing what I would wake to.

It was a relief when Neil and Zach stepped out of the honey house carrying Our Lady. They carried her under their arms like a tube of carpet, with the chains slapping against her body. You'd think they would use the wagon again, something a little more dignified than this.

August said, 'Well, here we are, and here's Our Lady.'

I looked her over, proud of how clean she was.

August read Mary's words from the Bible: '"For behold from henceforth all generations shall call me blessed—"'

'Blessed Mary,' Violet interrupted. 'Blessed, blessed Mary.'

'Today, we're celebrating the Assumption of Mary,' August said. 'We're celebrating how she woke from her sleep and rose into heaven. And we're here to remember the story of Our Lady of Chains, to remind ourselves that those chains could never keep her down. Our Lady broke free of them every time.'

August grabbed hold of the chain around black Mary and unwrapped a loop before handing it off to Sugar-Girl, who unwrapped it a little further. Every one of us got to join in taking off a loop of chain. It made a clinking noise as it uncoiled in a pile at Mary's feet.

'Mary is rising,' said August, her voice concentrated into a whisper. 'She is rising to her heights.' The Daughters lifted their arms. 'Our Mother Mary will not be cast down and bound up. And neither will her daughters. We will rise, Daughters. We . . . will . . . rise.'

June sliced her bow across the cello strings. I wanted to lift my arms with the rest of them, but they hung limp by my sides. Inside, I felt small and abandoned. Every time I closed my eyes, I saw the Trailways bus.

The Daughters stayed with their arms reaching into the air. Then August picked up a jar of Black Madonna Honey from behind June's chair, and what she did with it brought everybody back to earth. She opened the lid and turned it upside-down over Our Lady's head.

Honey oozed down Mary's face, across her shoulders, sliding down the folds of her dress.

I looked at Rosaleen as if to say, *Well, great, we spent all that time cleaning honey off her, and here they go putting it back on.*

The Daughters swarmed around Our Lady like a circle of bee attendants and rubbed the honey into the wood, working it into the top of her head, into her cheeks, her neck and shoulders and arms, across her breasts, her belly.

'Come on, Lily, and help us,' said Mabelee.

Rosaleen had already dived in and was coating honey all over Our Lady's thighs. I hung back, but Cressie took my hands and dragged me over to Mary, slapped them down in the muck of sun-warmed honey, right on top of Our Lady's red heart.

I remembered how I'd visited Our Lady in the middle of the night, how I'd placed my hand on that same spot. *You are my mother*, I'd told her then. *You are the mother of thousands*.

'I don't get why we're doing this,' I said.

'We always bathe her in honey,' said Cressie. 'Every year.'

'But how come?'

August was working the honey into Our Lady's face. 'The churches used to bathe their special statues in holy water as a way to honour them,' she said. 'Especially statues of Our Lady. Sometimes they bathed her in wine. We settled on honey.' August moved down to Our Lady's neck. 'See, Lily, honey is a preservative. When we bathe Our Lady in it, I guess you'd say we're preserving her for another year.'

'I didn't know honey was a preservative,' I said, starting to like the feel of it under my fingers, how they glided as if oiled.

'Well, people don't think about honey like that, but it's so strong-acting people used to smear it on dead bodies to embalm them.'

This was a use for honey I hadn't considered. I could just see funeral homes selling big jars of honey for dead people, instead of coffins. I tried to picture *that* in the drive-through window at the funeral home.

I began to work my hands into the wood, almost embarrassed at the intimacy of what we were doing. Once Mabelee leaned her head over too far and got honey all in her hair, but it was Lunelle who took the cake with honey dripping off the ends of her elbows. She kept trying to lick it off, but of course her tongue couldn't reach that far.

The ants started a single-file parade up the side of Our Lady, drawn by the honey, and not to be outdone, a handful of scout bees showed up and landed on Our Lady's head.

Queenie said, 'Next I guess the honey bears will be joining us.' I actually laughed and, spotting a honey-free place near the base of the statue, worked to get it covered up.

Our Lady was covered with hands, every shade of brown and black, going in their own directions, but then the strangest thing started happening. Gradually all our hands fell into the same movement, sliding up and down the statue in long, slow strokes, then changing to a sideways motion, like a flock of birds that shifts direction in the sky at the same moment, and you're left wondering who gave the order.

This went on for I don't know how long, and we didn't ruin it by talking. We were preserving Our Lady, and I was content—for the first time since I'd learned about my mother—to be doing what I was doing.

Finally we all stepped back. Our Lady stood there with her chains spilled around her on the grass, absolutely golden with honey.

One by one the Daughters dipped their hands into a bucket of water and washed off the honey. I waited till last, wanting to keep the coating of honey on my skin as long as I could. It was like I was wearing gloves with magic properties. Like I could preserve whatever I touched.

We left Our Lady in the yard while we ate, then returned and washed her with water the same slow way we'd washed her with honey. After Neil and Zach carried her back to her place in the parlour, everyone left. August, June and Rosaleen started doing the dishes, but I slipped off to the honey house. I lay down on my cot, trying not to think, and failing.

Twenty minutes later, August tapped on the door. 'Lily, can I come in?'

'Sure,' I said, but I didn't bother to get up.

She breezed in holding a gold and white-striped hatbox. She stood for a moment looking down at me, seeming unusually tall.

She has brought me a hat, I thought. For one second I guessed it might be the hat Lunelle had promised to make for me, but she wouldn't have had time to sew up a hat this soon.

August sat on Rosaleen's old cot and placed the box on her lap. 'I've brought you some of your mother's belongings.'

I stared at the box. When I took a deep breath, it stuttered strangely as it came out. *My mother's belongings*. I didn't move. I smelt the air coming through the window, churned up by the fan. I could tell it had turned thick with afternoon rain, but the sky was holding back.

'Don't you want to see?' she said.

'Just *tell* me what's in it.'

She patted the lid. 'I'm not sure I can remember. I didn't even remember the box till this morning. I thought we'd open it together. It's just a handful of things your mother left here the day she went back to Sylvan to get you. I finally gave her clothes away to the Salvation Army, but I kept the rest of her stuff, what little there was. It's been in this box ten years, I guess.'

I sat up. I could hear my heart thudding. I wondered if August could hear it over there across the room.

She set the box on the bed and removed the lid. I stretched up a little to see inside it, unable to glimpse anything but yellowed tissue paper.

She lifted out a small bundle and peeled away the tissue. 'Your mother's pocket mirror,' she said, holding it up. It was oval and in a tortoiseshell frame, no bigger than the palm of my hand.

I eased off the bed and slid down onto the floor, where I rested my back against the bed. August acted like she was waiting for me to reach out and take the mirror. I practically had to sit on my hands. Laying it on the bed, August reached into the hatbox and unwrapped a hairbrush with a wooden handle and offered it to me. Before I thought, I took it. The handle felt funny in my hand, cool and smooth-edged, like it had been worn down by excessive holding. I wondered if she'd brushed her hair a hundred strokes every day.

As I was about to hand the brush back to August, I saw a long, black, wavy hair threaded through the bristles. I brought the brush close to my face and stared at it, my mother's hair, a genuine part of her body.

'Well, I'll be,' August said.

I could not take my eyes off it. It had grown out of her head and now perched there like a thought she had left behind on the brush. I knew then that no matter how hard you tried, no matter how many jars of honey you threw, no matter how much you thought you could leave your mother behind, she would never disappear from the tender places in you. I felt tears coming. The brush and the hair belonging to Deborah Fontanel Owens swam in my vision.

I handed the brush back to August, who dropped a piece of jewellery into my hand. A gold pin shaped like a whale with a tiny black eye and a spout of rhinestone water coming from its blow-hole.

'She was wearing that pin the day she got here,' August said.

I closed my fingers around it, then walked on my knees over to Rosaleen's bed and placed it alongside the pocket mirror and the brush, moving them around like I was working on a collage.

When I looked up at August, she was pulling a black book from the box. 'I gave your mother this while she was here. English poetry.'

I took the book in my hand, leafing through the pages, noticing pencil marks in the margins, not words but strange little doodles, spiralling tornadoes, squiggles with eyes, pots with lids, pots with faces, pots with curly things boiling out, little puddles that would suddenly give rise to a terrible wave. I was staring at my mother's private miseries, and it made me want to go outside and bury the book in the dirt.

Instead, I placed the book on the bed with the other things, then turned back to August, while she reached down into the box again, causing the tissue paper to whisper. 'One last thing,' she said, and she drew out a small oval picture frame of tarnished silver.

When she passed it to me, she held on to my hands for a second. The frame contained a picture of a woman in profile, her head bent towards a little girl who sat in a high chair with a smudge of baby food on the side of her mouth. The woman's hair curled in forty directions, beautiful, like it had just had its hundred strokes. She held a baby spoon in her right hand. Light glazed her face. The little girl wore a bib with a teddy bear on it. A sprig of hair on top of her head was tied with a bow. She lifted one hand towards the woman.

Me and my mother.

I didn't care about anything on this earth except the way her face was tipped towards mine, our noses just touching, how wide and gorgeous her smile was. She had fed me with a tiny spoon. She had rubbed her nose against mine and poured her light on my face.

Through the open window the air smelt like Carolina jasmine, which is the true smell of South Carolina. I walked over and propped my elbows on the sill and breathed as deeply as I could. Behind me I heard August shift on the cot, the legs squeak, then relax.

I looked down at the picture, then closed my eyes. I figured May must've made it to heaven and explained to my mother about the sign I wanted. The one that would let me know I was loved.

CHAPTER TWELVE

AFTER AUGUST AND I went through the hatbox, I drew into myself and stayed there for a while. August and Zach tended to the bees and the honey, but I spent most of my time down by the river, alone.

The month of August had turned into a griddle where the days just lay and sizzled. I plucked leaves off the elephant ear plants and fanned my face, sat with my bare feet submerged in the trickling water, felt breezes lift off the river surface and sweep over me, and still everything about me was stunned by the heat, everything except my heart. It sat like an ice sculpture in the centre of my chest. Nothing could touch it.

People, in general, would rather die than forgive. It's *that* hard. If God said in plain language, 'I'm giving you a choice, forgive or die,' a lot of people would go ahead and order their coffin.

I wrapped my mother's things in the falling-apart paper, tucked them back in the hatbox, and put the lid on it. Lying on my stomach on the floor, I pushed the box under my cot.

When I woke up in the mornings, my first thought was the hatbox. One night I had to get up and move it to the other side of the room. Then I had to strip off my pillowcase and stuff the box inside it and tie it closed with one of my hair ribbons. All this just so I could sleep.

I gave myself pep talks. *Don't think about her. It is over and done*. The next minute I would be picturing her in the pink house, or out by the wailing wall, stuffing her burdens among the stones. I would've bet twenty dollars T. Ray's name was squashed into the crevices out there. Maybe the name Lily was out there, too. I wished she'd been smart enough, or loving enough, to realise everybody has burdens that crush them, only they don't give up their children.

In a weird way I must have loved my little collection of hurts and wounds. They provided me with the feeling I was exceptional. I was the girl abandoned by her mother. What a special case I was.

We were deep into mosquito season, so a lot of what I did by the river was to swat at them. Sitting in the purple shadows, I stared at things until I seemed to melt right into them. Sometimes I would forget lunch, and Rosaleen would come and find me, bearing a tomato sandwich.

After she left, I would throw it in the river. I felt the same way I did right after May died, only multiplied by a hundred.

August had said, 'I guess you need to grieve a little while. So go ahead and do it.' But now that I was doing it, I couldn't seem to stop.

I knew August must have explained everything to Zach, and June, too, because they tiptoed around me like I was a psychiatric case. Maybe I was. Maybe *I* was the one who belonged on Bull Street, not my mother.

I wondered how much longer it would be before August had to act on the things I'd told her—me running away, helping Rosaleen escape. Rosaleen, a fugitive. August was giving me time for now, time to be by the river and do what I had to do, the same way she gave herself time there after May died. But it wouldn't last for ever.

It is the peculiar nature of the world to go on spinning no matter what sort of heartbreak is happening. June set a wedding date, Saturday, October 10. Neil's brother, an African Methodist-Episcopal reverend from Albany, Georgia, was going to marry them in the back yard under the myrtle trees. June laid out all their plans one night at dinner. She would come walking down an aisle of rose petals, wearing a white rayon suit that Mabelee was sewing for her. Lunelle had been commissioned to make her a wedding hat. Rosaleen offered to bake the wedding cake, and Violet and Queenie were going to decorate it with a 'rainbow theme'. All I can say is how brave June was.

One afternoon I went to the kitchen, nearly dying of thirst, wanting to fill a jug with water and take it back to the river, and found June and August clinging to each other in the middle of the floor.

I stood outside the door and watched, even though it was a private moment. June gripped August's back, and her hands trembled. 'May would've loved this wedding,' she said. 'She must've told me a hundred times I was being stubborn about Neil. Oh, God, August, why didn't I do it sooner, while she was still alive?'

August turned slightly and caught sight of me in the doorway. She held June, who was starting to cry, but she kept her eyes on mine. She said, 'Regrets don't help anything, you know that.'

The next day I actually felt like eating. I wandered in for lunch to find Rosaleen wearing a new dress and her hair freshly plaited.

'Where did you get that dress?' I said.

She turned a circle, modelling it, and when I smiled, she turned another one. It was what you would call a tent-dress—yards of material falling from her shoulders without benefit of waistband and darts. It had a bright red background with giant white flowers all over it. I could see she was in love with it.

'August took me into town yesterday, and I bought it,' she said. I felt startled suddenly by the things that had been going on without me.

'Your dress is pretty,' I lied, noticing for the first time there were no lunch fixings anywhere.

She smoothed her hands down the front of it, looked at the clock, and reached for an old white vinyl bag of May's that she'd inherited.

'You going somewhere?' I said.

'She sure is,' said August, stepping into the room, smiling at Rosaleen.

'I'm gonna finish what I started,' Rosaleen said, lifting her chin. 'I'm gonna register to vote.'

My mouth came open. 'But what about you being . . . you know?'

Rosaleen squinted at me. '*What*?'

'A fugitive from justice,' I said. 'What if they recognise your name? What if you get caught?' I cut my eyes over at August.

'Oh, I don't think there'll be a problem,' August said, taking the truck keys off the brass nail by the door. 'We're going to the voter drive at the Negro high school.'

'But—'

'For heaven's sake, all I'm doing is getting my voter's card,' said Rosaleen.

'That's what you said last time,' I told her.

She ignored that. She strapped May's bag on her arm.

'You wanna come, Lily?' said August.

I did and I didn't. I looked down at my feet, tanned and bare. 'I'll just stay here and make some lunch.'

August lifted her eyebrows. 'It's nice to see you're hungry for a change.'

They went onto the back porch, down the steps. I followed them to the truck. As Rosaleen got in, I said, 'Don't spit on anybody's shoes, OK?'

She let out a laugh that made her whole body shake. It looked like all the flowers on her dress were bobbing in a gust of wind.

I went back inside, boiled two hot dogs, and ate them without buns. Then I headed back to the woods, where I picked a few bachelor buttons that grew wild in the plots of sunshine before getting bored and tossing them away.

I sat on the ground, expecting to sink down into my dark mood and think about my mother, but the only thoughts I had were for Rosaleen. I pictured her standing in a line of people. I could almost see her practising writing her name. Getting it just right. Her big moment. Suddenly I wished I'd gone with them. I wished it more than anything. I wanted to see her face when they handed her her card. I wanted to say, *Rosaleen, you know what? I'm proud of you.*

What was I doing sitting out here in the woods?

I got up and went inside. Passing the telephone in the hall, I had an urge to call Zach. To become part of the world again. I dialled his number.

When he answered, I said, 'So what's new?'

'Who's this?' he said.

'Very funny,' I told him.

'I'm sorry about . . . everything,' he said. 'August told me what happened.' Silence floated between us a moment, and then he said, 'Will you have to go back?'

'You mean back to my father?'

He hesitated. 'Yeah.'

The minute he said it, I had the feeling that's exactly what would happen. Everything in my body felt it. 'I suppose so,' I said. I coiled the phone cord round my finger and stared at the front door, imagining myself leaving through it and not coming back.

'I'll come and see you,' he said, and I wanted to cry.

Zach knocking on the door of T. Ray's house. It could never happen.

'I asked you what was new, remember?' I didn't expect anything was, but I needed to change the subject.

'Well, for starters, I'll be going to the white high school this year.'

I was speechless. I squeezed the phone in my hand. 'Are you sure you wanna do that?' I said. I knew what those places were like.

'Somebody's got to,' he said. 'Might as well be me.'

Both of us, it seemed like, were doomed to misery.

Rosaleen came home, a bona fide registered voter in the United States of America. We all sat around that evening, waiting to eat dinner, while she personally called every one of the Daughters on the telephone.

'I just wanted to tell you I'm a registered voter,' she said each time, and there would be a pause, and then she'd say, 'President Johnson and Mr Hubert Humphrey, that's who.' This went on even after dinner. Just when we'd think she had it out of her system, out of the complete blue, she'd say, 'I'll be casting my vote for Mr Johnson.'

When she finally wound down and said good night, I watched her climb the stairs wearing her red and white voter-registration dress, and I wished again that I'd been there.

Regrets don't help anything, August had told June, *you know that*.

I ran up the stairs and grabbed Rosaleen from behind, stopping her with one foot poised in the air, searching for the next step. I wrapped my arms around her middle. 'I love you,' I blurted out, not even knowing I was going to say this.

That night when the katydids and tree frogs and every other musical creature were wound up and going strong, I walked round the honey house, feeling like I had spring fever. It was ten o'clock at night, and I felt like I could've scrubbed the floors and washed the windows.

I went over to the shelves and straightened all the mason jars, then took the broom and swept the floor. I still wasn't tired, so I stripped the sheets off my bed and went over to the pink house and got a set of clean ones, careful to tiptoe around and not wake anybody up. I got dust rags and Comet cleanser in case I needed them.

I came back, and before I knew it I was involved in a full-blown cleaning frenzy. By midnight I had the place shining.

I even went through my stuff and got rid of some things. Old pencils, a couple of stories I'd written that were too embarrassing for anybody to read, a torn pair of shorts, a comb with most of its teeth missing.

By now I was starting to get tired, but I took my mother's things out of the hatbox—her tortoiseshell mirror, her brush, the poetry book, her whale pin, the picture of us with our faces together—and set them up on the shelf by the fan. It made the whole room look different.

Drifting off to sleep, I thought about her. How nobody is perfect. How you just have to close your eyes and breathe out and let the puzzle of the human heart be what it is.

The next morning I showed up in the kitchen with the whale pin fastened to my favourite blue top. A Nat King Cole record was going. 'Unforgettable, that's what you are.' I think it was on to drown out all the commotion the washer was making on the porch. August sat with her elbows on the tabletop, reading another book from the bookmobile.

When she lifted her eyes, they took in my face, then went straight to the whale pin. I saw her smile before she went back to her book.

I fixed my standard Rice Krispies with raisins. After I finished eating, August said, 'Come on out to the hives. I need to show you something.'

We got all decked out in our bee outfits—at least I did. August hardly ever wore anything but the hat and veil.

Walking out there, August widened her step to miss squashing an ant. It reminded me of May. I said, 'It was May who got my mother started saving roaches, wasn't it?'

'Who else?' she said, and smiled. 'It happened when your mother was a teenager. May caught her killing a roach with a fly-swatter. She said, "Deborah Fontanel, every living creature on the earth is special. You want to be the one that puts an end to one of them?" Then she showed her how to make a trail of marshmallows and graham crackers.'

I fingered the whale pin on my shoulder, picturing the whole thing. Then I looked around and noticed the world. It was such a pretty day you couldn't imagine anything coming along to spoil it.

According to August, if you've never seen a cluster of beehives first thing in the morning, you've missed the eighth wonder of the world. Picture these white boxes tucked under pine trees. The sun will slant through the branches, shining in the sprinkles of dew drying on the lids. There will be a few hundred bees doing laps around the hive boxes. From a distance it will look like a painting you might see in a museum, but museums can't capture the sound. Fifty feet away you will hear it, a humming that sounds like it came from another planet. At thirty feet your skin will start to vibrate. The hair will lift on your neck. Your head will say, *Don't go any further*, but your heart will send you straight into the hum, where you will be swallowed by it.

August lifted the lid off a hive. 'This one's missing its queen,' she said.

I'd learned enough beekeeping to know that a hive without a queen was a death sentence for the bees. They would stop work and go around completely demoralised.

'What happened?' I said.

'I discovered it yesterday. The bees were sitting out here on the landing board looking melancholy. So I searched through the combs, and sure enough she was gone. I don't know what caused it. Maybe it was just her time.'

'What do you do now?'

'I called the County Extension, and they put me in touch with a man in Goose Creek who said he'd drive over with a new queen some time today.' As she lowered the lid, she said, 'I just wanted to show you what a queenless colony looked like.'

She lifted back the veils from her hat, then lifted mine back, too. She held my gaze while I studied the gold flecks in her eyes.

'Remember when I told you the story of Beatrix,' she said, 'the nun who ran away from her convent? Remember how the Virgin Mary stood in for her?'

'I remember,' I said. 'I figured you knew I'd run away like Beatrix did. You were trying to tell me that Mary was standing in for me at home, taking care of things till I went back.'

'Oh, that's not what I was trying to tell you at all,' she said. 'You weren't the runaway I was thinking about. I was thinking about your *mother* running away. I was just trying to plant a little idea in your head.'

'What idea?'

'That maybe Our Lady could act for *Deborah* and be like a stand-in mother for you.'

The light was making patterns on the grass. I stared at them, feeling shy about what I was going to say. 'I told Our Lady one night in the pink house that she was my mother. I put my hand on her heart, and for a while after that I really did feel stronger. Then I seemed to lose it. I think what I need is to go back and touch her heart again.'

August said, 'Listen to me now, Lily. I'm going to tell you something I want you always to remember, all right?'

Her face had grown serious, intent. Her eyes did not blink.

'All right,' I said, and I felt something electric slide down my spine.

'Our Lady is not some magical being out there somewhere, like a fairy godmother. She's not the statue in the parlour. She's something *inside* you. Do you understand what I'm telling you?'

'Our Lady is inside me,' I repeated, not sure I did.

'You have to find a mother inside yourself. We all do. Even if we already have a mother, we still have to find this part of ourselves inside.' She held out her hand to me. 'Give me your hand.'

I lifted my left hand and placed it in hers. She took it and pressed the flat of my palm up against my chest, over my beating heart. 'You don't have to put your hand on Mary's heart to get strength and consolation and rescue, and all the other things we need to get through life,' she said. 'You can place it right here on your own heart. *Your own heart.*'

August stepped closer. She kept the pressure steady against my hand. 'All those times your father treated you mean, Our Lady was the voice in you that said, "No, I will not bow down to this. I am Lily Melissa Owens, I will not bow down." Whether you could hear this voice or not, she was in there saying it.'

I took my other hand and placed it on top of hers, and she moved her free hand on top of it, so we had this black and white stack of hands resting upon my chest.

'When you're unsure of yourself,' she said, 'when you start pulling back into doubt, she's the one saying, "Get up from there and live like the glorious girl you are." She's the power inside you, you understand?'

Her hands stayed where they were but released their pressure. 'And whatever it is that keeps widening your heart, that's Mary, too, not only the power inside you but the love. And when you get down to it, Lily, that's the only purpose grand enough for a human life. Not just to love—but to *persist* in love.'

She paused. Bees drummed their sound into the air. August retrieved her hands from the pile on my chest, but I left mine there.

'This Mary I'm talking about sits in your heart all day long, saying, "Lily, you are my everlasting home. Don't you ever be afraid. I am enough. We are enough."'

I closed my eyes, and in the coolness of morning, there among the bees, I felt for one clear instant what she was talking about.

When I opened my eyes, August was nowhere around. I looked back towards the house and saw her crossing the yard, her white dress catching the light.

The knock on the door came at 2.00pm. I was sitting in the parlour writing in the new notebook Zach had left at my door, setting down everything that had happened to me since Mary Day. Words streamed out of me so fast I couldn't keep up with them, and that's all I was thinking about. I didn't pay attention to the knock. Later I would remember it didn't sound like an ordinary knock. More like a fist pounding.

I kept writing, waiting for August to answer it. I was sure it was the man from Goose Creek with the new queen bee.

The pounding came again. June had gone off with Neil. Rosaleen was in the honey house washing a new shipment of mason jars, a job that belonged to me, but she'd volunteered for it, seeing how badly I needed to write everything out. I didn't know where August was. Probably in the honey house, helping Rosaleen.

I look back and wonder: how did I not guess who was there?

The third time the knocking came, I got up and opened the door.

T. Ray stared at me, clean-shaven, wearing a white shortsleeved shirt with chest hair curling through the neck opening. He was smiling. Not a smile of sweet adoring, I hasten to say, but the fat grin of a man who has been rabbit hunting all day long and has just now found his prey backed up in a hollow log with no way out. He said, 'Well, well, well. Look who's here.'

I had a sudden, terror-stricken thought he might that second drag me out to his truck and hightail it straight back to the peach farm, where I would never be heard from again. I stepped back into the hallway, and with a forced politeness that surprised me and seemed to throw him off stride, I said, 'Won't you come in?'

What else was I going to do? I turned and forced myself to walk calmly into the parlour.

His boots clomped after me. 'All right, goddamnit,' he said, speaking to the back of my head. 'If you want to pretend I'm making a social visit, we'll pretend, but this ain't a social visit, you hear me? I spent half my summer looking for you, and I'm gonna take you out of here nice and quiet or kicking and screaming—don't matter which to me.'

I motioned to a rocking chair. 'Have a seat if you want to.'

I was trying to look ho-hum, when inside I was close to full-blown panic. *Where was August*? My breath had turned into shallow puffs.

He flopped into the rocker and pushed back and forth, that got-you-now grin glued on his face. 'So you've been here the whole time, staying with coloured women. *Jesus Christ*.'

Without realising it, I'd backed over to the statue of Our Lady. I stood, immobilised, while he looked her over. 'What the hell is that?'

'A statue of Mary,' I said. 'You know, Jesus' mother.' My voice sounded skittish in my throat. I was racking my brain for something to do.

'Well, it looks like something from the junkyard,' he said.

'How did you find me?'

Sliding up on the edge of the cane seat, he dug in his trouser pocket until he brought up his knife, the one he used to clean his nails with. 'It was *you* who led me here,' he said, pleased as punch to share the news.

'I did no such thing.'

He tugged the blade out of the knife bed, pushed the point into the arm of the rocker, and carved out little chunks of wood. 'Oh, you led me here, all right. Yesterday the phone bill came, and guess what I found on there? One collect call from a lawyer's office in Tiburon. Mr Clayton Forrest. Big mistake, Lily, calling me collect.'

'You went to Mr Clayton's and he told you where I was?'

'No, but he has an old-lady secretary who was more than happy to fill me in. She said I would find you right here.'

Stupid Miss Lacy.

'Where's Rosaleen?' he said.

'She took off a long time ago,' I lied. He might kidnap *me* back to Sylvan, but there was no need for him know where Rosaleen was.

He didn't comment on Rosaleen, though. He seemed happy to carve up the arm of the rocking chair like he was eleven years old, putting his initials in a tree. I think he was glad he didn't have to fool with her. I wondered how I would survive back in Sylvan. Without Rosaleen.

Suddenly he stopped rocking, and the nauseating smile faded off his mouth. He was staring at my shoulder with his eyes squinted almost to the closed position. I looked down to see what had grabbed his attention and realised he was staring at the whale pin on my shirt.

He got to his feet and walked over to me, deliberately stopping four or five few feet away, like the pin had some kind of voodoo curse on it. 'Where did you get that?' he said.

My hand went up involuntarily and touched the little rhinestone spout. 'August gave it to me. The woman who lives here.'

'Don't lie to me.'

'I'm not lying. She gave it to me. She said it belonged to—' I was afraid to say it. He didn't know anything about August and my mother.

His upper lip had gone white, the way it did when he was badly upset. 'I gave that pin to your mother on her twenty-second birthday,' he said. 'You tell me right now, how did this August woman get it?'

'You gave this pin to my mother? *You* did?'

'Answer me, damn it.'

'This is where my mother came when she ran away from us. August said she was wearing it the day she got here.'

He walked back to the rocker, shaken-looking, and eased down onto the seat. 'I'll be goddamned,' he said, so low I could hardly hear him.

'August used to take care of her back when she was a little girl in Virginia,' I said, trying to explain.

He stared into the air, into nothing. Through the window I could see the sun beating down on the roof of his truck. It was spattered with mud, like he'd been trolling the swamps looking for me.

'I should have known.' He was talking like I wasn't in the room. 'I looked for her everywhere I could think. And she was right here.'

The thought seemed to awe him. He shook his head and looked around, as if thinking, *I bet she sat in this chair. I bet she walked on this rug.* His chin quivered slightly, and for the first time it hit me how much he must've loved her, how it had split him open when she left.

Before coming here, my life had been nothing but a hole where my mother should have been, and this hole had left me always aching for something, but never once did I think what he'd lost or how it might've changed him. I thought about August's words: 'I don't doubt he started off loving your mother. In fact, I think he worshipped her.'

I had never known T. Ray to worship anyone except Snout, the dog love of his life, but seeing him now, I knew he'd loved Deborah Fontanel, and when she'd left him, he'd sunk into bitterness.

He jabbed the knife into the wood and got to his feet. I looked at the handle sticking in the air, then at T. Ray as he walked around the room touching things, the piano, the hatrack, the drop-leaf table.

'Looks like you're here by yourself?' he said.

I could feel it coming. The end of everything.

He walked straight towards me and reached for my arm. When I jerked away, he brought his hand across my face. T. Ray had slapped me lots of times before, sharp smacks on the cheek, the kind that cause you to draw a quick, stunned breath, but this was something else. This time he hit me full force. I heard the grunt of exertion escape his lips as the blow landed. And I smelt the farm on his hand, smelt peaches.

The impact threw me back into Our Lady. She crashed onto the floor a second before I did. I didn't feel the pain at first, but sitting up, gathering my feet under me, it slashed from my ear down to my chin. It caused me to drop back again onto the floor. I stared up at him.

He was shouting. 'How dare you leave me! You need a lesson, is what you need!'

I filled my lungs with air, tried to steady myself. Black Mary lay beside me on the floor, giving off the overpowering smell of honey. I lay there afraid to move, aware of the knife stuck in the arm of the chair across the room. He kicked at me, his boot landing in my calf, like I was a tin can in the road.

He stood over me. 'Deborah,' I heard him mumble. 'You're not leaving me again.' His eyes looked frantic. I wondered if I'd heard him right. 'Get up!' he yelled. 'I'm taking you home.'

He had me by the arm in one swoop, lifting me up. Once on my feet, I wrenched away and ran for the door. He came after me and caught me by the hair. Twisting to face him, I saw he had the knife. He waved it in front of my face.

'You're going back with me!' he yelled. 'You never should have left me.'

He was no longer talking to me but to Deborah. Like his mind had snapped back ten years.

'T. Ray,' I said. 'It's me—Lily.'

He didn't hear me. He had a fistful of my hair and wouldn't let go. 'Deborah,' he said. 'Goddamn bitch.' He seemed crazy with anguish, reliving a pain he'd kept locked up all this time. I wondered how far he'd go to try and take Deborah back. For all I knew, he might kill her.

I am your everlasting home. I am enough. We are enough.

I looked into his eyes. They were full of a strange fogginess. 'Daddy,' I said. I shouted it. '*Daddy*!'

He looked startled, then stared at me, breathing hard. He turned loose my hair and dropped the knife on the rug.

I stumbled back and caught myself. I heard myself panting. The sound filled the room. I didn't want him to see me look down at the knife, but I couldn't help myself. I glanced over to where it was. When I looked back at him, he was still staring at me.

For a moment neither of us moved. I couldn't read his expression. My whole body was shaking, but I felt I had to keep talking. 'I'm—I'm sorry I left like I did,' I said, taking small steps back.

He looked away, towards the window, like he was contemplating the road that had brought her here.

I heard a creaking floorboard in the hallway outside. Turning, I saw August and Rosaleen at the door. I gave them a quiet signal with my hand, waving them away. I needed to see it through by myself, to be with him while he came back to his senses. He seemed harmless now.

For a moment I thought they were going to ignore me and come in anyway, but then August put her hand on Rosaleen's arm and they eased out of sight.

When T. Ray turned back, there was nothing in his eyes but an ocean of hurt. He looked at the pin on my shirt. 'You look like her,' he said, and him saying that, I knew he'd said everything.

I leaned over and picked up his knife, bent the blade closed, and handed it to him. 'It's all right,' I said.

But it wasn't. I had seen into the dark doorway that he kept hidden inside, the terrible place he would seal up now and never return to if he could help it. He seemed suddenly ashamed. I watched him pushing out his lips, trying to gather back his pride, his anger, all that thunder-clap he'd first come striding in here with.

'We're going home,' he said.

I didn't answer him, but walked over to Our Lady where she lay on the floor and lifted her upright. I could feel August and Rosaleen out-side the door, could almost hear their breathing. I touched my cheek. It was swelling where he'd hit me.

'I'm staying here,' I said. 'I'm not leaving.' The words hung there, hard and gleaming. Like pearls I'd been fashioning inside my belly for weeks.

'What did you say?'

'I said I'm not leaving.'

'You think I'm gonna walk out of here and leave you? I don't even know these damn people.' He seemed to struggle to make his words forceful enough. The anger had been washed out of him when he'd dropped the knife.

'*I* know them,' I said. 'August Boatwright is a good person.'

'What makes you think she would even want you here?'

'Lily can have a home here for as long as she wants,' August said, stepping into the room, Rosaleen right beside her. I went and stood with them. Outside, I heard Queenie's car pull into the driveway. It had a muffler you couldn't mistake. August had called the Daughters.

'Lily said you'd run off,' T. Ray said to Rosaleen.

'Well, I guess I'm back now,' she said.

'I don't care where the hell you are or where you end up,' he said to her. 'But Lily's coming with me.'

Even as he said it, I could tell he didn't want me, didn't want me back on the farm, didn't want to be reminded of *her*. Another part of him—the good part, if there was such a thing—might even be thinking that I'd be better off here. It was pride now, all pride. How could he back down?

The front door opened, and Queenie, Violet, Lunelle and Mabelee stumbled into the house. Queenie stared at my cheek. 'Everybody all right?' she said, out of breath.

'We're all right,' said August. 'This is Mr Owens, Lily's father. He came for a visit.'

'I didn't get an answer at Sugar-Girl's or Cressie's house,' Queenie said. The four of them lined up beside us, clutching their bags up against their bodies like they might have to use them to beat the living hell out of somebody.

T. Ray sniffed hard and looked at the ceiling. His resolve was crumbling all around him. You could practically see bits of it flaking off.

August saw it, too. She stepped forward. Sometimes I forgot how tall she was. 'Mr Owens, you would be doing Lily and the rest of us a favour by leaving her here. I made her my apprentice beekeeper, and she's learning the whole business and helping us out with all her hard work. We love Lily, and we'll take care of her, I promise you that. We'll start her in school here and keep her straight.'

I'd heard August say more than once, 'If you need something from somebody, always give that person a way to hand it to you.' T. Ray needed a face-saving way to hand me over, and August was giving it to him.

My heart pounded. I watched him. He looked once at me, then let his hand drop to his side.

'Good riddance,' he said, and moved towards the door. We had to open up our little wall of women to let him through.

The front door banged against the back wall as he jerked it open and walked out. We all looked at each other and didn't say a word. We seemed to have sucked all the air from the room and were holding it down in our lungs, waiting to be sure we could let it out.

I heard him crank the truck, and before reason could stop me, I broke into a run, racing into the yard after him. Rosaleen called after me, but there was no time to explain.

The truck was backing along the driveway, kicking up dirt. I waved my arms. 'Stop, stop!'

He braked, then glared at me through the windshield. Behind me, August, Rosaleen and the Daughters rushed onto the front porch. I walked to the truck door as he leaned his head out the window.

'I just have to ask you,' I said.

'What?'

'That day my mother died, you said when I picked up the gun, it went off.' My eyes were on his eyes. 'I need to know,' I said. 'Did I do it?'

The colours in the yard shifted with the clouds, turned from yellow to light green. He ran his hand across his face, stared into his lap, then moved his eyes back to me.

When he spoke, the roughness was gone from his voice. 'I could tell you I did it. That's what you wanna hear. I could tell you she did it to herself, but both ways I'd be lying. It was you who did it, Lily. You didn't mean it, but it was you.'

He looked at me a moment longer, then inched backwards out of the driveway, leaving me with the smell of truck oil. The bees were everywhere, hovering over the hydrangea and the myrtle spread across the lawn, the lemon balm clustered at the fence. Maybe he was telling me the truth, but you could never know a hundred per cent with T. Ray.

He drove away slowly, not tearing down the road like I expected. I watched till he was gone from sight, then turned and looked at August and Rosaleen and the Daughters on the porch. This is the moment I remember clearest of all—how I stood in the driveway looking back at them. I remember the sight of them standing there waiting. All these women, all this love, waiting.

I looked one last time at the highway. I remember thinking that he probably loved me in his own smallish way. He had forfeited me over, hadn't he? I still tell myself that when he drove away that day he wasn't saying good riddance; he was saying, *Oh, Lily, you're better off there in that house of coloured women. You never would've flowered with me like you will with them.*

I know that is an absurd thought, but I believe in the goodness of imagination. Sometimes I imagine a package will come from him at Christmastime, something inspired, like a fourteen-carat-gold charm bracelet, and in his card he will write, '*Love*, T. Ray.' He will use the word 'love', and the world will not stop spinning but go right on in its courses, like the river, like the bees, like everything. A person shouldn't look too far down her nose at absurdities. Look at me. I dived into one absurd thing after another, and here I am in the pink house. I wake up to wonder every day.

In the autumn South Carolina changed her colour to ruby red and wild shades of orange. I watch them now from my upstairs room, the room June left behind when she got married last month. I could not have dreamed such a room. August bought me a new bed and a dressing table, white French Provincial from the Sears and Roebuck catalogue. Violet and Queenie donated a flowered rug that had been laying around in their extra room going to waste, and Mabelee sewed blue and white polka-dot curtains for the windows. Cressie crocheted four eight-legged octopuses out of various colours of yarn to sit on the bed. One octopus would have been enough for me, but it's the only handicraft Cressie knows how to do, so she just keeps doing it.

Lunelle created me a hat that outdid every other hat she'd ever made, including June's wedding hat. It reminds me a little of the Pope's hat. It is tall, just goes up into the air and keeps going. It does have more roundness than the Pope's hat, however. I expected blue, but no, she sewed it in golds and browns. I think it's supposed to be an old-fashioned beehive. I only wear it to the Daughters of Mary meetings, since anywhere else it would stop traffic for miles.

Clayton comes over every week to talk to us about how he's working things out for me and Rosaleen back in Sylvan. He says you cannot beat up somebody in jail and expect to get away with it. Even so, he says, they will drop all the charges against me and Rosaleen by Thanksgiving.

Sometimes Clayton brings his daughter Becca over when he comes. She's a year younger than me. I always picture her like she is in the photograph in his office, holding his hand, jumping a wave. I keep my mother's things on a special shelf in my room, and I let Becca look at them but not touch. One day I will let her pick them up, since it seems that's what a girlfriend would do.

Becca and I watch for Zach in the lunchroom and sit with him every chance we get. We have reputations as 'nigger lovers', which is how it is put to us, and when the ignoramuses ball up their notebook paper and throw it at Zach in the hallway, which seems to be a favourite pastime between classes, Becca and I are just as likely to get popped in the head as he is. Zach says we should walk on the other side of the hall from him. We say, 'Balled-up notebook paper—big deal.'

In the photograph by my bed my mother is perpetually smiling on me. I guess I have forgiven us both, although sometimes in the night my dreams will take me back to the sadness, and I have to wake up and forgive us again.

I sit in my new room and write everything down. My heart never stops talking. I am the wall keeper now. I keep it fed with prayers and fresh rocks. I wouldn't be surprised if May's wailing wall outlasted us all.

At the end of time, when all the world's buildings have crumbled away, there it will be.

Each day I visit black Mary, who looks at me with her wise face, older than old and ugly in a beautiful way. It seems the crevices run deeper into her body each time I see her, that her wooden skin ages before my eyes. I never get tired of looking at her thick arm jutting out, her fist like a bulb about to explode. She is a muscle of love, this Mary.

I feel her in unexpected moments, her Assumption into heaven happening in places inside me. She will suddenly rise, and when she does, she does not go up, up into the sky, but further and further inside me. August says she goes into the holes life has gouged out of us.

This is the autumn of wonders, yet every day, every single day, I go back to that burned afternoon in August when T. Ray left. I go back to that one moment when I stood in the driveway with small rocks and clumps of dirt around my feet and looked back at the porch. And there they were. All these mothers. I have more mothers than any eight girls off the street. They are the moons shining over me.

SUE MONK KIDD

One of Sue Monk Kidd's most vivid childhood memories is of the bees that visited her family home in Georgia each summer. 'They lived in a back bedroom and actually made honey inside the wall. Now and then it would leak out through the cracks and create a mess on the floor. No one ever considered exterminating them. As my mother said: "What kind of terrible people kill honeybees?"'

Although she had always dreamed of becoming a writer, Sue Monk Kidd chose to study nursing at college. A decision she puts down to 'watching too many episodes of *Dr Kildare*!' But she never lost the desire to write and, in her thirties, she began to write articles and essays, drawing on personal experiences. She became a contributing editor to *Guideposts* magazine, and published two successful nonfiction books, but her ultimate goal was to write fiction. 'It was a longing I couldn't ignore. It was very scary; I couldn't imagine having any success.'

The Secret Life of Bees started out as a short story, but the author was certain that one day she would develop it into a novel. '*The Secret Life of Bees* grew,' says Sue Monk Kidd, 'out of my Southern background and my intimacy with the racial wounds and tensions of the 1960s. I needed to do something with my memories of that time, to psychologically and spiritually digest those experiences and put them into a narrative.'

Although the author had quite literally lived with honeybees while growing up in Georgia, she admits to knowing 'nothing about bees or beekeeping before writing this book. I'd never even seen a beehive close up.' But as she set out to discover more about them, she became captivated. 'There's a mystique about bees and the making of honey that's fascinating, full of lore and imagery. It weaves a spell around you, if you begin to explore it. It's beautiful for a writer to play with.'

The mother of two grown children, Sue Monk Kidd also wanted to explore the roles of the mother and the family in her novel. 'I think the book is about the search for home, family, bonds, loving. What is family? Where do we find that haven? Sometimes it's in unlikely places. In the course of looking for a home, for a mother, Lily has to find something in herself and understand a lot more about herself. So I surrounded her with wise women who taught her.'

Sue Monk Kidd revelled in the joy of writing her first novel, but when she was halfway through it she suddenly realised that she had no idea how it was going to end. Then she had an amazing dream in which one of her characters, beekeeper August Boatwright, came to talk to her. 'She was complaining about my ideas for an ending. They were all wrong, she said, and proceeded to tell me the ending. I've always been a great dreamer,' the author admits, 'but that sort of thing's never happened to me before!'

Jane Eastgate

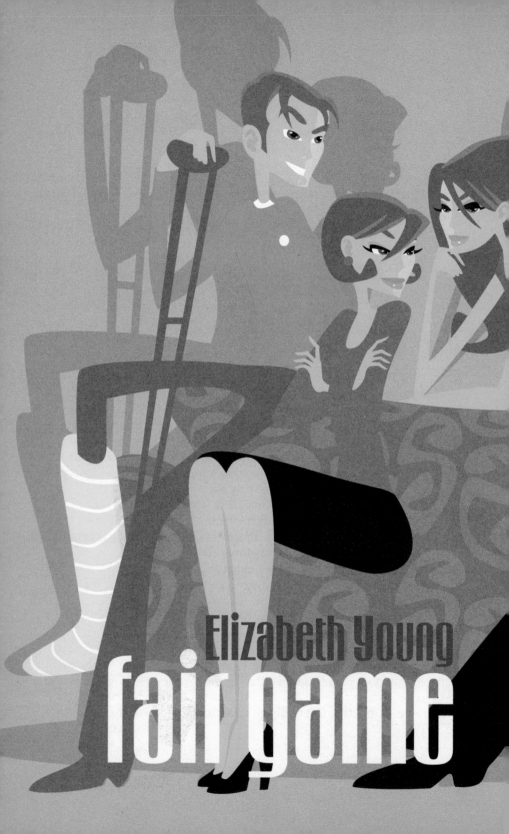

Elizabeth Young

fair game

Harriet Grey does not have time for a life of her own—she's too busy sorting out everyone else's problems. First, there's Sally, a penniless, unmarried mother, worried that her baby's father will turn up and upset everything. Then there's Jacko with a broken leg, and Helen from next door with a broken marriage.

What time does poor Harriet have for love? The only man she's fallen for in ages is involved with someone else and when he asks her out for a drink, she knows she should say no. But surely one little drink won't hurt, will it?

Prologue

MY SINS CAUGHT UP with me outside the deli, on one of those January afternoons we hardly ever get in London. It was arctic, ear-biting cold; the air smelt of coming snow.

Not that I cared; my personal central heating was on Dangerously High. Next door to the deli the travel agent's window was offering long-weekend cheapies to the Gambia, but even they couldn't tempt me. I was popping in for some fresh pasta when I almost collided with Rosie.

'Harriet! I was just on my way to see you! I hope you weren't after any of that tomatoey salady stuff, because I've just had the last of it.'

'No. Why were you coming to see me?'

I don't know why I asked. Rosie was a lovely person but if she'd had a website the address would have been *don'ttellanyoneItoldyoubut.com*. She had round brown eyes, full of what I can only describe as guilty relish. 'I just *had* to tell you the latest in the Nina/Helicopter saga.'

Rosie, Nina and I had all been at school together. 'Helicopter' was what Rosie called Nina's ex, and since he *was* ex, and had been for about a week, I didn't quite follow. 'What do you mean, the latest? He dumped her!'

'Yes, but she was just a teensy bit put out, remember?'

I hadn't witnessed the scene but Rosie had passed on every gruesome detail. Nina had ranted and demanded to know if there was someone else, and he'd said no, there wasn't, and she'd shrieked that he was a lying bastard and who was she, the bitch?

'Of course, she never believed there *was*n't anybody else,' Rosie went on. 'So no prizes for guessing what she's been up to now.'

I have special sensory equipment for occasions like this: antennae finely tuned to pick up 'oh shit' situations. 'What?'

'She's put a private dick onto him!'

'*What?*'

'Yes, that's what I thought. Bit OTT, isn't it? It's not as if they were engaged or anything.'

Maybe the Gambia wasn't a bad idea, after all. 'Since when?'

'Since right after he dumped her.'

Forget the Gambia—maybe a cheapie to Ulan Bator?

'It's costing a bomb but she said she had to know,' Rosie went on. 'The bloke said it might take a while to catch him with whoever she is.'

'They'll see him. Some furtive bloke in a grubby raincoat . . .'

'Oh, come on! He's a *pro*! Mega-zoom paparazzi lenses, you name it. I hope they keep their curtains drawn, that's all.'

They most certainly would.

'She's got a fair idea who it is,' she went on. 'Some dopey blonde she sacked a few weeks back. She had to introduce them at some do and Dopey was eyeing him up. She's done it to get her own back, Nina says.'

I moistened my lips. 'How would she know? The girl's no dopier than the average, either.'

Rosie's eyes popped wide. 'Are you telling me you actually know her?'

'I do, actually,' I said. 'Intimately.'

'You're *kidd*ing! Why the hell didn't you tell me before?'

Actually, Rosie's not that thick. As she gaped at me I saw her brain furiously working back, going whirr whiz bang. When it finally went 'click' her eyes popped wider still, if such a thing were possible.

'You do realise she's going to kill you?'

One

I DON'T QUITE KNOW why I said 'sins' back there. I never set out to pinch anyone's bloke, let alone Nina's. The day it all started, picking up a bloke was the last thing on my mind. Even I don't go out on the pull in manky old combats, a sweater that's seen better days, and hair sorely in need of Frizz-Ease. All I was thinking of, that drizzly afternoon, was finding a cab home. Since it was early December I was laden with what was supposed to be highly organised Christmas shopping. I'd made a methodical list saying *Mum, Bill, Sally, Tom, Jacko* . . . so I could go round the shops efficiently ticking them all off.

With customary efficiency I'd only ticked off Tom. My bags were full of impulse buys for the house and two bottles of ready-mulled wine to put me in the Christmas mood—the weather certainly wasn't. Mild and damp, it felt more like October.

Having started off in mist-like fashion, the drizzle had moved up a gear, as if it were thinking about turning to proper rain, instead. At this point I was just up the road from Covent Garden, with drizzled-on hair, arms coming out of their sockets, and a jumper starting to smell of wet Shetland sheep. That was when I saw Nina, coming out of a restaurant, with a bloke on her arm.

If I can misquote Jane Austen here, it is a truth universally acknowledged that if you bump into someone like Nina when you haven't seen her for four years and don't want to ever again, you'll be looking like a pig's breakfast. While she'll be looking like, well, like Nina.

Like a *Sunday Times* fashion shoot of some taupey thing in silk and cashmere, a snip at only £799. That dark-haired bob as sleek and glossy as ever. A face like an airbrushed L'Oréal ad.

Only about six paces away, she was talking and laughing in her silver-tinkle way to the bloke, who was holding her umbrella.

If she'd seen me, and recognised me, she'd have been over before you could say 'sick as a pig', with a delighted smile (delighted to make me sick as a pig, I mean) and a '*Harry!* How *are* you!' Then there'd be a couple of *mwah-mwah* kisses, and a 'This is Gorgeous Bloke—Gorgeous Bloke, this is Harriet—we were at school together and I used to be terribly nice to her on the surface but laugh behind her back because she had size eight feet and looked like a scarecrow.'

So before any such daymare actually occurred, I turned round and pretended to be riveted by a shop window. I heard tinkly laughter, with stuff like, '. . . and don't you *dare* be late—tinkle tinkle,' a kissy noise, and the sound of a car door slamming.

Of course I'd never intended to lurk there, eavesdropping, but something in that window detained me. When you're hiding from the Ninas of this world you don't expect to find yourself gaping at a massive wooden willy.

No, it wasn't a sex shop; the window was full of ethnic art. And the pride of the display was a six-foot-ish twisty chunk of tree, carved into a misshapen man: a primitive Jesus and fertility god combined. I was just searching for a price tag when someone said, 'Different, isn't it?'

And lo, there he was. Standing quite casually about three feet away, hands shoved in his trouser pockets. They were grey trousers, if you're interested: the bottom half of a quietly pricey suit.

It took me a second to get over the shock, but I said, casually enough, 'That's one way of putting it. I suppose you can't see a price tag?'

He peered a bit closer, then turned to me. 'Fifteen hundred quid.' And I took my first, proper, full-face look.

My first thought was: Just the sort of bloke I'd expect to see attached to Nina, followed swiftly by: On the other hand, maybe not.

The last time I'd seen her (at a wedding four years back) she'd had some tall, dark, good-looking specimen in tow, with an eligibility rating of eleven and a half out of ten. To me, though, he'd seemed a bit *plastic*. It had been quite a boost to my ego to realise I didn't fancy him, when everybody else was saying, 'Trust Nina to get a bloke like that.'

I don't quite know what it was with this one—he wasn't good-looking, exactly, but there was definitely no plastic and the spark hit me at once. His eyes were greeny-blue, his hair the colour of old, polished oak. He was taller than me by half a head (and I'm five foot nine) and marginally heftier than is currently fashionable.

I said, 'Oh, well, I suppose it's a bit steep for a cat scratching-post,' and he laughed.

Well. His spark had practically turned into a fire hazard, most of it coming from those greeny-blue eyes. For some reason I thought of those corny old films in which Lady Arabella's carriage is held up on the Great North Road. '*I will never part with my jewels!*' she says hotly to the rough-looking fellow in the mask. '*I would sooner part with my virtue!*' And the fellow drawls, '*Then I will have your virtue, my lady*,' and she sees the wicked glint in the eyes behind the mask, and thinks, '*Well, actually . . .*'

Thinking, trust bloody Nina to get a bloke like this, I said hastily, 'Well, better hit the road, if I can find a cab,' and readjusted my shopping. In addition to five carrier bags, my bag was slung over my shoulder, and I suddenly realised the zip was open and my purse wasn't in it.

I went cold and gaped at my bag. I said, 'My purse has gone,' like an idiot, and he said, 'Christ—are you sure?' and I hunted through my bag, as you do, but I knew it wasn't there.

I said, 'Yes, God, what a *fool* . . .'

He said, 'When did you last have it?' and I thought back, and realised it was twenty minutes ago, in some shop called Expensive Useless Stuff That Seems Like A Good Idea At The Time.

In a frozen panic I said, 'My credit cards—I must ring and cancel them . . . God, I didn't even bring my mobile . . .'

'Use mine, then. And let's get out of this weather.' In the relative shelter of the shop doorway, he handed me his mobile.

Of course I hadn't a clue what numbers to ring, so I phoned Sally at home, asked her to dig out credit-card statements and cancel for me. Then I said, 'If Jacko's in, ask him how much cash he's got. I'm laden with shopping—I want to bum a cab fare.'

'He's just gone out. And I've only got about six quid.'

'Never mind. See you later.'

I handed the phone back. 'Thanks so much. If I had any money, I'd buy you a drink.' I only said this because I'd just noticed a little wine bar two doors away. I certainly wasn't expecting the reply I got.

'Look, I can let you have a cab fare.'

I was appalled. If he thought I'd been dropping hints . . . 'No, really, I don't need a cab.' From the thigh pocket of my tatty old combats, I dug out my One-Day Travelcard. 'See? I'll take the tube.'

He glanced at my bags. 'With that lot? How far have you got to go?'

'Putney, but it won't kill me.'

'Christ, that's miles!' Almost before I'd blinked he'd whipped his wallet out and extracted a couple of notes.

I gaped at the proffered thirty quid. 'Look, it's very kind of you, but I really couldn't.'

'Why not?' He sort of smiled and added, 'It's Christmas.'

And I thought: God, it's not *fair*—I could fancy you rotten. But since I hadn't fancied anyone even half rotten for months, I decided I might as well make the most of it. Waste not, want not, as my Great Aunt Dorothy used to say when she was saving the oval tops off Kleenex boxes. (Handy for shopping lists, you see.)

Besides which, a cab beat the tube any day, especially with four tons of shopping and a ten-minute walk the other end. 'I'll only take it if you let me pay you back. Give me your address and I'll send you a cheque.'

'It's really not necessary.'

Great. I could see I'd put the wind up him. If you dished out your address to drizzled-on messes, they might turn up on your doorstep.

'But you could maybe buy me that drink some time.'

Er, sorry? I waited for him to grin, 'Only kidding—my girlfriend would kill me,' but there was just a little half-smile.

Well, I can be as cool as the next drizzled-on mess. 'Do you actually know anywhere that does thirty-quid drinks?'

'A couple of drinks, then.' The smile turned into three-quarters. 'And a packet of pork scratchings?'

I have to say, a wicked little *frisson* went through me. All I could think was: God, if Nina could see this, she'd go ape. 'Give me your number, then, and I'll give you a call.' I scrabbled in my bag for my organiser, only I was so organised I'd left it at home. All I could find to write on was a Tesco's receipt, so I gave him that.

It was while he was scribbling that I went all frozen again. Because in a sudden flash I knew exactly where my purse was.

I'd bought a cast-iron wart hog in that Expensive Useless shop (because he looked cute and it seemed like a good idea at the time) but after paying I'd ended up with my hands full and my purse tucked under my arm. And because I couldn't be bothered to put the bags down and my purse away properly, I'd let it drop in a carefully aimed manner into the Expensive Useless carrier bag, with the wart hog.

Only just as he'd stopped scribbling, and I was about to open my mouth to tell him, a cab hove into view. Two seconds later he'd not only grabbed the cab but put that thirty quid and the receipt into my hand, and I just didn't know how to come clean. I'll admit I didn't altogether want to, either. He might have put me down as a worrying case of pre-senile dementia. So all I said was, 'Thanks again—bye.'

I waved, and once he was out of sight peered sheepishly into the Expensive Useless carrier bag. There it was, battered brown calf, saying, are you mad, or what? Credit cards cancelled all for nothing, all that hassle, just for a ride home and a drink with a bloke of Nina's?

Sally said much the same, moments after I was in the door. 'You dope! After I'd gone mad unearthing Visa numbers, too.'

However, I hadn't got to the best bit. Once we were in the kitchen I tipped one of those bottles of mulled wine into a pan. 'Remember Rosie? Ex-school Rosie who came round the other week?'

'Yes, she was nice. She had two helpings of my gone-wrong veggie lasagne and pretended it was lovely."

'Well, she was talking about someone called Nina, remember?'

'You were both talking about her—or was it bitching about her.'

'Well, anyway. Her bloke just gave me his phone number.'

A couple of minutes later, after I'd related every juicy detail, she said, 'So what's his name?'

I realised I hadn't a clue.

'**H**ad a good day, dear?' said Sally, when I made it home two days later after my nightly game of District Line Sardines. 'It's been so exciting here, I can't tell you. There were terrible ructions on *Home and Away*—I needed a good strong cup of PG to settle my nerves.'

Sally was 'unwaged', as they like to put it, and had been for months. She didn't feel any more brain dead or useless than the rest of us, but was sensitive about other people thinking she was.

While spooning coffee into the filter I started telling her about my day, to perk her up. 'I gave Rosie a call this morning and we met for a sandwich. I told her about Mr Cab Fare and she's met him.'

Sally's green eyes widened instantly. 'And?'

'At least, I suppose it's him,' I went on. 'Nina's been seeing him for a couple of months and thinks he's the *cojones del perro*.' This had a more sophisticated ring than 'the dog's bollocks'; we'd used it almost since we'd met, which was eight years ago now, on a bus from Malaga Airport.

Having clicked immediately, Sally and I had never unclicked since. She could be unbelievably pig-headed but so could I. We'd had masses in common. Both heading for English-teaching jobs in Granada, we were also both recent graduates with no idea what we wanted to do, except that we didn't want to do it in England, and both thought teaching English would be a brilliant way to travel and get paid at the same time.

We'd soon discovered even more similarities. Both only children, we had the kind of parents who'd made tutting noises about offspring who were putting off getting 'proper' jobs. (Actually it was my mother who'd said stuff like this. Dad had said, 'Do what you want—I wish I had,' and slipped me a cheque, bless him.)

I'd done the TEFL bit for five years, since when I'd had more jobs than you could shake a P45 at. Frequently I'd had two at once, while frantically saving for six weeks' scuba-diving in Sulawesi or whatever.

Back to Nina and Mr Cab Fare, though. Rosie had met him at Nina's flat-warming only last week, having been dragged there by Suzanne, another old contemporary from school. Rosie was staying with her on a temporary basis while Suzanne's co-sharer was 'doing' India.

Rosie had talked about Nina's do all through our lunch. 'She was up to here with Nina even before they went,' I told Sally. 'Even Suzanne was, and she's supposed to be best buddies with Nina. Nina had been swanking on about this bloke's five-star gorgeousness, his corporate high-flying-ness and all that. She'd even chucked in a snippet about some flight the other week being forty minutes late, which would have been a disaster had it not been for his personal helicopter waiting to whisk him off to an urgent meeting with God.'

'Well, I suppose God gets a bit hacked off if people are late.' Sally poured two coffees and came to join me at the battered pine table.

'Even Suzanne was browned off with all this helicopter swank,' I went on. 'So by the time they left for Nina's do, Rosie was hoping this

Helicopter'd turn out to be a pompous prat, at least.'

'Can't blame her.' Sally rubbed at what looked like dried sick down the front of one of Jacko's grey Liverpool FC sweatshirts. She had exhausted circles under her eyes and her chin-length blonde hair had that mind-of-its-own look, telling me she'd let it dry itself again.

'But she had to admit that he was at least four-star gorgeous and seemed really nice, too,' I continued. 'Not only that, but the flat was a state-of-the-art loft conversion with acres of blond-wood floors, and the Roquefort cheese tartlets were ambrosial."

'And Helicopter's the one who gave you his phone number?'

'Looks like it, doesn't it?'

'So what's his name?'

'John,' I said, tasting it on the way out. 'I rather like "John". Conjures up a sort of what-you-see-is-what-you-get nice-bloke-ish-ness.'

'Harriet, nice-bloke-ish-ness doesn't exactly tie in with kissing your girlfriend goodbye and chatting up someone else the minute she's gone.'

'It was hardly a chat-up. I've got a horrible feeling he *was* just being a nice bloke. He wasn't bothered about the money, but didn't want me feeling bad about taking it. Anyway, I was looking like a pig's breakfast.'

'OK, but if she's always that perfect, maybe he's sick of perfection.'

This gratifying notion had occurred to me already.

'Or maybe he just likes pigs' breakfasts,' she added.

Great. She'd be saying maybe he fancied a bit of rough, next.

'Especially if they've got legs up to their tonsils,' she went on. 'But are you sure your bloke *is* Helicopter? Maybe he and Nina are just old mates.'

Before talking to Rosie, I'd been exploring this minute possibility, too. And not only 'old mates' but 'old exes', fourteenth cousins twice removed—anything that would mean he was potentially available.

But even without the evidence of my own eyes, everything Rosie had told me fitted. 'Sally, I think I know "old mate" behaviour when I see it. She was all tinkly and flirty like she always was, and Rosie said she's obviously obsessed with him.'

Sally fetched the jug and poured me another coffee. 'So when are you going to phone him? You are *going* to phone him?'

'Of course! There's the little matter of that thirty quid, isn't there?' There was also a weird little flutter in my stomach. It was a cocktail of guilt and that *frisson* you get when you're even just thinking about a brand-new object of prime fanciability. Which explains the guilt, of course, because he was Nina's object of PF, damn it.

'I wish someone'd give me thirty quid,' she grumbled. 'There's some mail for you, by the way.'

There were two credit-card statements, which I didn't open, and five Christmas cards, which I did. The first four were from Mum and an assortment of friends. It was the fifth that gave me a jolt.

'Nina's sent me a Christmas card! Rosie must have got pissed enough to give her my address.' I was seriously spooked, I don't mind admitting it. I showed Sally the card. '"Much love, Nina. Maybe I'll pop in sometime!" It's a bit weird, when we were never even third-best friends.'

'Some people send much gushy love to everybody,' Sally yawned. 'It's a good old Christmas tradition, like rowing with your entire family and pretending you like Brussels sprouts.'

Talking of family . . . I re-read the card from my mother, who was no longer married to my father. Under 'Lots of love, Mum and Bill,' she'd written, 'I do understand about Christmas, but I'm sure Sally's parents will be very hurt if she doesn't go home, even if they don't show it. If you change your mind we'll be very pleased to see you, of course.'

I handed this to Sally too.

'Why does everybody have to make me feel guilty?' she groaned. 'OK, they might be a bit hurt but they'll be relieved, too, even if they won't admit it. All their loathsome friends'll be popping in and out nonstop for drinks; I'll just be rubbing their noses in it.'

Sally's relationship with her folks had been a mite strained since the minor bombshell she'd dropped in May. I should explain here that Sally's parents are somewhat 'proper'; having married late they'd produced Sally when they'd just about given up. In fact a much less 'proper' aunt had once confided to Sally that she thought they'd never quite got to grips with that messy conjugal stuff in the first place.

Back to that bombshell, though. Unlike me, Sally had continued to capitalise on the global English explosion and was by then working in Muscat on the Gulf of Oman. Home on leave for a couple of weeks, she'd been staying with me, trawling the London shops for new summer stuff to take back and trying it all on in my bedroom.

It was the black bikini that did it.

With a frown she'd said, 'I'm getting positively lumpy around the middle. Look at this!'

I'd seen only a marginally thickened version of the usual Sally. I was about to make soothing noises when she'd added, 'Anyone would think I was pregnant!'

'I almost wish you were,' I'd retorted. 'Then at least you'd really have a massive gut to bitch about.'

'It's not funny! I could hardly do my jeans up yesterday! My tits have got bigger, too!'

'I wish mine would,' I'd grumbled, until I'd seen her face.

In a weird, frozen voice she'd said, 'They were tingling the other day, too—is that a sign?' Putting her hands to her stomach, she'd said in a panic, 'I *can't* be. Please, let me wake up . . .'

She'd gone on hoping to wake up until four and a half months later, when eight-pound Tom put in an appearance. She'd known at once who the proud daddy was: a certain Steve she'd met at an overnight beach party on Bandar Khayyam, a little island half an hour by speedboat from Muscat Yacht Club. I know this because I'd been a reveller at that party, too. My feet had been itching badly at the time, so I'd got a cheap ticket and invited myself to stay with Sally for a fortnight.

There had been around twenty of us at the beach party, and the setting was lethal. The stars were like diamonds on black velvet, the sea lit with silvery phosphorescence. As Sally had said, when you've just met someone you fancy rotten it certainly beat Bognor.

This Steve had not been one of her usual crowd. Working in Singapore, he'd been on an en route visit to friends of Sally's. Barely twelve hours after their little twosome (once in the sand, once in the sea) he'd carried on to Singapore and the wife he'd somehow forgotten to tell her about. Sally had only given her folks the blunt details a couple of months ago, when they'd demanded for the thirty-eighth time that she contact the father and make him 'face up to his responsibilities'.

Catatonic shock had ensued. 'You'd known him *how* long?'

Going back to Muscat had been out of the question; so she'd stayed with me from then on.

Tom was now six months old, with Father Christmas scheduled to make his first visit down a London chimney, rather than his grandparents' one in Chester. Apart from Sally and Tom, the other residents of our house were Frida, a Swedish girl who was hardly ever in, Jacko, who usually was, and Widdles, a geriatric cat of dubious personal hygiene.

'Where's Jacko?' I asked.

'God knows. He had a physio appointment at three, so he's probably crawling home via half a dozen pubs.'

Just as she said it a faraway bang announced the front door. Seconds later the kitchen door opened and Jacko hobbled in.

Sally said, 'Shut the door, Ape-Face, it's blowing a gale from the hall.'

He gave the door a whack-bang with his crutch and flopped noisily into a chair at the kitchen table. He had short, sandy-brown hair, non-designer stubble to match, and a Scouse accent that had been thicker than Cilla's when I'd first met him, although he'd toned it down now. We'd both been nineteen then, sharing a grotty student house. He'd been the most outrageous, foul-mouthed and instantly likable boy I'd ever met. He'd inhabited one of my best soft spots ever since.

'How's the itching?' I looked at his right leg, which was in plaster.

'Murder,' he said pathetically, turning hazel eyes on me. 'I'm dehydrated from drinking myself to death last night, to get some sleep. Harry, my angel, stick that kettle on, would you?'

I obliged, if only because of said plaster and an arm that was similarly recovering from a fair old mashing. Jacko was still based in Liverpool but since I'd been in London he'd come down often, usually for some football match. On the last occasion, ten minutes after leaving, he'd collided with a joyrider. He'd been in hospital for three weeks; his frantic mother had stayed with me. Once he'd been discharged she'd been desperate to get him back to the nest, so she could fuss him to death.

Still too weak and wobbly to manage alone, Jacko had nevertheless amazed me by putting his foot down. He told her he wanted to stay if I'd have him, and would go for his follow-up to the hospital that had sorted him out. Sorry, Mum, but her fussing would do his head in.

While I made him a cup of tea, Jacko was inspecting my mail. 'Who's Nina, then?'

'An old friend she can't stand,' Sally said. 'Her bloke tried to pick Harry up on Saturday—even gave her his phone number.'

He put on his hurt-puppy look. 'You never told me!'

'It wasn't *exactly* a pick-up.' I went on to explain briefly, playing it right down.

'Why can't you stand this Nina, then?'

'She was a little cow,' Sally said.

You will gather that I'd been having another bitch about Nina. 'That's a slight exaggeration. She just used to make me feel like one of those *Blue Peter* things built from bog-roll tubes that's supposed to be a dinosaur, but just looks like bog-roll tubes falling apart.'

'Why?' he asked.

Well, if he really wanted to know . . . 'Because she was five foot five and perfect, with silk-curtain hair and size three feet. And I was all awkward and gangly, with a mouth full of braces and feet I hadn't grown into, tripping over everything and blushing like the Revenge of the Killer Tomato and feeling a prat. And even when I was past the killer-tomato stage, she *still* made me feel like a bog-roll dinosaur, OK?'

Apparently satisfied, he went back to inspecting my mail. 'So are you two off home for your turkey after all?' he added, scanning Mum's card.

'No way—I'm staying put,' Sally said. 'But I wish Harriet would. Her mother's going to blame me for depriving her.'

'She won't,' I said. 'She'll be too busy to miss me and I'm not sure I can face those kids again, anyway.' I got on fine with Mum, and Bill was great, too, and the Devon long house lovely, but it would also be full of Bill's son, plus son's wife, and three kids, two of whom were little pains.

'Maybe I'll stay too, then,' he said. 'The mistletoe between two prickly bits of holly.'

'God help us,' said Sally.

As Frida had already booked her ticket home, I'd been hoping he'd stay. He'd be gone for good soon enough, and more was always merrier. 'Won't your folks be put out if you don't go home?'

'Probably, but you don't know Christmas in our house—Auntie X bitching about what Auntie Y said thirty years ago, Granddad snoring with his mouth open, and Mum wishing she and Dad could just piss off to Barbados for once.'

'Then why don't they?' Sally asked. 'They're not exactly skint.'

'They're going in February,' he said. 'So they have to suffer first. It's the rules.'

Just as he said it, a faint whimpering came from the baby alarm. 'Oh God, not *again*,' Sally groaned, heaving herself to the door.

'She's knackered,' Jacko said, as she departed.

'She's been knackered for a week.' Tom was teething on top of a bad cold; poor Sally had hardly slept for several nights.

Jacko was rereading Nina's card. 'So you're going to see her bloke?'

'It's not exactly "seeing", is it? Just a little thankyou drink.'

'Sounds like "seeing" to me. Speaking from the enemy camp, I can tell you that dishing out emergency dosh is one thing. Dishing out phone numbers is something else.'

'Jacko, he was just being nice.' I said this largely to fool Fate, who was bound to be listening. Privately I was wallowing in the piquant possibility that he wasn't just being 'nice'. Even more piquant was the off-chance that he was also, after all, a fourteenth cousin of Nina's.

I started tidying up, though the kitchen never looked tidy even when it was. The house was one of those six-bedroomed Edwardian jobs that fetch bombs when done up, and lesser bombs even when they're not. This still possessed 'a wealth of original features', including prehistoric chain-pull loo and built-in, wall-to-wall draughts. It had been the family home of my father's crotchety old Auntie Dorothy.

And poor old Dorothy was still here, tucked up in an urn on the dining-room mantelpiece. I felt bad leaving her there, especially as she'd left half the house to me, but she was waiting to be scattered off a particular cliff in Dorset. Only Dad knew where it was and he was in Turkey.

Sally came back, with Tom on her hip. He was pale, poor little sausage, but he gave us a dribbly grin. 'Hi, stinker,' I said. 'Keep Mummy at it, there's a good boy.'

Jacko said, 'Start the way you mean to go on, mate. Treat 'em mean.'

Sally shifted a pile of washing, flopped onto the sofa, and yanked up her sweatshirt to give Tom his comfort food. I'd made the kitchen into a living room with a sofa and a fourteen-inch all-in-one TV and video. Since October we'd hardly used the sitting room, because although it would soon be described by estate agents as a 'well-proportioned and elegant drawing room', it was perhaps best suited to defrosting a chicken over six weeks or so. It contained the only truly modern item Dorothy had ever lashed out on: a massive Sony television, as her main pleasure in life had been the racing and her eyesight had been getting dodgy.

As always when Sally was feeding Tom, Jacko watched in unashamed fascination. If any other bloke had been gawping like that, Sally would have felt uncomfortable. With Jacko it was impossible; there'd always been a certain disarming innocence about him.

Tom soon drifted off, and Sally crept away to put him down.

'It's enough to make you wish you were six months old again,' Jacko sighed. He picked up Nina's card once more. 'So when are you going to phone this bloke?' he went on.

'Now,' I said. 'Might as well get it out of the way.' Which sounded nicely casual, I thought, as I delved in my bag for mobile and receipt. Not even Fate would realise I suddenly had a stomach full of baby pterodactyls.

My call was answered almost at once with a crisp 'Hello?'

'Oh, hello—I do hope I'm talking to the right person—did you give me a cab fare on Saturday?'

He laughed. 'Yes. And I don't even know your name.'

Phew. 'It's Harriet—hideous, isn't it? Most of my friends call me Harry. Or Aitch.'

'At least it's not boring. Mine's the most boring name in the book.'

'I'm sure I couldn't guess,' I lied.

'I bet you could. It's John.'

Shit. It was Sod's Law, wasn't it? Sod's Law Section V, subsection iii(a):

'When you haven't particularly fancied anyone in ages it follows that when you do, the object of fanciability will not only be involved with someone else, but that someone else will be the person who always had everything you previously coveted, inc. one of those leather skirts you begged your mother to buy, but she said certainly not, they were tarty. (See also subsection iii (c): "People who get new Suzuki Jeeps for their seventeenth birthdays.")'

But I just said, 'John's hardly common any more. After all the Dans and Lukes, it's supposed to be an endangered species.'

'I'll take your word for it.'

Even his voice sent a buzzy little tingle through me. It made me think of melted dark chocolate. Not that I let it show. 'It's payback time, remember? Drinks and pork scratchings, if you're still up for them. Or I'll send you that cheque after all—I promise it won't bounce.'

'I think I'll go for the drinks.'

Just like that? Was Fate taking a sickie or something?

'Unless you're tied up and it's going to be a pain,' he went on.

Well, yes, it was going to be a colossal pain, fitting a bloke like him into my non-hectic social round. 'How about Thursday evening?'

'Sorry, I can't do Thursday.'

Damn it. Already I was imagining three more regretful 'sorrys', whereupon I'd offer that cheque again and he'd say, 'No, have it on me, take care.' And then he'd say to Nina, 'I think I wriggled out of that one with commendable skill, darling.'

Might as well make it easy for him. 'Pre-Christmas is a nightmare, isn't it? I could manage an hour on Friday, seven thirtyish.'

'Yes, I can do Friday. Where would suit you?' he went on.

I hadn't even thought that far. 'Er, how about that little wine bar? The one near old Wooden Wally?'

'Fine. See you there, then.'

I hung up feeling nonplussed, in a guiltily chuffed sort of way. 'Well, that's a turnup,' I said to Jacko. 'I never thought he really meant it. I was looking like something Widdles dragged in.'

'Yes, my angel, but beneath the old tat he saw this vision of ineffable gorgeousness.'

Much more of this and I'd make him another cup of tea and a fried-egg sandwich, too. It wasn't often that Jacko got all poetic.

'Plus he could tell a mile off you fancied him,' he grinned.

'Who said I fancied him?'

'Oh, come on, Harry. I could see it in your face. It went all pink and girly. And you'd never have taken the money if you didn't fancy him.'

Unfortunately there was no arguing with this.

'Sounds like he's a bit of a naughty boy,' he went on, 'if he's seeing this non-mate of yours, and he's trying to get *you* out on the side—'

'It's just a drink, for God's sake. He gave me thirty quid!'

'He's planning on giving you another little something, if you ask me.'

'Oh, grow *up*!'

Now, I'd almost go so far as to say Jacko was the brother I'd never had. And, like a real brother, he frequently made me want to thump him, and he had some deplorably laddish tendencies.

'Every bloke isn't like you,' I added acidly.

'No,' said Sally, who'd just come back and flopped down on the sofa. 'Some of them are possibly even marginally worse.' I filled her in on John.

'Maybe he's just going off Nina,' she yawned, which made me realise how infinitely more perspicacious and high-minded your average female friend could be than your average male ditto, even when half asleep. 'Which would serve her right for being a two-faced little cow.'

'God, you girls can be so nasty,' Jacko tutted. 'Just look at this card: "Much love", she says. She's even talking of popping round.'

'She'll have heard I've inherited half an expensive house,' I said. 'She's preparing the ground for a good old nose. I know it doesn't sound very nice,' I added, seeing Jacko's face, 'but it's probably spot-on.'

With another yawn, Sally announced that she was going to have a bath. Once she'd gone, Widdles decided to wake up and stretch himself. Then he jumped down from the sofa he now considered his personal throne, waddled fatly over to me and jumped onto my lap.

Widdles was another of Dorothy's goods and chattels. He'd actually been christened Tiddles, but as he watered his litter tray every hour the change had seemed apt. My mind was not on him, however. Having psyched myself up for a 'nice' fob-off, I wasn't sure what to think about John. He certainly didn't strike me as Jacko's in-with-a-chance-there type, looking for a pig's breakfast on the side. On the other hand, Sally's going-off-Nina bit was surely overoptimistic. Which left me with the hyperoptimistic fourteenth cousin.

It was all very unsettling, in a *frisson-y* kind of way.

Evidently sensing this, Jacko was fixing me with an uncharacteristically penetrating eye. 'You know your trouble? All you've thought about in months is non-drip emulsion, Sally and the baby. When did you last go out with a bloke you really fancied?'

'What the hell's that got to do with anything?' I asked, stroking Widdles's tabby old fur.

'Everything. You hardly even go out any more. All you and Sal talk about are Tom's poor ickle toofies and did that curry the other night go into the milk and give him funny-colour poos.'

This was a monstrous lie. Sally and I had animated discussions about whether we could get a passable highchair from a car boot sale, and the relative merits of Tesco's versus Sainsbury's lasagne. We debated long and hard about whether to get *Pride and Prejudice* from Blockbusters for the fourteenth time, and if so, whether we were entirely sad or merely intellectually superior to those people who got *Ace Ventura—Pet Detective* for the fourteenth time. (We'd only had it six times.)

'You used to be a right live wire,' Jacko went on. 'You just haven't got a life any more. The most exciting thing you've done lately is murdering those poor little woodworms in the chairs.'

'I'm only trying to make the place habitable. We can't all have brand-new warehouse conversions on the Liverpool docks.'

It had been a godsend that I *had* somewhere to make habitable. Half a house could hardly have come at a better time. Never married, Dorothy had left everything to be divided between her nephew David (my father) and her great-niece Harriet, who'd put up with a cantankerous old woman far better than she would have herself. And if anyone spent good money on flowers for her funeral, she'd haunt them.

I'd been almost appalled, at first. It was Dad who'd gone to see her every fortnight, attacked the garden and taken her out for Sunday lunches. I'd called in now and then, but not as often as I might have. I'd fetched her gin from the offie, put her bets on the horses, and done my best not to cringe when she'd asked me to cut her toenails.

Dad, however, had recently retired and was about to go abroad to indulge a long-cherished dream. The prospect of sorting out mountains of junk and putting the house on the market had filled him with the sort of helpless dismay that had prompted Mum to leave him for no-nonsense, hands-on Bill.

When he'd suggested I live in it for now my first thought had been *no way*. The house had been so big, so chill, so full of that musty-fusty smell you only get in really old people's homes. The kitchen still had one of those pulley-operated clothes-airers, and on the wall was a glass-cased thing saying drawing room, bedroom one, etc, so the skivvy knew who was ringing for tea. The actual bells were still intact.

However, at the time I'd been living in a grotty flat in one of the few untarted areas of London, sharing with people who wrote 'Chris' on their eggs to stop people nicking them. So I'd moved in, intending to find a nice home for Widdles, sort out the junk, and finalise plans for a trip to Oz. I should have been off by November at the latest.

Famous last intentions.

Jacko said, 'It won't be woodworms getting murdered if Sal ever finds out what you've been up to.'

'She won't unless you tell her, and if you do you're dead.'

What he meant was this. After that ClearBlue test, when Sally had still been in shock, I'd urged her to stay. I'd said probate would take for ever and I wanted the company, which was true. However, since probate had come through two months ago the house could have been on the market already, maybe even sold. If Sally had known this, though, she'd have gone into prime pig-headed mode and insisted on moving out, so I could get my half of the loot and zoom off on my trip. And since even the grottiest of flats would stretch her precarious finances, I'd told her there were problems with probate, if I got the house on the market by March I'd be lucky. By that time she'd be back on her feet—she already had work lined up for January.

Jacko's stomach let out a rumble even I could hear. 'Right, I'm going to phone the takeaway,' he said. 'What do you fancy?'

'We're always having takeaways! I'll throw something together—there should be some fresh pasta if you and Sally haven't pigged it all.'

I didn't object to takeaways on any purist grounds, but as Jacko sent out so often and usually insisted on paying as well, I felt guilty. The fact that he could afford it was rather beside the point.

Jacko had been a bit like me, without a clue what he wanted to do except that it had to include plenty of laughs. After grasshoppering from job to job, he'd done what he'd said he'd never do: gone to work for his old man, who had sundry businesses on Merseyside. Having startled everyone, especially himself, by discovering a feel for it, Jacko had been his old man's number two for the last eighteen months. He should have gone home by now, but he was dragging it out till after Christmas.

As I was checking the fridge for that pasta, the doorbell rang. Like just about everything else in the house it was antique, and also deafening. I found Helen on the step.

'Sorry, but I was feeling a bit low,' she said. (Helen always preceded her opening remarks with 'sorry'.) 'You're not eating, are you?'

'Not yet, and even if we were it wouldn't matter. Come in.'

Helen lived next door, in a house much like Dorothy's, except that it had been done up with a colossally expensive vengeance. Over the months I'd got friendly with her. Her husband was a solicitor with a lucrative practice in Wimbledon. Four months previously he'd left her for his accountant, who was eight years younger than Helen and had a doll's-house cottage in Wimbledon Village.

'Hi, pet,' said Jacko, when I took her through. 'Found a nice bloke yet to get your own back with?'

She produced a wan little smile. 'At the moment I'm so fed up I'd have a fling with the first man who asked me.'

'Well, I get my plaster off next week,' he grinned.

'Have a glass of wine,' I said.

'I can't.' With a glance at her watch, she sighed. 'I've got to pick

Matthew up soon—he went home with Sam after school.'

Helen was thirty-nine, but could have passed for twenty-eight. She had smooth, fairish hair, lovely pearly skin, and one of those faces that look mousy and ordinary until a particular expression makes you realise that it's almost beautiful, in a quiet, diffident way. Having married very young, she had three boys. Eighteen-year-old Oliver had just started at Exeter University and she missed him desperately. Toby and Matthew were twelve-year-old twins, and by now I was familiar with their habit of treating their mother like a doormat.

While I was making her a coffee instead, Helen said, 'I'm so fed up—Lawrence is taking the boys on some adventure weekend thing with mud and dirt bikes and they're over the moon. It's barely a month since he took them to EuroDisney, for heaven's sake! And it was wretched Francesca who suggested it, so now they think she's the bee's knees.'

'Is she going with them?' I asked.

'Into *mud*? Of course not!'

Francesca had suffered the twins for a couple of weekends, on her own terms. She'd made them take their trainers off, and there was no telly or PlayStation in the titchy spare room, and she'd made them eat 'horrible veggie stuff with no ketchup'. So what Helen was feeling, but not saying, was that she wanted them to go to Francesca's again, so they'd hate it and long for home and Mum, instead of which they were thinking she was cool, because she'd suggested the adventure weekend so she wouldn't get boy-muck over her cream carpets.

'You should tell Lawrence he can have custody of the twins,' I said. 'That'd sort Francesca out.'

Jacko hooted, but Helen looked as if I'd just suggested running a couple of old ladies over, for a laugh.

'Well?' I went on, regardless. 'He never asked whether you wanted custody, did he? He just assumed!'

Jacko hooted again. 'She'd kick him out like a shot, I bet.'

I was warming to this theme nicely. 'They're his kids just as much as yours. She'd screech, "*Kids?* Who said anything about kids?"'

'She'd have them, I bet,' Helen said wanly. 'She'd never give Lawrence up that easily.'

Her mobile rang just as she was finishing her coffee, and for once a furrow of irritation creased her brow. 'Toby, you've *had* your tea!' (Pause.) 'I don't know! Look in the fridge!'

She hung up so abruptly, I was startled. 'I'm sick of it! Phoning me from next door because he's still *hun*gry! He's twelve, for heaven's sake!'

'Good on you, pet,' Jacko grinned. 'You sort the lazy little tyke out.'

On Friday night I left work bang on time for once and charged home for a panic shower and change. While I was throwing on my best grey suit and a pale pink sweater, Sally came in with Tom. 'I just had to get out of the kitchen—Frida's making her Swedish meatballs again.'

'Her meatballs are lovely!' I was trying to find the eyeshadow that was supposed to make my eyes all smoky and alluring.

'I know, but Jacko's making me want to puke. He's saying stuff like, "Oh, Freeds, Viking princess of my dreams, will you marry me and make me meatballs every night?" He just never *stops*.'

Whether it was the stitches, hormones or Steve (probably all three), ever since Tom, Sally was about as interested in men and sex as Jacko was in needlepoint. 'It's just the way he is,' I said, trying not to get exasperated. 'If Frida didn't like it, she'd soon tell him.'

Frida wasn't quite your stereotypical Swede, in that she wasn't blonde. She was typical in having virtually perfect English, however, and in being incredibly tall and gorgeous: two inches taller than me, which made a nice change. She said it was all the herrings.

I found the eyeshadow, made a mess of applying it, and cursed.

'Why don't you put something a bit flasher on?' Sally asked. 'That looks rather workish.'

'It's *supposed* to look workish, dopey. I don't want him thinking I've charged home to change, on purpose.'

'Poor old Helicopter's going to get a bit of a shock after last time.'

'That was the general idea.' The suit was beautifully cut and short enough to show off my best feature, and the pale pink sweater made my skin look delicately creamy. I'd hot-brushed my hair into controlled waves (sort of) and my face was looking reasonable. I have a wide, slightly lopsided mouth, which I'd hated at the gangly stage, but someone I would now love for ever had recently asked whether it was the product of plastic surgery, it was so quirkily attractive.

Sally said, 'What if he wants to see you again?'

'I haven't even thought that far.' This, of course, was a massive lie. I'd thought endlessly about what I'd do if he did (still out on that one), whether I'd really care if he didn't (yes), and just how sick I'd feel if he told me about his wonderful girlfriend. 'Anyway, he won't,' I added, in case Fate was lurking at the keyhole.

'He might. I bet Jacko a packet of giant Smarties he's going off Nina. So I'd better be right.'

'How am I supposed to find out?' I demanded. '"Excuse me, but are you going off that woman I saw you with on Saturday, who just happens to be a non-friend of mine?"'

'Bit awkward,' she conceded. 'Jacko still thinks he's a potentially two-timing arsehole. Which is a bit bloody rich, the way he's carrying on with Frida lately. It'd serve him right if Erik Bloodaxe came over and duffed him up.' (This was Frida's boyfriend in Stockholm, who was apparently about six foot five and built like a tank.)

'It's just Jacko! He's always been like that!' I misted myself with CK1 and grabbed my bag. 'I've got to dash—enjoy your meatballs.' I charged downstairs, yanked the front door open, and found Helen on the step. 'Are you going out?' she asked.

'Well, yes.' I peered at her in the half-light. 'Are you OK?'

'Fine. I was just going to ask you something, but it'll keep.' With a bright 'Have a nice time,' she departed.

En route to the station, I felt a bit bad about Helen. She hadn't exactly looked fine. Ever since Lawrence had left, she'd come to rely on us as a sort of support system. Most of her friends were also his friends and she hated forcing anyone to take sides. However, once on the train I almost felt as if I were escaping, zooming down a runway to a world where other people's problems just didn't exist. It was close to that exhilarating sensation you get when the plane breaks through the murk and suddenly you're in a world of brilliant blue and cotton-wool clouds.

Jacko was right. I'd hardly thought about men in ages, or even having a wild night out. While queuing at supermarket check-outs I never picked up *Cosmo* any more, I'd started picking up *Mumsy World* instead.

I'd planned to arrive at around twenty to eight, so I wouldn't have to sit on my own if he was late. But the wretched underground was playing up, so it was nearly ten to eight by the time I reached the bar.

It was very busy. He was there, sitting in the far corner, with a blonde who was laughing at him as if he were the best thing since takeaway sushi.

I know I said I was an only child, but I lied. I have a prissy elder sister who comes visiting now and again, but only in my head. When I was younger she used to say smug, bossy stuff like 'You'll get found out,' and 'It's no use hiding your school report under your bed.'

'I knew this was a bad idea,' she said triumphantly. 'You're only fifteen minutes late and he's picked up someone else already. Just look at him.'

I was.

'Silk-curtain hair, too, only blonde,' she went on smugly. 'Push off quick before he sees you and you look a complete prat.'

I would have, once. However, I was grown-up now. I had instant bottled cool. Applied with care, like instant tan, I defied even a Helicopter to tell it from the real thing.

It was the blonde who saw me first, when I was still three tables away.

She gave him a little nudge and he looked up instantly. He stood up, too, which made me hear another voice in my head, my mother's this time: 'Nice manners do go a long way in a man.'

'Harriet!' he said. 'I'd just about given you up.'

Evidently. Wearing my best unfazed smile, I said, 'So sorry—it's been one of those days.'

'Don't tell me.' He turned to his companion. 'This is Amanda,' he said. 'Amanda, Harriet.'

She gave me a friendly enough smile. 'But I'm on my way. I was just going when John came in, but as I hadn't seen him for ages I thought I'd keep him company.' She gave him a peck on the cheek. 'I'll give you a call—you *must* come for supper. I'm dying for you to meet Miles.'

'I'll look forward to it,' he said.

'Be good.' With another smile she departed and I sat down, remembering what else my mother had said about a million times: 'Do sit up *straight*, Harriet. It's so unflattering to slump like that.'

'Amanda got married three months ago,' he explained. 'I was away and missed the wedding, and I haven't seen her since.'

Well, it was just typical of my prissy elder sister to jump to nasty, suspicious conclusions.

Belatedly he was giving me an appraisal that told me my panic tart-up had been worth it. 'Let me get you a drink,' he said.

'No, this is my shout, remember?' I glanced down at a glass of what looked depressingly like mineral water. 'Are you ready for another?'

'Yes, I'll have a gin and tonic.'

Thank God for that. I'm not exactly a piss-head, but I just can't relate to abstainers. I ordered a large glass of red burgundy, too.

Until then I suppose I'd been wondering whether I'd worked him up in my head into a bigger 'thing' than he merited. Well, I hadn't. I liked the wrappings, too. I liked the dark grey suit. I liked the navy and white striped shirt and gold cuff links. My trusty in-built bloke register was quivering instantly into life, saying *Action stations!*

'I hope there wasn't anything vital in that purse,' he said. 'Like a winning lottery ticket with your perennial lucky numbers on it.'

Feeling guilty, I was almost tempted to confess, but what was the point now? 'Only a dry-cleaning ticket and I always lose those anyway. It was really very kind of you,' I added quickly.

For some reason he seemed to find this funny. He gave me an amused facial appraisal that allowed me a good chance to return the favour. And since we were crammed together, this was a *frisson*-y sort of exercise.

'I was feeling mellow,' he said, as our drinks arrived.

After lunch with Nina? This was not a good sign. In fact it was so depressing I needed a good swig of Jacob's Creek to wash it down. 'Everybody at work thinks I made you up. Men just don't dish out cab fares to strange women.'

His mouth gave a minute quiver. 'I wouldn't say "strange". Weary and bedraggled, OK.'

Great. I couldn't think of a witty, alluring reply, either. Just as I located my tongue, he beat me to it. 'The fertility god's still in the window, but he's looking a bit down in the mouth.'

I wasn't surprised. Passers-by were probably making coarse remarks about his equipment. 'He'll be homesick,' I said. 'Maybe we should start a campaign to send him home.' I nearly added, 'You know, like *Free Willy*', but bit it back as too puerile.

'Yes, maybe he could do with a change of residence,' he mused.

'Are you thinking of giving him one?'

'If I can work out a foolproof ram-raid strategy. As you said, fifteen hundred's a bit steep for a cat scratching-post, especially when you haven't got a cat.'

I laughed. 'I have.' I found myself telling him about Dorothy and the house and Widdles. 'And then a friend moved in and I'm still there. I was supposed to be off to Oz for three months, but that's on the back burner.'

'Three *months*? You must have a chilled-out boss.'

'I'd have given in my notice. That's what I used to do—work for a few months and take off.'

'Permanently itchy feet?' he asked.

'And restlessness. After three months anywhere I was bored.' Suddenly I felt I'd talked about myself quite enough. I found a safe topic. 'What are you doing for Christmas?'

'Sailing in the Grenadines.'

'God, you lucky devil,' I said, thinking, if you're taking Nina, I'll really hate her for ever.

'Actually, I'm not,' he went on. 'That's what I'd like to do, but I have tribal rituals to attend.'

That was one way of putting it. 'Or the tribal elders'll be offended?'

'No, but they need a referee. Our rituals tend to turn into tribal warfare. Blood could be spilt,' he added, in mock-doom tones.

I burst out laughing. 'If you go ahead with ram-raiding old Wooden Wally, you might get banged up in time to get out of it.'

'Now there's a thought.' It went on like this, light, silly stuff, with lots of laughs and eye contact (plus another couple of drinks), but I still didn't feel I was getting anywhere, one way or the other.

Nothing in his demeanour said categorically either 'spoken for' or 'available', let alone 'up for a bit on the side'. Once or twice I thought I caught a hint of undercurrents, but they were so fleeting I decided I'd imagined them. As for 'accidental' brushings of fingers, or thighs under the table, no such luck.

And I could have done with a morsel of such stuff, I can tell you. Close up, he was exerting the kind of pull you learn about in physics lessons. It was unbelievably frustrating, especially as I was feeling on top form: witty, sparkling and desirable. I usually do, though, after one glass of anything on an empty stomach.

Beginning to see merely a 'Bye, then, take care,' looming at the end of the evening, I was getting desperate for a signal, whether red or green. I thought I might as well contrive some 'accidental' brushings myself. The bar was getting noisier, so it was perfectly acceptable to lean slightly closer, as if to hear him better. In fact I managed this so cunningly that my hair fleetingly brushed his cheek. Even better, someone pushed past me rather roughly and I could shrink closer without it looking obvious. This made me go so warm and fluttery I almost wished some semi-drunk would bash right into me, send me slithering gracefully off my stool half into his lap, and really send my flutters into orbit.

Seconds later, it very nearly happened. A semi-drunk's elbow jabbed into my shoulder blade so hard that my arm jerked sideways and knocked my glass over.

And half a mega-glass of red went flying into John's lap.

Two

WHO SAYS TIME TRAVEL doesn't exist? In half a second I was fifteen again, all legs and elbows, wishing I could die and evaporate, in that order.

Semi-drunk was mumbling apologies, but I wasn't listening. I was too busy saying, 'God, I'm so sorry—how stupid—quick, get a cloth—'

A cloth was procured and he mopped up the worst, but any fool could see that no amount of Wunda-Stain would ever save that suit from the bin.

'I'm so sorry,' I said. 'That suit's going to be a write-off.'

'It couldn't be helped.' With a wry little smile, he dumped the cloth on the table and glanced down at the massive red stain. 'Just as well it was red—white would look as if I'd peed myself.' Nodding at a table that had just been vacated, he added, 'Let's shift over there.'

I felt more like shifting out of the door, but he still had half a gin and tonic left.

I ordered an espresso. After all that Jacob's Creek, I needed it. I must have been half pissed already, trying to get up close and personal like that. And now he was making hideously polite conversation. 'So what are you doing, while your trip's on hold?'

'I work for a high-street recruitment agency. I started as a temp, but they offered me something more permanent. It suited me to be settled until Sally's back on her feet.' I'd already told him she had a baby. 'How about you?'

'I work for a development bank. It funds capital projects in the Eastern bloc countries, or doesn't fund them, as the case may be.'

'So you get some travel chucked in?'

'Now and then.' After a pause he added, 'You said your old man was abroad—is he working overseas?'

'No, he's wallowing in antiquities. He always wanted to be an archaeologist.'

'Then why wasn't he one?'

'His father was a solicitor. He was expected to go into the practice, but his heart was never in it. So now he's poking round the ruins of Troy and so on, hoping to find a stone tablet saying "Helen's diary, 1256 BC. Dear diary . . ."'

As he chuckled politely, I thought how sickening it was that I could find absolutely nothing wrong with him. According to Sod's Law this meant that even if he wasn't Nina's, he'd be somebody else's. But I made a polite effort in return. 'Why are you expecting tribal warfare over your Christmas dinner?'

He raised his eyebrows in a God help us fashion. 'My old man has an elderly aunt who's going gently demented and has been staying for the past year. My mother has an elderly ditto who is what they politely call "eccentric" and traditionally comes every Christmas. Between them these two work my old man into the kind of state where he threatens to shoot one or both of them. Added to that, my younger sister winds him up at every possible opportunity, and between all these my mother goes quietly crazy and threatens to run off with the dog. So what are *you* doing for Christmas?' he asked.

I told him briefly, adding the Devon rituals I was getting out of. 'So I'm going to be cooking my first turkey. I dare say it'll end up like Mr Bean's, but nobody'll care. Mind you, I might have minor warfare on my hands, too. If the fourteenth rerun of *E.T.* clashes with the fourteenth rerun of *Top Gun*, Sally and Jacko'll be at it like a pair of kids.'

'*The Great Escape*'s the only film I'll be thinking of.' With that, he glanced at his watch. 'It's five to nine—don't you have to go?'

'My God—is it?'

'I should be off, too. If only to change out of these trousers,' he added, as we headed for the door. 'On second thoughts, it does look as if I've peed myself.' He shot me a little wink as he said it, as if he knew how bad I felt and was trying to make me feel better.

It was still unseasonably mild; the fresh, damp air was sobering me up fast. He nodded along the road, where cab-hunters were hugging the kerb. 'If you need a taxi, we'll have a better chance further down.'

I'd intended to take the tube, but what the hell.

'Where are you off to?' he asked, as we reached a likely corner. 'You've got something else on, I take it?'

I'd prepared a lie earlier, but if I stuck to it and he suggested cab-sharing it might be awkward. 'I was going to a do in Battersea but I don't suppose they'll miss me—I might just go home.'

Two cabs went past in quick succession, both occupied.

He stopped suddenly. 'Look, if you're really going to duck out of this Battersea thing . . .' He paused. 'Have you eaten?'

If I hadn't written him off by then, my first reaction would have been *Yes! Yes! Yes!* As it was, I realised just how thick I'd been. We were standing right by a street lamp, and I saw in a flash that I hadn't imagined those undercurrents; he'd merely been playing it super-cool.

'Well, no . . .'

'Neither have I. So if you'd like to come back to my place and wait while I change, we'll go and eat.'

I was horribly tempted. The trouble was, I knew I'd never enjoy it properly unless credentials were on the table, which would be a terrible waste of the best flutters I'd had in ages.

'You're looking dubious,' he added, with an utterly disarming little smile that very nearly worked.

But I had to know. On an impulse I said more or less what was in my head. 'Dinner's fine with me. Only I saw you before you saw me the other day, you see, and I can't help wondering whether dinner with me would be fine with, well, whoever she was.'

His reaction was exactly what I'd been hoping not to see. Momentary, caught-in-the-act shock, which disappeared almost before I'd blinked.

I was beginning to wish I'd never asked. 'Look, I'm sorry, it's really none of my business,' I said quickly.

'No, it's OK. But since you ask, yes, I have seen her a couple of times. But it's no big thing,' he added. 'It's really not going anywhere.'

He said it with such convincing candour I'd have believed him like a shot if I hadn't known the background.

'So how about that dinner?' he went on.

Half of me was saying sod it, just go. The other half was telling me here was a smootharse *extraordinaire* and I wasn't that desperate. Still, I like to give people the benefit of the doubt, especially when I fancy them rotten. If he was about to dump Nina, or already had, Rosie would be full of it. There was no harm in playing it cool, however, so I produced an apologetic expression. 'I'd love to, but I really should be getting home. A friend next door was in a bit of a state when I left—I ought to go and see her.'

'Maybe another time, then?' he went on. 'Buy me another drink. A pre-dinner drink, this time, and I'll get the dinner.'

Yes! 'No, I'll get the dinner. I still owe you most of that thirty quid, never mind that suit.'

'Well, if you give me your number, I'll give you a call,' he said.

As he wrote it on the back of a business card, I told myself matches could always be found later, if boats needed burning.

Then an unoccupied cab appeared. Just as I was about to get in, John caught my wrist. 'Take care,' he said. 'And thanks for coming.'

'I enjoyed it.' I enjoyed the next bit even more. He put a finger under my chin in a way they should teach at evening classes in How To Make Women Go All Fluttery, tilted my face up, and kissed me very lightly.

On the cheek, damn him.

He stood on the pavement as the cab pulled out, and waved, and I waved back. Once he was out of sight I sat back, put my finger to my cheek where he'd kissed me, and thought, What the hell am I getting myself into?

Not that I was exactly into anything yet. Ten per cent of me, of course, had still been hoping he'd say, 'Oh, *Nina*!' with a little laugh. 'Oh, she's just an old friend/a pain-in-the-arse second cousin I felt obliged to catch up with.' On the other hand, if he'd given a 'correct' reply, would I have believed him? After all, 'pain-in-the-arse second cousin' was exactly the sort of thing an on-the-ball smootharse *would* say.

Maybe it really *was*n't going anywhere. Maybe he'd wanted to say, 'Actually, she's a bit of a pain and I'm going to dump her,' but had thought it would sound callously ungallant and put me off. This gratifying notion perked me up all the way home.

The instant I was inside, Sally came from the kitchen, shutting the door behind her. 'Thank God you're back,' she whispered. 'Helen's here—you'll never believe what she's done.'

Helen was sitting at the kitchen table with a nearly empty bottle of wine. She looked up at me. 'I did what you said. I told Lawrence he could have custody of the twins.'

'*What?*'

'Well, I didn't tell him to his *face*.' She spoke with the careful enunciation of someone who's had a few, and is trying to sound as if they haven't. 'When he came to pick the boys up I said I wouldn't be here on the Monday night, so he'd have to have them after school.'

'So you haven't actually said it?'

'I have.' She took another mouthful of supersave Lambrusco. 'I wrote him a letter. I was going to ask you about the wording, but you were on your way out so I just posted it before I changed my mind.'

'Helen, I didn't mean you to take me literally!'

'Maybe not, but once you said it, it seemed so unbelievably rational. I suppose I'd thought of it before, but not really seriously.'

'You said yourself Francesca'd never give Lawrence up that easily!'

'I'm not doing it to get him back. He doesn't love me any more—what's the point?' she went on, with the same semi-drunk control. 'He's planning to sell the house, so the boys and I can move into something smaller and *he* can get something better than a doll's house with bloody Francesca. Why the hell should I get the short straw?' She knocked back another mouthful. 'If she wants Lawrence that much, let her pick up the bloody football kit and run round after the boys.'

'Helen, those kids are your life! You'll miss them like mad!'

'Not like I miss Olly. If I thought for a minute they'd care I'd never do it, but they won't. They've never once said, "Poor Mum, are you all right?" It's always just the same old "I'm starving," and "Where are my swimming things?" and moans because I was no use with their maths homework and they had to fax it to Lawrence.'

What could you say to that?

'So he'll get my letter on Monday morning,' she went on. 'When he'll think he's done his fun-father bit. I'll move out this weekend.'

I'd just found out what shell shock feels like. 'Where will you go?'

'To an old friend in Muswell Hill. Felicity never liked Lawrence anyway and he'll never think of her. I'll take most of my stuff—he'll probably be so mad he'll have the locks changed.'

'He can't!' Sally said.

'He can. He'll be furious. He'll probably stop the credit cards too, but I thought of that. I took the maximum amount of cash out on each of them. And then I'll get a job. I'd have got one years ago, but he said I'd only earn peanuts so it wouldn't be worth it. He doesn't think I'm good for anything but cooking and shopping, and buying presents for his bloody mother, and managing just about everything in his life apart from his practice. And his fucking sex life,' she added bitterly.

I was shattered. Not once had I heard her say 'fucking' before.

It was midnight before Helen left. Once the door had shut behind her, Sally said, 'What a turnup! Talk about the meek little worm turning.'

I put my head in my hands. 'Why did I ever say it? Why the hell didn't I wait to find out what she was up to?'

'You'd have been late for Helicopter. What happened, anyway?'

Even if Helen hadn't put John right out of my head, I couldn't deal with this just now. 'Nothing happened, for God's sake!' I said irritably.

'Really?'

'Of course not.'

Relenting, I told her every last detail. 'Maybe Jacko's right, and he's a two-timing smootharse. Even if he is, I almost feel like having a little fling anyway, but I know I'd feel bad afterwards. I never liked Nina, but—'

'You'd hate anyone doing it to you. It's super-bitch stuff.'

'Hyper-bitch. Plus I couldn't face being a side order to Nina.'

'If she's still the main course, and not leftovers. You never know, you might even hear from Rosie that he's binned her. She phoned earlier, by the way.' She paused. 'She'd told Suzanne you were seeing him.'

'*What?* Suzanne's best buddies with Nina!'

'Yes, but it probably sounded reasonably innocent. Just a little drink to say thanks for charging to the rescue . . .'

'And that's how it's going to stay, as far as she's concerned,' I said, with feeling. 'I like Rosie, but she never did know how to spell discretion.'

'Well, you'll find out soon enough.' Stifling a yawn, Sally got up. 'What if there's still no sign of leftovers when he phones?'

'I'll say I'm tied up, I suppose. I'm more worried about Helen at the moment. I bet you anything she'll be in tears tomorrow, asking how the hell she can get that letter back before he sees it.'

'Well, she can't, so don't lose any sleep over it.'

I lost quite a bit of sleep that night. When I got downstairs at a quarter to ten next morning, the first thing Sally said was, 'Helen's gone already. She left a note.'

It said only, 'I'll call you. I won't give an address—Lawrence'll probably try to bully it out of you. If he asks you can tell him you don't know with a clear conscience. Love, Helen.'

'At least she's not in tears on the step,' I said.

'Not on our step, anyway.' She dumped Tom on my lap. 'Do your auntie bit while I shove some washing in.'

So we played bouncy babies, and blowing raspberries on tummies, which was Tom's favourite game. He laughed a lot, showing his perky little tooth.

Rosie popped in around eleven. 'So what happened?' she asked, wide-eyed, the instant she was in the door. This was one reason why you couldn't help liking Rosie. Anyone else would have pretended they'd just come to see you, and said, 'Oh, by the way . . .' ten minutes later, as if they'd only just thought of it.

So I dished out my 'innocent' lie, adding, 'Well, it was too much to hope that it'd be anything else,' in a suitably wry, jokey manner.

'Might have known,' she sighed. 'Anyone else's bloke would have been up to no good, I bet.'

'Why on earth did you tell Suzanne I was seeing him, anyway?'

Having just plonked herself in a woodwormy chair in the kitchen, Rosie looked a bit sheepish. 'I never would have, honestly, only she was really browned off the other day, because she'd just been at Nina's, and Nina was planning a nice little trip to the Maldives with you know who. Or maybe it was Mauritius. Somewhere that costs three grand each with no meals, anyway.'

A nasty little green snake had suddenly appeared in my stomach. Called *Serpentus jealousissimus*, it was closely related to *Serpentus sick-as-a-pigus*, but more poisonous. 'Only three grand?' I said lightly, catching Sally's eye. 'Slumming it a bit, isn't she?'

'Mind you, she hasn't asked him yet,' Rosie went on. 'But it still made Suzanne sick. All she had with her bloke was a rainy weekend in the Lake District and he dumped her on the way home. She said she wished, just once, Nina would bite into a peach and find she'd eaten half a maggot. So I felt a bit sorry for her, and I said, well, you never know, Helicopter might just turn out to have a little maggot. It's OK, she'd never *tell* her,' she added defensively. 'Nina's your archetypal Scorpio, you know. Jealous and possessive. Suzanne said she once went absolutely ape when some bloke tried to dump her. Shoved his mobile in the freezer, parked his car in a towaway zone, you name it.'

'That was a maggot, then,' I said, putting a packet of blueberry muffins on the table. 'Have a nibble, Rosie.'

'No, I mustn't. Are they low-fat?'

'No, but high-yum.'

'Oh, go on, then.'

Rosie was what Jacko would call 'cuddly', with brown curly hair and round brown eyes to match. She was permanently on the kind of diet that features no breakfast, two Twixes on the way to work (on account of no breakfast), salad for lunch, half a skinned chicken breast and three mangetout for dinner (on account of the Twixes) and a massive pepperoni pizza at ten to midnight (on account of the dinner). This then accounted for no breakfast, and so it went on.

'I'll tell you something, though,' she went on, 'if old Helicopter did have a maggot, I wouldn't mind luring it out.'

Sally made a face. 'Listening to this lot makes me thank God I'm right off sex. Give me a baby any day. They never turn out to be married, and if they wake you up in the night at least you don't have to fake anything.'

How long was it since anyone had woken me up in the night? I wondered. Apart from Widdles, of course, and Sally trying not to make a noise with Tom, and Jacko thumping down the landing to the loo . . . Feeling suddenly confined and restless I went and peered out of the window. The sun was shining on a window box of snowdrops that had amazed me by actually coming up and showing a few buds already. 'It's a gorgeous day. Anyone fancy Richmond Park?'

'Brilliant,' Sally said. 'We could take Tom to feed the ducks.'

Just as Rosie was saying she would too, she needed the exercise, Jacko came in, unshaven, unshowered and unbrushed, saying, hi, everybody, God, he felt rough. Sally said, yes, we could see that.

Having put the kettle on, Jacko hobbled over to a pinboard where an Advent calendar hung. Sally had officially bought this for Tom, but if you ask me she secretly still loved snowy-glitter woods with lots of exciting little windows. So did Jacko, but he didn't care who knew.

'If you dare open any more of my little windows, you ginger ape,' Sally said, 'I'll put itching powder down your plaster.'

'You're a mean old hag,' Jacko grumbled, hobbling back to the kettle, 'grudging me a couple of poxy little windows—I've got a good mind to take your Christmas present back to the Oxfam shop.'

'They're worse than a pair of kids lately,' I said to Rosie.

'*I'll* buy you a calendar, Jacko,' Rosie giggled. 'With chocolates.'

Eventually we made it to my car, a nine-year-old Escort bearing various battle scars from arguments at lights, etc. 'I wish I'd moved in with you lot,' Rosie said, as we stowed ourselves.

I had offered, only Suzanne had offered first. And, as I'd pointed out, at least Suzanne's flat probably had post-Jurassic heating and a shower that understood its job description.

'I mean, Suzanne's really nice but she's permanently stressed,' Rosie went on as we headed for the A3 in milky, pale blue sunshine. 'And half of it's Nina, still expecting her to drop everything and come over every time *she's* stressed. They were like that at school, remember?'

All too well. Nina had only ever been really intimate with Suzanne, and that had been a sort of princess/slave relationship.

As we crawled into the park's Robin Hood Gate, Rosie said, 'By the way, Nina's having a girly lunch thing soon—Suzanne said she's going to send you an invitation. Will you come?'

'I think I'm going to be horribly busy. Or dead, or something.'

I parked at the Isabella car park. It was packed, which was not surprising as it was more like spring than December. Along with the world and his wife and dog we pushed Tom's buggy down the path to the Isabella Plantation, licking ice-cream cones. We stopped to admire a huge stag whose massive head of antlers had bits of bracken festooned on them. They hung over his face and eyes, giving him a raffish but dopey air.

'Looks like he's recovering after a really wild party,' Sally said.

'Talking of parties . . .' Rosie started giggling helplessly. 'I forgot to tell you something I said at Nina's flat-warming—she was *livid*. I made some daft crack to Helicopter about his helicopter being dead handy for nipping to Tesco's when the roads were gridlocked, and he looked a bit taken aback, and Nina shot me a Look, but then he laughed and said he'd only got a lift in the helicopter because his chairman was on the same plane.' She paused for breath. 'But Nina felt a fool, I could tell, because he knew she'd been swanking about him.'

I enjoyed the thought of Nina feeling a fool, but I felt entitled to. If she'd only had the consideration to get involved with some pompous, arrogant prat, I wouldn't be feeling sick already, thinking of the polite excuses I'd have to make when he phoned.

There were no calls on the Monday night, but Helen's friend Felicity phoned on the Tuesday evening. 'She's gone for a walk—I'm afraid I got your number from her mobile memory,' she said. 'I'm a bit worried about her, actually. She had a furious text message from Lawrence, saying if that's what she wants, fine. I know she's regretting it already, but she won't admit it. I can see why she did it, but I'm sure she's only going to be even more bereft without those boys.'

My heart sank.

'I was wondering if you might talk to her,' she went on.

I tried, half an hour later. Helen sounded on the brink of tears, but she was adamant. If she gave in now, Lawrence would only think she was more pathetic than he already did, and what little self-esteem she had left would be down the pan with the rest of it.

I slept really well that night, as you can imagine.

At half past ten on the Wednesday night, Sally said, irritably, 'Harriet, you're really getting on my nerves. Every time the phone goes you say, "Oh God, *now* who?" as if you weren't dying for it to be Helicopter, and then try not to look disappointed when it's only your mother.'

It had just been my mother, saying would I please give her *some* idea what to get me for Christmas, and by the way had I heard from Dad lately? She was getting a bit worried in case he'd fallen off a Turkish cliff or something. (They were still friends and kept in touch.)

'If you ask me, he's priming the plum,' Sally went on.

'Sorry?'

'Getting you in a state, thinking he's not going to phone, so that by the time he does you'll be a ripe plum, ready to plop into his mouth.'

'I am not in a state,' I said testily. 'And I'm not about to do any plopping, all right?'

On the Thursday night I came home to find Sally in a state of her own. She'd had a Christmas card from Tamsin, a friend in Muscat. Tamsin had written, *Remember Steve? He passed through again ten days ago and was asking after you. And guess what? He's left his wife!! He's heading for the UK around Christmas, and I gave him your address—well, you said to forward any mail, ha ha.*

Sally was as churned up as I'd ever seen her. 'I just can't cope with this. I don't *want* him turning up.'

Not so long ago, I'd have thought it was exactly what she did want. 'You're afraid he'll take fright once he sees Tom, you mean.'

'Harriet, I don't want him coming at all! OK, I liked him, but it was just a fling. How would I tell him now? It's been fifteen months! He'd never believe Tom was his, anyway.'

'I don't see why not. If you'd just wanted maintenance, you'd have told him before. And you liked him a lot more than you let on at the time. You were devastated when Tamsin said he was married.'

'It was shock! I couldn't believe what a bastard he was.'

'Maybe it was on the rocks already.'

'He still should have told me.'

'Sally, you'd only just met him! I don't suppose he set out to have a fling. Whether you want to see him or not, he has a right to know about Tom. And sooner or later, Tom's going to want to know who his daddy is.'

'Some daddy,' she said, looking down at Tom's downy head. 'Some mummy, come to that. She was a bit of an old slapper, wasn't she?'

I only laughed because she expected me to. Typically, she was trying to shrug it off, pretend she wasn't in a state at all.

I woke up that night at ten past two and heard her creaking along the landing and down the stairs. I found her in the kitchen with Tom, saying she couldn't sleep and would I please not start all that do-you-want-to-talk-about-it stuff, because she didn't. Would I please just go back to bed, she was going to watch a corny old film.

Since there was nothing corny on, however, I drove in my pyjamas to the video machine at the petrol station (I got some funny looks) and came back with *Chicken Run*. I finally went back to bed at four thirty, got up at seven and went to work to find that some virulent bug had descended on the capital. Half our temps were sick, and it was chaos.

So I went home exhausted and thoroughly ratty to find Sally equally exhausted and ratty, because Tom had been whingy all day, and Widdles had sicked up on her bed. Jacko was also ratty (for Jacko) because Frida had gone to some fancy-dress hen night and refused to take him along.

'He offered to dress up as a guardian eunuch,' Sally said scathingly.

'I might as well be a bloody eunuch lately,' he grumbled.

'If Erik Bloodaxe ever gets to hear half the things you say to Frida, you will be a bloody eunuch,' she said. To me she added, '*And* he nicked the last bit of my squirty cream to have on his Weetabix.'

'You nicked all my Smarties!'

'Only because you nicked my M&Ms!'

That was when I exploded. 'Oh, grow up, the pair of you!' I banged out, but the door rebounded instead of slamming shut and Jacko's summing-up wafted after me.

'She needs a bloke,' he said to Sally. 'A bloke and a life, in that order.'

'I—do—not—need—a bloody—bloke! OK?' Having yelled this from the fourth stair, I then ran up to my room and banged the door.

So when John phoned twenty seconds later, I was ready for him. In fact I'd never been readier for any plum-priming smoothcarse in my life.

I answered like snappy bullets. 'Hello?'

'Harriet?'

My God, it's him. 'Oh, *John*! Hi, how's it going?'

'Is it a bad time? You sound a bit stressed.'

'No, not really. I'd literally just charged upstairs after a day from hell.'

'Sounds as if you could do with a dinner out, then,' he said, in those melted-chocolate tones.

Too right I could.

'Could you make Sunday night?'

Damn it. Still, just as well he hadn't said Saturday, as I had something on, for once. 'Er, yes, I think so.'

'What nationality do you like to eat?'

'There's a new Middle Eastern place someone's recommended not far from my office in Fulham—I can't remember the name but I can find out.'

'Let me know, then, and I'll book it. Eight-ish?'

'No, I'll book it. And this is on me. I still owe you for that suit.'

He didn't argue. 'If you insist. Shall I pick you up?'

With Jacko and Sally nosing? 'No, I'll see you there. I'll ring and give you the details, all right?'

I hung up, and suddenly I didn't care if he was Nina's. Buried for months in *Mumsy World* and non-drip emulsion and other people's problems, I was desperate for some excitement.

Just one night of it. One night with vibes swirling like hot mist (because I knew they would be) and no faffing or dithering, or wondering whether I should be doing this because it wasn't very nice . . .

What would it matter? Nobody was going to find out, because I wasn't going to tell them. Jacko would only grunt about smootharses. Sally would tut, and remind me what I'd said about side orders.

But I had to tell them something; you couldn't just say 'going out' in this house. On the Saturday night I was going to a do thrown by an old friend from Athens. If I 'met' someone there, he'd do very nicely.

I don't know what it was, but two passable blokes made considerable efforts on the Saturday night. Maybe I was giving off an aura of Tantalising Hidden Depths. At any rate, I came home with a perfect alibi, only as everyone had gone to bed, he had to wait.

'Andy what?' Sally said, in the morning.

'Travers. He was nice.'

'And where are you going?'

One little white truth wouldn't hurt. 'That new Middle Eastern place near the office. How was your evening, anyway?'

'Not bad. Rosie came round. And later on Jacko rolled in with a massive pizza and that Czech au pair from number fifty-three. Another to add to his list of "in with a chance, once I get my plaster off".'

Some of her digs at Jacko were beginning to get to me lately. 'He probably just felt sorry for her!'

'OK, I didn't *mean* it!' she huffed, as if I was supposed to know.

She was vaguely huffy for most of the day, but it didn't stop her coming and flopping on my bed with Tom while I was getting ready for takeoff. She always liked to supervise the operation.

'So what does he do?' she asked, as I wriggled into a silvery top.

'He's a journalist on the *Independent*.' It was actually *DVD Choice* or something, but the *Indie* sounded better.

For a minute or two she kept quiet, as I sat at Dorothy's dressing table, hot-brushing my haystack into something passably attractive.

Then she said, 'It's Helicopter, isn't it? He's phoned and you haven't told me.'

'Don't be stupid.'

'It is. I knew he'd got to you. You're like a fish on a line, just begging to be reeled in.'

I half turned on my stool. 'It is not—bloody—Helicopter! All right?'

'OK, OK!' Other things were already on her mind. Her brow creased with anxiety as she gazed at Tom, who was restless and fretful in her arms. 'I think he's starting another cold—he hardly ate any tea and he's a bit hot. Come and feel, will you?'

I put a hand to his forehead. He might have been marginally warmer than usual, but I couldn't be sure. 'Where's that thermometer thing?'

'I can't find it. Do *you* think he feels hot?'

'Well, a bit, maybe, but babies can get temperatures even from teething, can't they?'

'Yes, I suppose . . . but I don't like to keep giving him Calpol.'

'See how he is in an hour.'

'Yes, but what if he's still hot?'

'Then give him some Calpol.'

'Well, you're a great help!' Getting huffily off my bed she gathered up her angel. 'Come on, *Mummy* cares if you're not a very well bubba.'

I could have shaken her. 'I *do* care! But it's no use getting all worked up if he's just being normally whingy.'

This was entirely the wrong thing to say. 'Are you implying that he's whingy and miserable nonstop?' she said, incensed.

'Of course not! I just meant—'

'Oh, forget it. I don't expect you to give a toss.' And she banged out, leaving me torn between guilt and exasperation. Mostly exasperation, actually. She was getting so bloody ratty lately. All right, part of it was down to Steve, but I also had a feeling she was vaguely resentful because I was having two nights out on the trot.

More than ever, I was dying to escape. I felt as if I was back on that runway, tingling with anticipation as the engines revved . . .

I'd ordered a minicab, and outwardly cool, I arrived at one minute to eight. The place was straight out of *Harems and Gardens*: marble, exotic plants and a fountain going tinkle-splash. I was half expecting Aladdin to appear when someone whispered, 'Come wiz me to ze kasbah.'

Whatever drug I was on, this gave it a massive top-up.

'I think we've strayed into *The Thousand and One Nights*,' he said. 'Are you sure you're not Scheherazade?'

'I hope not. Wasn't she in nightly fear of getting chucked into the Bosporus in a sack?'

'Or getting her head chopped off. Here comes Ali Baba,' he added *sotto voce*, as the head waiter came scurrying up.

I managed to say, 'Harriet Grey—table for two,' without erupting into fizzy giggles. He showed us to an intimate little corner; the air was delicately scented with incense and jasmine, and evocative, Middle Eastern music was playing quietly in the background.

He looked even better than last time, which was saying something. Fresh from shave and shower, his hair was still slightly damp and the scent of shaving things and clean shirt were combining with incense and spices into a lethally seductive concoction.

After ordering two gin and tonics, I said, on impulse, 'I have a confession to make.'

'Go on, then. But bear in mind that I'm very easily shocked.'

His mouth quivered as he said it, in a way that made me think, stuff dinner, I'll just eat you. 'I lied,' I said, with mock penitence. 'I hadn't lost my purse after all. I thought I had, but I remembered almost at once that I'd put it into one of my carrier bags.'

'So why didn't you say so?'

'You'd have thought I was a complete idiot.'

'No, I wouldn't. I'd have thought you were only half an idiot. I already thought you were a complete idiot for leaving your bag open in the first place.'

'Then why didn't you say so?'

'Because I was well brought up. And I thought you might hit me with your handbag.'

I stifled a volcanic giggle. 'I wouldn't have had the energy.' Deliciously teasing banter, with more quivery stuff and eye contact to kill for. 'So, are we going to look at these menus or not?'

Once we'd ordered (meze and lamb with plum sauce), I said, 'How are the ram-raid plans going?'

'I'm not telling a shocking liar like you. How do I know you won't phone *Crimestoppers* and grass me up?'

'How could I?' I asked, all innocent. 'I don't even know your surname.

The Old Bill wouldn't be very impressed with "A tall, darkish bloke called John", would they?'

'It's Mackenzie.'

Well, it was a vast improvement on Helicopter. 'Scottish roots, then?'

'My old man was, originally. I'm still expected to put on a dress kilt occasionally and pretend I'm not a Sassenach.'

This was just another plus. I've a bit of a thing about dress kilts.

From then on, vibes swirled nicely. They were subtle, grown-up vibes, behaving themselves under a veneer of civilised conversation. I was enjoying them like nobody's business until I nearly suffered cardiac arrest.

From where we were sitting I couldn't quite see the entrance, but some woman in a cream jacket had just come in. All I saw, in the first sick instant, was a swinging silk curtain of hair as she turned, obviously looking for someone. 'Magda! There you are!' I heard, as she swung round—and I saw her face.

Phew! As if it could have been Nina. It was ludicrous.

Or was it? What if Rosie had popped round again? What if Sally had told her? And Rosie, unable to contain this hot, tasty morsel . . .

What had she said about Nina? '*Jealous and possessive . . . she went absolutely ape . . .*' No, surely even for Rosie this would be a mouth-opening too far. Surely Sally wouldn't open her mouth, either, even if she still suspected I'd been lying about Andy . . .

My mouth went dry. Why had I told Sally where I was going? What if a venom-spitting Nina was even now heading our way? I suddenly had a vision of that evil, sledge-travelling witch in *The Lion, the Witch and the Wardrobe*, who made it always winter and never Christmas. I saw her cracking a whip, screaming, 'Faster, faster, fool!'

This was where prissy big sister came back. 'It'd serve you right if she did catch you,' she said smugly. 'What sort of cow are you turning into?'

I really hated that girl sometimes. 'I owe him a dinner, don't I? It's just one night! I'm not trying to pinch him!'

I'm afraid to say that twenty minutes later any guilt I felt had been drowned by another glass of wine. As I dithered between fresh mango and baklava, John said, 'Why don't we get one of each and share?'

Lovely. There's something deliciously intimate about forking delicate morsels from someone else's plate.

By then we'd got onto how I'd bumped into Sally and my TEFL era.

'If you've got the travel bug, why didn't you stick with that?' he asked. 'You can go virtually anywhere and teach English.'

'Yes, but one day, when I was teaching the third conditional for the four-hundredth time, I decided it was about time I did something else.'

He picked up a piece of my mango on his fork. 'What the hell is the third conditional?'

'You really don't want to know.'

'I wouldn't have asked if I didn't want to know.'

Well, he'd asked for it. I said, 'If I *tell* you the truth about my purse, *you'll think* I'm an idiot—that's the first conditional. If I *told* you the truth, *you'd think* I was an idiot—that's the second. If I *had told* you the truth, you'd *have thought* I was an idiot—that's the third.'

For a quivery moment he took this in. 'If I tell *you* a barefaced little truth, will you promise not to hit me?'

My God, I thought. He's going to come clean about Nina.

'You've got a bit of baklava on your lip.'

No he's not. 'Have I?' I said unsteadily. 'Where?'

'Hold still . . .' Touching a fingertip to the corner of my mouth he removed a morsel, which then stuck to his own finger. 'Lick,' he said.

As if hypnotised, I opened my mouth, touched the tip of my tongue to his finger and licked the crumb off. And his eyes never left my face.

For tantalising starters I defy anyone to beat it. But we got back to grown-up conversation. And five minutes later, as little cups of Turkish coffee arrived, he glanced at his watch. 'It's still relatively early. Do you fancy doing something else afterwards?'

I'd been expecting it, but that weird, unnamed little organ still gave a wild involuntary lurch. 'Like what?' I asked, casually.

'We could maybe catch a late-night film?'

'Yes, lovely,' I said, thinking of sitting close to him in a cosy little art-house place, while vibes built up like that electric tension you get before a really spectacular storm. Except that it was Sunday night, which meant we'd probably be restricted to stuff like *Blair Witch II*, rather than *Le Plot Noir avec Soupçons de Hanky-Panky Dangereusement Erotiques*. On the other hand, Blair Witches would provide brilliant opportunities for pretending to be scared out of my wits, having to hold his hand tight and cuddle closer. 'How about the Trocadero?'

'Just off Piccadilly Circus?'

'That's it.' I tried to catch a waiter's eye for the bill, but they all seemed to be deliberately avoiding me. Feeling the effects of a high fluid intake I headed for the ladies, instead. Even the steamiest vibes can go right off the boil when all you want is the loo.

Suddenly remembering Sally, I felt a bit bad for thinking she'd have blabbed to Rosie. I felt even worse for rowing with her: she had a lot on her mind. Feeling a quick 'sorry' was called for, I gave her a call.

I let it ring for ages, but there was no reply. She'd hardly be in bed yet, but she could be in the bath. After the loo I adjusted my hair, reapplied my lipstick and tried Sally again.

I let it ring even longer. Again there was no reply, but if she was in the bath, she'd hardly get out and go all the way downstairs in a towel.

On the way back I stopped at the head waiter's station. Paying now would save any tedious arguments. Despite our agreement I had a feeling he might be awkward when it came to the crunch.

'May I have my bill, please?' I said. 'Table fourteen.'

From the way the waiter was looking at me, I was beginning to wonder whether it was a sackable offence to dish out bills at the desk. Suddenly appearing relieved, however, he looked over my shoulder and said something in Arabic to the approaching head waiter, who produced a professional beam. 'Is not necessary, madame.' He spread his hands in a gesture of expansive generosity. 'Is free, today!'

'Free?' I gaped. 'Since when does any London restaurant dish out free dinners? Are we your five-thousandth customers since opening?'

'Is a special, madame,' he beamed. 'Just for you.'

The penny dropped. 'Are you telling me he's already paid?'

The head waiter gave a deprecating little smile and an almost Gallic shrug, as if to say, 'What could I do?'

Well, if he thought he could put one over on me, I was well up to playing him at his own game. I was just in the mood for piquant little games; at a time like this they only added an edge.

With a brilliant game plan up my sleeve, I headed for our table.

'Sorry I've been so long,' I said brightly. 'I was trying to ring Sally, only she's not answering. I'll try again on the way to the cinema.' I added a bright, expectant smile. 'Shall we go?'

A momentary start didn't escape me. 'Well, if you're ready . . .'

'I am if you are. Oh, the *bill*.' I pretended to have suddenly caught on. 'I paid it just now, at the desk.'

For about a millisecond I saw it going through his head: Just what the fuck is going on? But he said, 'Give me two minutes—I need to check the plumbing . . .'

I gave him precisely half a minute before following; I didn't want anyone outraged by accusations of dishonesty. At the desk he was already sounding heated in an even, controlled way. 'Yes, I *know* I paid it, but one of your staff must have been half asleep—'

This was quite enough. I tapped him on the shoulder. 'Funny place for a pee.' It was barely a nanosecond before he twigged. His eyes closed briefly in an 'Oh shit' fashion. '*Now* shall we go?' I said sweetly.

He said nothing till the door had closed behind us.

'All right, I'm sorry,' he said, holding up his hands as if to ward off a frenzied bashing with a handbag. 'If it really bothers you that much, you can pay me back.'

'I don't carry that kind of cash!'

'A cheque, then. Look, can we continue this argument in a cab? It's brass monkey stuff out here.'

It was, too. My coat was designed more for looks than thermals but it was a good deal better than his, which he'd evidently left at home. 'I haven't got my chequebook. I hardly ever carry it.'

'Then you pay next time. I swear I'll play ball.'

'Who said there's going to be a next time?' To tell the truth, I was enjoying this little game. I even thought I'd take it a bit further. After all, a brief chase would make it all the sweeter when I eventually let him catch me.

Accordingly I started a fast walk towards the underground, which was a good five minutes away, even the way I walk when I'm pretending to be mad and it's freezing. I will fully admit that I knew he'd follow.

He kept up manfully. 'It's starting to rain, in case you hadn't noticed.'

'It's not rain. It's sleet.'

'So it is,' he said, in determinedly cheerful tones. 'Thank God I didn't bring a coat—I haven't felt this close to the elements in weeks.'

We carried on past shop windows full of Christmas displays and twinkly lights. 'Where are you off to, just out of interest?' he asked.

'The underground—where do you think?'

'All the way to Piccadilly Circus? Wouldn't you prefer to be stroppy in a cab?'

'You call this stroppy? Wait till I really get going. And who said I'm going to Piccadilly Circus?'

'You did. Before you decided I was a sexist bastard.'

'Well, you said it.'

Apart from the fact that even I was getting cold, it was time to let him catch me. I wanted to try Sally again, anyway. Diving into the shelter of a shop doorway, I got my mobile out.

'If you're trying your friend again,' he said, 'it's a little-known fact that mobiles work far better from inside cabs.'

I bit my lip. Just as I was about to say, 'John, I was winding you up,' he said, 'Look, can we start again?'

I thought you'd never ask.

'Give me a good slap, if you like.' Inclining his head, he tapped his left cheek invitingly. 'Go on, before I chicken out.'

I did laugh then. 'It'll hurt.'

'I thought that was the general idea.'

'Hurt *me*, I mean. I did it once before and it hurt like hell.'

His mouth flickered in a lethally wooze-making fashion. Added to which, it isn't often a bloke can look down on me when I've got two-and-half-inch heels on. I was hoping he'd move in for starters there and then, but he just said, 'Stay there while I hijack a cab.'

Funny how a black cab can look like heaven; in these conditions I'd have expected to wait ten minutes. Once he was in beside me I shot a guilty glance at his trousers, where splodges of sleet were still melting. 'I'm sorry, I didn't intend you to get quite that wet.'

'Yes, you did. You're a merciless, cold-hearted woman.'

His mock-sorrowful tones made me laugh. 'That'll teach you to renege on an agreement.'

He brushed a splodge from a substantial-looking thigh. 'If you hadn't been so long in the little girls' room, I mightn't have done it.'

'If Sally had been answering, I wouldn't have *been* so long.'

He was giving me another of those deliciously lingering appraisals. 'You wouldn't have lasted long as Scheherazade. You'd have been slung in the Bosporus in ten minutes, in a sack labelled "Stroppy concubine—handle with care, she bites".' As he said this, he took my hand and gave it a gentle squeeze.

It's one of the great mysteries of life how, at twenty-nine, something like this can still make you go as gooey as a fourteen-year-old.

'Your hand's cold,' he said.

'Yours isn't.'

'It takes more than a bit of sleet to mess up my thermostat.'

Even in the semidark, I could see his eyes. 'Just as well,' I said unsteadily. 'I wouldn't want you going down with a nasty chill.'

'I don't think there's much chance of that.'

Added to his eyes, and a minute caress with his thumb on the back of my hand, this was quite enough to get vibes swirling wildly.

And when he spoke, his voice was subtly different. Rough and soft at once, like an old Shetland sweater. 'If you're going to try your friend again, why don't you do it now?'

Clear the decks for action. Get it out of the way.

'God, yes, I'd almost forgotten . . .' Wondering whether my thumping heartbeat could be heard in the Mile End Road, I fumbled in my bag for my mobile. I let it ring for ages, but again there was no reply.

'Gone to bed?' he suggested.

'Sally hardly ever goes to bed early.' Suddenly I was becoming uneasy. She was alone in the house. What if she'd done something really stupid, like touching a light switch with wet hands when too tired to think?

On an impulse I tried Jacko. He might well be in a pub just round the corner—he could check on her. His bloody mobile was off.

Telling myself I was getting as bad as my mother, imagining all sorts at the drop of an unanswered call, I looked out of the window. We'd just hit the river, on the Chelsea Embankment. The Albert Bridge lights were reflected in the Thames, but the night looked so black and icy cold, you couldn't imagine summer ever coming. 'I should have been diving off the Great Barrier Reef by now,' I said, 'saying hi to a few sharks.'

'Don't you mind the sharks?'

'Of course I do. I was petrified the first time, but they're an occupational hazard. Just when you're thinking this is the most beautiful coral you've ever seen, something comes looming out of the depths.'

'As they say, every Eden has its serpent.'

I wished he hadn't said that. Not when I was already uneasy about Sally. I wasn't sure I wanted this buzzy little Eden any more, not with maggots and Nina-serpents lurking under rocks. If he was going to evict that particular serpent, OK, but he hadn't. And what about me? What sort of rock-lurker was I turning into?

Still, surely the Trocadero wouldn't hurt. And I might allow myself just one really toe-curling kiss. God knew I needed a little treat.

I tried Sally again as we were coming up to Parliament Square. Still no reply. I heard her voice, though. Like an accusation, it was suddenly ringing in my head. *'Forget it! I don't expect you to give a toss!'*

Oh God, I thought. Tom.

Three

THE UNEASE I'D FELT before was nothing to this. It crawled over me like iced spiders. I'd read all Sally's baby books, you see. *'. . . respiratory infections . . . pneumonia . . . small babies can succumb within hours . . .'*

'The baby wasn't well,' I said, my mouth suddenly desiccated. 'What if he's got worse? What if she's taken him to hospital?'

'Surely she'd have phoned you?'

'My phone was off!'

Why hadn't I left it on? Why the hell had I gone out at all when she was worried? 'There's a really nasty flu bug doing the rounds.'

Twenty yards further on I came to a decision. 'Look, I'm sorry but I've got to go home.' Without waiting for a reply I rapped on the driver's partition. 'Forget Piccadilly Circus—could you make it Putney, instead?'

'I'm sorry,' I added to John, 'but there's no way I can sit watching films at the moment.'

'Harriet, it's fine.'

It wasn't fine at all. While the driver did a U-turn I replayed everything Sally had said, feeling sick with guilt. I'd hardly even listened.

Tom had been under the weather for ages. If he'd picked up full-blown flu on top of all that . . . Recent news bulletins flashed through my mind: hospitals being overstretched, the elderly and babies especially vulnerable '*. . . a particularly virulent strain . . .*'

As the cab crawled in heavy traffic neither of us spoke. Perversely, though, as my tension grew, I almost wished he'd come out with something irritatingly soothing, so I could snap at him.

I tried Sally again, but I knew there'd be no reply and there wasn't.

With a hideous feeling of foreboding, I fixed tense eyes on the road. Then I saw the meter, clocking up by the second. God, I couldn't let him pay this, too. Scrabbling in my purse, I dug out all I had in notes, and thrust it at him. 'That's for the fare.'

'Harriet, it's really not—'

'Take it! I was supposed to pay for the dinner, wasn't I? Have you got some big macho thing about having to pay for everything?'

He looked at me a moment, before putting the cash in his pocket. 'I haven't analysed my motives, but I expect that's it.'

His dry, controlled tones cut me down far worse than overt sarcasm. 'Look, I'm sorry.'

'So am I.'

For what? I thought. For paying? Or for finding yourself with a snapping turtle?

But we were nearly there. Leaning forward, I rapped on the driver's partition and he slid it back. Dry-mouthed, I said, 'Next right and second left.' Thirty seconds later, perched on the edge of my seat, I added, 'Number forty-seven, just past the lamppost.'

As the cab pulled into the kerb and I was hunting for my key, John broke his silence. 'Do you want me to wait? In case you need to go on?'

'No, I've got wheels. Thanks for the dinner.' Already I was opening the door. 'Good night.'

I ran up the path, key in hand. As I pushed the door open, the house felt cold and silent. 'Sally?' I called, racing to the kitchen.

The light was off. Only Widdles was there, curled up on the sofa.

I raced upstairs. The room Sally shared with Tom was at the back of the house, next to mine. I flung the door open.

Tom's cot was empty. I felt sick.

In fact I could have thrown up, but only with relief.

Sally sat up with a startled jerk. 'For God's sake, Harriet!' she said, in a hissy whisper. 'You'll wake him!'

Tom was cuddled up beside her, the cot pushed against the side of the bed to stop him falling out.

'I was trying to ring you!' I whispered back. 'I thought maybe he was really ill!'

'No, but he was being such a miserable little whinge-bag I got sick of running up and down stairs—thought I might as well come to bed, too. Hope I've not started Bad Habits here,' she added, looking down at the small head beside her.

'Why on earth didn't you answer the phone? I was getting frantic, thinking you'd rushed him off to hospital!'

'I was in the loo! At least I was the first time, and by the time I was out it had stopped ringing. When it went again, I just couldn't be bothered to get out of bed.'

'I phoned four times!'

'I didn't *hear* any more! I expect I was asleep by then. Until you had to crash in and wake me up. Honestly, my one early night . . .' Suddenly her expression changed. 'You didn't charge home just because of Tom?'

'Of course I did! I was worried!'

'I hope Andy wasn't browned off.'

I had to tell her now. 'It wasn't Andy.'

She made a *God, I knew it* face. 'Why the hell didn't you tell me?'

'You'd only have had a go at me. I never intended to go, but I was so up to here . . .' I sat on her bed and related the whole farcical saga.

If nothing else, it brought back a ghost of the old, pre-Tom Sally. 'Harriet, I'm appalled,' she said, with mock shock. 'Planning to throw yourself at him like some brazen old slapper—you're getting as bad as me. Did he say he'd call again?'

'Are you kidding? After I snapped at him like some hormonal nutter? Look, can we change the subject?' In some perverse way, those electric vibes had changed the way I felt. Although nothing had really happened, we'd been within a heartbeat of fuses blowing. To me it felt as if we'd shared a certain intimacy already, so the thought of him blowing fuses with Nina, or anyone else, was increasingly difficult to stomach.

So I asked Sally what she was going to buy Jacko for Christmas, and we talked related rubbish until a quarter past eleven, when I said, 'I suppose I'd better let you get back to sleep.'

'Yes, but I wouldn't mind a hot chocolate first.'

'You're getting addicted to that stuff.'

'With squirty cream,' she called, as I left the room.

I came back with two hot, overfull mugs, but just as I'd kicked the door shut my mobile rang. As my hands were full she answered it.

'Hello?' she said. There was a pause. 'No, it's Sally—Harriet's got her hands full. IT'S HIM!' she mouthed at me.

Needless to say I slopped a bit of hot chocolate, but she was talking again. 'No, he's fine, thank you.' (Pause.) 'Yes, Harriet said. She'd got herself in a bit of a state.' (Pause.) 'Well, it was really kind of you to call. Shall I pass you to Harriet?' (Pause.) 'You too. Good night.'

I felt relatively calm as I took the phone. I even sounded calm. 'Hi, John. You'll have gathered that it was a panic in a teacup, thank God.'

'I'm glad. I guess it's a bit late to call, but I thought I'd check.'

'Well, it was very kind of you. I'm sorry I had to dash off like that, but I wasn't in any fit state for sharing a box of Maltesers in the Trocadero.'

He chuckled quietly. 'We can do the Maltesers another time. Shall I call you back in a couple of days?'

This was it, then. 'Actually, it's probably better if I call you. The thing is, I'm going to be really tied up for the next few weeks. I've got to put the house on the market soon and it's a terrible tip—you just wouldn't believe how much junk there is and I've hardly started.'

In the minute pause before he replied, I knew he hadn't been expecting this. I knew he was wondering why the hell hot vibes had suddenly gone lukewarm. 'Sooner you than me,' he said, pleasantly enough. 'Have a good Christmas then, if I don't see you.'

'You too. Enjoy your tribal warfare. And thanks for the dinner.'

As I shoved the phone back in my bag, Sally was wide-eyed. 'Harriet, I never knew you could lie so convincingly. And you haven't even burnt your boats to bits. Mind you, after a pretty categorical "sod off" like that I should think he'll pass out with shock if you *do* ever call him. I almost feel sorry for him,' she added, reaching for her mug. '*I* thought he sounded really nice.'

'He does. That's just the trouble, and you haven't seen him. It's no use, if it's not on the level I just don't want to know.'

'Ask Father Christmas, then. "A no-strings Helicopter, please, because I've been a very good girl except for tonight, when I was planning to be a very bad girl."'

'He'd better bring me a Bad Girls' manual, too. It's been so long, I've probably forgotten how you do it.'

'You've been cooped up with me too long.' Rather awkwardly she went on, 'Look, I'm sorry if I've been a miserable cow lately, but what with one thing and another . . .'

Steve, for starters. And the prospect of leaving Tom with a childminder when she went back to work, and all the other preoccupations of single mothers who aren't earning ninety grand with a live-in nanny.

'It's all getting on top of me,' she went on, in mock-woeful tones. 'There was a programme the other day about colour-theming your Christmas presents, and now I'm in a terrible state about whether to go for midnight blue paper with silver ribbon, or forest green with gold.'

For once, I wasn't going to be fobbed off. 'Try pink with purple. As for really trivial things, like where you're going to live once I get rid of this place, I've made up my mind to buy a flat before prices shoot up any more. I'd be mad not to. At least a two-bedroomed one. So while I'm off on my trip you can keep it warm for me.'

I'd mentioned this before, but I hadn't got very far.

'Harriet, I've told you often enough, I'm not having it.' Not sponging off me, she meant. 'And I'm not living with you, either,' she went on. 'Not after you sell this place, anyway. You don't put enough chocolate in the hot chocolate, you're too skinny for me to borrow your clothes, and you lust after illicit Helicopters and wake me up.' She stuck her tongue out. 'So push off and let me get some sleep.'

Flu-chaos still reigned on Monday, and Tuesday was worse, if anything. I came home that evening to find Jacko in the sitting room with the useless little fan heater on, watching some European League game on Dorothy's mega-TV. 'Why don't you watch it in the kitchen?' I asked. 'It's freezing in here.'

'It'd get on Sal's nerves. This picture's better, anyway.'

Sally was in the kitchen, folding some washing neatly, which was a pretty ominous sign. 'How did it go with that woman?' I asked. She'd had an appointment to see a childminder: about the sixth so far. With five mornings a week of classes lined up, something had to be sorted out soon.

'She seemed all right,' she shrugged. 'They all *seem* all right . . .'

'But you didn't take to her?'

'I don't know! Tom was upset when she picked him up, but he's been like that with all of them, the awkward little devil . . .'

On an impulse I said, 'Look, why don't we go out?'

'How can I?' she demanded. 'Frida's out and I'm not leaving Tom with Jacko. Bombs could drop and he'd still carry on watching football.'

'I'll get him to turn the volume down.'

'No, thanks,' she said flatly. 'I'm going to have a bath. Admire the pearly opalescence of my stretch marks and really cheer myself up.'

She was still in the bath when Rosie came round.

'Thought I'd just show you this,' she said, unfolding one of those free local papers. 'Suzanne and I were gobsmacked!' She pointed at a half-page article publicising the opening of a new gym called Scott's, with a rather fuzzy black and white photo, showing the proprietor Stuart Scott.

I couldn't believe it. '*Stuart?*'

'Exactly,' Rosie said, with satisfaction. 'Done pretty well for himself, hasn't he? This is his third Scott's, but his first in London.'

Stuart! Stuart and I had been an item in my last year at school. Decidedly nice-looking but on the shy side, he'd been the first boyfriend I'd really been keen on, and not merely grateful for.

A nostalgic little pang washed over me. 'Well, I'm glad he's doing well, even after our non-happy ending. I really liked him, you know.'

'I know,' Rosie said. 'You nearly didn't come on holiday, you were so upset.'

With half a dozen others, Rosie and I had booked a September fortnight in Skiathos. It was to be a last fun fling together, before we all went off to various institutions of higher education, to learn more about sex and drugs than we'd managed so far. But the holiday package wasn't going to be quite the girly thing our fond parents imagined. Four of us had arranged, on the quiet, for our assorted boyfriends to get cheap flights and join us.

Three weeks before we were due to go, Stuart had phoned me and mumbled that he was terribly sorry, he didn't think he could afford it after all. I'd said not to worry, I'd give him some money.

He'd mumbled that no, he couldn't—sorry—and hung up.

I wasn't stupid. I knew it was nothing to do with money; he was giving me the elbow. After ten minutes I'd phoned him back. I'd said, 'If this is your way of telling me you've had enough of this relationship, you could have just said so. I was going off you too, you know.' Then I'd run upstairs, thrown myself on the bed, and cried a river into my pillow.

As I gazed at fuzzy Stuart, it seemed like another age. In another way, though, it seemed like last month.

Rosie said, 'Suzanne thought you might pop along and see him, for old times' sake, at the opening night.'

'Are you kidding? He'd only be embarrassed. Especially if I asked him why he went off me like that. At least, that's how it seemed. Maybe he'd been going off me for ages and I was just too thick to see it.'

'I don't think so,' Rosie said.

'How would you know?'

She hesitated in an awkward, most un-Rosie-ish way that alerted my antennae instantly. 'Rosie, what?'

She made a wincey sort of face. 'The thing is, he didn't go off you, exactly. He thought you'd gone off *him*. Suzanne told me last night.'

I gaped at her. 'Why the hell would he think that?'

'Someone told him. Someone who fancied him.'

I could have strangled her. 'Rosie, *who*?'

It gushed out like one of Thames Water's best leaks. 'For God's sake, Harriet, who the hell d'you *think*? It was *Nina*!'

I don't know what my face looked like, but it can't have been a pretty sight.

'God, I knew I should never have told you,' Rosie said fearfully.

I suppose it was about fifteen minutes later that Sally came down. 'Oh, hi, Rosie,' she said. 'Anyone mind if I watch *Peak Practice*?'

I said, 'If you want dramas, how about *The Tale of the Scheming Witch*?'

Needless to say, Nina hadn't been part of the Skiathos party. She hadn't been in my immediate circle, besides which she'd had something swankier lined up than a self-catering cheapie. Some relative had a flash villa on the Italian Riviera; she was going for a whole month with some cousins, Rob (her then boyfriend), and Suzanne. But Rob was playing hard to get, thought he'd rather go surfing in Cornwall, so Nina, piqued, decided it would just serve him right if she took someone else.

Then, one day, while she was filling her Jeep at the petrol station where Stuart had a summer job, it occurred to her that Stuart was decidedly nice-looking. For some weird reason, though, he'd never made a move on her. So she'd set about correcting this glitch in the universe. She'd started chatting, fluttering her eyelashes. She'd somehow implied that she'd heard I was going off him, I didn't really want him coming to Skiathos as he'd cramp my style with the beach bums.

'Suzanne thinks she almost believed it, at the time,' Rosie had said. 'She can convince herself black is shocking pink if it suits her.'

Having stuck her poisoned arrow right in she'd waited a day or two before going to fill her Jeep up again, and Stuart had said he'd saved me the bother of dumping him. So Nina had fluttered her eyelashes again, and said what a shame about Skiathos, but as it happened . . .

Oh, and I nearly forgot the best bit. Nina had felt *bad*, afterwards.

And Suzanne, to her eternal credit, had said, 'Oh, come off it—you just wanted to get him to prove you could do it.'

I was warming to Suzanne considerably.

'Shame Helicopter never made a move,' Rosie said plaintively, once Sally had been genned up. 'Lovely poetic justice, or what?'

I almost felt like filling her in anyway, but already she was going on, 'Suzanne says Nina's got this psychological thing—she just *has* to have what she wants.'

'Psychological thing?' Sally snorted. 'It's called being a manipulative bitch.'

I thought back to my tart 'I was going off you too, you know.' I couldn't have played into Nina's hands better if I'd tried. 'If you still go to her girly lunch and pretend to like her after all this, I'll kill you,' I said.

'I'm not!' she said, all hurt. 'I made an excuse about having to help my mum do her Christmas shopping. So I'll *have* to go home now,' she added crossly. 'And traipse round the shops with her saying how about this for so-and-so?' She stopped and looked from me to Sally and back again. 'Sorry,' she added, a mite sheepishly. 'I know we're in the middle of a major drama here; that was the commercial break.'

'I wish you'd said,' Sally tutted. 'I'd have put the kettle on and dashed off for a pee before part two and the really exciting bit. Where Harriet's eyes go all scary and glittery as she plans her fiendish revenge.'

She shot me a conspiratorial little look, but I ignored it. 'How the hell can Suzanne still be friends with her, when she knows what she's like?'

'In a funny sort of way,' Rosie said, 'I think she feels sorry for her. Nina hasn't really got any proper friends except her.' A moment later she added, 'Anyway, the latest Nina bulletin might cheer you up: she's a bit upset with Helicopter at the moment.'

My antennae pricked right up. 'Why?'

'She was hoping he'd invite her to his folks for Christmas. They've got a nice little country place, apparently, but he said other people's families are a pain and she'd be bored. Which *she* takes to mean that he's not sufficiently serious to want to take her home. So she's booked a week's skiing in Aspen with somebody from work,' Rosie went on. 'Which is supposed to make *him* jealous in case she picks up some Silicon Valley billionaire on the chair lift.'

'Knowing Nina, she probably will,' I said.

When Rosie finally left, Sally said the one thing she'd been dying to say for the past hour and a half. 'For God's sake. *Now* she tells you.'

'Sod's Law,' I said. 'Plus she only found out last night.'

'It makes me sick. Talk about fair game—you should tell him you've found half a dozen slots in your diary, after all.'

It was hideously tempting, but for one thing. 'Don't you think I'd love to? But being a side order would really make me sick after this.'

'OK, I can see that. You wouldn't fancy being a side order to a snake.'

I wouldn't even call her a snake. They got a bad enough press anyway. The Witch of Narnia was far more appropriate.

This discussion got no further, though, as the football was over and Jacko had just joined us. I didn't want him in on this. Besides, he had a gripe of his own. His mother had been on the phone, doing his head in.

'She wants *me* to talk to her!' he said. 'As if she's going to listen to me! They should just let her get on with it.'

All this referred to Jacko's much younger sister, Tara, who was giving her parents grief with a highly unsuitable boyfriend. While Jacko was in hospital, I'd heard every detail from his mother. Not only was Lee far too old (twenty-four), he played in an unsuccessful rock band ('nasty, druggy types') and was distracting her from her A levels.

'That's another prime reason for staying here for Christmas,' Jacko grunted. 'Tara and the old lady'll be at it like a bag of cats.'

Two days later Jacko got his plaster off at last and celebrated by trying to burn the house down. To be strictly accurate, he announced that it was bloody freezing in the sitting room and he was going to make a fire. First he rolled sheets of newspaper into sausages, twisted them into zigzags. Then he arranged sticks on the newspaper, lumps of coal on top of those, and applied a match.

It burned beautifully for twenty seconds, whereupon it went out. After he'd repeated the process Sally said, 'For God's sake let me do it, you ginger ape. You'll burn the house down.'

'Fires are boys' stuff,' he scoffed. 'It's a law of nature. So toddle off and polish your stretch marks.'

'Oh, for God's *sake* . . .' Sally stomped out crossly, probably because she couldn't think of anything to cap his last remark with.

'Stretch marks is hitting below the belt!' I said. 'You know she's sensitive about them. And if you dare say "She started it", I'll thump you. She's still in a tizz about bloody Steve, if you ask me.'

'She's in a tizz about bloody something. What was he like?'

'I told you!' I said. 'Didn't I?'

'Don't think I ever asked.' He put a match to a newspaper zigzag. 'Didn't want to be a nosy bastard.'

'Well, I suppose you'd say he was good-looking, confident, a bit full of himself. To be quite fair, though, before we found out he was married I might have said good-looking, confident, quite a laugh.'

Jacko's mind was back on pyromania, however. 'Get a load of that,' he grinned, as the flames began to take at last.

I then went after Sally. 'He'll be gone for good after Christmas—can't you stop having a go at him?'

'He's always winding me up,' she said irritably.

'It doesn't mean anything!'

'Come on, we're going out. No excuses. Frida's in for the next couple of hours; she'll keep an ear out for Tom and I'll take my mobile.'

For once she barely argued and we headed for the Drunken Dragon, the nearest walking-distance pub. It was naff as you like, with an over-dressed artificial Christmas tree, a proper fire, and a barman who said, 'All right, love?' To be honest, I was rather fond of it.

We stayed an hour and a half and Sally actually seemed to relax, which was partly due to two glasses of mulled wine. On the way home the air was sharp and frosty, tingling our cheeks and making puddles glitter icily under street lamps. It was so unusually cold we stopped for bags of chips and ate them walking along, giggling like a pair of sixteen-year-olds.

When we finally made it to the gate, she said, 'Whose is that?' There was a shiny BMW sports parked outside. 'Maybe Father Christmas sent Helicopter early, with your Bad Girls' manual,' she giggled.

My stomach gave a drunken lurch. Suddenly I was back in that cab, with vibes swirling like hot mist and my fantasies going into orbit.

As soon as I'd opened the door Sally charged upstairs to check on Tom. As I slung my coat over the banisters, Frida came from the kitchen bearing mugs of coffee. 'Your friend's here—I was about to give you a phone.'

My stomach gave another drunken lurch.

She nodded towards the sitting-room door. 'Could you open it?'

I opened. Widdles lay flaked out fatly in front of the fire, which was burning so merrily it would have got an A plus in inviting glows. On the sofa sat Jacko, and on his lap sat Tom, happily eating a rattle.

And next to Jacko sat the Witch of Narnia.

My first thought was that she'd found out and come to kill me, but murderers don't smile at you like that. This was followed instantly by furious disbelief. How dared she sit there like a welcomed friend?

'You've got a nerve,' I said. 'And by the way, your BMW just turned back into a broomstick, so your cover's blown.'

I said it in my head, at least. What I actually said was, 'Nina! Goodness me, what a surprise! Long time no see, and all that . . .'

Yes, I can be as loathsomely hypocritical as the best of them.

Her voice was just as I remembered: the kind-to-lesser-mortals tone that had always irked me. 'Well, I'm only a couple of miles up the road—I expect Rosie told you—and I thought I'd pop round and give you an invitation to my little lunch. Did Rosie mention it?'

Before I could answer, Sally burst in. 'You might have told me!' she expostulated. 'I nearly had a fit, seeing an empty cot!'

From Jacko's lap, Tom gave his usual Mummy-greeting beam.

'You didn't give us a chance!' Jacko retorted, as she snatched him up.

I shot Sally a private Look. 'Sally, this is Nina. We were at school together—I might have mentioned her.'

Sally's taken-aback flash was only momentary. 'I've heard all about you,' she said, in tones so dangerously demure, they spelt incipient wickedness.

But Nina had turned to me. 'How are you, anyway? It's been yonks—I don't think I've seen you since Tina Sinclair's wedding.'

As always, everything about her was immaculate, including that hair, which still hung like a black silk curtain round her perfect, neat-featured little face. I'd forgotten how big and navy-blue her eyes were, how thickly lashed. I thought of her using them on John, and began to realise just what five-star, fully paid-up jealousy feels like.

Not nice, I can tell you.

Frida was sitting on an ancient leather pouffe Dorothy had used for putting her feet up. 'If you and Sally want coffee, I need more cups.'

'I'll get them,' Jacko said. Still limping slightly, he went out.

'*Such* a nasty accident, poor man,' Nina said, once he'd gone. 'I gather some old auntie left you half this house?' she went on.

I began to think she'd just come for a good old nose, after all. As she cast an appraising eye at original mouldings on the ceiling, I could see her thinking, 'Seven hundred grand or so, less fees and death duties and divide by two—not bad for the likes of Harriet Grey.'

I have to say the room didn't look too bad with only table lamps and the firelight. Square and high-ceilinged, it had a massive bay window curtained in ancient maroon velvet. The sofas and armchairs were ancient chintzy stuff; the floor was polished wood, covered with a faded old Oriental carpet, which was probably still valuable. The fireplace was the original, of the type specialist burglars nick to order.

Jacko limped back with the cups. 'Does it still hurt?' Nina asked, all concerned sympathy as he reseated himself beside her.

'No, he just wants sympathy,' Sally said.

Frida said, 'Sally! How can you say that? His leg is still stiff, poor Jacko.'

'Yes, but I'm playing it for all I can get,' he grinned.

Nina gave the kind of tinkly laugh I remembered all too well, and bestowed on him the kind of smile that had always gone with it. I'd seen her do it at parties in my teens, when flirting with some boy I'd have loved to flirt with, if I hadn't thought he'd ask where my paper bag was. The formula still seemed to be working. I wouldn't have thought she'd try it on Jacko, though: he wasn't flash enough. Maybe it was sheer habit. On the other hand, because he was just Jacko, I often forgot that although he'd never stop traffic, he was passably nice-looking.

And if she was flirting, he was lapping it up. It made me livid to see him fall for it, but that was blokes for you. I imagined John lapping it up in exactly the same way and instantly my stomach was full of green snakes again, writhing. Why *had*n't he said the odd night out wouldn't hurt? Wasn't I worth making an effort for?

Nina was giving another tinkly laugh. 'Goodness, I nearly forgot!' She handed an envelope to me. 'The invitation—do hope you can come.'

Thinking, oh shit, I opened it and thought, thank God, instead. 'I'm terribly sorry—it would have been lovely—but I've just accepted another invitation for next Sunday lunchtime.'

'Oh, well . . .' Nina gave a regretful little smile. 'Another time, then.'

'Yes,' I smiled, loathing my own hypocrisy.

As Tom was getting restless, Sally yanked up her jumper and fed him.

Just for an instant Nina looked startled, as if she'd heard that in the distant past breasts had another function apart from man-bait, but had never quite believed it. Maybe she realised I'd noticed, because almost immediately she said, '*Sweet* little baby,' as if to cover up.

'Yes, isn't he?' Sally said. 'How's your boyfriend, by the way? Rosie said you had a fantastically yummy boyfriend with a helicopter.'

Nina gave a little laugh. 'Oh, it's not *his*—just a corporate thing, you know. But yes, he is pretty "yummy",' she added.

'Jacko has a plane,' Frida said. 'His own one.'

'Really?' Nina was all wide-eyed again, but at Jacko, not Frida.

'Just a little Piper—fifty-fifty with the old man,' he said, almost apologetically. 'Dead handy for nipping to Blackpool for a night out, though.'

Nina produced a silver-bells peal. 'Isn't he a hoot?'

Frida said, 'Will you take me for a fly in it?'

'Of course, my angel.'

'You wouldn't catch me in it,' Sally retorted. 'I used to go out with an airline pilot once. He said weekend pilots were all lethally overconfident and skipped their checks.'

'I'd never take you anyway,' he replied. 'You'd be a right back-seat driver, all "Slow down a bit, can't you?" and "Watch that UFO, dickhead!"'

Nina gave another silver-bells peal.

Then Sally said, innocently, 'I hear you're going skiing in Aspen, Nina. Isn't that the really smart place where all those *Hello!* types go?'

While I tried not to laugh, Nina did a good job of trying not to preen. 'Well, I suppose it *is* pretty exclusive. Of course, John would have loved to come, but he feels obliged to do the family thing.'

'I must go,' Frida announced.

Jacko watched as she rose in a lithe, fluid movement to her feet. 'Where are you off to in those leathers?'

'Tramp,' she said. 'Cecilia met someone who can get us in.'

Jacko watched her fluid-leather exit. 'Clubbing,' he sighed. 'God, she makes me feel old. I can get overexcited just watching the Teletubbies these days.'

Nina let out another tinkling peal. By the time she left, half an hour later, I was beginning to wonder how many more I could have stood without slapping her. Jacko and I saw her to the door.

Once we'd watched her broomstick zoom off, I turned to him. 'If you even *think* of saying it, I'll thump you.'

'What?' he said, all hurt.

'You know what. "I don't know what you were on about, I thought she was really nice." And before you say God, I can be really nasty, I'll tell you something about Nina. She nicked a bloke of mine, years ago. Someone I liked as much as you liked Michaela. She didn't really want him—she only nicked him to prove she could do it.'

He looked as if someone had just told him Liverpool had been relegated to the Fourth Division. 'Why didn't you tell me?'

'Because she did it so cleverly I only just found out.'

Leaving him to un-daze himself, I took the cups to the kitchen, where Sally joined me once she'd put Tom back in his cot. 'I thought she was a friend of Frida's!' she said. 'I nearly had a fit!'

'*You* nearly had a fit?' I put the dishwasher on. 'I thought she must be onto me, but it was just a good old nose, checking out the house.'

'Maybe she came to check out Jacko, too, 'cos the other night I told Rosie he was loaded,' she said, a trifle sheepishly. 'Or that he's been half running his old man's empire—it's much the same thing. I mean, he looks so scruffy and acts such a dickhead, so when she asked if he had a job to go back to I couldn't resist telling her, just to see her face.'

And Rosie, of course, had passed on every detail of William 'Jacko' Jacques, of Jacques Loadsamoney Enterprises.

'No wonder she was practically flirting with him,' I snorted. 'Did you see him lapping it up like an idiot?'

'Given that he fancies just about everybody, he was bound to fancy her,' Sally pointed out. 'Who was Michaela?' she added.

'A consuming passion, years ago. It was a nightmare when she dumped him. He hardly came out of his room for days.' Just before his finals, too, which was one reason he'd only got a third. Attending only about fourteen lectures in three years was the other.

Even Sally looked touched. 'Poor old Ape-Face,' she said, and a second later he came in.

'I wish you'd told me she'd nicked your bloke,' he said, still sounding hurt. 'I didn't think she was that great, anyway. That laugh of hers'd get right up my nose in five minutes.'

'Jacko,' I said, 'I love you.'

On the Thursday night I came home to find that Santa's little elves had called. There was a huge holly wreath on the front door. A round ball of greenery and mistletoe hung from a velvet ribbon in the hall. An evergreen garland was twisting up the banisters.

The sitting-room door was open. Another fire blazed in the grate. And in the corner, nearly brushing the ten-foot ceiling, was a massive Christmas tree. I stood and gaped like a four-year-old.

'Great, isn't it?' Jacko enthused. It was draped in dozens of tiny coloured lights and decorations in every style and colour.

'Sal thinks it's not *Homes and Gardens* enough,' he went on. 'Wanted me to do it all arty-farty white. She thinks it's naff.'

'I don't!'

'Yes, you do, Stretch Marks. I think it's great, anyway.'

'It's lovely,' I said, shooting a Look at Sally.

'I *do* think it's lovely,' she protested. 'My mother would never have a real tree, because of all the needles on the carpet.'

'I am going to make some *glogg*,' Frida announced.

'I'll help,' Jacko said. 'And then we can all get Swedishly rat-arsed.'

Once they'd gone I said to Sally, 'Did you have to throw cold water on it? Why do you always have to have a go at him?'

'I never said it was naff! He took it the wrong way on purpose!'

Jacko and Frida came back with mugs of hot *glogg*, which had raisins and God alone knows what alcohol in it, and was lethally moreish. By now the room smelt like a whole pine forest—I could almost have got drunk on the scent. Jacko had bought a corny Christmas CD, too, and we sang along and got merrily festive by the fire. After the second round of *glogg*, Jacko said, 'There's only one more thing that tree needs. Presents!'

As we eventually staggered up to bed, Sally said to me, 'I hope to God he's not been spending a bomb on presents. I can't afford much just now and I'll feel awful if everybody else does.'

'Sally, he's not going to compare costs.'

'That's not the point! I hope you haven't either—I'll kill you.'

With Widdles snuggled beside me, I lay under my duvet, trying to work out whether it was the *glogg*, or whether I actually was feeling marginally more content than I had for the past couple of weeks. Helen, at least, had kindly taken herself off the 'urgent preoccupation' list, having phoned that afternoon. She and Oliver were spending Christmas in Saffron Walden with her sister, who had a son much the same age. Lawrence and the twins were going to his mother, who adored the twins as they were so like her only son. Francesca was going to friends of her own, but there was no question of her and Lawrence splitting up. Did I know she'd moved in next door already?

Yes, I'd gathered as much, from the Renault that had appeared. Helen had seen Lawrence at her solicitor's office, and he'd made neither scenes nor threats. She'd sounded so calm, I began to think she'd done the right thing after all. Then I thought about Christmas, instead. Dear old Jacko. He was just a big kid at heart, and so was Sally. I'd do stockings for both of them, with daft little presents and a satsuma in the bottom.

In fact, I was going for the whole corny bit, including a box of spectacularly tacky crackers. We'd watch the usual festive stuff on the television and play daft games. In short, the kid in me was looking forward to the whole thing more than I had for years. So naturally it followed that only days later, Harriet's Perfect Christmas started falling apart.

Four

IT BEGAN WITH A CALL from Jacko's mother that lasted twenty minutes and left him more exasperated than I'd ever seen him.

'I *told* them,' he said, in up-to-here tones. 'If they'd kept their noses out she'd have got fed up with him by now.'

It was Tara. There had been a huge row over Lee. Parental feet had been firmly put down. He was a Bad Influence and distracting her from her A levels; he was absolutely forbidden to come to the house.

And after saying, '*OK*, don't go on,' with sufficient sulks to fool them, she'd disappeared, taking a few clothes and her building society cash card. She'd left a note saying she was eighteen, she could do as she liked. She was going with Lee into the wide blue yonder, which was nowhere near Liverpool, so they needn't bother looking for her. She would phone, just so they knew she wasn't dead.

All this had happened three days previously. Jacko's folks hadn't dared tell him at first, thinking he'd say 'I told you so' (which he had). However, Tara still hadn't phoned and they were frantic. She'd be doing heroin, catching HIV, getting pregnant, getting arrested.

'They want me to go home, in case she calls,' he said. 'They think she might listen to me—that's a joke, for a start. She'll be home once she's out of money. She's never had to rough it, not even for a day.'

'She's probably having a ball,' I said.

'Try telling them that. I'd better go, though, before the old man's blood pressure goes through the roof and the old lady overdoses on Prozac. They've spoilt her rotten, you know. It's probably the first time in her life they've ever put their feet down.'

I tried not to care that my perfect Christmas was going down the pan; it just wouldn't be the same without Jacko. 'When will you go?'

'The day after tomorrow. I've got a physio appointment tomorrow.' He gave a ghost of his usual grin. 'The physiotherapist's a cracker—I've got to give her a Christmas kiss before I never see her again.'

Once he'd disappeared to the DD for beer and sympathy, Sally said, 'I bet they spoilt him rotten, too.'

'I don't think so,' I said. 'When I first knew him he didn't have much more money than the rest of us. His old man made him work for his pocket money—he had to go and polish the cars in the showrooms. He was a bit sick because Tara's never had a job. At least, she went life-guarding at the swimming pool for two whole Saturdays, but they made her mop the floors and it was too much like hard work.'

'Brat,' Sally said, with feeling.

Frida left early on the 22nd; Jacko was leaving on the 23rd. And on the evening of the 22nd, Sally had a call from her un-proper aunt that threw her into an orgy of guilt.

'It's Mum and Dad,' she despaired. 'They're terribly upset that I'm not going home. They think *I* think they're ashamed of me.'

'Well, you do,' I pointed out.

'The neighbours have been asking why I'm not bringing Tom home for his first Christmas, and Mum thinks *they* think she doesn't want us.'

Knowing what was coming, I kept quiet.

'And I know they were a pain at first, but I can't help wondering how I'd feel if Tom didn't want to come home,' she went on.

To save her asking, I answered first. 'Look, don't feel bad if you want to go. I honestly don't mind a bit—I'll go to Mum's after all.'

She looked positively relieved. 'Are you sure? I'd truly much rather stay here, but I think I would feel bad.'

I phoned Euston and booked her a ticket on my credit card.

Since there was little doing in the office, I took the following morning off to drive Sally to the station. Jacko left first. He and Sally had called a truce by then; she'd even let him open the twenty-third window on the Advent calendar.

'You needn't think you're getting rid of me for good, though,' he said. 'If you feel like tarting yourselves up for a wild night out, I'll come back for New Year.'

'Are you kidding?' Sally demanded. 'What sort of a wild night can I have with no baby sitter?'

'We could get one. From an agency or something.'

'It'd cost a bomb. I hate New Year's Eve, anyway. It depresses me.'

'God, you're a right little ray of sunshine, aren't you?' Jacko said. 'Let me spark you up with my famous magic touch.' From his pocket he produced a mangled bit of mistletoe.

She received his kiss with reasonable grace. 'Happy Christmas, Ape-Face. Be good.'

'Happy Christmas, pet. Try not to murder your folks—I'll probably be murdering mine and I don't want you sharing my headlines.'

Then it was my turn. 'Good luck,' I said. 'If Tara shows up, give her a good slap for me.'

'I'll probably be murdering her, too. Come and visit me when I end up in Broadmoor. Smuggle me a couple of beers in your bra.'

He then kissed Tom, perched on Sally's hip. 'Bye, mate. Smile a lot at the wrinklies and say hi to Father Christmas for me.'

Although he'd have left after Christmas anyway, I hated seeing him go. After several weeks he'd begun to feel like a permanent fixture. He'd be down for the odd weekend, but it wouldn't be the same.

After we'd waved him off, and while Sally was collecting her things I went into the sitting room. It felt chill and forlorn, with cold ashes in the grate. Even the tree looked dejected, all its glory about to be wasted on thin air and Widdles. However, there were things under it that had not been there an hour before. When Sally came down, I showed her.

'Oh, my God,' she said. 'What the hell has he done?'

There were identical, normal-sized presents for me and Sally, and a huge one for Tom. The card read, 'It might be a bit big for you just now, mate, but at least you won't need a licence. Love, Jacko.'

'You can't take it on the train,' I said. 'Are you going to open it now?'

'I suppose so,' Sally said fretfully. 'I wish he hadn't done this . . .' She ripped the paper off, to reveal a blue, toddler-sized Thomas the Tank Engine. It was dual purpose: push along with the handle, or sit on and ride. Sally stared. 'For God's sake, it's miles too big for Tom!'

I was hurt on poor Jacko's behalf. 'He'll grow into it in no time!'

'And what the hell's he got me?' Picking up the present, she stared at it. It was rectangular and floppy. 'I hope it's not some horrible tacky nightie.'

'Don't be such a cow! Poor Jacko—I wish he hadn't got you anything!'

'So do I!' Impatiently she tore the paper off.

'Well, thanks a lot,' I said. 'He's got me exactly the same—you've spoilt my surprise now.'

'He won't have got you the same colour!' From its neat folds, she was shaking out a soft, fine-knit sweater in palest pink. 'It's bloody cashmere!' Her eyes were suddenly wet with leaks. 'Why did he do it?' she choked. 'All I got him was that stupid fart pot and a paperback!'

Feeling awful, I tried to comfort her. 'He'll love the fart pot! I bet nobody else'll get him one!' In case you're wondering, the fart pot was a tub of green goo you stuck your fingers into. It made wet-fart noises, and Jacko was something of a connoisseur in that department.

She was still fretful on the way to the station. 'Whether she's been upset or not, I just know Mum'll be having a go before I've been there an hour. I'll get tensed up just waiting for her to do it.'

Happy Christmas, ho ho ho.

I didn't get round to phoning Mum till after work and barely got a hello in before she launched into a hurried monologue: 'I'm up to my elbows in stuffing—we've got people tonight as well so I'm trying to get on top of everything—Bill's very good of course, but he's been entertaining the children—all five of them now, would you believe—Juliet phoned last night to say their central heating boiler had packed up.'

Juliet was Bill's daughter, who had two kids.

'So she asked if they could come too, and we could hardly say no,' she went on. 'The children'll have to sleep end to end, though I'm sure they won't mind—Juliet and Mike'll have to share that single bed in the little room—Oh Lord—hang on—something's boiling over—'

It was just as well; those ten seconds gave me time to think.

'Wretched cranberries,' she said, half panting as she got back to the phone. 'I've got sticky red goo all over the hob now. By the way, did you know it's best to take your turkey out of the oven a good half-hour before serving? It carves better.'

'Yes, I'll do that,' I said brightly. 'Have you got that special brandy butter recipe, by the way? That's why I was ringing, actually.'

'Oh Lord, I haven't made brandy butter for *years*. I should go to M&S if I were you. I'm sorry, darling, but I really must dash—I'll phone on Christmas Day, all right?'

Of course there were people I could have phoned, but I didn't want people feeling sorry for me. In any case, everyone I knew was either going to family or opting out and heading for the ski slopes, like Witch Nina. Ridiculously I began to think it was her fault that my perfect Christmas had fallen apart. Like her Narnia counterpart, she was making it always winter and never Christmas.

I didn't tell anyone at work that my Christmas was down the pan. After packing up at twelve thirty, we went for drinks and when I got home I put Capital on, to cheer myself up, but by about seven thirty it was only making me feel that everyone in the entire universe was out partying, except for me. I thought of Jacko, probably out somewhere with a crowd of friends. I thought of Mum and Bill's house, stuffed with food and drink and people, and wondered why I hadn't told her.

And then I thought of the Witch of Narnia, who'd made my perfect Christmas fall apart. Skiing. The Witch of Aspen, ha ha.

Of Aspen.

In Aspen . . .

The thought sneaked up when I wasn't looking.

Phone him.

What, now?

Why not?

He's still seeing her.

Not just now, he isn't. What do you care, anyway?

He'll be busy.

He might not.

Before another twenty seconds had elapsed I was pinging his number.

Brrrr . . . Brrrr . . . Brrrr . . .

He's not going to answer, is he?

Brrrr . . . Brrrr . . .

Yes, but what if he does?

I jabbed 'off' in mid-ring and would like to make it perfectly clear that this was not due to any onset of sudden, irrational panic in case he answered, after all. It was Christmas Eve, for God's sake. I could hardly say, 'Hi, John, fancy going for a pizza?' I shoved my phone back in my bag. 'This is what you call getting desperate,' I said to Widdles, who was actually awake for once. 'While the cat's away, he's hardly going to be sorting out his stamp collection, is he?' I said. 'After all, he had no qualms about playing, even when the cat was only just down the road.'

I went to bed at ten, with Widdles and one of Dorothy's collection of ancient Regency romances. I'd never have thought she'd be into this sort of thing, which just goes to show you should never judge by appearances. Had she secretly dreamed of a lusty Sir Tarquin? *'I can never marry you,' wept little Dorothea, 'for I am fated to grow old and arthritic in Putney and moan about the government. O, pray unhand me, sir! Have the goodness to remove your hand from my placket fastener!'*

Poor old thing. By page ten I was almost beginning to fancy lusty Sir Tarquin myself, but then my mobile rang. It was Jacko, bless him. 'Hi, pet—how was your drive to darkest Devon?'

I wasn't going to tell him there hadn't been one. 'Not bad—how was yours?'

'Diabolical. Still, I've calmed the wrinklies down a bit. She still hasn't phoned, though.'

After we'd talked for a couple more minutes I switched the light off. And just as I'd drifted into sleep, my phone rang again.

'Hello?' I said dozily.

'That was quick,' the voice said. 'I thought you might have your rubber gloves on and be doing unspeakable things to turkeys.'

I was still groping for my brains. 'Er, sorry, who is it?' Even as I said it, though, a massive flying jelly hit me in the guts.

'John. John Mackenzie. You weren't asleep, were you?' he added.

Help. Think. 'Erm, no, not really, just sort of nodding . . .'

'I think you called me, earlier,' he said. 'Only there was a hell of a racket and by the time I got to my phone . . .'

My brain kicked in just in time. 'Well, it didn't matter. It was only going to be a quickie, to say good luck with your tribal warfare.'

'Let's hope I don't need it. Plying the old man with enough single malt might help. At least he won't be able to shoot straight.'

I laughed, while checking the clock. Only 10.47?

'If you weren't attacking turkeys, I'd have thought you'd be out partying,' he went on.

From the sounds of it, he still was. I had to keep my end up. 'I *was*! From lunchtime! I rolled in half an hour ago and fell into bed.'

'Just as well, if you're cooking tomorrow. Don't head cooks have to be up at the crack, shoving the stuffed sacrifice in the oven?'

'Not now, I don't. I'm not cooking, after all. They've all gone home.'

'Sorry?'

'Gone home. Last-minute changes of plan.'

'So you're all on your own?'

'Well, yes, except for Widdles.'

'Not tomorrow too?'

God, was I sounding plaintive? 'Yes, but to be honest, I'm really looking forward to the P&Q. Nothing to do all day long but eat and drink.'

'Think of me, then,' he said wryly. 'You need a United Nations peacekeeping force at our dining table.'

From the mixed voices in the background, one suddenly stood out. 'John, we're about to go—are you coming?'

Female, wouldn't you know it.

'Yes, hang on . . .' To me he said, 'I have to go. Enjoy your P&Q.'

'Good night.'

I lay back on the pillow, my eyes suddenly pricking with miserable tears. 'Bastard,' I said to Widdles. 'Why did he have to phone back at all, if he was only going to get me all worked up for nothing?'

Widdles woke me at ten to eight, by patting my cheek with his paw. Knowing I'd slob all day in my dressing gown otherwise, I went straight for a bath, as I couldn't face our dribbly shower. There were advantages to being on your own; at least the hot water wouldn't run out. I then dragged on jog bottoms and a sweatshirt and went down to the sitting room. Despite the tree it didn't feel very festive.

I opened Jacko's present first. As I'd thought, it was just like Sally's, except that mine was scarlet. It wasn't a colour I wore often, but I tried it on and studied the effect in the ancient gilt mirror over the fireplace.

Why didn't I wear scarlet often? It suited me brilliantly. In fact, it looked pretty damn good altogether. *Thank you, dear old Jacko, kiss kiss.*

Next I opened my mother's. Another sweater, but a chunky, dark grey mohair mix this time, with one fat cable down the front. I rather liked it. She'd added some pink grapefruit Body Shop stuff, too, and a best seller. *Thank you, Mum, kiss kiss, hope those kids aren't driving you mad.*

Sally's, next, which gave me heart failure at first. A couple of months back I'd seen a scarf in a magazine: Kenzo or something, price £179. I'd said, 'I wouldn't mind that, if it was ten quid instead.'

She'd put in a note. 'Old Dorothy's knitting needles came in useful after all. I've made a few bums but I don't think they're too obvious.'

Somehow she'd reproduced it: broad, irregular stripes in gloriously clashing shades of red, pink and purple. It must have been a yard long.

My eyes misted to think how many hours she must have spent while I was at work, or even at night, in her room. I didn't even know she *could* knit. I put it on: one of the reds matched Jacko's sweater exactly.

I sat in a sea of paper, suddenly miserable as sin. It was no fun just *opening* presents; you needed the donors there to say thank you to. You had to dish them out, too, and see people's faces, even if they weren't as ecstatic as you'd hoped.

I poured myself a massive Baileys. Might as well get pissed. Might as well start now. Might as well cook that turkey, too: the lovely roasty smell might make me feel a bit Christmassy. Just as I was looking for the cookery book, the doorbell rang.

'Hi,' said the chap on the step. 'I just called to say Happy P&Q.'

'John!'

'And sorry for waking you up last night. I'm on my way to the tribe, but I made a minor detour.'

Still in shock, my brain had been in better working order. 'Well, that's what comes of partying from lunchtime till nine o'clock.'

'I know the feeling,' he said. 'Although I didn't start till three-ish.'

I suddenly realised that his spark had lost some of its edge. He was showered and shaved, wearing a casual, bluey-grey jacket, but his face indicated serious partying. 'And finished about three-ish, I bet. If you don't mind my saying so, you look just a bit rough.'

'I feel just a bit rough. You wouldn't have a coffee, would you? I found an empty packet when I got up. I'm afraid I uttered a foul curse or two.'

Even at 90 per cent spark level he was still pretty effective, especially when he chucked in that lethal little smile. 'I expect so. Come in.'

By now, of course, flutters that had been temporarily displaced by shock were getting going again. However, I had a stern word with them. From now on they would be required to behave in a circumspect manner. If he was warming up an old possibility while the cat was away, or had just thought I'd make a convenient pit-stop . . .

The kitchen was less of a tip than usual, no maternity bras strewn on the sofa for once. 'Take a seat,' I said, nodding at it while spooning Rich Roast into the filter. 'How far have you got to go, to the tribe?'

'West Sussex—only about an hour's drive. Do the bells still work?' he added, evidently noticing the glass case on the wall.

'Oh, yes. Jacko was very tempted when he was just out of hospital, but Sally would have thumped him.'

While the coffee was filtering I collected mugs and milk, as if he were just anyone. I felt quite pleased with my casual demeanour.

'How do you like your coffee? Milk?'

'Just a splash, no sugar.'

This was when I heard him get up from the sofa. 'To tell the truth,' he said, coming over to the worktop, 'I didn't just come to say sorry for waking you up.'

Something in my stomach gave a violent lurch. Only about a foot away, he was leaning against the worktop, arms folded, his eyes on me.

'I thought you sounded a bit down last night. A bit hacked off at being on your own.'

This was so unexpected, I had no trouble looking taken aback. 'God, no! I'm really looking forward to the peace.'

Since the coffee was now ready, I could turn away from him to pour it. 'Sally and Jacko have been squabbling like a pair of nine-year-olds lately. There you go,' I added, turning round to hand him a mug.

But that was when my bluff ran out. There was something so weakening about the way he was looking at me. 'Well, I was a bit,' I confessed. 'I was really looking forward to it and suddenly, *phut*, it was all gone.'

'Why didn't you go to your mother's, after all?'

'I was going to, but she was already panicking about unexpected hordes. So I just didn't tell her.'

'You could come with me. To my war-zone Christmas dinner.'

It took me a moment to locate my voice. 'You're not serious?'

'As serious as I'll ever be after a heavy night.'

Which evidently wasn't saying much. 'Look, it's very kind of you, but I couldn't possibly. They don't know me from Eve!'

'So?'

'Won't your mother have a fit if you turn up with a total stranger?'

'She'll probably be relieved. The old man's far more likely to behave himself with a total stranger.'

He had a point. 'OK, but aren't you staying over?'

He shook his head. 'I've got some work to catch up on tomorrow. Look, I'll give my mother a ring, if you like.'

Masses of things were racing through my head. I thought of being on my own all day, and the next. I thought of hitting the Baileys, talking to Widdles like a nutter. And last, but far from least, I thought of Nina, deliberately setting out to steal Stuart . . .

'Actually, I'd love to come,' I confessed. 'I only said I wouldn't to be polite. I can't think why—it's not very polite to turn down invitations just to be polite, is it?'

He suppressed what might have been a lethal smile if he'd let it out.

'But ring your mother first,' I went on. 'And if she says, "Oh, *please*, I'll have to hoover the stairs," you will tell me?'

'She won't.' Taking a mobile from his jacket pocket, he pushed buttons rapidly. It was answered almost immediately. 'Hi, it's me,' he said. There was a short pause. 'Of course I'm coming!'

Was that telling? I wondered.

'Look, would you mind if I brought a friend?' he went on. 'She's unexpectedly on her own.' There was another pause. 'Harriet,' he said. After a further pause he added, 'No, just a friend.'

Well, he had to say that, didn't he?

Another pause. 'Yes, I've told her all that.' Giving me a brief up-and-down check that ended with a little wink, he went on, 'Yes, I think she's bombproof.' (Pause.) 'She thought you might throw a fit and think you had to hoover the stairs.' After another short pause, during which he was laughing silently, he turned to me. 'She says there is rather a lot of dog hair on the stairs, so please try not to notice.'

Thank God for normal people.

Into the phone he said, 'All right, we're on our way. Bye-bye.'

Shoving the phone back in his pocket, he looked at me. 'Ready?'

Was he kidding? I looked down at my jog bottoms. 'Can you give me two minutes?'

I charged upstairs, yanked off the joggers, yanked on a black skirt but left Jacko's sweater. Not only was it Christmas-coloured, it was also clean and not lying at the bottom of a bone-dry heap of ironing. I just added lip gloss and mascara, a squirt of CK1 and charged down again.

'Christ, that was quick!' he said, evidently impressed.

'I did say "two".' All I had to do now was leave lunch and afternoon tea for Widdles and grab a jacket.

We headed south in his lovely dark green Saab convertible in typical English-Christmas weather, i.e. cloudy, mild, and wondering whether a spot of rain mightn't be a good idea. I couldn't help wishing for proper Christmas weather: snowy and crisp, the trees prettily frosted.

After a while he said, 'What made your friends decide to desert you at the last minute?'

'It wasn't their choice.' After telling him a little about Sally's 'proper' parents and even more proper neighbours, I got onto Jacko, terminally indulged Tara and the Lee ructions.

'They should let her get on with it,' he said, a good deal more drily than I'd expected. 'I'm only surprised my sister never did anything like that. I suppose I shouldn't say it, but she can still be a bit of a pain.'

'How old is she?'

'Twenty-two, but still acting fourteen and a half now and then. She dropped out of college, went au-pairing, generally titted about for years.'

'Sounds a bit like me,' I said.

'She's nothing like you! You were paying your way. She's actually in her first year of a media studies degree now. I swear she only picked it to brown the old man off. She might as well have said she was doing a combined BA in Political Correctness and Woolly Lefty Liberalism. He's just a tad old-fashioned,' he added wryly. 'If you want to see an interesting display of facial veins popping, just say you think it'd be a jolly good idea if that nice Mr Blair allowed gays to marry in church.'

I laughed. 'I get the message. We keep off politics.'

'You might—Lucy won't. She winds the old man up on purpose.'

'Well, it's better than nightmare family dinners where people just say, "I think I might cut the grass later," and "Did you pay the gas bill?"'

He laughed, but I couldn't altogether join in. 'I was speaking from bitter experience,' I confessed. 'I sat through some awful meals like that when my folks were about to split up. There would be these hideous, tense silences, punctuated by trite remarks that were supposed to sound normal, for my benefit. It made me want to scream.'

It had all come to a head that summer after my first year at university. They'd taken separate holidays the previous year, which should have warned me. At the time, though, I'd told myself it was just because they liked different types of holiday. Dad liked ruins and museums; Mum liked flaking out on a beach with a Jilly Cooper. She had been sitting in a beach café when a man had said, 'Do you mind if I take this chair?' He'd sat at an adjacent table, and that, as they say, was it. Bill's wife had died three years previously so she wasn't breaking anything up there, but she'd agonised over Dad.

She'd told me almost exactly a year after first meeting Bill. I'd cried for Dad. He'd looked so lost and bemused, but after a few months he had realised it was for the best. He could spend months of evenings learning Middle Egyptian for his trip to the Upper Nile, without anybody saying, 'Don't tell me you've forgotten we're going to the Tuckers' tonight?'

I was glad they were friends again, but I still often wondered what had brought two such incompatible people together.

John said, 'When my parents were going through a bad patch, throwing things or not speaking, my sister and I used to retreat to the garden shed and work out ways to get ourselves adopted. That was my other sister, Anna. She's in Sydney now, hitched, and about to produce her first sprog.'

Neither of us spoke then for a bit, so naturally I started thinking again. I thought of that night in the cab, vibes swirling like mist. I dare say it made a difference that it was daytime, he was hungover and we were heading for a family do, but he hadn't made one remark that held any hint of anything. To be honest, it was a bit of a letdown.

I was dying to somehow bring up Nina, but I couldn't bring myself to do it, in case he said, 'Oh, she's ancient history,' and I knew it was a smoothArse lie. On the other hand, *would* it be a lie? What if he'd done the deed already and Nina hadn't told Suzanne?

As the soft cushions of the South Downs came closer and the sky brightened to milky pale blue, I realised there was something I should have done already. 'Do you mind if I make a pre-emptive phone call? If my mother tries the house phone and finds no one answering, she'll think we're all dead from a gas leak.'

'Go ahead.'

It was Mum herself who answered. After I'd said Happy Christmas and thank you for the lovely presents, it was her turn. 'We haven't opened ours yet—we're saving them till after dinner, though goodness knows what time that'll hit the table. The children are all crotchety already—they didn't sleep very well. Bill waited till one o'clock to do their stockings and can you believe that little devil Robert was still awake and said, "Is that you, Grandpa?" Six! I ask you.' Here she paused for breath. 'Have you heard from your father lately, by the way?'

'I had a card. He said he'd be spending Christmas in Cyprus.'

'Yes, but did he say who *with*? I had a letter the other day—I forgot to tell you. He said he's met an "extremely nice woman called Kathy" and they're spending Christmas together!' She sounded almost affronted.

'Well, that's lovely for him, isn't it?'

'Yes, but I'm wondering what *sort* of woman. He said she adores Cyprus and now he's talking about buying a house there! I can't help thinking she's seen him coming.'

'Mum! He was a solicitor! He's not going to be taken in!'

'Yes, but it sounds as if this Kathy's exerting an undue influence. He said he might go skiing with her! *Skiing!* He'll crash into a tree and kill himself. What if she's got him to change his will?'

'Mum, I'm sure she's done nothing of the sort.'

'Well, I'm not so sure about that. Anyway, I must go, darling, I haven't even done the potatoes yet.'

I pressed 'end call'. 'Well, that was good for a laugh on Christmas morning. My mother thinks some scheming gold-digger's got her painted claws into my father.'

After I'd given the gist he said, 'You don't sound so entirely certain it's good for a laugh.'

On reflection, I wasn't. 'He probably *is* susceptible. I don't think there's been anyone on the scene for years.'

I thought back to how lost and rejected he'd looked, like a lanky old dog taken to the rescue home because his owners had become fed up with him and got a puppy, instead. I thought of him looking like that again and couldn't bear it.

It was partly because of Dad that I'd stopped working abroad. He'd had a minor heart attack: so minor he hadn't even realised what it was until he'd gone to the doctor, but it had put the wind up me when a neighbour had phoned me in Athens to say he was in hospital. I'd been spending at least ten months of the year away, and even when I was back I was all over the place, seeing old friends. Mum and Bill had been in Bali at the time, and I'd had a horrible vision of getting another phone call one day to say he'd been found dead by the microwave, with his dinner all dried up inside it. I'd thought that if I were working at home for a few months at a time, at least I'd see him more frequently.

As it turned out I'd seen him most often at Dorothy's on the Sundays when Dad had come up to tidy the garden and take her out for the statutory roast.

I realised John had turned off the main road. 'It's not far now. Only a few more miles.'

We were in South Downs country; the cushions rolled gently on all sides, some ploughed, some grassland dotted with sheep. He drove through one of those villages that have probably been there since long before the Domesday Book or even the Saxons: clustered higgledy-piggledy round a church with a square Norman tower and a pub.

The lane wound on like a meandering river, past long-gone obstacles. Or maybe there never were any obstacles. Maybe it was a case of the rolling English drunkard making the rolling English road, like the poet said. You could imagine the Ancient Brits staggering home after four pints of mead, wondering whether 'er indoors would have given their pottage to the pig.

John turned at a T-junction into a road leading through woods, and we'd just rounded a bend when a mud-splashed Land Rover coming in the other direction hooted and braked sharply.

'It's the old man,' John said, braking likewise as the Land Rover pulled up. They both wound their windows down.

I saw a man with hair turning from red to grey, a beard to match, and a shaggy Dulux dog on the passenger seat. 'Flora's gone walkabout,' he barked. (The man, not the dog.) 'I'm taking the clockwise route—take the anticlockwise, will you? She can't have gone far. Morning, Harriet—get weaving, John, chop chop—though with a bit of luck the old trout might have got herself run over already.'

Five

As Mackenzie senior shot off, Mackenzie junior shot me a look of comic resignation, fifty-fifty with apology. 'Well, I did warn you.'

I was doing my best not to laugh. 'Are we talking batty old aunts here? I hope we won't meet your old man coming the other way with a mangled old dear on the roof rack.'

'He doesn't mean it.' He bore left round another bend that struck me as positively lethal to a wandery old aunt. There were no pavements, of course. After we'd gone another couple of minutes, however, his phone rang in his pocket. The call lasted all of three seconds. 'Panic over. The old man's found her.'

He stopped, reversed into a muddy field and headed back the way we'd come, except that he turned off again, down a lane you'd miss if you weren't looking. On the left were fields, on the right, about 100 yards down, was the house, lovely mellow old brick, double-fronted, probably Georgian, set well back in what looked like square miles of garden. There was a curving, irregular front lawn and a gravelled sweep leading to the front door. There were several parked cars, including the Land Rover. Having just pipped us, Mackenzie senior was helping a very elderly lady out. As John was parking, the front door opened.

I saw at once where he had got his looks, though his mother was paler, with lighter hair, and an expression of anxiety mixed with relief.

We got out to a cacophony of 'Flora, where have you *been*?' followed immediately by 'Harriet, how nice—' and a woofing mass of Dulux dog, which came at me like a Scud missile. I fielded him, catching his front paws in my hands in what I hoped was not an ungracious fashion. Almost before he'd hit me, however, there was another cacophony of 'Horace, get *down*!' from his father, and a sharper 'Down!' from John.

'It's fine, really.' One thing about dogs, they do break the ice.

'John, for heaven's sake take her in to wash her hands,' said his mother, in a harassed voice.

'Get her a large gin,' grunted his father. 'She's going to need it.'

The object of the trout hunt, meanwhile, was looking worried. 'Margaret, I can't find my bag.' Suddenly aware of me, she peered at me suspiciously. 'Who's that girl? She hasn't taken my bag, has she?'

'It's in the *house*, Flora. You left it in the house,' Mrs Mackenzie soothed, while Mr M. muttered, 'Christ on a bicycle . . .' John led me inside, and I tried not to crack up.

After that it was relatively civilised for a bit. We had drinks and chat in a large, light room overlooking a garden. There was a log fire and a discreet, six-foot Christmas tree in the corner, lots of antiques, but nothing of the opulent variety.

After proper introductions, I was asked to call his folks Angus and Margaret. I explained why I was unexpectedly solo and we did the usual 'And what do you do?' bit. Angus was a vet, but semiretired; Margaret had been a registrar of Births, Marriages and Deaths

Aunt Beatrice, grand and portly in some flowing caftan thing, looked me up and down. 'Kept you quiet, hasn't he?' she boomed.

'She's just a friend, Beatrice,' said Margaret hastily.

'I'm beginning to wonder about you,' she said darkly to John. 'Thirty-two and losing your grip already?'

John shot me a little wink. 'Beatrice still has a kingsize grip. When she's drunk enough she might tell you about a certain sixty-five-year-old at her Tai chi class.'

'He's sixty-eight,' she retorted. 'And I'm never going to get drunk at this rate. I'll have a large whisky, John. And no—'

'—bloody soda,' he supplied. 'Beatrice, I wouldn't dare.'

'Margaret, that dog's slobbering in the nuts!' she said, in a terse boom.

Quietly hoovering up assorted nibbles from a bowl on a side table, Horace was told to behave himself and I had a minute to myself. Of course I'd been dreading someone saying, 'How's the lovely Nina, then?' but nobody had, and just as well. Throwing up on the carpet would have been highly embarrassing.

Lucy eventually appeared. Slim, about Sally's height, she had long, dark red hair, almost chestnut, and was dressed in baggy grey trousers and a top that might have been lying on her bedroom floor for a week.

'Lucy, you might have made a bit of an effort,' Margaret tutted. 'It's Christmas Day.'

'So?' She gave me an enquiring but friendly enough smile. 'Has he got it in for you or something?'

'Sorry?'

'Bringing you here. He hardly ever brings anyone, especially not girlfriends. Thinks they'll take one look at his genetic base and get put off.'

'Lucy, do stop it,' Margaret tutted.

John had just come back from topping up glasses. 'About time too,' he said to Lucy. 'I was about to come and haul you out of your pit.'

'No, you weren't. You were hoping I'd stay there and not embarrass you.' There was a kiss, however, of the reasonably affectionate variety. 'Where's my present, then?' she asked.

'In my wallet,' he said. 'So if you want it, behave yourself.'

Margaret said, 'She's doing media studies, you know. In London.'

Angus gave a bristly snort. 'Media studies, women's studies—the academic world's gone mad.'

Lucy said, 'I *am* doing a women's studies module, Pa. I'm using you as a case study of traditional patriarchal attitudes that all stem from a primitive fear and loathing of female sexuality.'

Margaret said, 'Lucy, *please*.'

'You should use Freud,' Beatrice boomed. 'All that rubbish about penis envy—personally I always thought the male organ the most singularly unattractive of God's creations. Looks like the neck thing they give you with the turkey giblets to boil up for gravy.'

The entertainment continued over lunch.

After goujons of sole for starters, Angus got stuck into carving a massive joint of sirloin, and Lucy got stuck into wind-ups. She was on my right, John sat more or less opposite me, next to Flora.

'What happened to that Natasha girl?' she asked, in demurely mischievous tones that reminded me of Sally when she got going.

A tiny frown creased his forehead. 'That was months ago.'

Lucy turned to me. 'He brought her to a cousin's wedding. TV presenter or something. Mummy said she was common.'

'Lucy!' Margaret remonstrated. 'I didn't!'

'You did. You said it was irritating, the way she wouldn't say her t's.'

'Well, it was, a bit,' Margaret said defensively.

'Lucy, get your elbows off the table!' Angus rapped, passing some delicately carved beef to Flora.

For a while there was relative peace as we devoured delicious rare beef, parsnip purée, roast potatoes and tiny Brussels sprouts. After the beef came a traditional flaming pudding and an orange soufflé.

John abstained from both, to Margaret's maternal concern. 'What's the matter? I thought you loved Christmas pudding!'

'I'm just full,' he soothed.

'You should be relieved he's not stuffing himself,' Lucy said. 'Last time he came you said he was getting a bit of a tummy.'

'Not enough exercise,' Angus barked. 'He ought to take up rugby again. Used to be a damn good scrum half.'

'I don't have time to train,' he said, with a trace of exasperation.

Lucy turned to me. 'Where did you meet him, anyway? Not on one of his boys' nights out at Lapdance Heaven, I take it?'

John's brow furrowed. 'Lucy, do you want your present or not?'

He said it so tersely, even Lucy looked taken aback.

'She really can be very silly,' Margaret said, as if Lucy were six. 'And it's none of your business anyway,' she added pointedly to Lucy.

John had taken me aback, though, too. I'd expected him to be mellow, at least, and I began to think he must still have a morning-after head.

Inevitably, I suppose, the conversation got round to politics, starting with fox-hunting. Angus was in favour, Lucy and Beatrice violently opposed. I kept well out of it. Having done with foxes, Angus moved on to other vermin, a.k.a. young offenders who trash cars.

'Pa belongs to the hang 'em and flog 'em school of political philosophy,' Lucy said. 'Thinks the country's going to the devil.'

'They say the devil's back on earth,' said Flora. 'I saw a programme about it. That's why we've got all these awful wars and things.'

'We always had awful wars and things,' John soothed. 'Only they weren't all over the six o'clock news every night.'

'They give me nightmares,' she said. 'All those poor little children. I'm knitting squares, you know. I've done nearly a whole blanket to send out to that awful place where all the refugees are.'

'Well done,' John said, and patted her hand.

'Thank you, dear.' Across the table she said to me, 'He was a lovely baby, you know. I used to knit him little jumpers with mittens to match. I'll knit yours a little jumper when it's born. No sense starting till I know what colour to get. When's it due again? You're not showing yet, are you?'

'Flora, dear, that's *Anna*,' said Margaret hastily. 'In Australia, remember? John isn't married.'

'Isn't he? Dear me, I do get so muddled lately . . .'

'Never mind.' John slipped an arm round her. 'You can knit me a jumper when you've finished your blanket.'

I added a couple of Nice Bloke points here; in fact I went a bit gooey. No grounds for adding any other points, though. In fact, the only undertones I sensed were general 'let me out of here' stuff.

Once we'd sat over coffee and fruit, chocolates and more coffee, it was nearly five o'clock. Margaret refused help in the kitchen, saying it was all going in the dishwasher.

John said to me, 'Do you fancy a walk?'

I did. Having had seconds of almost everything, not just to be polite, I felt uncomfortably full and disgusting.

The sky had cleared so there was moonlight, which was just as well on the route John took. It led through woods, where carpets of dead leaves at least cushioned the mud. He was walking very close, the sleeve of his jacket almost brushing mine. After a few minutes he said, 'I have to hand it to you. You bore it all with remarkable aplomb.'

'It was a nightmare,' I retorted. 'I don't know when I've suffered such excruciating discomfort, trying not to crack up. But I do see what you meant about Lucy—'

My heel had caught in a root; I stumbled badly and would have gone inelegantly flying if he hadn't caught me.

He held onto my arm. 'Are you all right?'

The moonlight was filtering through bare branches, a little cloud scudding across its pale face. 'More or less,' I said unsteadily. From somewhere in the leafy undergrowth came the scream of an animal. It sounded eerie, almost primeval. 'What was that?' I asked.

'Probably a rabbit getting hard luck from a fox.'

I shivered. Suddenly the whole place felt primeval. There was no artificial light. There was no traffic noise. There was nothing but night, and nature getting on with her bloody business. I knew it was stupid, but I was getting the creeps. Part of me wanted to do the pathetic girly bit, admit it, and have him say 'There, there', and put his arm round me.

But he said, 'Come on, it's getting cold.' Letting my arm go, he gave me a brisk pat on the back, instead.

I'd never have done the girly bit anyway, but I didn't quite care for that pat. It felt as if he were trying to get a sluggish horse moving.

Once in the mood for mental bitching, I soon found something else to bitch about. Why was it all right to inflict his lunatic family on me, but not on Nina? Did he think her too delicate to take the strain? And how dare he call me 'bombproof', earlier? It was positively insulting.

'I thought we'd hit the road in about an hour,' he said. 'After the secondary rituals of cups of tea and presents.'

It would still be only around half past six. 'Won't your mother be upset if you shoot off so early?'

'Probably, but I can't hang around until nine o'clock, stuffing ham and pickled onions.'

I could bet she'd cooked a ham specially, made mince pies and a Christmas cake, and he was just going to disappear. 'That's not very nice. She's probably gone to a lot of trouble.'

'I know!' His tone changed immediately, however. 'Look, to be honest, I'm a bit knackered.'

We arrived back to the predicted cups of tea and dishing out of presents. To my acute embarrassment, Lucy gave me a beautifully wrapped little gift containing Belgian chocolates. I thanked God I'd bought some narcissi at the petrol station on the way down.

As we took tea things back to the kitchen, John announced that we had to hit the road, and as I'd feared, his mother's face fell. 'I've got some lovely ham! Aren't you staying for supper?'

'Mum, I've eaten far too much already.'

'But it's Christmas!' She covered her disappointment with a smile. 'But I'm sure Harriet's endured quite enough of this clan for one day.'

'It's not that.' I hated her to think we were leaving on my account; on an impulse I regretted almost at once, I added, 'John's feeling rather tired.'

'Well, I might have known,' she tutted. 'He works far too hard.'

He shot me an exasperated glance. 'No harder than anyone else.'

It was another twenty minutes before we actually left, and even as we drove away I knew John was browned off with me. I thought a pre-emptive strike was in order. 'I'm sorry, but I had to say it. She thought it was me, wanting to get away.'

He changed gear sharply. 'Well, didn't you?'

'I wasn't in any hurry! I certainly didn't want her thinking you were leaving early on my account.'

For a couple of miles he uttered not a word, and I felt increasingly cross and upset. If he was going to sulk all the way home, I'd start to wish I'd stayed with Widdles. In fact, what on earth was I doing in a car with a pathetic, sulky bloke who'd ever fancied Nina? Any bloke I fancied should possess the discrimination to see right through her. I was just starting to compile a list of Perfectly Valid Reasons For Going Off John when he slowed down and pulled into the side of the road.

'Won't be a tick,' he said shortly.

Well, there was another reason to add to the list. Why did blokes who'd only just left entirely adequate facilities at home have to stop to pee up against trees? Jacko had once told me he loved peeing out-of-doors, given sufficient space. He'd take aim at some particular target (as in darts) and see if he could score a direct hit.

I'm ashamed to say I glanced over my shoulder, to see whether John was into grass-verge target practice. He hadn't even got his dart out.

Grabbing tissues from my bag, I almost ran from the car.

'Harriet, get back in the car,' he said tersely.

'You've just been sick!'

Instantly he threw up again, all over the grass verge.

As he stood there, trembling with cold and aftershock, I passed him a tissue. 'Are you all right?' I asked, like an idiot.

'Brilliant.' He wiped his mouth. 'Will you please get back in the bloody car?' He then threw up again. 'Shit,' he said shakily.

'Couldn't you have got this out of the way last night?'

'It's nothing to do with last night. I didn't drink that much.'

Light was dawning fast, particularly in relation to quietness and refused Christmas puddings. 'Were you feeling ill all afternoon?'

'I don't know . . . I wasn't feeling great over lunch—I guess I felt a bit rough this morning, but I didn't think it was anything.'

Full of compunction now, I said, 'Are you going to be sick again?'

He shook his head.

Once we were back on the road, I said, 'Are you OK to drive?'

'When I'm not, I'll tell you.'

'Why didn't you tell your mother you were feeling rough, instead of pretending you were just shattered?'

'How could I? First, she'd worry, second, I couldn't face the fussing. I just wanted to get home and hit the sack.'

'You've probably got this bug.'

'I never get bugs,' he said. 'I never even get colds.'

'Well, you've got something. Do you think you've got a temperature?'

'God knows. I feel more cold than anything.' He turned the heating up. 'If you really want to know, I feel like nonspecific shit all over. Whatever it is, I'll sweat it out tomorrow with a game of squash.'

Might have known he'd react like this. On the other hand, the most unlikely blokes could be appalling babies, wishing their mummies were there to make that special eggy pudding they only ever made when they were sick. Then you had type B, who'd go to work even if he was dying of plague, and say it was nothing, putrid pustules all over your body never killed anyone, a hot whisky and lemon'd soon sort him out.

Or a game of squash. Definitely type B.

I glanced across at him. His face looked whitish-grey, but so did mine, probably, in that light.

It seemed a quicker journey than on the way down. As he finally turned into Dorothy's road I said, 'How are you feeling?'

'Pretty bloody rough,' he said wearily, pulling into the kerb.

I was amazed that a hard-core type B had admitted it. 'Have you got any paracetamol at home?'

'Probably not.'

'I should have. Do you want to come in while I find them?'

I'd expected a short 'No, I'll be fine.' In fact I saw him hesitate, but then he said, 'I guess they're worth a try.'

I'd left the heating on high for Widdles, so at least the kitchen felt moderately warm. I said, 'Take a seat, then, while I find them,' and he sat heavily on the sofa, where Widdles was curled up, as he probably had been all day. He raised his head in an affronted fashion, to see who was invading his throne.

I charged upstairs, where I rummaged around, eventually finding a packet gathering dust on an ancient chest of drawers in Jacko's room.

I charged down again, about to say, 'Here you go,' but it died in my throat. Slumped against the back of the sofa, he was asleep.

He looked awful. His face was pale, a sheen of sweat on his brow. His forehead felt cold and clammy. I shook him gently.

He opened his eyes.

'I don't think you should go home on your own—why don't you stay the night?'

Still half asleep, looking grey and groggy, he made an effort to collect himself. 'Christ, Harriet, I'm not quite dead on my feet yet . . .'

I had a Cunning Thought. 'All right, but why don't you go to bed for a while? You might feel a bit better when you wake up.'

He hesitated, but I knew the magic word 'bed' had done it. 'I wouldn't mind,' he confessed.

'I'll wake you up in a couple of hours.' I took him to my room, as it was reasonably tidy and the sheets were more or less clean. It was chilly, though, so I lit the archaic but extraordinarily efficient gas fire. Then I gave him two Panadol, told him where the bathroom was and left him to it. By the time I went up again with some hot honey and lemon he was tucked almost completely under my green checked duvet cover fast asleep. I could barely see his face. I glanced at my watch. It was still only twenty past eight. This meant waking him at say, half past ten. I turned the fire right down and tiptoed out.

'Only I'm not going to wake him,' I said to Widdles. 'What's the point? Just so he can drive home and get into another bed?'

Funnily enough, prissy big sister was back in my head. 'You can't fool me. You just want to keep him here. Play Florence Nightingale. I bet you're hoping John'll be so sweaty and fevered and weak tomorrow you'll have to give him a cooling sponge down.'

Honestly. As if any such thing would ever have entered my head.

Before I was two minutes older, I phoned Sally.

During the telling she went from sheer *What?* to old-Sally mischief. 'Looks like Father Christmas brought your Helicopter after all.'

'Yes, but he's still got strings attached.'

'Maybe you should come clean. About Nina, I mean. He might just tell you he's got shot of her already.'

'No chance. I'm sure I'd have heard. I'm hoping he's just putting it off. Too nice to dump her.'

'Keep me posted, anyway. I need something to perk me up.'

'How's it going?' I asked.

'Better than I thought. Tom's not whinged much, and Mum's doing her damnedest not to say, "If you pick him up every time he cries . . ."' She paused, but when she spoke again I heard a telltale wobble in her voice. 'I've been feeling really bad, actually. They've decorated the little spare room like a nursery—bought a lovely new cot and everything. Apparently they did it weeks ago, assuming I'd be bringing him home. And you'll never believe what wallpaper they used.'

'Not Thomas the Tank Engine?'

'Hole in one. So between them and Jacko, I've been feeling like mountains of really smelly nappies.'

'You can talk—how do you think I felt when I saw that scarf? When did you do it? Half the night, every night?'

'Well, sometimes. I was doing quite a bit during the day, but Jacko said at the rate I messed up, Tom's first words would be "Oh, big fat hairy *bollocks*."'

I woke at ten past seven, in Sally's bed. Except for Widdles snoring, it was horribly quiet. I lay for a minute wondering whether I should go and check in case John had died of some flesh-eating plague. However, eventually I heard giveaway creaks. I went and tapped on his door.

'Harriet?'

I went in. Clad only in a pair of white boxers, he was sitting on the side of the bed with the bemused look of a man who's woken up in someone else's bed and can't quite remember how it came about. 'Weren't you supposed to wake me?'

'I tried,' I lied. 'You were out for the count. How are you?'

'I don't know . . . All right, I guess.' Evidently still half asleep, he looked around. His hair was damp and dishevelled, his face flushed.

'You don't look very all right to me. Get back into bed—I'll put the fire on.'

'Where did you sleep?' he asked, as if it had just hit him.

'In Sally's bed.'

'Well, I'm sorry to have been sweating in your sheets all night, but you should have woken me. Given me a good whack on the head or something. It's high time I was out of here.' He went to the chair, started pulling on his trousers.

'God knows what I was thinking of,' he muttered.

'You were sick! You looked awful!'

'Yes, and I still feel bloody awful, but this thing's picked the wrong host.' He reached for his shirt. 'I'll sweat it out on the squash court. That'll teach the little bastard . . .'

Not only did his voice suddenly die on him, he actually swayed. I was there in an instant, holding him. 'For God's sake, go back to bed!'

Even for a type B, he was impressive. 'For crying out loud, Harriet, stop fussing. I just need something to eat. A piece of toast or something.'

From experience, I knew type Bs needed careful handling. 'All right, if you'll get back in bed to eat it.'

Already buttoning his shirt, he stopped. With an exasperated expression he held his hands up, in that warding-off-evil fashion. 'I'll be fine, OK? Run along and stick a piece of toast on, like a good girl.'

I knew he was saying it on purpose to infuriate and therefore get rid of me, but that didn't stop me. 'Get it yourself!'

I banged out and flounced downstairs, where Widdles instantly started yowling at the cupboards. 'Oh, shut up,' I said irritably. 'Bloody males—you're all the same.'

However, I gave him some duck'n'rabbit, put some coffee on and grabbed a mango-flavoured yoghurt from the fridge. Five minutes after finishing it, it occurred to me that John should have been down by now. God, what if he'd fallen and fractured his skull?

I ran upstairs two at a time.

There was an old armchair near the fire in my room. With his socks on but no shoes, he was sitting back in it, his eyes closed.

They soon opened, however.

'Get weaving, John, chop chop,' I said, with more than a trace of acid. 'You're supposed to be off to the squash court to sweat that little bastard out. Only pathetic people get sick, don't they? If they didn't give *in* to it, the entire NHS would be out of a job.'

He produced a faint smile.

Lighting the fire, I added, 'To save arguments, can we agree now that you're hardly fit to get down the stairs, let alone drive home?'

'OK, I'll go back to bed for a bit. Sweat some more in your sheets.'

'Not yet, you won't. I'll change them first.'

Entirely the wrong thing to say; it galvanised him. 'Harriet, if you're going to start changing sheets on my account, I'm out of here now.'

'You can't. I've hidden your car keys.' They were actually exactly where he'd left them, on the kitchen table.

He sat back, half-closing his eyes. 'Great,' he said weakly. 'Imprisoned. You haven't got cellars, have you? Fitted out with implements of torture?'

There *were* cellars, full of the junk of ages. 'Yes, but only for my paying customers,' I said sweetly.

With another sick-ghost smile he started to rise from the chair.

'Stay put, will you? Until I've changed those sheets.'

'Harriet, I'm going for a pee. Feel free to come and watch,' he added, with wraithlike sarcasm. 'Make sure I don't make a run for it.'

He'd have a job. He moved gingerly, as if every joint, muscle and cubic centimetre of brain were aching. I was beginning to revise my type B diagnosis. I suspected type C instead: the man who had never been ill before, and couldn't believe it was happening to him.

I stripped off sheets, listening for sounds of skulls crashing onto lavatory pans, but all I heard was a flush. While he was gone, however, I thought maybe I *had* gone a bit OTT. Also I was aware that I was not acting from purely saintly motives.

When he came back, still as gingerly as a fresh green root, I said, 'Look, if you're really desperate to get home, I'll drive you.'

'*Now* she says it.' He flopped into that chair by the fire. 'But I don't think I've even got the energy for being chauffeured across London.' He closed his eyes again. I went over, put a hand to his forehead.

'You're burning up!' Dropping the sheets, I grabbed another couple of Panadol and thrust them at him. 'Get these down, now.'

He didn't argue.

I remade the bed at top speed before ransacking Jacko's room for pyjamas. When I gave them to him he actually winced. 'I haven't worn pyjamas since I was at school.'

'I don't care. Put them on and get back into bed.'

'Are you always this bossy?' he asked faintly.

'This is nothing, I can tell you.'

I went downstairs, made some more hot honey and lemon and took it up with a jug of water on a tray. He was back in bed, nearly asleep again.

Call me daft, but suddenly I really felt like doing the Florence Nightingale bit. Despite the generally grotty appearance (or perhaps because of it) he looked oddly vulnerable. 'I've brought you some honey and lemon,' I said. 'You ought to get some fluids down. Do you still want that toast? Or anything else to eat?'

He shook his head and winced.

'You've never had anything like this before, have you?' I asked.

Much more gingerly, he shook his head again. 'Even my eyes are aching. But I'm sure you've got better things to do than play nurse.'

Funnily enough, I couldn't think of anything. 'Masses. But I still owe you at least fifteen quid, remember? Never mind that suit.'

'I'd forgotten that. But now you've brought it up, there's one little thing you could do for me.'

'Yes?'

'I feel sweaty and gross,' he said. 'You couldn't manage a bed-bath, could you? I think I'd sleep better.'

Heaven help me. 'Well, erm, I've never given anyone . . .'

Too late, I realised I'd been had. Even in that state, an ember of his spark was glinting. He actually started laughing, which turned rapidly to a racking cough, as if he were on forty fags a day.

'That sounds positively terminal to me,' I said tartly. 'Don't expect the kiss of life, will you?'

He quickly got it under control, however. 'No, Nurse Fearsome. Would you pass me my mobile? It's in my jacket pocket. I need to check my messages and make a couple of calls.'

After a shower, I decided to roast the turkey before it went off. After ramming ready-made stuffing up its backside, I found from the 'poultry' section of the *Clueless Cooks' Book* that I should be stuffing the other end, 'pulling the flap of skin firmly over to tuck underneath'. After which I should 'truss neatly with a trussing needle and string'.

'What normal person has trussing needles lying about?' I said to Widdles. I shoved the untrussed turkey in the oven, poured myself a large glass of wine, and phoned Sally.

'So how long d'you think you'll be playing nurse?' she asked.

'I can't imagine him staying beyond tomorrow morning. You weren't thinking of coming back just yet, were you? I'd hate to think of him passing it on to Tom.'

'I said I'd stay until just before New Year, so let's hope the sweetness and light lasts that long. I think Mum's beginning to crack. This morning she said, "I hope you're going to give him *proper* food, not just those lazy-mother jars."'

The doorbell rang while I was in the middle of peeling muddy potatoes. On opening the door in my rubber gloves I was hit by a) a temperature that had plummeted since yesterday, and b) Helen on the step.

'I thought you were in Saffron Walden!' I gaped.

'I was, but I came to pick up a few of my things while Lawrence is away. Are you busy?' she added, eyeing the potato peeler in my hand.

'Not exactly. I'm cooking the turkey for me and Widdles.'

Her eyes widened. 'Where are the others?'

'Come in and I'll tell you.'

Over coffee for her and a glass of wine for me at the kitchen table I gave her the gist of Harriet's Revised Christmas, telling her I'd gone home with a friend who'd felt rough on the way back and was sleeping it off upstairs.

She accepted it without a murmur, making me think her mind was half elsewhere. She looked strained, as if she'd had several sleepless nights on the trot. 'How's Olly?' I asked.

'Worried about *me*, bless him. Still, he's having a good time with Laura's boy. He asked me to pick up a few of his things, too.'

'Have you been in already?' I asked.

She nodded. 'It was weird, seeing her stuff hanging in the wardrobe. She'd cleared what was left of mine into the spare room.'

She spoke almost mechanically, but I felt sure she was on the point of bursting into tears. 'Have you spoken to Lawrence again?'

She gave a little sign. 'Briefly. He's going to try to get the twins into boarding school. He said it would do them good. He said I spoilt them.'

She was still speaking in a curiously detached way. 'And I suppose I did. They won't care, anyway, as long as they're together.'

'Have you spoken to them over Christmas?' I asked.

'Not for long. They couldn't drag themselves away from their new PlayStation. They couldn't be bothered to talk to Olly for more than ten seconds, either.'

I just didn't know what to say, but the silence was filled by a jolly London Live weatherman telling us to expect overnight frosts.

'I suppose I spoilt Olly, too, but only because I loved him. Spoiling didn't *spoil* Olly, if you know what I mean. He never treated me with indifference.' She smiled wanly. 'So you needn't worry that I'm agonising over having done the wrong thing. I'm not. Not about that, anyway.'

I picked this up at once. 'What do you mean?'

An odd look crossed her face, like a kid who's been up to no good and is about to get found out. At the same time, there was a hint of *but I don't care*. 'I've done something incredibly stupid,' she said.

'You haven't trashed Lawrence's suits?'

She shook her head. 'Worse.'

'Not *Francesca's* suits?'

She shook her head again. 'I think I'm pregnant.'

'*What?*' I gaped. 'But I thought you and Lawrence—'

'It wasn't Lawrence.'

'*What?*'

'I knew you'd look like that,' she said, with a despairing sigh. 'As if you thought I didn't have it in me.'

I was too shell-shocked to utter a syllable.

'Lawrence would never think I'd have it in me, either,' she went on.

I found my voice. 'Who was it?'

'A man on a train.'

'*What?*'

She looked almost offended. 'We didn't *do* it on the train! We did it later. In a hotel room.'

I think I'd have been less shocked if she'd told me she'd joined some New Age travellers. 'What hotel room? What *train*, for God's sake?'

'The Eurostar, to Brussels. When Lawrence took the boys to EuroDisney. I was so low and miserable, I suddenly thought, why shouldn't I have a break, too?'

God help us. At this rate Widdles would be telling me he'd like a tossed green salad for dinner. I topped up my glass. 'Go on.'

'And there he was.' Cradling the coffee mug in her hands, she went on, 'He asked if he could borrow my *Telegraph*. After a few minutes I realised it was an excuse to talk to me. *Me!* The boring wife and mother who's only good for picking up socks and chauffeuring!'

I could have shaken her. 'Helen, *why* do you say things like that?'

'Because it's how Lawrence and the twins see me! I'm invisible! But he was talking to me as if I were a *person*. Gradually it dawned on me that he was attracted to me. But I could see him looking at my wedding ring, so I told him I was separated.'

'Well, you were.'

'Yes, but I said *legally* separated. And I told him masses more lies. I didn't want him thinking I was just a housewifey bore. I told him I was running a catering business. I even gave it a name: Cooking to Go. I said I was taking a break because I'd been working so hard, and he believed me. He said why didn't I meet him for dinner?'

Who needed the *EastEnders Christmas Special* when you had this? 'And one thing led to another?'

She nodded. 'I didn't even have to ask him up to my room. He knew. I think we both knew that it was going to happen.'

What could you say? 'Was it lovely?'

She gave a reminiscent little sigh. 'I swear, if I'd ever realised it could be like that, I'd have done it before. When he left, first thing in the morning, he asked for my phone number.'

Something in her tone told me we were getting to the cold-light-of-day bit. 'But he hasn't rung?'

'I don't know. I gave him the wrong number.'

I gaped at her. 'Why?'

Sighing, she ran a despairing hand through her hair. 'I thought of one of the boys answering the phone—they use mine so often—and I panicked. I just gave him the first number I could think of.'

Honestly, shaking was too good for her.

'But he gave me his number, too,' she said.

Now she told me. 'So have you phoned him?'

'How can I? I'd told him all those lies, and now this . . . I told him it was safe! I thought it was safe!' She gave another despairing sigh. 'I still can't believe I did it . . . but I don't regret it,' she added, with a touch of defiance. 'I found out what I've been missing.'

Suddenly she looked over her shoulder. 'Maybe you should turn the oven down—it's spitting fat like mad. You should put some foil over that turkey. And weren't you doing some potatoes when I arrived?'

'Helen, will you stop talking about bloody potatoes? Have you done a pregnancy test?'

'I don't need to. I'm late, and I'm hardly ever late.' She paused. 'But I don't want to. If I do a test I'll know for certain.'

I must have been utterly thick, but it was only then that I realised how her mind was working. 'You want this baby, don't you?'

She didn't even have to nod.

She left half an hour later, leaving me to reflect again on the monumental power of hormones. Or maybe she just wanted someone to love her, to have her as the centre of their universe.

After seeing her off I poured myself another glass of wine. 'At least I can't say I've had a boring Christmas,' I told Widdles.

When I checked John five minutes later, he was out of bed. 'What on earth are you doing?' I gaped.

'I need some fresh air.' Minus his pyjama top, he was shoving the window up. A Siberian blast tore into the room.

'OK, *OK*! I'll turn the fire off, all right?' I pulled the window down a little, leaving a few inches open at the bottom. 'Go back to bed, for heaven's sake, before you get pneumonia.'

'No! I need a bath first. I feel disgusting.'

I could tell without touching him that he was still feverish. He looked hot and dry as Sahara sand. His pillow-rubbed hair might have graced a hedgehog at the adolescent punk stage and his stubble was increasingly impressive. 'You look pretty disgusting, too,' I agreed, reasoning that this would go down better than old-woman fussing. 'But have something to eat first. You've had nothing since yesterday.'

He sighed. 'I could force some scrambled eggs down, if it's not too much like hard work.'

At least it wasn't Mummy's special eggy pudding for the not-vewy-well lickle soldier. 'I could just about manage that.'

'But I need that bath first.' He ran a hand over his chin. 'And a shave, if I can borrow a razor.'

'You can borrow mine. I'll find you a towel.'

Knowing how long blokes can take over a bath and shave, I gave him forty minutes. I did two eggs, scrambled more or less reasonably, on wholewheat toast. I wondered whether to cut the crusts off, but this struck me as OTT, as if I were cunningly trying to impress a bloke I fancied rotten. I mean, absolutely *nothing* like that was anywhere near my mind. I took it all up on a tray, and tapped at the door. 'John?'

As there was no reply, I entered and went instantly ballistic. He was asleep, lying face down on the duvet, naked except for a towel that was coming adrift. He'd opened that window wide again; the room felt like a freezer. Since that coming-adrift towel was revealing most of one olive buttock, I slapped it, hard.

'Jesus!' Starting violently, he jerked to a sitting position. In the process his towel came further adrift, revealing glimpses of a respectable-looking dart and etceteras. I was almost too mad to look, however, which just goes to show how mad I was.

'Are you actually *trying* to give yourself pneumonia?' I demanded furiously, yanking the window closed. 'It's like Siberia in here!'

I might as well have saved my breath. The only effect was to bring back more than a glimmer of his temporarily indisposed spark. 'I'm beginning to see what your "paying customers" are paying for,' he said, with an edge of wry amusement that almost made me want to slap him again. 'Not that I'm into that kind of thing, of course.'

'Oh, for God's sake . . .' It was grossly unfair, sparking like this when he'd only just been exposing buttocks and darts. Irritably I chucked his pyjamas at him. 'Put those on and get back into bed.'

I went and drew the curtains. When I turned back to him, he was sitting up in bed, buttoned into Jacko's pyjamas and wearing an expression I had a horrible feeling was a feeble attempt to suppress laughter.

'At least you don't look quite so disgusting now,' I said, in grudging tones. 'Which is more than you can say for your scrambled eggs. They'll be stone cold.' I plonked the tray on his lap. '*Bon appétit*. If you throw up again, please try to make it to the bathroom first. I'll leave you to it.'

But as I turned to go, he gripped my wrist. 'Harriet . . .'

Something in his tone made my heart turn over. '*Now* what?' I said, like Snow White's Grumpy.

'Sorry if I've been an awkward, ungracious bastard.'

As if that weren't enough in my suddenly wobbly state, he pulled me down and brushed my cheek with his lips. 'Thank you.'

I think I avoided audible wobbles. 'Don't mention it,' I said briskly, and cleared off downstairs, where I could wobble in private over yet another glass of wine. The strength in his grip had amazed me; what on earth would he manage when he was fit? Never mind his voice, gently husky, though maybe that was down to a sore throat, too. Between them, these were enough to make a girl go as gooey as something out of a corny old film. *'Oh, John,' she whispered, melting in his arms. 'Take me now before that beastly doorbell goes again . . .'*

Because it just had. 'Shit,' I said to Widdles. 'I can't even have a pink fantasy in peace. Who the hell's visiting on Boxing Day?'

I thought it was one of those tea-towel vendors, at first. The girl on the step was scruffy and unkempt, with a bag slung over her shoulder.

But then I saw her face. Grubby, wary and defiant, all at once.

The picture of Runaway Love.

Six

'TARA!' I GAPED. 'If you're looking for Jacko, he's not here!'

'I know! Do you think I'd have come otherwise? I phoned home yesterday,' she added, in answer to the question I was about to ask. 'Can I come in, or what? I need somewhere to stay for a couple of nights.'

I was still taking it in. 'If you like. Where's Lee?'

'In Leicester.'

Once she was inside, I bit back fifty nosy questions about what the hell was going on. She looked positively dirty and there were dark circles under her eyes. However, I guessed from her defensive body language that any questioning would make her clam right up.

'I thought William was supposed to be staying here for Christmas,' she said, dumping her bag on the kitchen floor.

Some instinct made me play it down. 'He was, but your mum and dad were a bit upset about you not being there, so he thought he'd go home after all. Take a seat,' I added brightly. 'Like a coffee?'

'OK.'

I'd met her several times over the years, on the odd visit to Jacko's. While I was filling the kettle she said, 'I only phoned home to let them know I was OK, but Mum started going on and on, and then William took over and had a go at me and I hung up.'

Well done, 'William'. I passed her a coffee. 'Lee's in Leicester, then? Will he be joining you?'

'Look, I got fed up with him, OK?'

He'd slung her out, then. Or something had happened to make her walk out.' Either way she'd die rather than admit it.

She was stroking Widdles, who was curled up on the sofa and didn't even have the courtesy to wake up. 'You work in an employment agency, don't you? I thought you could get me a job. And maybe I could stay here for a bit, too. William's not coming back, is he?'

I should have seen it coming. 'He might be back for New Year.'

Her face fell. 'Then I'll go somewhere else.'

Feeling my way, I said casually, 'Now you're here, it might be an idea to give your folks a call—just let them know where you are.'

'Are you kidding? They'd only be on at me again.' Sudden suspicion dawned. 'You won't tell them I'm here, will you?'

I suppose I hesitated.

'*Please!* They'd be down here in five minutes! Promise you won't?'

'All right, I promise!'

'It's none of their business anyway. I was eighteen three weeks ago—I don't have to tell them anything.'

'Look, I've got a turkey in the oven—it's just about ready. Would you like some?' I said, changing the subject.

She gave a not-bothered shrug. 'I wouldn't mind.'

So gracious.

'Where's the one with the baby?'

'Sally went home too.' After telling her briefly about my 'friend' upstairs, I thought he might still be peckish; two scrambled eggs wasn't much in twenty-four hours. 'I'll nip up and see if he fancies any turkey.'

When I tapped on the door he called, 'Come in,' dozily.

I sat on the end of the bed. 'How are you feeling?'

'On a scale of one to ten, about three better than this morning. But I still feel as if someone's taken half my stuffing out.'

I said, 'I shoved that turkey in the oven earlier—it's just about ready. Would you like a bit with some mashed potato?'

'I could murder some.'

Definitely feeling better. I told him about Tara's arrival, ending, 'She's asked me to get her a job and to promise not to tell her folks she's here.'

'But you're going to do exactly that?'

'Of course I am, having sworn I wouldn't. But I'll have to talk to her first, make her see I don't have much option.'

'Harriet, just call them. It's what she wants. She won't crawl home admitting they were right—she wants them to do the running.'

It annoyed me a good deal that I hadn't thought of this myself. 'You seem to have it all well sussed!'

'You forget Lucy.' He started a fit of coughing but quickly overcame it; he lay back on the pillows, exhausted. It was very unsettling. I was overwhelmed with a sudden desire to do caring-nursey things, eg tuck the covers round him, plump up his pillows, in fact, any excuse to get up close and personal. But I fought the impulse womanfully. 'Back to the turkey and Tara, then,' I said briskly.

Tara was nearly asleep on the sofa when I went down, but she roused instantly, looking almost guilty, as if I'd caught her up to no good.

After peeling an extra couple of potatoes for John, I set about manhandling the turkey out of the oven and making gravy. I did some frozen peas as well, for want of anything else, and when I finally put a plateful in front of her, Tara fell on it like Jacko used to when he'd just come back from water polo.

I said, 'Look, I've got to go to work tomorrow and John's probably going home in the morning but he's still not very well—could you make him some breakfast? Scrambled eggs or something?'

She nodded. 'Is he your bloke?'

'No, just a friend.'

Over another couple of mouthfuls she gave me a rather searching look. 'Mum was thinking William might fancy you,' she said.

I could almost have laughed. 'What on earth made her think that? Jacko and I have only ever been mates.'

'That's what I told her.' She shrugged. 'But she thought it might be a reason why he hadn't come home, anyway. Dad's been really pissed off. He relies on him more than he admits.'

'He was just recovering and enjoying some slobbing. Mind you, he does have a bit of a thing about Frida—and his physio at the hospital. He doesn't usually limit himself to one passing fancy at a time.'

'He never has more than passing fancies,' she snorted. 'Dad reckons all those EU grain mountains are William's wild oats.'

After devouring seconds she asked if she could have a bath, so I showed her the bathroom by way of Jacko's room, where she'd be sleeping.

Feeling like a bed-and-breakfast landlady, I went down and hacked off a couple of slices of breast for John, added a portion of mash, peas and gravy, and took it up with some freshly squeezed orange juice.

He was awake, listening to the London Live news.

'There you go,' I said, depositing the tray on his lap.

He sniffed appreciatively. 'It looks great. How's the runaway?'

'In the bath.' I hadn't intended to, but I sat on the bed. 'I wish she'd run somewhere else, to be honest. I've already had one major drama today.' I hadn't intended to do this either, but I told him about Helen.

'Is she the one you had to get back to after we went for drinks?'

I was surprised he remembered. 'Yes, and I came home to find she'd done the deed, after I'd more or less put the idea into her head. Still, at least I'm not remotely responsible for a pregnancy.'

'You're not responsible for runaways, either. Get on that phone and pass the buck back where it belongs.'

'I will. Only I've got to talk to her first.' It was much more tempting to stay and talk to him. For a few minutes the relationship had seemed more like a heart-to-heart between friends. However, I left him to eat in peace. Since Tara was still in the bathroom as I passed the door, I went downstairs rehearsing convincing arguments about parents worrying themselves into heart attacks or other dire conditions. But by the time I'd loaded the dishwasher and vaguely tidied up, I became aware that everything had gone ominously quiet. I went back up to find that both she and John had crashed out already.

Downstairs again, cross with both of them, I phoned Sally.

She was stunned to hear about Helen, of course, and as for Tara: 'Brat,' she said, with feeling. 'She just went to bed without even saying good night or thank you for the dinner?'

'Yes, and now I've got to phone her folks, after swearing blind I wouldn't.'

In the event I phoned Jacko on his mobile, and his main reaction was apology that I'd been landed with her. However, the folks would be profoundly relieved. He'd call them (he was in some pub, of course) and get back to me.

When he eventually did, it wasn't quite what I'd expected. Yes, they were overwhelmingly relieved, but turbocharging straight down might not be wise. First, if she refused to come home they could hardly force her to. Second, if she *was* expecting them to do the running, it might not be a bad idea to let her think they weren't going to. Let her sweat. So they hated asking, please feel free to say no, but if I wouldn't mind terribly having her . . .

'OK,' I said to Jacko. 'It's not as if there isn't room.'

'Thanks, pet. Don't so much as make a coffee for her, though, will you? She's used to the old lady waiting on her hand and foot.'

No, there'd definitely be no more 'waiting', I thought. I might even tell her she could clean Widdles's litter tray, for starters.

Since they were both still asleep, I didn't see either of them before I left in the morning. I scrawled a note for Tara: 'Help yourself to anything and please feed and water John if he's still feeling rough. Tell him I've washed his clothes. They're in the airing cupboard. Back around six.'

Underneath I added, 'If you're bored, the kitchen floor could do with a wash.' I was pleased with that. Neat, I thought.

I needn't have bothered going to work at all: the phone only rang twice. At twelve fifteen I phoned John's mobile. He answered after four rings and any rumours that I was going fluttery just waiting to hear his voice are a malicious slander. 'John Mackenzie,' he said.

'It's Harriet,' I said. 'How are you feeling?'

There was a minute pause. 'Oh, hello, Graham. How's it going?'

It took me only half a second to catch on. 'Tara's with you, I take it? Is she talking?'

'It's possible. Look, can I call you later? I'm a bit tied up just now.'

I was bursting with curiosity until he called back about an hour later.

'Sorry about that, but she was in the middle of a tearful flood about Lee. Plus she'd just been saying you'd probably told her folks she was here already, she should never have come.'

'I have told them. Where is she, anyway?'

'Just nipped to the shops. Look, I've sworn not to tell you any of this, but she walked out on Lee. He'd taken her to some scruffy house in Leicester, where half a dozen of his friends were living. At least two of them were women he obviously knew very well—she felt uncomfortable from the word go.'

I could just imagine it.

'She soon sussed out that one of them had been more than just mates with Lee,' he went on. 'Nothing happened till the other night, though. She found Lee on the verge of having a pretty good time with this woman. So she threw a fit and walked out.'

I felt for her. I really did. 'Poor Tara. After that little lot, you'd think she'd be dying to go home.'

'Well, she isn't. I got the impression that it's not just losing face she can't stomach—something else has been going on. Maybe you should ask her brother—see if he's got any pointers.'

Maybe. Then I asked belatedly, 'How are you feeling?'

'A damn sight better, thanks. I'll see you later—I won't leave until you're back.'

When I got home they were sitting at the kitchen table, over empty plates.

'I made him a baked potato with some cold turkey and salad,' Tara said. 'We'd have waited for you, but we were starving.'

'That's OK,' I said brightly, and went to put the kettle on.

'I washed the kitchen floor,' she added.

'Yes, I can see that. Thanks a lot.'

Tara looked like a different animal from last night. For a start, she was clean. She wore a soft grey fleece top and her hair hung in a rippling, corn-silk mass. 'I hope you don't mind, but I borrowed your hair dryer,' she said, still slightly defensively, as if I were the enemy in disguise. 'And I put all my clothes in the wash—they were minging.'

'No, that's fine. And thanks for looking after John. I take it you're feeling better?' I added, to him.

'About seven points up on yesterday. Tara's been great—I couldn't have had better service at five hundred quid a night in the London Clinic. At least she didn't yell at me,' he added, in mock-hurt tones. 'I tell you, Tara, if your average NHS nurse were like Harriet, the hospitals would be half empty overnight. People would be too terrified to get sick.'

Turning back to the worktop to make my tea, I heard Tara quietly giggling, and suddenly felt acutely hurt that he was making jokes at my expense. I might have been fifteen again. It felt as if they were ganging up against me.

Telling myself for God's sake to get an adult grip, I joined them at the table.

After shooting John a glance, Tara turned to me. 'I suppose you've already told my mum and dad I'm here?'

From the way she said it, I knew there was no point lying. 'I'm sorry, Tara, but I had to. They've been out of their minds. But you needn't worry that they'll be charging straight down. They said there wasn't much point, as you'd probably refuse to come home and they couldn't very well force you.'

If this startled her, she covered it instantly. 'Just as well, because I wouldn't be here. John said there's a flat I can stay in, till I get myself sorted.'

'It belongs to a friend of mine,' he explained, in answer to my *What the hell?* expression. 'He's in Abu Dhabi—won't be back for a bit.'

'Won't your friend mind?' I asked John, with a trace of acid.

'He won't know,' he soothed, and Tara stifled another giggle.

'And what do I tell her folks if they ask for an address?'

'You'll be able to tell them with perfect truth that you don't know,' Tara said. 'I'm not obliged to tell them anything. John agrees with me,' she went on, giving him another glance. 'I'm eighteen, not a kid.'

'She does have a point,' he said, glancing at his watch. 'We ought to be making a move. Tara, go up and get your things together.'

She went off like a lamb. Once the door had shut behind her, I said, exasperated, 'What the hell are you up to?'

'I didn't have much choice!' Lowering his voice he went on, 'She'd have left by now if I hadn't offered. Look, do you think I need this? Believe me, I've got enough on at the moment. I will give you the address,' he added.

'Even though you evidently told her you wouldn't?'

'I had to, didn't I?'

He'd lied beautifully, then. So beautifully she'd believed him utterly. My stomach contracted, as I suddenly thought of what other beautifully believable lies he might have told. 'You're a pretty convincing liar, then.'

'You can talk,' he said, in drily amused tones. 'Little Miss, "Oh dear, I've lost my purse . . ."'

'I thought I had!' I said it more tartly than I'd intended, because something else had just hit me. Even if Tara's parents didn't ask who this friend was, gaily dishing out flats like Smarties, Jacko certainly would. What the hell was I going to tell him? *'Remember Smootharse? Well, I did see him again, even though he's still seeing Nina, and I went home with him for Christmas—and he just happened to get the flu . . .'*

Suddenly I knew exactly what was meant by cans of worms. 'You should have kept out of it! It was none of your business!'

'OK, and what if she'd just taken off? Nobody would have a clue where she was!'

Tara came back just then, with tension still hanging in the air and me looking decidedly browned off.

'Can I use your mobile to make a quick call?' she asked.

'Go on, then.'

As she went off, out of earshot, he gazed across at me. 'You look seriously hacked off.'

'I just hope she won't trash your friend's flat.'

'She'd better not. It's mine. It's between lets.'

I gaped at him.

'It seemed expedient,' he said, in apologetic tones. 'An Abu Dhabi friend liable to come back at, say, forty-eight hours' notice . . .'

Another lie. They were popping up like Kleenex from a box. 'I hope you can cope, that's all. Jacko says she's an arsey little madam.'

'I have years of experience with arsey little madams. Lucy was arsey from the word go. She used to whack me with her rattle.'

Of course he said it in that trying-not-to-laugh tone that melted me, which was just what he'd intended. 'Harriet, thanks for everything.' As we heard Tara's feet in the hall, he added, 'I'll give you a call.'

Tara handed back his mobile. As she looked up at him, I suddenly saw him through her eyes: an older man, not old enough to be remote, but properly grown-up. Relaxed, but with that indefinable aura of substance and savoir-faire. She'd have snorted in derision if I'd actually said it, but he was the eternal white knight, galloping up just as the dragon was about to have you for breakfast.

He picked up her bag. Well, that's what white knights do. They never expect you to carry them yourself.

We paused by the front door. 'Thanks again,' John said.

Now he was about to go, I was perverse enough to have misgivings about my misgivings. He still didn't look much more than 80 per cent. I wanted to say, 'Look after yourself,' but strangled it at the tonsil stage. 'Wait till you get the bill,' I said. 'Take care.'

'You, too.' His lips brushing my cheek, he added, 'I'll be in touch.'

Looking rather awkward, Tara said, 'Thanks for having me. And for the dinner and everything.'

'You're welcome.' I opened the door to a blast of cold air, watched the car disappear down the road, and went back to the kitchen.

'I wish she'd never come,' I said to Widdles. 'Is there some massive sign out there I haven't noticed? "Please feel free to come and foul up Harriet's life a bit more—she can't do it fast enough herself?"'

He gave a huge yawn.

'Fat lot of use you are,' I said crossly. I rang Tara's folks. I told her mother I'd had a friend staying over. While I was at work he'd somehow got her talking and this was the result. I asked what she thought the 'something else' John had mentioned might be, but she couldn't think of anything. Tara never told her anything anyway.

Eventually she went on, 'I'm praying she'll come to her senses before school starts, but I must say it was very kind of him to step in like that. I just hope she won't turn his flat into a pigsty in two minutes.'

After she'd hung up, I thought a similar line might do for Jacko. Tara was staying at a flat belonging to an old friend I hadn't happened to mention. I thought I'd get Sally's opinion; I was just about to try her number when the phone rang. It was Rosie.

This was a wee bit spooky. Since I hadn't heard from her for a week,

I'd been thinking of ringing her for the past forty-eight hours, hoping there might be some little news items she'd forgotten to pass on.

Rosie was still back home, and bored. 'We have to take the whole week as annual leave so I thought I might as well stay. Besides, I have to help Mum out of a dire personal crisis.'

'What crisis?'

'About fourteen boxes of Belgian chocolates. I have to keep eating them to take temptation out of her way. Did you get any exciting prezzies? I've ended up with a pair of those massive furry-dog slippers that make you walk funny, and some bath stuff that smells like strawberry puke—whereas Other People end up with colossally expensive earrings from Helicopters.'

This was another reason I hadn't rung her. In case any news items turned out to be ones I'd rather not hear. 'Typical. Diamonds?'

'I don't know, but they were really nice. He gave them to her the night before she left. So much for her paranoid imaginings.'

My antennae pricked right up. 'What paranoid imaginings?'

'Oh, didn't I tell you? She'd been getting in a bit of a tizz, thinking he was cooling off.'

'Not taking her home for Christmas, you mean?'

'Oh, it wasn't just *that*. He'd been *working late*—her italics. But she'd got this idea he might have someone else on the go.'

I wasn't sure I wanted to hear this. How many times had he been 'working late'? And which dates, exactly?

'But Suzanne thinks she might well be right,' Rosie went on. 'She said colossally expensive earrings smelt of guilt offerings to her. Mind you, she never quite took to Helicopter in the first place. Says she never trusts blokes with pulling power coming out of their ears. It's too easy for them, like picking up Mars bars in Tesco's.'

I gave a carefree little laugh I thought came off rather well. 'What a nasty, suspicious mind.'

'Yes, that's what I thought. He never made a proper move on you, did he? Not real Mars bar stuff. Maybe he thought it'd be too much like hard work to get your wrappings off.' She started te-hee-ing helplessly.

We nattered for another ten minutes until a 'call waiting' took my mind right off Mars bars.

It was Dad. He'd tried to phone on Christmas Day, but no one had been answering. Maybe we'd all gone to walk our dinner off. (Dad, wasn't the type to think *'Gas leaks!'* and call the fire brigade.) I said yes, more than likely. Yes, I'd had a lovely Christmas—had he?

'Extremely nice, thank you, dear.' He then got to the point. 'I don't know whether Mummy told you, but I've met a very nice woman.'

'Yes,' I said brightly. 'I heard you were thinking of going skiing.'

'Yes. As a matter of fact, we're in the mountains now.' He sounded positively tickled with himself. 'Kathy's quite the expert, she's rather younger than me, of course, but I've had a few goes. It's fun, isn't it?'

I tried not to think of what Mum said about susceptible old fools.

'But the reason I was ringing was to say I'll be back in the next week or two,' he went on. 'Kathy'll be coming, of course; she wants to go and see her family. I thought we could all have dinner together.'

'That'd be lovely,' I said. 'Will you be staying here?'

'Oh, no, dear, I wouldn't want to put you out. I'll book a hotel. I do hope you'll like her,' he added anxiously.

There's a technique to sounding bright over the phone. You force your mouth into what in low circles is called a split-arse grin, and believe me, mine was stretched ear to ear. (My mouth, I mean.) 'I'm sure I shall. How long will you be staying?'

'Oh, only a few days, then we'll be off to Egypt. We'll stay in Luxor a week or so, and then on to Aswan. Kathy's got a yen for the Old Cataract Hotel; it's rather famous, you know. Very scenic.' He paused. 'Actually, dear . . . it's not *quite* going to be just an ordinary holiday.'

No flying jellies hit me; I'd seen it coming. Or rather heard it, in a voice you could only describe as besotted. I did a split-arse extreme enough to require surgery. 'Are you telling me it's your honeymoon?'

'Well, yes,' he said, sounding half embarrassed but chuffed at the same time. 'I do hope it's not too much of a shock.'

'No, it's *lovely*! Have you told Mum?' I added, knowing full well he hadn't, or phone lines would have blown up by now.

'No, dear; I'm not going to tell her till after the event—that'll be next week. She'll only think I'm rushing into it.'

'How long *have* you known her, by the way?' I said.

'About seven weeks,' he said, almost bashfully.

God help us.

'I know Mummy thinks I'm a bit clueless,' he went on, in wry tones I'd hardly ever heard him use, 'but I know I'm doing the right thing. I'm really very happy.'

I don't quite know why that changed anything, but it did. My eyes were suddenly misting, my throat pricking. 'I'm happy for you, too.'

After hanging up I was straight into another quandary. If Mum wasn't forewarned she'd have a fit. So I phoned her, and her reaction was entirely predictable. 'He's *what*?' she almost screeched.

'Mum, calm down!' I'm only telling you so you'll be prepared! If you dare say anything horrible I'll kill you! He sounds really happy!'

'Of course he does! God knows what she's been doing, flattering him and heaven knows what in bed—dear Lord—how old is she?'

'I don't know. Younger, anyway.'

'I guessed as much. Did he say which hotel he's staying at?'

'No.' And just as well. I wouldn't have put it past her to get on a plane and sort the scheming Jezebel out.

'And they're going to Egypt? Not one of those Nile cruises, I hope. She might be planning on pushing him over the side.'

This was becoming ridiculous. 'Mum, will you just stop it? You're working yourself up into a positive hate thing about this Kathy!'

'I can't help it. I'm sure he's making a terrible mistake.'

'So what if he is? You're not responsible for him!' Something in me was flipping, fast. 'For God's sake, can't you just be happy for him? He deserves to be happy—when was he ever properly happy with you?'

'Harriet! That was uncalled for! I'm only thinking of—'

'You think he's stupid—you always did! You were impatient with him for years! Why the hell did you marry him in the first place?'

There was an awful silence. When she finally spoke, her voice was shaky, as if she were about to cry. 'I really don't think there's any point prolonging this conversation. I hope he'll be happy, believe me. I'm more fond of him than you'll ever know.' And she hung up.

I went to bed thoroughly miserable.

Lying on a pillow that smelt of John didn't help either; no, of course I hadn't changed the sheets. I was fully expecting to wake at seven with a sore throat and shivery aches; but I went to work feeling fine.

My phone rang while I was on the train home after work the next day.

'Oh, hi,' said a bored voice. 'It's Tara. I just thought I'd say thanks for having me.'

Having done an instant vertical takeoff in case it was somebody else, my spirits crash-landed into a mangled wreck just out of Parson's Green station. 'What have you been up to?'

'Not a lot. It's a lovely flat. A sunbed and everything. I tried it earlier—I've got a little bit of colour already.'

She sounded as if she were lying on a sofa, examining her nails.

'Have you looked for a job yet?'

'Give me a chance! I did buy an *Evening Standard*, though—there are millions of jobs. Look, I'd better go—John said he'd pop in about now.'

Did he, indeed.

Before I'd even got off the train, I had a horrible smell in my nose, worse than Rosie's strawberry puke. It smelt of Mars bars, a.k.a. bruised little plums called Tara, suddenly faced with white knights who might well have started out with purely knightly motives, but who were, under the shining armour, but mortal men.

By the time I got home the smell had grown so strong, I was seeing Tara in tears again, saying she must be hideously ugly or Lee would never have fancied that slag. And mortal man would melt again, and say, 'Tara, you're as lovely as the rosy-fingered dawn, come, let me stroke your hair and dry your little tears—oh, what the fuck . . .'

I was so wound up, it took me an hour to notice that Widdles hadn't come to greet me. He wasn't even on his throne. I looked everywhere, but there was no sign of him.

Beginning to be worried, I walked up the road, praying not to see a bedraggled tabby corpse in the gutter, peering into every front garden in case he'd been injured and crawled under a shrub. Then I went home and started phoning local vets.

After three vets I gave up, and that was when John called.

'I hope you're not in bed with my bug,' he said.

'I hardly ever get bugs.'

'I can imagine,' he said, in drily amused tones. 'Any bug hoping to breach your defences would need to be armed to the teeth. Kalashnikovs and Semtex, at the very least.'

Well, thanks a lot. More 'harridan' stuff was all I needed just now.

'Have you spoken to Tara's folks?' he went on.

'Of course. Her mother said it's very good of you, but she's worried she won't be back in time for school.'

'I'm not surprised. She told me she's got her mocks coming up and the thought makes her want to yak up. She was talking of modelling.'

'She's not tall enough!'

'I wouldn't know about that. I said it was a tough business, and she got upset and asked if I was saying she wasn't pretty enough.'

Almost worse than my imaginings. 'To be honest, John, I couldn't care less at the moment if she wants to do exotic dancing with a python. She's a spoilt brat.'

'Maybe, but she's had a bit of a rough time.'

'*Rough?*' I said, incensed. 'Have you any idea what kind of home she's come from? And she's worried her parents sick and couldn't give a toss!'

'Harriet, I know all that, but she's just a kid.'

'Not that much of a kid!' Hearing myself doing the snapping-turtle bit again, I tried to calm down. 'Look, I'm sorry—I've had rather a bad day. Could you give me your folks' address, for a thankyou letter?'

Having dictated that, he said, 'Unless anything earth-shattering happens, I'll call you in a couple of days, all right?'

'All right.'

After hanging up, I realised I hadn't even asked how he was.

Not that I cared. Did he care that I'd had a bad day? Of course not, when he was so busy caring about poor little Tara. Harridan Harriet was fine for mashing sodding potatoes and changing sweaty sheets, but she could look after herself.

Sod him.

For the fourteenth time, my eyes wandered to the cat flap. I'd have given anything to see Widdles ooze fatly through it. At least he loved me. Or used to love me, if he wasn't dead.

By the time Jacko phoned, all I could see was a pathetic little corpse under a bush. He was so upset for me, saying he wished he was there to give me a cuddle, that I got a bit weepy. So my 'friend' with the flat turned into something of a secondary issue: Jacko just said good luck to him, he was buggered if he'd lend Tara a flat.

The doorbell rang just as I was going to bed. There was a woman on the step, her arms full of Widdles. 'Is he yours?' she asked anxiously.

'Yes—where on earth was he? I've been looking everywhere!'

'In one of my armchairs, I'm afraid, at number fifty-nine. I did try to send him home earlier, but he just wouldn't go. He does pop round now and then—I often have little nibbles left from dinner parties. You naughty boy, I *told* you your mummy would be worried!'

Unmoved, the faithless beast jumped like a ton of lard to the floor and waddled kitchenwards.

'Quite a weight, isn't he?' the woman said brightly. 'I asked my husband to bring him, but he's got a bad back.'

I changed the John sheets before I went to bed, and then wished I hadn't. I told myself I'd be very nice when he phoned again, sympathetic about Tara, so he wouldn't think I was a cow. I told myself I'd be sparkly and amusing. And then I thought no, I'd be merely polite in a coolish sort of way. Sod him. Sod him and fuck him.

And then I thought about that, too.

The doorbell rang again at ten to eight. I found a boy on the step, looking embarrassed. About fifteen, he lived a few doors down.

'My mum asked me to bring these round,' he said. 'They came yesterday but you were out, so they brought them to our house.'

'I was looking for my cat,' I said, feeling suddenly sick. 'Thank you.'

I closed the door and looked down at an armful of spring. Scented narcissi, hyacinths, freesias—I could almost have got drunk on the scent. What must he have thought when I didn't even say thank you?

Assuming it *was* him—I tore the little envelope open.

The card read simply, *Thank you, John.*

Well, what was I to make of that? I hadn't expected a '*love*', but would '*Thanks so much for everything*' have been more encouraging? Or was simplicity somehow more eloquent? You can tell the kind of pathetic wreck I was turning into, agonising over three words on a florist's card. When I eventually phoned he wasn't answering, so I left a message thanking him and explaining about Widdles.

He phoned back when I was on the train home. 'Glad they turned up, I was beginning to wonder.'

'You can blame Widdles. He's found someone who gives him nice little leftovers from dinner parties. How are you feeling?'

'About ninety per cent, thanks.' He paused. 'I was going to call you anyway. Tara's got an interview, with some modelling agency. On the 2nd. She's fizzing with it.'

'Her mother'll have a fit. I spoke to her earlier—she's getting really worked up about her not coming back in time for school.'

'The only thing in her head at the moment is this interview. I said I'd meet her afterwards for something to eat.'

On the 2nd? Four days away? 'Won't you be seeing her till then?'

'I thought I'd leave her to her own devices for a few days. If you feel like coming, I could make it a table for three. You'll be able to give her folks a first-hand report. Whatever the agency tells her, I thought this might be a good time to bring my Abu Dhabi friend back. Landing at, say, seven ten on the 6th might be good.'

I was beginning to wonder how I could ever have had mortal-bloke thoughts at all. What sort of jealous, suspicious cow was I turning into?

'Will you come?' he went on.

Wild elephants wouldn't stop me. Already I was buzzing at the mere thought of seeing him again. 'I could probably make it. Where?'

'I'll give you a call tomorrow.'

'Tomorrow' was the day before New Year's Eve. He gave the name of a Mexican place Tara had chosen. Then, although I'd promised myself I'd do no such thing, I said, 'Doing anything exciting tomorrow night?'

'Possibly even dangerous,' he said. 'I made a wild promise a couple of months ago to dust off my sporran and skeandhu. I think there might be a few bets on as to whether I go for orthodox Highland freestyle underneath. How about you?'

'Oh, out raving,' I lied brightly.

'Happy New Year, then. Have fun.'

'You, too.'

Shit. Dress kilt. Black velvet jacket with silver buttons. Ravening hordes of champagne-soaked, giggling women trying to see up his kilt to check out his freestyle accessories. Nina in a slinky dress with her tits out, or someone else ditto. Almost certainly Nina, though; she must be back by now.

Sally returned that evening, and if not exactly ratty, was quiet and twitchy. Jacko had phoned to say he was in bed feeling 'like shite' so another one down with flu. In the end, our New Year's Eve wasn't a bundle of laughs. Sally made a Thai green curry that went wrong, but we ate it anyway and watched some *Ally McBeal* Sally had taped. And all the while I was watching the clock for midnight, thinking of John kissing Nina, or some other cow with a four-inch cleavage he'd been drooling into all night. How I was going to last until the 2nd, I couldn't imagine.

The restaurant was in Leicester Square, which didn't surprise me. Leicester Square was exactly the sort of place you'd gravitate towards if you were eighteen and new to London. I arrived a few minutes early. John was there already, in a dimly lit corner, on his own. My heart and stomach did a drunken little *pas de deux* when I saw him. God, what an obsessed wreck.

'How's it going?' he asked.

'Oh, brilliant,' I said, in a sparkly, non-wreck fashion, sitting opposite him. 'Apart from the fact that my father's about to marry this Kathy and my mother thinks she's planning to drown him in the Nile.'

He started laughing, but Tara had just arrived. I saw at once that she was underwhelmed with joy to see me. She said, 'Hi, yes, he said you might be coming too,' in a tone that said . . . *and I suppose I'll just have to put up with it*.

'So how did it go?' John asked, as she sat next to him.

'Pretty good,' she said, perking up a bit. 'They said I had good potential but I'll need to get a portfolio done first.'

'How much will that cost?' John asked.

She shrugged. 'About a hundred and fifty quid.'

John shot me a tiny, conspiratorial little wink that did possibly illegal things to my vital organs. Casually he said to Tara, 'How are you planning to get hold of a hundred and fifty quid, then?'

'A job, of course. I'll have to save up.'

After we'd ordered (tortillas and fajitas, plus beer for him, Coke for her and a margarita for me), John turned to Tara. 'Have you done anything on the job front? My Abu Dhabi friend emailed me this morning. I'm afraid he's coming back on the 6th.'

I hadn't expected him to come out with it so quickly, nor so briskly. Her face lost about 30 per cent of its perk instantly, but regained most of it almost at once. 'I could stay with you for a bit.'

'I don't think so, sweetheart.'

'Why not?'

'I work a lot at home. You'd distract me.'

'I'd be very good,' she said, in tones that managed to be simultaneously demure and pertly flirty.

I realised that at least half my imaginings had been spot-on. She'd worked him into some fantasy romantic hero who'd fallen for her instantly but wasn't admitting it because he'd feel like a dirty old man.

'Tara, it's just not on,' he said, a good deal more firmly.

All the sympathy I hadn't felt for her suddenly came upon me in a rush. If he'd intended to crush her, he'd certainly succeeded.

A waiter brought our drinks. Once he'd gone John said in kinder tones, 'Tara, I'm not sure you've really thought this through. Have you any idea, first, of what it costs to live anywhere in London, and second, what you might expect to earn in the kind of job you're likely to get? You'll be hard pushed to find a shoebox to live in and eat in, let alone save a hundred and fifty quid.'

'Other people manage,' she said.

'Most people your age are still living at home,' he said. 'Which is a bloody sight cheaper, even if you're paying your folks something. You'd save your hundred and fifty quid a lot faster if you went home.'

'I'm not—going—home!'

John wasn't even mildly taken aback; it was as if he'd been testing the water one last time. 'OK, OK,' he soothed.

The food arrived then: colossal, American-style quantities on yard-wide plates. Tara got stuck into her fajitas as if she were about to go on a crash diet for a month. Maybe that agency had told her she didn't look anorexic enough. But I could have sworn I saw her eyes welling up. Feeling for her more than ever, I said, 'You could come back to me for a bit.'

'No, thanks,' she said, as if I'd offered a nice cup of poison.

After what could barely have been ten minutes, having shovelled most of her food down, she mumbled, 'I'm going to the loo,' grabbed her little rucksack, and departed.

Once she'd gone, John's eyes met mine across the table. 'Oh shit,' he muttered. 'I didn't want it to come to this.'

I realised then that he knew exactly what had been going through Tara's head.

'She'd somehow got the wrong idea,' he went on, in wryly apologetic tones. 'I've been trying to ignore the signs in a "tactful" manner, but maybe I've been too tactful.'

'It's not easy,' I said, wondering just what the signs had been.

'No, but I didn't want to be brutal.'

His eyes were suddenly so warm, so utterly nice-bloke-ish, I had to finish my margarita to fortify myself. 'You weren't exactly brutal.'

'That's how it came across.'

'You were only trying to help.' I was getting so gooey by this point, I nearly put my hand across the table to take his.

'The balance of my mind was temporarily disturbed,' he said, looking me right in the eye.

Something in the way he said it made my heart and stomach do another drunken little salsa together. Suddenly my vibe sensors were back on red alert. *Meaningful eye contact!* they were screaming. *Undertones!* But a millisecond later he was only eyeing my empty glass. 'Another margarita? Or something else?'

I glanced at the drinks list, and then wished I hadn't. Restaurants should be banned from putting things like 'Sloe Comfortable Screw' and 'Screaming Orgasm' on their cocktail menus when people like me are trying to cope with overdoses of flutters in a public place.

However, I managed to say, 'Yes, same again, please,' as if I weren't thinking a 'Sex on the Beach' would go down very nicely, too.

Or maybe not. He was nodding at my plate. 'If you're not going to eat the rest of that tortilla, pass it over.'

Typical. My stomach doing Latin American dancing, his merely thinking of food. There was probably a whole section to that effect in *Women Are From Venus, Men Are Basically Just Greedy Buggers*.

After a few reflective chews, however, he stopped. 'Maybe you'd better go and check on Tara. She's being a hell of a long time.'

I hurried to the *Señoras*. There were three cubicles, a queue of six, and a couple of girls standing at the mirrors. I stood hesitantly a moment, before calling 'Tara?'

There was no reply.

'Tara, are you all right?'

Again there was no reply. A girl in the queue said, 'Someone's been in there for ages.' She nodded towards the furthest cubicle.

I tapped on the door. 'Tara? Are you all right?'

'Do you mind?' said an irate voice.

'Sorry,' I said. Almost immediately, the doors of the other two cubicles opened. Neither woman was Tara.

I went back to John. 'She's not there!'

His expression sharpened. 'Oh shit,' he said. 'She's done a runner. I'll get the bill.'

Seven

'SHE'LL BE HEADING BACK to the flat, first, to get her things. We should catch her. Have you got wheels?' I asked, as we exited.

'No, and just as well; the traffic'll be a bitch. It'll be quicker on the underground.' As we hurried through the crowds in cold, mistlike drizzle, he glanced at his watch. 'She can't have got much of a start.'

'Where the hell can she be thinking of going?'

'God knows.'

He said nothing as we dashed through tunnels to the trains, but I knew he was thinking much the same as me. He was thinking of just what type of person a naive girl with hardly any money, who thought she knew it all, might meet, wandering on her own with a backpack.

As we waited on the platform amid heaving crowds I said, 'I'm sorry I landed you with all this.'

'You didn't land me. I didn't have to get involved.'

But he had. And now, like me, he felt responsible. When he was busy and had just been ill, and could do without it. *I* could do without it. I had an adolescent father to worry about.

'Look, in the circumstances, maybe I should go on my own,' he said suddenly, as the train whooshed out of the tunnel. 'Go home. I'll call you later.'

Eventually, at ten past eleven, he did.

He sounded raggedly up to here. 'I found her two hundred yards down the road from the flat, heading for the main road with her stuff. She was planning to hitch to Colchester. Some ex-schoolfriend moved there a year ago. She didn't even know what road to take.'

'What did you do?'

'Told her to phone the friend first. And when she did, the friend said she couldn't have her anyway, there wasn't room. Eventually I got her back to the flat and square one. I told her I'd sort something out, but God knows what. Look, I'll call you tomorrow—I've got to hit the hay.'

At work next morning I told my colleague Sandie the gist of the Tara problem, while not going into detail about John. 'I'd have her back with me for a bit, but I know she won't come,' I said.

Oddly enough, it was Sandie who came up with a possibility. Her sister's friend Rachel had a room spare. It was a pretty grotty house in a pretty grotty area, but it was really cheap.

I got the address and phoned Tara as soon as I got home.

'Thanks, but John's found me somewhere to live,' she said, in her former bored tones. 'And a job thrown in.'

I was gobsmacked. 'Already?'

'He's got a friend who manages some flash country club in Wiltshire or somewhere,' she went on. 'I can live in. It's got a health club and gym and everything. He's going to take me down on Saturday.'

Mad that he'd sorted it when I'd been trying to sort it, to save him the trouble, I forced a smile into my voice. 'I hope you'll at least tell your folks where you're going.'

'I will! It's a seriously flash place, you know. They get stacks of celebrities. Even film crews on shoots.'

Suddenly her voice held a thread of excitement and it didn't take a genius to figure out why. She saw herself waitressing, serving some Merchant Ivory director, and him saying, 'Honey, you're wasted here. How would you like a part in my movie?'

She bounced back, I'd say that for her. 'Well, good luck.'

John phoned forty minutes later.

'Yes, I heard,' I said, as he started to tell me. 'Why the hell didn't you phone me first? *I'd* found her somewhere to stay—a nice grotty place with hot-and-cold running burglars—perfect for making her miss her own en suite bathroom. Why a flash country club, anyway? Wouldn't a crummy dive in Paddington have been more appropriate?'

'I don't know anyone who manages crummy dives in Paddington!'

Well, of course not.

'She won't last a week,' he said.

'Are you kidding? She's seeing wall-to-wall *Hello!* types and Leonardo DiCaprio popping in for—'

'Harriet, will you give me credit for a little intelligence?'

A little intelligence was precisely what I'd just been lacking. 'You've built it right up, haven't you? So it'll be a massive letdown?'

'Not exactly. It is pretty flash and they do get the odd celebrity, but she won't get anywhere near them.'

The kitchen, probably. Scullery-maid stuff. 'You're a pretty devious so-and-so, aren't you? And does this friend of yours actually need any unskilled staff at the moment?'

'Of course not. It's low season.'

'And you've agreed to pay her wages, I suppose? How much?'

When he didn't answer I went on, 'I can't have you shelling out!'

'All right, we'll split it. I haven't got the energy for arguments.'

Since he was still probably suffering from post-bug fatigue, this made me feel bad. 'I could drive Tara down.'

'No, I said I'd take her, but I was going to ask you to come along for the ride. I thought you could keep me awake on the way back. I have to go away on the Sunday morning, so I'll probably be knackered after catching up with the work I should have been doing last night. Could you make it?' he asked.

'I should think so. I can't have you falling asleep on the way back. You might splat a poor little bunny. I'd never forgive myself.'

'Harriet, do I strike you as a malicious bunny-splatterer?'

'No, just checking. I could drive, if you like. Then you could put your seat back and snore all the way home.'

'You never know, I just might. I'll pick you up about three, all right?'

I wasn't looking forward to passing on this latest development, but Mrs Jacques had already heard from Tara herself. 'I just hope she'll come to her senses before school starts,' she said, in resigned tones.

Half an hour after she'd hung up, Frida was on the phone. 'D'you want picking up from the airport?' I asked.

'I cancelled my ticket. I had a big fight with Erik. He said if you go back that's it, finish. So I said OK, go and boil your big fat head.'

'But you're staying anyway?'

'Of course.' Her voice took on a mischievous note. 'He went to the travel agent. Two weeks in Jamaica. So I think I love him again!'

Somehow I'd half expected it, but I was still deflated. 'Jacko, Frida—this house is going to feel horribly empty,' I said to Sally.

'Don't tell me. I'm almost missing Ape-Face already. I've only got you to bitch at now, and you don't even nick my squirty cream.'

Straight after getting home on Friday evening I indulged in what magazines laughingly call 'pampering yourself'. Personally I call it sheer hard work: face mask, manicure, pedicure, exfoliating everything and stinking out the bathroom with hair remover. All this was purely because I was long overdue for such treatments, of course: nothing to do with the fact that I was going to be seeing John the following day.

Rosie turned up around half seven. I took her into the sitting room, which was warm for once. Sick of sitting in the kitchen like a pair of below-stairs domestics, Sally and I had raked out the ashes like another pair of below-stairs domestics and got a fire going.

'So what have you been up to?' I asked.

'Not a lot, apart from work,' she said, in between cootchy-cooing at Tom. 'Suzanne's friend's come back early from India. She's with her folks for now, but she's going to want her room back so I've got to find somewhere else sharpish.'

'There's always here,' I said.

'I know, thanks a lot, but I guess I should find something more permanent if you're selling soon. You should get a garden flat. Great for barbies in the summer. And for Tom to play in, of course.'

Sally made an *Oh Lord* face. 'Rosie, I won't be living with Harriet.'

'Won't you?' She looked startled. 'Why not?'

'Because I'm going home. To do a PGCE.'

I was dumbfounded. 'Since when?' I gaped.

'I've been thinking about it for ages,' she said, defensively. 'I discussed it with Mum and Dad over Christmas.'

'Teacher training?' Rosie asked. 'Won't that take years?'

'*One* year. I've already got a degree.'

I still couldn't take it in. 'You always said you'd never teach!'

'Harriet, what the hell else have I been doing for the past eight years?'

'Yes, but that's adults! *Motivated* adults! You always said you could never hack kids!'

'I know, but I wouldn't mind little kids. And it'll fit with school holidays and all that. Don't look at me like that,' she added. 'My mind's made up.'

'Your mother'll drive you mad!' I said.

'I'll just have to put up with it. They offered to have me; they weren't obliged to. Mum even offered to do some of the baby-sitting. I'm doing it for Tom, not me,' she went on doggedly. 'I didn't give him a very brilliant start, but I'm damned if he's going to suffer for it.'

From bitter experience I knew that once Sally had made her mind up, you might as well ask the sun whether setting in the east mightn't make a nice change. And I knew it was the sensible, practical course, but somehow it depressed me to think of Sally being sensible and practical. It felt too much like growing up, a thing we'd both been putting off.

Suddenly I felt bereft. Jacko, Frida, Sally . . . 'When will you go?'

'At Easter. I'm committed to these adult classes till then. I've already spoken to a college near home,' she went on. 'I've left it a bit late, but they're going to contact me about an interview.'

I spent the next hour in a sort of shell-shocked daze, while Sally and Rosie did most of the nattering. In fact I left them to natter while I went and made some pasta with tomato sauce and mozzarella. We were washing this down with robust Tesco's red when Rosie suddenly said, 'Gosh, I nearly forgot!'

'What?' I said.

'Helicopter dumped Nina!'

My heart did a perfect backflip. 'Oh, really?' I said casually, avoiding Sally's eye. 'When was that, then?'

'Just after she got back from Aspen, but Suzanne only found out the other day. Nina's really convinced he's got someone else now. She can't accept that any bloke can just go off her. There has to be some poisonous slag of a Jezebel, enticing him away with her fiendish wiles.'

'Well, maybe there is a Jezebel,' Sally said deadpan.

'Yes, that's what Suzanne said. I mean, he'd hardly *tell* her—she'd go round and stick dog poo through the poor girl's letterbox or something. Mind you,' Rosie went on, 'the official line is that she dumped *him*. The other way round doesn't suit Nina's image.'

It was half eleven before Rosie left. Once she had, Sally said, 'Well, hallelujah. All hail to the queen of the jungle telegraph.' She gave me one of her shrewd looks. 'It's not just buzz, is it? You really like him.'

That depended on how you defined 'like'. If you counted total obsession, I suppose 'like' might do. I nodded. 'But I feel a bit bad now,' I confessed. 'Sometimes I'd look at him and think, yes, you're a smootharse *extraordinaire*, and all the time he was only telling the truth when he said it wasn't going anywhere with Nina.'

'Well, he took his time about it. Just watch yourself. I'd hate you to get hurt.' Less grudgingly she added, 'Still, at least you can dream of him tonight with a clear conscience.'

I had a nice little fantasy shaping up already. The car would break down on the way back and he'd phone the RAC, who'd say they couldn't come for at least four hours, so could we just sit tight and hang on . . .

'Why the hell didn't you tell me about this PGCE?' I said, as we went back to the dying fire.

'I was going to, but I knew you'd only say I was mad.'

'Only because it is such a shock—the thought of you turning into a proper, grown-up alien.'

'Harriet, it's about time I grew up. Tom's only got me. If I don't do my best for him . . .' There was suddenly a crack in her voice. She looked at me, her eyes misting. 'What if something happened to me?'

I was appalled. 'Nothing's going to happen to you!'

'It might! If it did, would you have him? Harriet, I need to know,' she went on, almost desperately. 'I know you love him, I haven't got any brothers or sisters, and Mum and Dad are too old and pernickety—what if he got taken into care?'

Suddenly I realised that this must have been on her mind for ages. 'Of course I'd have him! But nothing's going to happen to you!' I was about to add, 'You've written Steve off, haven't you?' but bit it back. I already knew the answer.

John arrived twenty minutes late the following afternoon. I'd known it'd feel different, seeing him this time, but I hadn't realised just how different. In fact it was a job not to charge straight at him, throw my arms round his neck and cry, 'Oh, thank you, thank you, for doing it at last.'

But it can't have shown, as he was disappointingly businesslike. 'Sorry, we're running a bit late,' he said, with a glance at his watch. He added a lopsided little smile, though, which was better than nothing.

I gave him one back. 'That's OK. I'm not in any rush.'

He gave me a brief up-and-down glance. If you're interested, I was wearing new grey flannel trousers of the smart-casual type, short black boots, and a black rollneck sweater of the casual-casual type.

I was giving him a once-over, too. He'd pinched my colour scheme. In fact, he was wearing exactly the same as that first day: dark grey jacket and lighter trousers. It seemed oddly apt, as if we were starting again. Back to 'Go', with ladders, but no snakes.

Someone was having a party; he'd had to park about ten houses down. Tara was in the front, trying not to look put out that I was coming.

'Are you all excited?' I asked, as he headed for the main road.

'Not particularly,' she said, with a shrug in her voice.

'Bloody miserable weather,' John grunted, switching on the wipers as a few drops of rain started to fall. It had gone really cold again.

'The weathermen have forecast snow,' I said.

'Expect a heatwave, then.'

'Where are you off to tomorrow?' I asked.

'Sofia.'

'What time's your flight?' Tara asked him.

'Twelve-ish.'

'Why didn't you book it for Monday morning?'

'I have a meeting first thing on Monday. Next question?'

It was a while before anybody spoke again, but once we'd hit the M3 Tara said, 'Is there an indoor pool at this place?'

'Probably,' he said. 'Why?'

'I'm a qualified lifeguard,' she said. 'I've got experience.'

Recalling what Jacko had said about her two whole days, I had to admire her nerve.

'And I've never done bar or restaurant stuff,' she went on.

'I wouldn't worry about that,' he said. 'I doubt you'll be seeing much of bars or restaurants.'

'Then what will I be doing?'

'Making beds, kitchen stuff . . .' he said casually.

'*Kitchen* stuff?' In the appalled silence that followed, I realised just how devious a devil he could be. Having let her think there was going to be some element of glamour, he was letting her down hard.

'But you don't have to go,' he went on. 'We can head back now and I'll tell them you've got the flu.'

'No,' she said quickly. 'I don't mind working in kitchens.'

After another five minutes' silence, I said, 'Which way are you going?'

'M3, A303,' he said. 'After that I'll have to consult my directions.'

'Haven't you been before?'

'No. Gisela hasn't been there long.'

'*Geez*ler?' Tara echoed. 'What sort of a name's that?'

'G-I-S-E-L-A,' he spelt. 'She's Swiss.'

There was a taken-aback silence. 'You mean *she's* the manager?'

'Yes.'

'I thought it was a bloke!'

'Really, Tara,' he tutted. 'That was a very sexist assumption.'

'I didn't mean that! I just assumed your *friend* was a bloke!'

So had I; I don't quite know why. But I realised at once that this had skewed Tara's ideas drastically. She'd been imagining someone like John, someone vaguely indulgent to a pretty eighteen-year-old.

'What's she like?' she asked, in a voice that said she already suspected the answer.

'A pretty tough cookie,' he said, in matter-of-fact tones. 'But I don't suppose you'll be seeing much of Gisela. You'll be under her underlings. Or her under-underlings.'

The traffic was relatively light; we were soon heading south in the dusk, the fields either side lightly frosted. John and I talked about general things; Tara sat in silence. We left the M3 and turned southwest, passing right by Stonehenge, just visible and looking creepy in the wintry dark. By contrast the inside of the car was luxurious, leather-scented warmth, but the atmosphere was something else.

Apprehension was coming off Tara like mist. Tension was also coming off John, partly, I guessed, because he felt bad for misleading her. Having turned onto a minor road he cursed as we approached about the third rural crossroads.

'Which road are we looking for?' I asked.

'The right one,' he said shortly.

'Which one's that?'

'I'll know it when I see it.'

Bloke-speak for 'I haven't a clue'. 'Why don't you give me the directions? You have *got* the directions?'

'Of course,' he said, even more shortly.

'Pass them over, then.'

'I can't, unless you want me to take my head off.'

I counted to ten. 'You mean you didn't write them down?'

'Only in my head.'

Typical. 'Then let's go back to that pub we passed and ask.'

'Look, I'll get us there,' he said, in that dogged tone men invariably use when they won't admit they're lost.

Tara gave an eyes-to-heaven tut. 'You're just like my dad.'

'Thank you, Tara,' he said drily.

'Well, you *are*,' she retorted. 'My mum always says, "Are you sure you know the way?" And my dad says, "Yes, stop fussing." And then he drives round in circles, and Mum says, "For heaven's sake let's stop and ask," but Dad never will. So they always end up half an hour late and not speaking.'

'Well, thank you for that,' he said. 'And that's enough from you in the back,' he added, over his shoulder.

'I didn't say a word!'

'No, but you do a good snort.'

I probably had, trying not to crack up. 'May I make a suggestion?' I said. 'I don't mind asking the way, so why don't you let me drive? You could pretend you're foreign, if you like.'

This produced a snort from Tara.

'Thanks. I don't think that'll be necessary,' John said. And to give him credit, he sounded as if he were at least thinking about cracking his face.

Then he gave an exasperated little 'tut'. 'Bloody thing,' he muttered, adjusting his rearview mirror. I looked up. And as he skewed it, I realised exactly what he was up to. As our lines of vision converged for a second, he shot me a tiny, conspiratorial wink.

This was quite enough to warm me up nicely for the next few miles, I can tell you. In fact, I was well into a thorough reworking of that breakdown fantasy, when, about ten minutes later, we passed a sign to the Haddon Hall Hotel and Country Club. Then, suddenly, round a bend, there it was, set in lawns, lit up in all its glory. It was the kind of house the nineteenth Earl of Muchacre might have built in 1683, after his countess had put her foot down. She didn't care if the castle had been in his family since William the Conqueror, it was freezing cold. She wanted a flash new place with forty bedrooms and an orangery. So the earl had torn down the castle, whacked up the house, and 250 years later the twenty-third earl had had to flog it to pay death duties.

It was freezing as we walked from the car park, but inside it looked and felt like the sort of place I'd choose if anyone offered me a stately home. No gilt or grandeur, just supreme comfort with unobtrusive minions to peel your grapes. As we headed for reception I saw discreet signs to the Pool and Fitness Suite, the Trellis restaurant, the ballroom.

'Is Gisela Koch around?' John asked at the desk. 'John Mackenzie.'

'Oh, yes,' the girl smiled. 'One moment.'

We were shown into an office near reception and if I'd had a smile on, it might have frozen. Around thirty-three or -four, Gisela reminded me most horribly of Nina: little and dark with sleek hair. Her eyes swept over you in an assessing instant. Her manner was spiky and staccato, like the peckier kind of bird. 'John, good to see you,' she said briskly, with more than a slight accent. To me she said, 'And you are—?'

'Harriet. How do you do?'

'Hello. And you must be Tara.' Her eyes darted over her rapidly. 'You may as well start now—they are short in housekeeping. Two are sick with flu, or say they are. It is very convenient, flu, when they have been partying. Someone will take you to Sue, who looks after housekeeping. We can sort out your paperwork tomorrow. Any questions?'

If Tara was fazed, it showed only a moment. 'I was wondering if you needed anyone at the pool,' she said. 'I'm a qualified lifeguard.'

After another assessing sweep, Gisela said, 'I have pool attendants. In any case, you would not be right.'

Tara was not so easily put down. 'Why not?'

'My dear,' she said, with the edge of sarcasm I associated with a certain kind of teacher, 'most of my pool customers are middle-aged women with money, cellulite and not enough to do. They don't want someone like you showing them up. They like big brown muscles to feed their fantasies.'

She picked up a phone on her desk. 'Michelle, Tara Jacques is coming. Please ask Maria to show her to her room, and take her to Sue.'

She then looked at Tara. 'If you go back to the office behind the front desk, Maria will see you there.'

My heart went out to Tara. She had the air of a condemned prisoner who's only just realised it isn't a bad dream. 'Good luck,' I said.

John patted her shoulder. 'I'll give you a call in a day or two.'

'OK. Thanks.' Without even looking at either of us, she exited. The door shut behind her. Gisela glanced at John.

'Well?' she said. 'Too nasty? Not nasty enough?'

I was shattered. Her whole demeanour had changed. She suddenly had the mischievous look of someone who'd be a really good laugh.

I wasn't quite sure I liked it.

I felt even more uncertain when I saw the way John's demeanour had suddenly changed, too. He was quietly cracking up. 'Christ, Gisela—you nearly had even me messing my pants.'

She laughed a rich, throaty laugh, and went up and kissed him. 'Poor girl,' she said. 'But don't worry, nobody will eat her.'

She motioned us to sit down. There were two easy chairs near the desk, which she perched on, showing elegant legs. 'In fact, Sue will be glad of extra hands,' she said. 'We have a conference starting tomorrow night. There will be plenty for her to do. After three days she will be very expert in cleaning toilets.'

'I don't suppose she's ever cleaned a toilet in her life,' I said.

'She will learn. It is very good for kids to work, I think. They get real very fast.' Then she turned to John. 'It's been too long,' she said, in playfully accusing tones. 'And then you only call me because you want something. I think I will go in a big sulk.' But she smiled.

Ever felt like a gooseberry? 'I'll go and have a wander around,' I said, rising to my feet. 'I'd like to see it properly while I'm here.'

'Help yourself.' Gisela gave me a friendly smile. 'I can find someone to show you, if you like.'

'No, it's fine.'

John didn't object, either. He even looked as if he'd been hoping I'd do exactly this, damn him. 'Don't get lost,' he said, glancing at his watch. 'I thought we'd hit the road in about half an hour.'

'Fine,' I said brightly.

So much for breakdown fantasies, then. Well, it served me right. Had they had a thing going, or what? An old flame? Even if she was an ancient ember, you didn't have to blow very hard to turn old embers into flames. Half an hour should certainly do it.

Heading back to the lounge area, I found a squashy armchair near the fire and a colour supplement. It was full of food and cookery, eg 'A perfect Sunday roast with a difference', followed by, 'Stuff the calories for once: sticky winter puds to die for'.

Suddenly I was starving. To hell with it, I would order something to eat. Tea and sandwiches would take my mind off embers. I looked around for someone to order from and saw John, heading briskly from Gisela's office.

'Ready to go?' he asked.

It was a relief to see no visible smirks, or any other signs that might indicate urgent 'other business' transacted across desks. 'More or less, but I was just thinking about ordering some tea.'

'If you're hungry we can stop at the services,' he said crisply.

About to object, I bit it back. He didn't want to hang about. He probably had things to do before tomorrow.

It was bitterly cold outside. 'So much for your heatwave,' I said, as we got back in the car. There was a film of ice on his windscreen already.

We sat for a minute waiting for it to melt. 'I have to hand it to Tara,' he said. 'She's got balls. Arguing the toss like that about lifeguards.'

'Especially as she only lifeguarded for two days in her life.'

Having explained that I went on, 'But Gisela was right: work makes you get real. And I think Tara could do with some getting-real time.' I paused. 'I felt sorry for her, though.'

'How d'you think I felt?' he said, setting off into the road. 'Like when I once took the dog to the kennels. He thought he was heading for one of those mega-walks you have to drive to.'

'Aah. Poor old Horace.'

'It wasn't Horace. It was Marmaduke, now buried in the garden. The old man planted a tree on top but it died. He said it was probably Marmaduke's ghost peeing on it.'

I laughed rather louder than I intended, partly to cover a rumble in my stomach. 'I thought Gisela might have offered us a sandwich or something,' I said, as another empty-pang seized my stomach.

'She did, but I said we should hit the road.'

'You might have asked me first,' I said, a tad irritably. 'I'm starving, and it's miles to the services.'

'We might pass a pub. Grab a baked potato or something.'

'Let's find one, then. That one we passed on the way, where you wouldn't stop and ask. The Royal Oak or something. It wasn't far.' I peered into night. 'Is this the way we came? It doesn't look very familiar.'

'Gisela gave me another set of directions,' he said. 'Quicker than even the last lot should have been if I hadn't cocked up.'

I wasn't so sure about that. The route he was taking seemed to be getting ever more minor. 'It looks to me as if we're getting buried in the country.'

'Don't fret,' he soothed. 'It's all under control.'

I fought an increasing desire to thump him. Men who tell me not to fret in that tone invariably bring out my violent side.

'I thought you wanted me to drive, anyway,' I said.

'I'll get you something to eat first. There's bound to be some baked-potato joint soon. Then I can lie back and snore with a clear conscience.'

'You'd better not.'

'You can talk,' he said. 'I can hear your stomach from here.'

'What the hell do you expect? Why didn't you let me order some tea?'

'Tea's a waste of time. We need proper food.'

'Whoa, that looks like a pub, coming up on the left,' I said. 'Quick, pull in.'

He slowed down. 'Doesn't look very brilliant,' he pronounced, speeding up again right past a sign I could have sworn said BAR FOOD.

'Why didn't you stop?' God, he was impossible. I sat fuming, my stomach doing empty-pangs every three seconds. 'And it's snowing now,' I said crossly, as a couple of little flakes hit the screen.

'It won't come to anything.'

'I bet it will. We'll get buried in a drift down some bumpkin lane and die of hypothermia.' I was too hungry even to see the possibilities of getting buried down lanes, which goes to show how famished I was.

A minute later he slowed down past a sign that said *The Hen and Peacock, next left, half a mile*. He turned to me and raised an eyebrow. 'Shall we give it a go?'

'We could,' I said acidly. 'But it might be simpler to nick a couple of frozen turnips from a field.'

He turned down the kind of rural road you tend to find blocked with sheep in the daytime. But at least the Hen and Peacock looked promising. It was one of those quaint old places you see on postcards: rambling, with crookedy timbers and funny little windows—and, when we made it to the entrance, a sign showing a couple of stars, awarded by the Pub Grub guide.

Feeling more mellow already, I pushed the door open. It was a larger than usual saloon bar, with comfortable seating, lots of blackened oak beams and a fire. Through one of those low timbered doorways was the restaurant area, with maybe a dozen tables. 'It looks pretty full,' I said dubiously, as lovely foody smells wafted out.

'No harm trying,' he said, as a white-shirted boy came up.

'Have you got a table?' I asked.

'Er, have you booked?'

Bugger it, I thought.

'Yes,' John said. 'Mackenzie. Table for two.'

'Oh, yes, sir. This way.'

I turned disbelieving eyes on Mackenzie.

'Gotcha,' he said. 'Gisela recommended it.'

It's weird, that in the space of fifteen minutes you can go from wanting to thump somebody to wanting to kiss them. When you've been wanting to kiss them for weeks previously the effect is naturally multiplied by forty-seven and you think about having their babies, too.

But I settled for laughing. 'Bastard,' I added in a whisper, as we followed the boy to our table. Next to a curtained little window, it was cosy and secluded. We sat opposite each other, the boy lit a candle, dished out menus and departed.

Already checking the starters, I almost started salivating. 'Coquilles St Jacques! God, I *love* Coquilles St Jacques—I haven't had it in ages . . .'

The boy came back for drinks orders. 'I'll drive the rest of the way,' I offered. 'I'm sure you could do with a couple of glasses of something.'

He shook his head. 'I need a clear head tomorrow.'

Accompanied by a large glass of house white for me and a beer for him, we ordered. On a seafood kick, I added linguini with mussels and prawns to my coquilles; he went for some fishy pâté thing and local venison. After that came the really heady bit: conversation and delicious, candlelit eye contact, while that wine shot straight to my head.

Not that my head could be described as entirely clear anyway; it was stuffed to the gunwales with fluffy little pink clouds. Why had I ever doubted him? Not that I ever really had, of course. All that stuff about Mars bars was just dreadful cynicism from people with no romance or poetry in their souls . . .

By the time the main course was cleared away I was in that delicious state that comes only from alcohol, lovely food and reciprocal vibes you could drown in. It wasn't just candlelight putting a glint in those greeny-blue eyes.

As we were looking at pudding menus, I became aware of the couple at the table behind John talking to the waiter while he topped up their coffee. 'I told him,' the woman was saying. 'Those people at the Met Office aren't all idiots.'

'It won't be much,' the man scoffed.

'Can I have that in writing? Just look at it!'

Realising what they were on about, I drew back the little curtain and glanced outside. 'Look,' I said to John. 'It's really snowing now.' Large flakes were falling softly, the ground outside already white.

'If it carries on like this, our lane'll be blocked,' the woman said.

The boy said, 'You could always stay here. Two rooms upstairs are going begging.'

'No chance,' the man said. 'We've got two geriatric dogs and a geriatric mother. They'll all be doing puddles on the floor.'

John and I both chuckled quietly. Nodding at the window, he said, 'Maybe you were right about bumpkin-lane drifts. I hope you've got your thermals on.'

'You could keep the engine on,' I pointed out. 'And the heater.'

'Profligate waste of fossil fuel,' he tutted. 'The heater wouldn't do you much good anyway. Not while you're outside, pushing.'

I stifled a cackle and threw my napkin at him, he ducked, and it landed on the back of the man's head, behind him.

'Sorry,' John said apologetically. 'My friend's getting violent.'

'We'd better push off, then,' the man replied, in genial tones. 'Before she starts with plates and glasses.'

They left shortly afterwards, and half an hour after that John asked for the bill.

'Mind how you go,' the waiter said, as we left.

We stepped out into a hushed winter wonderland. The ground was carpeted white. The trees and shrubs were softly iced, every leaf laden. An old-fashioned street lamp stood near the door, its light making every tiny crystal sparkle like diamonds on white velvet. It was still snowing but not as hard. The flakes were drifting down in a gentle hush.

I had to stop and take it in. 'Don't you just love it?'

'Brings out the kid in you,' he agreed.

'Makes me think of Father Christmas.'

'Makes me think of sledging.'

'And snowmen.'

As we approached the car park at the side, I thought of snowballs, too. Walking just behind him, I scooped up a handful and moulded it rapidly. 'John?' I called sweetly.

It was a brilliant shot, she said modestly. I slung it while he was still turning and his reactions weren't quite fast enough. It hit him on the side of his neck, half of it going down the collar of his shirt.

'Right,' he said, in mock-mad tones. 'This is war.'

We might have been back in the playground. There was ducking and darting behind cars and rapid rearming from snowy bonnets. I remember my taunt of 'Rubbish!' as he missed me by a whisker. I remember him saying, 'Right, I'm playing dirty now . . .' I remember finding myself cornered and shrieking as he grabbed me from behind. Most of all, I remember the exact moment when I stopped pretending to fight, his grip relaxing as I turned round. There were snowflakes on his hair. I looked at him, and he looked at me, and suddenly neither of us was laughing any more. In a rough-soft voice he said, 'Do you surrender?'

What a question.

I felt my heart rate rise as he brushed a snowflake from my cheek. I remember exactly how it felt: the quivering electricity in his fingertips.

We came together like two irresistible forces held apart for too long. To be frank, it was the kind of kiss that used to make poor old Dorothy go all embarrassed and say she was going to write to the BBC about all the smut and filth on the television. We devoured each other as if our lives depended on it.

I don't know when I'd ever felt such an instant explosion of desire. It welled up in me like a hot volcano, unstoppable.

I suppose it was a couple of minutes before we came up for air. He drew back a fraction. 'That'll teach you to play dirty.'

There was laughter in his voice, but only 10 per cent. The rest was the rough echoes of his own volcano. And I thought, now what?

Ten yards away a car was passing tentatively down the lane, snowflakes fluttering in its headlights. Half turning away from him, I said lightly, 'I hope you've had a session at the skid pan.'

'Afraid not,' he mused, his breath warm on my hair. 'I can never remember whether you're supposed to drive into a skid or out of it.'

About to say *liar*, I stopped. Suddenly I knew exactly where he was heading. 'In that case, maybe I'll stay here,' I said, in supposed-to-be-casual tones. 'I don't want to end up in a ditch.'

'But it's all right if I do, is that what you're saying?'

'I suppose I might feel a bit bad,' I conceded. 'When they're digging you out tomorrow morning, half dead from hypothermia, while I've been snuggled up nice and warm all night.'

I was still half turned away from him. It seemed easier like that. I mean, I wasn't the type to come straight out with it, eg, *'Can we just stop messing about and get a room?'*

Neither was he, evidently. 'Now you've really put the wind up me. Given the treacherous state of the roads, do you think I should risk it?'

'Maybe not,' I said unsteadily. 'Perhaps we should do the sensible, prudent thing.'

'I think it might be wise.' As he brushed his lips against my hair, I felt a tiny vibration of suppressed laughter. 'Shall we go back inside?'

When we went up to the bar and John asked the landlord whether we might have a room, he just said very wise, sir, the roads'd be terrible. Would we mind waiting ten minutes while he checked with Annie, though? She might not have got fresh sheets on after the last lot. Would we care for a nightcap while we waited?

I can't even remember what we talked about, sitting by the fire with a couple of cognacs. Tara, I suppose, while wondering how the hell Annie could take so long with those sheets.

Eventually the landlord called that we could go up, second on the left at the top of the stairs. Annie was still there, smoothing a candlewick bedspread, telling us anxiously that she was sorry the bathroom was a bit old-fashioned, but they were having the rooms refurbished in the spring. We could have breakfast any time after seven, just give her a shout. Oh Lord, she'd forgotten the bits and pieces for the tea and coffee tray—

John said, no, everything was fine, thank you. I smiled nicely and she looked relieved and said, well, good night, then—oh Lord, she'd forgotten to check the clock radio—it had been playing up—click—yes, it was working, thank heaven—well, good night, then.

And she shut the door.

From opposite sides of a small double bed, draped in pink candlewick, John and I looked at each other. Quite frankly I'm surprised neither of us died on the spot from spontaneous combustion.

'I thought she'd never go,' he said.

Eight

ALAS FOR ANNIE'S nice smooth candlewick.

There was a lot of unseemly haste, I'm afraid, as garments were flung aside, and much of it was from me. I dare say I was behaving like a desperate old slapper but it had been so long, a caveman quickie would have gone down fine. Still, as it didn't say in the old *Girl Guides' Handbook*, when a man not only has an expert knowledge of erogenous zones, but also possesses the equipment and stamina for a really efficient ravishing, a girl should count herself lucky and enjoy it.

By the time he thought I'd suffered enough, I think I made the kind of noises that used to cause Dorothy to switch to the snooker on BBC2. Right afterwards he followed suit, and all I heard for a bit after that was the mutual thumping of hearts.

We were still conjoined, as it were, when he rolled onto his side. I like that. I don't care for prompt withdrawal once business is transacted, as if you were a bloody cash machine. As we lay entwined, still drifting back to planet earth, I gave him an intimate little squeeze.

He kissed my forehead. 'Was that a "hi" or a wake-up call?'

'Just a "hi". I don't expect miracles.'

He followed the kiss with another. 'Give me half an hour.'

That was a laugh. I could tell that he was drifting off already, not that I minded. I mean, I'm not greedy. I don't expect a repeat performance inside a few hours. Some cuddle-up talk would have been nice, though. I might even have got round to Nina-confessions.

'Speaking of wake-up calls . . .' Rousing himself briefly he set the alarm for six thirty, which made me wince, but twelve o'clock flights meant ten thirty check-ins and he had to get home, pack . . .

Sliding back under the covers, he wrapped his arms round me. 'I'm falling asleep already,' he murmured. 'Lousy manners.'

'It's all right. Go to sleep.'

Moments later, he had done so. I lay for a while, wondering when I'd last felt so warmly replete, so like the moggy who'd got the cream. Certain he was asleep, I ran my fingers down over his chest and stomach. I don't know why his mother had said rude things about 'a bit of a tummy'. Perhaps it wasn't quite reinforced concrete, but who wanted to snuggle up to building works?

I suppose I drifted off soon afterwards. The next thing I knew was suddenly finding myself awake in the dark. First I wondered where the hell I was, and when I remembered I thought I must be dreaming.

He was still sleeping like the dead. I raised my head and looked at the clock. It said 4:53. lifting myself from his arm, I tiptoed starkers over to the window and drew the curtain aside. There was condensation on the pane, so I eased the sash half open.

The room faced onto the garden. It had stopped snowing. There must have been security lights on as the garden was all lit up, sparkling white and silent. The snow on the lawn was pristine. Then I saw what had alerted the security lights. From under a hedge to the side, a fox padded across the lawn. Probably from instinct, it looked up. 'Hi,' I whispered. 'How's it going?'

'I thought you were asleep!' Turning round I saw him propped on an elbow, watching me.

'I was.'

'I hope you're not fraternising with burglars,' said a voice behind me.

With the snowy light from outside, I could see him well enough, propped on an elbow, watching me. 'There's a fox in the garden,' I explained. Then I felt daft for talking to it, and slightly self-conscious to be scrutinised in my full-frontal glory, so I turned back to the garden, where the fox was sniffing around a wooden bench. 'It's lovely outside,' I said. 'Come and look.'

'I've got a lovely view from here, thank you.'

All right, it was corny, but I liked it.

'Come back to bed,' he said.

'In a minute. I'm watching the fox.'

I heard the bed creak as he got out. He came to stand right behind me, his arms stealing round my waist. 'Shut that window,' he said.

'Certainly not. It'll all be melted by morning.'

'You're getting cold.'

I was, a bit. 'No, I'm not.'

'You are.' He ran his hands down for an exploratory stroke. 'You've got goose pimples on your bottom.'

After all that exfoliating, too. 'I have not!'

'Yes, you have.' Then he traced a lazy, upward curve. 'Dear me, what have we here?' he tutted. 'A pair of frozen raspberries?'

Suppressing a violent giggle, I felt the stirrings of another volcano.

Particularly when he went on, in softly wicked tones, 'I'd better warm them up before they get frostbite.'

Well, if you insist . . .

During the next twenty seconds, as he applied delicate first aid, I felt as if the bones had been filleted right out of my legs. There was an armchair by the window, with a back at just the right height. I will say no more, except that I got my caveman quickie after all. And believe me, no Cavewoman Slapper of the Year ever enjoyed it more.

'You'll be fit for nothing tomorrow,' I murmured as we cuddled up again under the covers.

He chuckled quietly. 'A couple of Shredded Wheat'll soon sort me out,' he said, and dropped a kiss on my hair.

And that was it: I was gone.

When I awoke it was light. I sat up in a panic, saw 8:47 on the clock and an empty pillow beside me. Then I saw the note.

'You were flat out—I didn't like to wake you. A taxi is coming at 9.45 to take you home. Annie will bring up breakfast at 9.15 if you haven't woken up by then. I'll call you from Sofia. John.'

There was a PS, too. 'Two things were lovely last night, but one of them was lovelier. And it doesn't melt by morning.'

Possibly the best start to a Sunday morning I'd ever had.

By the time the taxi dropped me off at home the snow had disappeared altogether. Sally too came as a bit of a dampener.

'Trust you to fire the first shot,' she said, when I gave her the details. 'A come-and-get-me tactic if ever there was one.'

Her less than fizzy tone rather took the edge off the telling. About to have a go at her on the subject of miserable cows, etc, I bit it back. If I were her, I don't suppose I'd be fizzing on my behalf, either.

'I could go to the deli,' I offered. 'Get some ciabatta and fresh pasta.'

Her face brightened. The only thing that ever brightened it these days was food. 'Brilliant. We've got some sauce Napolitana.'

So I wound her rainbow scarf round my neck and headed for the deli.

Which is where I began this whole saga. I almost collided with Rosie, who, if you remember, was on her way to see us, but had stopped at the deli for some of their tomato salad. She was coming to pass on the latest bit of gossip: Nina had put a private dick onto John. So I sort of confessed, if you remember, and she said Nina was going to kill me, and we ended up in the Drunken Dragon.

'I can't believe you didn't tell me,' she said for the fourth time, over a glass of Pinot Noir. She sounded so hurt, I felt really bad.

'I didn't even tell Jacko,' I pointed out. 'He doesn't have a clue, either.'

This seemed to mollify her. 'I wonder if this dick realises John's away till Thursday? He might be watching his flat for nothing. Are you sure nobody was tailing you on Saturday?'

I'd been thinking of that ever since she'd told me. 'I'm sure we'd have noticed.' Would we, though? Would anybody? 'What the hell's the point, anyway? I could just about understand her having him spied on *before* he dumped her, but afterwards?'

'That's what I thought, but Suzanne said that's Nina for you. He said there was nobody else; she knew there must be. She's got to prove herself right. What on earth will you do if he catches you? Shows Nina a shot of the pair of you together?'

Naturally I'd already thought of that. I'd been thinking of nothing else for the past twenty minutes. 'Then I'll go and see her.'

Rosie's face was suddenly horrified. 'If you tell her I told you about Stuart, Suzanne'll go mad! Nina'll kill *her*!'

'Rosie, calm down! I could say I found out ages ago. Bumped into a friend of Stuart's or something. In any case, Stuart's got sod all to do with it. I'd never have got involved just to get my own back. Nothing really happened till after John had dumped her, remember?'

'Yes, but she's going to think he dumped her for you.'

'It's just tough,' I said, draining my glass. 'Come on, Sally'll be wondering where on earth her lunch is.'

This latest news perked Sally up, at least. 'I wouldn't even wait for the photos,' she said. 'I'd tell Nina now. Serve her right.'

After lunch I phoned Tara's mother, told her how it had gone. Angela Jacques sounded wearily resigned. 'I dare say it'll do her good.'

'Will you ring her?' I asked.

'Maybe I'll leave it a bit. We've run after her far too much. It won't do any harm for her to think we're not tearing our hair out.'

John phoned a couple of hours later, and I tried not to sound as if I'd been dying to hear from him. 'You should have woken me,' I chided.

'I didn't have the heart. You were curled up like a warm puppy.'

It was enough to make me go gooey again. 'How was your flight?'

'No delays, at least. I've got to get stuck into some work now.' He paused. 'I'm going to be really tied up for the next few days but if I don't catch you before, I'll ring you on Thursday night, all right?'

'All right.'

In a softer voice he said, 'I have to go. Take care.'

'You, too.'

No way could I have mentioned the tail. That would have meant the whole Nina bit, and how on earth could I do that over the phone?

It started snowing again that night. I watched little flakes drift onto the pavement and thought I'd never feel quite the same about snow again. It was still there next morning, only about an inch, but enough to lighten the grey. I was positively overflowing with feel-good all day.

At lunchtime I switched my mobile on and found a message from Helen: 'I have some news—I'll ring you later.'

Realising that I hadn't given her a thought for days, I called her.

'I thought you'd like to know, I'm not pregnant after all.'

If it had been me, I don't think I could have been more relieved.

'It was probably stress,' she went on. 'And I am relieved really, but I can't help feeling a bit sad.' She paused. 'But I might just have another "baby" soon. I'm thinking of starting that catering business, after all. Felicity's got some friends who want a silver wedding party done on the fairly cheap. Only twenty people. She said why didn't I give it a go?'

This was the second-best news I'd heard all month. 'Go for it, then. You're a brilliant cook. Have you phoned your demon lover yet?'

'No, but I'm thinking about it,' she said sheepishly.

'Then do it!'

I didn't hear from John that day, but on Tuesday he left a message. 'It's pretty hectic. I might not be back until Friday now, but I'll call on Thursday anyway. I've failed to reach Tara. If you get hold of her, say hi for me.' More softly he added, 'Take care. Bye.'

Later that evening Dad rang. He and Kathy were landing at Heathrow on Thursday. I hadn't forgotten about Saturday night, had I?

On Wednesday evening I tried phoning Tara but there was no reply till a quarter to ten. 'How's it going?' I asked brightly.

'OK, I suppose. Fine,' she added quickly.

'Have you made friends?'

'Not what I'd call friends. Most of them live out, anyway.'

I got the impression she was pathetically glad to talk to anyone, but trying to pretend she wasn't. 'What's your room like?'

'OK.'

Can we have another adjective? I thought. 'Titchy, I expect.'

'Yes, but I wasn't expecting much else.'

Suddenly I thought I heard a muffled sob. It appalled me, but then I thought I'd imagined it, because she was going on, in a reasonably normal voice, 'Do you know I have to make beds? With sheets and blankets, I mean. I've only ever had a duvet.' Now I knew I wasn't imagining it; her voice was cracking. 'The under-housekeeper had such a go at me, she made me do them all again . . .'

Feeling her fighting a river of tears, my heart went out to her. Was this breaking point at last? Delicately, feeling my way, I said, 'Tara, you don't have to stay. Not if you really hate it.'

'I can't leave!' she sobbed. 'What'll John say if I let his friend down?'

How could I tell her the truth? 'He won't care,' I soothed, 'not if you really hate it.' Was this the time for a gentle strike? 'You don't really want to make beds, do you? Let alone clean loos . . . be bossed about . . .'

There were more sobs, unmuffled, this time. 'Where would I go?'

If the iron wasn't hot now . . . 'Home,' I said. 'Home's not really so bad, is it? I know school can be a pain but you'll be finished in the summer, and you'll have such a laugh at university . . .'

'I can't go home,' she wept.

'Why not? If it's Lee, your mum and dad won't say anything, I'm sure.'

'It's not him! It was never just him—I can't—' For a moment there was nothing but the sounds of rivers bursting their banks. 'Mum and Dad are going to kill me . . .'

I hung up twenty minutes later, feeling overwhelming relief, and phoned Angela Jacques. Then, over a large glass of wine at the kitchen table, I filled Sally in.

'She hardly did any work last term. She had something like seven essays outstanding; the school were saying that if she didn't get up to date over the Christmas holidays they wouldn't let her sit her A levels. But there was so much, she just didn't know where to start.'

'Well, I know the feeling,' Sally said.

'Me too. There was a parents' evening, but she didn't tell her folks. So the school wrote to them. She checked the mail every morning and grabbed the letter. It said if she didn't change her attitude soon they'd prefer her to leave. She didn't dare tell her folks, so when Lee said he was off to Leicester she tagged along.'

'So where have you left it?'

'Hang on, I haven't finished. That model agency she went to? It was some dodgy bloke with a camera, wanting her to get her kit off.'

Thinking back to her welling eyes in that restaurant, I felt for her all over again. John's straight talk must have been the last straw.

'No wonder she didn't tell you,' Sally said.

'I wouldn't have told us, either.'

'So where *have* you left it?'

'Her folks are going down on Saturday, to stay the night. They'll phone once they get there, and tell her they know what's been going on and it's all right. With a bit of luck she'll burst into tears, and they'll say they just happen to be there, so if she wants to grab her things . . .'

For the first time in ages, Sally wore a mischievous little smile. 'How many Brownie points does that make, then? You can phone John now and tell him smugly that you've sorted it.'

'Yes,' I said, glancing at my watch. 'But not now. It's one o'clock in the morning in Bulgaria.'

I tried John at Bulgarian lunchtime on Thursday, but all I got was his voicemail. I left a message anyway, giving the gist about Tara. Next I phoned Gisela and filled her in. She said she was glad that it was all sorted out.

I left work feeling like a diplomat who's just averted a Middle Eastern war. But then I got home.

I felt the atmosphere as soon as I opened the door: cold, crackling tension. 'Sally?' I called.

'In here.' She was in the sitting room. It was chilly; there was no fire. She was standing with Tom on her hip, and she was not alone.

He stood apart from her. Tall. Good-looking. Light brown hair streaked with blond. But not quite so full of himself as before.

'Oh,' I said. 'Hi, Steve.'

He had no time for the niceties. 'Were you in on this? Did you know she'd used me like some bloody sperm bank?'

Before I'd even drawn breath, Sally cut in like the avenging angel's sword. 'What the hell do you care? What was I to you but a quick, opportunistic shag?'

'I don't recall you complaining at the time!'

'No, and I'm not complaining now!' she flared. 'You could have been anybody passable, I just wanted a baby! You weren't the only one!'

Heaven help me, I thought. What the hell was going on? Apart from wounded vanity coming off Steve in waves, I mean.

'How many?' he demanded, hands on his hips.

To wounded vanity please add righteous affrontedness.

'It's none of your business!' Sally retorted.

I felt I had to do something. 'Look, Sally—'

'Harriet, please keep out of this. Steve was just going.'

'Like hell I am!' The waves were turning to bristles, but suddenly I realised that they were at least partly due to shock. 'You can't just tell me I might have fathered a child and then tell me to clear off!'

'Oh, can't I? Who says?'

There was a long, tense silence.

Steve was staring at Tom. 'He looks like me.'

'For God's sake, he doesn't look like anybody!'

'He does. I've seen pictures of myself at that age, haven't I?'

Tom started whimpering. Sally, shushing him, said, 'Steve, please, look what you're doing . . .'

'I have a right to know,' he said flatly. 'I want a blood test.'

'You don't have the right to anything!' she burst out. 'You were bloody married!'

'It was on the rocks! I want a blood test. I'm entitled to it. I'll go now but when I come back I want that test. I'll go to court if I have to.'

And he went. The front door banged behind him.

I looked at Sally. 'What the hell did you tell him that for?'

'He just turns up after fifteen months, assuming I'll be over the moon—he's been back three weeks!' she burst out. 'Three *weeks*! And you know why he came? He's going skiing tomorrow—he thought he'd pop in and see me! Pop *in*! Get another quick shag and a bed for the night, nice and handy for Heathrow!' And she burst into tears.

I suppose it was about two minutes later, while we were in the kitchen, with Sally still in floods and Tom coming out in sympathy, that my phone rang. Perfect timing. 'John, I really can't talk now,' I said, nipping into the hall. 'Tom's father just turned up—Sally's in a hell of a state. I'll call you later if I can—are you back home?'

'Yes, but don't worry—tomorrow'll do. And well done with Tara.'

'Thank God she's sorted,' I said, with feeling. 'I just wish I could sort Sally as easily. Look, I'm sorry, but I've got to go . . .'

I knew exactly why Sally had done it. He'd swanned in with a grin on his face, after months and months and months. After conveniently forgetting to tell her he had a wife. She'd wanted to wipe that grin off his face. Make him think he wasn't so bloody irresistible, just marginally more attractive than artificial insemination.

He'd turned up only ten minutes before I'd got home. She'd been stunned. She'd had Tom on her hip, but it hadn't even occurred to him that he was hers. He'd said, 'Whose is the sprog?'

That was when she'd said, 'He's mine.'

He'd looked at Sally and then at Tom; she'd seen his mind working back like a calculator. He'd said, 'For God's sake, don't tell me he's mine?'

That had cut her to the heart. Not for herself, but for poor little Tom. She'd retorted, 'I couldn't tell you, Steve. Probably not, but I couldn't give a toss who did the honours.'

And so it had gone on.

By the time we eventually got to bed, around midnight, I was getting seriously worried about Sally. Somewhere she'd still had that little dream tucked away. If and when he'd turned up, her heart would have given a leap, and she'd have known it wasn't just lust and opportunity, after all. As it was, she'd been faced with a stranger she'd once had sex with on a faraway beach, with stars like diamonds on black velvet and silvery phosphorescence in the sea. On a doorstep in Putney he was just another bloke.

I slept badly, and I knew from up-and-down creaks that she wasn't doing much better. I didn't see her before I went to work. I felt like a rag, except for the thought of speaking to John.

He called shortly after one. Having done with Sally and Tara, we got onto other matters.

'How are you fixed for tomorrow night?' he asked.

Saturday. *Oh, bum.*

'I'm afraid I can't do tonight,' he went on. 'I've got a long-standing dinner thing—if I back out feelings will be wounded.'

Swallowing my disappointment, I said, 'It's all right. I really ought to stay with Sally tonight—you'd think half a dozen vampires had been at her. But I can't do tomorrow night. My father's coming with his blushing bride. I've got to check her out for Mum and take notes. How many horns she's got, and so on.'

He chuckled. 'Good luck. I'll give you a call on Sunday morning. You're not tied up on Sunday, are you?'

'No.'

'Then I'll see you then.'

I couldn't wait.

In Kathy's honour I tidied up, vacuumed and dusted, lit a fire in the sitting room, put tonics and wine in the fridge, and nibbles in little dishes.

By the time the doorbell went, at two minutes to six, I was sick with apprehension. I opened the door with my split-arse smile glued on, and it fell straight off again. Was this the parent I'd last seen five months ago? What the hell had she done to him?

It wasn't just the tan. He'd filled out. He was even standing up straighter. He'd lost that almost apologetic, lanky stoop.

'This is Kathy,' he said, with loving pride.

With one glance I knew she was right for him. During the next hour, over drinks and nibbles, I made notes for Mum. Fifty-four, which wasn't a guess, as she told me she'd taken early retirement last year at fifty-three. Quietly well dressed, attractive, looking younger than her age (I was beginning to wonder whether Mum would go off her after all) with a quiet sense of humour. She'd been a history teacher (I could just hear Mum saying, 'Well, no wonder') and had three children, all grown-up. Her husband had left her when they were six, eight and eleven, yes, it had been a bit of a struggle. But they'd all turned out well.

Best of all, though I wouldn't tell Mum this, she looked at Dad in the way Mum looked at Bill. With that quick, serene, just-us happiness that only lovers use when they know they've hit the big one.

As for Dad, well, I could only think, 'He's in love.' Bless him.

I phoned Mum when I got back after dinner. She said thank God for that, and I went to bed thinking ditto, one major worry off the list. I just wished I could feel as happy about Sally. She was thinking the fun was over for ever; she needed something to look forward to.

'We'll go on holiday in the summer,' I said to her, over breakfast. 'Somewhere nice. You, me and Tom.'

She stared at me. 'What about your trip?'

'I'm not sure I want to do backpacking and staying in grotty hostels any more. We could go to Greece. Think how Tom'd love the sea.'

'He'd get burnt,' she said flatly. 'It'd be far too hot for him. Anyway, I wouldn't be able to afford it. And if you were thinking of paying, thank you very much, but no way. I just hate sponging.'

I had a good mind to book something anyway and tell her when it was too late to cancel. It wasn't noble self-sacrifice when I said I'd gone off the thought of my trip, either, I *didn't* want to do the overgrown student bit any more. Above all, I didn't want to do it alone.

'Anyway, what about John?' she asked, a minute later. 'You might want to go away with him.'

Sometimes I thought Sally was telepathic.

'Wasn't he supposed to phone today?' she went on.

Already tingling with anticipation, I tried to look as if I wasn't. 'Yes, but he won't yet, will he?' It was barely half past nine.

When the phone actually rang, at twenty past eleven, I tried not to swoop on it like a gannet. 'Hello?'

'Harriet, it's me.'

'Oh, hi, Rosie,' I said, trying not to sound disappointed.

'I had to ring you, I've just been talking to Suzanne. She was at Nina's last night—she's got the photos. From the private dick.'

'Don't tell me he caught us last weekend?'

'It's not you.'

One of those flying jellies hit me, but this time it was a killer. A cold green lump, right in the guts.

'I'm really sorry, but I thought you ought to know,' she went on. 'It was Thursday or Friday night, Suzanne said. There are at least four shots, and it's obviously not his granny.'

I felt sick.

'Harriet? Are you OK?' Rosie asked anxiously.

'More or less,' I lied.

'Are you sure? I thought you really liked him!'

My throat felt like cat litter. 'Look, it's not a massive big thing. OK, the other night was nice, but I don't have any claim on him.'

'Thank God for that. I'm not sure I'd be OK, though. I think I'd be in a bit of a state. Nina was in a right old state, according to Suzanne. She thought it was going to be dopey blonde, remember?'

As if I cared who it was.

'But it wasn't her at all. Still blonde, though. Looking up at him all sweetly adoring. Suzanne said they were pretty good shots. They were on their way from some bar to some restaurant.'

That jelly had turned into a cold green snake, winding itself round my guts. 'Was that it? Drinks and dinner?'

With a wince in her voice she said, 'They went back to his place.'

'For how long?'

'Well, the bloke waited outside till five o'clock in the morning . . . You are upset, aren't you?' she went on anxiously.

'I'm not!' I even added a light little laugh. 'It's not as if I've been seeing him for six months.'

I thought she'd never get off the phone. When she eventually did, Sally said, 'For God's sake, *what*?'

It's weird how in the space of hours, roles can be reversed. Sally was now the comforter, while I felt like a lump of frozen sick.

She did her best, pointing at every reasonable explanation. 'He might have arranged to see her even before anything happened with you.'

'Yes, but couldn't he have stopped at dinner?'

'Maybe she was just staying the night.'

'Yes, and maybe Jacko just signed up for a *passementerie* class.'

'What the hell's *passementerie*?'

'Tassel-making,' I said, like a numb mechanism. 'As in soft furnishings.' I'd never have known this either, only Mum had been to just such a class, so she could make nice tiebacks for the bedroom curtains.

'He told you he was going out on Friday night, didn't he?' she pointed out. 'You didn't exactly throw a fit then.'

'It was a dinner party!' At least, that's what I thought he meant.

'Maybe it was a long-standing dinner *date*,' Sally said. 'An old friend who'd come up from the sticks, who'd have to stay the night.'

The more she came up with reasonable explanations, the more I couldn't accept them. Every shred of suspicion I'd ever held about him was suddenly combining into a tidal wave. 'Working late', the ease with which he could lie . . .

'Sally, Suzanne *saw* the photos. You can tell "old friend" stuff a mile off, and this was not "old friends".'

'OK, maybe it wasn't. Look, I'm not making excuses for him, but if you couldn't see him three nights in a row, you can hardly expect him to stay in watching the snooker. You had one night with him, not a joint mortgage. You've got to get this in proportion.'

'You don't get it, do you? It meant something to me, the other night!'

'Of course it did! You'd let yourself get obsessed with him, and you hadn't had sex in ages!'

'It wasn't just sex!'

That was when my phone rang. I stared at it, green snakes having babies in my stomach. 'I can't speak to him! I just can't, not yet . . .'

She picked it up. 'Yes, she's here,' she said, ignoring my frantic faces, and passed it over. 'It's Angela Jacques.'

Phew. I did my best to sound brightly normal. 'Hi, how did it go?'

They were in the car, on their way home; everything was sorted out. She went on for ages, and all the while I was expecting a call waiting that would send my stomach into knots.

There was no call waiting. He phoned twenty minutes after she'd hung up, by which time I knew exactly how I was going to play it.

'How did it go with your old man and his blushing bride?' he asked.

'Oh, fine,' I said brightly. With a glued-on smile it was actually quite easy. 'She was nice. I was so relieved, I got a little bit pissed.'

'I hope you're not still in bed with a hangover.'

'No, not that pissed. I've been up for ages.'

'How about some lunch, then? If I come in, say, forty minutes?'

On the other end of that Nokia, I could almost see his face, expectant. Much more clearly, though, I could see his face that night as he'd brushed a snowflake from my cheek. I could see it in that pink-candlewick room, just after Annie had left. Then I saw it as he'd been falling asleep, when I'd been thinking life couldn't get better than this.

And then I saw him doing it all over again, with someone else.

This was the best way. Nice and bright and casual. 'Actually, John, I don't think I can make lunch. I'm a bit tied up, after all. I'm sorry, but something came up.'

I knew he'd expected nothing like this. 'Dinner, then?'

'Probably not. I'm really sorry, but you know how it is.'

Keeping that smile glued on was harder by the second, but if I let it slip for an instant I knew I'd start dissolving, instead.

'I thought I knew how it was,' he said. 'But I'm not so sure any more. Why don't you tell me?'

I put a puzzled note into my voice. 'What d'you mean?'

'Oh, Harriet, come on. We've been here before, haven't we? Off, on—hot, cold—is it just me, or do you have thermostat trouble?'

I couldn't keep this up much longer. 'Look, John, I think we might have got our wires crossed. It was just a bit of fun. I had Tara's mother on the phone earlier, by the way—she said thank you so much for everything and be sure to let them know how much they owe you. Oh Lord, I still owe you for the hotel bill and my taxi fare, don't I?'

His reply was cool and sardonic. No melted chocolate at all. 'No, Harriet. Not this time. Have them on me.'

As he hung up, my glue was already dissolving. 'Bastard.' I slammed my phone on the table in tears. 'That'll teach you.'

Two minutes later I was blowing into the third soggy tissue. 'Sally, I *had* to. I had to make him think it meant sod all to me, too.'

'You don't *know* it meant sod all to him.'

'It didn't mean much, did it? Not if he could do it with someone else inside a week. You're the one who said "don't get hurt", remember?'

'I'm the last one you should listen to when it comes to relationships. Just look at me. A walking disaster area, with stretch marks.'

Something in her tone alerted me. Her eyes were welling up. 'Sally, what is it?'

She wiped them with her sleeve. 'Nothing.'

It obviously wasn't. Had I read her all wrong? 'It's not Steve, is it?'

'No. It's not Steve! How many times do I have to tell you?' But she forced a smile. 'I'm just being daft. End of subject, OK?'

I lay awake for ages that night, thinking of my own burnt boat, of his cool, sardonic voice saying, 'Have them on me.' Where had the melted chocolate gone, once I wasn't melting? Could he turn it on and off like a tap? I thought of that night, of how warm it had felt, how utterly right, as if every other man had been a mere rehearsal. I thought of the post-script on his note, and my heart contracted painfully. Maybe it was second nature to him to write stuff like that. A few little words, to make you go all warm and gooey. Maybe he'd even meant them at the time. It wouldn't surprise me. I knew I'd done the right thing. How could I have ever handled a relationship with someone like that?

All the following day, I tried to put him out of my head. I told myself it was just as Sally had said: obsession and frustration combined. On Tuesday I managed not to think about him for about 32 per cent of the day, but by the following evening I was a churning wreck again. 'I'm going to see Nina,' I told Sally when I got home.

'You're not going to tell her?'

'I have to! This whole business is eating away at me like some horrible parasite. I have to get it out in the open.'

I went at around seven thirty the following evening, hardly expecting her to be in. Her flat was about two and half miles away, a conversion from one of those huge houses that used to have butlers and fourteen under-housemaids flirting with the footman. There was an entryphone, of course; I pressed it.

'Nina, it's Harriet. Have you got half an hour?'

'Harriet!' There was a taken-aback pause.

'Nina, I have to see you. It's about John.'

'John?' This taken-abackness was different. 'What on earth would you know about—'

'If you let me in, I'll tell you.'

After a momentary silence she said, 'Take the lift to the fourth floor. It's on the left.' *Bzzzz* . . .

Inside it was quietly up-market, smelling faintly of polish. Her front door was substantial panelled wood and my first thought, when she opened it, was that she'd shrunk. She was wearing a soft grey robe thing, like a long dress, and her feet were bare, which was why she seemed to have shrunk. Her face, devoid of make-up, seemed almost vulnerable, which is a word I thought I'd never use in the same breath as 'Nina'.

With heels on, I towered over her. And not for the first time since I'd grown into my feet, I felt the advantage of height.

Still at the door, she was eyeing me with guarded suspicion. 'What's this about John? I finished with him a couple of weeks ago.'

'No, you didn't. He finished with you.' As she opened her mouth for outraged denial, I went on, 'Nina, it's no use. I know what happened. I came to tell you I was seeing him, too.'

I don't think I'll ever forget her face. Take two parts of shock mixed with one of disbelief and you wouldn't be far wrong.

'Can I come in?' I asked, before she got her voice back.

Wordlessly she showed me through. As Rosie had said, it was all blond wood and uncluttered cream. 'You can't have been seeing him,' she said in disbelieving tones, after I'd sat on a cream sofa without being asked. 'Where on earth would you have met him?'

I ignored the implication that someone like me just wouldn't meet someone like him. 'It was in the street, not long before Christmas—nothing really happened,' I added quickly, seeing stirrings of outrage. 'Not until I knew he'd finished with you.'

'I don't know how you've got the nerve to come and tell me this.'

'At least I waited till he'd dumped you,' I said. 'Which is more than you did with Stuart.'

I do recommend this tactic. Before your first bombshell's worn off, drop another. She actually had the grace to look awkward.

'I was wondering whether you ever found out about that,' she muttered. 'Who told you?'

'Does it matter? It was years ago. And before you ask, anything that happened with John had absolutely nothing to do with it.'

By now she was looking so much like someone wanting to crawl away and die, I almost felt sorry for her. But she soon recovered her composure. 'I gather Rosie's been busy.'

'Can we just leave Rosie out of it? Everything she told me was perfectly innocent. She hadn't a clue I'd been seeing him till the other day.'

Obviously about to argue, she bit it back. 'I'm not making excuses, but has it ever occurred to you that Stuart must have been attracted to me, or he'd never have played along?'

'I didn't come to talk ancient history,' I said, with an edge even I could hear. 'I came to talk about John, and the fact that whoever your spy caught him with wasn't the only one. God knows why, but I thought you might like to know you're not the only one who got hurt.'

After a tense silence she said, 'I never felt sure of him, not even at first. There's something about him women just can't resist. He's got a way of looking at you as if you're the only woman in the world.'

As if I needed telling. My throat constricted painfully. For the first time I felt some real empathy with her.

'But I'm over him now.' She looked up. 'Do you want to see the photos?'

I couldn't hold back the next question. 'Why on earth did you do it? What was the point, when it was over?'

'I had to know,' she said flatly. 'I knew he was lying and I had to know. I can't imagine what on earth he sees in her, except that she's looking up at him as if he's the only man in the universe.'

She disappeared for a moment, and came back with a brown A4 envelope. 'There are six. He had a good camera, I'll say that for him.'

All taken at night, they were sharply focused black and white shots. As I looked at the first, then the second and the third, my stomach felt as if it were being sucked into a vortex, like water down a sink.

I'd known I'd feel sick. I just hadn't realised how sick.

Nine

WHATEVER MY FACE BETRAYED, Nina noticed. Suddenly sharp, she said, 'Don't tell me you know her?'

My voice came out dry and weird. 'It's not him. It's not John.'

'Of course it's John! What on earth are you talking about?'

'It isn't! It's nothing like him!'

Some flash of realisation crossed her face.

'What?' I demanded.

'Where, exactly, did you meet him?'

I told her, more or less.

'Well, I should have guessed,' she said, in almost matter-of-fact tones. 'That was *John*-John. Not *John*.'

Now I felt I really was going mad. But before I could say anything it was her turn to drop a bombshell. '*J-O-H-N*-John. As in John Mackenzie. As opposed to *J-O-N*-Jon. As in Jonathan King.'

'All right, I'm not particularly proud of it,' she said, tucking her bare feet underneath her. 'But as I said, I never felt sure of Jon. I had to have another iron or two in the fire.'

An iron or *two*? 'You're not still seeing him? John Mackenzie, I mean?'

'God, no. I only saw him three times, maybe four—I really can't remember.' Suddenly her eyes narrowed, her expression sharpening like a lead pencil. 'You weren't thinking *he* finished it?'

My face evidently said it for me, because she gave an incredulous little laugh. 'He was quite sweet,' she added, in tones that suddenly made me want to slap her, 'but he really wasn't my type.'

My mouth was desiccated. 'I don't believe you.'

I'd expected a furious flash, but I should have known better. In almost pitying tones she said, 'Ask him, then.'

Until then I'd thought my green snakes could not possibly get any worse. I don't know when I'd so desperately wanted someone to be lying, but known they weren't.

Twisting the honeyed knife, she went on, 'He was very keen, I can tell you. I didn't like hurting his feelings but it would never have done.'

Like a masochist I asked, 'What was wrong with him?'

She shrugged again. 'He just wasn't quite up to the mark.'

He might do for me, in other words, but he wouldn't do for her. I remembered her once talking to me almost exactly like this in Home Economics, when I'd produced a reasonable cheese soufflé: 'Oh, well *done*, Harriet,' when she knew perfectly well hers was miles better.

Unable to take any more, I rose to my feet. 'I think I'd better go.'

'Well, if you must . . .'

I don't know why I bragged about height advantage, earlier. On the way to the door she managed to make me feel like that bog-roll dinosaur all over again. At the door she said sweetly, 'Do give my love to John.'

Slapping was too good for her. I wanted to ram her head down the loo and pour a bottle of Toilet Duck on top. That would have sorted her sodding silk curtain out.

Back home, Sally said everything a friend should say, eg, 'I *would* have shoved her head down the loo,' and 'Well, how were you to know? If it didn't occur to a cynic like me that she was seeing two at once . . .' This was followed by 'Come on, have some lasagne. It'll be all dried up.'

Since she'd actually slaved over it herself I tried, but it might have been cat litter. I said, 'I'm sorry, I'm just not hungry,' and poured myself another glass of wine, about the fourth since I'd got home.

'What did he look like?' Sally asked.

'Like any other good-looking bloke. But nothing like John.'

An edge of exasperation came into her voice. 'Why the hell don't you just phone him?'

'How can I?' I asked miserably. 'I'd have to tell him everything—what kind of devious, screwed-up bitch will he think I am? First I pretended I didn't even know her, then I've told him to sod off twice.'

After a minute Sally said, 'Are you sure it's just having to confess you can't handle? Nothing to do with him being one of Nina's rejects?'

'All right, it galls me. It sickens me. I mean, how the hell could he possibly not be "up to the mark"? What mark, for heaven's sake?'

'Look. she was just trying to piss you off,' she said. 'And it looks as if she succeeded. Shouldn't you be ringing Rosie, before Suzanne gets it in the neck from Nina for blabbing, and Rosie gets it in the neck from Suzanne?'

I was dreading telling Rosie, but when I spoke to her she was more concerned for me. 'I feel awful,' she fretted. 'I never imagined . . .'

'Neither did I. I'm just worried about you getting hell from Suzanne. If she does go off her head you can always move in here.'

'Thanks,' she said. 'You never know.'

Helen rang shortly afterwards. 'I phoned him,' she said. 'My demon lover from the train. I thought you'd like to know.'

About time too. 'And?'

'I've seen him twice.'

I was so pleased for her, it almost took the edge off my own mess. 'How's everything else? Have you seen the twins?'

'Yes, last weekend. Lawrence dropped them off and I took them to Burger King and the cinema afterwards.'

The old, unloved note had come back to her voice, almost making me wish I'd never asked. 'And?'

'Nothing,' she sighed. 'I don't think they're even missing me. All they were concerned about was whether they could have double fries.'

'Talking of chips, how's the cooking going?'

'I'll let you know after this party tomorrow night.'

'At least the cooking and the bloke are taking her mind off those kids,' Sally said afterwards. 'She's obviously regretting it, but she'll never just call Lawrence and say she's changed her mind.'

She gave me a pointed look. 'Like you won't call John and say *you've* changed your mind. Don't come crying to me after you've taken two weeks to psych yourself up and then he's got somebody else. OK, I know you can't phone him now, you're half pissed.' She picked up the bottle; there was about an inch left at the bottom. 'I wouldn't *want* you to phone him now. You need a clear head.'

A clear head was precisely what I didn't have next morning. I woke up feeling like something decomposing behind the sofa after Widdles had dragged it in. By nine o'clock that evening I looked and felt like something that's been in a morgue for six weeks.

Sally said, 'For God's sake, will you please just *phone* him?'

'Like this? Just look at me! What if he came straight round?'

This was an unlikely scenario, but I couldn't risk it. I had rings under my eyes and my skin looked like wallpaper paste.

'He won't notice,' she scoffed. 'Have a shower. We could light a couple of candles and pretend all the bulbs have blown.'

Eventually I did phone him, at half past nine.

I got the answerphone. I tried at ten to ten and got it again.

My green snakes might never have gone away. 'He's out,' I said miserably to Sally. 'I might have known. He's out with some non-screwed-up cow who doesn't look like something out of *Prisoner: Cell Block H*.'

'He's probably taken his blooming auntie to see *HMS Pinafore*,' she soothed. 'Phone him tomorrow.'

I tried to ignore my snakes, but they wouldn't go away. In fact, they were turning into pythons. 'I miss Jacko,' I said forlornly.

'Call him, then.'

So I did. He was actually at home. 'How's things?' he asked.

'Crap,' I said, and felt myself dissolving.

I was on the phone for over an hour. I lay on my bed, telling him everything I'd never told him about John, and all about Sally and Steve. 'I'm a daft cow,' I sniffed.

'Yes, but you always were a daft cow and I love you anyway. You'll feel better in the morning. Phone John then—I bet he's just having an early night. He's probably been crying into his beer nonstop.'

Then I passed him to Sally, who said, 'Hi, Ape-Face, why aren't you out on the piss?' She seemed perkier afterwards. I think she'd been missing all the squabbling.

I went to bed feeling better, woke up at eight and still felt better, until I looked in the mirror. My skin was still wallpaper paste, but I didn't notice that. You don't notice wallpaper paste when there's a huge red mountain on your chin.

All thoughts of phoning John went out of the window. It was going to go purple, I just knew it. I hadn't had a purple mountain in years. It was just typical sodding bloody Sod's Law that I was getting one now. It leered at me evilly in the mirror, saying it had a good mind to turn septic and infect the whole lower half of my face.

It was a horrible day, too, drizzly and depressing. For want of anything else to do, I made an overdue assault on Dorothy's junk. Although I'd already got rid of masses, there was still enough to sink the Isle of Wight, but this was stuff that needed careful sorting: books, letters, photos.

An hour after I'd started Sally brought me a coffee and since Tom was taking a pre-lunch siesta, she stayed. I was going through the photos. Most were ancient, of people I dare say even Dad wouldn't have a clue about, but there were later ones, too. Even one of me, aged six or so. Then I found something else to show Sally.

'Aah,' she said. 'Your mum and dad?'

It was their wedding group, with old Dorothy looking sprightly enough at sixty-five or so. Mum was wearing a traditional, frothy white dress, Dad a morning suit; they both wore happy-ever-after smiles.

'Sad, isn't it?' Sally said, echoing my thoughts exactly. 'Or poignant, perhaps. All those naive expectations. I wonder what went wrong?'

'Incompatibility,' I said. 'I often wonder how the hell they hit it off enough to get hitched in the first place.'

I soon found out.

As waking-up noises were wafting up the stairs from Tom, Sally went to see to him while I got on with the letters. In bundles according to the writer, some dated back to the twenties; some, however, were much more recent. I recognised the writing on one little bundle: my grandmother, Dad's mother. The first three were pretty mundane: the dreadful weather, poor Muriel's sciatica, whoever Muriel was.

It was the fourth that caught my attention. '. . . I can't pretend to be pleased, but of course there's no alternative. David's perfectly happy, anyway, and Pat's a nice enough girl. They've arranged the wedding for April 17. She'll be nearly five months gone—I hope she won't show. . . '

Something inside me went weird and frozen, until I read it again.

It didn't make sense.

I ran down to Sally. 'Look at this!'

'So they "had" to get married, as they used to say. Because of you.'

'Not *me*, dopey! I was born nearly two years after their wedding!'

I phoned Mum half an hour later.

'I've been sorting out Dorothy's letters,' I said, without preamble. 'Why didn't you tell me you were pregnant when you married?'

There was an awful silence. 'Oh, dear heaven,' she said, in despairing tones.

It was a good forty minutes later when I finally hung up.

She hadn't been pregnant, as it happened. She'd had a miscarriage a fortnight before the wedding. She'd hated even thinking about it afterwards, it had been so awful . . .

Eventually she'd got round to the rest. She'd met Dad when she was just getting over someone. She'd been devastated and Dad had been like a safe haven after the storm. She certainly hadn't married him just because of the pregnancy. They'd both been distraught over losing that baby. All she'd wanted, at the time, was to try again. She'd been 'happy enough' for years. That's exactly what she said; I thought it very telling.

It wasn't till I was about twelve that she'd realised she should never have married Dad, because safe havens just weren't enough any more. But she'd never intended to leave him, not until she met Bill and found out just what she'd been missing. She'd hated hurting Dad, which was why she'd been so worried that he was doing the wrong thing with this Kathy. She wanted him to be happy more than anything.

I said to Sally, 'I can't bear to think of them staying together all those years because of me.'

'She didn't say that.'

'No, but they obviously did.'

All this was still on my mind until around five o'clock, when we heard the front door open. 'Anyone home?' called a familiar voice. 'Thought I'd better come and cheer you up,' Jacko grinned. 'Here. For my two favourite girls.' From behind his back he produced two identical bouquets of flowers.

'Oh, Jacko . . .' I was almost dissolving again, and even Sally wasn't as rude as usual.

'I missed you, Ape-Face,' she said, giving him a kiss.

It was quite a good evening, after that. We made a fire and a massive curry, and enjoyed a thoroughly cultured evening. That is to say, we played Monopoly. Sally and Jacko argued, of course. They both wanted the little silver doggy, and Jacko said Sally was cheating and she said he couldn't have Mayfair, he'd lower the tone.

After that things could only go downhill, culturally speaking. Jacko started a game we'd played as students, called Choose or Die. What you did was this. You chose two of the most disgusting substances/activities you could think of and said to your victim, 'You have to eat (insert first disgusting substance) or (insert second). And you have to choose or die.' The sole object of the game was to produce the loudest shrieks of disgusted laughter known to man. It follows that the substances that did the best drew largely on bodily waste, particularly of animals or ninety-five-year-olds; I'm sure you can imagine the activities.

After initial eyes-to-heaven stuff, Sally entered into the spirit of the thing and it soon turned into a battle between her and Jacko to come up with the most disgusting things. I hadn't seen her like this for ages. Her face was flushed with laughter, her eyes picking up the light from the fire.

Wanting an early night anyway, I left them to it and went to bed. I was out like a light till seven fifteen. The first thing I did, naturally, was inspect my purple mountain in the dressing-table mirror. No worse, anyway. Possibly even a bit better. Nominally cheered, I went to the bathroom, padding softly so as not to wake anyone.

Sally's door was ajar, Tom's early-morning gurglings wafting out. Then I heard, 'Well? Some of that leftover curry? Weetabix? I used to like a nice boiled egg with soldiers, me.'

I pushed the door open.

Jacko was lifting Tom out of his cot. 'Here's Harry,' he said to him. 'She was a boring old hag last night, but we'll pretend she wasn't.'

I looked from him to Sally's neatly made bed. 'Where is she?'

'Asleep,' he said.

'Don't tell me she crashed out on the sofa again?'

Jacko turned to Tom, perched in the crook of his left arm. 'Poor old Harry's a bit slow, isn't she?' he said to him. Then he turned back to me.

A killer jelly hit me, but it bounced. I gaped at him.

There was no hint of a smirk on his face.

'Why do you think I stayed here so long? I love her,' he said simply. 'I loved her from the word go.'

I was so stunned, I couldn't get anything out.

'I was asking Tom what he wanted for breakfast,' he went on, as if he hadn't just been launching airborne jellies. 'I heard him talking to himself, but I didn't want to wake Sally.'

I located some sort of voice. 'She usually gives him a bottle first thing. She's had to get him onto bottles, for when she goes to work. But he'll need his nappy changed first.'

'I thought he might. Like to give me a few pointers?'

Still stunned, I put the changing mat on the bed, handed him baby wipes. I watched as he cleaned him up competently enough. Eventually, handing him a clean nappy, I said, 'Why didn't you *tell* me?'

'I couldn't,' he said. 'I thought I might as well tell you I wanted Madonna. Which way up does this thing go?'

I showed him, and he managed the rest himself. With Tom back in his arm, he said, 'Could you give me a hand with his bottle?'

I followed him downstairs, wanting to ask fourteen thousand questions, but unable to get any of them out. In a way, Jacko was carrying on as if nothing unusual had happened, but in another way he was different: an aura of placid, warm assurance hung about him. After helping him with the bottle and feeding a yowling Widdles, I sat with Tom, while he made breakfast for Sally.

Once he'd gone upstairs with Tom in one arm and a tray in the other, the thoughts I'd been refusing to think came to torment me. What if Sally had just got carried away? What if she'd just felt her urges coming back like a landslide? It was so easy to think of Jacko as a multi-fancying dickhead; hardly anyone realised how hard the real thing could hit him. And this was a hard hit, I just knew it. If we were in for Michaela all over again, I couldn't bear it. I couldn't bear it for him.

After two cups of coffee and a shower, I went back to bed, but I didn't sleep.

From the word go, he'd said. It had hardly been a laugh-a-minute 'go'. He'd first met her three days after that ClearBlue test, when Sally had been in no frame of mind even to notice he was there. He'd come again for the occasional weekend, but there had always been a reason. Liverpool playing West Ham, rugby at Twickenham: I'd never thought it odd, I'd always been glad to see him. It was after a stag night that he'd had that accident, and it had only been sensible to stick with the consultant who'd patched him up. As for Frida . . .

A blind? A smoke screen? Or just Jacko being Jacko?

I went downstairs at five to nine and found the three of them in the kitchen. Something told me at once that my fears for Jacko were needless. I looked from him to Sally. 'I've got a good mind to sue you two,' I said. 'I had to go back to bed to get over the shock.'

'Any excuse,' Jacko grinned. He was fully dressed, and Tom was muffled up in his all-in-one. Jacko shot me a wink, but it was Tom he spoke to. 'Right, mate, let's get out of here.' In a whisper he added, 'I think they want to talk about me.' He dropped a kiss on Sally's cheek.

'Bye, Ape-Face. No speeding with that buggy.' To me she added, 'He's just popping up the road. We're nearly out of milk.'

Like Jacko, she looked different. A pink, contented aura hung around her. 'Maybe you'll believe me now,' she said. 'About Steve, I mean.'

'But since when?'

'Ages. I suppose it started dawning on me when he had his accident. And then when Frida came, and he started all that daft flirting, only I wasn't so sure it was just daft . . .'

I sat at the table. 'And last night it all just happened?'

'If you put it like that,' she said sheepishly. 'We were still playing that stupid game and I was laughing my head off, but suddenly he was looking at me and I wasn't laughing any more. I just knew. And he said, "We can be just mates or I'll love you for ever. And you have to choose, or I'll die."' Suddenly she was wiping a tear from her eye.

My throat constricted. 'Oh, Sally . . .'

'He kissed me. It's been so long, it was like the first kiss I ever had.'

I was a bit wet round the eyes now, I can tell you. 'But bed? I thought you couldn't face the thought.'

'That's just it. I thought I couldn't. And he said, "Never mind, we'll just have a cuddle." He was so sweet . . .' She wiped another tear away.

The old Sally soon came back. 'But then I wanted to, after all,' she continued, with a wicked little grin. 'I'll tell you something, though. All that practice has paid off. He knows what he's about.'

We laughed, and suddenly things were normal again. As normal as they'd ever be. After a minute I said, 'I still can't believe you didn't tell me.'

'I couldn't. I thought you might tell him and he'd start something just to be nice. There was the bloody money factor, too,' she added. 'I couldn't bear anyone thinking it was just a bit too convenient, a broke single mother falling for a bloke with money.'

Jacko was a long time getting that milk, but he did possess a certain amount of tact, when required. Eventually we got back to Steve.

She hadn't wanted him showing up, for various reasons. First, she'd thought he wouldn't want to know and she didn't want to *know* that he didn't want to know. She didn't want poor little Tom having a bloke like that for a father. Second, if he did want to know she'd feel she should get together with him, but knew she couldn't. It would really have been easier if he'd stayed away.

Except for my mountain, I went through the rest of the day in a sort of rosy haze. After all, your two best friends in the world getting it together is something only the Emmas of this world dream about.

Jacko left around nine thirty. He was coming back on Friday night. Once he'd gone Sally busied herself with preparations for starting work the following morning.

It was only then that the last of my rosy haze wore off. My mountain was subsiding, but I still wasn't sure I'd be anything like presentable tomorrow. Assuming I needed to be presentable, of course. What if he wasn't answering again? I went to bed with a mass of nervous butterflies in my stomach. When I woke up they were still there, but at least my red mountain was more of a pink hill.

Sally refused a lift to the childminder's. It was walking distance, she needed the exercise. I said good luck as she went off at a quarter to eight, had another coffee, and left the house at ten past.

I stepped outside to a mini-drama: Matt and Toby in their school uniform, dawdling out of their front gate, and Francesca standing by the car, looking harassed. I don't know what I'd imagined: someone like Nina, I suppose, or even worse. But she looked just like any other reasonably smart and attractive woman.

'Will you please hurry *up*?' she said, as Matt dropped something and picked it up with maddening slowness.

I hadn't even seen the boys since before Christmas. 'Hi,' I said.

'Hi,' they mumbled.

As Francesca registered me, I had to say something. 'Hello. I'm Harriet.'

'Hello.' She said it awkwardly, which didn't surprise me. 'We're running late,' she added hurriedly. 'Lawrence is down with flu so I'm doing the school run. *Now* what?' she asked Toby. Having half got into the car, he got out again. 'I've forgotten my swimming things,' he muttered.

Something in her seemed to snap. 'Right, that's it. I *told* you to be ready—I'm late as it is. You'll have to get the bus.' She shot me an exasperated look. 'I'm sorry, but they've got to learn. I know their mother ran round after them like a slave, but I'm not prepared to.' And she got into the driver's seat and zoomed off.

Matt said crossly to Toby, 'Now look what you've done, dickhead! We'll be late now! The bus takes ages!'

I'd never felt much for either of them till then, but once I saw Toby's face I felt awful. His lip was trembling as he went back into the house. He suddenly looked like a little kid whose world's just fallen apart.

I said to Matt, 'Look, I'll run you to school, if you like.'

He suddenly looked very young, too. 'You'll be late for work.'

I couldn't believe he'd even thought of it. 'Not much. It won't matter.'

Toby came back, stuffing a towel messily into a plastic bag. Matt said, 'Harriet's going to take us, dickhead. Get in, quick.'

The traffic was dreadful, as usual on a Monday morning. They sat in the back, not uttering a word, but after a few minutes I could have sworn I heard muffled sniffs. I looked in the mirror and saw Toby wiping his eyes on the sleeve of his blazer. Matt hissed, 'Shut—up!'

While stopping at the fourth set of lights I said casually, 'Apart from this morning, how are you getting on with Francesca?'

'OK,' said Matt, in dull tones.

Toby said nothing. A hundred yards further on, though, he said in a wobbly voice, 'I wish Mummy would come back.'

Something in me dissolved. I'd never heard him call her Mummy before.

'Well, she won't, will she?' Matt said. To me he added, 'Dad says it's our fault she left. He said we treated her like a doormat.'

Bastard, I thought, changing viciously into third.

'I wouldn't treat her like a doormat if she came back,' Toby said tearfully. 'I'd make her cups of tea and tidy my room and everything.'

'Well, she won't,' Matt said doggedly, but some tiny timbre in his voice told me it was only a cover.

On the point of saying, 'She might, if you asked her,' I bit it back.

I was late for work, of course, but it was just tough. I'd had enough of this place, anyway. I made a mental note to buy a paper later, scour the Appointments pages. Not that jobs were the main thing on my mind. At lunchtime I phoned Helen. 'How did your party go?' I asked first.

'Quite well, actually,' she said, sounding almost bushy-tailed. 'One of the guests even asked if I'd like to do her mother's eightieth. I shall have to move out of Felicity's place, though, if I'm going to do it seriously. She's only got a little freezer and not much fridge space, either.'

I thought of her acres of Smallbone kitchen at home, of her cubic miles of fridge and freezer. 'I saw the twins this morning,' I said.

Her voice changed at once. 'How were they?'

I got off the phone ten minutes later feeling emotionally challenged, but knowing I'd done the right thing. What was the point of making points, of striking blows, if she was never going to be properly happy. She was going to ring Lawrence and say she was going back.

All afternoon I got steadily more sick with nerves over ringing John that evening, but it was easy to put it off. For a start, I had to ask Sally about her day. It hadn't gone badly, quite a nice class. She'd had to phone the childminder three times to check on Tom, of course, but the woman had said that he was fine.

Then she peered at my chin. 'I can hardly see your mountain any more. If you don't phone him tonight, I'll kill you.'

He answered after only three rings. 'Mackenzie,' he said crisply.

'John, it's me,' I said, like an idiot. 'Harriet, I mean. Please don't hang up—I really need to talk to—'

'Harriet, I'm sorry, but I can't do with any—'

'*Please*, listen a minute! I didn't mean what I said the other day—there were all sorts of complications I didn't tell you—I knew Nina, you see—I should have told you before but—Oh God, this is awful . . .'

After a pause for breath I went on in a gabbly rush, 'I really can't tell you over the phone, it's all so tortuously involved—I could come to you—right this minute if you're not tied up . . .'

There was a short, agonising silence.

'I'm afraid that's not going to be possible.'

Ten

THAT WAS IT. 'No, of course, not. I'm really sorry—'

'Harriet—'

'No, it's all right, honestly, we'll leave it there, I knew—'

'Harriet, will you listen to me? When I said it wasn't possible, I meant not possible. I'm in Prague.'

I hung up ten minutes later, in a jelly-splatted daze.

Sally was grinning all over her face. 'He told you to sod off, then.'

'I can't believe it! He told me to come! Only he said I'd have to get my skates on, he wasn't sure what time the last flight leaves.'

'What about work, tomorrow?'

'Stuff work—everybody else takes sickies.' Suddenly I was in action-stations overdrive. 'Right, get moving, Harriet—could you call a taxi while I phone Heathrow—see if there's a flight I can make—God, where the hell did I put my passport—?'

If I didn't make *The Guinness Book of Records* that night, I demand to know why. Checking airlines, fuming through recorded messages, slinging things in a bag, phoning man of seventeenth-heaven dreams back to say I should be on the twenty-one fifteen with a bit of luck, frantic ablutions of underarms, no time for teeth but could do this on plane, panic as taxi crawled in traffic—what if flight closed just as I got there?

Add to this charging like demented madwoman through terminal looking for right airline desk, cursing everyone in way, subsequently rushing to shop with boarding card in teeth to buy deodorant as realised had forgotten to apply or pack any, abluted underarms therefore probably smelly again already, especially after charging like further demented madwoman to gate, as departure board flashed 'last call' . . .

Phew. It invariably happened. You break Olympic and possibly entire solar system records and find nine shuffling people ahead of you.

While I still could, I phoned man of seventeenth-heaven dreams. 'Just made it. I'm on.'

'I'll be there.'

I boarded in a radiant, dopey daze. There was no celestial blue to climb into, of course, no fluffy bouncy castle, but I didn't care. All the way I gazed down at the blanket of European night, cities dotted like gold fairy lights in the darkness, and felt sorry for everyone else in the entire universe, because they couldn't possibly be as happy as me.

He was there as I came out of customs. He wore a dark grey overcoat and a smile that made my heart turn over.

Like an idiot, I almost felt like crying. 'Are you sure you haven't changed your mind? Do you still want a lunatic, screwed-up prat like—'

Mouth-to-mouth silencing is invariably the most effective.

Taking my arm, he whisked me to the exit. 'You could do with those thermals after all. It's brass-monkey stuff outside.'

It was, too. Subzero, diamond-frost stuff, sparkling wherever light shone. And real snow. Not that poor relation that melts by morning.

He had a car waiting, and we sat close together in the back. As the driver moved off, he took my hand. Just like that other night in the cab, he gave it a minute caress. 'Your hand's not cold now,' he said.

So then I knew he was thinking of that night, too, and how I'd gone cold on him, and how I'd done it again, only so much worse. 'That's because I got my thermostat fixed.' I hesitated, but had to ask. 'Did you think I was a complete bitch?'

It was a moment before he answered. 'I thought maybe you'd had some crushing experience that made you want to dish out exactly the same to anyone who looked as if he needed his ego squashed.'

A bitch, then. I felt awful.

'Before that, I just thought you might have someone else,' he went on.

'I thought it was you who had another option, that's all.'

It was another moment before he replied. 'Is Nina a friend of yours?'

I hadn't gone into detail over the phone, just the blurted-out basics. 'Not exactly. We were at school together. I know it sounds pathetic, but that first day I met you I was hiding, praying she wouldn't see me.'

'Why?'

'She used to make me feel a mess. Badly put together. And even then, in Covent Garden, she still did.'

In the dark taxi, his eyes were unfathomable. 'Go on.'

So I went. It was such a relief. I told him everything: Stuart, Rosie, and every bit of gossip I'd misinterpreted so spectacularly. I told him about Jon, the private dick and going to see Nina and feeling sick.

Eventually I said, 'Had you any idea she was seeing someone else?'

'No, but it doesn't altogether surprise me.' After a pause he added, 'What did she say about me?'

Just as a nasty little green snake was about to worm its way back into my stomach, it evaporated. His mouth was definitely quivering.

'What did she say? She did say something, I take it?'

'Well . . .' I mean, how did you say it?

'Go on,' he said. 'I need to know. However much it hurts.'

I knew he was laughing now, if only on the inside. And although my relief was profound, I didn't get it, whatever there was to get. 'John, *what*?'

'Hang on, we're here. We'll just drop your bag . . .'

The taxi pulled in at a hotel. John paid the driver and we went inside. It was one of those gracious old buildings that might have been a stinking rich merchant's house back in Mozart's day. He left my bag at the desk. 'Have you eaten?'

'Yes, on the plane—what were you going to say?'

'I need fortification before I hear the worst. We'll go to the Old Town Square.'

It was only a couple of minutes over cobbled streets to the Stare Mesto: the Old Town Square. On the way I told him I'd been before, a few years ago, but it had been summer, the square filled with people sitting at café tables and crowds milling round the medieval clock, where Death and Justice popped out on the half-hour.

It was not only midwinter now, but late. There were few people scurrying in the cold. We ended up in a typically Czech café bar, the type where you can get everything from apple dumplings to schnapps, with someone playing the violin.

He ordered a beer; I ordered a coffee and a schnapps chaser. After a mouthful of best Pilsner, he said, 'Right, my upper lip is stiffened. Massacre my self-esteem and tell me what she said.'

There was a wicked glint in his eyes now. 'She said you weren't quite up to the mark,' I said, plaintively. 'I'm dreadfully sorry.'

His mouth quivered a fraction. 'Is that it? Dear me,' he tutted. 'I don't know how I'm ever going to get over this.'

I could contain myself no longer. 'John, if you don't tell me—'

'All right, all right!' he said, seeing me about to burst. 'I'm afraid I was a bit of a naughty boy. I met her at a wedding in Scotland. We were thrown together for the entire weekend. We were even on the same plane home. She talked virtually all the way. And I listened, as you do. You talk back a bit. You take an interest.' He paused. 'But the trouble is, you do it too bloody well.'

At last, I was beginning to get it.

'It never occurred to her that I wasn't interested, so by the time I was yanking her bag off the carousel, she was talking about lunch.'

'And you didn't like to say no?'

His eyebrows gave a wry little lift. 'It seemed slightly brutal. By the end of that lunch, though, I knew I was going to have to be either brutal or devious.'

Devious, then. I wished he'd told her to sod off, but there you go.

'I said lunch again,' he continued. 'I said I'd pick her up. I thought I had her sussed by then. So I borrowed Lucy's car.'

Light was beginning to dawn. 'A beat-up old wreck?'

He shook his head. 'That would have been overdoing it. It's just a bog-standard Ford, getting on a bit.'

'What did she say?'

'Nothing at first. But once we were moving she said, "Is this your car?" I said oh, yes, I didn't believe in wasting money on fancy wheels when they only got nicked.'

'What did she say to that?'

'Nothing. But I felt her freezing round the edges. And that was when I got the wind up and took it a bit further. I started telling her I'd been suffering from stress and was thinking of buying a smallholding in Wales and keeping goats. I said I was going down at the weekend to look at a couple of places, and I'd really love her to come along.'

By now I was giggling helplessly. 'You wicked, devious bastard . . .'

'It worked. She said brightly that she was tied up at the weekend, but it was a lovely lunch, thanks a lot. Oh, and I mustn't bother dropping her home, she'd take a cab. So I stood on a bloody freezing pavement for five minutes, finding her one.'

'So that was your first official date, then,' I said. 'Just before we collided in front of old Wooden Wally.'

He nodded. 'And there was this woman.' Here he shook his head. 'She's been a sad trial to me, I can tell you.'

'That'll teach you to pick women up on pavements. Especially shameless trollops who pretend they've lost their purses.'

'Disgraceful,' he tutted, but his eyes were glinting so wickedly I had to lean across the table and kiss him.

It was snowing softly as we eventually left the bar and walked across the Old Town Square. I told him about the bog-roll dinosaur and he laughed, but kindly. We stopped to look up at the twin Gothic spires of the Tyn church, covered with new snowfall, and I said it was like fairyland, they reminded me of the Disneyland Castle. And he brushed a snowflake from my cheek and kissed me, and I knew exactly how old Walt's Cinderella felt when she found her prince. And then he said as we couldn't get much colder we might as well carry on to the Charles Bridge and do it properly. So pressed up together we walked to the bridge, and gazed down the river at all the bridges in the lamplight, and back at the Old Town, all its fairyland roofs white with new snow, and he said he'd never feel the same about snow again, and kissed me.

By the time we arrived back at the hotel I was thoroughly warmed up, if you know what I mean. On the surface, however, I was still chilly. So I said, 'I might warm up in the shower. I didn't have time before I left.'

'Maybe I should join you. Foreign showers can be awkward little cusses—I could come and twiddle the knobs for you.'

I have to say, I've never had such wonderful room service in my life. Nor such an unbelievably thorough shower, bits I never even knew I had soaped to lazy perfection. I returned the favour, of course, and I think I can safely say that no lovely smut and filth was ever cleaner.

Wrapped in fluffy towels we lay afterwards on the bed, talking delicious post-coital rubbish, eating chocolate from the minibar. Seeing the time, I said, 'Haven't you got to get up in the morning?' and he said, 'Yes, but I'll worry about that when I come to it.'

'This time, wake me up before you go.'

I sold the house in early April. I bought a lovely garden flat a couple of miles further into town. It had to be a garden flat for poor old Widdles; besides, as Rosie had said, it was great for barbies. Rosie found a nice flat eventually and is out nonstop. She rarely sees Suzanne any more. It was a mite fraught after all the spilt gossip came out, but Suzanne had the grace to admit that she could hardly blame Rosie for passing on confidences when she'd done exactly the same herself.

I changed jobs around the same time as moving, so it was a hectic period. I went to one of the multinational recruitment companies, so my mother'll be able to swank in her next Christmas letters that I now have a really good job.

Tara did a computer course for a month, went temping till July, and actually saved enough money to go to Greece. She started at an A-level crammer in September. Jacko said she's doing all right so far.

Helen has a little blue van with 'Cooking to Go' painted on the side, and it goes quite a lot. Whenever I see her, she's up to her elbows in filo pastry and has long since stopped running around after the twins: she just doesn't have time. She told Lawrence she wasn't prepared to move out of her home. If he and Francesca wanted something better than a doll's house, that was their problem. And Lawrence was so relieved she was going back, he barely argued.

She carried on seeing her man from the train for a couple of months but then he got transferred to Frankfurt and it sort of died the death. He did her a colossal service though. She recently mentioned some other chap, whom she met at some fortieth birthday-party bash. He was called Philip, she said; he loved her Stilton-and-celery nibbles.

Exactly as planned, Sally went home to her folks at Easter. She stayed until mid-July, by which time it wasn't so much a case of them driving her crackers as Tom driving them. He was toddling by then, into everything, trying to climb everything. Both grandparents were constantly agitated, in case he fell—about germs, getting cold, getting hot, sharp objects, and the fact that he wasn't yet potty-trained at thirteen months.

All of which had soon turned Sally into a nervous wreck, too.

So eventually, after Jacko had asked her forty-eight times to move in with him and save him coming to fetch her every weekend, and she'd said forty-eight times that she wouldn't until she was earning a proper salary, she did. It meant kissing goodbye to her place at that college, but she managed to get another through clearing at a college in Liverpool. She started at the end of September and is enjoying it so far. She still calls Jacko Ape-Face now and then so I hope she won't forget herself and say, 'I take thee, Ape-Face,' when they get married next March.

Steve did come back. It wasn't the cosiest of meetings, but they parted on reasonably civil terms. There was talk of finance and visiting but since he's in Hong Kong now I don't know how that's going to pan out. Tom adores Jacko, anyway. And as Sally says, it's the one who gallops round the kitchen at six thirty in the morning, giving 'horsey' shoulder rides, who counts.

Dad and Kathy bought their house in Cyprus. They're planning to spend half the year there and the other half back home.

I saw Nina again towards the end of September. It was a beautiful, breezy, golden Saturday morning. Off to see my mother, I'd just bought a bunch of flowers and a packet of Polos at a petrol station a couple of miles down the road when I saw her going in to pay.

'Nina! Hello again.'

There was a moment's awkwardness, but she broke it. 'Been somewhere nice?' she asked, looking me up and down.

I was wearing pink shorts, sandals, and a little white top. And the reason she asked was because I had a lovely golden tan.

'Very nice, actually,' I said. 'Sailing round the British Virgin Islands.'

'Really?' Her smile suddenly got slightly tighter.

The breeze was blowing my hair. I was glad of this, because it allowed me to carry on holding it back with my left hand. I knew she'd notice and I don't mind admitting I wanted her to. Ninas always notice such things. Like a homing missile her eyes zoomed in on my finger. 'Are you engaged?' she asked, as if I'd just had a sex-change or something.

'Yes,' I admitted, holding my hand out for her inspection. 'I always thought getting engaged was a waste of time, but when you're moored in a little harbour and someone suddenly produces something like this, you don't like to tell him to take it back to the shop.'

She gave another tight little smile. 'Very nice.'

I was almost expecting her to add, 'Is it real?' but she didn't go that far. It was a square-cut emerald, surrounded by diamonds that nearly knocked you out when the sun caught them.

'So who's the lucky man?' she went on, just as John appeared.

'You've met him,' I said, but she'd already twigged.

I have to say he looked absolutely gorgeous: browner than me, his eyes like the Caribbean in those deeper-water bits, glinting bluey-green in the sun.

He behaved with perfect aplomb. He said, 'Nina, good Lord!' in an entirely agreeable fashion, and shook her hand. 'How's it going?'

'Very well, thank you. And congratulations.'

'I'm taking him to meet my mother,' I said.

'Yes, and we'd better get a move on,' he said. 'Lovely to see you, Nina. Take care. Hop in, Harriet.'

He opened the passenger door of the car. The hood was down and he'd had it cleaned the day before, so it was all nice and shiny dark green.

She didn't quite gape, because Ninas never do, but she got as near as damn it. 'Is that yours?' she said to John.

'I hope so,' he said. Suddenly he pretended to catch on. 'Oh, the other one! Well, it was about time I got some respectable wheels. Harriet said she couldn't have that thing lowering the tone outside her new flat.'

She gave a silver-bells little peal, but the silver sounded definitely plated to me. 'What about the goats?' she asked.

'*Goats?*' I gave him an askance look. 'What goats?'

'Oh, that,' he said wryly. 'It was just a bad patch. I had plans for a rustic idyll. I soon changed my mind.'

I looked at Nina, raising my eyes to heaven. 'Honestly. This is the first I've heard of it.'

'Well, you won't hear it again,' he said. 'Hop in.'

So I hopped. I said, 'Bye then,' and smiled at her as we drove off.

For half a mile neither John nor I uttered a word. We didn't even look at each other. Eventually, though, I said, 'Stop it.'

'Stop what?' he said, deadpan.

'Laughing. It's not very nice.'

'I know it's not very nice,' he said. 'That's why I'm not doing it.'

'Yes, you are,' I said, suppressing my own eruptions. 'I can always tell. You won't be laughing in a few hours, when my mother's showing you hundreds of photos of when I was two and seven and eleven, and making you wonder what the hell you're letting yourself in for.'

'I know what I'm letting myself in for, my little bog-roll dinosaur.'

Call me soppy, but it still made me go gooey every time he said that.

At the lights he leaned over and kissed me. 'The sun, an open top and thou,' he said. 'What more could anyone ask?'

'How about a Polo?' I popped one in his mouth.

Except for lack of snow, it couldn't have been a lovelier day.

ELIZABETH YOUNG

'Think Pink and Earn a Mink' was the arresting headline in an old copy of *Good Housekeeping* magazine that grabbed Elizabeth Young's attention. She had always wanted to try her hand at writing romantic fiction, but she just hadn't known how to get started. 'After reading the article,' she told me, 'I thought, "What the hell" and began writing, accumulating dozens of rejections along the way. After a couple of short stories, I eventually had a "short and sweet" novella published, and won a prize in a romantic novel competition run by *Woman's Weekly*.' Elizabeth then had two Mills & Boon style romances published, which gave her the confidence to embark on her first full-length novel, *Asking for Trouble*. 'I guess I wrote *Asking for Trouble* for me,' Elizabeth said with a laugh. 'I wanted to prove to myself that I could do it.'

In the years before she started writing, Elizabeth lived in a variety of different places and had an odd mixture of careers. In the late sixties she dropped out of a Russian degree to follow her boyfriend, Andrew Young, to Cyprus, where she found work modelling for television and cinema commercials. 'We were really, really broke at the time,' she told me, 'and the commercials paid five pounds per day, which was a fortune to us then. The director, Andreas, would phone me and say, "Bring hot pants, bring bikini" and off we would go in his old Bedford van. It was really good fun.'

After Cyprus, the couple returned to England for eighteen months and Elizabeth started to work for British Caledonian Airways as an air stewardess. 'Remember the tartan uniforms?' she asked me. Then, in June 1974, Robert and Elizabeth were married and went to live in Muscat. 'We lived in a tiny prefab with orange plastic floors. The temperature rose to more than a hundred and thirty degrees in the summer and the power often failed. However, it was an exciting country to explore—people in remote villages would invite you in for coffee and feed you dates.' After the birth of her daughter, Philippa ('she was born in England as no expat had yet dared to have a baby in the local hospital'), the family moved on to Abu Dhabi, where a second daughter, Alexandra, was born.

In 1987 the Youngs returned to their home in Kingston upon Thames and that is when Elizabeth read the *Good Housekeeping* article and began to write. Having taken so many interesting twists and turns in her own life, it is no wonder she is able to produce such wonderfully fresh romantic comedy. 'In *Fair Game* I started out with the idea of the very last person you want to see and the novel just evolved from there. When I began I didn't really know where it was going. Writing is like travelling from London to Newcastle: you know the general direction but not the direct route.'

Jane Eastgate

PICTURE CREDITS: COVER: Bill Ling/FPG/Getty Images. Barbara Taylor Bradford photograph, and page 147: © Deborah Feingold. Sue Monk Kidd photograph, and page 325 © Linda L. Ruggles. Elizabeth Young photograph, and page 479: © Jerry Bauer. THREE WEEKS IN PARIS: pages 6 & 7: Martin Barraud/Gettyone Stone. THE SECRET LIFE OF BEES: pages 148 & 149: illustration by Anthony Robinson @ The Organisation. FAIR GAME: pages 326 & 327: illustration by Roman Greay @The Inkshed.

Printed and bound by Maury Imprimeur SA, Malesherbes, France

601-016-1